Remedy

Remedy

The Forgotten Legacies Series
Book Three

K.J. Simmill

Titles by K.J. Simmill

Fiction:

The Forgotten Legacies Series:
Darrienia
The Severaine
Remedy
The Dreamwalker

Non-Fiction:

Herbal Lore

To my wonderful husband, without your support none of this would have been possible.

Thank you.

Contents

Chapter 1

The Treasure Hunter

Dawn approached, not caring for those who would be bound by its spell. Most would celebrate the first glimmer of light as it cast hope upon a new day, others would mourn the losses of the night; and then there was Rob. For him the encroaching dawn was like the sand of an hourglass, trickling away precious seconds. Where he stood when the final grain fell, and light touched the unseen horizon, would decide his fate. Life or death. Victory or defeat.

Time was of the essence, and too much had slipped away since he had first entered this domain. Even now he found himself being driven deeper into the twisting labyrinth, rather than seeking an escape. But still, he had to hold on to the belief that a portal was within reach. He would not survive being sealed within The Depths of Acheron.

The pressure of every passing second bore down on him with crushing force, adding to the fatigued burning that spread throughout his exhausted legs. His lungs screamed for air as he ignored his body's desperate cries for rest. How could it ask that of him when to stop would be to die? Those things, the ones living within the tunnels, were close behind. The scraping of their dull claws on the stone surface echoed through the warrens. But there was light ahead, an opening. He could but pray he would find himself somewhere familiar.

His momentum should have sent him plummeting to his death. It was only by sheer luck the ore lining the ledge's edge had caught the flickering light from his torch. But it had left very little time to react. His feet skidded, giving those precious few seconds required to turn and grasp at the stone ledge as he fell. His knuckles turned white under the exertion. Digging his feet into the wall his gaze turned downward, tracing the path of his torch as it spiralled through the air to leave a glowing trail of smoke and cinders. Despite the countless journeys to this domain, and the horrors witnessed, he was somehow unable to accept this scene. Below stood the abandoned ruins of a stone city, larger than anything he had before encountered. The creatures hissed and snarled from within their darkened shelter, yet did not continue to pursue him. They remained within their territory as if they were fearful to trespass further.

Below, the city's spired buildings and domed roofs stood tall, draped in moss and vines causing the once pale stonework to grow dark with age. The area seemed undisturbed in what, he hoped, was an indication of its long-standing abandonment. Straining his ears he listened for sounds of life, for evidence of things dwelling below. The silence was unnerving. Either this city had been deserted as its first impression implied, or something silent prowled the ruined and darkened streets.

Even at their greatest the craftsmen of his own domain could not construct such beauty. The stonework shimmered with metal, yet woven within, like mortar or binding, vines and roots burrowed. They secured large blocks together in such a manner that deliberate construction was the only plausible answer.

The city had been crafted in natural balance. Its design sung of an affinity between magic and man. The people who had once dwelt within the walls, those who could combine opposing forces and marry them in grand displays of harmony, possessed a talent that would leave wielders of the arcane in awe. Rob wondered what had become of these grand architects; it was unclear if they had been driven from their homes or simply been seduced by the bestial nature of all within this domain. Had they cast aside the final shreds of their humanity, leaving their structures to become one with the darkness?

This city had been left to ruin. With its masters' absence nature had once more grown dominant, slowly reclaiming parts of the land. The weight of heavy vines and fungi causing stone to collapse and metal to rust. The city was growing, yet at the same time was plagued with decay.

Narrowing his eyes Rob studied the rooftops. Dark smears revealed silver shimmers of reflected light, some scattered with stripped bones suggesting his concerns about the silence were founded. A nest, perhaps, but certainly a hunting ground of some description. But to what he couldn't be certain. There were no clear marks to allow him to formulate an educated guess. Rob swallowed, recalling his pursuers' reaction to this area. He suppressed a shudder, trying to imagine the predators of those from within the tunnels. Those creatures had evolved into carnivores, everything about them had indicated dominance. Yet it seemed there was something here even they had cause to fear.

Distant sounds echoed through the darkness causing him to turn his focus upwards. Bioluminescent fungi grew in crevices and hollows found within the sheer cliffs, crudely and poorly casting light and shadows. The minimal lighting revealed only towering walls of darkness where the large glowing spores became pinpricks of light, like stars on a clear night, stretching up into an expanse he could not even begin to fathom.

He tried to relax, telling himself the gruelling chorus of shrieks coasting on the almost undetectable breeze were far away, carried to his alert senses by the echoes they rode upon. But the tightness spreading across his chest, and the prickling of the hairs at the nape of his neck, warned him his instincts believed otherwise. For the briefest moment the area seemed darker, like a cloud had covered the sun; but here there were no clouds, no sun, no sky, at least none that he had seen.

His grip trembled, his body flinched in response to a strange, eerie cry. The natural flickering light from above was masked by a shadow almost as haunting as the noise which now filled the air. Of all the sounds within the world he could attribute this to none. The shriek contained an almost bestial roar within its guttural depths, as if more than one creature cried from the throat of the being.

Pinpoints of light continued to fade as more complex and ear-piercing screeches echoed their response. Rob felt his tense limbs spring into action, carrying him down towards the rooftops below. There, he could at least seek shelter. With every downward step his chest and stomach grew tighter. His heart pounded with a deafening roar, one almost loud enough to conceal the ever-nearing cries. If he had any hope of escaping he needed to be heading upward, not being forced constantly lower. If he failed to reach an exit before dawn he, like his fate, would be sealed. He would not survive the twenty-eight days it would take for the portals to once more materialise.

Horrific wails reverberated, announcing that the circling creatures had seen him. Their large leathery forms swooped closer before veering away from the wall that briefly deterred them. It would not be long before they adapted their approach. He quickened his descent, his eyes burning from his refusal to blink. He could not die, not down here.

Rob adjusted his position as the first of their talons fixed upon the wall, twisting its enormous frame to begin a vertical pursuit. He aligned himself with the closest rooftop and braced for impact as he pushed himself away from the stone cliff face. He would be exposed for a short time, but if he picked his route with care the shadows and spires could be used to his advantage. Louder, more excited cries, filled the air at his sudden and unexpected movement. Twisting as his body struck the roof he attempted to roll, losing traction against the coat of thick green residue which seemed to cover a smooth surface beneath. He heard the unmistakable sound of a crack before his eyes caught sight of the webbed damage spanning out from the place he had first impacted.

Regaining his footing he carefully began to move, his mind warning him of the dark circling forms above. He fixed his vision to the expanding fractures. His disruption of the algae revealed nothing but darkness below and, perhaps, a slight hint of reflected light. Each shift of his weight caused the cracks to expand further.

Rob looked upwards, readying his crossbow as he lifted it from the clasp on his belt. Its tether momentarily twisted around his arm as he tried to find the correct bolt. He dared not avert his eyes from the descending creatures. The walls rippled with their movement, their numbers immeasurable through the darkness, and more circled overhead. He loaded the bolt, feeling the floor physically shudder beneath his feet. Cries echoed from above and, with no salvation in sight, Rob closed his eyes launching himself upwards, using his momentum to land heavily on the fractured roof.

The glass shattered beneath his feet, cascading with him down into the large open space below. He prayed, to any who would listen, that his eyes had not deceived him.

The shadows of the circling creatures grew larger, their clawed talons scraping on the rooftop, scratching new paths for light to penetrate as they fumbled to find their footing before taking to the air once more. He saw the ripple of thick algae-coated water below him, the source of the slight reflection of light he had seen from above. The heavily decaying stench caused bile to rise in his throat as his form broke the stagnant surface. He fought his way through the thick fluid, gasping for breath, gagging as the odour penetrated his nostrils.

All fell silent, except for the sound of Rob pulling himself from the dense and putrid waters, and onto the slate floor. His hand stirred the sleeping moss, which grew in thick and sporadic blankets, causing shimmers of light to expand outward from his location. For the briefest moment it illuminated the area as its light chased throughout the temple, extinguishing as quickly as it spread until only the area in contact with him remained aglow. Each leaf and capsule activated those within its mat, bathing the area with a gentle green light in a display of nature's own magic. His movements sent invisible spores to pass along silent communication between the capsules, ensuring the gentle blooms lit his path whichever way his feet staggered.

Rob's eyes fixed on what he hoped would be an exit. He needed to get out of here. The darkness that shrouded the room bordered on the unnatural and, in this realm, darkness truly was a thing to fear. It was the flesh and blood of nightmares.

Shadows played as light from above was obstructed by the still-circling hunters. The area was enormous. The tall ceilings were supported by thick columns, larger and wider than most modest dwellings he had seen. The giant cylinders, embossed with images he could not discern through the gloom, made him feel tiny, insignificant. He leaned against the nearest pillar, resting for a moment. He could see very little, but there were enough implications to suggest it could be a place of worship. The grandeur, and time such a construction would have taken, was likely only to be the result of dedication, or servitude.

Rob swallowed, his eyes narrowed almost certain that the darkness had become more tangible. His rising fear was a subtle reminder of his predicament. The familiar glow of moss once more chased throughout the temple before centring on a distant point, adding a depth and length to the room he had not thought possible. The subtle illumination became overpowered by the shifting darkness, as if the shadows themselves worked in twisted unison to quell the light. But the more this spiralling mass advanced, the larger the guiding carpet became. He felt his chest tighten as the mosses' influence expanded further, quicker. Something was coming. His feet slipped in the dank fluids pooled around him as he began his retreat. Turning his back on the moss, but unable to ignore its growing luminescence, he forced his trembling legs into action.

His elongated shadow began to expand before him, warning of the closing proximity, but he dared not glance behind. He knew to behold his pursuer would be to seal his fate. Fixing his sight forwards, he focused on the small ray of light he hoped marked his escape.

Each rapid breath was perfectly timed with the hard impact of his boots upon the floor. The light at his own feet was slowly being overpowered from the increasing glow behind him. A light that was not fading, but growing ever larger to become visible in his peripheral vision.

The glimmer of metal reflecting in the expanding light caught his attention just moments before his damp hand slid down the surface of an overly large door. Within it, clearly illuminated, lay a smaller, locked door. Taking his dagger he wedged it between the securing bolt. The trembling of his hands forced him to muster control over his panicked breathing, but fear warned him of the increasing darkness of his shadows. The three perfect copies, one from each angle of expanding light, were growing more solid, darker, warning him how near his pursuer drew.

With great effort he forced his gaze to remain steadfast on the bolt. Tensing his muscles against the tremors he prised it from the wooden structure.

The echoing sound of metal set his nerves further on edge. He shoved the door, surprised how easily it opened as he tumbled forwards into what would have once been a street. Scrambling to his feet he hastily slammed the door, pressing his body firmly against it until his commonsense caused him to question the use of such an action.

Rob's frantic vision searched the area before him. Whilst he could have marvelled at the eloquence and beauty of the buildings, which lined the cracked paved streets, his mind had turned to survival. He beheld only shelter and shadows, where brilliant structures and architecture were in abundance. His footsteps echoed, the only sound through an otherwise silent tomb.

Dark buildings towered over him, their blackened windows not quite concealing the flickers of movement his mind warned him came from within. The hairs on the back of his neck began to prickle again, causing him to glance upwards as he took shelter beneath one of the many archways that littered the winding streets.

The small voice in the back of his mind, the one he often trusted to keep him safe, told him the portal was higher, that he needed to gain height, and quickly. He called this voice commonsense. The portals were always close to the surface. But he was a stranger to this area. With the vast monuments he could see little before him, although the roaring of water cascading down from one of the aqueducts became increasingly more prevalent.

He followed this sound until his sight fell upon a central reservoir. The amount of water being deposited was a clear indication that only a small portion was visible above ground. Edging forwards, confident the roaring of water would disguise his rapid footfall. He worked his way up what appeared to be a stone staircase beside the thundering torrent. It was only on closer inspection that he noticed the water descended an identical structure, separated from this one by a small channel. He looked above, hoping the dry texture of this stone signified its lack of use.

Crouching near the top of the aqueduct he surveyed the area. The bridges were joined, creating a complex outer ring to the basin this city had been constructed within. Several channels, similar to the one he had just climbed, descended in various locations, all depositing the water collected as it cascaded down the basin's cliffs from numerous sluice gates. Small sections of the outer ring had crumbled away, sending waterfalls crashing down into unseen depths.

He walked the stone canal, keeping a constant vigil on his surroundings as he followed his new path over the city. As yet he could not discern a way to scale the basin; but there was bound to be something near the outer ring, a means to access the sluice gates in case of failure. He just needed to find it.

The aqueducts forming the outer ring were larger and wider than the one he had so carefully walked. He felt safe upon its thick stone platform, but still his pace never faltered. He felt the staggering clumsiness of each hurried step. His body visibly recoiled as the familiar wail sounded from above.

He forced his limbs to work harder, his stomach tightening as the roar of water from the damaged bridge before him grew louder. The waterfall, seeming so small from his initial vantage point, now appeared in all its splendour, ever growing, monstrous. The cries from behind forbade him from rethinking his path, but the almost inaudible churning of heavy waterwheels below warned of an equally fatal danger. He would rather attempt this jump than offer himself as a feast.

His feet left the bridge. Every muscle tensed, adding extra force to the leap, but still he knew it would not be enough. Grasping his crossbow tightly he let out a cry, drawing the attention of his pursuers, spurring them into action before they lost their prey to the depths. He released the bolt as the first shadow sailed above him. The agonised cry came as audible evidence his aim had been true. He rotated his hand, securing the tether as the rope grew taut. The struggling efforts of the creature lifted him higher as it attempted to flee. Water whipped around him as he was dragged through the spray, his grip remaining firm as the creature continued its frantic flight.

Gasping for breath Rob scrutinised the area below, noticing for the first time the thick heavy chains which operated the counterweights to open and close the sluice gates. They had cleared the break, and covered a surprising distance given the obvious fatigue of his carrier. Pulling himself up he unhooked the tether before uncoiling it from his grasp, hoping his judgement was correct. He braced himself for impact, rolling as he struck the ground. With barely enough time to confirm his path he rolled again. Putting extra force into the movement he propelled himself from the aqueduct towards one of the chains, hoping he had gauged it correctly. He fell several feet before his extended arms impacted with the chain. He could but hope his pursuers had thought him lost to the currents below.

He dared not pause to catch his breath. He had to push onward and upward to what appeared to be a dark ledge above the sluice gates. Reaching it was his only hope of escape. Grasping the thick chain in his hands he used the large links as a ladder, knowing if negotiated correctly it would shield and protect him while he climbed.

When he had scaled half the chain's length he felt it shudder beneath his weight. From above the sound of grinding gears began to echo. He closed his eyes briefly before redoubling his efforts. The leathery beating of wings and the flurry of movement below caused his stomach to lurch in time with the chain.

Whilst some sluice gates seemed to remain permanently open, others appeared to release when the pressure reached a required force. Their timing most likely calculated to ensure the continued movement of the great waterwheels he had seen within the aqueducts. It made sense, people with the ability to erect such a place would also incorporate a method to ensure water could gather to the strength needed. It also made sense that a newly opening source would attract predators. Not only water would be carried from the land above.

Rob tightened his grip as the mechanism shuddered once more before dropping slightly. He turned his attention to the chain running parallel to his own. His had lowered as that one had risen. With a deep intake of breath he tentatively transferred his weight across to the rough surface of the corroded wall, not fully releasing his grasp until he was certain it was safe. As quickly as he dared he edged across, his fingers and feet utilising water-worn ridges and crevices.

The grinding sound echoed again, sending a flurry of shadows from below up into the air, racing upwards past him as the wall at his fingertips began to grow damp. A second wave followed, the force of their movement knocking him off balance and into the flock. Their rapid movement battered him as he fell, knocking him aside until he felt the force of the chain strike him. He clawed desperately at the metal, wrapping his limbs around the link and tightly interlocking them until all movement from below had halted. His body protested against the prolonged exertion and injuries, while his adrenaline, coupled with his mind, channelled it away to be dealt with at a later time. Right now he could only focus on surviving.

It was only once he fully regained his balance he became aware of the roaring sound of the water, and the gradual rising of the chain as the gate opened the remaining way. The creatures played, delighting in catching their live prey as they raced up and down the cascading waterfall feasting on all caught within its currents.

When the chain's movement stopped he was still several feet from what he had thought was a ledge. His stomach tightened as he realised the darkness had been formed by a change in the rock's stratum, giving the impression of depth. That left him only one option, the water tunnel. If the water was, as he believed, channelled from above, it had to enter from a portal of some description. If he followed the tunnel perhaps he could find an escape.

The water had begun to slow, indicating its resources had been depleted. Rob was certain this meant the gate would soon close once more. Before he had time to reconsider he reached out towards the wall, working his way across towards the gated opening. Like the city below it was large, the gaps more than adequate for him to force himself through and land arms first in the shallow water that remained undrained. He waded through the ankle deep water. Its gentle current, while forceful, was not enough to delay him.

The tunnel was short, ending abruptly with a stepladder leading down into a cylindrical passage. His heart hammered in his chest as relief swelled through him, looking down he could see the night sky, and a familiar arrangement of stars. He scratched his head for a moment, frowning. He had never seen a portal such as this one before, one where his own world was inverted. Jets of water erupted, entering the tunnel in small angled sprays as he wondered how he could escape the portal when the gravity of his own world became the dominant force. That was something he could address shortly, for now, there was no more time to delay. With a deep breath, and still weighted with concern, he jumped.

Rob saw the sky rushing towards him. His arms flailing in panic, not even realising the sky was a reflection until he broke the water's surface. The portal had exited near the churning paddle blades of an old waterwheel, sending him tumbling into the river below.

The raging currents battered and pulled him towards the turning wheel. Surfacing, he gulped for air trying desperately to break free of its snare and swim to the shore. The currents dragged him down, the churning motion of the mill audible even through the silence of the water. He struggled against the seething undertow. His limbs burned and energy rapidly diminished as he fought the slow, painful battle until his knees struck the incline of the riverbed. His fingers clawed at the river's bank as he pushed himself forwards until his trembling arms gave way beneath him.

Rob dragged himself up, still lying partially in the river as his strength faded. He was aware of the icy coldness of the lapping water, but lacked the strength to move. Then finally, with great effort, he managed to turn over. His eyes became transfixed on the rhythmic turning of the waterwheel. The strange sound of the moving water gripped his attention as it cascaded from the paddles to fall into the portal he had only moments ago emerged from.

He let his head fall back onto the muddy riverbank, savouring each painful breath as his gaze lingered upon the softening shades of the sky. The sounds of the dawn chorus sang in harmony to the water's own music as it returned to its natural rhythm. Relishing the morning's cold touch upon his damp and shivering skin he placed his right hand on the pocket of his battered tan jerkin. Feeling the weight of the bounty within, he let out a deep, throaty chuckle.

* * *

It had been many years since Rob had last stepped foot in Elpída. There were as many reasons to avoid this temple as there were that drew him to its door. Yet here he stood, overlooking its grand design and marvelling at the gardens and out-buildings, all of which had thrived in his absence.

Elpída was now the size of a small town. Once nothing more than a broken down temple had stood here. Now it had been revived, expanded, and its purpose adapted to give a home to the lost and orphaned, as well as becoming a respected schoolhouse.

The silence was unnerving, but it was not the first thing he became aware of as he stood, arm outstretched, at the temple's main doors. There was a reason he had not returned, why he sent his donations, or left them without crossing the threshold. Why had he thought today should be any different?

17

Lowering his arm he pushed his hand deep into his jacket's pocket, removing a small coin pouch. He gauged its weight, nodding to himself, before lifting the lid of the metal donation box and placing it inside. The lid closed smoothly without the betraying groaning sound of metal he had come to expect.

Rob's hand moved down the door, feeling the smooth grain beneath his touch. Part of him had hoped the box would betray his presence and see him welcomed within the walls. He wasn't sure he had the strength to enter alone. Reminded of the strange silence, he moved closer to the door, straining to hear the telltale signs of life as a sense of foreboding washed over him.

At this hour the temple should be busy. The morning prayers should have recently concluded, and the temple was normally filled with the unmistakable bustle of life. It was a schedule rarely deviated from. Yet it stood shrouded in silence. As he listened, he could hear but a single sound. The rhythmic scraping of a blade being sharpened on leather. Its never faltering pace warning of a well-practised hand. His stomach tightened as his deft fingers instinctively loaded a bolt into his crossbow before quietly placing it back on his belt. Whoever was inside would have realised someone had approached from the initial noise, but he hoped his silence assured them they had been left undisturbed. He closed his eyes, listening for the children, for any sound except for the one he heard.

Slowly he moved to the windows, attempting to peer through the plain glass. The drapes were drawn, obstructing his view of within. Surprise would be his only ally. With a prolonged exhale he braced himself before forcing his weight against the door, surprised when it gave with ease. The resounding impact of the wooden doors against the walls forced more adrenaline to race through his system as he prepared himself for the image he feared he would behold.

The echo of metal clattering across the floor immediately drew his attention to the rapid movement of the figure before him as she dropped to her knees. His fingers quickly slipped from his lever trigger as he beheld the scene before him. The metal pail, sent tumbling from her fearful reaction, rolled, soaking the wooden floor with its dirty contents. Kneeling in the spilt water, with her gaze fixed upon the floor, was a woman. Everything about her posture signalled submission. Her body was rigid with fear with startled breaths being drawn in quick succession. Despite her alarm she did not raise her head to look at the figure who had entered the temple so violently.

Rob allowed himself a moment to regain his composure. His own breathing calmed as he realised the danger had been imagined. He took these moments to study the figure before him. She was unfamiliar. Her white dress—now turning partially transparent around her knees as the water absorbed through the

19

thin cloth—revealed her to be a novice. Dark stains and dirt blemishes told tales of her tireless labour.

Her fear of him was understandable. People like her were often the focal point of aggression, and his entrance would have done little to put her at ease. She sat in silence not daring to move, barely daring to breathe, as she awaited his approach. Rob saw her cringe as he slowly began to advance. Realising she flinched at the sound of each step he paused to study her further, aware that her reaction was the result of many years of conditioning.

Her long black hair had been carefully braided into a single plait. This once tidy presentation had become slightly unravelled by her labours, freeing small wisps from their bindings. Her hair was a dark contrast to her ivory complexion, an enchanting combination, especially when paired with her strong feminine jawline. Even Rob, who had travelled extensively, was unable to place her origins. But, aside from making her mysteriously beautiful, these traits were not the cause of her fear. It was unlikely, given her more obvious heritage, any would look on to see the beauty before them. This young girl was Méros-Génos. But never had Rob seen one with a feature as prominent as hers.

Most Méros-Génos—often referred to as Demi-humans or Demies by those trapped in archaic beliefs of superiority—possessed a trait of the creature their essence was bound to. This was normally a subtle quality. The pure, those thought to belong to bloodlines preceding the Titanomachy, could walk amongst humans unseen. Whilst the others were once dubbed Demi-human, and thought of as lesser beings by Méros-Génos and humans alike.

It was said the fusing of man and beast was a mistake in the release of souls ready to be reborn from the underworld. It was rumoured these souls, in life, had somehow tethered to another creature, drawing on its instincts and traits. When their souls were united at the Gate of Shades it caused the merging of the two.

Once this new soul was ready to be reborn it was different, no longer fully human. From the moment the life-force entered its intended vessel the fusing of it and the bestial essence altered the growth of the child, causing it to possess strange and unnatural characteristics which belonged to the animalistic aspect.

The joining of two Demi-humans, or Méros-Génos, often resulted in the birth of a child sharing the traits of both parents. There were, however, rare occasions when two human parents would give birth to one of these 'impure' souls. Some would love the child. Others sought to be free of the burden through abandonment or sacrifice, and hope that their next child would not be tainted in such a manner.

The Demi-humans possessed more pronounced features, such as scales, claws, a tail or even bestial ears. But often such things could be hidden to shield their nature from those who would persecute them. The Méros-Génos, seeing in them a partial likeness, came to understand the Demi-humans. They realised that while created initially by magic and mistake they were no different in essence to themselves. Eventually they welcomed them as kindred spirits, hoping to be rid of the derogatory term. But such was not to be. Hate is far harder to quell than acceptance is to give. Their label was shortened further by the uneducated and used as a term of degradation. A word uttered to describe the most worthless and detestable of Mankind.

The Méros-Génos, where possible, hid amongst the humans, concealing that which made them different. Some thought humans to be the lesser-species and created settlements of their own where they could live unburdened. But this young lady had no hope to walk amongst humans unseen. She had something Rob had never seen their kind possess before, wings. She would be an outcast to all. Destined to be labelled a harpy and shunned by both races. These large appendages mirrored the darkness of her hair, and whilst almost Moiraic in their feathered appearance, their shade would ensure no one would confuse her with the benevolent beings thought to watch over and guide the people of this world.

"Good morning." Rob spoke softly, the deliberate gentleness of his tone causing the woman before him to raise her gaze to meet his. Her smoky grey eyes reflected the deep fear his presence caused; a fear still mirrored by her posture as she struggled to breathe. He offered her the warmest smile he could muster before continuing to speak. "I am Robert Raymond. By chance does Iereía Sunniva have a moment to spare on a weary traveller?"

Cautiously rising to her feet the young woman folded her arms across herself. Offering a slight nod she began to back away, never taking her eyes from him until she reached the door. Only when her hand firmly grasped the handle did she turn, quickly making her departure.

* * *

Rob had not been left waiting too long, but even a few seconds alone with the statue of this temple's patron deity, Artemis, was enough to see him question his presence. The Iereía was a busy lady. She had better things to do than waste her time with him. He was beyond redemption anyway. His pacing steps had halted briefly, before continuing with fresh purpose as he made his way towards the exit. He could leave a note perhaps. His business was not so important that he should request an audience with the person who had constructed this haven from nothing.

"I see you are still adventuring." Rob cringed, his departure stilled as the familiar voice caught him in the act of retreating. He turned slowly, turning the corners of his mouth in a forced smile, but as soon as his sight fell upon her all falsities drained away. Sunniva, as always, carried herself with the grace of a queen. Her elegant steps created the illusion that she glided towards him, rather than walked. Without pause she approached, extending her slender arms around his torso to pull him into a warm embrace.

The silk of her dress whispered against him as he raised his arms, returning her affection.

The welcome was brief. She pulled back wrinkling her nose, critically scrutinised his dishevelled appearance, and looked down upon her own once flawless attire. She shook her head slightly, picking the small pieces of debris from her own white dress, which had been transferred during their embrace. "I swear, Brother, it was not too long ago you announced the world was void of such escapades. 'Everything has been discovered and all that can be plundered has been.' Or words to that effect." She recited mimicking his voice terribly.

"True," he grinned, ruffling a hand through his brown hair. "But that was *before* the Severaine unsealed The Depths of Acheron. So much has happened in the last six years." Everything had changed the day the Severaine had broken free of its seal. Until then few had even known of its existence. By the time the true danger was realised so much had already been lost. Lives had been destroyed, and cities had been razed to the ground under its unrelenting power. The world had lived in fear, and the Gods had all but abandoned them.

His gaze turned heavy as he shifted his vision to stare beyond her, into a place only he could see. His face grew shadowed by torment. The glaze of his eyes showing the distance his mind had travelled even with such simple words. Sunniva allowed him this moment. It had been so long since last she had seen him, yet the past still haunted him relentlessly. "Oh well." He forced out the words with a heavy sigh, trying to dispel the regret. "Is it just the two of you today, you and—" Rob grasped for a name he now felt he should know. "Who was that Méros-Génos anyway?" he questioned. When he had first seen her there was nothing familiar, yet now he had the strangest feeling he should have recognised her.

"Yes just us. There's a traders' market in Estarc. Such things are good for the children. Some may earn apprenticeships, and the younger ones enjoy the festivities," she explained.

"And the Méros-Génos?" He glanced towards the door, through which the young lady had made her escape. A small tugging sensation in the back of his mind caused his eyebrows to knit tightly together in a frown. He returned his attention to Sunniva, awaiting her answer.

"You truly have been gone too long if you fail to recognise your own niece. That was Taya, and shame on you." She waved her index finger as she scolded him lightly. Rob felt his stomach knot and his shoulders slump as her mention of the young lady's name brought a flood of remembrance.

"Taya Ethelyn, as I live and breathe. But she was just a—" he gestured the height of a child. "My word, Sunni, have I really been gone so long a girl could become a woman?" Sunniva was unable to ignore the self-depreciating tone of his voice. She reached out gently stroking his arm as his gaze returned to the door.

25

His mind filled with memories of the sickly child his sister had raised as if she were her own. But the woman he had met seemed far older than such memories would allow. Then again, he knew her life had been anything but easy. He scratched his chin in contemplation. He had stopped seeing his niece as a Méros-Génos long ago, but the sight of her in adulthood had come as a surprise. So much so he had been unable to recognise her.

"Sadly yes. It has been a long time since last you graced us with your presence, Brother. Last I recall you departed for Oureas' Rest, hoping for news. We haven't seen you since..." Sunniva's tone, like her eyelids, lowered with regret before her words trailed off into silence. She knew better than to bring up a past her brother so clearly still fought with. These tragic events were the reason he had distanced himself from these walls.

Even after all this time it seemed he was still unable to forgive himself, or perhaps he blamed her. Why else would he willingly keep so much distance between them? He had been distant for some time, but she knew her actions were as much to blame for their estrangement as his were. There had been times when she had seen him approach her door, but never had she opened it to welcome him. She had simply let him leave. There was part of her, in earnest, that understood his grief and willingly accepted the burden of his blame. He had sacrificed so much for her as they grew. His commitment to her had seen she could meet the required donations needed to train at the Acropolis. If not for him, she would have been unable to accept the destiny fate had placed before her.

"Six years," Rob's voice once again reduced to a whisper as he realised exactly how long had gone by. His fingers instinctively sunk deep within his jacket pocket, brushing the cool metal of the small object within. Its texture upon his flesh brought him both comfort and distress. "It seems like only yesterday," he reflected, quickly removing his hand from his jerkin as the dull flame of anger began to burn within the pit of his stomach. Six years. It had been six years and still he was no closer to finding what he sought.

Each month he risked life and limb on the whim of nobles, and not once had he even found the slightest indication he was close. Six years, wasted. He felt his nails digging into the calloused flesh of his palms, his fist tightening slightly before he forced his hands to relax. "That would make Ethelyn what, twenty now?" He forced his mind away from his previous thoughts. They were dangerous, especially if fed. He needed to stay calm. Think and plan. The answer was waiting for him, he just hadn't come across the right person or rumour yet. There was still time. As long as he drew breath there was still time to make amends.

Rob avoided Sunniva's concerned glance, taking the opportunity to divert his attention towards his backpack. He rummaged through its contents, focusing anywhere but on her.

"There about. It's hard to say for certain, she was so young when she was left at the door." Rob nodded slightly, he remembered the day well. His sister had been little more than a child herself when she became responsible for this temple, and Taya had been left at her door soon after.

"Is she staying with you then?" Sunniva knew exactly what her brother was asking. She ran an orphanage, and the children housed were expected to be self-sufficient by the age of seventeen. She would often help them find work their skills were suited for, and failing that, see them to Albeth Castle. Oureas' Rest was always grateful for labourers, and provided food and shelter for those who aided them. But Taya would not be welcomed in such a place. Whilst the Méros-Génos were accepted within their borders, they would not see her as such. She would be viewed as a monster, a threat.

"The situation with Taya is difficult. I think of her as my own and she is family to both of us. I raised her from an infant, how could she be anything else? I think of her as my own. Besides, even if I were to find somewhere willing to overlook her obvious disadvantage, how long do you think they would continue to tolerate her presence when her hallucinations returned? Most are not equipped to deal with one touched by the Maniae." Sunniva gave a heavy sigh. "I truly thought we were about to begin a new era, that at least some good would come from the devastation.

"I thought we would build a new world on the ashes of the old. A world where Demies and humans could unite. They worked together so well to rebuild after the Severaine. They stood united, shoulder to shoulder. How quickly the banner of unity was burnt when difference once more became the focal point. It seems relationships cannot be reforged as easily as iron and timber can."

"You're wrong. So many have willingly embraced the Méros-Génos. There are still extremes, and they fall to both sides. Unfortunately this island is one of them," Rob lamented, shaking his head slightly as he spoke.

"I honestly don't feel she would fare well. The people in this area alone show so little tolerance. Given the chance, they would see her drawn and quartered before suffering her presence. Mothers scream at the sight of her, the young seek shelter behind the closest adult, and those are the more tolerant of attitudes." Sunniva glanced towards the door as she bit her lower lip. She could imagine Taya stood just on its other side, listening to their every word, probing their conversation for evidence of lies.

The precursors to a relapse had been evident for some time now, and her paranoia was unquestionable. The traders' market had come at an opportune moment. It allowed Sunniva the time she needed to try to quell the rising storm, but Rob's arrival here, as wonderful as it was, had only served to worsen things.

There would soon be little choice but to have her returned to *that* place. They could work the miracles she could not. She was but one person. Her ability to repress the unwanted thoughts was limited, but her stay with them was not yet due. She had to endure. She had to pray for the strength to hold the Maniae at bay a little longer. The safety of everyone under this roof depended on it.

"It must be difficult, for both of you," Rob acknowledged softly, his fingers seizing the item he had been searching for within the backpack. He presented the pouch to Sunniva with a smile less joyful than that he had managed before being reminded of the burden his sister bore.

Sunniva opened the draw string slowly and marvelled at the small figurine within. The pearl figurine was delicate and beautiful. The crafter had paid so much attention to detail that she could almost see the moon's reflection in the wolf's eyes. It sat in a baying position. Its pose indicative of once being part of a larger display, one no doubt involving Selene, as this was clearly intended to represent her wolf. "I retrieved this from one of my adventures. I thought it would be more at home in a temple than gathering dust on a collector's shelf."

"It's remarkable. We'll keep it safe. Thank you, Brother." He gave a dismissive shrug as if to imply she should think nothing of his gesture. If she was aware of what he had endured to obtain it, he would be more likely the recipient of another scolding rather than the gratitude she currently offered.

"You can always sell it on if you find yourself in hardship. Such things fetch a good price on the market. On that note, I've added my donation to the box out front. It's overdue, like my visit. I'll stop by again once I've completed my current errand at the Plexus. I'm really proud of you, what you do for these children is remarkable." He encouraged the conversation to a point where his departure would be accepted, knowing if he didn't he could easily lose the day in her company and both of them had things they needed to attend to. He felt so at ease in her presence he questioned why he had postponed his visit for so long.

"Thank you, Brother, you have no idea what it means to me." She placed her hand on his, squeezing it gently before he turned to leave.

"Well, it grows late and I still have to report to the Plexus. Since there's the market in Estarc I'm best heading to Riverside Quay." He began to walk away, raising his hand in a parting gesture at the door. "I'll stop by again before I leave," he reaffirmed before pulling the door closed behind him.

After Rob had left, Sunniva lowered herself to her knees before Artemis, closing her eyes in silent prayer as she tried to gather her strength. Her conversation with her brother had exhausted her more than she had expected. So much had changed since last they spoke and it was essential he remained unaware of all of it. She was not in a position to answer his questions, and so, she had guided their conversation. In return she had been reminded of exactly how precarious the situation with Taya had become. Her next appointment at Mirage Lake was not scheduled for over a month, and despite her needs the escorts were unable to retrieve her any earlier. Perhaps, with her brother's arrival, there was another option. Assuming he stayed long enough.

Sunniva tried to force her mind into a state of calm, and allow feelings of peace and tranquillity to wash over her. A task made almost impossible by her awareness of Taya's presence near the threshold of this sacred space. Sunniva's training at the Acropolis had gone beyond that of those normally chosen by the Gods. She had been designated to a special purpose, and as such had been given her own private blessing. She had been privilege to insights others remained oblivious to and central to all was Taya.

The oppression of Taya's presence made recovering from her exhaustion more difficult. It left her weaker, and thus diluted her own attempts at treating her. In turn this resulted in Taya's unwanted behaviour gaining dominance. It was a vicious cycle, and one which often resulted in injury.

On more than one occasion Taya had nearly been successful in taking Sunniva's life, and would have been, if not for the intervention of those living within Elpída. They knew the dangers. Those within this temple had been carefully chosen to help with not only its normal operations, but the extra burden of Taya's condition.

Closing her eyes again she tried to find the recharging energy of peace, but instead found only silence. A silence which only served to remind her she was alone with Taya. For that brief moment, instead of the confidence and strength she felt just moments before Rob's visit, she felt only fear.

Chapter 2

The Plexus

Riverside Quay had once been a thoroughfare. Owing to the port's location a small tavern had been constructed by the roadside when trade agreements between Estarc, Albeth, and Therascia had been finalised. The subtle greasing of palms saw the boats docked only at twilight, and travellers were ushered towards the tavern, the sole resting place before the long journey to the city. It had stood two stories tall, a beacon offering shelter to all, and turning profits into expansion.

Over the years the tavern grew to twice its height and size, offering games where coin could be gambled away on the wings of luck. But those seeing the fruits of this labour sought to turn their own hand to profiteering. There was no ownership of the land surrounding the inn, and soon traders established small ramshackle huts and offered games of chance, rumbustious encounters, and more, to those willing to pay. Gamblers' dens and houses of iniquity snaked through the surrounding area. The more sordid of which were often hidden behind the facade of honest trade.

Merchants arrived, preying on those of good fortune or high spirits, setting up their own trading posts to complete the maze of temptation and sundries. When the Plexus was finally requested to bring order, what had once been a simple roadside inn had become a town.

Riverside Quay, inheriting its name from the founding inn, soon became the second largest town on the island of Livingstone, and was second only to Estarc. While Estarc was more of an esteemed trading town, specialising in raw materials, crafts, and tradesmen, Riverside Quay blossomed into the gathering place of merchants.

The Lords of Livingstone, seeing the rapid and unsavoury expansion, enforced a boundary by acquiring the surrounding domain. When the lack of unclaimed land denied further expansion, prospectors employed frames and platforms to support haphazard constructions in place; elevating their own establishments above their competition in bizarre and curious fashions. Seemingly dangerous wooden walkways linked the structures, creating a second town interlinked with one below. With space now a rare commodity people burrowed beneath the ground, employing the skills of local miners to create subterranean dens and parlours.

The streets heaved with mercantile presence. Those not possessing stores pushed carts through the busy streets. Often lingering before the more affluent traders in hope to tempt a passerby before being forcibly moved, by members of the Plexus, to the market square, where all the carts should gather.

The inn remained larger and more majestic than any other building, the central feature of an intricate web. There was a perplexing, chaotic order to the town, but the enforcement of laws was without reprieve, and there was but one punishment. Those causing disorder, or owing an unpayable debt, were sent to Estarc to perform hard labours in the mines or refinery, until all obligations had been settled in full.

As Rob reached the town he was greeted by a few vaguely familiar faces. The Hunters' Plexus here offered the island some measure of security. They donned the robes of law enforcement and possessed a more obvious presence in time of high business, such as that brought by the traders' market. Whilst hosted in the neighbouring city the whole island benefited from such events, more noticeably, the inns and taverns.

The sun hung low in the sky, casting elongated shadows across the land and bringing premature darkness to the lower streets before the skies above grew black. Visible to those still strolling the higher tiers, the light's final glow sent hues of red, crimson, and purple across the darkening sky in a brilliant display.

Rob took a deep breath of the cool air, the scent of roasting meat stirring his hunger. Light began to illuminate the streets, drawing the eye to places whose business thrived in the darkened hours. Merriment and laughter filled the night chorus as proprietors closed their shops for the evening, fending off the last minute bargain-hunters who tried to barter a lower price for perishing wares.

Briskly Rob side-stepped a young couple who were lost in flirtatious conversation, seemingly unaware of his presence as they continued their unbroken stride without even a passing glance in his direction. The creaking groan of a cart drew his attention. The young merchant hid within the shadows. Covering himself and his wares with a dark tarpaulin, he concealed himself within an alcove in the hope of remaining undetected until first light, when he could once again ply his trade.

This town attracted those from all walks of life, the rich, and the poor. Those not living or granted lodgings within the borders were removed as last orders were called, with no heed or quarter granted for weather or distance. Most traders were not fortunate enough to be able to cover the cost of residing here, and found themselves evicted without mercy. Unless, as this young merchant hoped to, they evaded the sight of the Plexus.

The brilliant, blue light emitted from a cylinder caught Rob's attention. It moved through the crowds, clutched within the hands of a middle-aged man, bathing him in a luminescent aura as he made his slow, ritualistic progression through the street. Halting frequently, he would raise the cylinder, the act releasing a small orb of light from within. Rob monitored its path, watching in silent appreciation as it snaked upwards before finding its home within one of the many lanterns to bathe the surrounding area in its cool glow. Once the orb had found its resting place his progression continued, stopping at each lantern or light-well.

Rob nodded politely as the figure stepped past him. The Bearer of Dynamism was an important and respected role. The Research Plexus had taught select few how to maintain the energy the town would need. There was much to the process. It involved the accurate alteration of reception devices, as well as the gathering and distribution of energy.

Their final task of the night was the lighting of the town's lanterns. A true master of their role had collected enough energy throughout the day to see this task empty the final cylinder, without waste or excess. From Rob's estimation, the fair-haired man was well-practised in such things. Not that any would be wasted if they had generated an excess, anything left unused would be stored for the next day, but the Plexus was said to offer incentives for those showing efficiency.

His familiarity with this town afforded Rob a certain knowledge, such as the places often forgotten by those passing through. Whenever he found himself here, he would follow the dark winding passages to an inn hidden beneath supports and shadows. Even during the busiest times the environment always adhered to a certain clientele, hunters and seasoned travellers.

To Rob, there was a beacon which betrayed its nature. Lost within the velvety shades it could still be easily identified by the small collection of merchants standing sentry near its doors. Rob often referred to such a gathering as a con of merchants.

Whilst seeming to work independently, haggling and counter offering their competition, they were all part of the same association. Their act ensured they got the best deal, rather than lose a sale. Buyers deeming the wares too expensive would be tempted by a rival's counter offer, believing it to be a bargain. A similar method was employed for the purchase of goods, ensuring they could be resold for a generous profit. A merchant recognised members of the Hunters' Plexus as easily as most people recognised an Elementalist. Hunters were easy prey. They sought to lighten their load as quickly as possible before moving on to their next quarry.

Rob took a slight step backwards as he found himself flanked by the merchants. Each cast their hungry gaze over him, mentally probing his pockets as if they could see the spoils within. There was almost a look of disappointment as he carefully unwrapped the leather cloth he had removed from his jerkin, to reveal an ornate dagger and a silver ring.

He felt their gaze burning into his breast pocket, as if the green jewel he had risked his very life for called to them. They anticipated his presence greatly.

He had been known to bring back items which provoked a physical response from even their most senior members. If nothing else, they knew he always had something for them.

Whilst he rarely stopped to gather treasures and trinkets he almost never passed by a weapon. With the uncertainty and dangers of The Depths of Acheron, being prepared could be the difference between life and death. The items he found were often small and well-forged, worth a few coin to any willing to part with them. There was little he retrieved he wouldn't part with, but on occasions, when he would find a familiar hilt or crest, he would return them to the Plexus to be passed along to the next of kin.

With his business concluded he pushed open the plain wooden door, leaving the merchants behind in the cool night air. The atmosphere within was alive with chatter, a stark contrast to what would have been discovered the previous night.

The full moon brought with it tidings of woe. People flocked in crowds, praying that numbers alone would ensure their safety. Parents slept huddled in the room beside their terrified children. Neighbours slept with neighbours and, despite the sheer volumes of empty abodes, even the bravest of criminals rarely strayed from their clan. Unrest had settled throughout the land. Once they had been safe from danger, yet now a terror stalked their plane, drawn into their world by the moon's own grace. The Goddess Selene, solitary in nature, now granted passage for unspeakable things to prey on those who, like her, thrived in isolation.

Fables had once warned children not to stray after dark, and now this truth made them fear even the moon's once comforting light. The Severaine had brought with it a new order, a new cause to fear. Those taken were lost. Hunters had once infiltrated The Depths of Acheron in force, hoping to rescue the abducted and stem the corruption of all that was good. Of thirty men just two returned, such was the horror of the darkened kingdoms. Knowing its terrors, none but fools would seek to enter.

Rob shuffled through the crowd. Regulars—recognising the hunter from the many solitary hours he had passed within these walls—parted, allowing him to approach the bar unhindered. His familiar tankard was waiting. The amber shade was somewhat paler than usual, a clear indication of the barkeep's intention to stretch his stock further during these busy hours. With a long exhale, Rob moved to lean with his back against the bar, his bottom perched on the edge of the stool as he surveyed the room.

The roar of laughter and the raised tones of heated debate echoed throughout his tired mind. There was still time to complete his task before the Plexus closed its doors, but he knew the moment his fatigued legs had carried him across this threshold he would not stray from the tavern for some time. One ale would be followed by several more, perhaps more than normal given its weakened state. It would do little to relieve the fatigue which weighed on both his body and mind. He had survived once more, yet he had still achieved nothing. Raising his hand to his breast pocket he reflected on the complete insignificance of it all.

Rob swilled the warm ale around his mouth, clicking his tongue with slight disgust at the diluted flavour. A small crowd had started to gather around a young man, his shrill tone filled with excitement. Placing his tankard down he signalled to the barkeep, before approaching the gathering mob. There were rare few occasions people attracted such attention. Those recipient to such a gathering were either brilliant, or fools.

The young man flicked his hair from his sparkling eyes, before he unrolled a parchment on the ale soaked table before him. The stale fluid caused small segments of the ink to smudge. Rob heard him speak, his tones now showing a calm anticipation as he spoke of the labour he sought in order to pursue the treasure detailed on the map. His finger prodded the parchment as he explained his intensive plan.

Moving closer Rob felt the quiet chuckle leave his throat and, catching the barkeep's eye again, gestured for another drink to be placed beside his own. He saw the proprietor cringe slightly as he nodded.

"Now that is impressive," Rob grinned to himself. He heard the quiet murmurs of awe as he approached to place his hand on the young man's shoulder. Rob's reputation of surviving The Depths of Acheron had earned him respect. Much to his frustration his trials below had not gone unmentioned, but few dared to broach such matters. Often he was left alone, hearing the whispers of speculation that he sought to rescue someone from within. He let them gossip. He didn't really care as long as they kept their distance. But on occasions such as these he was happy to shed his solitude. "I've heard tales of these ruins, of the treasures within."

Seeing his approach an older man moved as if to stand, prepared to offer his seat to the hunter. The respectful gesture was stilled by a raise of Rob's hand as he continued talking. "I can see you've put much thought into your retrieval of the relics." Rob fought back the smile which caused the edge of his lips to twitch slightly. He knew full-well this treasure had already been claimed and relocated. "Tell me, what are your plans for passing the sentries?"

"Sentries?" The young man questioned in amazement, once more inspecting the map. He knew he would require labour to dig down to the ruined shrine, but he had not imagined any safeguards to still be in place. "What kind of sentries are we talking about?" The man frowned.

"From my understanding the security is immense. I have to say, there have been several attempts to do what you are suggesting, and all have met with failure." Rob shook his head slightly. "You do realise that parchment won't help you right? It doesn't grant you any legal ownership."

"But if I claim it—"

"You can try. The thing is, if they let anyone possessing a treasure map enter the museum and stake a claim they'd soon have an empty building, wouldn't they?"

"Museum, no I—" he gestured towards the map, his face clouded with confusion.

"Yes, you *are* talking about a heist, right?" Rob grinned.

"What? No I—oh." Rob saw the alarm on the man's face become disappointment. He patted him on the back in a consolatory fashion before he approached the bar collecting his tankard and the additional glass.

"I guess the only one lining their pockets tonight is the merchant. Sorry, lad, but he saw you coming." Rob placed the drink before the disillusioned youth. He took a long sorrowful gulp as he tried to conjure an explanation to give his wife about where this week's wage had gone. He slammed his hand onto the table, scrunching the parchment into a ball.

"Looks like I'm sleeping on the floor tonight. If the wife even lets me in that is. Ah well." He rose to his feet, thinking it better to excuse himself now.

"Here." Rob approached the bar, pulling a few of the flowers from one of the displays under the scrutiny of the frowning barkeep, despite the fact he knew he would be compensated later. "It'll soften the blow."

"You know, one day someone really will be planning a heist." The barkeep smiled refilling Rob's tankard as he relaxed once more in his familiar seat.

"Not that one, he's a good lad. I didn't want to see him chasing debt." Rob knew all too well how some of the less than savoury merchants operated. They sold a dream and offered to finance it. They'd supply tools and labour at no upfront cost in exchange for a signature on a loan agreement. But when they reached their destination, no fortune or glory awaited, only debt.

The treasures had long been plundered, but the dreamer still had to find the means to pay for services rendered. The merchant would reclaim their loaned equipment and, since the would-be adventurer had no means to repay the contracted amount, they were sent to the mines. Their labour became extra coin in the hands of the loan trader. It was a longstanding, underhanded operation. But as soon as the contract was signed it was impossible to renege on the agreed terms.

* * *

As the first ray of light fought its way over the horizon Rob was already walking the streets. Traders began to cross the borders, tired from their long walk from the neighbouring villages. Quiet conversations were carried on the wind, the lowered tones almost appearing considerate to those who still slept.

The paling light of Dynamism was starting to fade. Its cool light slowly extinguishing as the wind, warmed slightly by the sun's first breath, dispelled its fading remnants. Darkness still chased beneath the twisted structures, hiding in corners to become shadows as the sun rose higher. Few paused to witness the final disappearance of energy, the turning of night into day, but Rob was one amongst them. Another night had passed, another day born. He shrugged to himself, hunching his shoulders against the still cool wind, and listened as the slow creaks and groans of timber became drowned out with the sound of life.

He had stayed at the tavern until last orders, retiring to his room with a bottle of spirits. The merriment of intoxication was a stranger to him now, no matter how often he tried to recall its numb embrace. He had waited until dawn stirred on the distant horizon.

He never slept well the night following his return. At first it had been the terror of what he had seen haunting his mind. Over the years such things had become more like figments of a nightmare, recalled in part, but not dwelt upon for any time. Something else caused his sleep that night to be fitful. The disappointment of further failure, and the growing pit of hatred that came with each unrewarded return.

Given there were so few who would venture into The Depths of Acheron, Rob often found his services in high demand. He—or more specifically the hunter named Aeolos—would today receive an influx of requests ranging from the pleas to find a loved one, to the materialistic demand for something of value. The latter were the quests he would often accept.

He ventured into The Depths of Acheron each month, so long as it was of benefit to him. He would research that which piqued his interest, and gather what little information he could before agreeing to a contract.

His clientele all had one thing in common, a knowledge of The Depths of Acheron beyond what they should possess. They knew of events, unearthing of treasures, and their insights into such things intrigued him. But none seemed willing to reveal their sources, and yet, each request so far had proven suspiciously fruitful. He had learnt a long time ago asking questions of their inexplicable knowledge served no purpose. The nobles were not forthcoming in the sharing of information, but occasionally, in excitable states, they had revealed the slightest hints of rituals and madness.

"Hey there, I've not seen you around for some time," hailed the gruff, familiar voice of the Plexus master as Rob pushed the door open to reveal the strangely busy room. The man behind the counter was not exactly what people had come to expect from one in such a role. He was a stocky, old man, with the broad shoulders of a lumberjack. His salt and pepper hair was short with unruly curls trying to make their appearance. His beard and moustache were kept short and tidy to frame his slightly rounding jaw line.

This man, in his time, had been one of the best hunters known. He had ranked second on the tables in the year of his retirement which, by some strange coincidence, was the same year Theron, who had been in the lead that year, had hung up his weapons.

The point system operated by the Plexus was originally designed to ensure those lacking the necessary skills could not be assigned work surpassing their abilities, but had soon become the means to host a friendly competition within their ranks. Each year those ranking first, second, and third within their field would receive a Plexus Star. It was a widely recognised decoration which, for the entirety of the year, afforded the bearer certain benefits. These included a small discount from merchants and craftsmen, as well as first refusal on high paid work.

Each year the star was of different design, and even once their year of glory had finished, it was a respected medal of honour. The points for any given job were determined by the Plexus master, based on the difficulty and danger. The higher the value the more difficult the task.

In the beginning the Hunters' Plexus had not been divided into subclasses. As time moved on, and the world changed, there became a clear divide between the types of requests passing through their doors. There were those who requested hunters to find or retrieve treasure, and those who sought wanted criminals. Thus the subclasses were born in order to create a more balanced reward structure, where each class had their own table.

"Hey." Rob raised his hand returning the greeting with a polite smile. Before lowering his hand he made an effort to brush the longer parts of his sandy-brown hair behind his ears. His hair, which was normally well-kempt and short, now looked a little on the untamed side. Not that such a look deterred the passing gaze of any woman. He was devilishly handsome, and even with little attention to his appearance somehow he seemed to pass from clean cut to rugged. He could apparently look clean, rugged, or dangerous but never, it seemed, scruffy or messy. Not that he himself put much stock in his looks, but he did appreciate other people noticing him.

Rob paused his approach to the counter, his sight passing down the volume of wanted posters which now lined the wooden walls. The last time he had visited this particular Plexus the pictures had been but a few. Now it was as if the Plexus master had decided to conceal any evidence of the wooden structure below.

"Thinking of switching to real work?" a voice challenged. The man was easily seven foot in height, with the stocky frame most hunters would covet. The figure's hair was tied at the nape of his neck in a scruffy, grey-brown ponytail. A few of the people paused their browsing to watch with interest.

"Nah, I think I'll stick with what I know." Rob waved his hand in a dismissive, lighthearted gesture. His eyes fixed on the broad back of the large figure who had addressed him.

"Yeah, but I dunna see much for flower arranging here. Then again, nothin's better than part time ay?" the hunter smirked.

"Just count your blessing, if you'd half my skill the Plexus'd already be destitute." The figure's laugh roared like thunder through a mountain range, reverberating through the room. He turned to face Rob, reaching out his thick arm in greeting. A thundering strike resounded as their flesh met in a friendly forearm shake.

"It's been a while, Aeolos. Been quiet without ya." The huge figure guffawed, calling Rob by his Plexus alias, before releasing their greeting. The forearm handshake was used by Plexuses and merchants as a standard greeting. It had replaced the hand-to-hand shake some time ago. After all this gesture made it easy to check for weapons or items concealed in the sleeve, it was easy to break away from, and most importantly it was a clean and idiot-proof display of camaraderie.

"What's it been, Iphios, a year? Of all the places I thought we'd meet I never expected it'd be here." Rob slapped the man on his shoulder a little harder than necessary.

"Well everyone says the Iereía of Elpída is something else. She's as succulent as honey, hair like gold, and a body," Iphios paused making an hourglass gesture with his hands accompanied by an appreciative 'mm-mm,' sound. "A body that should in rights belong to a goddess. She's a real bellibone. Maybe you should take a look. Just a glance was enough to recharge my battery... now what was her name?" He mulled it over as he scratched his chin. The sound of his nails meeting stubble grated like sandpaper.

"Sunniva?" Rob questioned with raised eyebrows as a bemused expression crossed his face.

"That's it!" He waved his index finger at him frantically, as if just hearing her name unleashed excitement. "So you've met her?"

"She's my sister," he retorted bluntly, his brows knitting together.

"Flosh." He gestured dismissively looking at Rob carefully for any sign he was teasing. There was none. The hunter gave a hearty laugh and slapped Rob on the shoulder hard enough to push him to the side. "Ya joking right?" Rob shook his head maintaining eye contact with Iphios. The burly figure stepped back slightly to regard him critically before shaking his head. "Nope, sorry, I can't see it. She obviously got the looks, the smarts and, well, just about everything." He roared in laughter, his huge frame shaking.

"Now, that's not what your daughter said if I remember correctly," Rob teased, invoking another hearty laugh from the man.

"Daughter? I've a fine-looking lad, bit of a pretty boy. Don't tell me yer the one who got away," he chuckled.

"Hmm, I guess I should've found the stubble suspect." Rob shrugged grinning lightheartedly.

"Ha, stubble, that'll be the day. Anyway, I'm on my way to Therascia, how 'bout ya?" he questioned brandishing a small parchment before Rob's face.

"I think I'll be resting up for a few weeks, you know, until the next full moon."

"Ya wanna be careful, ya'll earn yaself a reputation." Iphios smiled reaching out for the door.

"I already have, haven't you heard? I'm the best." Rob smirked playfully, approaching to give the figure another hearty slap on the back, one which sent searing burning pains through his hand but did little to move the great weight.

"Ya'll never fill my shoes." He gave a deep throaty chuckle.

"I don't know, three more, and I have beaten your record, shame you chose to turn bounty hunter on me, you were my only real bit of competition."

"Between ya and me Aeolos, there was no competition," he retorted.

"Yeah, I suppose you're right. You've long past your prime, I still have my youthful spring."

"And childlike wit. Besides, did ya not hear? A month ago I seized the Opik Blue." His hand pulled open the door as he turned back to face Rob, making no attempt to conceal his beaming grin. A grin which only broadened to see the look of utter bewilderment on Rob's face. He turned back towards the door, raising his hand in a parting gesture.

"What?" Rob almost choked in dismay. The shock of the news striking him with more strength than any of their friendly exchanges. Rob swore he could hear the hunter's rumbling chuckles as the door swung closed behind him. "Is it true?" Rob demanded spinning to address the Plexus master, shock still lining his features.

"Afraid so," he answered with a smile and tone contrary to the expected apologetic mannerisms of one delivering such devastating news. In fact, the Plexus master was smiling so intently that each of his wrinkles had become visible and his moustache threatened to meet his eyebrows. "One of his marks had it in their possession."

"Of all the dumb luck!" Rob exclaimed before giving a hearty sigh. He tossed a small pouch on to the counter. Attached to it was the Plexus emblem that most in their service wore, with pride, as a badge. "I guess I better cash this in and see what you've got. Dirty cheat, I thought he'd given up on the treasure hunting," he chuntered in good humour.

Rob searched through his pockets before finding the parchment with his most recent request. He slid the paper across the desk as the Plexus master tipped the green stone from the pouch. His brow wrinkled slightly as he studied the writing from the latest missive before taking both the parchment and jewel into the rear area for verification.

The Plexuses possessed the ability to communicate across vast distances. Their operation, in some ways, was similar to how seasoned Elementalists had described the silent exchange between trees. These scholars of nature had spoken of a fungus, buried deep within the soil, creating a network which was used to communicate, and even pass nutrients, to others. Similarly the Plexus had some undisclosed method of communication, one which was thought to connect to some form of repository where impressions of all Plexus members were preserved.

Even Rob, who had known things in operation beyond the understanding of this time, could not fathom how it worked. He, like any other hunter, would simply present his emblem, and leave the rest to the Plexus master.

When the Plexus master reappeared the pouch held in his possession seemed considerably heavier.

"Everything seemed to be in order. It'll reach them no later than this afternoon. We've added the completion to the records." Rob gave a slight smile as he slipped some of the payment into a secondary pouch concealed within his inner jacket pocket.

"Was there anything new for me?" he prompted, leaning forward on the counter. He bit his lip slightly, anticipating a reply, while wondering the best way to regain his lead.

"Demon Marauder?" The Plexus master gave a hearty chuckle. One which became a full-blown laugh when he saw the horrified expression on Rob's face.

"No!" Rob grimaced, the disgust in his voice apparent. Plexuses, unlike most businesses, never exchanged personal names. When someone entered their service, and passed the trials needed to earn the emblem, the Plexus assigned them a generic name. One usually fitting to their skills and talents. As they found their expertise their aliases sometimes changed to reflect their calling. No two Plexus names were ever the same, and on occasion people were dubbed with terrible titles such as the one the Plexus master had just uttered.

"Demon Marauder, really?" Rob questioned, wiping his hand down his face in an attempt to conceal his frustration. "Why, when did they change it?"

"They haven't, yet." The Plexus master roared in amusement. He knew this young man would be good for a chuckle or two.

"Thank the Gods, don't do that to me old man. I thought you were serious." Rob, despite the frown meant to reinforce his words, failed to hide the relief. He liked his current name, Aeolos, meaning quick moving. It had a nice ring to it, and he wore it well.

"Well, from what I've seen they're reorganising things. It's only a matter of time looking at the requests you've been taking." He shook his head, his eyes still sparkling with amusement.

"They wouldn't would they? Not to something like Demon Marauder. Would they?" he prompted again when he met with no response.

"Unlikely, something like that would be no better than assassin hunter Victor. An alias like that is just asking for trouble. But he did insist on naming himself." Hearing the name Rob heard himself tutting, feeling the slow shaking of his head which accompanied the noise.

"I heard about him, poor fool."

"There were rumours of an investigation. They still don't know how he managed to pass the trials. He may have been broad and strong, but we all know he was skating on the wrong side of the ice. That's what got him killed." The Plexus master shook his head.

"Enough on such things, pass me your insignia, I'll go check."

Every Plexus member, regardless of which branch they were aligned to, was presented with their Plexuses' emblem. Most saw it as a symbol of honour, a means to announce to any who looked that they were of the Plexus. But it served another purpose. In the hands of a Plexus master, by way of sacred and shielded ritual, it called upon the reflection of its owner, allowing them to confirm the member was who they claimed, and pair them with any assignments currently held. It was a functional tool, but given the difficulty of the trials it was also a symbol of great accomplishment. It was for this reason most chose to display theirs with pride. But Rob's badge weighed heavily. It was nothing more than a painful, unrelinquishable burden.

As Rob waited, he became aware of the silence. All the noise associated with everyday life, the traders readying their wagons, the sellers preparing their wares, even the early morning shoppers, had fallen abruptly still. This eerie quiet lasted for easily a minute, perhaps two. It was always hard to tell in such prolonged unnatural moments. Then, without warning, sound returned; the volume seemed almost deafening as one noise was indistinguishable from another. The only clarity to it was the tone of hatred.

It took Rob a moment or two to decide to investigate. Given the hostile tones it appeared someone had become recipient to the town's malice, and no one within the Plexus—who all seemed content to observe from the windows—made any attempt to intervene.

* * *

Taya dismounted her steed. The chestnut stallion whinnied, complaining as she secured the reins with a quickly executed clove hitch to one of the posts. There were only a few horses and mules secured in such a manner. Merchants, and those spending prolonged time at Riverside Quay, were required to pay for stabling in order to leave the hitching posts solely for the use of quick business, which Taya was certain this would be.

The complex maze of streets and buildings loomed before her. She pressed her lips together tightly as she beheld the towering monstrosities stretching on rickety walkways. She had reconsidered entering countless times. Wondering whether she should proceed, or simply return to Elpída before anyone realised she was missing. The weight of the parchment in her pocket reminded her of her task. If she could prove to Sunniva she could be trusted, perhaps they would see how hard she tried to conform to their needs.

Steeling herself slightly, Taya crossed the boundary, marked by a worn, two rail, post fence. The shadows of the taller structures bathed her in imposing darkness, sending goose-pimples chasing across her flesh. She felt herself duck slightly as she passed under the first walkway, despite it standing far higher than any pedestrian.

Her cheeks flushed with colour as her presence attracted strange looks and curbed whispers. Glancing behind her she was almost certain she was being followed. Swallowing, she lowered her head towards the uneven ground, aware how most of the world viewed 'her kind'.

Pain shot through her wrist as a calloused hand reached out from the shadows. It grabbed her with such force it wrenched her arm back, causing her to spin to face the rosy cheeks of a drunken man. His breath reeked of stale ale, his grip tightening further as she tried to pull away.

"You're a long way from home harpy," he slurred. "It's like you're begging for trouble. You know what they'll do if they catch ya." He released her from his grasp, sending her staggering backward a few paces. Regaining her balance she turned, quickening her stride, her gaze flickering backwards towards the dark figure as she retreated. Turning the corner she caught her breath, pressing her back firmly against the wall. Her right thumb and index fingers tugging gently as they turned and traced the ring on her left hand in a habitual movement she displayed whenever she felt anxious.

Passerbys slowed their pace to cast disgusted looks in her direction, but not all of them continued on their way. Some stopped to stare, whispering behind raised hands as they studied the harpy.

"Your kind aren't welcome here, scat!" hissed a female voice from the gathering crowd.

"It's too late for that. It's not the first time she's entered these borders." A tall figure made his way forward. "Who knows what she's doing here, she could be hunting for children, or sowing foul seeds. If we let her leave unharmed what message does that send? How long before she returns with her sisters and snatches your children from their beds?"

The gathering stood a little straighter, paying attention to his words, his resounding voice causing others to stop and listen. "No, she needs to be taught a lesson. Her kind are not, and will never be, allowed to walk these streets." A small cheer rose from some of the groups, chorused by a small applause. "You've all heard the tales, children and babies snatched from the arms of loving parents. Whisked away only to be found desecrated while the parents are blamed.

"They are evil creatures, and I say we take a stand, here and now, let us cast a clear message to the world. The island of Livingstone will *never* welcome evil." A louder cheer rose up. Mothers gathered their children closer, some with the foresight to retreat from the crowd.

Taya moved slowly, trying to make herself small against the shadows as she edged along the building, hoping to reach the corner and make her escape. The figure lashed out, coiling his hand around her hair, dragging her before him and casting her towards the ground. She scrabbled in the dust, trying to pull herself up. Her attempt meeting with a solid strike to her back from the figure's heavy boot. He pressed down on her spine, fixing her in place. "For too long have we tolerated this creature. She befouls our temple, taints the air we breathe. We must do what our honourable Sunniva could never. We must rid ourselves of this tiresome burden." Cheers met his words this time, his foot shifting from her back to force her face back to the ground.

"I hear their kind don't feel pain like us," boomed a deep voice.

"It's true." He grabbed Taya's hair once more, dragging her to her knees before him. "There's only one true way to cleanse the spirit of its evil." He produced a blade from its sheath, pulling her hair until her neck was exposed. Tears streaked her panic-stricken face. "Decapitation, would do little more than kill the body, and fire could carry her evil to safety so it may return." He released her again. "We must unite. Ensure her tainted form is cleansed through the punishment of pain. Such is the only way to ensure her befouled spirit finds peace and never returns.

"There is but one method I know, I speak of course of lapidation." Excited murmurs echoed through the crowd. Those captivated by his speech already searched the ground, securing stones and pebbles, some even prising them from beneath the ground. Small round objects were passed forward, as if someone had stood in wait, ready to supply the need.

The advocate stepped aside, raising his hand, readying his followers. With a single gesture they released their projectiles, leaving him free to vanish within the crowd to watch in satisfaction as another tainted life was cleansed. He relished in each of the rising cheers which signified a projectile had struck its mark.

* * *

Rob forced his way through the unruly crowd. Those recognising him quickly shuffled aside as murmurs of the Plexus' interference passed between them. He reached out, grasping a hand, applying enough pressure to see the woman drop the stone to the ground. His angry glare alone caused her to retreat into the shadows, her own child clutching the back of her skirt as she fled.

He stepped forward, his hands balled into fists. His jaw was clenched so tightly it was a moment before he could force words through the anger. His nostrils flared as his gaze met with each member of the lingering rabble.

"Leave. Now," he growled through gritted teeth. His hands began to tremble and his fury was a tangible force that caused the crowd to dissipate quickly. But three remained, their hands still grasping the rocks tightly. His cold glare turned towards them, causing two to silently slink away, while the remaining figure stood steadfast.

"You've no right to interfere," The fair-haired man challenged bravely. His hand lowered slightly as he turned to find himself without support. "Their kind are a blight, and like any scourge it needs to be purged."

"You make me sick. What gives you the right?" Rob advanced, the figure faltered slightly. "Does it make you feel strong, attacking a woman?" He gestured towards Taya, who still lay curled upon the ground, her arms protecting her head. "You're not even man enough to make it fair, hiding your face in the crowd."

"Yeah, well, you've no authority over me!" he yelled. He once more glanced over his shoulder, as if to seek support. He released his stone, noticing the approach of two hunters from the Plexus. "Do you know who my father is?"

"He could be a god for all I care. You lost any stature the moment that rock found your hand." Rob grabbed the youth, shoving him towards the others. "Get him out of my sight." They did as they were bid without a word.

Rob watched them lead the youth away, forcing himself to take a long, deep breath, his head almost hanging in shame. He turned his gaze to Taya, who had managed to push herself to her knees, despite a bleeding head wound. She winced, wrapping her arms around her stomach protectively. Tears mingled with blood to streak her face. When Rob extended his hand, she flinched. "Don't judge us all by their prejudice." He forced a softness to his furious tone, offering a weak smile as she accepted his help.

Her balance faltered, causing her to raise a shaking hand to the bleeding wound. Retreating backwards she found the wall at her back and used its strength to support her weight while her head spun. For a moment she thought she saw movement in the distant shadows, but the distortion of her sight made it impossible to be certain. "Here." Rob slid the top from a small silver tin he had taken from his belt. Inside was a ground powder. When she didn't move Rob placed his fingers within, grabbing a pinch of the powder before applying it to the bleeding wound. Taya's eyes scrunched closed in pain, her sharp intake of breath detecting the scent of yarrow and salt. "It's a styptic powder. It'll stop the bleeding. Do you have any—"

"I can take care of myself!" she snapped sidestepping to place some distance between them. She paused for a moment, her fingers interlocking. "I mean, thank you."

"What brought you this way?" Rob questioned, aware that his sister was all too familiar with the attitude of this town towards the Méros-Génos. Their prejudice against Taya surpassed any display he had witnessed, but she too was unlike any Méros-Génos he had seen before.

"The priestesses were in prayer, so I brought this for you myself." Taya placed her hand into the folds of her short cloak, her trembling fingers producing a crumpled parchment. Once rolled and sealed with care it had been crushed flat, the wax breaking away from its damaged edges.

Taya had seen the parchment on the table, and with no one around to prevent her from doing so, she decided to capitalise on a moment of freedom by delivering the message to its intended recipient. By doing so, and returning safely, she could prove to

Sunniva that she didn't need such close observation, and perhaps earn a little more freedom. Although she would be lying if she failed to admit that, once upon the steed, she had considered fleeing, never to return.

Rob extended his hand. No sooner had he touched the parchment Taya released her grasp on it, placing yet more distance between them until she turned her back towards him, retreating quickly towards the town's borders where her horse stood waiting.

Rob looked at the parchment, frowning slightly when he failed to recognise the scrawl which had written his name. He unrolled it carefully, his frown deepening as he turned it over a few times. His eyes narrowed as he scrutinised its surface. The parchment itself, except for his name, was blank. An uneasy feeling began to tighten his chest. The same feeling he had just before things went horribly wrong. Rob glanced behind him, surveying the strangely empty streets. The hairs on the back of his neck rose, someone had been watching them.

* * *

Sunniva was worried. A few of the acolytes flitted about the temple, clearing away after morning prayers, a task normally left for Taya's attention. When Sunniva had sent one of the acolytes to summon her, they had found that she, along with the horse, was no longer on their grounds. Pacing, Sunniva looked pleadingly to the statue, as if beseeching it to talk and impart wisdom. Yet Artemis remained silent, her unaltered features maintaining vigil over the temple.

Enquiries revealed the children had not seen her either, suggesting she left before the cook had prepared breakfast. This did not bode well. Taya knew better than to leave Elpída. But there was more to this restriction than simply her appearance. There were so many reasons she should never leave the grounds, her safety being only one of them.

Forcing her shoulders back to adopt a strong and confident posture, Sunniva approached the window that looked out over the forest and plains surrounding Elpída. She rubbed her shoulders, her sight nervously panned the dirt track, willing for Taya's figure to appear.

By the time the scent of lunch filled the air Sunniva had resorted to pacing again. The clicking of her heels marked each passing second. Doubts and fears haunted her. If Taya failed to return, or if she couldn't be recovered, then Sunniva would be held accountable. This was not a fury she wished to face. She had been charged to watch over Taya, to ensure her condition was managed to the best of her ability. The stakes of losing her were beyond measure, beyond recompense.

Wringing her hands she questioned where Taya would run. The harbour knew better than to offer her passage, and the towns here would show her no favour, but what if she knew of Collateral? There was no telling how far she could run should she enter the travellers' city. If she reached this haven all her work, all her sacrifice, would be for nought. Taya would be lost to them.

Her vision shifted to the door, as if staring at it would see her clerics return. Even now, after so many hours, they still searched for her. But with each prolonged minute the inevitability of her return grew more doubtful. Sunniva scolded her own negligence for becoming too accustomed to the children keeping vigil on Taya. But this morning they had been preoccupied with the preparations for the first day of the harvest. The seasonal crops were ready to be picked and stored. It would have been easy for her to slip away unnoticed. Sunniva heard herself sigh, and once more straightened her posture. She would have to enforce Taya's presence in prayers again, regardless of how uncomfortable it made some of her clerics. That was assuming she returned.

Sunniva's focus snapped towards the door as she heard the hurried footsteps of an approaching figure. Her mind raced with thoughts of the ill-tidings being brought at such a pace. The door flew open to reveal Taya's breathless figure. Her bloodshot eyes and reddened cheeks betraying the shedding of tears. Sunniva breathed a quiet sigh of relief, quickly hurrying to embrace her wayward child. She clutched her tightly, whispering thanks to the Gods for her safe return before finally expressing her relief aloud.

"I'm so glad you're safe," Sunniva breathed, stroking Taya's shoulders lightly taking in her dishevelled appearance. She cupped her face, pausing to assess each of the dark wounds marking her pale skin. She studied the injuries intently. The bleeding from her brow had stilled to form a large scab surrounded by dark, unsightly bruising.

It was clear to Sunniva what had happened. She had seen these types of injury before and had little doubt there would be many such abrasions on her flesh. But she was home now, and the damage seemed superficial. "You look terrible my child. What happened, whatever possessed you to leave without a word?" Sunniva's hands moved to Taya's neck, checking for signs of fever. "You're burning up." Her words caused Taya's body to flush with a sickly heat. "Come, we must get you to bed."

Taya allowed herself to be led; her mind strangely clouded as her vision blurred. She raised her hand to her forehead as a wave of dizziness passed through her. Her fingers traced the throbbing wound. The stones must have struck her harder than she had thought.

"I wanted to help," Taya whispered, struggling to focus her gaze on the floor before her. "There was a letter—" Sunniva guided her to the edge of her bed, gently encouraging her to sit before starting to undress her. Her cool fingers pressed firmly on the bright, angry-looking blemishes which marked Taya's pale skin. Sunniva studied each wound carefully before applying a witch hazel balm. It would heal the bruises. Within days they would have faded completely. She was fortunate there had not been more damage, someone had clearly intervened.

After Sunniva had helped her into her night gown and tended to her injuries, Taya pressed her hands to her forehead, trying to gain some clarity. "What did you ask?" Taya questioned frowning slightly, certain Sunniva had just asked her something. Everything was becoming unclear. The world around her grew faint, dream-like. She heard a strangely familiar voice call her name, causing her to startle. Squeezing her eyes closed several times she attempted to concentrate on Sunniva's words. Each movement caused flushes of heat and nausea to swell within her.

"Come, lie down. Rest, and I'll begin your treatment. You'll soon be feeling better," Sunniva assured, lifting Taya's legs onto the bed after slipping her boots off. Carefully, she tenderly wrapped the covers around her tucking them beneath the mattress firmly.

"I'm sorry I left," she apologised weakly, her eyes growing heavy.

"Left?" Unable to see her face Taya could only hear the confusion in Sunniva's voice as her gentle touch caressed her temples.

"To Riverside Quay," she whispered.

"Oh, my dear, you've not been out," Sunniva cooed.

"But... I thought—"

"Shush now, you're sick. Close your eyes. I'm going to start now, and when you wake you'll feel much better."

Chapter 3

Escape

Taya was unsure how long she had sat staring unseeing into the mirror placed upon the dressing table, but her awareness slowly began to return. Her mind felt sluggish, and her head throbbed. All indications suggested she had received one of Sunniva's more intensive treatments. They were worse on waking. Often she would find herself gaining awareness partway into a morning routine, such as cleaning her teeth, or brushing her hair. Her body responded to any summons on instinct, while her mind remained clouded. She saw she was already dressed, and had a vague recollection of eating before being escorted back to her room.

A figure at the door cleared their throat, reminding her of their long-forgotten presence. It seemed to be time for evening prayers. Since her last treatment Taya had lost the freedom Sunniva's trust afforded. She was now expected to attend each prayer session and, except for the time she spent in isolation within her room, was never unaccompanied.

It took a few moments before Taya's body responded to her demand for it to move. Her limbs felt strangely heavy. She knew part of her body's response was from the dreadful anticipation of what loomed in her future. Treatments only became this intense before Sunniva thought it necessary to send her away. Taya felt the slow tingle of fine hairs as they stood upright upon her flesh, sending an icy chill deep into her core at the thought of returning to Mirage Lake.

In the temple, as Taya knelt with her head bowed to mirror the posture of those in service of the Gods, her mind drifted. She had spent almost the entirety of her life within these walls, and had been raised from infancy by Sunniva to worship her deities. Yet kneeling and praying to these gods seemed wrong, somehow unnatural. She felt no warmth or comfort, no connection to those who ruled over the mortal realms. She simply felt empty, lost.

When all was still, and the barely audible breathing of the clerics had become as one, Taya raised her head. She stared at the statue of Artemis. Questions she dared never voice circled her mind until she felt the teasing fingers of a soft breeze through her hair. She turned slowly, seeing the temple door had been left ajar, and instantly berated herself for wondering if she could leave unheard.

A flash of movement caught her eye. The glass of the lantern reflecting the light from within as it was thrown, with precision, through the opening. She heard herself gasp in foreknowledge of what was to come. The echoing sound of the shattering cylinder was almost concealed by the roar of fire. The brilliant flames snaked across the ground as if igniting invisible oil. It burnt without mercy, devouring all within its path.

The clerics sprung into action. Each one casting a glance in her direction, as if believing she was somehow responsible. The panicked chorus quickly changed to organised instructions as they tried to bring the spreading flames under control. They rushed through to the kitchens to fill pails with water. Some doused the flames, while others pulled the curtains from the plain windows, using the cloth to smother the fire. But nothing seemed to sate its relentless hunger.

Taya stood staring, rooted to the spot captivated by its slow, almost hypnotic dance as it consumed all it touched. She watched it sway with the breeze from the door, until she heard someone calling her name.

"Taya!" Sunniva called again, relieved when her posture finally stiffened in response. "Take the children to safety and wait until I send word," she commanded before continuing to issue instructions to those around her.

At her words Taya seemed to regain focus. She shook her head as if to dispel the trance and, returning to her senses, nodded. She picked her way through the winding fire towards the rear door. Its blistering heat singed the fine hairs on her arms as she was forced to pass too close to its insatiable heat. A splash of water drenched the bottom of her dress as it was flung in her direction. The fabric clung to her ankles, yet her steps showed a grace her disorientation should not have allowed. Through the commotion no one noticed the dark figure slip quietly through the temple's door, concealed by the thickening smoke.

Taya hurried through the rear door, using the small corridors and connecting buildings to reach the children's sleeping quarters. They were the furthest from the temple and were interspaced with smaller rooms belonging to the clerics and acolytes. If there was a design to their room assignments it was one Taya had not discerned. She ran as quickly as she could, rousing the tiny figures one at a time. She checked their numbers repeatedly to ensure they were all present and accounted for. She tasked the older children to do the same, in case her own count could not be trusted. By the time she had gathered them everything was blanketed with thick smoke. Echoes of tiny, gasping coughs filled the air as Taya led them outside to safety.

The youngest amongst them was barely a toddler. She cried against the forceful stirring of her sleep and pressed herself closer to Taya as she sobbed. Her tiny voice calming only to cry out louder as the cold night air forced her to wake further.

The other children, seeing where they were heading, now pushed their fear aside. Never had they been permitted entry into the place Taya led them.

The small building had been constructed with a stone foundation. As it rose it became panelled with wood, the grey stones still set at uniform intervals until its composition was lost beneath a heavily thatched roof. The structure lacked any windows and allowed access through a single, heavy wooden door. The door, Taya knew, could be locked from within, but there were also a number of wrought iron hasps fitted to the outside.

Set on the furthest border of their land, beyond the crops and gardens, it seemed to stand as a lone sentry before the forest. It was thought to have been constructed around the time the land had been purchased, but none of them remembered seeing it constructed. The children all swore it had simply appeared one day, but when they spoke of this miracle to the clerics they were warned against the harm of lies and living in a world of make-believe. These words had caused great unrest, and when Taya heard she had taken them aside, quietly explaining that most adults could no longer witness miracles and magic.

Fortunately her words never reached Sunniva's ears, and the children were happier for believing in a magic lost to all but them.

The children had always wanted to explore this small building. Taya had, and she loathed it. For all the intrigue the children displayed, she felt an equal measure of dread. The memories of it alone were enough to bring the stinging taste of bile to her throat. She had spoken of magic and fantasy but, given the time she had spent here, this place had become her own personal nightmare. She would admit it to no one, but she still awoke soaked in sweat, having dreamt she had once more been imprisoned within. In her dream she had never been alone. Another had come to her, twisting her to their purpose. Regardless of her own personal feelings and experience she knew the children would be safe here.

The inside of the room was just like she remembered, empty, except for a few woven mats which were placed at intervals upon the floor. There was one for each of the temple's clerics, and an additional one at the front, a place Taya assumed Sunniva would sit. Just to its right, near the rear wall, stood a small wooden altar. The children seemed disappointed to see the bland nature of this structure, but bringing them here had indeed silenced their sobs and questions.

"I'm going to need you all to be very brave," Taya whispered softly, swallowing her own fear as she placed the youngest child down on one of the mats. "There's nothing to be sca—" Taya froze. An image of terror filled her mind with such vividness she felt her stomach tighten. The children, who moments ago looked to her with fear-filled eyes, now lay dead. Their tiny bodies slashed and mutilated beyond all recognition. It was a scene of carnage, complete and merciless slaughter.

"You can't hide forever Daimon." A cold steely voice called out through the fragile silence. For a moment she saw an image of the temple, reduced to its bare bones, devoured completely by the now sated flames. She knew, without a doubt, the unseen figure was the one responsible for this horror, and that he had come for her.

"Taya?" a small voice questioned cautiously. She blinked, seeing the worried looks of the children as they all focused their attention on her trembling body. They all knew she walked a different reality. Just as she watched over them, they too had been given instruction to keep vigil on her. They didn't see her differences in the same light as most. They loved her like family, after all, she had been here as long as any of them could recall and, although she was often taken ill, she told tales of magic and wonder.

"It's okay. I'm okay," she reassured through gasping breaths, unable to hide the relief at seeing the figures once more animated with life. Although perhaps her relief was premature. Whilst Sunniva referred to what she had just experienced as a relapse, Taya knew in her heart that if she failed to act such things would come to pass. She had stopped so many terrors and disasters by acting on such images, or at least she thought she had.

Taya twisted her ring as she chewed her bottom lip in consideration. She knew what was happening now. Her mind was trying to convince itself that such things were real. If she allowed herself this belief she would sink deeper into the madness, and be consumed by the disease that thrived within her blood. She knew she should not believe the images, but with such potential consequences how could she deny them?

"Taya?" the voice questioned again, seeing the concern crossing their big sister's face. Taya gave a reassuring smile. She knew what had to be done.

"Holly, you're the eldest so it falls to you to take care of everyone. If anything happens, or you get really scared, there's a crawlspace behind the altar." Taya knew this crawlspace well. Had it been lighter she had no doubt the children would see the claw marks etched within the walls from the times she had been imprisoned here. Times when she had relapsed so violently there had been no choice but to detain her within these walls. Here she could cause no harm to anyone but herself, and here she would remain until the escorts arrived to attend to the situation. Sunniva always said that believing the things she saw, and her impossible fantasies, was the first step of decline. Her fear of such things usually caused her to lash out, hurting those who only wanted to watch over her.

"Taya, aren't you staying?" Holly questioned, her big brown eyes fixed on Taya pleadingly. At ten this young girl was the oldest of the orphans, and with the fiery temper attributed to all red-heads none questioned her seniority. Even the boys never challenged her. She was fierce and loyal. Taya knew she would protect them. The young girl had proven her ferocity numerous times when the older children visited for lessons from nearby towns. They had thought they could exploit those without a home or family, that they were weaker, and no better than the Demi-human they cohabited with. They had been wrong.

"No, beautiful, I can't." Taya kissed the top of her head affectionately. "I have to help the clerics. There's someone here who means us harm." Taya stilled her words, her mind warning against pulling the children into her own imaginings. "The fire is a nasty predator, he must be doused," she added in haste. "I need you to be brave. I'll be back soon, but if you get really scared, lead your brothers and sisters to Herne's Rock. Do you think you can do that?" The young girl nodded. "Okay, good. Now, lock the door behind me. Do not open it for anyone but the clerics."

With these words of parting Taya left the young children secure in the small sealed building, while her hurried steps propelled her towards the temple where billows of smoke could still be seen. She leapt the small fences and shrubs with ease, unaware they even blocked her path. Her sole focus was the building before her.

The glow of fire saturated the air with its orange hue, and the light from the windows caused unearthly shadows to flicker across the surrounding land. The sun was setting. Its own glow a mirror of the brilliant colours. Billows of smoke rose high into the air, only to be quickly dispelled by the wind before the beacon of disaster could be seen.

Taya stood at the doors, twisting her ring as her stomach tightened. She knew there was someone within the walls who did not belong, and the silence of the clerics served only to fuel her growing fear.

Her premonition had suggested the figure came for her, so surely her presence would put an end to this horror. Her hands trembled as she raised them towards the door. She inhaled deeply, steeling herself to face whatever lay within. The huge wooden structures swung inward, releasing fresh clouds of smoke from within. The fire swelled, growing and roaring as it feasted on the fresh air. It appeared almost as if her presence excited it.

The clerics and acolytes sat huddled, cowering at the feet of their goddess. Their fearful eyes never strayed from the burley figure before them, not even to see if it were friend or foe who had entered. The smoke shrouded figure turned, dragging Sunniva's weight with him. His thick arm was coiled around her waist while his other held a blade to her throat. She shielded just half of his wide form, but he knew no one within these walls would risk her life.

"Ah, the Daimon appears," he chuckled. His weapon's pressure on Sunniva's throat increased, causing her to let out a stifled cry.

"Stop!" Taya screamed. Her voice carried an authority few would dare ignore. One so absolute the figure had eased the pressure on Sunniva's throat instinctively, before the smoke had even cushioned the echoing command.

Heat from the fire distorted the smoke-filled air further as the clerics looked on in horror. The glimpses of unnatural movement were seen only as shadows, dancing and twisting as they caught the plumes of smoke.

Taya stood hunched as she stifled her cries. Where once the feathered wings could be seen the horrific bones of a skeletal frame now danced in the firelight. They appeared to bleed, shedding thick viscous fluid between the fine web of bones to create the most macabre, yet hauntingly beautiful, wings they had ever seen. Unlike those she once bore, they were segregated into two parts, the lower protruding from her lumbar region. These downward arching hindwings expanded, relishing in their liberation. Her silhouette cast across the haze. The shadowgraph reminiscent of a butterfly caught in the light.

Taya screamed internally against the mental agony of this somehow familiar sensation. Her mind warned how deep into her delusion she was being drawn. She looked to Sunniva through the haze. Her own horror was mirrored on the face of the Iereía.

The figure watched her closely, his weapon still held firmly against Sunniva's throat as Taya hesitated. She looked on in uncertainty, her choice unclear. What if she were to act on these images, charge forward to defend those she cared for, only to find later she had been the one to inflict scars upon those she thought she was saving? But if she were to believe her eyes, believe the familiar power and comforting sensations that now washed over her, she would also have to accept everything she had been led to believe as truth was in fact the lie. And all which she had been told were lies, were in fact truths.

There was certainly nothing about the way she felt which seemed remotely Méros-Génos. Her awareness, her power, it was almost recognisable. She shook her head, trying to dislodge some of the confusion. Sunniva had been warning her for days now of her deteriorating condition. As if in response to this recollection, she looked once more at the captive figure as if to seek her guidance. Begging for Sunniva to once more help her to distinguish the truth between reality and delusion.

"Run," the hoarse voice commanded before being silenced by the increase of pressure upon her throat. Taya was more confused now than before. Was she to believe those words had really been spoken?

"Run and she dies," the figure warned. "You think yourself clever disguising your blood-soaked heritage with the appearance of a Demi-human. My eyes see through your cheap visage. How you broke the moonlight seal is beyond me Daimon. You even dare to bewitch those in service to our gods. It would be a mercy to kill them. I must purge your taint from their souls. Immolation or death by my blade, these are the choices you have left me with should I wish to spare them." He turned, casting his gaze back towards the fear stricken clerics ensuring they dared not attempt to escape.

There was something villainous in his eyes, a glint emphasised by the glow of the firelight. Taya knew his intention. He was about to make an example of their Iereía. He was going to kill her, ending the stalemate between them.

"No!" Taya heard the cry leave her lips before being aware she had spoken. Her reaction instinctive as the figure moved, tugging Sunniva's hair to fully expose her bared throat. Taya struck him, the sword falling from his grasp when the blow to his temple was followed quickly by another to his wrist. The figure stumbled. He had not expected her to be able to move so quickly. She had covered the distance from the temple's entrance to him in the blink of an eye, or so it had seemed. But such was an enchantment for his eyes only. Taking advantage of his disorientation she struck him again. Her blow firmly connecting with his jaw, knocking him from his feet. She didn't even pause to question how one of her frame had the strength to fell such a large hunter.

Sunniva, no longer supported by the hunter's grip, sank to the floor. Her legs unable to hold her weight. Giving the attacker but a cursory glance Taya rushed to her side. The clerics seemed to retreat further at her approach.

"Are you all right?" Taya draped her arms around Sunniva's shoulders as she sat before her trembling. The hunter still lay to their side. Taya regarded him carefully for a moment, she knew she had not struck him hard, her only ally had been surprise. She was relieved to see he remained motionless, allowing her to concentrate solely on the Iereía. Sunniva looked to Taya, offering a warm smile.

In that instant, as Taya returned the relieved gesture, she heard the flurry of movement behind her. Every instinct warned her of the coming strike, warned her to dodge, or roll aside. Yet she froze. Perhaps in realisation that the victim of this blade had no relevance to the hunter. He cared only that his strike met with blood. She felt herself tense, holding her position. She cleared her mind. If this was all a delusion then she had nothing to fear. If, however, this was real the blow seemed too clumsy to be deadly, and she would have a physical reminder of the truth. A wound which would prove without a doubt her sanity was not lacking.

The burning heat of the metal blade scalded her as it pierced her back. She leaned forward, her arm extending to thrust Sunniva to the floor in a further attempt to protect her. Taya's agonised cries were not the only ones to be heard. She felt a part of herself extending into the blade, taking hold of this hunter's remaining time and claiming it for her own. An act ensuring she would live as she severed his lifeline. The sword withdrew in a sharp painful motion. His blow had barely inflicted the damage he had intended before his fate had been sealed.

Taya felt the sticky warmth of blood flowing from the wound. Her head grew light with a confusion that threatened to steal her consciousness. In her peripheral vision she could see her familiar, black feathered wings, not the monstrosities she thought had replaced them. A weakness began to consume her, her arms trembled as they refused to hold her weight. Yet still her eyes looked to Sunniva, who still lay upon the floor below her, supported by her elbows. Sunniva pushed herself into a sitting position as she assessed the damage. She knew Taya had deliberately shielded her, yet still could muster no guilt for what would have to be done.

"I'm okay." Taya forced the words in answer to Sunniva's concerned stare. Yet she questioned this very notion as she heard the hunter's final words.

"You're marked now, more will come, your time is—" Taya blinked free some tears as she fought the darkness shrouding her vision. The clerics still cowered, huddled together in fear despite the hunter's obvious passing.

"By the Spirits, what are you doing?" Taya snarled. "Put out the fires." They continued to stare at her, fear's invisible snare still rooting them in place. "Now!" she ordered, moving with great effort to kneel. As she moved, Sunniva reached forwards, placing her cool hands on either side of Taya's head as she looked her in the eyes. "He called me a Daimon," Taya whispered as the world around her began to fade. Sunniva released her grip, allowing the unconscious figure to fall into her arms.

* * *

A messenger sprinted through Riverside Quay. His pace unaltered by the greetings called out to him. Within his hand he held a parchment, one sealed with silver wax and marked as urgent. The runner kicked up a trail of dust, almost losing his footing as he found himself closer to the Plexus than he had expected. His gasping breaths betrayed the exertion of his journey. Sweat ran in rivulets from his face as he forced open the door to the Plexus.

All conversation within fell silent as the request was presented to the Plexus master. His hands rotated the scroll, finding the seal and the name of the addressee. He gave a nod, allowing the man to relax and sink into one of the chairs to catch his rasping breath as the Plexus master took charge of the document. With the parchment in hand he lifted the counter, his steps quickening until his pace nearly matched that of the messenger.

Requests from Elpída were rare, but rarer still were those sealed in silver. A silver seal meant a matter of grave importance. It was reserved for urgent situations, time sensitive. Such specialised undertakings would not normally be recorded until completion. They required immediate and swift action. Nothing good would come of any delay in its delivery.

Without a knock the Plexus master barged into Rob's room, not even pausing to reflect on the damage he would have caused had the door not been left ajar.

Rob glanced up from his book, subtly aiming his crossbow towards the door as he leaned back in his chair. Seeing the familiar figure he released the pressure on the lever trigger, allowing the weapon to rest in its place once more. His face filled with concern, one which mirrored the Plexus Master's own urgency, causing his attention to shift towards the silver wax upon the parchment. Rob had never seen a request sealed in such a shade before. He couldn't even fathom its priority or perhaps, given the Plexus master's personal appearance, he could.

His heart thundered in his chest as he rose, quickly closing the distance between them to seek out the identifier. He knew it intimately, the impression marking the wax was from the temple, and that meant there was trouble.

"We've an urgent job." The Plexus master placed the paper firmly in Rob's hand. The Plexus processing fee for this job would have been sent with the messenger. As for the reward, if there was any, it would be settled between hunter and client directly.

"So urgent you'd seek *me* out?" Most here knew of his relationship to Sunniva, but that would not alter the task assignment. For this to come to him there must have been no one else available.

"It's marked for you," the Plexus master explained gesturing towards the scroll, before allowing his eyes to roam the modest room. The bed was made, perhaps even unslept in. The burnt out candles and collection of tomes spread across the table, along with the countless empty spirit bottles, told the tales of sleepless nights lost to research. He knew this man to be one of their best. There were few who would undertake the tasks he did. It suggested a talent which its owner did not fully apply. The Plexus master was certain that with the right motivation the man before him could become a legend; then again, in some respects he already was.

"Is Sunniva all right?" Rob's weighted stare was still fixed on the rolled parchment within his hand, barely daring to open it in fear of what may be within.

"It comes to you first. Even I don't know the details." As he spoke Rob broke the seal. His eyes passed over it hurriedly before returning to the top, and reading it again, with care. His shoulders visibly sank a few inches as he gave a sigh of relief. Several long moments of silence passed while the Plexus master stood awaiting a response. When the silence continued to extend, he spoke again. "I assume you'll take the job?" Rob, remembering himself, gave a nod. The thundering of his heart had not yet calmed from the danger he had imagined.

"Mark it down as a standard task would you? And maybe reeducate her in the colour-coding system." He shook his head. "I can't believe she'd ask this of me," Rob groaned, pinching the bridge of his nose as he released a long, drawn-out sigh. He read the parchment again, shaking his head. Even now he was unsure if he could, in good conscience, complete this request.

* * *

Taya's eyes opened slowly as awareness seeped back into her aching body. She sat up with a start. Her mind nervously flitting over the last events she recalled before settling on a single vivid image. Her panicked gaze fixed on Sunniva, who sat resting in a nearby chair.

"Iereía, are you all right?" Taya gasped, wincing against the pain radiating from her back. The wound was still there. The wound which confirmed everything she had experienced had been real. Her mind filled with suspicion as she looked upon the figure who had moved quickly to perch herself on the edge of her bed. She seemed more tense than normal, her posture unusually rigid.

"I am fine. The important question though, is how are *you* feeling?" Taya carefully slipped herself out of the bed, testing her weight on her legs before dressing quickly. Each movement sent waves of fire through her treated injury.

"And the children? What of the temple?" Taya questioned. Sunniva had risen to her feet and was regarding her cautiously, but Taya's coordinated movements as she dressed saw her attempt to approach fail as she retreated.

"All fine. What's gotten into you?" This time Taya saw her advance too late, Sunniva's cold hand pressed tenderly against her face. Taya felt her body's conditioned response as she leaned into the comforting sensation. Her shoes were forgotten, left unlaced as all movement stilled and she felt herself draw comfort from the delicate aroma of Sunniva's rose scented hair. As if remembering herself Taya pulled away quickly, regaining her momentum.

"What of the fire, the hunter?" She felt the doubt creeping back. Her injury was the only reassurance that the events she recalled were real. They had to be, how else would she have obtained such a wound?

"Fire?" Sunniva questioned softly. "Oh, my dear, you've had another one of your turns. You've been sleeping for the past few days. You must rest." But Taya was no longer listening. Her hurried steps carried her towards the temple. If she could see the damage Sunniva could not question her sanity, not with the evidence clearly before her.

Her anxious steps halted abruptly as she reached the middle of the temple. Her eyes panned desperately for the damage she knew should be present. Her head swam and balance faltered as she sunk to her knees in confusion. The temple was pristine. There was no sign of fire or smoke damage. Everything was immaculate, right down to the drapes she knew had previously caught alight.

Sunniva's hand on her shoulder startled her as she ran though her memories. This didn't make sense. How could she still possess an injury when no further evidence of the altercation could be found?

Taya felt the bile rise in her throat as her fingers nervously twisted her ring. If this was all in her mind her actions had only one consequence. She had been behaving so well, fighting back the images of what she believed. She knew it was better to accept Sunniva's reality over her own. All so that she would not be made to return to *that* place. A place commissioned by the Acropolis, yet the acts within were anything but sacred. She could not go back there, not again. She had sworn to herself that her previous visit there would be the last, that she would do all within her power to be compliant to what was expected of her. She couldn't survive it, not again.

"Taya, what is it, what's wrong?" But the words Taya intended to say were not those she found leaving her lips. She intended to speak of nightmares, and confusion on waking. All acceptable things, if acknowledged. Yet instead, the words spilling uncontrollably from her mouth betrayed her.

"You've moved him. You've cleaned it." She rose to her feet, frantically examining the temple in disbelief. Her subtle steps placing distance between herself and Sunniva as she made a steady retreat towards the temple's doors. She would not be forced to return to Mirage Lake. Not now, not ever. Her compliant self spoke words of warning, *'Still your tongue,'* it whispered, yet the words would not be silenced. "I don't know how you've managed it. But I see through your deception, your games. Well I am done. I want to go home. I am going home." Sunniva reached out, grabbing her arm pulling her close. For a moment Taya did not resist.

"You're just confused. You *are* home Taya. Don't you recognise me, don't you recognise Elpída?"

"Liar!" Taya spat, showing more strength than expected as she broke Sunniva's grasp. During their brief embrace Sunniva had turned her from the door. Realising this Taya glanced around desperately, seeking an escape. "This is a prison. You're doing this to me, you're keeping me here. But I know the truth, I see it clearly now, dretch! What I don't understand is why. You're trying to use me for something, but what?"

"Taya, see sense child." Taya matched Sunniva's steps, adding her own twist, in the hope Sunniva would mirror them perfectly. Any minute now she would have a clear path to the door. "I've watched over you since you were a baby, since your parents abandoned you on my doorstep." Sunniva extended her hand comfortingly towards Taya. It took everything she had not to accept it. "I raised you, remember? Every weekend we would visit Herne's rock and make an offering, remember?" Sunniva prompted, gaining a step towards her as Taya hesitated in taking her retreating one.

"We... we would make daisy chains, and place them over it." With the memory came a feeling of serenity, one which calmed her panicked breathing slightly.

"Good, you remember. And now, we still go to the rock don't we? And when daisies aren't in season," Sunniva prompted.

"We use other flowers. The roses were so pretty. We made you a crown from them last time. The red went beautifully with your pale hair." Taya gasped, feeling Sunniva's arms once more embrace her.

"Good, you're doing fine. Hold on to that memory a little longer." Sunniva made a gesture to the acolytes who had appeared at the temple's rear doorway. Quietly, without a word, they slunk back to leave the two of them alone.

"It started to rain. You covered me with your cloak so I wouldn't get wet."

"I've always protected you. I do what is in your best interest, even if it doesn't seem that way at the time." Taya felt herself relaxing further into the embrace. She felt safe, loved, she raised her arms returning the gesture. But as her hands touched Sunniva's back her body grew rigid, the trance broken as she realised what was happening. She pushed forwards, knocking Sunniva from her feet. Taya's unexpected movement caused her to tumble backwards, her head striking one of the pews.

"No, you're tricking me," Taya snarled as Sunniva pushed herself into a sitting position, raising her hand to nurse the injury. "You've cleaned the damage, hidden his body, but you can't disguise my wound." Taya placed her hand expressively to the burning injury on her back. She stepped backwards towards the door. She had to leave here, nothing good would come of her staying. While freedom was a possibility she had to run. What was the worst that could happen? If her attempt failed, then there was no doubt she would be returned to Mirage Lake, and should she stay, she had no doubt the same fate awaited her now. She would run. She would rather choose the hope of freedom than spend another second here.

"You mean the wound on your back?" Sunniva questioned, her voice freezing Taya's hand upon the door handle. "You left us with no choice. If Priestess Claudia hadn't acted you would have killed me." Sunniva stood slowly, supporting her weight on the seating while raising her other hand to remove the silk scarf, which Taya had previously failed to notice. Beneath were dark purple and black bruises where it seemed someone had attempted to choke the life from her. Taya looked to the injury in horror, unable to find the wound made by the hunter's sword. Her mind reeled at the sight. She glanced briefly to her hands, questioning if she had really done this.

"No, I won't believe it," she answered both Sunniva's statement and her own thoughts.

"I wouldn't want to either," Sunniva agreed with a few small, understanding nods. Taya's hand turned the handle pulling the door inward. Sunniva was still too far away to stop her. She could make it, she could be free. Her legs moved of their own accord, propelling her through the doorway.

Her vision remained fixed on Elpída as she ran, seeing nothing of the land before her. Not daring to watch for anything but her captor's pursuit. Had she focused on the path she would have seen the person standing in her way before her small frame collided with his solid one. He grabbed her tightly, she kicked and screamed trying to force herself loose as he moved to hold her from behind. His voice whispered soothing words into her ear, calming her until she dared a glance over her shoulder. It was the Iereía's brother. She took a slow and steady breath. There was still hope to be free of this place yet.

"Taya Ethelyn, it's nice to meet you again." He released her, offering a greeting now he was happy she was calmed. By the time he had looked up from studying the parchment his sister had sent, their collision had been inevitable. Still, he had not expected such a violent reaction.

"You'll find your sister in the temple," Taya offered, forcing a calmness to her voice she hoped would mask her building hysteria. She had to be very careful, one wrong word would see her back within the prison. This man did not know she was not permitted to leave. The fact he had seen her in the town only aided her case. If she remained calm she could still be free.

"She usually is." He smiled. "But I'm not here for her. I'm to be your escort, or your tail. Either way you're stuck with me for a while." There was no mistaking the fear he saw within her eyes at his words. For a minute, he feared she would run. Her body tensed as if in preparation.

"Escort?" Taya questioned, allowing herself a glance towards Elpída. There was still no movement. If Sunniva had sent for her brother then she must have somehow known she had planned to run. Taya questioned how she could have predicted such a thing when she herself had been unaware of her intention.

"To Mirage Lake." Rob barely brought himself to speak these words. He still had not decided whether he was accepting his sister's request or not. Taya twisted her ring as she inhaled deeply, chewing on her bottom lip as she thought over the options. There was still hope. Normally, when she was sent there, she would be collected by carriage, but he was walking. He didn't even have a horse. She shook her head in decline.

"Thank you, but I am in need of neither an escort nor a tail," she stated sharply, stepping around him to begin walking. As expected he began to follow.

"So you would rather die out here?" She turned to look at him as he kept pace a few steps behind her. She bit her lip again, preventing her desired response. Would she rather die? What kind of question was that? Given the choice then yes. She would die a thousand times before being forced to return there.

"I can look after myself," she snapped. "I can use magic. I have studied it for many years." Even as the words left her lips she wondered if they held any truth. She paused for a moment, looking inside herself to see if she could find the seed of power. She felt nothing. Delusion or not, she knew one thing for certain, she needed to find the answers for herself. Answers away from medicine, away from treatments, an opportunity to think for herself instead of being conditioned in how to behave. And if it turned out she was delusional then, maybe, she would prefer to stay that way.

"Would that be the same magic that protected you from the blade," Rob chuckled, his eyes fixed upon her back. Taya gasped, turning her burning gaze towards him. "Calm down, I can see the wound." He gestured towards the injury. Turning to glance over her shoulder she saw the bloody dressing clearly showing through the white garment. "Sunniva told me you'd been injured. She just wants to make sure you get there safely. Besides, I can't leave you now. I've already been paid."

"If you've been paid, then surely you need not worry further."

"But that brings my honour into question." Taya slowed her steps allowing him to approach. Until she saw the opportunity to be free of this man, perhaps it was better to accept him, until such a time he thought her amenable. It would be better to have him believe he had won, at least then her escape may be unpredicted.

"How far must you take me?" she questioned dryly.

"To me, it will seem too far," he sighed drawing level with her. "Shall we?" Taya gave a reluctant sigh and a nod. The sooner their journey began the sooner she could be free of him. Besides, maybe if she walked slowly enough he'd grow bored and seek his excitement elsewhere. Given the direction they were heading she was certain, if she caused enough delay, they wouldn't reach a town by nightfall.

Sunniva watched the two distant figures from the window. The gravity of the situation had weighed heavily upon her shoulder, but she had known Rob was nothing if not punctual. Most of the time anyway. As she stood watching them disappear she reached out, sharply grabbing the hand of one of the passing acolytes, her gaze never leaving the window.

"When I say this place needs to be spotless, I mean spotless. Imagine what could have happened had she seen that. Everything we've done would be for nothing." Sunniva released the hand from her firm grasp to gesture towards a small area of charring, barely concealed beneath one of the pews. It had been no small feat to return the temple to its pristine condition, taking longer than she would have hoped. She knew Taya would not dare to question the change in the lunar phase, if she was even aware of it.

"I'm sorry, Iereía." The acolyte bowed.

"Do not let it happen again. Too much time has gone into this for it to be unravelled by carelessness. If I have to find too many excuses even she would start to question my word, and *that* is the last thing we want. We have been charged with a task of the utmost importance. Failure is not an option."

Chapter 4

Surrender

The silence was absolute. For years they had called out. Their cries pierced The Stepping Realm from The Betwixt, a place where all those wishing to venture between planes must pass. Their ritual never varied. Four would sit, four would rest. Their minds extending to touch the gateway to the waking world, hoping to relay their message and receive an answer. The silence was deafening.

There had been minor successes. The implantation of thoughts or ideas, but nothing had given the desired result. The one they sought remained beyond their grasp, captured only in fleeting glimpses. It was yet another confirmation that powers of old were indeed weakening. It was even noticeable in The Betwixt, a plane which adjoined all others, a place where dream and reality met.

It was through The Betwixt that The Stepping Realm could be found. Its form like stepping stones across a turbulent ocean, granting safe passage to any who used it. Allowing travellers to traverse the realms in safety. But the flow of energy had altered. Where once the astral images of the four could glide, weightless and free, they now fought turbulence never before present. A change was coming. Something on the distant horizon which caused even the oldest foundations unease.

Eadward slowed his pace, noticing Daley was once more finding this journey particularly difficult. It was the second time in as many days that he had witnessed the dark and oppressive energy. Once again it seemed to be drawn to Daley, enshrouding him in its dark aura. Eadward, with no other option, gave the signal to return. Once acknowledged he focused on the feelings of his body, the slow motion of each breath, the pressure of the stone floor, the quiet, rhythmic beating of his heart. He felt himself being drawn back until his sight rested on the familiar image of his three companions.

Daley, as the one intended to attempt the communication, had sat in the room's centre. Eadward, Cafell, and Sybella surrounding him, channelling their energy into him in both physical and astral forms.

The room itself was beautiful, yet its purpose ensured it was almost always in complete darkness. This was the chamber of scrying. The place the Kyklos were at their strongest. A place of focus and solitude, of safety and power. The very design, each crystal and mineral found within the walls, served only to ensure their safety and success. Yet something had clearly gone awry, for despite all their protection Daley did not stir.

"What was that?" Eadward turned to the central figure, noticing the concern on his companions' faces. His voice caused a gentle glow to radiate from the core of several crystals, generating colourful refractions of light in a scene intended to relax and soothe. But he gleaned little comfort as he approached Daley. The rise and fall of each breath was clearly visible, his body had life; but the most integral part, his consciousness, had not returned. "How is this possible?" The slight tremor in Eadward's voice caused the two women to draw nearer. Sybella, the youngest and newest addition to the Kyklos, reached out to place her hand upon Eadward's arm.

"What was that darkness?" she questioned, her voice betraying her own fear and inexperience.

"It happened last time as well," Cafell recalled. She pulled a beautifully adorned headdress from her dark hair, keeping her distance in fear of disturbing something which could provide further insight. Such an occurrence was unheard of. No one had ever failed to return from The Betwixt, not in the history of the Kyklos. She took a single hesitant step forwards. "I can't sense his tether. Eadward, what could do such a thing? Should we return, attempt to find him?"

"No. We must inform the Regent. He connected briefly before the disruption. *She* was unprotected but we must act now. As for Daley, Cafell, see if Meredith and her Kyklos have encountered anything similar. Whatever did this needed him alive, and yes, I am saying this was deliberate. I doubt it is a coincidence it occurred the instant we reached her. But I'm at a loss to what possesses such power. Not only to ensure life remained within the body, but to breach this protection." Eadward gestured widely at their surroundings. "This does not bode well."

* * *

Rob and Taya walked in silence. She had to suffer his presence, but not his conversation. It was just as well. He didn't seem too intent on talking either. There was something unnerving about the glances he kept casting her way. His eyes were not filled with the same animosity she had come to expect from those outside Elpída.

Her heritage had seen her the focal point of much aggression, even within the temple walls. People, outside the watchful eye of the Iereía, had gone to great trouble to ensure she knew she was unwelcome, a stain on their existence. They may have been morally outraged at the thought of hitting a woman, but as they had so often stated, she was no woman. She was an abomination, a blight. Taya knew where she stood with them, but this man was different. She was unclear of his motives, and that made her uneasy.

Taya was rarely seen when the temple was busy. She remained unobserved, concealing herself cautiously within the shadows. Her presence agitated Sunniva's followers. Many commented if not for her being under Iereía's mentorship that she would have been cast from Livingstone or, more realistically, executed.

Sunniva had informed her that most people within this world shared these views. That Demi-humans had no place among humans and were often exploited for menial tasks or labour. They suffered at the hand of humans, and most accepted them as their masters. Such talks would end with Sunniva offering her comfort, saying that she was safe from such servitude thanks only to her, and that, unlike her, the world would never welcome her. But the words she had overheard Rob speak during his last visit implied this was not so.

The clerics in Elpída weren't too different from the people who paid homage there. They simply concealed their intolerance better. Their fear towards her was unusual, especially since the Acropolis welcomed and trained people from all walks of life. Taya was certain Sunniva had once mentioned a few of the seniors there being Méros-Génos, but when she had once challenged her she had denied ever making such a claim. Insisting that Demi-humans were servants and slaves, and could never hope to be anything more.

The sun hung low in the sky, casting long shadows towards them as they walked. With another sidewards glance Rob confirmed what he already knew, Taya was exhausted. He had known of her pretence, of her attempt to slow their journey in hope he would reconsider his option to leave her. But he doubted she had become aware that the mimicked fatigue had become a reality.

Her injury, coupled with the fact she was unaccustomed to such walking, had slowed them considerably. There was little point in continuing further, not if they planned to make any progress tomorrow. He caught himself glancing towards her again. Once more he was met with the mistrust in her eyes and quickly refocused his attention on their surroundings.

He found his niece intriguing. He had never had the opportunity to get to know her, and the tales Sunniva had spoken of stirred in him an interest he could not repress. He had allowed her to slow their progress. He was in no hurry to reach their destination. Not when there was still, perhaps, another option.

"Ethelyn." Rob's steps came to a decisive halt as he turned to address her. He had allowed her to fall behind, knowing she was too exhausted to attempt an escape just yet. "I know you intend to run." Her eyes met with his in alarm, surprise tracing her pale features. He passed her a leather skin, knowing dehydration was a factor to her fatigue. He had not offered it her before simply because it had worked to his advantage. "Who wouldn't?" he answered her unspoken question. "The place I have been asked to take you..." He let his gaze stray from hers as he shook his head repressing a shudder.

He was no stranger to the world, nor to the stories regarding Mirage Lake. Cries of its prisoners were said to echo through stone tunnels where no man could hope to escape. The imagery conjured by tales of its terror were the seed of nightmares, and those hearing them suffered so little compared to those found within the sealed rooms and hidden crevices. People whispered outlandish accounts, but their imagination was lacking.

"If you claim to know its horror, how can you be so insistent on ensuring I reach there?" Taya snapped. Mirage Lake had only one purpose, to break people until they would do anything, be anything, rather than be subjected to any more of their treatments. The depressed found a smile; the angry found their calm. Most people entering those walls were cured within days. Just a few days of that hell either cured someone or drove them deeper into madness.

"Sunniva is my sister," Rob answered finally. "I am bound to her by blood. I cannot afford to question her until evidence makes me." Rob looked to her with hidden meaning, almost begging her to produce some proof of his sister's deception. He was a hunter, he knew when he was being manipulated. He could see there was more to this situation than the information her request had revealed.

"Then you have doubts?" There was an almost hopeful lift to her voice as she raised her eyes from the floor to briefly meet his, before turning her attention to the surrounding area. The sky above the canopies was softer, indicative of dusk's approach. Areas of darkness formed within the stretching shadows, shadows that could possibly even conceal her.

"Ethelyn, I must take you as I promised." As she shot him a look of haunting repulsion his face grew stern and serious, as if in weighted thought. "I can't let you escape, and without a weapon you have no hope to do so." She took a moment to study him, his tightly pursed lips and knitted brows confirming his commitment to a task he himself despised. Without some means to deceive him she knew she could not hope to outrun him. Perhaps he could be swayed with words alone. He was looking for a reason, could she create one he would trust? She shook her head as if in answer to her own thoughts. There was nothing she could offer this man that he would believe. He knew all too well of her affliction, and she could give him no cause to overlook any doubt.

"Why?" she whispered, the sadness in her voice ringing through. Her burning gaze fixed upon the woody debris lining their path. "Why would you do this to me?" She wanted to question how he had realised she was unarmed. Her departure had been so desperate she had fled without pause. Taya sat on the grass with a sigh, giving her legs a chance to rest. It was only as she pulled the coarse material over her knees she realised there was no place within this garment to conceal a weapon.

Sunniva had insisted she always wore the same style clothes as the novice priestesses, insisting such attire would lessen the people's prejudice. Even hatred had a way of knowing who, and what, to respect. If nothing else it granted her a little immunity from the people's intolerance.

"I've already told you, I'm bound by my word." He met her eyes as he spoke, offering her a hand to her feet. As their eyes briefly met he saw a reflection of the burning shades cast across the sky by the sinking sun. He had no doubt she could see things others could not. She had a look often seen on those raptured and enthralled by things no ordinary mortal could hope to glimpse. An enchanted sight whose dreamlike gaze implied sight beyond the planes of reality to a world he could only imagine. He thought about the delusions she was said to suffer, and found himself wondering exactly what she had seen with those eyes. "Talk with me a while as we walk. Sunniva says you have such wondrous dreams."

"My delusions?" Rob nodded, pausing to gather some fallen branches from the nearby area. Taya mirrored his actions, giving a slight snort before speaking again. "I doubt she used the word wondrous. I dream of a place far beneath the land. Untouched by the sun and sealed by a barrier broken only by the magic of the year's end moon."

Rob looked to her in astonishment. He knew the barrier she spoke of intimately, but had cause to wonder how *she* knew of it. Such a fable was spoken of only between treasure hunters and those who study legends. Then again, with the rising fear spread by abductions it was possible she had heard rumours, but most people were unaware of the barrier and believed the moon itself released the predators. But if she had overheard people talking of such things, surely she would know it was now a monthly occurrence, not an annual one.

"You're talking about the demons, The Depths of Acheron?"

"We are Daimons, not demons!" she snapped, calming as she realised that this man was willing to hear her tale without attempting to silence her. It was something she had never known. A topic she had never been permitted to indulge in. "I'm sorry. Our world is immense, and grants passage to many buried fiefdoms and treasures. Both those with value, and those which could destroy life. Some treasures were entrusted to us for safekeeping. Others we have retrieved on our own when the moon allowed.

"There are some things too dangerous to be in the hands of man. We attempt to regulate such powers, ensuring things with such devastating potential are not left unprotected. Where possible we destroy them, otherwise we seal their powers." She raised her hand to her breast as she spoke, feeling the truth of her own words calling to her.

"Why would you do that?"

"A war between humans has little concern for us, but when their disregard threatens the planet, a place we all must live, that is not a species war, it is an act against life itself. In days long past we were guardians, thought of as a race between human, spirits, and gods, possessing both knowledge and divine powers. With our freedom long lost there has been so little we can do to prevent your wars."

"But did the demons—I mean Daimons—not wage such a war themselves?"

"A war of magic?" Rob gave a nod. "Strange how such things are remembered. Many cycles ago, beyond the time of your records, there was such a thing. But magic affects the world differently to the devices made by man's hand."

"How so?"

"To use magic you must give back what you take. Gaea is powerful, and our magic, the Moirai's magic, even that of the humans, all added to the strength of the world's protector. The Severaine would feed on this energy, repairing the damage such a war created. But then, the humans took the conflict too far and designed an item of catastrophic potential." Taya stopped, her shoulders slumped as she looked away from Rob. It was no wonder Sunniva had insisted she be sent to Mirage Lake. Just listening to herself recite the past of her people brought understanding. She knew these tales, this history, by heart, clearer and more vividly than any of this world. She knew these fables better than her own childhood. She gave a sigh. "But none of it is real. Sunniva would scold me for speaking of such things."

Taya knew the danger. If she continued to immerse herself in this fiction things would only be worse for her if she somehow failed to make her escape. They had already taken so much, but this small awareness had been shielded and remained intact, despite their efforts. She had faith she would not lose herself while safeguarding this secret, but those watching over her would say it was for this very reason she would never be well. She clung to her madness as if it were a lifeline.

"Please, I am interested. You say you have many items from eras past, do you have none made by your own hand?"

"*You* are a bad influence." She shook her head, grinning despite her fears. "There are a few, but most would be of no use to your kind. Although I heard rumours of one much sought after in your fables. We call it The Seed of Nzin." Rob's posture noticeably stiffened as she spoke its name. "It was believed to be a tear of crystallised magic." Taya paused as the image of something long forgotten had flashed into her mind. She had spoken before realising the danger. Real or not she knew better than to speak of such things.

"Is it a great treasure? I imagine something like that is very safely guarded," he pried. Taya could see the enthusiasm within his eyes, perhaps his interest had revealed a means to escape him.

"It is well protected, but not for the reasons you might think." Taya shook her head. "No, sorry. This is no good for me. I should not speak as if such things are real." She felt the confusion washing over her as pillars of light illuminated the twilight sky. They rose high above the trees, conjuring an image of the trail left by a shooting star, except these lights did not fade. They extended upwards, reaching far into the heavens as if they were a beacon to guide her home.

She could not always see this wonder, but when she did she spent the time, between dusk and the sun's complete disappearance, admiring their unearthly beauty. The silver lights cast halos of rainbows in a mesmerising display that it seemed was beheld only by her. She tore her gaze from the sky, looking anywhere but towards these heliographs. Sunniva had been right, things were getting worse.

"Hey, Ethelyn, I have a proposition for you," Rob revealed, dropping his collected firewood to the ground in the small clearing. She looked up, giving him her full attention. "Before I take you to Mirage Lake, let's have an adventure of our own."

"I don't understand."

"I am trying to find a reason not to fulfil this contract. If you can take me to this Seed of Nzin you mentioned it will prove there is more to your troubles than Sunniva believes. That in itself is enough to warrant further investigation. I give you my word, if you do this I *will* protect you."

"Do you really think she will care?"

"I do. If we find it, it implies everything you've seen is true, perhaps even suggests a link between you and another realm. It would mean I can reject this request and Sunniva would seek The Acropolis' guidance.

"But one thing is for certain, if even part of what you know is the truth your insight could be used to protect people. They would not risk you losing such insight by sending you to Mirage Lake," he explained, removing the two blankets from his backpack before igniting the firewood using his tinderbox. He glanced up, seeing the uncertainty in her features. "Let's rest here tonight. You can sleep on it and let me know your decision in the morning. If nothing else it would delay your arrival and give you more opportunity to escape my watch." He forced a lightness to his tone as if to imply he was joking, but the seriousness reflected in his eyes suggested otherwise. She gave a slight nod, before sliding herself inside the blanket with her back towards him.

He watched her for a moment. The deliberate alteration of her breathing implied she was attempting to feign sleep. Rob chewed thoughtfully on a piece of dried meat from their travelling rations. Her actions alone suggested she still harboured hopes on a retreat rather than accepting his proposition. He stared into the fire questioning if, when the time came, he would let her escape his grasp. His moral scales weighed heavily. He knew he couldn't, but not for the reasons he had expected.

As her breathing altered, and sleep claimed his charge, Rob relaxed beneath his own blanket. He had been both gifted and cursed as a light sleeper. Tonight it was a blessing. He could feel the weight of someone watching from the shadows, but he had not yet found the source of his unease. It could be something as simple as wildlife, or perhaps there was something more sinister lurking. He glanced around once more, his focus resting on the moon as he lay on his back, his arms crossed behind his head.

With the moon in its current phase there was no cause to fear demons this night. Although if his thoughts about Taya were true, it was possible her strange insight could be a double-edged blade. Could they, or even one amongst them, know of her existence? The crackling of the wood upon the fire brought anything but comfort as his mind wondered how far, and to what extent, the influence of The Depths of Acheron extended into his own world.

* * *

Upon the cradle of the wind rode an unnatural dust. Not fairy pollen, but magic in a way. It drifted over the two figures as they lay sleeping near the fire. Released from the hands of the one who had been tracking them. He was skilled in his craft. A hunter born and bred. But not the type who made an allegiance with the Plexus. He hunted a different prey altogether. Normally he sought the kill, but tonight there was a prize to be claimed.

* * *

Rob's eyes were open, staring transfixed into the firelight as he heard the footsteps approaching. Whoever it was had no concern for their footfall being heard, but anyone who crept into a camp at night would not have honourable intentions.

The steps were heavy, yet not quite human in gait. A Méros-Génos perhaps, but even at this thought his mind warned him otherwise. He had heard too many tales of the monsters who stalked the darkness. Creatures spawned from a town thought to have been made by Hades himself. Creature or not, it was getting closer. He had to act now, while he still possessed the element of surprise.

Rob counted each step, waiting until the intruder was close enough. He willed his muscles into action. Nothing happened. His body refused to move, refused to obey even the simplest command as his mind warned of the increasing danger his inaction wrought. He tried to blink, realising his eyes were dry and gritty, and even this small movement was halted. He watched helplessly as a silhouette crossed before the firelight, to venture deeper into the small camp. Its slow steps hesitated briefly as it walked past him towards Taya.

The figure left his line of sight, leaving him unharmed. His heart sped, fearing now for the young woman who slept mere feet from him. Rob felt his stomach contract. He had to do something. He had to move.

* * *

Taya had been dreaming when the sound of movement through the camp had first awoken her. She sat now, locked in eye contact with the surprised figure who towered above her. She wished she had feigned sleep, perhaps then they would have simply raided their supplies and left. But something in the way he looked at her warned otherwise. She was his intended target.

Using her hands she slowly began to push herself away, freeing herself from the blanket, hoping the figure's surprise remained such that she could escape. She felt the solid force of what she hoped to be a tree at her back, hindering further movements as the figure continued to stare.

"Rob," she hissed glancing in his direction. She felt the icy vein of terror flood through her as the firelight illuminated just some of the features hidden by the hooded robe. She tried to speak again, but fear stilled her words. For a moment, with her eyes once more transfixed on the figure, she questioned if he could be her salvation. A calmness washed over her, ordering her to do as he bid. If she went with him at least she was not on her way to Mirage Lake. It was after this thought rationality seized control. She was in danger. She chanced a glance across to Rob, his sleeping figure huddled in the blankets, peacefully unaware of the danger she faced.

"Taya Ethelyn." The voice was more bestial than human as it growled her name. The words had been intelligible but possessed a subtle difference unrelated to its monstrous tone.

"H-how do you know me?" She felt the tremors of fear start deep within her core. A terror which was stilled suddenly by a calmer, more powerful, part of herself. The same part that had allowed her to survive the shared, and unwitnessed, transgressions of those seeking to alleviate their boredom within Mirage Lake.

"You will come with us," he ordered, bending to wrap his claws around her throat. The pressure of his grasp pushed her upward against the tree as he forced her to stand. She pressed herself back against the bark, shrinking away with her eyes squeezed tightly closed.

Whatever touched her, as the firelight had already revealed, was not human. It couldn't be real. It was not a Daimon, nor was it one of the creatures roaming the labyrinths and catacombs below. It was something she had not seen before, a child of Hades. It was filled with a dark magic, not that it could wield it. She opened one of her eyes slightly as she wished it away, willing the delusion from her reality. This was not real, it couldn't be.

Sunniva had always insisted that any creatures she imagined possessed no power, but for that which she gave them and, at this moment, she willed it to be weak. But deep inside she knew as long as she feared it, feared what it would do, its touch would remain solid at her throat. Hearing Sunniva's voice within her mind, telling her to wake from her delusion and seize control while she still could, she squeezed her eyelids tighter. But the grasp remained firm.

Through the darkness, the ring of a weapon parting from its scabbard pierced the air. It was a sound which brought her comfort. If someone was arming themselves it meant she was not alone in perceiving the creature. Unless, while she believed she stood immobilised by its grasp, she was in fact attacking someone who now chose to meet her in combat.

Reluctantly, she opened her eyes, finding herself relieved to see Rob. His normally soft features hardened. When they had walked together she had considered how gentle he appeared. Now she saw through his facade, to a deeper, concealed aspect of himself, appearing through the fractures as a contrast to the image he worked so hard to maintain. He looked almost as intimidating as the monstrous creature. His eyes burnt with threat as his short sword's tip extended to her captor's throat.

"Sorry to disappoint you, but this young lady is staying with me," he stated coolly, his narrowed gaze burning into the creature. Taya closed her eyes, realising Rob was unphased by its unnatural appearance. The pressure from her throat released as it turned its attention to him. "You're wondering why your dust didn't paralyse me?" His dark smile caught in the fire's glow, twisting it into something more sinister. "That's my little secret. Now, kindly step away." Rob always liked to imply such things had no effect on him, it meant they were less likely to use it a second time.

"Do you think that blade can hurt me?" it challenged, adjusting its position to stand beside Taya, ensuring she could not escape.

"Shall we find out?" His smile through the darkness made her shudder. "I think you will find yourself *deathly* mistaken. This, is the Holy Blade of Paion." He tilted the blade slightly to reflect the minimal light from the fire.

"Heh, do you really expect me to believe that?" the figure spat. Its claws seized Taya's arm possessively, almost as if realising her intention to run.

"Can you afford to doubt it?" Rob maintained confident eye contact as they stood in deadlock. The creature's narrowed eyes briefly glanced to examine the weapon. There was no doubt this man could impale him if he attempted to flee with his prize and, if his sword was truly the Blade of Paion, even a single wound would be enough to kill him. He had seen the result of such weapons before, in Abaddon, and the Blade of Paion was one of the most feared.

Paion was rumoured to have been an enforcer from the Gods, yet he had no place or mention in historical texts. His deeds were told only through song and tale, and his existence debated by philosophers of old. There were those who claimed he was a hunter, others labelled him a Moirai, but all agreed his purpose was to deliver the sinful to Hades. His weapon was poised for justice, his heart pure, and thus, over time his blade became endowed with the righteous energy of the acts it performed. Then one day, new tales of him simply ceased. The man himself, to this day, remained the threads of legend.

The creature lowered its hand. The release of pressure causing Taya's limp body to slide weakly to the ground, supported only by the thick tree trunk. Rob cast a concerned glance towards her. She stared blankly ahead, but aside from the violent tremors of fear she was otherwise unharmed. His eyes had lingered on her for only a second, but it was ample time for her attacker to return to the cover of the shadows.

"Are you all right?" Rob crouched beside her. Placing a reassuring hand on her shoulder he checked for any sign of injury. Surprisingly, despite the power of the creature's grasp, not a mark had been left upon her flesh.

"That thing... it wasn't human," she whispered, resisting the urge to throw her arms around him in search of comfort. He may have just saved her but he was still her enemy. A fact she needed to keep in the forefront of her mind. Especially now, when she almost felt she could trust him.

"Neither are you. What's the problem?" She looked to him in disbelief, but he was too intent on examining their surroundings to notice. Unsure how to answer she diverted his attention by asking a question.

"Is that really the Holy Blade of Paion?"

"You tell me," he shrugged, sheathing it before she could examine it further. "We have to leave. Now." Rob seized her wrist pulling her to her feet in a hurried motion. His eyes flitted from her to the shadows surrounding them.

"What about your things?" Taya questioned shakily. Rob cast a quick look towards the fire where his backpack lay abandoned. He shook his head, pulling her along behind him.

"No time, we need to move. It said us," he observed, his palms growing damp as he finally became aware of a faint scent on the breeze. He cursed under his breath before looking over his shoulder to Taya. "Cover your nose."

"Why?"

"Just do it," Rob snapped, covering his nose and mouth with his jerkin. His grasp on Taya increased as he heard the scuttling movement from the canopies above. He knew that scent. He had spent too long around the unspeakable not to.

"What is that?" Taya whispered inhaling the sweet odour. She pulled against his grasp as she tried to follow the enticing aroma.

"Pheromones. Quickly, this way. We need to break cover." Glancing above them, searching the canopy, he willed his mind to remain clear. He pulled Taya aside, guiding her protectively past a long silken thread suspended from the branches above. Careful scrutiny revealed more shimmering in the twilight, marking the path which would lead them from the dense woodland. He felt his gaze lingering too long on the reflection of light emanating from large orbs at the base of the silken threads.

"What is it?" Taya whispered, her voice seeming distant. Her free hand left her nose to reach out in an attempt to touch the luminescent pearl.

"A lure," Rob concluded, his surroundings becoming hazy as he pulled Taya back. She tumbled into him forcing him off balance, and causing his head to spin. He looked around, trying to regain his bearings. But he could only see the orbs, hovering in the air like suspended rain. They caught the light of the approaching dawn, beckoning him towards them with the promise of warmth and comfort. He shook his head, trying desperately to dispel the confusion, and spoke aloud in hope it would somehow ground him. "Some are responsible for the release of pheromones, the others are bolas, intended to snare us. We need to focus, tread carefully. The arachnid is counting on our disorientation."

"A spider did this?"

"I'm not sure what to call it. Neither animal nor man, but I've caught a glimpse of it in the trees." He continued in hushed tones. "It seems to hunt like the bolas spider, with some deviation. We're being drawn to these. We have to get past them." Rob motioned towards the scent sacks, taking care not to disrupt them in any way as he led Taya around them.

"We should turn back," she suggested, seeing the sheer number of threads surrounding them.

"That's what they want. If we don't fall prey to this they'll assume we'll retreat. If we don't make it outside the forest under our own power, we're not going to make it out. As long as we're here the trees will allow the pheromones to pool. It'll just be a matter of time until one of us makes a mistake." He gestured before them. "It's not far, I can see the forest's edge."

He looked back to Taya, aware her gaze was focused solely on the shimmering orbs. He drew her towards him, securing her so close he could feel her warmth. He covered his nose once more, aware of his own ragged breathing as his mind began to wander to the place he had first learnt of such monsters existing. He looked to one of the orbs, seeing himself within it before his reality shifted. For the briefest moment he found himself looking at a reflection of himself within the forest, accompanied by an unfamiliar woman.

* * *

Rob placed the beaker down, disrupting his reflection in the silver fluid. His brow furrowed as he regained his bearings. This small white laboratory had been his home since he had been recruited. If such a term was accurate for what had occurred.

While his sister trained, he had worked as an associate in the Hunter's Plexus planning one day, when he was old enough, to take the trials in order to become a fully-fledged member. But his tasks had advanced beyond those issued to one of his level, and he was being requested personally. This alone gave him the hope of being allowed to take the trials earlier than most. He had gone to sleep with such thoughts. But when he awoke he was no longer under the blanket of canopies, he had been in The Courts of Twilight.

"I thought we'd lost you there for a moment." Came the honeyed voice of his mentor. "I warned you they were strong didn't I?"

"What just happened?"

"Exposure. Did it have the effect you wanted?" Emily, the dark-haired beauty who worked alongside him, questioned. "You're still a bit disorientated, huh?" She slipped her hand on top of his, allowing it to trace up his arm until he pulled away. "I hear you're getting your tikéta soon," she mused, her fingers caressing her own ink marking. It was a ritual all those deemed worthy were granted. It was proof of their servitude to The Courts of Twilight. A high honour extended only to those who had proved both worth and loyalty.

"Tomorrow." Rob raised his hand, brushing his fingers through his hair.

"I had my doubts when they gave you to me. I've seen you adventurer types before, but this time I recant my preconceptions. I'm not sure what I did to deserve someone like you, but your aptitude for learning is remarkable.

"Your kind normally come in all brawn and no brain. It'll be a shame to see you move on." Emily gave a slight sigh, placing her hand upon his shoulder. "I wanted to keep you, but it seems they have other areas in mind. I hear they expect you to be working in research. I've told them you'd be better suited to arcane, but what can I do?" She gave a slight shrug, releasing another sigh which showed her frustration to be genuine. "I've never seen someone work with binding like you, or have such success in dispelling it. You've still not told me your secret." She leaned forward, pulling one of the fine needles from his belt. She toyed with it, not quite breaking her flesh with its sharp point.

"Nothing to tell. I guess I've just got lucky aim."

"Hmph! Fine, don't tell me. I swear, if I didn't know better I'd say you could see the web."

"Honestly, there's nothing to tell." He was lying, and she knew it, but there was nothing more he could say on the matter. He had been entrusted with secrets she could not even imagine, and his purpose here had altered over the passing years. He felt he was being prepared for something, but he was unsure exactly what.

"You should get some rest, tomorrow will be a tiring day." Emily slid herself from the table, taking the phials with her to place them into one of the large cabinets lining the walls. He left the laboratory without so much as a backwards glance. He had been dismissing her advances for some time now, knowing there was nothing sincere about her flirtation. She was the same with everyone. Some suggested the prolonged exposure to the pheromones had taken their toll.

"You are late." The familiar voice greeted him firmly as he closed the door to his assigned quarters. She had visited him many times, cloaked by shadows. "My father intends to secure your loyalties tomorrow. You have proven yourself, but he continues to underestimate your worth." He could hear the slight hint of a smile in her voice. "I have other plans. I can already sense your growing discontent.

"You recognise The Courts for what they are, a prison disguised by trinkets and trappings. You do not belong here, but have realised escape is not viable. Having seen through the ruse it is clear what awaits should your doubts be recognised. Swear allegiance to me and I will ensure you remain unaffected by my father's domestication."

"And what would you ask of me?"

"Time, patience, and obedience. I will teach you how to negate his training. In exchange, there is something you must do for me. Something that will earn you the freedom you so desperately crave."

"And how would we keep our alliance from Lord Blackwood?"

"Leave my father to me. He is not the influence he believes himself to be."

* * *

Rob became aware of an encouraging grip guiding his every movement as his mind slowly began to clear. The light of the dawn sun before them had grown darker than when he had last seen it reflecting his image upon the orbs. Dark and heavy clouds began to obscure the sky. The heavy rain to come was preceded by the gentle, refreshing caress of a light drizzle upon his flesh. It was a few moments before he realised it was Taya who led them. Her flesh shimmered with the drizzle that clung to her.

The oppressive air had been somewhat dispelled, and before him he could see their escape. He was only grateful Taya had somehow resisted the thrall he himself had been drawn into. It had been a long time since he had reflected on those days. His departure from The Court had been a turning point in his life, one from which he had never looked back. He had done his best to put those years behind him, and forget the many things he had seen and done.

Taya's pace stopped abruptly as they broke free of the tree line. Rob's partially dazed state causing them to collide. He looked up, realising his attention had been solely on the movement of his feet. The drunken haze dispelled in an instant as he saw what awaited them. He reached forwards grasping Taya's dress to guide her behind him, and shielded her with his own body. They had thought themselves fleeing a trap, instead they had walked straight into the awaiting ambush.

Enormous forms, in numbers matching those of a small battalion, stood awaiting their arrival. Rob glanced behind him, confirming what he already knew to be true. They had been surrounded. Led expertly to this place by design, to face monsters in greater numbers than he had dared to imagine.

The dawn sky was dark, concealed fully by the approaching rain. A lone shadow stepped forwards, its form concealed by the combination of distance and the misty rain. Despite this obstruction Rob could see it moved with an unnatural gait.

"The girl for your life." The figure opened negotiations with a single statement. But Rob knew all too well they had the numbers to simply take her. He could feel the weight of their many eyes upon him as they awaited his response. He guided Taya further behind him, feeling the warmth of each rapid, fearful breath upon his back. He grasped the hilt of his weapon, taking no comfort in its presence.

"Our freedom for yours," Rob retorted, drawing himself up to his full height. He squared his shoulders, focusing on projecting an air of confidence, hoping the trembling of the weapon in his hand went unnoticed. The sight of this battalion had been sobering, bringing him to a level of fear and awareness he had hoped to never again experience.

There was clarity on the borders of hysteria, where each horrific visage became burned into the mind. Whilst their forms cast a dark blemish across the land, he saw each one. Each heart-stopping, blood-freezing horror in perfect clarity. These *could* be creatures born of Hades as fables told, but more likely they were children born from the union of Echidna and Typhon. With both, or either, as their parents. He felt the fear begin to expand from his core, fighting it with all he was. He was one man against a battalion. Their negotiation only served to humour him. But the painful grasp of Taya's hand on his back, as she buried her head between his shoulder blades, urged him to resist.

"Make no mistake, human, she does not belong with your kind. We will take her by force if need be."

"The lady has no desire to accompany you." Rob swallowed with difficulty, steeling himself before speaking again. "I invoke Champion Warfare." A roar, of what he assumed to be laughter, echoed across the open plain with the force of the thunder promised by the blackened clouds above. It was silenced abruptly by a single gesture from the one who had addressed him.

"We accept your terms." The sound of the figure's hands striking each other caused movement to stir within the ranks. Rob braced himself, taking slow, deep breaths in an attempt to calm his pounding heart. Before him stood monsters. Images akin to those written of in texts of old. Things he had seen in only tome and composition. Yet he knew those surrounding them, closing their ranks to form the area of battle, to be so much more. More powerful, more primal. The one to face him would be a champion, perhaps the second in command of this scare.

Rob felt Taya's grip on him intensify. He turned his head slightly, whispering in a tone so quiet only the slight increase in pressure, caused by her body tensing at his words, confirmed she had heard him.

He had told her to run. Knowing as soon as she could, the moment their attention was diverted to the challenge, she would. He knew how hard, how fast, she would flee. There was no doubt she would outrun any who attempted to pursue her. He had seen the lust for freedom in her eyes, and there was little that could subdue such a thing.

Rob stepped forwards, the action pulling his clothing from Taya's grasp. He drew his sword. These creatures would know by now of his earlier deception. There was nothing wondrous about this blade. It was forged of steel, and nothing more. He thrust the weapon down, embedding it into the soft earth before releasing his sheath to fall upon the ground. He was no swordsman. He had to rely on his own talents, his speed, his skill, and his luck, which often defied belief.

The weapon was for show, and its holding would only serve to slow him. Given the skill he imagined the one to face him would possess he knew better than to take this combat lightly. He glanced over his shoulder to Taya, giving her a slight nod as she backed slowly into the scare.

A lithe form emerged before him. Approaching its commander briefly it offered a show of respect. Rob's gaze was drawn to the pincered arm and traced the long limb, trying to study the chitinous armour forged from its flesh. It was human in but part. The masculine figure possessed a thick torso, visibly altering in shape to become the segmented abdomen of a scorpion, supported by many pairs of short, thick, chitinous legs. It stood shorter than the commander, perhaps shorter than Rob himself.

The figure's eyes all seemed to be fixed on him. Rob attempted to ignore the black beady orbs running parallel to its jawbone, disappearing behind its ears, and instead concentrated on its more humanoid features. The figure, seeing his fear, smiled menacingly, baring carnassial teeth with an extended gap between them and its canines to allow its chelicerae to extend in front of its incisors.

The commander placed a bone horn to his lips, unleashing the low, deep tone. The figure raised its pincered left arm to mimic the defensive stance of a shield. Protecting its right almost human limb.

Rob felt the cool path of sweat tracing his flesh as the horn silenced. He readied himself, widening his stance ready to react. The force of the creature's armoured pincer struck him before he had registered its movement. It was fast. It propelled itself forwards with the same speed and agility as its arthropod brethren. The blow sent him forcefully backwards, to land on the ground, winded and breathless. Rob rolled aside, briefly seeing a flash of movement as the creature attempted to strike its fallen prey. It twisted with speed, knocking him to the ground again before he had the chance to fully rise.

Rob's fingers fumbled at his belt, removing one of his longer spiked needles. He was well-practised in throwing them. They were his main defence, but required distance. A commodity which he was severely lacking. He rolled again as the pincered arm bore down, tearing through the delicate grasses. Thrusting himself up, Rob angled the needle to penetrate between the plates of his attacker's natural armour, and forced the tip deep into its shoulder. The figure drew up to its full height, its immobilised arm hanging limply in temporary paralysis from his precise attack. But its retaliation was instant.

Rob felt the burning pain radiate through his arm before his mind had even registered the whistle of movement. The creature's tail retracted from its prey. The venom sacks hidden within its stinger only partially depleted. His arm rapidly grew heavy as the spreading numbness expanded from the point of impact. He saw the stinger draw back, preparing to strike again. No longer able to support his weight he fell crumpled to the ground. The hunting horn sounded once more, accompanied by loud screams that pleaded for his life. His body convulsed as he tried to force his waning attention towards the source of the noise, towards the place he had last seen Taya standing. The altercation had lasted mere seconds. Her escape had been impossible.

* * *

Tears streaked her face as Taya fought desperately to reach Rob before the second strike could land. She fought against the arms, now coiled around her torso, holding her back. She kicked and screamed, begging his attacker to stop. She pleaded for his life, unaware if it was already too late. The horn sounded again, indicating the battle's end and Rob's clear defeat.

Taya thrust herself forwards, as if trying to pull herself through the air to escape the powerful grip. She watched the convulsing figure as his adversary stood over him, looking towards his commander for instruction. A slight nod was offered as the commander's eyes briefly met with Taya's, in a way suggesting they had claimed their intended target. Now that she was within their possession nothing else mattered. She found herself paralysed within his stare. An unnatural silence descended and, for the briefest of moments, all resistance stopped.

She felt the rush of movement as a figure hoisted her over its shoulder. An action which broke their gaze, resulting in her struggle resuming once more.

The group began to reenter the forest, giving no heed to Taya's continual resistance, or the fact her once prominent wings had disappeared from sight.

She reached out. Desperately grabbing at passing fauna in hope to wrench herself free but finding only a flower caught within her grasp. Her fear pooled, flowing within it, transferring everything she protected of herself deep into its cells. Her mind shifted, the familiar escape seemed almost a relief. Never had she managed to assert it outside of Mirage Lake. The colour of the pink petals grew more intense, more vibrant, as her examination magnified the delicate veins within its silken surface.

Her perspective altered again. She felt the cool breeze. The refreshment of food carried by the petals' veins as they became her own, and the pressure of something crushing her stem. With this awareness the pressure relaxed. She felt herself floating on the gentle breeze, falling to rest near a silver ring lost in the struggle. The earth vibrated, moving beneath the march of heavy footsteps leaving her behind. There she stayed, in her mind, pretending that all she was, and all she loved, remained safe within the flower. A flower lost in the clearing, not far from where Rob's convulsing body lay.

* * *

Rob watched through clouded eyes as the figure restraining Taya rendered her into submission. He watched the rain as it streaked the air, catching rays of light, leaving shimmering trails in his distorted vision. Streams of sunlight, penetrating the thick clouds, focused his mind on a flash of movement. A rapid trail leaving Taya's possession as she fought desperately.

He clawed at the ground. The movement triggering convulsions that he convinced himself would help drive his body forward. His niece's screams penetrated the air as the shrouded forms vanished from view. Her cries possessed such piercing clarity that they sent painful spasms through his ears. His fingers clawed through the mud, seizing the silver ring to somehow hook it upon his own finger. No matter the cost he would return it to her, somehow.

This would not be the end. If they thought he would die here they clearly had no concept of how much he had already suffered. He was too close now. The darkness came for him through spasms of agony. But he swore he had heard a voice, carried upon the wind, drawn to him by Taya's screams.

Chapter 5

Amaranthine of the Mystics

Stacy pushed back the strands of wet hair clinging to her damp flesh. The voyage had been less than pleasant, but the call from the ship's watch signifying land had driven her to the bow to watch their approach through the rain and ocean spray. She had spent most of the journey huddled between crates, seeking shelter from the battering winds, and attempting to distract her mind from the turbulent currents.

Drevera was currently experiencing what was referred to as its green season. The entire island was shrouded in thick, heavy rain clouds. Their presence would be constant over the next few months, never breaking away, and rarely allowing the sun to penetrate its thick barricade. The sailors aboard the vessel had warned Stacy, on multiple occasions, that the inhospitable conditions were mild compared to those she would face from those living upon the island.

It was a small island, and required little in the way of commerce from outside sources. The quartermaster aboard the ship had warned there would not be another trade vessel this way for at least a month. Whilst they were on a tight schedule he implied they could delay, perhaps an hour, if she could attend to her business within that time. He was a burley fellow, his well-toned physique revealing the extent of his labour aboard the vessel. He spent his days alongside his men, attending to the loading and unloaded of crates as well as more serious concerns. There was always something requiring his attention, and he was not one to idle, which made his offer seem uncharacteristically out of place. He had shown her kindness and courtesy, but had little time to make conversation, and for this Stacy was glad. She preferred to pass the voyage in silence. Her nerves were already frayed at the thought of what was to come.

When the ship docked the quartermaster had taken her hand in his to escort her down the gangplank. Probably assuming the tremors passing through her were due to the damp and cold, rather than the fear of what this island may hold. He raised his hand, his bellowing voice calling out a greeting to an approaching man. He was a sorrowful looking figure, water ran off him in rivulets and his mood seemed only to add to the clouds above, that was, until he saw the vessel had docked. He stood a little straighter. His pace became a little quicker as he guided the horse and trap into the docking area.

"This here's the last of it. You've made good time 'sidering there's a storm on its way." He patted the horse gently as it drew to a halt, allowing him to begin unloading the remaining crates. The unmanned dock was filled with them, each baring the seal designated to this outpost by the Plexus.

"How long you been here now, the locals treating you any better?"

"Near a year, and no. Although I've managed repairs on the leaking shack they so generously issued as home and Plexus." The quartermaster shook his head solemnly as the Plexus master spoke. "Hey, don't worry. They're warming to me a little more for each time they don't have to deal with you." He forced a strained laugh.

"Hey listen, lass," The quartermaster petitioned Stacy's attention as she began to leave. "If you need to charter a vessel this fine fellow here will see you right. I can't see what a place like this has to offer." Stacy turned, approaching the Plexus master as he beckoned her towards them.

"I'll spare you some suffering. If you tell me what you want, maybe I can help and you can be on your way with this unsavoury bunch of rapscallions. I'd take months of hard labour on the sea with this rowdy crew over two days here with them." He made a gesture over his shoulder towards, what Stacy assumed to be, the direction of the town.

"I'm looking for a woman. She goes by the name Amelia."

"Ah, another outcast, a native one too. Though you wouldn't think it how they talk about her. Course, that all changes when they need something. You won't see her in town. She's easy enough to find, just look for the only house looking like it has been shunned. That's to say, she lives on the far borders, a good ways from the town.

"I guess I'd be out there too if it wasn't for me being the lesser of two evils. They tolerate me because they don't want to deal with this lot." He gestured towards the quartermaster. A slight alarm crossed his features when he realised he had started to help his men load the vessel.

He continued talking, but Stacy's attention had wandered slightly as she slowly began to edge away. It was cold, wet, and she couldn't afford to spend her time here. Not when she had been summoned in such a manner. Her journey here had already taken her longer than anticipated, and she feared the welcome she would receive. Stacy offered an awkward smile as he noticed her subtle retreat. He nodded his head in a polite gesture, his speech never stilling as he spoke to any who would listen.

* * *

Stacy looked upon the door. Her pale blue eyes showed clear signs of her apprehension, while the dark emerald rings surrounding their iris only serving to make her pale features seem more ashen. Her pupils further dilated as she once more raised her hand to knock. She feared that the sound of her striking the wood would summon the beast from within, yet it was this person she sought.

Despite her fear of the woman behind these doors, of the berating she expected to receive given her past mistakes, she knew she had no choice. Six years ago she had made a mistake. Now, having awakened to the truth of her abilities, she feared the repercussions of her actions, of all their actions.

She hesitantly moved again, pushing her hand through her brown hair. Her determination evident in the setting of her jaw, but once this blow had been struck her life would be irreversibly altered. She wasn't sure she was ready for all this could entail.

Stacy heard an exasperated sigh from inside as her hand lowered once more. A sound followed by quiet mumbling before the door was snatched inward to reveal the silhouette of an elderly lady. The figure's sudden appearance caused Stacy's breath to catch as she stepped backwards quickly, in a partial retreat.

"Enough of this procrastination. I'm not getting any younger you know," the figure scolded. "The pot has just boiled, again. Now wipe your boots and shift your backside. You're letting the cold in." The elderly figure stepped aside, allowing Stacy to enter. Her vision wandered the room. The walls were lined by a few bookcases, and gentle light from the far window filtered over a collection of wicker furniture. Central to the room stood a table, its worn, stained, and battered appearance giving it the impression of great age. Upon its mottled surface stood two delicate looking teacups. The warmth from the room was as much from the atmosphere as the small fireplace holding heated stones. "Boots!" Amelia's voice startled her, but she saw a slight smile turn up the corners of her lips.

"Thank you. Sorry, I'm—"

"Yes, yes, Stacy, Holder of the Sacred Chord." She waved her aged hand in a hurried motion before inclining her head towards the doormat. "Now if you'll be so kind." Once Stacy had obliged, and closed the door, the figure gestured her towards the table. "I'm not one for too much formality, but still, some things just have to be said. Be at ease, I, Amelia, Amaranthine of the Mystics, bid you welcome."

"You were expecting me?" Stacy's features still showed her confusion. Whilst their paths had never crossed, there was some part of her which recognised the elderly figure before her. Everything about this woman was familiar. Her image alone was enough to soothe her frayed nerves. Amelia's long white hair had been secured in a strangely regal fashion, held in its messy bun by hair pins and combs. Whilst her tone had held impatience, she looked upon her now with only warmth and recognition.

"Of course dear. Who do you think brought you here once your gift had awoken. But the fact you heeded my call speaks of the untold dangers we now face." Amelia always recognised her kin. Often she sought them out, watched over them as they led their mortal life unaware of the unique abilities which lay dormant within them. Abilities which were sealed away, triggered only by foreknowledge of some catastrophic event, for which their skills would be needed.

There had been times, over the countless cycles, where one, or even two, had stirred and sought her. But in her bones, Amelia felt the reforging of destiny. The path before them was no longer as clear as it had once been. A change loomed on the horizon, and her links to the kindred souls were beginning to stir. This time, they would all awaken. The threat to come was unlike anything they had seen since the purpose for which Gaea had first created them.

"I don't understand."

"You will." Amelia gestured towards a chair, smiling as she heard Stacy's steps halt suddenly.

"Holder of the Sacred Chord?" she questioned, realising Amelia had already named her. It was one of the reasons she had come here, to receive her title. The other was to be guided, taught all she should know, and awaken the part of her which held the ancient memories of her abilities.

"That's what I said." Amelia smiled gesturing again towards one of the chairs. Stacy complied without hesitation, startling slightly as its uneven legs wobbled under her weight. Amelia stepped through the opening into the kitchen, disappearing from view for but a moment before returning with a teapot. "I have much to offer you here. Your awakening means time grows short and disaster approaches. We have much to do and will begin immediately, after tea." She poured some of the amber fluid into the cups before joining Stacy at the table.

"But I thought—"

"I see," Amelia interrupted. "You thought your skill had something to do with the psychokinesis." Stacy gave a nod, her head remaining bowed to study the contents within the teacup. "That is just a part of you, but your strongest skill is one no sceptre can strip and it lies within your voice." Amelia's eyes narrowed as she scrutinised the woman before her. The sceptre had indeed done lasting damage. She could see its blemish on her essence. Her key skill remained un-tainted, but her actions had diminished her power, of that there was no doubt.

Amelia silently scolded herself as she completed the silent examination. She had been so preoccupied with protecting Rhea, the Chosen, and the Oneirois, she had failed to realise the threat to her kin. Now, only her own and Eiji's power remained unaltered. She could only hope it would prove to be enough. Especially if the danger she feared came to pass.

"What's the verdict?" Stacy questioned, she knew that look well. Amelia's eyes had misted with magic and no longer looked upon her but the aura revealing the power she carried.

"I will help you unlock your talents, but first we will focus on your key skill. It is essential, especially for the near future. I can see you have spent some time learning control over your more volatile trait."

"I have," Stacy confirmed with a firm nod. When she had taken the sceptre in her hand she had wanted nothing more than to be rid of her curse. Free from a power which controlled so many aspects of her life. When she had regained consciousness she, along with Peter, Marc, and Helen, were all being cared for in a small hospital wing in Albeth Castle, and she had instantly regretted her actions. Where the power had once nestled felt empty and hollow, as if a key part of her had been irrevocably stripped away. She felt a sensation of loss greater than any she had experienced before. Never had she felt so alone and afraid, so vulnerable. As soon as she could she left, hoping to somehow ease the emptiness within her, and find a purpose.

It was a year later, almost to the day, when the echo of her lost skill resurfaced. This time instead of fearing it she welcomed it, and her acceptance alone saw her gain control. Yet its power was but a fraction of that it had once been.

"What exactly is the Holder of the Sacred Chord?" she questioned, tearing her thoughts from the past. It was only as her eyes found their focus once more she realised she was staring at the hypertrophic burn scar across her right palm.

"A person whose song is so beautiful it can calm even the most violent of beasts, lulling them to submission or sleep. Some once called you a dragon charmer, but I'm a stickler for the old names. They command a respect and power often forgotten. Just like the truth of dragons thanks to Kadmos Rosu."

The wyrms had long ago been tainted with the name of dragon, yet the two species were different

in more ways than one. Whilst wyrms and dragons bore some similarities, the dragons were savage,
hateful creatures. Impossible to tame or reason with.
Holders of the Sacred Chord were the only means to
subdue them.

A single dragon could bring the world to ruin, and
there had once been a time where too many had darkened the skies. The wyrms had been the guardians
of humanity, teaching those with the skill the songs
needed to exploit their enemies. But to grant a person the means to control the most powerful beast,
allowed them dominance over every weaker species.
But when the last of the dragons had been defeated,
and their bones long buried by dust, the humans still
held this power, and some turned it to corruption.

The Gods, those long fallen and now forgotten,
were forced to intervene. They feared this ancient
and powerful music would be used to exploit their
own kind. But such a heritage could never be lost,
and so the potential to use it was expunged from all
but a single soul, one Gaea had created when there
was nought but life and magic. This soul belonged to
one of only six she created, and these six were known
as the Mystics.

"A sacred chord, such a thing exists?" Stacy felt
her hands trembling nervously as she took a sip of
the amber fluid from the wooden cup before her.

"Yes, and once mastered, it is possible your voice
could charm through speech alone. Come now dear,
finish your drink. We have much to do and the words
are old and complex. In time you will find your own

words and music. For now, I can teach you those I know, those your earliest incarnation taught me, so that I may return them. Then when you are ready, we will test your skills."

"In Kalia?" Stacy questioned, a small flash of a faded memory resurfacing. When they had been rescued after taking the sceptre within their hands she had faded in and out of consciousness. She was certain that one of the people who had rescued them had advised they would return to Kalia and request the aid of the wyrms and Eortháds.

"No." Amelia smiled, extending her hand across the table to place it comfortingly on Stacy's arm. "It will be a field experience I'm afraid."

* * *

Stacy sat at the unmanned port staring out across the sea, watching a storm on the distant horizon, lighting the turbulent waves beneath it. Another storm closed in from the south. The dark clouds twisted into each other, slowly merging to become one until no divide could be seen. It was a sight to behold. The flashing of forks from the sky struck the water in quick successions. Granting any who watched a display of violence only mastered by nature. The angry roars of thunder carried on the tempest, almost inaudible against the wind's force as it rushed across the ocean to the land.

Today had been one of reflection. She had been with Amelia for a month now, perhaps more. They had studied persistently, and she was making progress. Albeit slower than she would have liked. Amelia had not lied about the complexity of the ancient tones and words. Even now, after so much practice, she feared she would forget them. Once a week Amelia would insist she took the day as her own, and today was such a day.

On a clear morning, looking out to the northwest, she was able to see the distant peninsular of Therascia. Today, however, all remained hidden, lost in dark clouds and the onslaught of ocean rain. On days like these Drevera felt isolated, and she became aware of how far from home she truly was.

After leaving Albeth Castle she had taken a journey of discovery, hoping to fill the void the absence of her powers had left. But when her psychokinesis once more stirred she found herself returning there, wishing to speak with Helen.

During their unperceived imprisonment at the hand of Blackwood, the small group had become close friends. All were seeking the means to have life free of complications. They became a family, sharing mutual feelings of kinship and belonging as they awaited the time when their individual curses could be lifted. During their recovery they had been placed in the care of Albeth Castle, and had even considered making a permanent home within the walls. When Stacy had returned she discovered both Peter and Marc had chosen to follow her path of solitude, returning to a semblance of the isolation they had known before being united with their friends. The city was busy, and over time had become too much for those used to peace and calm.

Being short of funds Stacy had taken work in exchange for bailiff tokens. Albeth Castle was the only known place to operate such a system. Labour was exchanged for tokens, which in turn could be presented for food and shelter. She worked diligently, and it wasn't long before she found herself in the permanent employ of the castle kitchens. She had been offered an apprenticeship, but she had politely declined. Even then, part of her had known this arrangement would only be temporary.

A longing sigh left Stacy as she watched the distant storm come to a head. She was homesick, and her parting with Helen had not been on the best of terms. Their final exchange had been hostile and accusations were spoken which could never be revoked. Stacy wondered if she too could have forced herself to ignore the truth, if doing so meant living a life thought only to be a desperate dream. But even now there was one thing she could not forgive. The cruel words, the ignorance, were nothing in contrast to the urgency which had accompanied the awakening. No matter how hard she tried, she could not forgive Helen for turning a blind eye to something so important.

Amelia stood behind Stacy, waiting for the young woman to return from her daydream. Startling slightly Stacy rose to greet her as she became aware of the Amaranthine's presence.

"I have a mission for you, dear," Amelia announced in a comforting tone, yet there was a clear glimmer of mischief within her eyes.

"A mission?" Stacy felt herself flush with a sickening heat.

"There's a wayward wyrm sheltering in some caves near Beranme. I need you to calm it so that I might treat its injuries." Stacy lost the power to speak and simply stared at Amelia in pure terror.

* * *

Daley took several slow breaths before bringing his awareness back to his surroundings. He had expected to still be within The Betwixt, but such was not the sight which greeted him.

Sunlight fell in streams upon fields of darkened wheat. It seemed healthy, yet lacking the sun-kissed shades he knew all too well. A small field-mouse fought to climb the sheaths, but aside from this small honey-coloured creature he seemed to be alone. The trees in the distance were dark and dreary. The world itself so alive, yet at the same time its shades were a tribute to death.

"Where in all the realms am I?" Daley questioned aloud. He watched a humanoid shadow pass. Its slow staggering movements occasionally quickening in short bursts of jerky energy. Watching it, and how the light seemed to almost penetrate the shape, Daley was almost certain it possessed no physical presence. If he reached out, his hand would surely pass through it. It continued on its path, showing no signs of seeing him.

Similar forms walked in the distance, oblivious to all within their sight. They were fragments, somehow incomplete, trapped in prolonged decay. He wondered how long one must dwell within this realm to become as they were. He had no intention of finding out.

Sitting on the floor Daley closed his eyes, reaching out towards The Betwixt so that he could find his way home. It was an uncommon, but not unheard of, for a Daimon to slip into another realm during their workings. A single lapse of concentration could see their ethereal form anchored to the nearest gateway and pulled through. But as Daley failed to touch The Betwixt he knew that this was not what had occurred.

"Any fortune?" Daley's alarmed gaze panned the surroundings. This single sound was the first he had heard since his arrival. With this realisation came an array of noise, the sounds of the wind rustling through the corn, and the whispering movement of distant leaves. "I say, down here." Daley's vision was drawn towards the small honeyed field-mouse he'd noticed earlier. It sat upon the tassel of the corn, its rear paws gripping tightly as it extended its twitching nose in his direction.

"Are you addressing me?" Daley questioned uncertainly.

"That I am, my good sir, a Daimon yes? Would you mind? This is not as comfortable as it might appear."

The mouse inclined its head slightly, its eyes looking towards Daley's arm.

"Erm, of course." Daley extended his hand to the creature, allowing it to jump from the wheat.

"Thank you. I'm Jude. I'm glad to see you've not forgotten how to converse with us."

"With... mice?" Daley asked uncertainly, his dark eyebrows raising in a perplexed manner.

"A bit slow aren't you my good sir. I'm an Oneiroi and this"—the mouse sat on its hind legs turning its head from right to left before returning to all fours—"is a nefarious place indeed. A realm within a realm. A curse within a curse."

"And where exactly *is* this realm?"

"We're in the Forest of the Epiales. And this is *his* domain."

"His?"

"You really are a bit slow on the uptake for a Daimon aren't you, my good fellow? Do you not study the ancient mythos any more? The forest of the Epiales has only one master. It has been so since he was banished here." The mouse's body tensed cowering slightly as a shadow soared overhead.

"You mean Íkelos?" Daley questioned, his eyes scanning the surroundings for shelter. His mind warned him against lingering. He fixed his gaze upon a small grove and began to walk, taking care to hold his new friend securely.

"If you wish, but our kind refer to him as the Melas-Oneiros, the black dream, The Father of Nightmares, Haunter of—"

"But why are we here?" he interrupted, knowing how many names a being as old as the one dwelling here would come to possess. There was little doubt in his mind this mouse, Jude, would have named them all.

"Well that, my good fellow, remains to be seen but," Jude once more sat on his hind legs, "nothing good will come of this. Nothing good at all." His dark beady eyes surveyed the surroundings, his form relaxing slightly as they entered the shade of the trees. "You were unsuccessful in touching either The Stepping Realm or The Betwixt, yes?"

"Yes," Daley said, his voice displaying his confusion.

"And how about your prison, have you managed to access it?"

"Prison?" At his question the mouse let out a sound which sounded remarkably similar to a little sigh.

"You and I, we possess no physical body like the humans and the other things he normally detains here. Yet part of us has to be present within the forest. He has not simply banished us here. It's a complicated undertaking, separating a conscious mind from a thing already formed only of energy, but this forest can do it.

"I am loath to admit its workings are beyond my understanding. Even I was oblivious to it at first, but on a few occasions I have managed to return to that part of myself, or perhaps he returned me. But, my esteemed comrade, what I saw was not good. No, it was not good at all." Jude shook his head.

"What do you mean not good?"

"He's searching for something. He was using my link to the land to extend his sight across Darrienia. But you, he could use you to view any plane he chooses," Jude explained, his eyes narrowing. This Daimon's presence here was a cause for great unrest, greater than that of his own capture. Melas-Oneiros required something from them, and Jude shuddered to imagine the fate that awaited them.

"I'm not sure I follow," Daley admitted, moving to take shelter beneath one of the darkened trees. He leaned back carefully, ensuring the solidity of the trunk before trusting his weight to it.

"The Daimons still use The Betwixt to convey messages through The Stepping Realm, yes?"

"Yes, but we only reach to the Hum—"

"Doesn't matter. You're the only beings currently capable of traversing the corridors of The Betwixt. He's searching for something, of that much I am certain, and he has failed to find it in Darrienia. I believe that is the purpose of your presence. You would provide a much broader scope, a wider window into any realm he could choose."

"What else do you know?" Daley questioned, raising the small form to eye-level.

"You won't like it. It is ill-tidings indeed."

"Tell me."

"He's using our forms to draw energy from our respective realms."

"I don't understand."

"Of course you don't, you've not experienced it yet." Jude's fur stood on end as his small body trembled. "We are both aligned to the energies of our respective worlds. Myself to Darrienia, and you to Kólasi. Both realms have a very old, very unique magic. Íkelos is using our connection to syphon some of that power."

Jude knew the energies being drawn through him originated from places other than Darrienia. His only theory, at this time, was that the disruption to the dreamers caused by Melas' generals allowed them to bring another energy through, one the newly formed tideway harnessed and attuned to Darrienia. Kólasi on the other hand, had links to older powers. When it had been sealed it had been invoked forces beyond measure. Due to the passage of time and deity alterations Kólasi's seal was, in some cases, the only place some imprints of former powers still existed. The Daimon, Daley, would be used to harness that energy, and in doing so create a weakness in the powers retaining Kólasi's very alignment.

"But he's not attuned to our energies, so even if it was gathered he couldn't use it. Could he?"

"That, my good sir, is the true horror of this forest. It feeds on magic."

"So it takes the magic he draws through us and then adapts it into something he can use?" Daley felt himself pale at the realisation.

"Precisely."

"So what happens now, how do we stop it?"

"I don't know that we can. He's got us on our back paw, so to speak. All we can do is try to discern his plan and relay a message."

"But you said we can't touch The Stepping Realm. How can we hope to achieve that?"

"My partner Aidan will be searching for me. If I can sense him I should be able to relay a message," Jude explained, a hopeful lift to his voice.

"But we're not in your realm, so surely you won't be able to sense him."

"No, not normally. But there's an intermittent window. When the energy is drawn into me, if I can access my prison, I can see into Darrienia, and any there can see here."

"And how do you know Aidan will come?"

"He's my partner, and the generals' actions have created a tideway. He will be drawn to investigate the strange nature of the gathering energies because he will sense mine amongst them." The mouse scurried up Daley's arm, perching himself on his shoulder. "Something monumental is occurring. Everything I have known has been a mere prelude. Íkelos knows something powerful is about to be unleashed and he is ensuring he can harness its energy."

* * *

"Rob, thank the Gods, you're awake!" He heard relief in the voice as he let out a groan. His body ached and his chest hurt with the effort of every breath. When he finally managed to open his eyes the sharp, blinding rays of light sent spasms of pain through his throbbing head. There were a few more minutes of fighting the tired darkness before his eyes finally remained open. His awareness returned in broken and disjointed fragments. It took several moments for him to remember someone had spoken, and longer still to identify the voice as his sister's.

Gaining a small amount of focus on the room around him, he realised he had somehow reached Elpída.

"Di-did she get away?" His voice was weaker than he had expected. It took a great effort to shuffle himself up into a sitting position. He pushed himself back to rest against the headboard and recover from his efforts. "I feel like I was caught in a stampede." He brought his hand to his face, before rubbing his pounding head. His body ached, even the smallest of motions triggered fresh discomfort.

"Drink this." Sunniva lifted a glass of water from the small bedside table. "You've been fevered for a week. The poison was a nasty one." As his trembling hands took the glass Sunniva leaned forward, checking his forehead and neck for any remaining signs of fever. Her touch brought comfort. She had always worried about him, ever since they were children.

"Did she get away?" he asked again, his voice holding a little more power now his throat was not so dry.

"You could say that," Sunniva scoffed. "I knew she was dangerous, but I never expected her to attack you." Sunniva stood from the bed with her back turned towards him. The ringlets of her golden hair swayed back and forth with the motion of her shaking head.

"Attack me?" Rob rubbed his head, images of Taya striking at him with a dart filled his mind as he was overcome by another wave of nausea. Sunniva grabbed one of the metal bowls from beside the bed in time to catch the water he had drank as it returned. He let out another groan, but found his head had cleared a fraction. He tensed his muscles, feeling noticeably less fatigued than just a moment before.

"Sip it this time," Sunniva warned, refilling the glass from the jug. For the first time, as he looked down, he realised he was wearing only a night shirt. He covered his eyes in embarrassment, thinking of all the acolytes would have done for him while he lay unconscious. He felt a coolness upon his cheekbone, only realising it to be out of place after a few moments. He pulled his hands from his eyes to study the silver ring upon his little finger. "This is Ethelyn's," he recalled. Fragmented images returned to him, overlaying the image of her with his stolen weapon. Memories resurfaced of the ambush, the challenge, Champion Warfare, and his devastating defeat. He searched mentally for bruising and broken bones, yet found none. Even the place he knew should be damaged from the stinger was strangely injury free. Yet still felt sore when he tensed his bicep.

"It is." Sunniva reached out, taking his hand in a controlled manner as she studied it. "I gave it to her." Her eyes narrowed, Rob could see her concern by the furrowing of her brow. She released his hand, retreating a few paces before turning her back towards him once more.

"How did I get here?" he questioned, looking around the room as if to enforce his meaning.

"A convoy found you. The toxin had already spread. Thankfully, Brother, you are nothing if not reactive. The tourniquet they applied, when combined with whatever manner of concoction you'd taken, may just have spared your life.

"They brought you to my doors and we used the serum we had been given in case the children were attacked by one of the more inhospitable creatures that roam our fields. It seemed to have the desired result." Sunniva cursed silently. When her brother had been brought to her she had panicked. His condition had been grave indeed, but she had left his care to the acolytes, while she and the clerics desperately sought Taya. If she had tended to him she would have seen the ring, and removed it before he had reason to question her tale.

"Gods." Rob pulled his hands down his face, his eyebrows knitted together as his sight returned to the ring. "Oh Gods, Sunniva, they took her!" Sunniva looked to him sharply. His injuries had been extensive, but she had been certain Taya had somehow been responsible. The memories she had manipulated had simply ensured Rob remained unaware of any confrontation between them, or the passage of time while he recovered. It was better not to have to explain what she herself did not fully understand.

She had lied to him. It had taken more than days for him to recover. More than an entire month had past and she had begun to fear he would never wake. She hoped by concealing this he would be vigilant in his efforts to find Taya and not, as many would given the passage of time, believe her to be lost. But if he feared someone had taken her, perhaps there was more to this than her pursuit of freedom. Perhaps the situation was still salvageable, but now Rob possessed something Sunniva needed. The truth of what had come to pass.

"Who took her?" Sunniva questioned trying to hide the concern in her voice. "Tell me, what do you think happened?"

"The Daimons?" Rob's voice held a questioning lift as he spoke aloud the name Taya had given him. Everything was still confused. He was having difficulty remembering the details. Whenever he thought he recalled something, his mind refocused on the clear and vivid memory of her attack.

"No, my dear, sweet Brother." Sunniva sighed despairingly, moving to sit on the bed. "That's the poison talking. Think back, after she incapacitated you were there, perhaps, bandits?" He saw again the image of Taya, and, was that movement? The image of the treetops altered. Humans watched them from the shadows, waiting until he was helpless.

"I don't know. Maybe?" He rubbed his forehead as the dull throbbing returned. "But someone *was* after her." He paused as a clear impression of a creature bathed in firelight reached the forefront of his mind. "They weren't human. Creatures from Abaddon maybe, or—"

"I'm sorry, Rob, there's something I have neglected to tell you. I should have told you before." Sunniva gave a reluctant sigh, as long as this remained unresolved for him it appeared she could not purge the unwanted thoughts and memories. "Taya comes from a troubled past. She was promised to the demons by her mother in exchange for a good harvest. Their crops had been failing, their family all but starving. She had just discovered her pregnancy and so offered the only thing she had of value.

"But it is easier to offer a life you have no real bond to, but such a sacrifice is a different thing altogether when you hold that child in your arms. She did the only thing she could, she left the baby here in hope they would not find her.

"Ten years ago now, Taya came across the crumpled note that arrived with her at my door. I curse myself for keeping it. It was soon after that she contracted the blood sickness. It has only been since then she suffered from her delusions. They think her mind fixated on the fear seeing the note stirred, making it a reality for her. Now she says they call to her at sunset. When the delusions become all-consuming, to the point nothing I can do will guide her back to reality, we have no choice but to send her to Mirage Lake. There they have the means to familiarise her with what is real again."

"Mirage Lake." Rob shook his head, snippets of his conversation with Taya returning through the confusion. "I can't believe you would send her there. You know all too well what goes on within those walls." Rob's face grew dark. He knew there was something his sister wasn't telling him, and now he had a suspicion he knew exactly what it was. But if that was the case his whole definition of the word demons—or Daimons as Taya had called them—needed to be called into question. "If she was promised to them, how do you know the stories she tells aren't the truth?" More images clouded his mind as he questioned Sunniva. Flashes of memories, Taya running from him as the bandits circled his camp after leaving him for dead. But there was something empty about what he saw. The scene was bland, distant, with no trace of emotion, or fear.

"Because I raised her!" Sunniva snapped before attempting to calm herself. She let out a slow breath placing her hand gently on his arm. "I know her better than anyone," she whispered softly.

"I'm sorry, Sunniva," Rob sighed placing his hand to his head once more. He had found a moment of clarity within the jumble of memories. A cornerstone grounded him as the cool metal of Taya's ring made contact with his clammy forehead, and once more called attention to its presence.

He knew continuing to question his sister would serve no purpose. He needed information, and her cooperation was the only way to obtain it. If he continued to press her, to question her, it would only alienate her, and his concerns would be left unanswered, perhaps even forgotten. "You're right,

I know you are. The toxin must have been potent, in truth, I don't know what I saw." He massaged his temples slightly. "I remember being aware of someone following us. I'm not sure when she managed to take my needle." His attention turned towards his belt, which had been left carelessly discarded on top of his folded clothes on the smaller bedside table. He lifted it, tracing his fingers over the holder for the missing weapon, before running them over the others applying just enough pressure to ensure they were all accounted for. "I guess I'm lucky she took the one she did."

"I don't know why you insist on carrying such things," Sunniva scolded.

"The same reason a warrior carries a sword, for protection."

"Well, maybe this will teach you a lesson. Who keeps their weapons coated in venom anyway?"

"Someone worried about being attacked. Honestly, Sunni, sometimes I wonder if we live in the same world." Hearing him use the familiar childhood moniker brought a smile to her face, her shoulders visibly relaxed. It was a name he only ever called her when he had been fully seized in her thrall. "But I think you're right. I've been a fool, I know demons can't breach the barriers.

"I guess, given what you've told me, I was worried the oath would allow them passage to claim their dues. I mean, we both know the relics here bathe the area in holy blessings which are clearly powerful enough to keep evil at a distance." His sister seemed to once again stiffen at his response. Her ability to mask the concern his thoughts had kindled wavered.

Seeing this alteration he continued, playing on the fears he had given rise to. "I imagine the convoy and Mirage Lake have such blessings in place as well. It just made sense that when she was with me she was unprotected, and they'd get the opportunity to—Sorry, Sunni, can you forgive me? I'm still not feeling quite myself, I let my imagination run wild." He paused for a moment, blinking slowly as he moistened his lips. "Does she require familiarising with reality often?"

"At first her needs were less. But things have been getting worse. We've had to increase her stay to one month for every three." Rob felt his throat constrict. He had not believed Taya when she had said such things, but his own sister had confirmed her words to be true. There was no wonder she had been so desperate to escape. "With things happening as they did I could not get a convoy here in time, but I *was* hoping you would reach Collateral before nightfall. What delayed you?" There was an almost accusatory tone to her voice, yet despite the implication Rob felt himself being compelled to answer.

"Her wound," he answered obediently. "Had I known the danger I could have taken precautions." A barrage of new images flashed in his mind, at once he understood what she was attempting to do. He cursed his foolishness, his naivety at thinking his own sister would not stoop to that level of manipulation with him. He felt her overbearing presence as she carefully weaved her newest deceit.

He forced the tension from his limbs, allowing his gaze to seem unfocused. He had been privilege to her talents before, and once he realised her presence in his mind he knew how to feign enrapture. He echoed the words he heard her place. Attempting to calm his growing anger as he wondered how long she had been toying with him in this manner. "Do you think the bandits will give her to the demons?" He was to remember about Taya being promised to them, and everything else was to be forgotten.

"It's possible. They could be agents. Evil's tendrils stretch far, its influence immeasurable. You must forgive me, Brother. I am so used to talk of demons being woven from Taya's sickness that I sometimes forget there *is* a danger."

"Maybe her suffering is finally at an end. Perhaps she will find freedom." He scolded himself for not questioning the need to send Taya to such a place. He was worse than his sister in some respects, for she merely orchestrated the visits, he would have delivered Taya himself. Perhaps fate had turned to favour the young woman in the only way it could.

"Freedom? Do you think she will find relief in the clutches of death? She is my daughter, the things they will do to her—" Sunniva stifled a sob. "She will find no peace, no freedom. She will be used for breeding, or to power their homes. We all know demons use the light of our essences to power their own blackened realm. At least with my intervention she had a chance at life."

"With such frequent intervention it is a wonder she's alive, let alone sane." He took a slow sip from the water, swallowing it with difficulty.

"She's not sane. What we do is all for her own good. Please, Rob, we can't leave my little girl in the hands of those monsters. We need to find her before the full moon, or risk losing her forever," Sunniva begged, reaching out to grasp her brother's arm firmly. Rob found himself unable to hold her gaze. It was true he had spent very little time with Taya, but aside from believing herself to be a Daimon she seemed in quite sound mind. Rob manoeuvred his legs from the bed as he reached out to seize his clothes.

"I must be leaving. I have things I need to do," he announced suddenly to Sunniva's surprise. He staggered to his feet, almost losing balance as he hastily removed the long nightshirt and slowly dressed himself. It took a greater effort than he had expected.

"You're still weak. Won't you rest a little longer?" He slid his feet into his boots, almost toppling as he bent to secure the laces.

"I'll be fine," he advised, securing his belt in place, aware that resting against one of the door jambs did little to support his words. He couldn't bring himself to look at her, not after what he had discovered.

"Are you going to attempt to rescue her?" Sunniva prompted, whilst simultaneously implanting the desire.

"To deliver her there? I would rather the demons keep her," Rob retorted bitterly.

"Please, Rob, if you do go after her, bring her home to me." Rob, with his back to Sunniva, felt his lips turn into a slight smile. Throughout their conversation he had been given snippets of truth. Those he was not allowed to remember obviously more important than those she attempted to implant. His own deception had ensured Sunniva was not the only one to gain insight into what had occurred. His sister always let her guard down when she believed people to be under her control, after all, she erased all she wished them to forget.

* * *

Grayson Bray passed his hand through his short mousy-brown hair. He had been sitting in the comforts of the large bamboo chair for some time now. A small white cat, with beautiful sapphire blue eyes, sat on his lap looking up at him expectantly. The room had long fallen into silence, and the tension within was immense.

The owner of the cat sat across from him, staring at him with same intensity Bray used to scrutinise the feline. Sweat beaded on her rounded face. Her fidgeting movements caused the chair to occasionally creak under the strain of her heavyset frame.

"So, you were saying," Bray prompted. As if on cue the cat unleashed a barrage of howling and meows, never once breaking its gaze from Bray's.

"Hmm, I see," Bray responded, slowly raising his gaze accusingly towards the owner with a slight disapproving shake of his head.

"What, what did my baby say?" she questioned, wringing her apron in her sausage-like hands. The chair gave a groan, protesting under the sudden movement.

The man who sat before her had no equal when it came to understanding the needs of animals. She had heard about him only by rumour and reputation. She couldn't believe her luck when he appeared in her town around the same time her own little darling had started to act so moody.

"It's not going to be easy to hear." He gave a slight tut, his head shaking slowly his gaze holding hers firmly with what appeared to be a slight hint of regret reflected in his intensely green eyes.

"Tell me."

"She says," he paused for effect. The chair once more groaned as she leaned in to better hear his words. "She feels neglected. You either make her feel trapped and smothered, or ignore her completely." He gave a pained sigh. "I'm sorry you had to hear that." The cat protested briefly before Bray ran his hand affectionately down the creature's soft fur, placating it.

"My baby hates me?" she shrilled, before choking back a sob. "I-is there anything I can do?"

"Well, in circumstances such as these..." he stroked the cat again. Appreciating the affection she raised her head, narrowing her eyes showing her enjoyment of the well-practised touch. "I usually recommend plenty of fresh fish and cream. It will help to rebuild the bonds your actions have damaged. In addition, give her freedom when she needs it, affection when she asks. Do this and you'll be on your way towards restoring your relationship." He heard the cat give a deep throaty purr, head-butting his hand gently. Her purrs deepened further as she brushed herself against Bray's hand one final time before she dashed towards the kitchen to await her upcoming feast.

"Oh thank you! Thank you so much," the cat's owner exclaimed, wriggling free from the chair to shake his hand firmly. "Are you sure you won't stay for a drink, some food? It's the least I can do."

"Oh, no thank you ma'am. I've already had my fill. Besides, I have other matters to attend to." He flashed a debonair smile, closing the door behind him as he left.

The best thing about being in his line of work was he could convince almost anyone they were in need of his services. It was easy money, and he never had to worry about sustenance. He had seen a number of villages during the last six years, and inside the houses of the richest and most elite. Despite this, he was still no closer to finding what he sought. Although, if he was to be completely honest with himself, he hadn't exactly been looking. It was so easy to get carried away. He was enjoying his freedom, perhaps a little more than he should be.

"I'll spread the word. Thank you again for your help." The woman called through the kitchen window. Bray chuckled to himself, people were so predictable.

He followed the path to his next destination, opening the wooden gate precariously seated within the five-foot masonry wall. The design was unique. Its foundation began with the perfect ashlar design, but soon displayed the constructor's ebbing patience. Seams and joins became non-uniform, stones became strewn together haphazardly and fixed with copious amounts of mortar.

Small battlements—or what Bray could only interpret as the builder's impression of such—lined the wall's top, irrationally spaced and precariously balanced. He felt himself cringe internally as the wooden gate dropped slightly under the pressure of his careful touch.

This protective boundary sheltered what would have once been a magnificent garden, filled with splendour and beauty, but now it lay withered. Large grooves had been worn deep into the ground, contrasted by raised mounds which Bray knew concealed a multitude of horrific trophies in an ever growing collection. He felt his stomach churn, wondering if the desecrated burrows which marred the once perfect grass were the sole source of the tokens hidden beneath the soil. Or if another predator also concealed its true nature within this inhospitable boundary.

This person was the last on his schedule before it was time to move on. Beranme had been the worst town yet. He had already worked his way through the attractive men and women. Single or married, it made no difference to him, and no one ever said no. He was just that irresistible. He grinned to himself, his thoughts lingering on his charm. His ego swelling as he recalled the arguments between men and women about who would be leaving on his arm. But this town was boring. He was done with it.

"Grayson Bray," a voice called drawing his attention towards the front door of the generously sized house. A well-dressed man stood waiting. His five thinning strands of hair brushed over his receding hairline in a vain attempt to preserve his lost youth. His balding scalp was a reminder of his own age, one he was not willing to acknowledge. Thus he normally kept it concealed by the elegant hat now held within his thick fingers. The hat itself was of fine cut, but appeared perhaps a size too large. A thought confirmed as the man replaced it on his head, where it sat untidily.

Despite the elegance of his clothes, he made no lasting impression. He was rather plain, and easily forgettable. His money came from trade, and despite the smile and well-practised etiquette he had greeted Bray with he was, by no means, a gentleman. Bray knew all of his secrets, his underhanded dealings in using his wares to smuggle contraband. He had no qualms whether his services were enlisted for items or people, as long as the compensation was adequate.

"Good day to you," Bray began forcing a smile. "I understand you require my services?"

"I'm so pleased you could squeeze me in before you leave." He extended a small pouch of coins to Bray who took it in his hand, weighing it before giving a nod. The man stepped aside to reveal an enormous, savage-looking dog. It began to growl, curling its lips in a clear display of its contempt. "This is Hirsute."

Bray held back a slight chuckle as he eyed the almost furless creature with the same contempt it beheld him. It was not that he had a dislike for dogs, but there was something about this particular one which sat uneasily with him. He knew it possessed the same foul temper and unscrupulous nature as its master. It was only a matter of time before it turned its sights to prey larger than the rodents and small wildlife it delighted in killing. No, Bray did not like this dog at all.

"Hirsute." He extended his hand, pulling it back as the creature tried to seize it in its powerful jaws. Raising his hand he struck the animal across its nose in a swift movement.

"'You see what I mean?" despaired the man, raising his arms in frustration.

"Hmm, do you have children?" he questioned, knowing the answer. He had already noticed the torn remnants of once loved teddy bears, barely concealed within the limp and darkening grasses.

"Two, young ones. Have they been tormenting him?" The man's hands found his hips as he cast a glance over his shoulder to the inside of his home.

His head already shook disapprovingly as he tried to devise a suitable punishment.

"'You *are* a savage beast, aren't you?" Bray spoke again after a moment of silence. He could see the path both the man and dog's thoughts led them towards. They were well-suited to each other. The dog's behaviour, however, could *still* be modified. Bray crouched, further scrutinising the animal. Its mouth was thick with foam, and its posture spoke in threats, but perhaps it *was* salvageable.

"What do you suggest?"

"Dogs like Hirsute can be sensitive when it comes to certain... behaviours. For instance, you've opted to use an antiphrasis for its name. But dogs like these are dimwitted. They don't understand irony or humour. You've named it Hirsute, yet it is aware its name fails to reflect its nature. Instantly ensuring it feels it has failed you, its pack leader." Bray corrected the slight curling of his lips in order to portray a more serious demeanour. Despite Bray's subtle amusement the situation here was a dangerous one. "Since it is unlikely this particular breed will develop fur, and the damage to his ego has already been done, there are very few options available." Bray could almost feel the bass of the creature's deep and rumbling growl. "I suggest plenty of exercise. A rigorous routine to burn off the unwanted aggression, along with swift punishment for lapses.

"If that doesn't work, if we are already too late, the only means would be castration." The dog let out a whimper, its tail moving instinctively between its legs as its owner's hand moved as if to protect his own manhood. "Whilst dumb, this breed is prone to violence. Castration has proven a valid method of subduing those whose tempers cannot be otherwise quelled." Bray glared at the animal, who cowered under the intensity of his gaze.

"Castration?" the owner questioned, his voice breaking slightly.

"Dogs like these go one of two ways. They protect, or they harm. The instant it harms another thing there's only one choice. I'd hate for something to happen to your children."

"Are they really that dangerous?" The dog turned its panicked gaze to Bray, hearing his master's words. Bray looked down upon the creature, once more extending his hand towards it. The dog nuzzled it affectionately, before rolling to expose its belly.

"Perhaps if you do as I've suggested there will be no need to pursue the extremes. But, if he so much as growls at something not intending harm to your family, you must act immediately and without regret. Ensure your wife and children know this too." The man extended his hand, thanking him in time with the dog's own perceived gratitude. It wagged its tail, appearing to understand it had no choice but to obey—unless of course its owners weren't watching. Bray paused, almost as if having heard the concealed threat. "On second thought, perhaps a preemptive strike *is* preferable. I'll make the arrangements. The gelder will be with you before nightfall. In the meantime, it would be best to keep him contained." The man wiped his brow with the sleeve of his fine suit before giving a sharp whistle. The door to his left opened revealing a timid woman. She shuffled towards her husband submissively, taking the chain from his grasp. Despite not raising her head, Bray noticed the deepening shade of her cheeks as she recalled their encounter.

Bray raised his hand in a parting gesture, unable to stop the spread of the smile forming on his lips. He wondered if the dog's owner had discovered the bite marks left on his wife during their tryst just a few nights before. With his business concluded he made his way back towards the inn to pack his belongings. He would be glad to leave this town behind.

* * *

Taya felt the wind rising around her. She clung desperately to the image of the flower, to the belief she had become all that it was. But the image was fading, jolted from her mind with each sickening thud of her body as she tumbled ungracefully down what appeared to be a stone staircase. She lay at the base, unmoving as she tried to gain her bearings.

Above her, down the long rising corridor, she could just about discern the sky. The clouds were still dark, thick and heavy with the approaching rain. The disquieting atmosphere began to bear down on her. There were no bars or gates to prevent her from simply ascending the steps, and yet she still felt bound, trapped, as if to leave would be her very undoing. She was lost in the silence of her own breathing. The sound of her finally moving, to slowly push herself into a seated position on the steps, seemed intrusive. Despite her apparent abandonment she knew she was not alone. Someone, or something stirred in the shadows.

There was an unnerving familiarity to whatever it was she felt. One which caused contradictions to rise and her mind to throb painfully. She felt on the verge of discovery, yet in the same instant a horrific sense of loss. The two forces within her swelled. Her mind was a battleground of confusion. She tried to focus on simple things; the stone workings, the beautifully carved, but seemingly out-of-place, archway supports. Each rapid and fearful breath caused her chest to heave as her heart raced. She felt herself falling, part of her mind rejoicing in the familiar etchings, whilst another warned of deception and lies to the feelings she now bore.

A hand reached out from the shadows. A silhouette formed before her gaze as it grasped her elbow, preventing her from falling. She pulled away. Retreating from the gentle contact, her eyes wide with shock. The sight brought her no comfort, instead it forced her to further retreat until she stumbled off-balance when her heel caught the base of the steps. Her mind warned her to flee, to ascend the stairs and never look back. But she could only sit and behold a figure so familiar to her dreams.

"Kitaia." The silvery voice was like music to her ears. His rich honeyed tones almost calming her panic with just the mention of her name. "I feared we had lost you."

She sat, barely daring to move as the figure of a male drew closer. She was both awestruck and terrified, as both parts of herself attempted to assert their reality. He was a lie, a trick, a delusion. He was hers. His silver-white hair reminded her of the colour of starlight. It was short, expertly fashioned to remain just clear of his crystal blue eyes, but long enough to be swept aside, away from his forehead in a motion which made him seem almost bashful.

Within his heavily lashed eyes she saw such an array of emotions it stilled her breath. Perhaps she was now face to face with part of herself. A living reflection in which she recognised her own confusion and fears, hopes and relief. The darkness of his lashes were a stark contrast to his pale hair and eyes. The familiarity with which he beheld her was more unnerving than anything which had occurred before this moment.

"You do not remember me." His head lowered, concealing his eyes as he dropped his gaze for just a moment. In that instant she saw the pain her silence had caused. He looked upon her once more and, closing the distance between them, dropped to one knee. Bringing his eyes level to her own he searched for any sign of recognition. He spoke softly, inclining his head as he studied her reaction. "Do you remember nothing of me at all?"

"This can't be happening." Her tremulous voice was barely above a whisper. She pushed herself backward, as far into the step as movement would allow until she felt the cold stone biting into her back. When the creatures had taken her she had prepared herself for anything, slavery, prostitution, death. But not this. Not being brought into *his* company. He was a delusion, a manifestation forged by sickness. "Yuri." Although she spoke his name under her breath his posture straightened. He rose to his feet as he heard her address him.

"Kitaia." He spoke her name so softly, pronouncing it, as the creatures had. A name with such familiarity she could hear it as nothing but her own. "Please, won't you allow me to escort you home?" He extended his hand towards her in a courteous gesture, waiting patiently to see if she would accept. As she stared at the proffered hand so many thoughts circled within her mind. Their demand for attention causing her to falter.

Sunniva had warned her of this moment. A choice between reality and delusion. She knew if she were to accept his touch, feel its substance against her own flesh, she would lose all she knew to be true. He was nought but a fantasy, an escape held buried within her mind.

"My home is with Sunniva," she stated weakly, suppressing the undeniable desire to place her hand in his. She could feel her fingers twitching as if they longed for the embrace he would offer.

"I am sorry, but you are mistaken. The memories you have of her are the lies. This is the truth. *I* am the truth." He took another step towards her, his hand still extended.

"No. I suffered a malady ten years ago, that was when my confusion started. But I remember clearly being abandoned as a baby, my mother hiding me in a basket, and leaving me at the—"

"Truthfully, Kitaia," Yuri interrupted. "What being remembers their infancy with such clarity? I understand your confusion. The Kyklos have witnessed but a fraction of what has come to pass. The bending of truth to lies, fiction to reality. I will only ever tell you the truth, but from the hands of one you fear a delusion I don't know what comfort my words could offer.

"Ten years ago, we made a decision to send you to their lands. Your immunity to the barriers saw you to be the only one capable of such an undertaking. With the Mystics' awakening upon us we needed to gather intelligence on those who possessed their dormant powers. On the last day of each month you would provide us with your accounts, your discoveries. Then, you told us you had found the Amaranthine. Months passed, and we heard nothing from you. At first we assumed you feared detection. But as time continued its endless flow, and still no word came, the Kyklos searched for you and discovered your fate.

"They were clever. They knew what forces would keep us, and other creatures of dark magics, away. We tried countless times to penetrate their protection, but it was too powerful. We watched and waited, but even when they sent you... away, there was never a breach in their vigil. Then, today, we discovered you had fled without their protection. We had made previous attempts using Typhon's children to secure you, but the temple's barrier is as effective against them as it is us. We had already completed payment for their aid. One of their sealed treasures, for the return of ours. When we reported your escape they were quick to act, and were true to their agreement."

She gazed at Yuri, knowing that whilst none of this could be real—hidden worlds and traded treasures to see her returned—that the reality embraced with him was better than any alternative. She willed herself onward, drinking in his image, forcing her mind to embrace that which she held protected.

She fought back the lingering aroma of roses which assaulted her senses, focusing instead on his subtle scent. A fragrance so familiar her mind could do nothing but be drawn towards him and, briefly, for one moment she saw simultaneously through both of their eyes. A small semblance of clarity returned re-aligning her perspective, as so often occurred when the madness claimed her. She felt the smile forming on his lips, and released their connection to place her hand in his without regret.

Chapter 6

The Gateway to Kólasi

Bray did not so much as cast a backwards glance as he left Beranme. He had no desire to capture one final glance of their desperate and ostentatious displays. The people paraded like peacocks. They flaunted material gains as if they were things of beauty, but it only served to add glitter to the decaying husks that bore them. The people here had long atrophied in all but body. They had become materialistic vessels to greed, each wanting to appear more prestigious, more worthy of being adored, than their neighbour. They would face hunger to acquire the latest fashion to enhance the facade of richness.

Bray had witnessed real wealth, and these people were severely lacking in all manners. He had heard whispers of this town, of the lavish lifestyle and fascinating people. He had looked forward to fine dining and a degree of etiquette, but the people here could provide neither. There was nothing that could ruin a good meal like the constant entitlement of spoilt people. Spoilt people made rotten food, and this was one town he would sooner forget than visit again.

They had paid him well for his services, although he knew most of them treated him as a novelty, a visitor to be bragged about. But coin was coin at the end of the day, and who was he to refuse paying work? The shiny gold discs were a source of fascination for him, and he'd made it a personal mission to see how many he could retrieve. Beranme had been fruitful, but it was not close to his record.

"Bray!" Two young voices penetrated the air, their shrill tones causing him to outwardly cringe as they called after him. With the adults here being such challenging company he had found himself passing some of his free time with the children. It was good for business. Children had pets. They were more sensitive when it came to the needs of their furry companions, and could convince their parents they were in need of his renowned services. Not that he needed the assistance, but the young loved to see him at work. They could perceive things adults could not.

He turned slightly, offering them a smile as they each grabbed one of his hands. Their feet scrabbled on the dirt track as they tried to pull him towards the town. He remained unwavering, his advancing steps almost undeterred by their efforts.

"The Governor has a job for you. We get to keep you longer right?" the young boy questioned, his face showing the strain behind his effort to forcefully drag Bray back. Bray's steps halted as he turned to regard the two children.

"Really?" he questioned. Thoughts of how much he despised this town were drastically overshadowed by his consideration of how adequately they lined his pockets. The children gave a slight giggle, unable to conceal their excitement. Whilst their reaction caused the briefest stir of curiosity his thoughts returned to the townsfolk. His stomach churned, almost to the point of making him nauseous. "No. Sorry, my business here is concluded. I have my rules and etiquette you know."

"But this job is the best!" the other boy replied, moving himself behind Bray and attempting to push him back towards the town. "Come on, please!"

"Dad says it's worth a whole pouch of coin." Bray looked to the children in turn. If the offer was genuine, then perhaps he could find cause to stay for just one more task, after all, how bad could it be? The children, with a skip in their steps, led the now cooperative Grayson Bray back into the town's borders and straight to the Governor's house. Their excitement as they waited caused them to skip eagerly from one foot to the other.

Bellowing protests preceded Bray's reappearance. The children's excited steps halted, their eyes widening in shock as their friend was dragged from the house by his arms. Their shock turned to disbelief, watching as two of their father's trusted protectors manhandled the protesting figure through the doorway. But they recalled Bray was nothing if not a showman.

From what they had seen of his previous negotiations they knew he loved to be dramatic, often resulting in additional coin being offered for his service. But they doubted such a display would work here. They had applied his techniques to their father recently, without success.

"Unhand me!" he protested trying to pull himself free of the two burley men. The Governor followed them outside. He took a brief moment to survey his town and offer a smile to his sons, who stood now looking slightly more apprehensive than they had when tasked to return this man to him.

"I don't see what the fuss is about. We've just paid you," the Governor mused, his grin clear evidence of his deception.

"Don't see what the fuss is about?" Bray growled, planting his feet firmly on the floor as he tried to shrug the guards away. An act which served only to intensify their already strong grasp. "It's a bloody wyrm. I deal with pets, not monsters."

"But you're *so* skilled." The Governor's monotone words seemed almost mocking.

Bray finally pulled his arms free of the two men, dusting his jacket in annoyance as he straightened the ruffled fabric. He gave a snort of derision, his eyes locking angrily with the Governor's.

"You can keep it!" he snapped. As he spoke he felt the tip of a weapon prod him gently in his back. The Governor had taken great pains to ensure Bray heard the agreement between himself and his two protectors. They were to escort him to the caves where the creature resided, and wait until either it left, or he didn't.

Bray cursed under his breath as his hunger burnt through his veins. He blamed himself in part for this situation. If not for his ravenous hunger he was certain he could have negotiated a far better, safer arrangement. But he just couldn't stomach the thought of any more local cuisine.

"We have a deal. I would hate to see your reputation sullied over this." The Governor almost sang, his grin giving rise to Bray's frustration. "Now, please ask it to leave. It's bad for business having a wyrm devouring traders you know."

"But it's a rogue!" Bray's voice faltered, the pressure of the weapon at his back forcing him now to begin walking. The Governor led the escort to the town's boundaries. His swaggering steps revelling the sheer pleasure he took from the task.

"And you, Grayson Bray, are the renowned beast talker. Don't worry, my personal guards will see you don't lose your way." He waved his hand dismissively, grinning as the young man was guided from his town. He strolled away, his face an image of self-satisfaction, as he continued to ignore the protests. One way or another his export would reach its destination this time. If that meant he had to sate the beast's hunger with the occasional meal, then so be it.

* * *

Kitaia heard the rich voice call her name as she emerged from the place she remembered as her home. It was a simple and modest structure. No grander or ignoble than any of the other homes found. In this underground city, each building was made from stone, and they were plentiful. Their design, whilst seeming simple, was enriched with intricacies and energies only their kind could truly understand and, like most of their structures, was a fusion of the different elements and powers.

The city was part of a larger structure and whilst their island had been known as Kólasi, the city itself was named Eremalche, after the wildflower its structure had been built to mimic. Like the flower, the central part of the city was circular, and its heart being the palace where matters for the council, tacticians, and royalty were addressed. Surrounding this, in a distant and uniformly spaced ring, separated by a great river of water, was the area in which Taya lived. Further, beyond the fields and cropland, were five additional districts, accessible now only through portals and passages.

In the same manner as the flower, their entire territory was protected by a curved wall. It consisted of five overlapping structures, not only reminiscent of the plant's curved petals, but as flexible and delicate in appearance. Despite this fragile guise they stood as solid and sturdy as any battlement. The Eremalche flower was known to close its petals when night fell. True to design, so too did the structure of these walls close around and above the city when bathed in darkness.

No one remembered the sight of these grand petals being open. The Mystics' had torn the Daimons' very existence from the human plane and sealed them within a realm which came to be known as The Depths of Acheron. A place only accessible through The Stepping Realm, from which they had been sealed.

Cycles beyond count had passed, and those who lived within had but memories shared and stored by long forgotten ancestors to recall the image of the sun. They were permitted only the facsimile granted by the Mystics own 'mercy' to ensure their crops would continue to thrive. They hadn't sought to destroy their race, merely remove them from what they had deemed to now be the humans' world.

The Daimons, as a race, possessed an almost consistent number of living. They were a people of balance, and there were a finite number of souls for their kind. Their equilibrium following territorial wars had been turned askew, with more awaiting rebirth than were living. Normally the souls undergoing restoration and those living were of equal number. Daimons were reborn into an endless cycle of rest and reincarnation.

There had been a time when their numbers had been greater. They had been allowed to grow by birthing new souls with willing human partners. They had built new cities and structures within the confines of their banishment, unaware this territory belonged to something else, another species who thrived in the ruins of buried civilisations. The results had eventually been catastrophic, a conflict in which many of their own kind were slain. With the infrequency of offspring, owing to a later age of fertility and maturation, their numbers had remained depleted, and those awaiting rebirth became higher.

Turning, Taya pulled her thoughts from her ever shifting perspective. Since arriving in Eremalche she found the part of herself haunted by the delusions had become dominant. All she had once known to be real, all the things Sunniva preached, seemed distant, akin to her memory of being a flower when first she had been brought here. Just as she had been one with the flower within her mind, she now accepted and became one with all that was here. The displacement was the only means she had to survive.

Yuri was walking towards her, his pace attempting to remain casual yet quickened by his desire to be near her. His very image causing a slight flutter in her chest as her breath hitched. Even now she could scarcely believe she was here. His smile brightened as she looked at him, his eyes a mirror of the happiness seeing her created.

* * *

Yuri felt the smile starting to form the moment he heard her name leave his lips. He had been giving her time. There was so much she needed to adapt to that he knew his presence would only serve to complicate matters. She didn't respond immediately, her fingers played idly with the empty space where her ring once rested. It was a habit he recognised in her, one which caused his smile to broaden. He attempted to keep his stride even, but the sound of his footfalls had noticeably quickened. He couldn't help his anticipation. They were bonded to one another, and he had pined for her each day.

He hungrily absorbed her every detail, committing them once more to memory. She had changed so little despite the passing years, but in many ways she was almost unrecognisable. He felt her aura, recognising the effort the alteration of her perspective, and the acceptance of her natural reality, was taking. Something which should have come so naturally to her was taking tremendous effort. The part of her forced to belong above now fought with the part of her belonging to him.

Ten years was not long in contrast to their own longevity, but for him it had seemed an eternity. Each night he would lie in silence, reaching out to her through their dreams. He would visualise the curves of her face, the sound of her laugh, the touch of her flesh, all the time hating himself for not being able to save her.

"I've been reading my journals." Taya reached out as if to place a hand upon his arm, pulling back before committing. She had been in Eremalche for some time now and, whilst uncertain of exactly how long, she was all too aware of the absence of one person. The one she had longed to see most.

It had been more difficult than she had expected to embrace this city. Harder to feel the solidity of the ground at her feet, to savour the familiar scents lingering in the air. But it was easier with Yuri nearby, as if she was grounded by his presence. When he was close to her everything seemed more natural, easier. She had often found herself hoping he would visit, almost wishing that every knock on her door had been by his hand.

The nights had been the most trying, the time when she felt his absence the most. This was when she heard Sunniva's voice the loudest. The intruding cries almost forced an alteration in her active perception. She could almost smell her perfume, and part of her felt compelled to obey the desperate pleads for her to release the delusion, and find the passages to freedom. This internal dialect begged her obedience, warning all she saw was but a manifestation of her madness. It was persistent, overbearing, and allowed her little rest until physical pain became the only way to regain control of her thoughts.

"Have you settled in?" Yuri questioned softly, his eyes lingering on the fresh bruises marking her pale arms.

"Of course, like you said, everything is exactly as I..."

"Remember it?" Yuri prompted when Taya failed to continue her train of thought.

"I haven't seen you since the night you brought me home." She remembered that night well. He had led her to the door, kissing her hand gently before they parted ways. She had expected him to visit, yet instead others, all of whom she knew by name, had come. They brought her food and well wishes as they welcomed her home. She had seen so many people, but not the only one who she had ached to see.

"Given the situation I thought it best you didn't feel pressured by my presence," he admitted honestly. Many times he had longed to visit her, or hidden in the shadows as she received yet another guest. He had known it was unfair to approach; she needed time to adjust, to find her natural alignment. He feared if he were present she would be unable to reach the understanding she needed to.

"Ah, but you come here now?" she teased, her voice filled with a playful lift. She leaned against the door jamb, giving a smile which sent butterflies racing through his chest.

"Sadly, I'm here in an official capacity." He resisted the urge to close the distance between them, to allow his arms to slide around to the small of her back and pull her closer. How he wanted to hold her, to be near her. But he would not, not until she was ready to accept him once more. "Lord Geburah has asked if you are well enough to grant him an audience."

"Geburah, you mean he has returned?" Taya paused, realising she had fallen into step beside him as he had begun to move away. She noticed, not for the first time, that everything, the ground beneath her feet, the coolness of the air, even the intoxicating scent from Yuri, had become more real, more tangible. She felt unnerved, yet invigorated at the same time. She clasped her hands, her fingers playing idly with the absent ring.

"So much has happened, it has been over six years since someone finally succeeded in releasing his seals. He was returned to us, and is now bound by the same rules as we are." Yuri explained, allowing their hands to touch briefly as he encouraged her to continue walking.

"What does he want of me?" She moved closer, closing the small gap between them. Her mind redoubled its effort to silence Sunniva's voice. She could happily stay here, free to explore this world and make new memories.

Here there were no treatments. She had no need to guard her words in fear of the ramifications. She could come and go as she pleased, a captive to no one. She glanced backwards briefly, her stomach churning at the absence of the wings she had known since birth. At first their loss had been concerning, but now she barely noticed.

"To meet with you, and perhaps to see if you have any insight into the Mystics."

"The Mystics?" Her voice held a genuine confusion, her brow wrinkling as she tried to understand what was to be asked of her.

"From your reaction I assume this is one memory they managed to purge in its entirety. Perhaps as we walk, you would like to hear a tale. It may help you recall what her trickery has sealed."...

...Life had once been blessed with peace and diversity. A long time ago when the world was first crafted by the Gods, and Nyx still danced within the heavens to create the stars to light the dark velvet canvas above, differences went unnoticed. Magic, in all its forms, was simply accepted.

There were those born from the soul of magic, Elves, Daimons, and Moirai, and even the Mystics, those who were meant to watch and guide. The Mystics were given their soul abilities from Gaea herself, and the first of the Misorian Watchers received their blessing from the Fates. All was as it should have been.

Amongst this array of life were the humans. A species who outnumbered all those born of magic, and they alone had unrivalled potential. For only the humans could learn to harness any power, unlock the mysteries of magic itself. Those who did, who studied and were faithful, laid the foundation for Hectarians and Elementalists. Soon followed the wizards, sages, and sorcerers before they discovered a magic only humans could wield. They had been created in diversity, a combination of all the magic which was and could be. But those without the patience and dedication did not see their potential, only their differences.

Animosity and envy spread throughout the humans. Those coveting power envied those who so easily were granted it, those who were born with the ability to manipulate forces which took the humans years to learn. Magic in their own kind was celebrated as a great accomplishment, but when displayed by those of other races it was scorned. They had not earned the right to wield the power. They had simply been born with the privilege. Other differences started to become noticed. Those born from the magic were also granted a longevity not afforded to the humans, and once more the hatred grew.

The humans continued to grow in numbers, whilst the extended lifespan of the magical races saw their numbers remained small in comparison. Humans quickly learnt to hate and fear. The Moirai, keepers of the prophecies and guiders of fate, saw the future their hatred would create. They withdrew their presence, raising their lands into the sky far beyond the reach of man. They forbade their kind from interacting with those outside of their own species again, unless to twist the future to their whims. The Watchers also fled, as so instructed by the Fates, and for the first time sealed the lands of Misora, sheltering it from the coming war. All, in their own way, distanced themselves from the humans, yet the Daimons still remained visible upon their lands.

As time passed the humans coveted the prolonged youth and life of the Daimons and sought a means to unlock their secrets. The Daimons would experience childhood on parallel with the humans. Matching them year for year in growth and development, that was, until they reached maturity and the passing years would continue to visibly age the human form.

Longevity became an obsession. Rumours of fountains of youth, alchemical formulae of rejuvenation, and immortality became a quest for truth. Mankind seemed destined not to be granted this boon by the

Gods, and so took it upon themselves to use the insights and knowledge they had to create their own. But as is often the case, experiments can discover possibilities unimagined.

Instead of finding the secret to the Daimons' longevity they stumbled upon a means the strip the life from their being and convert it into a source of energy. They were certain they would eventually find a means to transfer this energy into themselves, thus granting them the years their own nature denied. They took without thought, killed without mercy, young and old, infants and adults, but the answer continued to elude them. Their hatred and jealousy grew, but in itself caused a shift in power.

The magic of the Daimons was more protective and worked on a spectrum opposite to that of the Moirai. The Daimon magic was heightened by the presence of negative emotions, and with such an abundance they began to grow in power.

It was during this time Eremalche was constructed. The Daimons required a sanctuary, a place of their own in which to be sheltered from the growing persecution. Their numbers were falling, their children were no longer safe, and so they sought isolation, hoping they would be left in peace. They knew a war between the two would have no victor. However, the humans remained relentless in their pursuits, first hunting those who did not relocate to Kólasi, before turning their focus to Eremalche.

The Daimons opted to retaliate, for humans often only saw reason when the consequences affected them. They hoped by applying the same tactics they would realise the error of their actions. But they saw only the wrongs done against them, ignoring that which they did to others.

At first the war was violent, magics collided, but such was a war the humans could never win. Whilst the Daimons were far fewer in number, the increasing hatred and animosity from the humans made them stronger still.

Both realised there could never be peace while the other lived, and weapons were crafted by both to ensure the complete eradication of the other.

It was at this point Gaea saw the need for her guardians to intervene. They were made from flesh and knowledge, and were to be known as the Mystics. She named them as her protectors, and yet, with their unlimited potential it was possible that the humans could even banish them. With this realisation came the need for self-preservation. For if a being crafted by the Gods could be banished by Mankind, this race could realise they possessed the means to reject the Gods themselves.

The Mystics, assessing the potential devastation, opted to align with the humans. Their intervention was kind and cruel. Whilst they saved many lives, they accomplished this by sealing Kólasi in a place of neither material nor spiritual design. The magic used was powerful, but one night a year the path to The Stepping Realm would open, allowing them to revisit the plane that had once been their home. As the full moon sank at the end of the year, the magic binding them would force them back to their land, where they would remain sealed.

The safeguard sealing the Daimons had held true for countless cycles. Their name became tarnished by the humans who had claimed victory. The truth twisted to ensure *they* were the righteous. It was a tale which survived the cycles, becoming a testament of how good could overcome evil. But when the Severaine was freed prematurely it set into motion an unpredictable chain of events. The powers suspending Kólasi between realms had weakened, allowing each full moon to grant them passage. Then one was discovered with the power to bring salvation, a means to traverse The Stepping Realm at will...

..."Does any of this sound familiar?" Yuri questioned, looking towards her hopefully. He had resisted the urge to reach out and take her hand, becoming aware of how close they were when her shoulder brushed against his as she turned to stop.

"Of course it does. I am not without memory," she explained, her words bringing a glimmer of hope to his eyes.

"Then, tell me what you remember?"

"About myself?" Yuri gave a nod as he escorted her towards a low wall that ran parallel to the river serving as their main source of water. He sat upon it, patting the area beside him in invitation. "That is a topic more confusing than most, but I'll see what I can recall."

She had given their stroll little thought, and only now realised they had walked parallel to their destination, along the residential border towards the river. This beautiful waterway flowed through their city to surround the palace. Large rocks, rich in minerals, protruded from the water's depths giving the flow a comforting whisper as it passed.

She sat beside him with her back to the water, looking out across the seamless stone paths. She concentrated so intensely that even the palace was unseen by her unfocused gaze. "My mother was Ethelyn Aldora, and my birth was a celebrated occasion. I think it was something to do with the colour of my aura. I was not named for weeks, and when my name revealed itself I became Kitaia Ethelyn, taking my mother's name as my last.

"As I grew, it became apparent that I was somehow able to pass through The Stepping Realm, despite the seal placed on Kólasi." Taya frowned, rubbing her temples, soothing her discomfort as she attempted to calm her quickening breathing. She inhaled deeply, reminding herself of the scents in the air, and the feel of her weight upon the rough stone wall. All was necessary to reaffirm she was where she saw, where she believed herself to be. Even so, speaking such words aloud caused her to tremble. Sunniva's voice rung within her mind and once more became deafening. She felt the pain through her arm as she pinched herself, her nails digging deep into her flesh.

"Do you need a moment?" Yuri placed his hand upon hers, forcing her fingers to relax their grip. He now understood why she bore so many bruises. He turned with a sweeping gesture towards the land behind them in an attempt to distract her. "The crops are faring well this season, soon the berries will ripen and I'll make you your favourite dessert."

Taya's lips turned upward in a soft smile as she surveyed the crops and fields which lay on the opposite side of the river. Closing her eyes, she tilted her head towards the light, seeking comfort in its touch, but found it possessed no warmth. This absence seemed unnatural, causing her heart to flutter. She swallowed, attempting to bring moisture to her dry mouth. A light disorientation returned, everything seemed wrong. How could a world exist where the sun knew no heat? She knew its touch, the true warmth of its embrace. With her rising confusion Sunniva's voice gained strength and spoke words of daisy chains, and Herne's rock. She buried her hands within her hair, seizing fistfuls in an attempt to fight back her distress, and then, her posture straightened and calmness descended.

"The roses were so pretty," she whispered, feeling the gentle touch of Sunniva's hands on her shoulders. "It started to rain..." Taya could see the rock before her, covered with a chain of seasonal flowers. She felt the coolness of the rain upon her flesh, the texture of the woven rose crown within her hands. She raised it, smiling softly as she moved to place it upon Sunniva's head.

"Kitaia!" Pain distorted the image of Sunniva before her to that of another figure, a man. She felt his firm grasp on her wrists. A grip that held her so tightly it stilled all movement from her raised hands.

They were empty. For the briefest moment she believed herself to have dropped something important, her searching halted as she realised Yuri now stood before her, his hands cupping her face. He pressed his forehead to hers as he closed his eyes. She leaned into him allowing her own eyes to close as she focused on his touch, the softness of his skin, and his warmth. The familiar scents flooded her senses. She opened her eyes, once more using his presence to ground herself.

"I-I went to find the vessels in which the sleeping Mystics waited." She continued as if the moment of confusion had never occurred. Moving away from him she sat back on the wall. "Should I find them corrupt then I would be their assassin. It was a premonition, something to do with their seals fading. If I could stop them from completing a new rite then our kind would be free, and all of them were needed for this." Yuri moved to sit beside her once more, his hand gently resting on her knee. His touch brought awareness to the severe tremors which passed through her body. "I'm all right," she assured blinking back the tears before raising her head to meet his concerned gaze. Taking a few long breaths she actively tried to regain her composure.

"Are you sure?" His arm slid around her shoulders so naturally that neither had noticed until he had pulled her close to rest her head against his chest. She listened to the rhythmic beating of his heart, drawing comfort and strength from his presence before speaking again.

"If I didn't choose assassination, then I was to return one to Kólasi with me so we might negotiate our future. You're concerned I have such clarity?" she questioned, noticing an unmistakable shadow of worry on his face.

"Well..." Yuri rubbed the back of his head, releasing her from his grasp as he looked away. He had often wondered how they had managed to retain such complete control of her, even when her resolve was strengthening. He knew some of their methods, but he had not expected this. He had felt the energy within her alter. Her mind retreated as her body began re-enacting conditioned responses of its own accord.

If he hadn't managed to break the recollection he had no doubt she would have been lost to that memory. She would believe herself within her envisioned place, her body autonomously responding to it until she found herself back within their clutches. She was under a strong thrall indeed. He knew of few who would be able to create such a deep-rooted cornerstone in order to force an alteration of perspective, and fewer who knew of the Daimons' ability to create genuine empathy with any they encounter.

Their race had once been tasked to stand between the Gods and humans, creating understanding between them. In order to do so they had needed the ability to completely embrace another person or thing's perspective. They could become one with anything, seeing, hearing, and feeling as it did. But how humans had come to learn of this was beyond his understanding. It troubled him greatly. "You did forget something, and it is perhaps the most important thing," he continued finally, pushing the concerns aside for the moment.

"What?" She linked his arm as he stood. The closeness of his presence filled her with relief.

"All did not go as planned. Somehow, a hunter possessing the gift of Katharí Órasi discovered your ability to breach The Stepping Realm. We believe they had planned to execute you, but instead, you somehow ended up hovering on the brink of death, in the possession of a priestess possessing the gift of Apallagí. It is a rare talent, intended to be used as a means to ease the burdens of others, relieve nightmares and guilt. But instead, it was used to confuse you, and take advantage of your weakened state to force an empathic bond with the life they wanted you to believe.

"The combination of the hunter's poison, her suggestions, and Mirage Lake, ensured the thoughts she implanted took root, and the dreams she gave became reality. One so real that even here it continues to haunt you. We still have no understanding of why this was done, or if the Mystics were involved, but for now we know of no way to reverse their hold." Taya opened her mouth as if to reply, but her words froze, stilling as her gaze fell upon a familiar sight. Without her even realising, she and Yuri had not only crossed the river towards the palace, but had continued their path until they stood on the threshold of its audience chamber.

The palace was a place of subtle grandeur. It had been constructed by the same means as the rest of the city. As its focal point it both generated and emitted more energy than any other structure within Eremalche. She relished in the beautiful craftsmanship of the chamber. It was forged from carved stone yet, as with all Daimon architecture, nature was a key part and woven deep within its very fabric.

Plants and trees embedded themselves within the stonework, growing as one with it to create a room of awe and power. Tree branches formed the magnificent archways, while bioluminescent flowers bathed the room with a gentle light. Neither stone nor nature had dominance here. They both simply coexisted, lending each other their support in a display of true unity.

Roots and vines pierced the ground, growing in majestic ways to form furnishings. The most magnificent of all being the audience chair, in which a large figure sat. Taya felt her steps falter. Seeing her hesitation Yuri placed his hand on the small of her back, encouraging her inside.

"You're here at last." The voice resonated through the room, filling it with echoes of the ancient power held by its owner.

Taya instinctively dropped to her knee before him, recognising his importance. He rose, an act which only served to make his enormous form more overbearing. Although he sat upon the throne of the Daimons he was not one of their kind, nor did he rule their land.

His Herculean figure was enough to intimidate any man, and in history he had been both feared and renowned. The clothes he wore drew attention to his sculpted muscles with each subtle movement. But Taya's gaze was fixed upon a different feature, away from his muscular physique and chiselled jaw line. She even seemed not to notice the hardened ash-shaded leather of his skin. Instead she saw but one thing. One prominent aspect which caused her to once more search her peripheral vision for her own feathered appendages.

His wings, unlike hers, were awe-inspiring. A combination of blues, purples, and greens which shimmered like breathing flames. They appeared not completely physical, as if they were made from ether, not just magic. They had not always been so spectacularly entrancing. They had been a simple white, like those possessed by all of his species. Geburah was a being like no other. He was once a Moirai, his banishment for knavery had seen him subdued to the most severe of punishments. One reserved solely for true enemies. Imprisonment in a place where death could only come if invited.

"Stand. You do not bow before me. It is I who should submit to you." Geburah was a valued adviser, a tactician, and, if need required, regent. The two figures rose, an act allowing Geburah to fully absorb every detail of the young woman who stood before him. He nodded to himself, as if giving a gesture to a thought he did not share. "Tell me, Yuri Kyne, has there been any progress?"

"It seems separating truth from reality will be a greater undertaking than we initially thought. It is difficult. Even now Kitaia is still partially held by the empathic thrall. Without severing the foundation I fear there is little hope of a full recovery." He looked to the woman who stood proudly beside him as she cleared her throat, alerting him to the error of discussing her as if she was not present. After ten years, speaking about her was something he had become accustomed to. He gave a slight chuckle seeing such a thing still frustrated her, and offered a quick apology.

"Separating truth from lie, a requirement too common to the everyday world," Geburah stated offering Taya a smile. His teeth shone a brilliant white in contrast to his dark skin.

"I'm here now, and where better to be imprisoned than a place I know as home?" Geburah and Yuri exchanged a brief, yet heavy look.

"Kitaia, *you* can leave whenever you choose. You are not bound to this land as we are. We are not like the temple, your movement here is your own. You are free to come and go as you please," Yuri stated, thinking to take her hand but deciding against it.

"Then I could leave now, and you would have no objections?"

"Yes, only, please don't. Won't you stay until the next full moon? I have barely seen you since your return. Stay, see if you can learn the truth for yourself. Is that alone not worth your time?"

"Of course, I'd only be—" Taya's eyes clouded over with heavy thoughts. The scent of roses intruded as, for the briefest moment, she lost her perspective and feared she did not truly stand here amongst them. "I'll gladly stay until Full-Moonday." She knew her response was selfish for more than one reason. She willed herself to subdue the flowery scent, and forced awareness to everything that surrounded her.

"Wonderful," Geburah's deep voice boomed, startling her as she once more became aware of his looming presence. "Now, if you don't mind, I would like to borrow Yuri for a few moments. Would you care to wait here?" Taya nodded, yet as he led Yuri away, Geburah heard her footsteps disappearing in the direction of the exit. Once inside the tactical room Geburah's posture noticeably relaxed as he approached his customary seat. It overlooked a large table, engraved upon its surface was a map relating to the first cycle. Despite the many changes this planet had undergone, the landmasses now differed in but a few details to the world he had once known.

"What can I help you with?" Yuri questioned, taking the seat Geburah's leg kicked out towards him.

"What are your thoughts?"

"I think come Full-Moonday she will leave and return to Sunniva. That Apallagí fleak has her claws in too deep. I almost lost her today. Even here the hold on her is strong. I assume you noticed the bruising?" Geburah nodded, he had seen it and he understood well the meaning of its presence. However, the fact she fought to remain here showed promise. Those who had visited her had reported her behaviour, and that the damage she was inflicting was gradually becoming more severe.

"You think bringing her to us was a mistake?" Geburah studied Yuri's body language intently as the silence extended beyond comfort. Finally Yuri's shoulders sagged, and he gave a long sigh before speaking.

"No, I believe your decision was correct. We know a little more about the empathic thrall, but as the full moon approaches the alternative is calling to her with more force. I think by the time the moon rises she will be unable to resist. She'll return to them, of that I have no doubt. The worst part is there is still nothing I can do, and no way I can keep her here safely." Yuri balled his hands into tight fists. "I either let her go, or watch her continue until—damn it!" He struck the table in frustration.

"I feared this would be so. I had hoped to be wrong, but—" Geburah's broad shoulders heaved a sigh. "Then there is little choice. I've had the opportunity to study her talent. When she leaves, be sure to pass through the portal with her. She can grant those in her proximity freedom for the span of a single moon cycle, but they will be sealed from Kólasi by the same magic which normally prevents exit. I have an uneasy feeling that our taking her will have made things worse. I fear she may need you close."

"She is my wife. I have sworn to keep her safe. Something thus far I've failed to do." Yuri gave a heavy sigh, unable to unclench his fists as he fought back the urge to strike out again. "The thought of abandoning her again is devastating... yet I know we cannot keep her here. Not if doing so means"—he threw his hands up in frustration—"damn it, I should be doing more."

"I understand your conflict. Please Kyne, trust in me. Things to come will not be easy, on her or you. Both of you must endure in your own way." Geburah placed his large hand upon Yuri's shoulder, causing him to wonder when exactly Geburah had rose.

"I would kill them all sooner than look at them," Yuri growled. "If I ever get my hands on that Mystic, or the Apallagí fleak, I will show them the monster they truly fear!"

"Endure," Geburah stated firmly, tightening his grip on Yuri's shoulder ever so slightly. "And be ready."

* * *

Yuri's steps from the palace were firm, fast, and angry. His thoughts returned to all his wife had been forced to endure. Even now, when he looked upon her, he saw but a fraction of the woman who had left. Her confidence, her presence, had been stripped. Despite being fully immersed in their world she still remained anchored to the other, and its toll on her had been a great one.

He watched with self-loathing as she subtly grasped her arm. Her fingernails now drawing blood when before the mere pressure had been enough to restore clarity. Kitaia had no cause to fear anyone, and as her husband he should ensure no harm befell her. He had failed in the worst way imaginable. Not only was she afraid, he had no means to protect her from the things she feared most.

His steps instantly softened as she looked up to notice his approach. She sat on the same wall they had stopped at on their way to meet with Geburah. A smile lit her features, her eyes coming alive with joy as she extended her hand towards him.

"Kitaia, might I walk with you through the fields? It has been a long time since I've had the pleasure." He took her hand in his, pulling her to stand and holding her close for a moment.

"Yes. Unless my memory deceives me the last time we did was on the night of our wedding." She looked to her hand at the place the ring he had given her should have been. She remembered the comforting weight it had possessed, how she had felt close to him even when they were apart.

Yuri had been hers since birth. Their families had instantly recognised the bond between them. Their soul's aura would align completely to create a seamless merging. Together they would be one, and no other union would ever be as perfect as the one between soul-bonded.

"Well, it seems you are not a completely lost cause after all." For a moment Taya thought she felt his steps falter. He released her hand, allowing her to place her arm in his as they walked.

They strolled together for a short time, enjoying each other's company. But as the artificial light began to pale, its brightness a mirror of that the moon would generate for the world above, Yuri felt the disappointment well within him. He hesitated outside her door, delaying her entry with a gentle touch. She turned to look at him, her eyes meeting his briefly before she coyly glanced away. Stepping aside, with a slight incline of her head, she welcomed him back into their home, to the place she knew he belonged.

* * *

Bray begrudgingly trudged onward, following the contours of the well-worn trade route. He watched with morbid anticipation as the small mountain range swelled before them. As they grew closer their trail veered from the trodden path to the luscious green lands that swept to the base of the rocky mountains.

The insistence from his escorts had kept their pace steady, yet even they faltered as they approached the entrance to the cave. Their once certain steps became hesitant. Seeing their trepidation Bray stepped forwards as if to examine the gaping maw which extended back into darkness.

"Hmm." He scratched his chin thoughtfully, noticing as he did so the short stubble on his normally clean-shaved flesh scratched against his nails. He took a few small steps, examining the outer edge of the cave before walking back. "Alas, it appears my reputation does indeed precede me." He raised his hands in a dramatic shrug, allowing them to slap against his thighs as they lowered. He heaved an over-exaggerated sigh. "It appears it learnt of my approach and departed. I thank you gentlemen for your escort, but I see no point in further delay and bid you farewell." He turned to leave, but their reaction had been quicker than he had expected, leaving him to turn straight into a weapon's tip.

"And how do you know this?" The escort's dark features hardened. Bray raised his hands, stepping back away from the metal blade.

"I am Grayson Bray, the great and famous beast talker, remember? *I* can tell." His raised hands moved to rest on his hips as he thrust his chest forward, offering a dashing smile. For a moment the weapon lowered before springing up once more with force.

"Get in there!" the man from behind growled, pushing him forwards. Bray, surprised by this sudden jolt, staggered a few paces towards the cave's hungry mouth. He complained silently, under his breath, dusting his dishevelled attire, and smartening his appearance. The two men advanced, their faces showed no sign of remorse for the act of murder they were about to commit. They forced him forward with their weapon's tips, watching with what appeared to be smug satisfaction as he took his first steps into the cave.

"You either do what you were paid for, or we do," the man threatened, brandishing his weapon menacingly.

"Yeah, the Governor was unconcerned if you left here in one piece, or at all," mused the other with a wicked snarl. Bray's shoulders slumped in defeat. He was too tired, too hungry, to protest. He caught a slight scent from inside the cave, one which, against his better judgement, tempted his curiosity.

"Okay, I'm going." He snatched the small oil lamp extended towards him.

His two escorts remained stationed outside the cave, listening as his footfalls faded. They were tasked to wait ten days. If after this time they had witnessed no fleeing wyrm, they could assume him dead. The Governor had ensured he had no supplies, and it was doubtful he'd find water within the caverns. Either way it didn't matter. Unlike Bray's, their bags had been packed with provisions, and the Governor had promised to resupply them every two days.

Bray would have preferred to progress without the lantern. Its light was more of a hindrance than an aid, but stalking through the shadows would only invite trouble. Especially when he caught up to the three people he knew walked within these caves. He could hear their footfalls, and whilst thieves and robbers made such networks their home, he knew approaching them unannounced would earn him no favour. He wondered if they knew exactly what they were getting themselves into.

He sniffed the air, through the earthy scent of rotten leaves, and the tinny vein of iron, he could smell the delicate scent of perfume. At least two of the group were women, their scent pleasing, clean. Not the kind of people who would normally be found lurking within such a location. The other odour belonged to a man, well-travelled with a tendency to-wards heavy drinking, perhaps he was leading the two beauties to their demise. He gave a shrug, there was no point dwelling on such things. He would just have to go and see for himself. Besides, he was hungry, perhaps one of them had something to his taste.

As he walked his thoughts returned to the wyrm. If it was here, and not just a story told by traders losing their supplies to rogues, then he was certain he would be fine. He always was. Besides, facing such a creature would only add to his endless repertoire of tales, and a wyrm was something he had not yet had the pleasure of experiencing. Another shrug left him with a slight chuckle. *'I'm so hungry I could eat a wyrm,'* he thought to himself, wondering if such a feat was even possible.

Bray disliked caves like these. Thus far there had been no deviation from the entrance, no side tunnels or nooks in which to conceal himself should the need arise. Such a route proved ideal for the laying of traps. He guarded each step until he finally saw the glowing aura of the light belonging to the people he had heard so long ago. He quickened his pace, announcing himself clearly so not to startle the three figures.

"Don't tell me," he began, his voice resonant. "They sent you as human sacrifices to appease it?" Stepping into their light he extinguished his own flame, shielding the glass with the heat-proof cloth formally wrapped around its handle. The three figures stopped their advance, each turning to regard him.

"You're seeking the wyrm also? Tell me young man, what cause have you to pursue such a thing?" The elderly woman eyed him critically, her tones filled with suspicion. Bray couldn't help but think, as she raised the lantern, that she scrutinised him a little too intently. But the gesture meant he too could study her.

Her pinched features softened, revealing a woman of aged beauty. Her white hair had partially freed itself from the constraints of its loose bun, dislodged in part by the large scroll strapped to her back. He noticed her eyes narrowing further as she continued to study him.

"I did not come by choice. It seemed Beranme hopes by feeding it, it will leave them be. You?" He kept his focus on the elderly lady, but remained aware of the shifting movements of the other two within her group.

"We're here to treat its injuries so it can return home. I'm also escorting this young man to Kólasi," Amelia answered in earnest. There was little to be gained by telling partial truths to one such as him.

"The Daimon lands, why would any seek them out?" Bray crossed his arms before himself, allowing his eyes to move across to the man within the group. He was definitely a hunter. The absent scent of blood, however, suggested his prizes lay in the more material gain.

"They kidnapped," Rob paused for a second thinking his next words carefully, "my niece." Rob was no fool despite what his sister may believe. He could tell one moon from another. She was mistaken to believe she could deceive him into thinking such a short amount of time had passed. Over an entire lunar cycle had passed since Taya had been abducted. She had been missing for over five weeks but, despite his fears, Amelia had assured him she would be safe. He only wished he was as confident as the old witch.

The crossing of Rob's path with theirs had seemed to be something more than a coincidence; but a coincidence was precisely what it had been. He had decided to check the Plexus for any requisitions relating to the area he needed to visit. He was once again heading into The Depths of Acheron, so checking for aligning interests, even purely for reconnaissance, seemed to make sense. The request had not been his normal forte. If not for the Plexus master he would not have considered accepting it. It was a petition for an escort. It said nothing of the full moon, but knowing the lay of the land before his journey's start was always of benefit.

It had been his initial intention to escort them without delay. But when he had arrived on Drevera, and found his stomach warmed by food and his tongue loosened by tea, his client, Ms Embers, had suggested they made but a single journey. She only required his assistance to reach the destination. After which she insisted he could attend to his own matters. She was confident her return would be trouble-free. The issue was getting to the creature, when those seeking to mount its head or capture it for sport may stalk the surrounding land.

Rob always seemed to possess a strange and uncanny instinct, an understanding of the portals leading to The Depths of Acheron. He rarely found himself mistaken, and when he had, it was often to some unrecognised advantage. He would take a request, and spend the night deliberating over the maps in his possession. He always ensured they were the last thing on his mind before being taken by sleep. When he awoke the next day he would know exactly where to find the portal, almost as if he was being guided by an unknown force. This time had been different. Almost as soon as he had left Sunniva's presence he had felt a strange sensation creep up his spine, and knew where he must travel.

"Daimons." Bray gave a few sharp sounding tuts. "Is it true they farm humans?"

"You should know the answer to that Misorian," the elderly lady responded firmly, finally lowering her lantern and signalling they should continue. "I am Amelia. The young lady with me is Stacy, the hunter is Rob, and you are?"

"Grayson Bray ma'am," he answered, his voice holding the utmost respect.

"Bray, you should leave, Psáltis will calm the wyrm, and Ms Embers will tend its wounds. There's no purpose to your being here." Rob seemed to regard him critically before once more focusing on their surroundings.

"Two armed escorts wanting my head would argue otherwise," Bray grumbled before turning to the one named Stacy. "Calm the wyrm, how?" Positioning himself at her side he gave a boyish smile. Despite the fact she wasn't his type, tonight anyway, there was always another day, and he found himself intrigued.

"Stacy is Holder of the Sacred Chord," Amelia revealed. She had no intention of deceiving anyone, and was still uncertain to the reasoning behind this young man's presence.

"The first born for... centuries," Bray mused, his voice filled with awe as his gaze regarded the woman in a new light. She did hold about her a certain beauty, perhaps he could be tempted.

"The first discovered," Amelia corrected. "Now hush, it awaits our arrival with little patience." She turned to give Stacy a smile, one the darkness masked. "Stacy, this wyrm is in a dangerous place, bordering on the transition to dragon. Our survival rests on you holding its attention."

"Wyrm to dragon," Bray interrupted. "Surely that transition is impossible. They were different species."

"The rules are changing, Grayson Bray. Things once lost are being reborn. When the conventional means are not open new methods must be formed, and a wyrm is the closest relation to the cursed species." She turned back to Stacy. "No matter what you see or hear, you must not stop. Are you scared?"

"Yes." Came her brittle reply.

"Good, that's how you should feel. It's what will keep you safe." Amelia nodded adjusting the lantern in her grasp.

"Close your eyes." Stacy jumped feeling Bray's breath in her ear, wondering how he had become so close without her realising. "Close them tightly and do not look." She felt his hand grasp hers, and in that moment she calmed just a little. Her focus turned to their hands. Realising his grasp felt somehow comforting, and how with him beside her she felt safe. She became aware of his delicate scent, and more tension drained from her until her breathing calmed and the swelling, which had threatened to steal her voice, subsided.

Amelia gave Bray a look of warning, understanding all too well the control he was exerting upon her. Seeing the fatigue this influence caused she allowed him to continue. It appeared there was nothing more to his action than a gesture of comfort, and *his* touch could offer more than most.

"Amelia, thank you. If not for you I never would have known there was a wyrm here, much less have devised a means of passing it." Amelia stepped closer to Rob, the words spoken shared just between them.

"Protect them with your life Rob, and bring her back."

Stacy's hand tightened on Bray's as they followed the turn in the path. Even through closed eyes she could feel the anger of the creature's gaze as it found them.

213

The light cast ghastly shadows, illumining the malicious twist of its jaws. Its size suggested it to be an adult. Its hunched form almost filled the alcove it had taken for its nest. It raised its head, eyes burning on the brink of madness, and its pain and loss were evident.

Amelia shook her head. She could see the severing of the bond between it and its chosen Eorthád. Given the extent of its injuries she could only imagine what had become of its rider. She could treat its physical wounds, but nothing more. She hoped it would prove enough. It tensed at their presence. Its tired muscles starting to move the enormous weight as a low growl erupted from its throat.

"When you're ready," Bray whispered, just as Amelia was about to encourage her to begin. She gave a determined nod, and began to sing.

It was a song like none other. Its ancient words unheard for longer than time could recall. The rise and fall of the delicate notes held tones known only to those who had heard the music of the heavens. It was captivating; a human voice lifting in power to harmonise with the sounds of life and the universe. A person able to achieve such a feat possessed a long forgotten understanding, a way to vocalise the sacred chord utilising the ancient powers of Grand Planetary Magic, an influence born with the universe.

The wyrm stepped forwards, emerging from its nest attempting to raise itself to its full height. To Amelia's relief there was still no outward indication of the pending transformation, except for the hunger reflected within its eyes. It stopped its advance, a throaty growl turning into the start of a deafening roar. Its open mouth dripped with saliva, but its heart was already touched by the soothing tones. Its eyes softened, betraying the effects of the hypnotic serenade as its salivating maw extended into an enormous yawn. Its large body began to sway, and its rage reduced with each note, calming the temper fuelled by the injuries those hunting it had caused.

The ground trembled as its large form was taken by sleep, and the song went on.

Amelia, seeing the danger had now past, moved to complete her purpose. With Rob's aid she began cutting free the steel bindings and wire. Given the methods employed it had no doubt been intended for a game hunter to subdue the beast and return with a living trophy. Weapons pierced the joins of scales, some of which were buried to their hilts embedded deep within its flesh. Slowly, carefully, they worked together, discarding all upon the cavern's floor. With each fragment removed the meridians flowing through the scales began to heal, but the damage it had suffered had been extensive.

Although wyrms obtained their energy directly from sunlight, this was done through exposing their wings, an act forbidden by the same chains which prevented its flight. The impending starvation had driven it closer to madness. Each unsubstantial meal from passing prey remained unsatisfying, giving rise to anger. This rage was the very heart of the power which fuelled the ancient dragons, and tempted its transformation. Amelia, given all she had seen, had cause to wonder if this had been a mere accident, or if someone had sought to deliberately revive the cursed race.

Amelia unwrapped the scroll from her back, applying thick smears of a green sap onto the wounds. Once treated she placed the large papyrus, which had been completely covered on one side with the sappy medicine, over the largest injury as if it were a bandage.

All the time, with her eyes tightly closed, Stacy continued to sing.

"The moon will rise soon. You should make haste from these caves," Rob warned. He knew once the melody stopped the creature would once more wake. With its injuries now treated he hoped it would seek only to return home.

"If we leave, Ms Amelia will have to contend with the wyrm. That is assuming it has not already been reborn as a dragon," Bray responded without delay. Given all he had seen, of both the woman and the wyrm, he had little doubt she would be safe. But it was her identity alone which saw him unwilling to take that risk. There was something about the lady he thought he should recognise, she was important. He just couldn't place how.

"If you stay you will be dragged into my business, and Ms Embers would still be here alone," Rob reminded him.

"Ah yes you said, a rescue mission. So be it then, I would be less of a man if I were to abandon those in need," he replied, his voice filled with bravado. The place Rob intended to venture was one like none other. Bray was already committed to embracing this experience. It was a once in a lifetime opportunity.

"Would you be so quick if you knew the one in danger was a Daimon?" A silence filled the air, one even Stacy conformed to. The ground began to tremble as the moon started to rise. Despite the fact the moon's light was unable to filter into the depths of the cave, the effect was the same as Rob had witnessed on countless occasions. The solid earth rippled from the place they had gathered, almost as if they stood on liquid, yet it remained firm to the touch, for the moment at least. "Quickly, you must leave now, you have no debt with me."

"This Daimon, she is important?" Bray questioned desperately as doubts began to surface. His hunger served only to remind him of how unprepared he was. He took a deep breath, willing the burning pain away.

"I think she possesses the power to destroy the world," Rob stated, repeating a warning he had heard through his fevered sleep when Taya had been taken.

"Ethelyn, Kitaia Ethelyn," Bray gasped. Rob turned to him in alarm. The name was close enough to that of his niece. But how could this stranger possibly know her?

"Who told you of her?" Rob demanded true to his thoughts. Questioning if this man was, in fact, someone sent by his sister to ensure he acted as she had suggested. No, it did not feel that way, but there was something else. Something he was hiding from them.

"As Ms Amelia said, I'm Misorian," he stated as if this should answer all questions. The cave floor rippled once more. The grating sound of rock on rock audible this time as the floor began to twist and reform around them, opening a burrow deep into the earth. It was too late for any of them to turn back. Escape was impossible. The darkness rippled beneath their feet as they looked down into the blackness below. They were slowly being pulled within, as if the void beneath them was made from quicksand.

Amelia's hand stroked the wyrm gently. The area surrounding them remained solid and unaltered as her three companions were drawn down into Kólasi. She whispered a silent prayer. She asked for forgiveness, understanding, and for their safe return. Her actions had wrought this, she knew that now, and feared the consequences to come.

Chapter 7

Geburah

Geburah sat in the audience chamber, studying the place where Kitaia had bowed before him. He closed his eyes to replay the scene in his mind, his head shaking slightly. He had not since requested her presence knowing this limited time was better spent with her husband. A heavy sigh escaped his lips as he tilted his head towards the ceiling. He watched the altering of shadows as they twisted through the twig and vine tendrils which had grown into aesthetically pleasing fixtures. Focusing on the weave of the wood his mind lingered on his latest dilemma.

Full-Moonday was upon them, and still, even after such a prolonged absence, she was still imprisoned. Yuri had been correct, purging the cornerstone of the empathic bond had proven impossible.

Even their most skilled professionals had been at a loss to explain how it had been so well established. The Kyklos had visited her, each performing their own assessment whilst speaking with her as a friend. They had worked tirelessly together. Sharing thoughts and attempting new methods to dissolve the hold Sunniva possessed. Geburah had hoped her presence here would have seen the task succeed. Without the need to enter The Betwixt they would be safe from the threat that had consumed Daley. The energy needed to locate her would be reduced and thus their effort would be strengthened. It had not been so.

The more he considered the strange occurrence with Daley the more unrest he felt. He would have been able to offer more insight, of that he was certain. Daley had spent much time with Kitaia as she grew. He had taught her to scry and harness her abilities. He was more familiar than most with her energy, and thus would recognise areas of concern more easily.

There was one other thing which troubled him greatly. The closer the lunar phase neared, the more the priestess' reality seemed to encroach. It was a call neither he, nor the Kyklos, had a means to silence and, as Yuri had predicted, she was using increasingly more dangerous methods in order to ground herself. It would only be a matter of time until the damage she did was beyond repair. He knew, for her own sake, there was little else he could do but to allow her perceptional shift to occur.

"Lord Geburah, the humans have come as you predicted." Meredith had entered the chamber without his notice to stand before him. She was a senior member of the Kyklos and, along with Eadward, responsible for keeping Kitaia under close vigil. They wove their power into her dreams and used their combined strength to force her eyes to behold what her mind denied.

There had been times when they had been successful. When they had thought it possible to bring her perspective back to its true alignment, but whenever they were close an overwhelming image of a rose crown would sever their connection to her, and further attempts to reach her would have to start anew. As long as they retained some manner of connection they believed she could never truly be lost to them, but there were some places even their abilities could not penetrate.

The woman's dark brown hair was braided and twisted into an elegant style. It was intricately woven to accommodate a magnificent headdress, almost crown-like, with carefully placed tines secured upon a single headband. Each member of the Kyklos wore one. Its sole purpose was to act as a tool to enhance their natural talents, ensuring a connection to the gemstones they used for their craft.

Iolite and lapis lazuli, used to enhance the dream and psychic workings, lined the upward pointing decorations and appeared like artistically crafted arrow heads formed from finely weaved gold and silver. Nine such decorations were present, but only the central one possessed merlinite, a stone imbued to allow access to the knowledge of all previous magic weavers and permit the wearer passage into the spiritual realms. These points were spaced equally to stop above the ears where the metal became the mineral vanadinite to ensure the wearer, when entering meditation, remained only aware of their internal world. Completing the careful design were two intertwined gold and silver links that positioned an amethyst crystal above the wearer's third eye chakra.

It took Geburah a few moments to realise she did not actually stand before him. Her message relayed the concern she and others of Eremalche felt. This was the closest that humans, other than those they had escorted personally, had been to the land of Kólasi. He had requested the Kyklos instruct the treasure hunter, Rob, where the entrance could be located. They had been watching him for some time, assisting his journeys. After all, his path crossing with Kitaia's had always been inevitable, and that was why they had allowed him so much success in the underground ruins of their kingdoms.

As their fallen and ruined cities bore testament to, they could not influence all of the creatures which lurked in The Depths of Acheron, but they could ensure he knew where to find that which he sought. To guide him, they had found the means to inform his would-be clients of things better suited for *their* possession.

"Humans." His gruff voice momentarily reflected his disdain for the events they had caused.

"Well, one if you wish to be technical."

"Life is all about technicalities. Without them I would not have been sealed, nor would I have found myself here now." He leaned forward, giving more focus to her image.

"Your orders, Regent? Should we seal the portals, confuse their direction and cause them to leave?"

"Yes. Keep them from Eremalche, but let them walk upon Kólasi's soil and allow them to take her."

"My lord?" The figure faltered.

"For the time being she is of more use to us there, and, given her difficulties, safer, it would seem." He stroked his chin thoughtfully as he considered what options were actually available to them at this time.

"How is that possible?"

"Seal the portals leading into Eremalche. Have the Kyklos use sensory illusions to conceal the walls and, most importantly, have Kitaia brought to me, quickly. I must explain what I need from her." The plan had already been on the forefront of his mind for some time. It would work, it had to. "We will reconvene later to discuss your other issue."

"Consider it done." Geburah blinked as her image before him faded.

"I can turn this to our advantage." His coarse hand rubbed his chin once more as he assessed their options. A smile turned the corners of his leathery lips. All he needed now was to await Kitaia. He only hoped she would forgive him for what he must do.

As he waited his thoughts turned back to the war, to the fate which had consumed him. He reached down, his fingers lingering over the beaten cover of his old companion. It was his journal, part of his story. He flicked through its pages, reminding himself of the past, and of how things began. His was a short tale. Mere footnotes in a grand history written long after the details had become hazy. But the facts remained, as did the powerful emotions they stirred in him. He read and reread this tome whenever he needed to find focus.

* * *

Geburah had once found much fulfilment in Talaria. He had lived and worked in the Tower of the Prophets and was a trusted adviser and tactician. The Seraphim made the decisions on which future was to be embraced, which forks to erase and which to accept. He was the one to devise the methods of enforcing their will. He found the easiest path to direct the future's flow, believing his work was for the greater good of all.

The Moirai pieced together the ancient scriptures and new predictions, creating the story of things to come. Deciding then the course the world must take for the betterment of man. Even if such things meant the termination of a life, or even an entire bloodline. They would completely, and without prejudice, eliminate anything and anyone deemed harmful to the future they chose. They thought themselves the protectors, and somehow no one ever saw them as the secret butchers they were.

Any born with the gift of prophecy, except for those of the Daimon bloodline, were brought to live within the crystalline tower. Often the humans were kept in states of minimal awareness, their gifts stimulated until their bodies became a mere husk. Few knew of the methods used to extract premonitions from seers, and many sought their wisdom. Talaria was thought of as the sacred lands. Their domain was small, comprising of many islands which stood around the tower like sentries. From this tower they recorded all prophecies, some spanning over countless cycles.

It was only when discussions of war filled the crystal halls that Geburah lost his faith in their ways, and he saw what his blinkered existence, and unquestioning conformity, had caused. He had been forty years of age when the whispers first came. In order to discuss such things in privacy he had been briefly brought into the inner sanctum, where only those gifted with prophecy should tread.

For the first time he witnessed the truth of how the human prophets were treated. He had always been led to believe that, like the Moirai prophets, they had an honoured existence, wanting for nothing and their every whim made flesh. But the reality was they simply had no desires at all.

They were kept on the brink of death, where it was believed their link with the spiritual plane was at its fullest potential. Their bodies were forced to endure great pain whilst their minds were denied the relief of unconsciousness, for those without awareness have no voice. Their predictions were forced by concoctions, crystals, and magic, and their reward for precognition was a brief reduction in the agony their sages deliberately induced and monitored. As time passed, the physical body could grow accustomed to pain. It was the sage's role to ensure this never came to pass.

The looming hostilities, and the need to know more about what was to come, saw countless seers exhausted and used. The Seraphim delved deeper into their sight and denied even the briefest moment of rest. The Moirai heard predictions of the endangerment of their race, and thus, after much deliberation, they turned their attention to devising a means to escape this fate.

Geburah, however, now understanding the wrongs of his own people, felt the need to right their actions, to protect those their hands would otherwise destroy. He formed allegiances with many species. All the time the Moirai's influence grew as they exploited those they needed for their own gains. They sought to ensure their own race's survival above all others. But privileged to their intentions Geburah worked from the shadows. He acted as a secret herald to the dangers, hoping people could safeguard themselves before the Moirai could execute their plans.

When the future turned once more to their favour a great banquet was held, viewed as a time of celebration preceding the undertaking of their greatest endeavour. All that remained was for their plans to be executed and their lands would be free from the reach of both man and Mystic. It was a night of heavy celebration, but of the glorious banquet Geburah had partaken in very little. The slight numbness of his tongue caused alarm. His panicked attempt at escape was foiled by those he had once mistaken as allies. The festivities increased in volume, creating the perfect distraction from what he feared was to come.

When the Underworld was first created it became apparent a barrier was required to shield any nearing its realm from the harmful effects of the dead. But one border had not been enough. There was need for a transitional location; a place where the lines between the realms of the dead and the living could slowly separate. The location would exist in both realms, but be of neither. Given the right conditions, man or shade could walk the path between the two. Those trapped within would suffer eternally. Burnt and tortured by the energies colliding from both realms until they themselves thought to invite death. This borderland was a place of still-time as it lay in between the planes of life and death, and it came to be known as Anámesa.

Anámesa served another purpose, one which crafted its image. It was the method Hecate and the Lampads used to traverse the lands. All looking upon it would see a dirt track, lined with trees, overlooking an orchard. This path for Hecate opened to any location, and so could be witnessed by places near and far. The image had become a tale of horror.

On moonless nights, when evil was at its strongest, those walking the path would recount stories. Tales of twisted corpses, suspended in grotesque positions from tree boughs, and the wind carrying the tortured moans of the dead. But the cries were not of the haunted souls who hung dead upon the darkened orchard trees, but of those beyond it. Those who still lived, imprisoned by the Moirai.

Those who gazed long enough upon the orchard of swinging bodies would gain awareness of its reality. A solidity granted to a once ghostly track which granted passage through the terrifying scene. Some would walk this endless path, risking entrapment and insanity. These few brave souls would bear witness to the horror beyond, the true source of the cries as they beheld the writhing bodies, suspended in iron cages. Few witnessing this spectacle could find their way home to speak of it. It was here, overlooking the images of death, where Geburah awoke.

He had not been expected to live, to find a means to claw to life and survive. But he had. The Seraphim had stripped him of his magic and imprisoned him in Anámesa. Within this prison, away from mortal hours, age would not claim its victims. Their body remained unaware of time's passage, whilst the mind suffered each eternal second.

Most imprisoned would beg for the God of Death to find them, beseeching him to end their suffering. Should their cry be heard their body would join the others, lifeless within the never-ending orchard. The hanging trees were the only means of death within this realm. Bodies lined their boughs, reminiscent of autumn foliage.

There was no reprieve from the anguish, none left within returned, and the Moirai had no cause to think

Geburah would be different. They had underestimated him, and his will to survive. He endured.

He was the first Moirai to suffer this sentence, and they had no knowledge, or care, how their own race would react. They had not foreseen the changes he would undergo, or the creature who would be created by their actions.

He was alone within Anámesa. Those before him had long succumbed to the relief of death. When he first became aware of the strange lights he had thought them an illusion. Small dark flames of blues, purples, and greens would sway in processions down the never-ending road, blinking in and out of existence. He would watch them, their quick movements reminiscent of fireflies playing within the night sky.

Over time the disjointed images grew closer, gained clarity. Finally he recognised them as Lampads, the nymphs who were escorts to Hecate. Whilst in the living plane they were found with their mistress, guiding her with their torches, or haunting the living, here was their playground.

The more awareness he had of them, the closer they drew, and the more interest they showed towards him. They would never speak to him, but often presented their torches. He thought perhaps in some way they had hoped to relieve his suffering. It was said the light from the Lampads torch possessed the power to drive a mortal insane, yet Geburah found comfort from the cold, flickering flame. At first he pleaded for aid, but soon he came to understand their inaction, and the reason for the crude, archaic structure of the cage. The Moirai had prevented such intervention, for spiritual beings were unable to make contact with iron. But he saw their pity. His prison ensured he was as much a manifestation to them, as they were to those they haunted. But their presence alone eased a fraction of his burden, but at first he did not understand why.

Over time the damage inflicted to his essence by the Moirai began to heal. But still the pain was insufferable. He was unsure how long he had endured, but he feared he could not do so for much longer. It was only as the first feather appeared on his wings he understood the Lampads' intentions. As he beheld the strange dark spark forming into a feather, burning and fading in constant motion, he finally understood. Their presenting of torches had not been intended to harm, but to heal. Each time he lost himself within the light he would absorb some of its power. That energy had been used to repair his essence, and fill the void created by the absence of magic.

The feathers of a Moirai were not akin to those found on creatures or beasts. They were a weave of magic, channelled and gathered through the exposed bone structures on their back, and converted into visible form by quills. All Moirai possessed wings of white, although the shade itself often varied. The whiter the magical manifestation, the stronger the possessor, the purer their magic. When Geburah had been stripped of his magic each fine wisp had become nothing, leaving bare bones and quill.

The loss of feathers was a symbol of the greatest dishonour. Those punished within Talaria bore their shame for all to see. Magic was thinned, but rarely removed. Those who had cause to be punished were often allowed to attempt to regain honour, and some even made amends in time. The change in Geburah, the appearance of new and altered magic, gave him hope. It was this hope that made it possible for him to persevere. But there was a heavy price to survival.

The result of opposing energies had seen his once fair skin burnt, charred, and healed times beyond count. His flesh was hardened and tempered until his skin became a toughened hide the colour of ash.

His wings became full, mirroring the shades of the Lampads' torches, as well as their ability to drive those who gazed too long upon his feathers into madness. He could see the images warped within the forever rekindling flames, terrors and fears woven from the very core of nightmares.

* * *

Whilst time for Geburah seemed both eternal and fleeting, the mortal plane had been ravaged by war. Once grand battles quietened into displays of force and power, all leading to one unthinkable result.

Seventy-five years had passed when the Daimons found Anámesa, drawn to his location by the magic now warped and burning within him. He was like no being they had ever seen, yet instead of fearing him, they freed him from his prison, returning him to Kólasi where they nursed him to health. They treated him with kindness, and in their presence the vibrancy of his wings diminished, merely making those gazing upon him uncomfortable, rather than maddened.

Having been lost in a world of silence had made understanding difficult at first. Skills he had once known no longer were executed at will. They spoke to him, knowing comprehension would come in time. Many of his waking hours were spent listening to conversations directed towards him, most aimed at encouraging a response. Eventually he began to understand. As they bathed and nursed him, and tended to his atrophied limbs with medicines and magic, they told him of the war, and of events his incarceration had kept from him. As he regained use of his limbs they encouraged him to read, write, and record all he could remember.

He remastered the written word far easier than speech. He wrote statements he thought to be true, opening the path for communication. He learnt that Talaria's prophets had forewarned that humans would seek to make the world their own. A place of no magic except for that they themselves could wield. It would become a place of intolerance, where those different would be hunted. Such news distressed the Moirai, who had always had their favour. The Moirai had always held a position of love, their predictions thought to inspire and give hope.

Fearing for their race the Moirai succeeded in lifting their lands, protecting their kind from the harm to come. But their actions served only to spur ha-

tred. For all the love the Moirai received the Daimons received an equal measure of hate. They were
perceived as beings on the opposite ends of the spectrum. The Moirai's magic was fuelled by the energies
generated by the emotion of love, but the Daimons
grew stronger in the presence of negative emotions.
This natural reaction was solely a means of protection, and yet, despite their solitude they were treated
as beings of evil. Those who sought them out found,
unlike the Moirai, they spoke no honeyed comforts,
only truth. People rarely liked to hear of their fail-
ings, and the dangers they could face, even when
asking of them. When the Moirai abandoned them
the humans needed to place blame, and where better
than those who appeared to contradict the nature of
the Moirai.

Their hatred grew, becoming a seed which spread
as younger generations aged, and soon there was just
one clear path apparent. The Daimons' evil must be
eliminated. Such a race could not be permitted to
survive.

Regardless of isolation and beliefs, no sentient race
would simply allow themselves to be driven into extinction by acts of unfounded slaughter. The result
was the predicted war.

It erupted first in a clash of magic, a battle which
raged on and permitted the Daimons time to construct Eremalche, a stronghold city which would sustain and protect them. But the Daimons had once
lived as neighbours to all races, and those who did

not immediately seek shelter within the city were hunted and slaughtered.

Whilst there was much fighting, and times when the air was permeated by the clash of steel and the thunder of cavalry, such was not the final battle. The final battle was not one of action, but of prolonged subterfuge. The poisoning of underground water sources, the kidnap and slaughter of children, and finally, peace talks concealing the development of Keres weaponry. The humans sought for a means to eliminate the Daimons without having to walk amongst them, and the result was the fearsome and terrifying weapon they named Remedy.

Keres weaponry was a matter discussed in whispered tones. Some thought the device brought this magic under their control, but the concepts were far more complex than most would come to understand.

Remedy exploited information and insight gained through the torture and execution of the Daimons. Even prior to the war, those seeking longevity had sought to learn their secrets and, in doing so, had inadvertently discovered a way to not only kill them, but to prevent their rebirth. It was a principle operating on resonation, and achieved by integrating and channelling old magics to create a force capable of negating their very existence. They just needed a means to expand its reach, and for that they needed time.

The Daimons used the diversion of peaceful negotiations to mount small-scale rescues on strongholds where their families were being contained. Within the Daimons' ranks operated an order of powerful scryers who, whilst communing with the spirits, were granted insights aimed to turn the tide of war in their favour. But the spirits' messages had changed, directing them to a place thought to be mere legend. They found themselves guided by the Lampads into the depths of Anámesa, and to a being the spirits believed could best secure their future.

As the facade extended both sides exploited the time to their own gains, and Geburah began to heal. As soon as he was able he swore his fealty to their queen, known by the title of Sfaíra Fýlakas. Geburah schooled them in tactics and deception. As he regained his health he saw the Daimons' magic was powerful, but having valued solitude and peace they had never learnt the art of warfare, only protection. Their attempts at rescue were also often hindered by the barriers the humans had created using the Moirai relics.

Through the execution of Geburah's suggestions the Daimons came to learn of Remedy. The threat of such a weapon was so great there was little choice but to create something of equal and devastating potential. They named this item Sunrise.

Remedy had been designed to erase all that was Daimon, and in the same manner Sunrise would abolish all human life. The Daimons' intention had been to force an end to the war where neither side would risk a possible retaliation. But instead, by the time both weapons were complete, both races were committed to their use.

It was then the Mystics intervened, for this new warfare had the potential to destroy all. Learning of these beings' intentions Geburah tried to seek out his own means to end the war. He knew the Mystics had little choice, tactically, but to side with the humans.

He sought a primordial tool. When something capable of great power, such as the Mystics, was created, a balance must be employed, and something of equal potential generated to coincide with their birth. This tool was not only equal to that of the Mystics, but would suggest enough force that his mere possession of it should still the war and reopen the table for genuine arbitration. He refused to allow those who had shown him such kindness to be the scapegoats the Mystics intended.

* * *

When Geburah entered the domain of the Mystics his fate had already been sealed. His purpose was to guide the Daimons into the future, but it was not the future he had expected. In order to fulfil his destiny his fate must first turn full circle. He had thought his time was now, that he would be a saviour to the race who had shown him so much kindness. He was mistaken.

The Mystics had as much to lose from the war as either side. Only they knew the true catastrophe the conflict between the humans and the Daimons would bring. Geburah had hoped to find them fair and just, willing to listen to reason. But they had no desire to mediate. They sought to ensure their own survival, which meant they had but one choice. They had to align with the humans. Even as he approached their awaiting council he felt the weight of defeat upon his broad shoulders.

The six figures stood tall. Their regal presence alone spoke of the power they could harness. Unlike other beings of magic they could manipulate not only the powers that were, but all that would be across the endless span of eternity. Their presence caused the large grove, which they called home, to bloom perpetually. The Mystics were open to all the forces of nature, the whispers of the world. Yet to Geburah's words they were deaf. When at last they chose to address him it was only the Amaranthine who spoke. Her words were few, yet their weight was immense, and her gift to him had been a glimpse into the future.

She had approached in silence, her frail elderly hands reaching out to gently caress his hardened flesh with her maternal touch. She looked upon him with tenderness and sadness, then showed him his awaiting fate, no matter the course the future would take.

Through her touch he beheld the fracturing and creation of realms as the Mystics drew upon a power even the divine would have cause to fear. The Daimons' land sank, pulled between fractures into an existence both unaligned and imperceivable. Ocean waters poured down gaping voids as stones and lands were moved to forge tunnels for this new plane; some of earth and stone, others from bone and death. Lands were lost to The Betwixt, forming islands adrift accessible only through that which would come to be known as The Stepping Realm.

The Amaranthine showed him the fate of the Daimons. How the Mystics would give life to things within their misaligned existence. They would create game, flesh to be hunted and devoured, and form life to sustain those trapped. They would ensure the races' survival and, in order to maintain all that would be needed, their world would draw power from many sources, inclusive of whatever means would be employed to keep the Severaine sealed.

Kólasi's plane would draw magic through The Betwixt, exploiting the infinite gateways of The Stepping Realm, and once each year the flow of magic would reverse, allowing those within to emerge until the dawn's first light.

Geburah saw the evolution of life within the realm, and the wars those he thought of as his people would face, their trials and hardships. But he witnessed the peace they would know, the alliances they would forge. He saw it all.

As the Amaranthine removed her hand he looked upon her with awe, his grasp slackening on the crystal in his hand. He turned his gaze towards it seeing, as the premonition had implied, it was incomplete, and that any attempt to engage them in conflict could have only one result.

"This is the only way they will survive." The elderly figure pulled a chain from around her neck, revealing the missing fragment of the crystal. Its absence from the one within his possession had sealed his fate the moment he had approached. It was now for him to decide how it would end. "Will you submit willingly?"

"I will." Geburah placed the crystal within the elderly lady's hand. "They deserve to know peace, and I will not be bound forever."

Chapter 8

Enthralled

The gentle flakes of snow fell to rest upon her flesh, neither melting nor altering in response to her presence upon the snow-laden hills. She had long lost track of whether she was in her own dreamscape or that of another person. She knew the intricacies of this world, and had bestowed upon herself the rune of boundaries, granting her accessibility to all of the dreamers' realm. She knew its dangers, and had unlocked many of its secrets in her years of wandering the ever-changing land.

She found the snow comforting, its silence was the closest to the peace of death she could embrace. Its cold touch chilled her flesh. But here there was no fear of exposure. Elly had cause to wonder if she should fear death at all.

"You're back again." The sound of a determined gait compressing the soft snow as its owner marched towards her caused Elly to close her eyes in despair, willing herself to sink deeper into the snow which embraced her body. "You do realise I could always wake you." With an exasperated sigh Elly pushed herself to a seated position, causing the blanket of snow upon her to crumble and fall.

"Better have tried," she assured him firmly; her tone, like the surroundings, lacking in any warmth.

"I suppose you're right." The figure sat heavily upon the snow beside her. He knew himself there had been many attempts made by his peers to expel her from these lands, but all had met with failure. Eventually they had been ordered to allow her the seclusion she sought, and leave her to her wanderings. She had proven herself capable of staying one step ahead of the darkness, and so they need not worry for her safety.

"Aidan, as much as I am flattered that you seem to have appointed yourself as my personal tracker, surely you have matters in need of attending. Can I not just be left in peace, is that really too much to ask?" She turned her vision towards the heavy snow filled sky.

Her image in this realm had altered from the one so often recognised. She had entered here of her own will, suppressing her ties to the mortal world, and yet now she appeared more mortal than she had for a long time. Her hair, in this existence at least, had shed the vibrant blue shades which had marked her as cursed, reverting to its former mousy-brown. But she knew the curse remained. Even in a world of imagination, where she could almost convince herself she was mortal, her eyes remained their strange violet shade. Such was a reminder to any who looked upon her that she remained tethered to both the curse and the waking world.

"It's a slow day." He shrugged non-committally. "Besides, you looked lonely."

"Not today, Aidan. Let me have my peace." There was an almost desperate tinge to her voice. One he had heard infiltrate her normally cool tones all too often. She wrapped her arms around herself against the cold, willing this figure away. But he remained.

"You can't mourn forever."

"And what would *you* know of such things?" Elly rose to her feet, turning her back to him as she made her retreat towards the shimmering light of the dreamscape's edge.

"More than you'd know."

"More than I would know? How dare you be so presumptuous. I have experienced more loss than you could fathom. What right have you to insert yourself into my—"

"What right?" Aidan rose to his feet, smiling inwardly at the show of hostility. "What right do you have to insert yourself into our lands? And as for presumption, you forget, *you* are the child here."

"Well on that note, I shall make my infantile retreat. I have neither asked for, nor wish your company." She stepped through the boundary, hastening her steps to ensure she walked the borders of multiple lands until, believing herself to be alone, she slowed her pace. She pushed her hands through her long hair, turning sharply as an unwelcome touch fell upon her shoulder.

"Childish indeed, to think you can out step me so easily." Aidan shook his head, smirking. His display of amusement deepened as her shoulders grew tense in annoyance.

"So you have been tasked to frustrate me until waking is better than remaining under your vigil?"

"As I said, you looked lonely. But, you know, I am beginning to think your other idea has merit." He nodded slightly, caressing his chin as if to give thought to this action.

"Do not mistake seeking solace in solitude with being lonely." She glared at him harshly, but her expression softened slightly as it met only with his disarming smile. "So you thought to befriend me, to ease my suffering?" Her voice was edged with sarcasm, yet the frustration had ebbed.

"Sure, why not. No one else wants to. Except maybe that." He jerked his thumb towards his right where, on the horizon, a dark shadow gathered in mass.

"An Ieró?" she requested, wondering if there was such a haven nearby.

"Oh, so now you want my help?" Hearing his words Elly turned away from the figure as if to leave. He reached out, taking her arm gently. "This way. Your prolonged presence in our realm is drawing them."

"Hmm, I would point the finger firstly towards yourself. I was under the impression they were only drawn to *your* kind in force. And you do have a habit of lingering. You really should know better."

"Often you would be correct, but not always. It must be a novel experience for you, being wrong. But if it's death you're seeking, why not stay and test your theory? I'm sure Melas-Oneiros would make far better company than an Outcast. Besides, why relinquish the opportunity to drink from his version of Lethe and forget your woes?" Elly looked towards the growing darkness, weighing her options. She felt the pressure of his grip begin to lessen as she began to accept his guiding touch.

"So you are an outcast?"

"Of sorts." He opted not to explain the word did not mean what she believed. In Darrienia, The Outcasts were a small division responsible for monitoring those trapped within the realm, and were tasked to investigate unusual events. "Why else do you think I've more interest in watching you sulk, sorry, I mean your silent contemplation, than in the role I was born to fulfil. I know they're not being drawn to me for one reason and one reason alone." Elly glanced to him questioningly. "*I'm* not doing anything to warrant attention."

* * *

Taya felt the quickening of her breath, and the beads of sweat pouring down her flushed face as she ran. How could she have been so foolish, how could she have allowed her perspective to be turned so askew? Sunniva's voice called to her louder than ever, begging her to return home. She felt shivers race through her body, her visible tremors causing her hurried pace to deteriorate.

Overlapped images created complex mazes before her gaze. Recent recollections took on a darker twist, where once humanoid figures had stood great monsters and demons had loomed, feeding from her as she lay trapped within their thrall. Tears streamed from her eyes, mingling with dirt and sweat as she pushed herself to run faster. She could not let them take her, not again, not when they held so much sway over her reality.

She tried to calm her breathing, force it into a rhythm to match the impact of her feet upon the stone. She tried to keep her thoughts on the sound alone, not even wondering where she planned to run. Such thoughts caused her pace to slow, her mind to falter, to question, and so she did the only thing she could. She forced her mind to relive the moment when everything around her had changed. When the images of those she had thought to be friends had altered, their welcoming smiles turning into famished snarls as they realised she had seen them for what they truly were.

They had planned to keep her, to use her life slowly. However, now she had breached their control there was no choice but to hunt. She could still hear their hungry, angered snarls as they closed in around her, but Sunniva's voice promised her safety. Fear overcame all, and she had ran. Lost in the back of her mind there was still doubt, but it was a doubt she could not afford to embrace. Not if she wished to live.

Distorted recollections reverted to familiar forms and kind memories, and so, as she had been told to do so often, Taya envisioned a rose, focusing her mind upon its red petals. Sunniva told her the rose held within it many secrets. Its petals were created from the blood and tears of the Gods and as such still held some of their power. Visualising its image alone possessed the strength to return her thoughts to the truth.

Taya knew herself to be close to the territorial border of Kólasi. The land across the unseen boundary was named Lemuria, and it was a place no living soul should linger. Whilst many generations ago this domain had once been theirs, other things had now claimed these territories.

The Depths were home to many creatures, ones that the Daimons often hunted for flesh, hide, and bone. But there were some things of sentience, and these were the ones Taya feared the most. They protected their boundaries like savage animals, killing all who attempted to trespass. The conflict between them had spanned generations. The Daimons were driven from their distant territories until they were forced back to Kólasi to take refuge within Eremalche. They ventured outside its protection solely when the need arose.

Taya searched desperately for the opening her mind told her would be there. Kólasi, when driven into this realm, had dragged with it part of the land's crust, forming vast and intricate mountains around what had once been their island. There were tunnels, caves, and catacombs which led to the places beyond, and whether it was Sunniva's voice within her mind, or the deeper one which seemed to whisper from the shadows, she knew it guided her to safety.

Taya paused at an intersection of tunnels. Movement, concealed partly by shadows, flickered in the distance. Conflicted, she wondered if she should retreat. Backtrack in the hope to evade detection, but the guiding voice within her mind insisted she advance.

Fearing exposure she pressed herself firmly against the stone wall, and silenced her laboured breathing as much as her fatigue allowed, still fearing it would betray her presence. She raised her hands, clamping one firmly over her mouth as she beheld, with disbelief, the gold-coloured knife clutched in her other. Her surroundings grew hazy, her intense focus bringing to her attention the intricate details of the familiar weapon.

Observing it now she could feel her grasp upon it, recalling images of it slicing through fruit as easily as it had flesh. She could almost hear Yuri's words as he scolded her for using weaponry in the kitchen. She took comfort in its weight, the feeling of its warm metal.

Her breathing calmed, allowing her to concentrate on the sounds belonging to her surroundings; the suggestions of movement, the instinctive feelings. She could make little sense of the jumbled sensations, but she knew for certain whatever approached was not human and, given its relaxed steps, it was currently unaware of her. She had but one chance, to strike before being discovered. Her muscles tensed, ready.

A dark shadow stepped into her line of sight. Without delay, without pause to examine its armour, she launched herself forwards, knowing her technique would pierce even the hardest of metal. She thrust her shoulder into the figure, her arm wrapping around him to place the dagger's tip to his side where the momentum, and weight of their bodies as they collided with the tunnel's wall, would drive it deep into his flesh. She heard the breath knocked from the figure as he lost his footing to her attack.

As the butt of the dagger touched the stone she felt the strong hands of another assailant upon her, forcing her against the wall as it pulled her intended victim back from harm. Her head throbbed before it even struck the wall as she felt an unfamiliar tugging sensation within her mind. She cursed her stupidity for not realising the figure was not alone. Through her fading sight she thought she saw the shadow reform to take on some familiar features. The dagger fell from her hand as her knees buckled. The world around her faded into nothingness. She never even heard the weapon strike the ground.

"Ethelyn," Rob gasped, recovering his balance as Bray flung him aside. He knew if not for this man's intervention her attack would have been fatal. He had seen enough altercations in his time, but never

had he seen that technique before. He had not expected her to attack him. When he had caught sight
of her at the junction she had looked panicked. He
had hoped approaching her alone would allow him a
chance to calm her. He looked to Bray, offering an
appreciative nod as their eyes met.

Bray inspected Taya briefly, feeling exhaustion
wash over him. Her impact with the wall had left
no lasting mark, but the efforts of his intervention
had been no small feat. He moved to sit beside her as
he tried to gather some energy. Such influence came
with a price, and now more than ever his hunger
burned. He needed to eat, and soon.

* * *

Taya, before being aware of anything else, felt the
cool caress of the wind across her face. It carried
upon it the sound of approaching footsteps. She saw
shadows moving through the darkness, and in the
distance the twinkling of stars as they emerged from
behind thick velvety clouds.

It was a moment before the fog within her mind
began to clear. She adjusted her position slightly,
feeling the cold stone at her back which supported
her weight as she sat leaning against it. The shadows moved again, and it was a moment before she
recognised the crouching figure before her as Rob.

"Rob," she whispered, expecting her voice to be far
weaker than it was. "What happened?" She moved

slowly, pushing herself backwards to sit more comfortably. Unable to meet his gaze she focused past him and across the darkened plains.

The occasional flicker of distant light suggested nearby settlements and, in an instant, Taya realised she did not know this place. She raised her hand, aware of the dull throbbing pain, and tentatively touched the wound on the back of her head. She shivered, only partly due to the chill of the night's air, and drew her hands down her face, trying to make sense of events as she recalled them.

Instinct alone spoke of the passage of many lunar phases, and yet, she was still with Rob, perhaps even still on their way to their intended destination. "I had one of my turns didn't I? Please, tell me I didn't hurt anyone." Her eyes searched his desperately. As he moved to stand she reached up, grabbing his arm tightly. "Please, tell me." Images of his death haunted her mind with vivid clarity, causing tears to burn her eyes.

"You didn't hurt anyone, Ethelyn." He offered her his best comforting smile, attempting to hide the confusion her words had brought. He had no idea what had happened to her. Nor did it seem he would be given the chance to learn the truth. Even now he could see his sister's influence clouding her tear-filled eyes. She leaned back against the rock, sighing in relief as the fear and tension drained from her. It was only as her gaze wandered she noticed the two people who stood watching them awkwardly.

"Erm, Rob," she whispered, making a small pointing gesture towards the figures. "Who are those people?" Everything was so confusing, she had no idea if she had wronged them, knew them, or owed them a debt.

"They are friends," he reassured her softly. "Bray and Psáltis." He gestured behind him to the place they stood. Hearing their introductions they stepped closer. "They helped to... to..." Rob looked at her again, his brows knitting into a tight frown as he noticed for the first time something which was so obviously amiss.

"What is it?" Taya shifted uncomfortably beneath his troubled gaze. She glanced just behind her to where he seemed to focus. There was nothing there. Taya felt herself flush with heat. A sickness burned in the pit of her stomach as she wondered if he saw it too, or more accurately, didn't see it. "Rob, I think I am hallucinating again. My wings they're..." but the next words failed to leave her lips.

"Hallucinating?" Bray shook his head. "You surely know they only appear in times of stress, or when channelling magic?" He approached Taya, crouching to examine her. He closed his eyes taking a slow breath in through his nose. His senses were overpowered by the scent of the night air, as well as the aroma of the woman who sat before him.

He could smell the fear which was so clearly reflected in her eyes, but there was something else. Releasing the breath he inhaled again, savouring the tastes of mingling scents at the back of his throat.

He felt Rob's firm touch pushing him backwards. It was only as he opened his eyes he saw the distress his strange actions had caused.

"No, I've always had them," she protested, finding her voice once more. Her words sounded alien to her ears, in fact, the whole conversation seemed out of place, disjointed. Bray turned his attention to Rob whose hand was still upon his chest from where he had encouraged him away. As Bray looked down to his arm he noticed, for the first time, the ring Rob wore. Now he had inadvertently brought attention to it he saw Taya's eyes were also trained upon it. It was too delicate to be his and the recognition in the Daimon's eyes led him to another assumption.

"Is that yours? I've not seen its likes for some time. I know a few ladies who would love to add it to their collection." He moved as if to grasp it. Rob pulled his arm away, but Bray's gaze remained transfixed. "Solon and Mika would love to see this little beauty. I bet—"

"A relic?" Stacy interrupted in amazement, moving in to study the ring closer as Rob removed it. She had heard this pair mentioned on a few occasions, and always in relation to this single topic.

"Yes, it's a glamour. I bet it was designed to react only to your—" Bray cut himself off, lifting the delicate item from Rob's grasp as the four of them leaned in to study it closer. There seemed nothing at all unusual about it. He became aware of the silence as they awaited the conclusion of his great revelation. "That's to say, it works just for you," Bray explained, opting to keep things in their simplest forms. There was little point to introducing unfamiliar concepts. "Here." Bray tossed the item towards her, no sooner had her fingers made contact when the dark black appendages appeared.

The sudden movement in her peripheral vision saw the ring slide from her grasp, the wings once more fading as contact was lost. She pulled her hands down over her face, stopping to cover her mouth as she tried to control her breathing.

"I-I need to see Sunniva." Her voice was brittle, on the verge of breaking. Reality washed over her in waves, causing dizziness to ebb and flow. She lowered her face back into her hands, passing them over her head to clasp behind her neck as she leaned forward. Her forearms positioned over her ears in hope to drown out the white noise which seemed to be all she could hear as they spoke. She closed her eyes tightly, unable to believe what she saw any longer.

"Are you sure that's wise?" Rob placed his hand on her chin, tilting her face to look at him as he spoke.

"Well look, it's been a great pleasure to meet you," Bray interrupted the heavy silence. "But I really must excuse myself, I'm famished." Bray patted his stomach, giving what could only be construed as a mischievous smile before he turned to leave. Eldnyng was the closest town, and despite its residence being somewhat of an acquired taste, he had a pouch full of gold, and a good mind to drink them dry.

"I'm afraid I too should be on my way." Stacy bent to give Taya's shoulder a reassuring squeeze. It was impossible not to see the young woman's distress, but she had the feeling their presence was doing little to calm her. "It was nice to meet you Rob, Ethelyn." Stacy took her leave. After a few moments Taya raised her head, rubbing her temples gently. She examined the surroundings finding herself alone, upon a seemingly deserted plain, with Rob.

"I guess that just leaves us then." Rob stood offering her a hand to her feet. "Come, adventure awaits."

"No. I have to return to Elpída," Taya said weakly, struggling for a moment to find her balance. The distant illuminations of the villages ahead were bathed in an aura of unfocused light caused by her fatigue.

"Ethelyn, are you sure?" He placed his arm warmly on her shoulder, pulling her trembling figure close.

"My sickness is getting worse. Would you believe I actually thought I was living amongst them?"

"Ethelyn, if your delusions are real would you still honour our agreement to help me find The Seed?"

"The Seed?" she paused for a moment before the memory became clear. Their conversation was the last thing she remembered with any definitive clarity. Everything that followed seemed like fragments of a dream she'd never had. "That's right, you said if we could find it you wouldn't take me." Rob gave a nod. "It seems like so long ago, but no. It's too dangerous." Her gaze stared over his shoulder, fixed on the rainbow aura that surrounded the full moon. She concentrated, deliberately ignoring the blackened shades of the grass and the colourless shadows which walked the land around them. The cold wind rustled through nearby trees, bending them beneath its gentle will, and bathing the land in darkness as a cloud obscured the brilliance of the moon. Taya fought back a rising shudder.

"I understand. Well, the least I can do is make sure you reach Sunniva safely. Once you're in better health, maybe we could try our adventure again?" he questioned hopefully.

"I cannot take you on that quest," she stressed pulling away from his warmth and crossing her arms in front of herself. Did he not realise what he was asking? Real or not, it was a journey she knew she should never make.

"For now, let's just get you home. Who knows, in time you may even change your mind."

* * *

Their journey back was made in silence. Rob, eager now to complete his task, decided the best course of action was to pass through Collateral and borrow a horse. The sooner he returned her to Sunniva, the sooner he could try to forget. He could turn his focus to his work, and pretend to be unaware of her suffering, unaware of his sister's manipulation and cruelty. It was the only way. Perhaps next time he visited, when things had once more reverted to Sunniva's will, she would be more open to their adventure.

He despised himself, the action he was taking, but a greater good would come from it. She knew of the item he had spent so many years searching for. She had provided his only true insight and, despite what he knew it would mean for her, he could not allow this opportunity to go to waste. He wouldn't simply abandon her to his sister's mercy, he would negotiate her safety first.

As they entered the portal into Collateral Taya's grip on his arm increased. He glanced towards her for the first time since their return began. Her eyes were tightly closed, her breathing laboured. She did not open them once, not to view the winding side-streets or seek out the source of nearby commotion. She simply trusted him to guide her path, and this unquestioning trust caused a wave of shame to wash over him. Especially when a darker part of his mind whispered he should play on her insecurities. They had, after all, just moments ago been walking an open plain, and within a single step had found themselves in the midst of a towering city's streets.

He silently berated himself for such thoughts. His actions were detestable enough without adding to her burden. He remained silent as his internal mono-logue castigated him, stirring a self-loathing so fa-miliar to him. Often his mind would remind him of his flaws, his failures, but there was always another voice, albeit a quieter one, justifying his actions and granting him a semblance of peace. Today that voice remained silent.

He hired a single horse from one of the stables, and lifted Taya to sit atop its bare back. Even then her eyelids never fluttered. She reached out, her breath-ing calming slightly as her fingers buried themselves in the steed's coarse mane. She let out a long breath, resting her head upon the back of its thick neck, and became alarmingly still. If not for being able to induce a similar state himself, Rob would have feared both her breathing and pulse had stopped. He led the horse slowly. He picked his path to the portal with care in an effort to ensure the horse's rider remained safe.

Once they had left Collateral it was a relatively short ride to Elpída. Taya showed no signs of emerging from her catatonic state. Not even when he mounted and pulled her to rest against him before spurring the horse into a gallop.

When they reached Elpída he would send the horse on its way, and enjoy the brisk walk to Riverside Quay. His mind was still in discord about the path he was pursuing, and a long walk would be conducive to restoring his balance.

* * *

Sunniva had been pacing before the statue of Artemis for longer than she cared to consider. Her anxious steps only halting as the doors opened. With barely a word from the Iereía, two of her clerics entered from the temple's rear, lifting Taya from Rob's arms, and encouraging her to her feet. Rob saw her awareness began to return, her breathing deepening, and the unmistakable slump to her posture showing a combination of shame and submission. She went without objection, her slow, unsteady steps made harder by the speed in which the clerics wished to remove her from sight.

Rob fell into step with his sister, matching her slow pace as they too made their way to Taya's room. Their conversation remained hushed as Rob recapped events. When nothing was left unsaid—except for his discovery about the ring, which still lay abandoned where Taya had dropped it—his sister spoke.

"We can never mention any of this to her. This experience will only loosen her precarious grasp on reality."

"I'll agree, but on one condition," Rob consented as they stood outside the young woman's room. Sunniva met his eyes questioningly, seeing the weight he held within she nodded, gesturing for him to continue. "You must *not* send her to that place, not again."

"Agreed." Sunniva responded a little too quickly for his comfort, her hand resting on the handle of the closed door.

"And," he added raising his hand before she could speak further. "Next time, I want to spend some time with her."

"I'm not sure that's—"

"I'll take whatever relics you require. Whatever it takes to keep the, the demons away." Rob knew he should have been ashamed of himself for bringing her back here. But it was the only way. When Sunniva had once more clouded Taya's grasp on reality she would be more open to helping him with his own quest. Sunniva's hold on her was fragile, and he knew he could easily penetrate her influence enough to have Taya once more wanting to seek the truth. He just had to be sure not to overstep the unseen boundaries. It seemed there was a fine line between her being willing to aid him, and feeling duty bound to deny his request.

The Seed of Nzin was a prize he had long sought, and this woman had been his only real progress after almost six years of searching. He knew this betrayal, this exploitation, made him every bit as monstrous as his sister. He was toying with her life, but there was too much at stake to give up now. Taya had already expressed her own desire to return. The least he could do was ensure she left Elpída occasionally.

"Fine, but tell me, why the sudden interest?"

"I've been so absorbed in my own problems I've not spared a thought to anyone else, to the burdens you carry. I see how much she means to you, how her suffering pains you. In all but blood you are her mother and that alone makes her worth my time. I've been a fool. She's family and we have so little left." Sunniva saw his eyes grow dark and reached out, stroking his shoulder comfortingly.

"If that's what you need, Brother, then by all means."

"I do have one concern though, whatever will you tell her about her wings?" Sunniva offered him a smile before entering the room. Taya, already dressed in her nightgown, was sitting on the edge of her bed, and seemed barely aware of the actions of those around her.

259

"Taya, you're awake. How are you feeling now?" As Sunniva spoke Rob was unable to conceal his expression of concern. She barely resembled the young woman he had only moments ago escorted inside. She appeared so frail and weak, as if she lacked the strength to hold even her own weight. Taya opened her mouth to answer as Sunniva moved to stand before her, but her inability to focus clearly robbed her of her words. "You've been unwell, you should lie back down."

Without giving her a chance to protest, Sunniva lifted Taya's legs onto the bed. Taya shuffled back slightly allowing herself to remain seated. Her eyes turned questioningly to Rob. "Thank goodness it happened when it did, you were all set to leave, your hand had barely touched the door when you fell ill." Rob could feel the force of the suggestion from where he stood in the doorway. Sunniva was being overly descriptive for his benefit, adding a voice to the images she tried to implant.

"My wings?" Taya extended her hand behind her, knowing it would meet only air where the black feathers had once been found.

"Wings? You must have been dreaming. Did you think that you could fly, is that why you went to the roof?" As Sunniva spoke he saw a fraction of the defiant spark in Taya's eyes flicker and fade. It was no wonder this young woman had been so confused. Every moment of her day was remade to suit his sister's needs. How was she to know the difference between fiction and reality when truth was a luxury frequently denied?

"The... roof? No, I went on an adventure with him." Her voice, which should have been so resolute, sounded uncertain. "Tell her, Rob, tell her. I was abducted by monsters, and you rescued me."

"I'm sorry, Ethelyn. We were discussing a trip, but then you took ill." With these words he finally felt it, the full brunt of the shame he should have known when returning her here for his own desires. He could feel the pull of Sunniva's apallagí on her. Its influence sinking ever deeper, until Taya was once more held in his sister's thrall. If he didn't do as she desired it was possible she could once again turn her talents to him. Such an attempt was inevitable, he had learnt too much truth. But being aware of this impending betrayal would grant him some protection.

"You really should rest now." Sunniva's fingers gently lifted Taya's hair, twisting it into a plait as she spoke. "I'm sure after a sleep you'll feel less confused. Rob needs to leave now, but if you're well next time he comes, I see no reason why you can't have a short adventure. I'll be back in a moment. Why don't you close your eyes and try to get some more rest?" With the plait finished Sunniva rose to her feet, taking Rob's arm to escort him away.

"It must be nice." Rob heard the harshness of his own voice, bringing himself to speak as they neared the temple's door.

"What?"

"To be able to manipulate someone so easily. To control their every thought, and bend them to your will." His knuckles turned white as he grabbed the handle. He had brought her back, subjected her to this uncertainty and manipulation, all for his own reasons; but what his sister was doing made him feel nauseated, as did his role. But the ends had to justify the means. Without Taya's help he had no way to save them.

"Taya is a very sick girl."

"Do you think having the truth so easily twisted saves her?" As if her demonstration hadn't confirmed his sister was indeed twisting Taya's mind to her own design, the fact she now prepared to utilise her abilities on him made it clear. One thing was blatantly obvious, Sunniva had more control on Taya whilst she remained in Elpída. Something here kept her weakened and susceptible. He stepped outside, scrutinising the area.

"I *have* to protect her, don't you see? There is no other way." Sunniva gripped her brother's hand.

"You call *this*, protecting her?" He pulled away, his arms gesturing widely to suggest the unseen boundary he knew encompassed the area.

"There's no alternative. You've seen for yourself what happens outside our protection. There's no other way to safe guard her, not yet."

"And what of the children, what will they think of Taya's change now?" Even as he asked he knew the answer. They would *not* remember. They would be oblivious to any differences.

"They know she's fragile. They will mention nothing."

"Careful, Sister, if you weave too many lies you may find yourself ensnared." Even as he spoke he heard her whispers, reforming the memory of his visit. He had left his donation, and never returned, until now to bid farewell. She played a dangerous game indeed but finally he felt her presence in his mind recede.

He forced his body to release the building tension, his furrowed brow relaxing as his face changed to host a gentle smile. "It has been great seeing you, Sunni, but I really must be off," he said, forcing cheer into his tones. Sunniva smiled warmly, offering a gentle nod to acknowledge his words. "If you or Ethelyn need anything—"

"I'll place a request. Thank you again for visiting, maybe next time Taya will be well enough to say hello."

"I'd like that. I don't remember when I last saw her." He said conforming to the suggestion. It seemed strange Sunniva would want him to retain some memories of her, perhaps she planned to use these seeds later. He began to walk down the path, his sister's arm in his own as she escorted him away.

"Iereía, the escort has arrived." An acolyte called from the temple's door drawing their slow amble to a halt.

"Escort?" Rob questioned.

"Yes, the Iereía from Therascia is coming to assess us. His escorts often precede him to ensure all is in order. If I can gain his support it means more funding for the orphanage."

"I see, well good luck. I'll try to visit for longer next time. Look after that niece of mine." She watched her brother leave, a smile forming on her face. He had never been able to resist her suggestions, even now he had forgotten everything of the last few weeks, his mind filled with only a memory of being plagued with a relentless ailment, keeping him confined to his room at the inn for too long.

* * *

Rob was barely an hour from Riverside Quay. His brisk pace did little to still the thoughts circling his mind. Sweat clung to his skin from his failed attempts to increase his physical burden to lessen his mental one. It had not succeeded. No matter how fast he walked, or on what distractions he focused upon, his thoughts would not still. They always returned to his sister, and the concerns about her hidden agendas.

There was more to what was occurring with his niece than he could see, but his mind could provide no answer. Even now the idea of what Taya had endured, what she would endure, turned his stomach. But despite the protesting of his morals he could not afford to regret his decision. He had ensured she would not be returned to Mirage Lake, surely that absolved him. He needed her aid, and the cost to her would be worth the weight of his guilt when he finally seized The Seed of Nzin. She had agreed to help him once, although unvoiced he was certain there had been acceptance in her eyes. He would make amends. He would right this wrong, eventually.

The thundering sounds of charging hooves sent tremors across the dirt track. The coachman, apparently as blinkered as the horses, made no attempt to slow his pace. He spurred the carriage past Rob, almost knocking him from his feet. Rob raised his fist, bedamning him in a language familiar only to those spending time in dark recesses of less than savoury taverns. But his crude words fell silent as his gaze saw the crest. He stood frozen until another single curse left his lips as he stared at the clouds of dust left in the carriage's wake.

"She lied," he snarled angrily, his body tense with rage.

"Who?" The sudden voice from behind startled him. He turned quickly to face its owner, his fisted hands raised as if to strike out. The figure raised his hands quickly in a placating manner, stepping back slightly as if startled, although Rob believed this gesture to be little more than an act.

Noticing the fine weave of the figure's attire Rob searched behind him for an escort. People of such standing rarely were found without some manner of protection, yet it seemed he was alone. Realising this Rob lowered his hands, turning his focus to study the man before him. He carried himself in a dignified manner, one which spoke of privilege. A noble, no doubt, but it was impossible to ascertain his standing within their hierarchy, and his lack of a crest made any assumptions impossible. His slender build suggested he was no stranger to some manner of combative training, or had yet to be married and sought to make a lasting impression.

"Never mind." Rob gave a dismissive gesture, still assessing the man, trying to place a linage with a similar shade of pale hair. There were many families with fairer features, but none he could recall with hair so void of colour in youth. The man before him was no older than he himself. Subtle movements suggested that, whilst the figure before him tried to portray the image of being relaxed, he was in fact, vehemently tense.

"I've been pursuing them for days but their fiefdom evades me." Rob gave an incoherent sigh, he was certainly a man of high-standing nobility, if not a lord. His mannerism and speech were too refined for him to be anything else. Rob straightened his posture, forcing himself to stand tall. He had much experience in dealing with those belonging to the noble classes. They were his main source of revenue, and he planned on gaining some information, or at least confirming his suspicions.

The figure gave a short sharp whistle as if to summon a horse. Rob waited expectantly until he heard the young man sigh, dropping his shoulders and gaze briefly towards the ground before whistling again. Still no mount appeared. He glanced around, shifting uncomfortably.

"You've been following them?" Rob broke the awkward silence. Those of Mirage Lake often moved at speed. To track them for so long was no small feat. The man's desperate gaze searched the area as if hoping to see a flash of movement from his returning steed.

"I've worn two horses to exhaustion trying to keep pace. It seems the third has thought to abandon me." He gave an amused snort shaking his head. "And they say beasts have no sense." The figure began to walk the track after the carriage, his pace quickening to a jog.

"You've been following them?" Rob called after him.

"That's what I said isn't it?"

"Did you see who they took?" Rob groaned internally whilst suppressing an impatient sigh, unsure if his words had been heard as the man's pace increased. It seemed he was intent on pursuing them by foot. There was no other choice, he followed the sprinting figure, aware of the hesitation in the man's stride. It was clear that although his mind was reluctant to accept it, his body knew he had lost his mark.

"I did." The figure's eyes looked desperately down the track, his run slowing to a jog and then a standstill. Desperation flooded his eyes as they searched the surroundings, but even the dust had now settled. He gave a resigned sigh. Defeat evident in his posture.

"And?"

"A young woman with raven hair. But she seemed subdued." The young man paced, pushing his hands though his white hair as he thought.

"Damn her!" Rob growled, glancing in the direction of Elpída. "What's your interest in Mirage Lake?"

"I'm not one to divulge personal information to strangers. I don't know who can be trusted." The man spoke with careful and guarded words, his vision fixed before him unseeingly as his mind weighed his options. Rob could feel the anger radiating from him, there was clearly something personal in his vendetta.

"I could say the same. I would offer to escort you, but fear a knife may find my back by a stranger's hand." Rob found himself amazed by his own words. Although presented to the contrary it had been an offer of assistance. There was something about this man, he felt a burning desire to aid him.

"I echo your sentiment but, perhaps, if you truly know of their destination then we need not be strangers." Rob looked to him sceptically, trying with difficulty to hide the effect this man's charisma had upon him. Although but a few words had been exchanged Rob could not help but like him. He was from wealth, that much was for certain, yet he possessed a charm most lacked. "I was named Yuri Kyne in my parents' honour."

"A pleasure Kyne, but bringing a noble with me would only serve to hamper my pace." Rob heaved a sigh. What was he thinking, how could he have even considered escorting another to their door? He would need more than a noble to pass their threshold, it was a task he was uncertain he could even accomplish. As these thoughts surfaced he realised, for the first time, his own intention to save Taya. He had been responsible for allowing her incarceration, he would find the means to correct his mistake.

"You will find my skills more than adequate I can assure you." For the first time Yuri regarded the man before him, turning his attention to him instead of the road.

"What purpose do you have with them?"

"They took my wife." Yuri clenched his fists, his eyes displaying the seething anger he tried so hard to conceal behind his eloquent manner.

"You had your wife committed?"

"Not I. She was abducted." Rob saw the muscles in the man's jaws clench as he tried to rein in his frustration. "I fear if they are successful in their scheme our very fiefdom could be at risk." Rob's features softened, the honesty behind his words was one few could feign. Yuri dropped to one knee, lowering his head. "I will owe you a great debt if you can assist me. If you will not allow me to journey with you, perhaps you could mark its location on my map?"

Rob looked at the kneeling figure in disbelief. Until now he had believed nobles were born with joints that had no concept of submission, yet this man bowed to him, a hunter, begging for his aid. Rob grabbed his hand, pulling him to stand. Yuri extended his map, his eyes hopeful.

"It's no good." Rob said after a few moments silence. He rolled up the parchment offering it back. "It seems your cartographer is without skill. Where did you say you were from?"

"I did not."

"Then might I enquire? Your accent is not one I am familiar with." Rob smiled realising he was now almost mirroring the man's speech. It was something he did by instinct. He found the adaption of his mannerism to mirror those he conversed with served to put them at ease, and a person's comfort sometimes allowed them to speak without thought.

"Would my answer alter your decision in any manner?" Yuri's eyes studied him intently.

"I guess not," Rob sighed. "Very well Kyne. Since I am on my way there perhaps we can be of aid to each other."

* * *

Stacy gave a gentle sigh, breathing out the tension. The door to the cabin beckoned. The small handle felt warm to her wind-chilled touch as if it welcomed her home. As the door creaked open she could hear the familiar sounds from the kitchen, the gentle clinking of crockery and shuffling of glassware which implied Amelia was preparing a warming drink.

Wiping her feet on the mat Stacy peeled off her cloak, shrugging off the rain water before hanging it on the old, twisted coat-stand found just behind the door. The warmth from the small fire penetrated her damp clothing, bringing relief to her fatigued body as she moved to sit at the table, closer to the source of the warmth.

"Did all fare well?" Amelia questioned placing a steaming drink on the table before disappearing back into the kitchen area. Stacy lifted the cup taking a slow sip to stifle the building yawn, and relished in the internal warmth the hot tea stirred within her. She had grown unaccustomed to going without sleep, and the last few days had been tiring indeed.

"We rescued the young lady. Well that's to say she came running to us. I've never seen fear like that, and I've seen many of its faces." Stacy rested her chin on her hands, allowing the table to sustain the burden of her weight.

"She was frightened?" Amelia's brow furrowed in concern as her head peered through the kitchen opening.

"Frightened doesn't come close. It was only thanks to Bray's intervention the hunter is still alive. She spoke of delusions, and was terrified by the thought she had hurt someone." Stacy sat upright, the recollection of the young woman's fear sending a brief surge of adrenaline through her tired body.

"These delusions, what did she say of them?" Amelia returned with a small plate holding a slice of cake drizzled with honey. She placed it in front of Stacy before taking a seat opposite her.

"Nothing, why?"

"She is a very gifted woman. There are so few born with the sight of complete prophecy."

"Prophecy? Then these delusions she spoke of could be warnings from the future?" Stacy became aware of the concern held in the Amaranthine's eyes. Something was troubling her greatly.

271

"Yes. Her bloodline always was skilled with such divination, but the fact she thought it a delusion concerns me." Amelia's brow wrinkled into a frown as she was lost in thought. She stared into the amber fluid of the cup before her, her chin resting on her hand as her index finger tapped her lips.

"Is she really a demon?" Stacy questioned after a prolonged silence. There was something heavy in the air, a tension radiating from Amelia.

"You'll remember it all in time, but her race is known as the Daimons, and it was we who sealed them."

"We created The Depths of Acheron?" Stacy asked in bewilderment. The revelation was almost enough to dispel her tiredness.

"Yes, it was a choice we made in great haste, and one I have long questioned. The war which persisted between humans and Daimons was a fearsome thing. I regret to say we chose the path of least resistance." Amelia shook her head slowly.

There had been times she had considered releasing the land, but the Severaine's constraint was intertwined with Kólasi's magic. To release the Daimons would have been to potentially unseal the Severaine, and so, she had opted against such actions, despite the rise and fall of many cycles. For as long as she had lived this choice was one of those which haunted her most, for she could see no other path they could have taken. There appeared to be no viable alternative, and such permanence troubled her greatly.

"Then how can she be unrestricted by the seal?"

"She must possess an unchallenged connection to The Stepping Realm. I intended to talk with her, but I was given little choice but to send her to Sunniva's temple on Livingstone. I was so busy with my guiding duties I failed to keep in touch, and to my shame I forgot her presence.

"Perhaps I grow senile in my age, to forget something of such importance. With magics altering as they have, soon the powers which shelter their land will dissipate, and we will have an important decision to make."

"Has nothing been learnt from them, has Sunniva not spoken with her in your stead?" Stacy took a bite of the cake, savouring the honeyed taste as her stomach growled its pleasure at finally being heard.

"I fear she may have aided my forgetfulness, for I have heard nothing from her. I think if not for meeting with Rob I never would have remembered her." She took a sip from her cup, annoyance flashing through her eyes at the thought of being manipulated so completely. If Rob had not spoken her name when first they met it was likely Sunniva's deception would never have been discovered. Something about his words, his presence, had triggered the forgotten memories. But what purpose did Sunniva's actions serve?

Amelia placed her cup down, staring at the leaves within in the hope to divine an answer. It was a few moments before she spoke again. "That Misorian's presence concerns me slightly. Their people do not

273

venture from their land lightly. I fear it is no coincidence he found us when he did."

"Then you think there is something Ethelyn can tell us about why we are awakening? Something Sunniva may wish to keep hidden?"

"Perhaps." Amelia was lost to her musings for a further moment, her gaze studying the shapes formed at her cup's base. "I am sorry Stacy, but I must ask one more thing of you."

"You wish me to speak with her?" Amelia nodded adding more fluid to the cup to swill the leaves away. There were no answers for her there today. "I will leave immediately."

"She has been waiting for ten years, a few hours for you to sleep will be of little consequence. I have my concerns about Sunniva's silence on the matter, it is best you be alert."

Chapter 9

Mirage Lake

Livingstone was easily accessible through Collateral, but even with the aid of a horse it still took almost half a day before Stacy found herself at her destination. She was certain her journey had been longer than it had needed to be simply because she was, as yet, unfamiliar with the many intricacies of the travellers' city. The sun was already beginning to set lighting the sky with its brilliant shades. Reds and oranges fought for dominance over the horizon, their long strokes adding depth to the sparse cloud cover as they burned in the evening's light. If the old rhyme was true, tomorrow would be a pleasant day.

She petted Amelia's dusty brown stallion gently as she secured him to the hitching rail. She had been unsure about riding him, especially given Amelia's revelation that she did not own him as such. Drevera was home to a number of wild horses. This one had taken a liking to her and allowed her his service when it was required. Stacy had spoken softly to the horse before mounting, in accordance with the disciplines taught in Albeth Castle. To her disbelief it had accepted her. Although still wild in nature, it had carried her with care.

The temple lay in silence. The prayers and tributes had finished for another day, and the children had long returned to their rooms to participate in shared reading before retiring for the night. Stacy found herself lingering outside for a moment as she took in the sheer amount the people here had accomplished. It was one of the largest temples she had seen.

The enormous farm to its rear was filled with crops, the fields seemed to be segregated into seasonal yields by low masonry walls or hedges. Smaller wooden fencing had been constructed to divide the different types of produce.

The gentle breeze carried with it the sounds of roosting hens, interspaced with the occasional braying of cows and goats. Unable to see their shelters, she assumed they were found further afield, beyond the schoolhouse and storage sheds which seemed to form a boundary around the farmland area.

It had been many years since Stacy had last stepped foot on blessed ground, and the sight before her gave rise to memories once thought forgotten. It was a few moments before she could bring herself to open the door. The coolness of the dusk air caused her to shiver. At least, she hoped it was the gentle breeze that invoked this response.

She entered cautiously, ensuring the doors closed quietly behind her. Temples often created much malaise within her. Even now, despite how long had passed, her body performed the habitual gesture of respect towards the temple's tutelary deity. All within the temple was still, and wishing to venture no further within Stacy took a seat. Her stomach tightened with memories of her own childhood within such a complex. Most orphanages treated children well, but she had not been normal in the eyes of her caretakers, and her differences had afforded her no comfort.

"Do you seek counsel?" Stacy was unsure when her eyes had lowered towards the floor to give the appearance of being in prayer. She had been unaware of the figure's approach and raised her head quickly, her eyes meeting with those of the acolyte before her.

She was a stout woman, the garb draped over her did little to complement her robust frame. Her brown hair was secured in a plain fashion which drew attention to the overly large, thick fringe which ran almost from ear to ear. She was heavyset, with a gentleness to her features that radiated warmth. The sparkle of her eyes offered a feeling of sincerity to her smile.

"I was hoping to meet with Ethelyn." Hearing this the young woman moved. Positioning herself to sit beside Stacy, she placed a friendly hand on her arm.

"Taya? I didn't realise she knew anyone outside of Elpída." The woman's eyes slowly moved from left to right as she surveyed the area, ensuring no one was in hearing range. When she spoke again her voice was little more than a whisper. "It's good she has friends, the Gods know she needs them."

"Is she here?" Stacy felt unnerved as the figure once again took a cautious glance over their surroundings.

"No. I'm afraid she won't be back for some time, but I know she'd do well to see a friendly face on her return."

"Then I may wait?" The priestess shifted uncomfortably, her hand moving to squeeze Stacy's knee.

"You could, but I would recommend lodgings at the town. She's been sent back to Mirage Lake." The woman shook her head, almost disapprovingly. But whether the gesture was towards Taya or the establishment was unclear.

Even after all this time the name of that place alone was enough to invoke a visceral response within Stacy. She felt her arms wrap instinctively around herself in an attempt to still the deep trembling which threatened to take hold.

"Mirage Lake?" Stacy felt the bile burn the back of her throat as she rose in partial retreat. It took incredible effort to control her breathing. Even after so long that place still invoked untold fear. The priestess stood, her hand once more on Stacy's arm, her eyes filled with concern.

"You must know, she suffers from the mind sickness." The priestess tapped her temple with her fingers as if to enforce the point. "There are days she will remain motionless, unblinking, others when she thinks herself some kind of demon. Although, seeing her in that fire I started to wonder. Oh it was terrifying, but you know what, I feared that man's intentions more than I did hers, he would have killed us all if not for her intervention, I swear. The thing is, it's funny, but we've always been told we have to be careful around her."

"Careful?"

"Well, I'm not one to gossip you understand, but—"

"Barbara, you should have told me we had a visitor." The curt voice echoed through the empty temple. Releasing Stacy's arm the acolyte took a step backwards. Adjusting her posture she bowed towards the blonde-haired woman, who had entered through one of the doors near the rear of the temple.

"Iereía, forgive me. The lady was just enquiring about Taya." Her head remained bowed as Sunniva approached, hoping she had not overheard their conversation.

"I'll see to our guest, I'm sure you have other duties to attend to." The dormant anger from the high priestess was unmistakable.

"Yes, Iereía." The acolyte gave a bow, hurrying away to attend to her duties.

Stacy turned her attention to the figure who had interrupted them, wondering what insights had been lost.

"I am Sunniva, Iereía of Elpída and high priestess of this temple. What has brought you to our doors this evening?"

Stacy extended her hand in greeting. When Sunniva did not take it she gave a slight placating bow.

The failure to embrace this greeting displayed that this priestess did not view her as an equal. It spoke volumes about her character. Amelia was correct, there was something untoward occurring here.

"I'm a friend of Taya's." Stacy amended the name she had heard Rob address her by, to the one used within these walls.

"A friend, how?" Sunniva's gaze narrowed suspiciously, taking a moment to absorb every detail of the woman before her. She had not seen her at the temple before, it gave her cause to wonder how their paths may have crossed, and when.

"I helped Rob rescue—"

"You must be mistaken." Sunniva raised her hand in a sharp gesture silencing Stacy abruptly. "Taya has not stepped foot outside Elpída for years. She is a very sick girl." Sunniva gave a melancholy shake of her head. The swaying motion of her golden ringlets seemed to amplify the gentle movement.

"I understand she's at Mirage Lake." Stacy failed to hide the slight quiver in her voice. She found herself inadvertently taking a small, distancing step between herself and the one who had condemned another person to such a place.

"That is correct," Sunniva affirmed, casting a sharp look in the direction the acolyte had vanished. "I know what you must think, but the girl tried to kill me. When she failed, she attempted to take her own life." Sunniva removed the silk scarf from her neck to display the faded yellowing bruises. "It was an extreme reaction, but with the children, and her attempts to harm herself or others, it was my only choice.

"She was dangerous, possessed even. I would rather she was helped than be cast out on the streets." Stacy looked to Sunniva in surprise, the memories of her own childhood surfacing. The temple had said, almost word for word, the exact same thing regarding her before she had been transported there.

Stacy's eyes met with Sunniva's. There seemed more to those words, an undertone of knowing. Somehow this woman knew of her own visit there. She was rekindling the fear, and deliberately stoked the faded embers of forgotten memories to invoke a reaction.

Stacy took a guarded breath. She could almost feel the bite of the cold, metal shackles upon her wrists as they had restrained her. Her breathing quickened, the taste of bile once more rising to the back of her throat as unshed tears burned her eyes. Memories of pain resurfaced and, for a moment, she swore she saw the Iereía smile. Stacy calmed herself, forcing back a past which threatened to consume her.

"I-I must be mistaken," Stacy whispered, swallowing with difficulty. "Perhaps it was someone else sharing that name. Forgive the intrusion." Stacy took another backwards step, closing the distance between her and the exit.

"Are you sure? You look pale, can I offer you a drink?" Sunniva smiled, motioning towards the rear of the temple in a gesture which lacked sincerity. She saw Stacy shaking her head slightly, her hand extending behind her to touch the door, almost as if she feared turning her back to her.

"No, thank you. Please forgive my mistake."

Sunniva smirked as the woman opened the door, quickly taking her leave from the temple. How convenient it was that Taya's only friend had also spent some time within those walls. There was no surer way to drive someone from her door than by rekindling memories clearly repressed. That woman was of no threat. With memories such as those none would take heed of any words she spoke, besides it was likely she would not give Taya another thought, not now.

Outside Elpída Stacy emptied the contents of her stomach. The memories she worked so hard to forget had resurfaced. She had been more fortunate than most, after two days she had managed to escape. Somehow her need to survive had focused her powers into aiding her. Two days there had felt like a lifetime, and something in the way the priestess had mentioned Taya's visit there made it seem like such an excursion was nothing out of the ordinary.

If Sunniva had hoped to drive her away by adding tinder to such volatile memories, she had chosen the wrong ones. It seemed this Daimon was in more danger from the people who should have been protecting her, than any threat she'd face alone.

* * *

The enormous body of water stretched as far as the eye could see, meeting with the skyline and reflecting the golden glow of the sun as it outlined the grey murky clouds. The effect Rob and Yuri now beheld was but one of the reasons Mirage Lake had received its name. The small island, appeared not to rest upon a calm lake, but float within the clouds. The reflection on the tranquil waters giving rise to such illusions. Many a traveller would stop in awe, entranced by the sight. The illusion brought pause to even the most hurried journey.

The island itself was small. The outer borders, surrounded by dark evergreen trees which stretched high into the heavens, cast dark and jagged reflections below, adding to the impression of the island's levitation. The dark reflections appeared like earth, supporting the weight of the island, while the small structure in the middle remained almost unseen in the water. Only the jagged peak of the watchtower disrupted the illusion. Even the smaller towers, where watchmen appeared to stand guard, remained sheltered. Their presence was barely noticeable over the wall that was protected with wire and brier. Sentries stood vigil, their silhouettes just discernible from Rob and Yuri's vantage point. It seemed their forces monitored both inside and outside of the barricade. The security, for such a small and sheltered location, seemed immoderate.

The island consisted of a single point of entry, a large gate, protected by two guard stations. From this station a grey stone path ran to the shoreline where, concealed below a few inches of water, was a stone bridge. The middle section of this bridge was controlled in a similar manner to the port access in Albeth castle. However, in order to gain entry to Mirage Lake, the centre section of the bridge needed to be raised to draw level with the rest, rather than descend into the water as it did at Albeth Castle.

This feature prevented any without invitation from approaching, and also became the second reason for the location's name. When the bridge was raised, those granted access, either by carriage or by foot, would appear to traverse the water's surface; or on a day such as today, seem to glide through the clouds to its shore.

Even from their vantage point only a small fraction of the building itself was visible. It was a humble structure, perhaps the size of a small family dwelling. Its only spectacular feature was the three-tiered stone watchtower that adjoined it.

Rob turned to Yuri, pulling a metal tin from their fire and sharing the contents between their two mugs. They were far enough away to be mistaken as resting travellers, and every action they took that could be witnessed was designed to reinforce that assumption. They sat in plain sight sheltered from the wind, resting, drinking, eating, and monitoring the changes in the distant patrols.

"Have you gained any insight on infiltration?" Yuri questioned. They had been here for some time and the one thing which seemed painfully clear was, without an invitation, there was no means to gain access. They *could* attempt to swim, but their approach would be detected, and there was still the issue of their barrier which would likely still their advance no matter how well they thought to conceal themselves.

"Security is actually quite light. Those three watch towers there only have sandbags in guards' attire. It's just another of their deceptions. And look," Rob gestured to the teams of patrolling guards. "The angle of the patrol is peculiar. I think we're seeing a reflection or mimic illusion of the ones who've just passed. My bet is they've only one genuine patrol walking the ground and the rest is residual imaging." Rob nodded his head at his own words. It made sense, they had no cause to rely on heavy guarding. There was no means to approach without being seen thanks to the natural environment.

"And the barrier?" Yuri questioned gesturing before them.

"Barrier?" Rob glanced across the area again looking for any indication of such protection. He narrowed his eyes. He was usually adept at detecting magical energies, which meant if there was something present, it was of unfamiliar design. It could perhaps be ancient in origin. Such a thing seemed unlikely, even the Acropolis did not have such resources.

"Oh, of course, you won't see it," Yuri whispered in realisation. Just as there were colours in this light his eyes could not perceive, so too were there spectrums that a human's eyes would remain oblivious to. Rob looked at him for clarification, Yuri cleared his throat before speaking again. "There is a barrier encompassing the land. From my understanding, when someone wants to approach the sentries have a means to create an access point."

"That's impossible. It defies logic." Rob frowned. If they had this protection employable he was certain it would have been placed elsewhere. Its presence here, protecting this small building, seemed strange. If not for the rumours of terror and horror that shrouded it, Mirage Lake looked like a picturesque, albeit over-protected, place of worship.

"Yet there it is none-the-less. Besides, it doesn't look like old technology," Yuri mused, narrowing his eyes as he scrutinised the strange field surrounding the area. It seemed to stem from the top of the watchtower creating, what he assumed would be, a spheroidal field encompassing the island.

"What then, magic?"

"No." Yuri shook his head, turning back towards Rob. "You claim this place receives funding from the Acropolis?" Rob nodded his affirmation. "Then perhaps the Moirai have intervened. They always did like to play heralds of the Gods." Yuri spoke in a tone barely above a mumble, and the hand covering his mouth made the words even less coherent.

"Moirai?" Rob questioned, but his query went unheard as Yuri continued his monologue and returned his vision thoughtfully to the barrier.

"No, surely they wouldn't risk exposure, not after what happened to Geburah and Semiazá. But it doesn't make sense otherwise. They could not have devised this without aid." There was a questioning lift to his voice, his scrutinising gaze returning to Rob.

"Maybe—Hey I think I know a way we can get inside," Rob announced suddenly. "But we'll need to stop by the Plexus." He had an idea, a good one. It would work, he was certain of it. He just needed the right tools.

* * *

Taya choked on her breath as her awareness returned. She felt the constraints of the familiar contraption holding her in place within the small darkened space. Despite the overwhelming hopelessness her compulsive desire to struggle was not stilled. She forced her muscles to tense, already knowing she had no hope to free herself. Her movements failed to even disturb the icy water which surrounded her.

She hated this place, it was dark, a dark that was never alleviated. With no sight came no hope of escape, just the painful awareness of all that was to come. Her breathing would have quickened in time with the panicked racing of her heart, but the apparatus she was attached to prevented control over her own body's functions. She could only lie motionless, in something no larger than a coffin, listening to the drip of icy fluid which had now chilled her to the point of burning.

This was not the first time she had awoken already immersed in what they called The Cleansing. Whenever Sunniva felt it necessary to send her here she was often forced to regain consciousness before being subjected to their methods. She would normally awake shackled, trapped within the centre of a stone room.

People dressed in protective burgundy hide, each with a cowl to conceal their features, came and went. Elongated masks, stitched of leather and bone, protected them from the incense and opiates they lit. Their procession continued until the air became dense with the sickly odour, and her mind struggled with coherent thoughts.

When they deemed her sufficiently unresponsive they would return, stripping the clothes from her near-catatonic form before transferring her to the cleansing chamber. They pierced her flesh with thin tubes and, whilst she felt the stinging burn of each, her body failed to respond. With every concoction administered there came heightened awareness, an increasing sensitivity to pain, and a daunting fear of what was to come.

Once she was suitably prepared they would secure the iatrical cuirass around her chest, ensuring all the tubes and fittings were secure. It was a contraption of cruel and torturous design.

The chest piece allowed the tubing to create vacuums and varying pressure. It was designed to mimic the body's natural pattern for breathing, and allow them control over it. Often they would spend prolonged periods in the pretence of adjusting the equipment, leaving her unable to draw breath until she hovered on the brink of unconsciousness. She had read of a magic once that induced a similar state, one thought to bring about compliance and suggestibility to prophets.

When her body was secured they affixed a mouthpiece, which fitted into place behind her teeth, preventing the possibility of her choking on, or biting, her tongue. Within this mask were also tubes, forced down her nose and into her stomach where, if the need arose, they could provide her body with the sustenance needed to endure.

They controlled her every breath, ensuring she remained at the correct level of consciousness for their methods to be most effective. Often, when the mask first released its gasses, she became aware of the subtle fragrance of roses.

Finally, they would seal the chamber, plunging her into a world of darkness and silence. Sometimes they would leave her for long periods before beginning The Cleansing, other times they would start immediately. They would lower the chamber down, through the floor, into the depths of the lake, causing her ears to re-pressurise several times before all movement stilled. She could hear each forced breath, then would come the sounds of the water.

Within the chamber were several minuscule valves, allowing small droplets of water to slowly fall, impacting with her exposed flesh. At first it would feel no more than a gentle caress, but as the hours passed each tiny droplet brought fresh pain. The frequency continually altering to be unpredictable.

They had designed their own form of torture, insisting that overfeeding the Maniae was the only way to expel them and return a balance to sanity. They said it was all part of The Cleansing. First, they would induce the correct state, and then, as she suffered, the messages pushed through her mental barriers became rooted.

This time there had been none of the ceremony, not that she recalled. She had awoken to the darkness. If not for the agony burning through her veins, she could have estimated her time in The Cleansing by the depth of water which almost completely covered her hands.

They had said this process was necessary. That the pain and water cleansed the sickness, made her body and mind open to being cured, and set the foundation for her recovery and return to normality. She had rarely awoken within this chamber. The times when she had almost always followed the infliction of severe injuries when some within these walls became too enthusiastic in the breaking of a person's spirit. This chamber was the ideal place to hide the evidence of their deeds. One phrase she heard, more times than she could count, was that in order to save a person's spirit it first had to be shattered beyond repair.

After so long of being subjected to their methods Taya no longer had the will to fight their control. But her acceptance did little to still their cruelty.

The prison jolted and lurched. The sound of the metal cranks used to raise her metal tomb lost through the pain caused by its movement. The sickly taste of gas assaulted her senses. Her tongue numbed as the opiates took effect, once more forcing her body to betray the resistance she had gained. Over time she had come to recognise their different tastes. This one made her compliant, aware of all that happened, but unable to resist whatever manhandling they chose to subject her to. All the time something forgotten in the far reaches of her mind would almost will her to fight back.

Water poured from the chamber as the two burly men released the seals. Once drained one removed the tube from the cuirass, unfastening it while the other removed the mouthpiece. Taya gasped and gagged while sucking in her first real breath of air. Her head felt light and her surroundings seemed to spin while she lay, unable to move. The conversation between the two figures who pawed at her echoed through her hazy awareness.

"Just 'ow many times are they gonna let this 'un go?" asked one as he released the straps. His shaved head shook, small shimmers of light reflecting from his scalp. He had seen this girl far too many times, not that he was complaining of course. This time, however, even he had to admit she looked sicker than normal.

"Funny you should ask, I hear *he* has come again. This time to try a new treatment." The other man's hair was not quite as short, whilst still shaved the mousy spikes stood several millimetres from his scalp. On the count of three they moved her from the chamber and onto a towel covered bed. The rough hemp fibres sent prickles of pain through her. She felt the pressure of her restraints being secured over her ankles with more force than was necessary, causing her to cry out.

"Hmm?" he questioned with intrigue.

"Yeah that's why she got out early, and we got to clean her up. She's going straight to the treatment room."

"What's it this time?" The bald man asked as he moved the limp figure to slip the gown over her.

"I'm not sure, but I hear it's a one-off thing and guaranteed to work." The man's lecherous gaze traced the pale body of the woman before him, his tongue moistening his lips as he savoured her every contour before it became concealed.

"Well ain't it it 'er lucky day, and 'e's 'ere to do it personally?" They each manipulated one of her wrists into the cuffs, securing them a little less forcefully than her legs.

"Apparently it's something to do with a long forgotten method, and he wants to make sure it works." The mousy-haired man took his position at the head of the bed frame, grasping the handles while the other did the same at the feet. They lifted the frame with ease and started the slow walk to the designated room. There was no empty padded prison for her this time. No opportunity for a quick distraction from their tasks.

"Sounds in'er'estin', well we bes' not keep 'im wai'in' tis. Shame though," he stated, his hungry gaze hovering on her as his co-worker's had just moments before.

"Yeah, we've got our orders. This time it's treatment, recover, monitor, nothing else."

* * *

Geburah sat in his tactical room with Meredith and Eadward, the two leaders of the Kyklos. For the last decade the situation had seen the need to have them operate in two separate groups. One would be in rest, whilst the other continued their efforts to help Kitaia. Having both of them together was unusual. It meant all activities had ceased. Recent events had caused a problem.

Geburah knew they now had a unique and limited opportunity. With Yuri watching over Kitaia he felt that they could utilise this time by directing the Kyklos' efforts to the retrieval of one of their more experienced and powerful scryers.

During her brief return Kitaia had spent much time in the presence of the Kyklos, and ensuring Daley's absence went unnoticed had been difficult, but necessary. She had been struggling enough without the addition of further concerns. But with her absence he knew they needed answers, and their departure had marked the perfect time to investigate further.

Daley's condition neither worsened nor improved. In order to ensure the Kyklos' tasks remained undisrupted Geburah had assigned a new member to Eadward's team. He lacked the experience of the more senior members but his aptitude had been proven. It would only be a temporary solution, but given the gravity of the situation they could not afford to reduce their efforts.

Until recently, reaching Kitaia and trying to dissolve the empathic cornerstone had been their primary focus. Even while she had been here their efforts had never ceased, hoping her proximity would somehow affect the results. But they had done little more than gain minor insight, and what they had learnt made them feel more hopeless. They had delayed on other matters too long. Recent events had caused distractions, but now their priorities needed to alter.

"It pleases me that Brice is proving himself useful. However, his adjustment is not the reason for this gathering. Tell me, has there been any progress with Daley?" Both Eadward and Meredith shook their heads. "I know it is unusual for me to assemble you both given your commitments but I must ask something from you." Geburah paused, expecting them to speak, when they did not he continued. "As you know, there has not been a moment until now, waking or otherwise, where we have not been attempting to resolve Kitaia's situation. But the circumstances surrounding Daley cause me great concern.

"It is my understanding that something was able to pull his ethereal form from The Betwixt. Is that a fair assumption?" Geburah leaned forward, first pouring himself a drink, then filling the goblets in front of his two guests, much to their obvious discomfort.

"It is, my lord." Eadward nodded solemnly as he spoke his affirmation.

"And have any other members of your Kyklos reported noticing anything unfamiliar?" He sat back down, keeping his gaze fixed on Eadward. Noticing the man shifted uncomfortably under the weight of his stare he made a deliberate attempt to soften his expression.

"No, my lord," Eadward confirmed.

"And yours, Meredith?" He looked towards her. Despite his many years in Kólasi they had shared but the occasional conversation. Generally, he left the Kyklos to their task, trusting he would be informed on any matters needing his attention. He was pleased with their work, and impressed with their skill. Yet they always seemed ill at ease within his presence. Rumours suggested they felt their failure to complete the given task had disappointed him.

"No, my lord." Geburah gave a sigh, leaning back into his chair.

"Please, let us drop the formalities. We are the only ones present, and such things serve no purpose here but to inflate my ego."

"Yes, my lord." The two figures echoed, their faces still solemnly serious.

"Very well. Onto the reason I brought you here. I want you to escort me to The Betwixt." His words finally brought a reaction to the motionless figures, transforming their looks of discomfort to ones of horror.

"But that would be dangerous," Eadward objected.

"You are unfamiliar with the intricacies of travel." Meredith too voiced her concerns over the act he was suggesting.

"My prison, whilst it was accessed via the crystal, was actually located within the complexities of The Betwixt. I am adept in mind-reaching, such was the means by which I was able to bind myself to a mortal in the hope they could liberate me. It is my intention to reach out to Daley," he asserted. The two figures before him exchanged a concerned look.

"But what you speak of is treacherous. We could lose you. Our people cannot be without a leader, not in a time like this," Meredith objected, her concern now outweighing the fear being physically within his presence caused. She found herself more at ease when only her astral form confronted him. She was almost certain this was why he had requested their physical presence.

"Your concern is noted, but I am *not* seeking your permission. I am asking you to perform Lathraía."

"Lathraía?" Eadward questioned in disbelief.

"Yes."

"But such a thing has not been attempted since the first war," Meredith interjected before Eadward could speak further on the subject. She felt her hands upon the table, wondering at which point she had risen to her feet. She sat down slowly, avoiding Geburah's gaze.

"Hence why I am entrusting myself solely to the leaders of the Kyklos," he explained.

"And when would you wish us to perform this rite?"

"Immediately."

"It will take time to prepare," Eadward acknowledged, his words supported by a subtle nod by Meredith.

"Then I shall delay you no further."

Chapter 10

Desperation

Amelia did not look happy. She had spent the last fifteen minutes hearing Stacy recap events at Elpída. Her expression was as dangerous as thunder itself.

"I've a good mind to go over there and show her what for. I blame myself, bloody fool that I am. I think myself above reproach, but could I really forget leaving Ms Ethelyn in her care, for ten years no less? I've questioned it since I first recalled her. The details around the event are still unclear. There's no question in my mind I was somehow tricked by her, but I never imagined her talents to be so strong."

"You believe she tried to use the same trick on you as she does on Taya?"

"From what I've just heard I think myself fortunate. A slight memory lapse is nothing compared to what I imagine she is doing to that poor girl. But to what ends I ask you?" Amelia stood from her chair. Her scowling face was wrought with concentration. Everything was still unclear, but she remembered more now. She recalled being watched from the shadows by a person who did not belong. She had thought no harm could come, she sensed no ill will.

If only she had approached her sooner, and now it may be too late. But there was information she was lacking, she couldn't understand the motivations behind Sunniva's actions. Amelia tapped her fingers on the table with a little more force than intended. "What purpose could such manipulation serve? I just don't understand. Perhaps if I could talk to Ms Ethelyn in person something would be revealed. But I don't even know what foul game is being played. Tell me something, how did she seem to you?"

"Taya?" Amelia nodded. "Confused. She spoke of hallucinations and turns. Amelia, I think she believed herself ill."

"And what were your thoughts?"

"It seems strange she wouldn't want to return home if she were ill, or stay there assuming that's where she was these last weeks. Surely her own people would be in a better position to treat her. We know nothing of their species. What heals us could be poison to them. But I got the impression she was running from them. What could make her own people turn on her in such a manner she seemed to fear for her life? It just doesn't make sense."

"I think Sunniva is playing a dangerous game, one we cannot risk entering until we have an understanding of the rules and stakes."

"That reminds me," Stacy spoke softly after a moment of silence. Before they had entered The Depths of Acheron Rob had said something which struck her as odd, but stranger still was the response it had received. She had meant to speak of it before, but the opportunity had not presented itself. "When Rob said she had the power to destroy the world Bray, that Mysore..." she trailed off, trying to recall the word which had been used to describe him.

"Misorian?" Amelia offered.

"Yes, when Rob said what he did, Bray spoke Taya's name. How could he know that, and why would Rob say she was capable of such things?"

"Master Bray is Misorian," Amelia reinforced as if it should explain everything. Seeing Stacy's confusion remained, she elaborated a little. "Their kind have knowledge outside of even our wisdom. What concerns me more is why Mister Raymond would think she had such potential, unless..." Amelia trailed off. It was several seconds until she spoke again, clear alarm in her voice. "Stacy, we need to post a job at the Plexus immediately. We must speak with Mister Raymond. If Ms Ethelyn is who I believe her to be, then the potential he spoke of may be something we unleash in her." Amelia grasped Stacy's arm tightly as she spoke, her thoughts cascading out of control as fear consumed her.

"What do you mean?"

"There's no time, head into town and post an urgent request. The Plexus won't know him by name, so use the words demon relics and Mirage Lake.

That'll be sure to get his attention. A description of him wouldn't hurt either. Time is of the essence. I have a very bad feeling about this. Go!"

* * *

When Taya next awoke, there was a figure standing with his back to her. His mercenary physique enhanced by the tightness of his clothes. Almost as if sensing the shift in her consciousness he turned to face her. His grey eyes seemed almost silver as they caught the light.

There was something about him which terrified her. Instinctively she tried to sit, to push herself away from the advancing figure. But as always nothing in this place was left to chance. She felt the metal restraints, unyielding as they prevented her escape.

His blond hair, while longer than those she was accustomed to seeing here, was combed back behind his ears to almost outline his angular jawline. His lips turned upwards in a smile, yet in his eyes she saw something she was more familiar with, a look of loathing. This hatred seemed to run deeper than most, but more terrifying than her imprisonment, than her being at his mercy, was the cold calculating gaze with which he beheld her.

"Ah, you're awake. Very well, we can begin." The figure leaned over her, passing a small crystal before each of her eyes in turn. She noticed the sickly sweet odour accompanying his movements as it stole her breath, sending bouts of dizziness through her as it became overwhelming. "Fear not, I'm here to repair you. I rarely take an interest in such cases, but you're special, aren't you? Adaptive to insanity and that is not a good thing at all." He shook his head, turning his back to her to lift a small object from the table. "There are great plans in the heavens for you. Tasks only you are fit to accomplish, and I shall ensure you are ready.

"By the time my work is complete, you will be as intended." His voice was calm, almost comforting in its hypnotic melody. He attempted to look stoic but she felt his disdain, his concealed oppressive nature. It was as strong as his pervading scent. There was something unpleasant in his eyes as he looked upon her, something that told her whatever was about to happen was far beyond her own best interests.

Every hair on her body prickled with fear as he reached out, seizing her with his gloved hand. His grasp was firm, painful, not something expected from a healer. But he had never said he was a healer, just that he was here to 'repair' her. Her body trembled uncontrollably as he secured a tourniquet in place.

"Please," she forced the hoarse whisper from her lips. It went unheard, lost in the sounds of the re-straints straining against the bed as she tried, in vain, to distance herself from him.

Her eyes fixed upon the large barbed stinger within his grasp. The sight of the affixed venom sac invoking fear, beads of sweat formed upon her flesh. She fought, praying to somehow break free of the bindings that fixed her firmly in place. He gave a half smile, standing back, watching in amusement as the truth of her situation became apparent. He could see the response of her adrenaline, her pupils had dilated, and the rapid movement of her pulse was accompanied by the heaving of her chest. The fear would serve to make his job far easier.

"Now, now." He raised a hand in a placating manner, his other, readying the stinger. "There's no need to be afraid. When you wake, you'll be better. You do want to be better don't you?" His voice became stern as he pressed upon her arm, searching for the vein he wanted.

"Please," she begged again. "Don't." Her voice was still barely a whisper. Tears leaked from the corner of her eyes as the contents of the venom sac emptied into her arm. He withdrew the stinger, releasing the tourniquet. Taya shuddered feeling the icy fluid flooding through her veins, numbing her senses.

His voice began to echo, his words only vaguely coherent.

"Perfect. You"—the figure clicked his fingers, summoning an attendant—"this will take some time, see that we are not disturbed." She saw a sinister smile trace his features as his gaze returned to her.

"As you wish, Lord Paion."

"Now, let us take a look at what we have." He raised a small, rectangular crystal to his eye, studying her intently.

Taya struggled to hold on to her lucidity. Time distorted as reality ebbed and flowed. A tightness enveloped her chest, and images flashed through her mind at such speed she could not distinguish one from another. Perhaps they were dreams, interrupted by her body's attempt to regain comprehension of what was occurring. Each time she regained focus she would see him standing above her. His gaze never altering from the crystal as he studied her. She couldn't help but feel he was taking something from her, something important.

She tried to fight, resist the pull of dreams, but the images always returned. Pain began to accompany the waking moments. An agonising pressure built within her skull, becoming more unbearable each passing second. She could hear her own tormented screams, aware through her more sentient moments that their volume gradually diminished. The sound became hoarse and raw, until only silence remained.

* * *

Paion left the room where the Daimon now slept fitfully. He had finally obtained all he needed from her, for now. For ten years he had been subjecting her to interrogations, and the detestable creature was too stupid to even realise what he was doing. His presence had been a mere shadow, imperceivable to those walking the complex. Glamour was but one of his many skills, and here it allowed him to operate discretely. Even those of this island knew nothing of his agenda.

The foolish girl was a means to an end. It was no accident that before The Cleansing a prophetic state was induced. The chamber she found herself in was nothing more than a crude adaption of that used by the Moirai. Her power of foresight was formidable indeed, and his use of her nothing short of genius.

He bore witness to all. Each time she found herself within their possession he was gifted with knowledge, and was able to formulate his plan. The mental stimulants fed to her were intended to provoke a cornerstone to tether her to Sunniva, but hidden within was the means to forward his own scheme. He compelled visions of his future, ensuring Taya herself remained oblivious to his actions.

Through her he witnessed the many failures he could face, and how his plan's execution would fail. Thanks to her gift he corrected the shortfalls and removed all unthinkable obstacles until success was his only perceivable outcome. His undertaking was vast. But with each visit, each new revelation, she brought him closer to success. It had been a time-consuming endeavour. One that now neared its end.

Last time he had known he was close. She had already revealed Remedy's location, and divulged weaknesses in his ranks and tactics. Last time there appeared but a single failing, and now only she herself had stood in his path. A problem easily remedied.

This visit with her would be his last until he had need of her services. Using his crystal he drew the prophecies from her mind, witnessing his almost all-encompassing success. It seemed she had one more insight to impart. A few adjustments were required to ensure all became as he willed it, and critical to its execution had been altering her perspective to a more beneficial one.

When next their paths crossed, she would adopt the role she was destined for. She would become all her birth prophesied, and so much more.

* * *

Elly, given her time within Darrienia, had committed to memory the location of many Ieró. They came in all manner of forms, from shelters made from canopies woven with branches, to small dwellings and caves. Their forms were as diverse as that of the Oneirois themselves. This particular location was one she had frequented often. Its border was nothing more than dappled light and shadow formed by unseen sources. It created a perfect circle, and whilst the surrounding area was often subjected to change, the area within remained consistent.

The tall grasses within were yellow, bending in the gentle current of a breeze she had never once felt upon her flesh. The rustling sound of movement was relaxing, almost hypnotic, like the tide upon a sandy shore as the grasses rustled and swayed. Small areas had been flattened, creating soft cushioned ground on which to sit, or lie, as those inside awaited the passing of a threat or took time to rest and gather energy.

Darrienia was a strange world. It was made of energy and the truth of its real image was known by few. Even Elly saw the land as solid, sculpted by the influence of the dreamers and understood solely by those glimpsing it. Where Elly saw the bending grasses forming an island within a mystical moat of streaming light, someone else may interpret the energy as something completely different. Reality was defined by the dreamer. Images were created by collective consciousness. All that was, despite how it appeared, possessed no true physical form.

"That's not strictly true," Aidan observed as if in tune with her thoughts. She looked at him questioningly. "You were thinking aloud. It's a habit you've developed," he explained with a slight chuckle. "The form of the land is determined by the strongest mind within a dreamscape, or area. But there are some areas which remain fairly uniform. I applaud your reasoning though. You are really quite thoughtful. I'll do you the service of correcting your misconception.

"The things that exist are as their intention implies. But they can also become anything. Everything is the same, formed of the same energy. That which you see as grass could as easily be shifted to stone or fire. This is the truth behind why our world forever changes. The potential within is limited only by the endless scope of imagination."

"The rest of your kind give me the courtesy of a wide berth. What must I do to afford myself that luxury with you?" Seeing the darkness beyond the Ieró begin to circle Elly sat, noticing the rough texture of the grass seemed to soften beneath her weight. She had not intended to remain in this man's presence longer than necessary, but for now it seemed there was little choice.

"Does their avoidance really come as a surprise? Your former ally nearly eradicated our race. It is not something one soon forgets."

"And yet you do not share their caution." Elly kept her gaze upon the shadows, trying to discern shapes within the swirling mass. Normally the Epiales took on forms to stalk their prey, but recently she had noticed their reluctance to do so. "Aidan, do you really think my presence is causing this unrest?"

"I did not say that."

"You have implied, countless times, that my presence is causing disruption. Not only to your kind, but now to that." Elly gestured towards the shadows, never removing her vision from them. The Epiales had become more audacious recently, venturing deeper into the areas of light. Darrienia, unlike the waking world did not turn, although to dreamers such rotation was implied. Part of their world remained forever bathed in light, another in darkness. Within these areas the land inside would alter, and those from the shadows and light would trespass upon each other's land in the hope to save or damn those within. But lately, the shadows had journeyed in force, casting darkness where none should fall.

"You have remained here since you were defeated by our prince, surely you have noticed the alteration. Although I don't think you're responsible for *all* the intricacies of change, your continued presence within our realm is drawing attention."

"From Melas-Oneiros? Let him come. I bore of such games. I am tired."

"This from one who chooses sleep to life?" Aidan shook his head in a manner which, despite his serious expression, implied amusement.

"There is little left for me. I have completed the purpose I was tasked for. I failed."

"Ah, so this"—he gestured towards her—"is because you're brooding?" Her brow furrowed in annoyance as he once again chuckled.

"I am *not* brooding. I do not brood," Elly asserted defiantly. This man unleashed such frustration and annoyance in her that she wanted nothing more than to be free of him. He made her feel like an indulgent child.

"Ha! For someone who doesn't brood you're doing an awfully good impression, my little snow-bunny." he patronised, grinning.

"I am *not* a child, do not epithet me." She glared in his direction, realising she had once again been voicing her thoughts aloud.

"I was not the one to make the comparison. Although, perhaps you forget who you walk amongst. You may have been old and wise in your world, but in mine you are an infant. And one who appears to seek release, why else do you think they come?"

"I am not—"

"*Twice* you have trespassed upon his land, and *twice* you left unscathed and a victor. Do you think he harbours no vengeance, no grudge?" Aidan questioned sternly. "Do you think he would ignore the weakness of his greatest adversary since being confined to his realm? He cannot enter these lands, but his minions can. I need not tell you that, to him at least, you are special."

"What are you neglecting to tell me?" Elly questioned sensing a faint hint of deceit within his voice. For the first time he did not respond immediately, bringing her to a sudden realisation. He pursued her for a reason. "You seek something from his domain. That is why you pursue me so obsessively. And what does your prince think of your fools-errand?"

"I *was* intending to investigate the cause of the energy fluxes we've been experiencing," he diverted. "But instead I was charged with—"

"Ah, so you *are* here on orders then? Your noble prince fears my intentions."

"You give yourself too much worth. He has given you little thought. It was his wife's instruction that we leave you in peace. She said you were a heroine without a quest, and you simply needed time to find a new purpose," he revealed, much to Elly's disbelief.

"I see. So you took pity on me and thought to offer me a purpose did you?"

"Not at all. I intended to exploit your grief for my own gain." A smile turned the corner of his lips as he heard her laugh for the first time.

* * *

Barnett was one of the most recognised Plexus masters in Collateral. He was a short balding man, his silver hair had long receded with the curse of age. Although if you asked *him* its cause he'd say it was the babysitting of hunters, not an affliction of his years. Seeing Rob enter he pushed his half-moon spectacles further up the length of his hooked nose, and offered him his full attention. Rob frequented the Plexus in Collateral more than any other. For him, it was simply more convenient than finding the nearest town with one in their midst.

Rob placed his emblem upon the counter. Taking it the old man disappeared for a moment, completing the formalities of identification despite recognising this man by appearance alone. As Rob began to explain what he needed the Plexus master's brows knitted together.

"Hmm, funny you should mention that place. When I checked your emblem I saw an urgent job, assigned to you and a few others by one Stacy Psáltis. Seems she is looking for one specific hunter. You know her?"

"Yeah, we did meet not too long ago."

"Then I think you'd better come take a look at this. I'll remove the other hunters since it seems you're the intended contact." The man raised the counter inviting Rob through. Unlike the less frequented Plexuses, this one possessed a few private areas that were situated through the door behind the counter. Collateral handled all the more sensitive requests, and thus when such arose any interested parties were directed here. Barnett raised his hand as Yuri attempted to follow. "Him only."

"Sorry, Kyne, could you wait here for me?" Yuri gave a nod as Rob disappeared into the rear briefing area with the old man. When he returned, he looked confused.

"We have to make a slight detour," Rob announced. He saw Yuri's posture stiffen. "Look, I know we're both impatient to reach there, but I think we need to do this first." Rob looked at the parchment the request had been transcribed onto. The only information given was a string of words; The Depths of Acheron, demon relics, Mirage Lake. Urgent. He did not like this, not one bit.

* * *

Rob guided Yuri at speed through the streets of Collateral. Given his lack of reaction to the city's grandeur, and the unique method of arrival, Rob assumed it was a place he had traversed before. Any seeing this metropolis for the first time always reacted with awe, not only to the portals, but the sheer scope of the land. Rob did not like introducing people to the travellers' city but here was the only Plexus which would handle his request.

Yuri had been strangely evasive on the topic of his past. Not even discussing his ancestry, which most nobles of honourable standing were more than eager to impart on any who would listen. He seemed humble, and such things made him easy to travel with. Rob hadn't even considered the implications of introducing him to Collateral. After all, knowing of it was indeed a high honour.

A predetermined number of Plexus members would come to know of this city. It was a privilege granted to those achieving a high reputation in their ranks. Some refused the introduction, but most accepted this boon gratefully. Once someone was introduced they could never be cast out, unless they were banished, so Yuri's lack of reaction brought him some relief.

Rob did not know the every twist and turn of this great city, quite the contrary. He knew but a few routes, those he commonly used. For anything outside his area of knowledge he would seek guidance from the taverns. Fortunately he still remembered the path needed to reach Drevera, mainly due to the many problems he had discovered in locating it the first time.

Yuri extended his hand as they emerged from the portal on the grassy plains of Drevera. It was raining. Rob watched him curiously as he seemed to savour the touch of the cool water upon his flesh.

"I assume you don't see much rain in..." Rob prompted, determined to learn something about his new friend. Yuri retracted his hand, giving a slight chuckle as they began walking. Realising he wasn't going to answer Rob continued. "Where did you say you came from again?"

"So you said this island is Drevera. What is our purpose here, and how does it aid us in the return of my wife?"

"I'm not certain. But we'll find out soon enough." Rob raised his hand striking the door firmly. He was not normally one to meet with clients, but given the requester he would make an exception; after all, like

313

it or not, he owed Psáltis a debt for her assistance. It surely was no coincidence they were both focused upon Mirage Lake. Rob could almost feel the guiding hand of fate upon his shoulder, spurring him onward. "Ms Embers." Rob nodded a polite greeting as the elderly woman opened the door. She stepped aside allowing him entry, stopping him as he drew level to her, her hand resting on his arm.

"Who is your friend?" she questioned sharply.

"This is Kyne," Rob stated. Amelia released him, gesturing him towards the doormat. She turned her gaze to the young man who lingered warily outside. He was soaked from the rain, but despite the obvious chill he knew better than to cross her threshold uninvited.

"Yuri, ma'am," he added as she stepped forwards. Her eyes narrowed as she scrutinised him. Her face flushed, he could not discern if it was a reaction caused by anger, or something else.

"Yuri is it? You shouldn't be here," she whispered, her scolding tones were not lost on him. He took a slight step away, adding a little more distance between them.

"Sorry, ma'am, I can wait out here."

"That is not what I meant and you know it!" she snapped, her tones still lowered. She bit her lower lip as if trying to decide what she could do about his unwelcome presence. She knew of one who could walk the boundaries unaffected by the seal, but he did not possess this gift. Everything she saw within his aura said he was bound like the rest of his kind. The fact he now stood at her door did not bode well.

"He's assisting me with a job," Rob called from the table he had very quickly made himself comfortable at. "Our interests align. He wants to break his wife out of Mirage Lake." Amelia cast a quick glance to Rob as he spoke. When her sight returned to Yuri he could see the shock register in her eyes.

"Then I suppose you'd better come in. I imagine we have much to discuss." Amelia turned her back to him, shaking her head as she walked to the table. Upon its wooden surface was a pitcher of freshly made lemon and ginger infusion, and three glasses, which Rob had taken the liberty to fill.

Yuri entered, wiping his feet and shedding his coat. "Please sit. First, tell me, what is your wife's name?" Amelia gestured to a chair which Yuri approached cautiously. He lowered himself into it, feeling the burden of her question.

"Kit—" his eyes turned to Rob as he stilled his words. He had been deliberately evasive of this topic, knowing his revelation could cause problems. Especially to the man who had been forced to consider his wife to be a member of his own family.

"Kitaia Ethelyn." Amelia, seeing his hesitation, took the liberty of revealing this truth.

"You can't mean Ethelyn!" Rob's posture straightened, his glass striking the table with more force than he intended. His face portrayed equal measures of surprise and confusion as memories of his conversation with Sunniva, following Taya's abduction, filled

315

his mind. Specifically one aspect of it. He felt his fists clench.

"I—"

"Of course he does. He has a claim on her." Amelia cast a curious gaze towards Rob. "Why, who do *you* think she is?" Her steely gaze made him nervous.

"My niece, not by blood of course, but Sunniva as good as raised the girl. She recently told me Ethelyn was promised to de—" Rob placed a hand to the back of his head, wondering how much of this was real, and how much Sunniva had managed to manipulate.

Taya had spoken to him of her glimpses into The Depths of Acheron, of the treasure he had spent the last six years searching for. He believed her delusions were a glimpse into their world, her sickness confusing the line between premonition and reality. But she was still his niece, the child his sister had raised, wasn't she?

"You're partly right," Amelia stated with an amused smirk.

"Then he's come to claim her?"

"No, he's a demon, or a Daimon to be precise."

"What!" Rob sprung to his feet, toppling the chair behind him under the force of his sudden movement. His mind conjuring images of the terror on Taya's face as she had fled from her captors. Memories of the bruises and cuts which had marked her skin when she had escaped caused him to seethe. This man, this thing before him, had been responsible for her abduction, her injuries, and most likely his own brush with death. "I'll not let you take her! Not after—"

"Sit down!" Amelia commanded sharply before Rob had a chance to lunge towards Yuri. "Is this how you behave in someone's house? Sit!" Rob's balled fists trembled as he glared at Yuri. His eyes never strayed from him as he righted the chair, before slowly sitting. Reining in his anger he attempted to organise his thoughts, instantly recalling Taya's words. She had also said they were called Daimons, a recollection which led him to question when Sunniva had once again managed to influence him. When had he confused the truth with her truth? "Daimons aren't monsters," Amelia continued. "They were simply made by the Gods from a different material to humans. You were crafted from clay, Daimons, from something else, this too is true of the elves, Moirai, and all other species of Man. And like your kind, there are those who are good, and those who are not." She turned to Yuri. "You, however, have some explaining to do."

Yuri was watching Rob cautiously, aware of his tensing muscles as he fought back not only the urge to defend his niece from him, but attempt to filter through the real and grafted memories to discover the truth.

"But I remember her as a baby." Rob frowned, recalling how Sunniva used to complain about the long and sleepless nights. For a moment, the image shifted to that of his own wife, Sunniva's voice distorting to the silvery tones of his own love.

"Are you sure, or was that connection implied, after all, is Taya not around your age?" Amelia raised her hand as Yuri intervened to speak. He closed his mouth.

"She used apallagí on her own brother?" Stacy questioned from the door, causing all at the table to turn to regard her.

"I thought I had deflected all of her attempts. Clearly I was too late realising what she was capable of." Rob rubbed his temples, trying to quell the cold rage he felt burning in the pit of his stomach.

"Well, now that's settled, we've more important things to focus on. Yuri, how *did* you pass the barrier?" Amelia turned her sharp gaze to him. He raised his hands as if to defend himself from her stare.

"I came through with Kitaia." There was little point to concealing the truth. This figure could sense a lie in the wind.

"Why?"

"It's complicated. We had those from Abaddon deliver her through the portal and return her home. The apallagí had begun to cause serious harm to her. She was truly starting to lose herself to their perspective. Until that night, for ten years, there had never been an opportunity to retrieve her.

"We hoped returning her home she would break the thrall's hold. The problem was, although she managed to return to us, she couldn't sever the link of the empathic cornerstone Sunniva had created. So the real her, fought against the one manifested by exploiting her empathic bond.

"We gave her time, hoping she would find a means to break the confines, but instead the thrall gained power. We had no choice but to let her leave, but we had to find a means to protect her real thoughts. To that end we stimulated an illusion to coincide with the perspective alteration. It was intended to see her to safety, guiding her from our lands without subjecting her to our enemies." He paused, shaking his head slightly.

He had not been pleased with the manner she had needed to leave, but it had been the only way to ensure her safety. "She left before I had the chance to give her this." Yuri produced a small ring. It was made of two parts, the first being the main body which rested firmly against the flesh, the second, possessed delicate carvings of symbols, resting upon the surface of the ring in a manner which allowed it to spin under manipulation. He had overseen its design specifically for her, it was the origin of her habit. She always spun the central section when lost in thought. "It is a facsimile of the ring I gave her when we pledged ourselves. The original was destroyed when she was captured.

"We managed to enchant this one to offer some protection to Apallagí's thrall. We hoped it could aid in her realignment. But it was completed too late. I pursued, hoping to get it to her, but that's when—"

"We stepped in thinking we were rescuing her," Stacy intervened taking a seat. Rob leaned forward on the table giving a slight groan as he realised his intervention had caused more harm than good.

"But why fashion something just to counter the Apallagí?" Rob questioned chancing a look to Yuri, his brow was heavy with concern.

"Her resistance was becoming dangerous. She was inflicting increasing amounts of pain to remain focused. We knew she couldn't stay, not while she still has part of her rooted to the empathic bond Sunniva created, but to return would be to subject her to that torture. She is *not* human, and it is detrimental to have her believing she is such. Given a chance, with this protecting her, I know she would have broken the hold. She would have come home."

"But why did she come here in the first place?" Amelia questioned. She disappeared into the kitchen, returning with an extra glass. Stacy took it from her gratefully and poured herself a drink.

"You should know, it was you she approached." Yuri tried to keep any animosity from his tone, making a constructive effort not to glare in her direction.

"But she didn't. She watched me for a while. Everywhere I went, she followed. Then one night I decided enough was enough, I went out to confront her, only, I encountered a hunter. It's a good job I came when I did. I don't know what his plans were, but she was already unconscious.

"When she came too she was wrought with fever. I did what I could to stabilise her and sent her to Sunniva until she was recovered. Only she used the same bloody trick on me. To think I could forget something so important. I may be old but I am a long way from senility just yet."

"Oh, so that's what happened." Yuri seemed to relax slightly, releasing a tension he was unaware of even carrying until now. "She was searching for you, the one who never sleeps. Countless of our kind have been born and died without knowing the touch of the sun, but this is the first cycle that the powers will remain weakened, and the first you will all awaken."

"What do you know of our awakening?" Amelia questioned, unable to conceal her concern.

"Taya had a premonition that it would be so. We knew it could only mean a great threat is coming, but we have been offered no insight. We thought perhaps you may know and, if so, in exchange for a promise of our aid you would be willing to reconsider our banishment."

"I'm afraid we have veered far from topic. Such things can be discussed later. We have more pressing matters at hand. If you are willing to take the risk, I can get you access to Mirage Lake. But I can only get you inside, the rest is up to you," Amelia announced, quickly restoring direction to their conversation.

"I'll do anything, whatever you need. Just tell me how to get to her." Yuri's voice betrayed his desperation. "I have an ill feeling about this. Its effect on her differs drastically from before. Something isn't right, I can sense it through our bond."

"You can feel her?" Stacy questioned uncertainly.

"No, it's more of an awareness. It's common with soul-bonded. But something isn't right. I feel like she's slipping away." He closed his eyes focusing for a moment on their fading connection.

"All we need is a way through the barrier, after that we'll be fine," Rob assured, reaching across the table to place a firm hand on Yuri's shoulder.

"Barrier?" Amelia looked surprised, it was an expression she did not wear well.

"Yes, it looks like something based on sundial warding. It surrounds the entire island," Yuri explained. There was a heavy silence, none knowing the answer to the unasked question of how they could achieve such a thing.

"Leave the details to me. Being my age you can't help but make a few influential contacts, and I know just the people to return my favour. Time is of the essence, I will come with you."

Chapter 11

Cured

Lathraía was a little-practised skill amongst the Daimons. Many talents used by the flitter-adepts had roots within the archaic skill, but on the whole the practise had long been retired. In The Depths of Acheron there was little need for concealment of that magnitude. Lathraía allowed a person to remain unseen by anyone, anywhere, both on the physical and ethereal planes; but the energy and concentration required to maintain it was exhausting.

There were many dangers associated with Lathraía. The toll upon the channellers was substantial, and those who performed the concealment could not afford the distraction of sight. Usually it was performed by two individuals, a concealer and a watcher.

Geburah sought more. He needed to ensure the strength of the workings were enough to allow undetected passage through The Betwixt, and such was a feat never before attempted. He required the two most powerful members of the Kyklos, and had to entrust himself to them completely. Their actions would protect him while he reached out, attempting to observe Daley, and his ability to mind-reach was the only reason this method could be executed.

The act itself would leave him vulnerable to any malicious forces. He understood the expressions of concern and hesitation he beheld. He had conceded to the use of their own chamber, agreeing that whilst the palace harnessed the most energy, this location afforded the most protection.

"This process will greatly deplete our energies. If you are committed to this you must know, it will take until Dark-Moonday to regain enough energy to continue our task," Meredith advised. Geburah stooped as she approached, allowing her to position the headpiece they had insisted he wear. He had accepted their council in these matters and taken into account their requests. She gestured towards the centre of the room, the very place Daley himself had sat.

"Yuri is watching over Kitaia. I can think of no better person to protect her." Geburah attempted to instil comfort, but knew his words did little. He adjusted his position until he sat comfortably with his legs crossed. He nodded, indicating he was adequately prepared.

"But even so, if something were to occur—"

"We would be unable to leave until Full-Moonday anyway," Eadward interrupted. Meredith's concerns were understandable, but their situation had not altered. They had already discerned there was no means to influence the cornerstone. Kitaia alone could overcome it. Their continued attempts would be nothing more than hope woven from habit. This, however, could prove productive. "We must trust Lord Yuri. It has long been my opinion their connection has the most chance of succeeding in dissolving the empathic bond. Perhaps his further time with her will turn events to our favour."

"Whilst Kitaia remains a priority, an attack such as this cannot simply be ignored. Already I delayed this course of action longer than necessary in order to give you the best chance at assisting her. But we cannot ignore that this could be a precursor to greater calamity." Geburah paused, lost in thought for a brief moment. "Regardless," he stated firmly. "*I* am the Regent. You have entrusted me to act in the best interest of your people. I cannot do that if I am expected to turn a blind-eye to things of concern.

"It is *my* duty to protect you, I cannot do so if you will not allow me to use what is at my disposal." Geburah's voice was lined with frustration. He could sense the hesitation and reluctance of the figures before him. "This attack on Daley could be a method of sabotaging our attempts to assist Kitaia, or it could be unrelated. Where would we be if we ignored this warning and all the Kyklos fell?"

"My lord, we are committed to assisting you, but we wanted to be certain you understood the dangers. What you ask of us will mean we remain blind to their plight and unconnected to the spirits until such a time we have recovered."

"I understand. Shall we begin?" he questioned, gesturing for their approach.

Meredith and Eadward positioned themselves to stand either side of Geburah. Moving forwards in unison they each presented him with a long vine woven with stones. Taking one in each hand he took a deep breath, closing his eyes as they walked around him thrice times widdershins. The vines trailed behind them, creating a spiral formation on the ground extending outward from where he sat.

As they took their seated positions he felt the pull on his essence and, for the briefest moment, instinctively resisted. Its feeling was similar to that he had experienced before being imprisoned. He attempted to take a deep breath, and realised all physical senses felt so distant.

He saw the vines within his hand disappearing deep into The Betwixt, and back towards The Depths of Acheron where his body sat in rest. If he hoped to find Daley he first needed to penetrate the protection of The Stepping Realm, allowing him to search through all the planes. Extending his wings he focused on movement while drawing upon his magic and feeling the fatigue such an action caused within this plane.

Geburah reached his hand to his back, feeling the soft, silky texture of the magic creating his wings. Carefully he traced his fingers through the feathers until he found the strongest, most suitable plume and pulled. He grasped the quill within his hand, and gazed deeply into the pulsating shades of the magic focusing his thoughts on Daley.

The light of the plume expanded around him as the feather's barbs extended. The intricate barbules reached throughout the expanse, seeking the target of his focus. The light traversed The Betwixt within a single blink, leaving but a solitary barb upon the rachis. Geburah followed its gentle glow. Its path twisted as it coiled through the darkened realm, passing landmasses and anomalies until it finally stopped, vanishing into a gateway.

With enough magic Geburah knew his ethereal form could penetrate The Stepping Realm, but doing so whilst engaged in Lathraía was dangerous, to both himself and those shielding him. He had known the chances of finding Daley lost within The Betwixt were minimal, and had the reluctant consent of the Kyklos to act as he deemed necessary.

Closing his eyes, he focused on the link formed to Daley. Holding the magic tightly within his grasp he concentrated, gently pushing his sight through the barb to the land beyond the gateway.

Daley's form was suspended beneath the nearly transparent bark of a tree. Before him was a window into the human world. The scene was ever moving, flitting from person to person, as if in search for something. Daley grew rigid, the image through the window blurring and distorting until finally reforming to display The Betwixt. Geburah could see the vine tethers that were attached to his unseen astral form through the window, and could feel the pull of energy from his realm. The window's focus honed in upon the tether, as if whatever watched had become aware of it for the first time.

Geburah took a sharp intake of breath as he was forced back within his body. Eadward and Meredith sat leaning forward gasping heavily. Pools of sweat stained the floor dripping from their exhausted figures.

"I'm sorry, my lord, we had no choice but to recall you," panted Eadward. "Are you... are you well?" Geburah nodded, feeling the weight of his limbs.

"How long was I gone?"

"Not long, but you shed your magic like autumn leaves," Meredith answered, taking a drink from the leather skin before her. She weakly tossed one towards Geburah, her exhaustion seeing it fall short. He reached out to take it, drinking deeply from the sweet liquid within. His wings were more quill than vane, but his reserves would replenish far quicker than those of the Kyklos.

"What did you discover, my lord?" enquired Eadward once the echoing pants of laboured breathing had calmed.

"Daley is being used to scry for something on the human plane. The place he is imprisoned feeds on magic itself, and yet it is somehow sustaining his energy through this realm," Geburah revealed. He pushed himself to his feet, carefully stepping over the coiled vines he rolled his shoulders and stretched his leaden limbs.

"A channel through his body perhaps?" Eadward asked, with a slightly perplexed frown.

"Its methods were unclear, but I could feel the intense energy being drawn towards and through him. Has there been any strange occurrences of late?"

"Not strange as such. One of the scouting parties reported the formation of a new tideway. They rise and crumble within this realm in correlation to Full-Moonday. We often harvest what energies we can from them. Unfortunately nothing more of its nature could be ascertained, it lies deep within hostile territory," Meredith offered as she carefully removed the headdress from Geburah.

"Then why mention it?" Eadward stifled a yawn, his heavy eyelids betraying the level of his own exhaustion.

"Because its appearance is either delayed, or premature. It shows a disruption of our realm's energy," Geburah summarised. Meredith nodded confirming her concern had been adequately voiced.

"So what can we do about it?"

"At the moment there is little that can be done. If we are to mount a successful rescue I must devise a method to reduce the fatigue caused by that plane, but it will take some time," Geburah stated thoughtfully, his distant gaze revealing the depths of his concentration.

"How much time?" Eadward asked curiously.

"We need to devise a safe means to infiltrate a realm that feeds on the very energy your ethereal forms would produce. What I am proposing has never been achieved. I will require your council. If we are to rescue Daley we must first nullify any dangers that realm poses to ourselves, and *that*, I am afraid, will take time. Leave me to my deliberations. Rest, regain your energy. Once I have devised a theory we shall talk more."

* * *

The rhythmic beating of hooves upon the ground altered as the dirt track made its slow transition to stone. Finally the two white stallions drew to a slow stop at the lake's edge, awaiting passage across the water to the small island. The two draught horses had moved without pause, pulling their ivory coloured carriage to its destination. These beasts were of fine breeding stock, powerful, capable, and the envy of many war commanders.

The envoy had been the recipient of much attention as it had made its long journey. Even trade wagons paused allowing them passage. Those walking the roadsides would remove their hats to perform habitual gestures of blessings towards the deep red insignia. This crest announced it not only belonged to the Acropolis, but housed a member of The Order. Children from nearby towns would pursue it with excitement, laughing and giggling until they grew tired and their legs would carry them no further.

A carriage like this upon the roads was not a commonly witnessed sight. Those belonging to the nobles paled in its grandeur. It was designed for comfort and privacy. Its smooth structure lacked windows, thus ensured no weakness in the metal casing.

It was rumoured many master blacksmiths had been enlisted to perfect its design. The Acropolis took the safety of their emissaries *very* seriously. Fused upon the carriage was a relic. One possessing a blessing so powerful, those in proximity could feel its benevolence enveloping them as it made its journey.

The interior had been crafted with the same meticulous care as the outer shell, but the internal design was one of comfort. Thick cushioned seats, of the same deep red of the outer insignia, were positioned carefully at the front and rear. It had been carpeted in luscious fibres mirroring the delicate shade of the carriage's outside. This durable, soft material lined the walls as well as the floors. It served to mute sounds and ensure the privacy of anything spoken within.

Feeling their movement stop Yuri glanced to Stacy. His hand tightened around the small charm Amelia had given him. If she spoke the truth, then this metal coin would protect him from the more painful effects his kind suffered when in proximity to, what most believed to be, holy relics. Something no doubt in abundance within their destination. He was inclined to trust her, especially since the protection belonging to the carriage had done little more than make him feel slightly fatigued.

There was, both in past cycles and present, still a misconception that holy items, those thought to be handed down to man from the Gods, caused injury to beings of evil. But as Amelia had said so aptly, Daimons were not evil.

This understanding was nothing more than careful and intentional deception. The Moirai, like the Daimons, had the ability to infuse items crafted by their hands with magic. Such things created lasting impressions on the material, causing them to become a fetish for the powers the beings themselves harnessed.

The Moirai favours would bestow feelings of great love and benevolence. Whereas those crafted by the Daimons caused the shedding of falsehoods, and the realisation of truth and understandings few were ready to accept. Both energies resonated on opposing sides of the magical spectrum. This resulted in the weakening or nullification of both when in proximity to each other. Such was also the reason Daimons and Moirai were rarely found within each other's presence.

Over time, the devout would present such relics to their temples. Those blessed by the Moirai would be housed within to extend their divine blessing to all. Those of the Daimons, were deemed cursed and sealed.

Stacy gave Yuri a reassuring nod and, although they were still unseen by the approaching guards, straightened her posture. She knew, from the almost inaudible conversation outside as the two men spoke to Rob, they would soon be opening the carriage door to confirm the identity of those within.

A sharp, firm knock sounded. Hearing this Yuri positioned himself between Stacy and the guards before opening the carriage door. He viewed them critically. His eyes assessing their threat and armaments. Satisfied, he stepped aside slightly to allow Stacy to look upon them, whilst still being shielded by his position.

"Please inform these gentlemen we are here to visit with one, Taya Ethelyn." Her voice held the authority her assumed role demanded, possessing accentual perfection combined with the appropriate infusion of snobbery. Her instruction into these mannerisms had lasted less time than expected, possibly given her existing aptitude for the Sacred Chord. She had mastered in mere hours that which took some nobles almost a lifetime to learn.

The guards, casting their cautious gaze past Yuri, assessed her every detail, scrutinising her appearance for any flaws. Her brown hair had been finely dressed and pinned by eloquent silver combs. Unlike many from the Acropolis, those from The Order never wore the uniformly tailored chitons of a cleric. Their clothes were made from a fine, rectangular cutting of silk, and wrapped in the appropriate manner. Such wrapping was an art taught only to those worthy, and although many tried to imitate the appearance, none could quite duplicate the results.

The iconic chiton was secured with fibula spanning at intervals from the shoulder to wrist, securing the fabric in place. These broaches mirrored the finery of the combs in her hair. The loose material was gathered and secured by a golden tie around her waist. The material spanning her arms had been draped to give the impression of sleeves. As expected it was a very specific vibrant blue in colour, and the front bore the embroidery of The Order. Her appearance was elegant and impeccable, as was expected from one of her standing.

The Order were highly respected. It was said those few who were selected for this honour could commune with the deities, and were granted their wisdom and prophecies. Those chosen were limited in number, and they were always well protected. Which brought their attention back to Yuri.

The Guardians of The Order were as well-presented as their charge, and Yuri appeared as regal as Stacy. He wore a navy, tailed jacket, dressed with golden buttons, each possessing the appropriate crest. His white shirt beneath was visible at only the neckline, and just below the cuffs of his jacket. A length to which it had been deliberately tailored. Around his waist was a sword, secured in its slightly decorative scabbard.

The Guardians always appeared dressed for formal dinners, but this attire served another purpose. Only those of skill were dressed so finely. The Order believed the man before them could easily, and without injury, defend his charge should the need present itself.

"Forgive me, I must see it." Spoke one of the guards somewhat hesitantly. He knew all too well that the trimmings and trappings did not mean they were who their dress implied. But a crest could never lie, they were impossible to forge. Yuri's eyes narrowed as he once again observed the figures before him. Stacy watched, waiting for his consent before placing her hand upon his in presentation. The two guards studied the crest with the scrutiny needed, and showed the respect due.

"May I?" The second guard questioned. Straightening his posture he took a single, respectful step backwards. Yuri carefully removed the ring from her finger, placing it in the requesting guard's awaiting hand. He held it for a long time, checking each engraving as he mentally weighed it. Finally he looked up, his eyes meeting Stacy's. "Apologies, my lady, I had to ensure it was no imitation or illusion." He returned the ring to Yuri, who once more placed it upon Stacy's finger.

"The protection of this facility and those within is your primary concern. To be anything but certain would be to do yourself an injustice. Your diligence has been noted. May we proceed?"

"Of course. Please allow us a moment to perform the blessings needed to cross the waters." With those words Yuri closed the door. Rob would now await their signal to proceed. Sure enough, within minutes, the carriage was once more on its way. Yuri resisted the urge to grasp the coin tighter as he felt the energy of the barrier closing around them. The strength of the items and magics within created a tangible force around him. He pressed the coin further into his palm, flexing his fingers slightly to ensure it remained in place, despite what his hand may do.

The horses once more drew to a stop outside the entrance to the small temple. The carriage door opened as news of their arrival saw the escorts approach to greet them. Stepping down onto the footplate Yuri surveyed the area and expertly assessed those before him. Once satisfied, he extended his hand into the carriage.

Taking it, Stacy emerged. Her presence causing the escorts to tense. Once Rob had secured the horses he moved to join them. Unlike Yuri and Stacy, the role he was assigned was that of himself, and thus he felt like a crow amongst peacocks as he followed them inside.

Their escorts, having not uttered a word, led the envoy down countless flights of stairs to the subterranean structure that was filled with long corridors and numerous rooms. They twisted deep into the bowels of the earth, encompassing an area perhaps as large as the lake itself. However, their guests would never behold the dark complexities within. There were places here even The Order had no knowledge of.

Even those of this employ were corruptible, and people of prestige paid handsomely for favours. Information could be gathered, or people could simply disappear.

Their pace never faltered as they walked the well-lit corridors until they reached the room where Taya resided. Even then, without a word, they simply offered a respectful salute and returned to their duties.

Having watched his every move, Rob could not help but feel Yuri was versed in such tasks. His very demeanour and every action, no matter how subtle, implied he had acted in this fashion before. Such tells were things no training could teach, they were developed by time and experience. He knew him now to not be a noble of their world, but questioned his role in the one he knew very little of.

Rob felt himself hesitate by the door, fearing what he would find within. He had heard much of their methods, and during his time in The Courts of Twilight he had seen more than his share of torture. But manipulated or not, his attachment to Taya felt genuine.

The doorknob felt warm to his cold touch and rattled in his grasp before the catch finally released. The fact there had been no lock made his stomach sink. Taya was not the kind of person to sit contently in such a room. His mind was flooded with images of restraint and sedation. He glanced to Yuri, wondering if he should request him to wait outside, but thought better of it.

"Uncle Rob!" He opened his eyes, unaware he had closed them as he stepped inside. The woman looked somehow younger than when he had last seen her. She wore a plain flannel nightgown and her face positively beamed as she bounded towards him before wrapping her arms around him tightly. The enthusiasm of her greeting surprised him. After a moment, when it appeared she had no intention of relinquishing her grasp, he moved his arms to stiffly pat her on the back.

"We are thrilled with her progress." Hearing the voice Rob stepped further inside, turning as much as Taya's grip allowed. He saw a figure standing outside, his long form-fitting attire typical of the practitioners within this establishment. "Please allow me to escort you to the seating area." They followed the dark-haired man who, in a nervous habit, seemed to be constantly brushing his long fringe from his eyes. "The physician is still preparing the papers."

"Papers?" Rob questioned, finally prising Taya from him. She looked up to him sweetly, her arm coiling tightly around his, refusing to be parted.

"For her release. When we informed Iereía Sunniva I had no idea she was so organised. Nor did I imagine we would receive such honoured guests." He gave a respectful nod towards Stacy and Yuri, who walked at a short distance behind them.

"We were close by on a rather discrete matter. This one, it seemed, took precedence," Yuri intervened before Rob could speak. "But there was no mention of papers." Rob found his gaze focused on the white-haired male once more. If he didn't know better he could have truly believed him to be a guardian. His mannerisms alone betrayed his authority. He looked to Taya, watching for any signs of recognition as she looked towards the man claiming to be her husband. There was nothing, except for the slight tightening of her grip upon his arm.

"Oh, it is standard practice. It ensures we keep track of our patients. I am sure you understand. Please, make yourself comfortable. I will see if the documents are ready. I think you will find the results most pleasing. *He* really does work miracles." The man stopped outside a large circular room. The walls and ceilings constructed of intricately carved arches and domes. Given that it was unlikely any relatives stepped foot within these premises it seemed more for those working than any other purpose. The central area remained vacant of comfort, as a place where those wishing to be heard would stand and speak. Be them orders or demands. "Please help yourself to refreshments, excuse me a moment."

There were several soft cushioned chairs around the circumference, intersected sporadically by a number of small tables. Upon the closest stood expensive looking tableware and a small selection of biscuits and cuskynoles. The teapot steamed, showing the freshness of the liquid within. Yuri approached a chair, using the handkerchief folded into his pocket to dust it down before pulling it out for Stacy. Taking her hand he guided her into the chair. He, however, remained standing. His fingers deftly refolding the handkerchief before replacing it. After a moment of silence, Taya spoke.

"So, Uncle, how's Mum, is she angry?" Taya lowered her head in what could only be interpreted as an expression of shame and regret. "I hope the news of my recovery made her happy." Rob glanced across to Yuri and Stacy, bringing Taya's attention to them once more. Releasing Rob she approached them hesitantly, her gaze barely daring to behold the beautifully dressed woman sitting before her. "Sister, forgive me, I feel I should remember you. Have we met before?" Her brow furrowed slightly as she tried to recall meeting with people of such prestigious standing, wondering if perhaps this figure had collected her previously.

"Yes, I am Stacy Psáltis." She extended her hand in greeting, and was almost unable to hide the surprise when Taya dropped to her knee to kiss the crest upon Stacy's finger.

"It is an honour to meet you, Sister." Stacy motioned for her to stand when it became apparent she would not do so uninvited. Taya turned to offer a gesture of respect to her guardian, her breath hitching uncontrollably for a second.

"Kitaia, I am glad to see you well." The gentle warmth in his smile brought a flush of heat to her cheeks. He was nothing like the burley old men she imagined to possess the title of guardians. He looked upon her with kindness.

"I don't believe I've had the honour." She gave what passed for a respectful curtsy.

"Kitaia, I am your husband, Yuri." The confusion in his voice seemed evident. Given that it was clear no one lingered close enough to overhear their words he was concerned by her commitment to the pretence. He allowed himself to study her carefully, his chest growing tight. Even with the coin pressed firmly in his palm there was still a residual effect from the relics in this location. He was unable to discern if this commitment went beyond mere pretence.

"I'm sorry, Sir, I've never left Elpída, I cannot be married." She paused for a moment, realisation dawning on her. "Do you mean to say we are betrothed?"

"Forgive my guardian." Stacy spoke before anyone else had the opportunity to confuse matters further. "You have met once before, but your health was failing. Iereía Sunniva arranged your marriage in exchange for the aid of The Order in regard to your treatments," Stacy explained.

"But I have no worth. Why would you agree to such a poor trade?" She looked to the man again, her eyes flooded with distress.

"We will explain the details once we have departed," Stacy advised, the room falling silent once more as Taya took a few paces backward to once more seize her uncle's arm. Rob's brow furrowed in confusion. It seemed Taya was committed to this pretence, perhaps she knew something of their surveillance they did not. He glanced towards Yuri, noticing the manner in which he beheld her implied he knew otherwise.

Time was unforgiving to the extended silence. Each second felt like minutes as they waited for their attendant's return. Each felt the pressure of unasked questions bearing down upon them. Doubt began to surface. Fearing their ruse had been discovered they mentally recounted their actions, attempting to find an error in their presentation or words, but they could discern none.

By the time the dark-haired man returned, with papers in-hand, the atmosphere had become exceptionally formal. Their host moved to present the documents to Stacy. His face registering concern as Yuri stepped before him, plucking them from his possession. He carefully examined both the papers and the quill, before passing them to Stacy with a nod. With his permission she scrawled a beautiful, yet illegible signature, before returning the items to Yuri. Who in turn presented them to the attendant.

The figure walked with them, leading them back through the long corridor and up the flights of stairs until they reemerged in the small temple. Again he walked in silence, offering only a respectful farewell as Yuri guided Stacy into the carriage, before stepping aside, motioning for Taya to approach. She did so hesitantly, flinching as he placed his hand on the small of her back to assist her up the extended steps and into the carriage. Once Yuri was inside, and the door had closed, their escort's posture relaxed. He seemed to shrink a few inches before Rob's questioning gaze as he turned to address him informally.

"Rob, isn't it?" The man enquired grasping Rob's arm gently as he escorted him away from the carriage. "Might I have a quick word?"

"Sure." Rob allowed himself to be led a short distance, his eyes trained on the carriage, watching for anything suspicious.

"I am glad it's a relative who came. It's better to tell such things to family, they have a better ear for such things compared to... those with no vested interest." He inclined his head towards the carriage meaningfully. "The procedure was successful as far as we can tell. *He* managed to isolate the delusions. I see no reason why your niece will need ever return, but should you notice anything unusual you must contact us immediately. It was a trial treatment, even we aren't sure of the potential ramification."

"Of course. So she remembers nothing?" Rob questioned, unsure if he could tempt some of the treatment information from his lips.

"Quite the contrary, her memory is perfectly intact. She should be able to continue living as if she were never ill. *He* simply stripped the delusions so she can be the person the Gods intended and not plagued by such terrors."

"And this is permanent?" His voice held the correct measure of scepticism to warrant the man giving a reassuring smile.

"We can't guarantee it, but we're fairly confident."

"My sister will be thrilled. Thank you again." Rob looked at the carriage critically. "I should get moving, you know what *they're* like if they're kept waiting."

"You don't need to tell me. The Gods forbid you get on their wrong side. Safe travels." With that, Rob climbed onto the driver's box. Taking the reins in hand he spurred the horses into motion.

* * *

343

The carriage began to slow slightly. The change in pace the agreed signal that Rob no longer believed them to be in danger of being discovered. Allowing herself to relax, Stacy leaned back against the soft interior. Their very success had hinged on the combined efforts of so many people. If even one had fallen shy then they would not be here now. She could scarcely believe they had managed to ensure everything fell into place.

The carriage they found themselves inside did indeed belong to the Acropolis. Any imitation, no matter how good, would have been immediately recognised. There were so many details, so many places their plan could have turned awry, but their luck had bordered on the divine. If she didn't know better, Stacy would have thought the entire thing had been orchestrated so they had the means required at their disposal.

The carriage they found themselves within had been the focus of a recent and hostile attack, and there was but one place with the skill to repair the damages. Amelia knew the Hackney Man well. He was a renowned wheelwright and spring smith and greatly indebted to her. He fashioned a temporary repair to the underside of the carriage's suspension using similar parts from his own. While he had seen to the adjustments, Amelia had left a work request for a young woman who went by the name of Chrissie, a cleric who traversed the lands offering aid to those in need.

Chrissie had met in private with Amelia, returning days later with a small package containing the clothes worn by members of The Order. Chrissie had many contacts, and amongst them was a line of descendants stemming from a Sister and Guardian who had married within The Order. Such a thing was not uncommon, often being assigned a single charge saw deep bonds develop, and marriage within the ranks was permitted.

On death, those who once served were burned in their attire as a final show of respect. However, these two had not died within servitude. They had left to raise a family, altering their names and living a simple yet blessed existence. The Order had thought them the victims of assassination. Their empty transport returning looted and bloodied, only served to support their assumption.

There was some truth to the events. They had indeed been set upon by rogues. But these bandits had not known who they had attacked. The mistake had been turned to mutual gain. The bandits received the cargo in exchange for secrecy regarding their newborn child. Chrissie had inadvertently discovered their secret. These clothes were the sole tokens retained of their past.

Rob also had his role to play in this grand facade. He knew himself of a request to find a stolen crest. The task had been simple, to track down a renegade operative and secure the crest by any means possible. Talking the hunter into temporarily parting with his recently acquired spoils had not been easy. But many owed a favour, or two, to Rob, and this man had been no different. After a long discussion the man had finally conceded, and would be amply rewarded for the inconvenience.

Even now Rob felt the dull ache radiating from the soon to be depleted coin pouch. His actions would cost him severely. There was little coin could not resolve, especially since it was only some bruising of ego and a slight delay in task completion.

* * *

Taya had almost instantly been lulled to sleep by the muffled sounds of the horses' hooves and the gentle rocking of the carriage. They had been on the road for an hour when she jerked awake, her breath momentarily panicked before a quick glance around the carriage saw her posture relax slightly. She rubbed her eyes, seeing that the guardian sat opposite her, watching her with a warm smile. She averted her gaze quickly, only to meet with Stacy's concerned expression.

"How are you feeling?" Her voice was soft, etched with the emotion clearly displayed in her eyes.

"Fine, thank you. Are we heading straight home to Mum?" she covered her mouth with her hand as she yawned. With the front communication window of the carriage now open Rob, hearing her question, called back to her.

"No, she asked if we would keep you with us for a while, to give you time to become better acquainted

346

with Yuri. She thought you may enjoy a small adventure."

"I see." She looked to Yuri once more, giving him a polite yet awkward smile.

"Sunniva arranged the betrothal some time ago," Stacy advised seeing Taya's clear discomfort. "In fact, you spent a while in his company not too long ago." Seeing Taya now, there was no doubt in her mind this was not a placating act to ensure her freedom. She truly didn't remember the man before her. Her words were an attempt to make this tense situation a little easier for the both of them.

"I'm sorry, I don't recall. There's so much from then I don't quite remember," she apologised meeting his eyes. She felt her breath catch, the way he looked at her sent butterflies coursing through her stomach and a flush of heat to her cheeks.

"The physician said such things are common. Do you really remember nothing of him?" Taya looked at the figure again. Leaning forward he took her hand in his, allowing her to gaze deep within his eyes. His eyes filled with delight as he realised, although weakened, he could still feel their bond. Some part of her still remembered him.

Taya reached out, unable to resist the urge to feel his silky hair in her fingers. Her hand gently closed around the hair at the base of his neck. Her delicate touch forced Yuri closer, his eyes closed briefly in an attempt to disguise his reaction to being so near to the woman he loved. Her uncertain touch moved from the nape of his neck, tracing down to feel the beat of his heart. Somehow she knew hers beat in time with his.

She reached up again, brushing a strand of his fringe away from his eyes. They were captivating, his dilated pupils bringing truth to Stacy's words of their closeness. She found herself lost in them, they were beautiful, each the shape of a perfect almond lined with heavy black lashes, and the colour, no man should have eyes that colour.

The carriage began to tremble and shake as the terrain beneath their wheels seemed to become less travelled, the sudden alteration almost propelled her from the seat. He steadied her, but the spell was broken. She pushed herself backwards, once more increasing the distance between them. She studied the contours of his face, his strong jaw line, and his pale pink lips, the corners raised in a slight yet distant smile. Part of her wanted to lean forward and feel the warmth of his kiss. She bit her lower lip, trying harder to remember, to pull even a fragment of his image from her mind. The carriage complained under the burden of the road, shaking so violently it sent powerful tremors through them all.

"Do not concern yourself." Yuri gave a gentle shrug as he reached out and squeezed her hand. His touch was so firm, his skin so soft. As he pulled away the road became smooth once more. "I've already committed my every breath to you, and I shall use each one to prove myself worthy." He gave her a charming smile, his teeth but a few shades duller than his hair.

"So where are we staying tonight?" Stacy called, reminding them of her presence. Even if Taya couldn't remember him, there was a definite attraction between them. She had never seen two people look at each other the way they did. It made her heart ache for someone of her own, for someone to look at her the way they looked at each other.

"Drevera," Rob called back. "There's someone Sunniva wanted Taya to meet. We're about to enter Collateral, I thought we could spend a few hours here. That way I can return the carriage and we'll grab some lunch. Although might I suggest you change into something a little less conspicuous?" Looking down at herself Stacy realised she was still in The Order's attire. Yuri turned, giving what little privacy the close quarters of the carriage would allow, while she changed into the clothes that had been stored in the under seat compartment.

Once changed, she and Taya extended him the same courtesy. By the time the carriage drew to a halt, with the exception of Taya, not one of them looked out of place. She only owned the nightgown in which she was delivered to them, but it could easily be mistaken as a priestess' gown given the cut and colour. They would have to address the situation of her clothing in the near future, but for now sustenance and rest was their first priority.

* * *

Grayson Bray wandered aimlessly. These last few weeks had been uneventful, bordering on boring. His mind had been preoccupied by thoughts of that Daimon. Even now certain fragrances in the air stirred his memories of her, and he found such thoughts occupied a large portion of his waking time. He had been lost to his reminiscing, unaware that his feet had led him to the temple where she had been known to reside. Since he had found himself within Elpída he had decided to take measures to quell this unnatural compulsion.

He had waited for the small crowds from the morning prayers to disperse before casually strolling through the doors. Several acolytes were busying themselves cleaning the temple. Clearing his throat he petitioned their attention, and was barely able to mask his frustration on discovering that Kitaia Ethelyn had been relocated to Mirage Lake, and was not expected to return for some time.

This knowledge did little to still his mind. If anything, knowing the truth of the establishment, it brought her to a more focal point. His every thought was consumed by her until he decided to take matters into his own hands. It had been a long time since last he played the hero to a damsel in distress. So, in order to finally shed his growing obsession, he would postpone his endless socialising and liberate her, perhaps earning in exchange her gratitude, and a good meal. Or such had been his plan.

He had been well received. The approaching guards were in no way immune to his charm. They spoke with him as a friend, revealing their darkest secrets, and also divulging the information he sought.

Their words weaved for him a new tale, one of miracles and a cure to insanity. They spoke of Lord Paion, and how The Order had personally collected her to witness the results of his work. They told him she had been cured, and presented full recovery. Bray knew such a thing meant trouble, and in no small degree.

Understanding all too well the implications, and the serious repercussions resulting from her 'cure', he vowed—after sating his hunger—to relinquish his decadent lifestyle until he had located her. He needed to reverse whatever damage had been done before she was forced into releasing her potential. The only problem was, he didn't know exactly where to start.

One final meal became two, and the endless stream of complimentary alcohol continued to flow. Each day he awoke full and content, swearing that this would be the day he'd seriously begin his search. But then would come the temptations and companionship. The meals here were second to none. He never had the same thing twice and still the menu seemed endless.

* * *

Once Taya had been forcefully encouraged into slumber by Amelia's apothecary skills, Yuri, Rob, and Stacy sat around the small table in an uneasy silence. Since eating in Collateral Taya had done nothing but empty the contents of her stomach, be it of food or water.

When Amelia saw her condition she had immediately insisted the young woman took her bed, and

351

had placed a metal pail beside it. After Taya had once more emptied the water from her stomach, Amelia returned giving her a small phial, to calm her nausea and help her rest. She had taken it with apprehension, accepting only due to her uncle's insistence.

Amelia had seen much in her time, but the appearance of the Mirage Lake temple was one memory which troubled her greatly. One she knew would be burned into her memory despite the passing years. Every cycle made its mistakes, its own horrific monuments, and this was but one of many. Eventually those of power sought out new means to govern the weaker minded, and she had seen many forms of conditioning; but never had she seen something completed so effectively and quickly as this. Taya's sickness concerned her. Hopefully it was nothing more than the result of whatever treatments she had been subjected to, combined with her body's own relief at being released.

Once Taya was sleeping soundly, Amelia moved from her position just outside the bedroom door to prepare a fresh pot of tea and some refreshments. They observed a few moments of uncomfortable silence while partaking in the offered hospitality. Rob divulged the additional information given to him before their departure, aware that he was not in full receipt of Amelia's attention. The atmosphere was apprehensive, but lacking in the tension of their last visit. Despite their many differences the small group were content in each other's company.

"So," Rob prompted. Amelia glanced towards him, removing her focus from the tome before her. It was written in a language none of them recognised. Closing the book she pushed it to one side, shook her head, and huffed a sharp sigh.

"Do you imagine there to be a scenario where I tell you something good?" Amelia snapped. They had taken too long assembling everything they needed for the rescue, and now Taya was paying the price. The tome she had been studying was a collection of information on iatric practises. Specifically, she had been searching for types of treatment which could produce such startling results. But even this text had been unable to provide further insight.

Amelia's compendiums worked in the same manner as the Oneirois' library. When held within her grasp a single book contained all the information she had ever been privilege to on a subject and, given the countless cycles she had seen, there was no shortage. However, even the wealth of knowledge at her fingertips could shed no light on what had befallen the Daimon.

"Well, is it fixable?" Rob stood, walking to the bedroom door, peering inside ensuring Taya still slept soundly. Seeing the figure in peaceful slumber he pulled the door closed a fraction more, so only a small glimmer of light could filter into the otherwise darkened room.

"From what I was able to observe I would hypothesise she was fed stimuli relating to her past, and some form of sensory diversion was implemented, likely surrounding the areas of her mind which reacted to the unwanted recollections," Yuri explained. A puzzled look crossed his face as he saw Amelia raise her cup to her lips to conceal her smile. It was only as he looked to Rob and Stacy, and saw their expressions of utter bewilderment, he realised why. It was easy to forget that, unlike his own people who were sheltered from the Severaine's wrath, those of this world lost every insight gained at the turn of a cycle.

"So... can you fix it?" Rob questioned, not really understanding the complexities Yuri had spoken.

"The only way is to find something to reconnect one of the memories, after that they should all eventually return."

"Something visual?" Stacy queried, glancing towards Yuri.

"No, or just seeing him would have reversed their work." Amelia inclined her head in Yuri's direction. "Daimons only take one partner. He is her husband, as such they share a connection created by the merging of their essence. Something similar to the ancient claiming rights, but not nearly as dangerous," Amelia explained. It had become apparent, from the moment she had seen them together, Yuri's relationship with Taya had been no manipulation.

"When she wakes I need some time with her, alone. As much as it pains me I cannot remain much longer. Full-Moonday is nearly upon us and my freedom here will be once more restricted. Besides, my presence here is likely to create more danger than assistance." Yuri masked a sigh, it had taken them almost a full lunar cycle to rescue her. He was grateful for their aid, and thankful his path had crossed with Rob's. He had not anticipated her being relocated. He had hoped to keep vigil and protect her from Sunniva's influence. He had failed. The protections of the many relics across Elpída were too powerful for him to breach, and her rescue had not been a task he could have accomplished alone. Unfortunately the enormity of the task had seen their rescue arrive too late, but at least she was distanced from Sunniva.

"What do you mean you're a danger?" Stacy questioned, looking to him curiously.

"Surely you felt it, the discharge of energy when she attempted to remember me? She now possesses little control over her magic, we are lucky she didn't tear the carriage apart."

"That was her?" Rob and Stacy exchanged concerned glances. "What do you mean she has little control?"

"Yes, it was. Daimon magic works on a different principal to other magics, we have to suppress it. It's probably for the best that I remain absent to avoid provoking such reactions." He paused for a moment, his gaze lingering on the bedroom door as concern marred his features. "What did you say you were doing the night she was brought to us?" He returned his focus to Rob, a small glimmer of hope returning to his eyes.

"I asked her to prove herself by locating a Daimon treasure," Rob answered honestly, while purposefully omitting the nature of the quest. Given Taya's reaction to his suggestion he was reluctant to state which treasure he had wanted to seek.

"Then that is what you should do. Go on an adventure, maybe she'll see something that will reconnect her to the past," Yuri announced. He would be unable to be close to her, but perhaps the proximity to their home would safely stir that which his presence could not.

"Am I correct in understanding you're giving us permission to enter your world and take your treasures?"

"If that's what it takes. Besides sparkles and baubles are hardly treasure, to us at least. Of course, within the darkness are those who would defend their gods with a ferocity you could but imagine." Yuri gave a slight shrug.

"Their gods?"

"You think all creatures have Gods like yours?" Amelia questioned before Yuri could speak. "Birds worship many a thing, such as the rain, for it unearths the worms and feeds them. They mirror its sound in homage, performing their own rain dance to lure their prey. It is no different to us performing the festival of Hades, or other rituals. On that note, did you think the Daimons would also share our gods when they have been sealed for cycles untold?" Amelia stood from the table gesturing towards Yuri. "A word, before she wakes."

* * *

Yuri, by instinct, slipped his arm around Taya's waist as he approached to join her as she looked out over the vast expanse of ocean. The sounds of the waves moving gently across the rocks below brought her a calm she never recalled feeling before. She watched as sea birds rose and fell in the wind, whilst others below them swam, their small forms bobbing up and down, drawn along by the gentle currents.

"It is beautiful here," she whispered, feeling small against the grandness of the world around her. The endless ocean reached past the horizon with the limitless sky falling to meet it. The sun warmed her skin and, for a moment she relished in the light touch of his arms around her. She closed her eyes, allowing both his warmth and that from the sun to envelop her completely.

"Might I speak with you a moment?" She turned towards him, his grip releasing her as she slid from his touch. He reached out, taking her hands in his. "I want you to know, I won't force you in to anything. Much has changed for you. You don't remember me, it's unfair to hold you to past promises." She opened her mouth to speak, but he continued before she had the opportunity. "I will ask only one thing from you. No symbolism, no commitment, it is simply a gift, but I would like you to wear this." He presented her with the ring, her eyes were drawn to the magnificence of the delicate item within his grasp. Before her mind had even completed a thought she had slid it onto her finger where it belonged. It fit perfectly and rested with a somehow familiar weight. She studied it, taking in every detail of its elegant design.

"Are you certain?"

"Yes." He took her hand in his once more, kissing it gently before releasing it. He smiled slightly as he saw the forefinger and thumb of her other hand moving to turn her ring in a manner that was so familiar to him. It was a habit she had developed when he had first presented it to her. Whenever she felt nervous, or was lost in thought, her hands would always find her ring, twisting it as if the action somehow cleared her mind.

"Thank you. There was something else?" She caught a flash of emotion in his eyes and knew there was something he still wished to say.

"Yes. I'm afraid I must leave soon, but I promise you, if you still don't remember me when I return, I will spend every minute of every day trying to once more win your affection." He gave her a smile which caused her heart to flutter. Somehow, she doubted this man needed to try very hard to win her heart, it seemed he already controlled it.

"Are you leaving now?" she questioned seeing his hesitance. Yuri glanced towards the sky, the sun was entering its final stage.

"Soon, would you like me to walk you back?" Taya shook her head, turning herself back towards the ocean. The thought of him leaving filled her with inexplicable sadness, so much so that she felt the warmth of tears as the ocean's wind chilled her face. "Then, my lady, until next we meet." In her peripheral vision she saw him bow in a gentlemanly fashion before taking his leave.

When he was far from sight she allowed herself to sink to her knees, releasing the tears which seemed to overwhelm her. All the time berating herself for such an emotional display over a man she barely knew yet, somehow, felt so lost without.

* * *

When Taya returned to Amelia's home the sun had set, and it seemed Yuri had departed. She was instantly aware of his absence within the house, and was once more overwhelmed by the feeling of loss. He had vowed to make her fall in love with him again, but as she had sat on the cliffs she had realised he needed to make no such effort. Whether she remembered him or not, she felt complete and safe with him beside her. She was his, and he was hers, and now she longed to stand beside him once more.

"Ethelyn." Rob, seeing her enter, approached. There was no mistaking the redness of long shed tears, the blemishes on her skin enhanced by her paleness. He wrapped his arms around her, feeling her tremble from more than just the coldness of her skin.

He escorted her to the table where Amelia lifted a teapot, pouring the warm fluid into a cup before her. Stacy took a blanket, wrapping it around her shoulders before giving them a comforting squeeze. There was something about the way they were looking at her which made her stomach tighten.

"I'm fine, Uncle, don't worry. I just lost track of time." She shivered as Rob rubbed his hands up and down her arms in an attempt to warm her.

"Listen, before you took ill we were planning an adventure. Sunniva thought it might be a good idea if we picked up where we left off. How about it?" Rob decided not to waste any time in broaching the topic. There was more at stake than trying to correct whatever influence Mirage Lake had used. Rob had almost managed to convince himself he was doing this solely for her benefit now, almost. His eagerness earned him a reproachful stare from Amelia as she studied them from across the table. She saw Taya's stiffened muscles begin to relax as the medicinal effects of the herbal tea began to take hold.

"I'd like that," Taya mumbled, struggling to keep her eyes open. Every part of her felt so heavy now, she wondered if she possessed the strength to stand.

"I don't know if she's fit to travel," Stacy objected, her tone more scolding than she had intended. If a few hours alone on the island had exhausted her this much there was no telling what an enormous undertaking, such as the one Rob was suggesting, would do.

"Honestly, I'm fine. It's nothing a good sleep won't cure." Her tired words were almost lost as she covered her mouth to conceal a yawn.

"You're still recovering," Amelia stated, seeming to mutter something under her breath which no one quite managed to hear before continuing. "Well if you're insistent. There's no stopping you youngsters these days. Do as you please," she grumbled harshly, throwing her arms into the air in a frustrated gesture as she disappeared into the bedroom to fold down the sheets. "What you doing child? Get in here," she scolded as Taya moved to make herself comfortable on the wooden floor where Rob had rolled out his blankets for her.

"Oh, I couldn't—"

"It's easy, you just get in here and lie down. Nothing to it."

"But—"

"Nonsense! You need it more than I do." To save further discussion Amelia emerged from the room, taking Taya's arm and guiding her inside. She pulled the door closed behind her as she left. "Rob, don't you dare push that child too hard you hear? We've no way of knowing the damage they did. Her fatigue is just not natural."

"Well at least her stomach seems to have calmed a little." Amelia glared at him knowing he'd avoided answering. She knew enough to see he was hiding something from her. "I'll watch out for her. She's my niece what do you think I'd—" Rob stopped abruptly, shaking his head. "Only she's not is she? Sorry I've still not got it all straightened out. I care for her like family, we'll take it easy." Amelia's narrowed gaze scrutinised him for a moment before she seemed satisfied with his words and left. She still had to gather some supplies from the town, and the hour was already growing late.

The morning mists rose in soft wisps from the ground, giving the impression of being lost amongst the clouds to any who looked through Amelia's windows. The incessant downpour had stopped for the first time in days. The silence almost alien, enhancing every sound previously unheard over the drumming of the rain.

The air, even inside the cabin, smelt fresh and crisp, and still held the delicious aroma of the cinnamon and fruit bread Amelia had prepared for them in the early hours.

Rob rolled up his blanket as Taya gave thanks to Amelia for her hospitality. They had stayed with her for a short time, long enough that she now seemed steady on her feet. Under the pretence of building her endurance, and judging her capabilities, Rob had frequently taken her to share morning tea with the Plexus master. It was the perfect excuse to see if there was something which required his attention.

The weathered-looking man, who ran the Plexus, seemed grateful, almost desperate, for the company. He happily relished in the tales Rob brought from those outside this isolated island. They spent many hours in chatter and, regardless of the tasks he needed to address, always welcomed them at his table with a smile.

Often, Taya would grow tired of such discussions and make her own way back alone. Sometimes she would rest, stopping to admire the majestic views this small island had to offer. She had been warned to give the people here a wide berth.

As if her own guardian, Stacy never seemed too far away. Whenever she felt the waves of fatigue encroaching Stacy's arm would slide into her own, and guide her back to rest. Taya had been grateful for their company, and saddened by the fact they were now departing.

As Rob reached the door Taya once more thanked Amelia, embracing both her, and Stacy as she bid them farewell.

"Could you wait just a moment, dear?" Amelia asked sweetly, her hand gently grasped Stacy's elbow guiding her into the kitchen to afford them a slight measure of privacy. "Why don't you go with them?" she asked softly, presenting a packed backpack from under one of the work surfaces. "I've a feeling Taya would appreciate a little female company." Stacy opened her mouth almost as if to object but Amelia cut her short. "Come now, you know how bull-headed men can be when they've got their mind set on something. Taya could use an ally, if only so you outnumber him if he gets a little... enthusiastic. We don't want her being worn out." Amelia peered towards the two waiting figures and smiled.

"I'd like that," Taya called, having heard her every word. She looked to Rob hopefully as Stacy appeared holding the backpack.

"I don't suppose I get a say?" Rob grumbled as Stacy flashed him an apologetic smile. "Fine, but we've got a task to complete. If you slow me down

I'll leave you behind." Rob had been patient, incredibly so. He understood the need for Taya to regain her strength, but the temptation from The Seed of Nzin had been growing stronger each passing day. He had waited so many years for this chance, and now it finally seemed within his reach. Each moment of delay pierced his soul, but its importance ensured he contained his enthusiasm, suppressing his impatience. He could not afford to jeopardise it by being too eager, but even acknowledging this did little to calm his restlessness.

"Well then, you're all set. Don't let me keep you, off you go, have fun." Amelia made a shooing motion with her hands as she hurried them quickly through her door. Closing it behind her she allowed herself a moment to lean against it, her dark thoughts reflected in the shadows of her eyes.

The Daimon's health concerned her greatly. She had found no reference for any means to undo the damage which had been done. But more concerning was that she wasn't even certain how this undertaking had been accomplished, or the real reason behind such an act. Their conversion had taken from Taya the very core of her being, her beliefs, her knowledge, and, for reasons unknown, they had invented a past which would somehow benefit their agenda. She knew one thing for certain, there was more to this than met the eye, and she would bet her teapot it had something to do with Taya's prophesied potential.

It had once been predicted that Kitaia Ethelyn could destroy the world, and given her current condition Amelia had no means to discern how.

Chapter 12

Talents

Hearing her laugh had come as a shock. For years Aidan had watched her wrestle with grief, but he had respected the wishes of their prince's wife. Thea—who Elly would have known by her mortal name Zoella—seemed strangely fond of the woman who had brought so much deceit and suffering to her life. More surprisingly was that she was genuinely pained by this woman's sorrow.

He had offered to watch over Elly when her grief had altered, and her attempts at staying ahead of the darkness had become more hesitant. There were many Outcasts who would have undertaken this task, but only he would do it for the woman who now sat beside him; albeit, he had his own motives, but there was an air of sorrow surrounding her he knew all too well. Unlike any of the other Oneirois who approached her, she responded to his presence. His attempt to engage her, and his constant intrusions, were the source of much frustration and annoyance, giving life to emotions he had watched all but fade. He was almost certain she enjoyed their exchanges, and with recent events had decided to use their relationship, she could be of help to him.

"So tell me of your grand plan, oh master exploiter." Aidan frowned as Elly addressed him, unable to discern if her words were edged with sarcasm or amusement. He noticed the smile lifting the corners of her mouth and, for the first time, appreciated the beauty her grief concealed.

"You're the seasoned adventurer, you tell me."

"Very well. Since it is apparent you have no intention on trespassing into his domain, despite your suggestion to the contrary, what is your aim?"

"Melas-Oneiros ordered the abduction of my partner, Jude."

"Then he is already lost. Do not tell me you seek retribution?" Elly knew Darrienia's lore. She also knew that the Epiales were the only beings the Oneirois had cause to fear. A single injury from one of these formless predators resulted in the corruption of their essence. A single wound was enough to turn them into one of the Epiales, the servants of Melas-Oneiros. If Aidan's partner had been seized by these creatures there was little question as to his fate.

"I said they abducted Jude. But it was not the Epiales, it was one of Melas' generals, and care was taken to ensure he was unharmed."

"To what ends?" Elly had heard a mention of these generals, spoken by those passing, in discrete conversations she hadn't cared to overhear. Her path had never crossed with one, and she went to great pains to ensure her privacy. Somehow, Aidan had always found her.

"And therein lies my question. Whilst it is true that Melas has been known to personally alter some of our kind to serve as his generals, enabling them to walk as neither Oneiroi nor Epiales, they have always been injured before being taken in order to begin the transition. *This* was different. They ensured no harm befell him."

"And these generals, what exactly is their purpose here?"

"Even now that is something which remains unclear. There is a definite alteration in the theta waves emitted by dreamers who have prolonged exposure to them, but their presence here is new. We have not had time to study the effects." There had been small forces assembled in order to investigate this strange breed of monster. They retained their original form yet were masked in shadow. They appeared to show no aggression to dreamer or Oneiroi, and their presence seemed to act as a beacon to certain dreamers. At this time they knew of two generals, and only one seemed to assert its presence here. The nature of their purpose had yet to be revealed. This alone was cause for great concern.

"And you believe there to be a correlation between the appearance of these generals, and the alteration of energy to this realm?"

"We can't be completely certain but we believe so. Much has altered in the realms, it would be foolish to believe we would be completely unaffected. I thought you claimed not to have noticed."

"I am many things, but ignorant is not one of them. How else would I still be alive?"

"But you're not, are you?"

"Alive? Of course I am. Do not be a fool." Elly took a brief moment of self-reflection. Her body still slept, and her vessel still awaited her return. She had suppressed her ties to both, ensuring she alone could choose if, and when, she would wake.

During their battle, all those years ago, Seiken's final strike had surprised her. He had utilised a power she had not anticipated, and created damage to her vessel she was unable to withstand. She had been forced into The Stepping Realm, forced to remain stranded between worlds until such a time Night repaired the damage to her golem.

As she had waited dark thoughts had clouded her mind. From the onset of their relationship Night had asked but one thing of her, that when the time came she would protect his daughter. She had been confident Marise could defeat Zoella. Seiken had been left unable to intervene, depleted of all his reserves, and yet a growing doubt had burnt within her. It was this doubt which had caused her to invoke, Algiz, which acted as the rune of boundaries. This permitted her to step into Darrienia in the same way she had so long ago, when her journey with Zoella had first began. But such actions took time.

When she found herself within the dreamers' realm she heard panicked tales of their prince's grievous injuries and tales of Thea, and the amazing feat of magic she had performed. When she felt herself being drawn back towards her golem she could not bring herself to return. She could not face Night, the father of the one she had failed. But this was not the sole reason she had chosen to remain. She had known more death than any mortal, but for some reason this particular loss seemed unbearable. She could find no reason to return, no purpose to continue. She had remained here, as Aidan had suggested, contemplating if death could take her in this realm.

"But your death is not mortal." Aidan's voice returned her from her thoughts. His presence once more grated on her as his words caused her to wonder if she had once more been thinking aloud. "It's unconventional, but not divine either. Here though, you believe yourself to be like the rest of them, is that not why you linger past your time?"

"My reasons are personal," Elly retorted impatiently.

"Your reasons, like my own, are self-indulgent. So will you indulge me? Help me to discover what has become of Jude."

"If I assist you in finding your answer, do you swear to leave me in peace?"

"By Darrienia herself, I give you my word."

"Then consider me at your disposal."

* * *

Grayson Bray leaned forward on the tavern's counter, resting his chin on his hand. A charming smile teased his lips as the bartender approached to place another drink before him. The man looked distraught. He twisted his wrinkled apron in his hands as he once more heard the words, 'On the house.' His brows furrowed in a deep frown and his jaws clenched as he looked at the man seated before him, wondering why he had spoken this distasteful phrase, again. Somehow, every time he opened his mouth to request payment, a message of gratuity left his lips.

"Much obliged." Bray raised his glass giving the man another smile before returning to his seat. It was only as he sat he noticed the woman opposite him. Her blonde hair was layered to gently frame her soft jawline. As he placed his drink upon the table, making himself comfortable, he felt the pointed toe of her heeled shoe trace the inside of his calf. Her eyes trained on him, awaiting his reaction to her invitation.

"I thought you looked lonely," she whispered huskily when he failed to acknowledge her advances. She leaned forward, reaching out across the table to stroke her fingers through his hair, her new position giving him a clear and unavoidable view of her exposed cleavage. "Can I, offer you some company?" Bray leaned towards her until his lips were almost upon hers, allowing himself to breathe in the vanilla scented perfume. She wore so much it became almost overpowering, overloading his fragile senses. He gave a sigh, slumping back down into his seat.

"Not tonight, honey. You're just not my type." He took a long drink from his glass before placing it back. She pulled herself from the table, her eyes still focused upon him as she sat back down, twirling one of her blonde locks in her finger as she tried her best, 'come hither' look.

"What do you mean not your type? I've seen the cocottes you leave here with," she countered, putting her free arm beneath her breasts as she leaned forward, giving them an extra lift. His gaze never so much as strayed in their direction.

"And needy too? No thanks." He felt the sting of her strike across his face, his angry eyes glared at her as she moved to stand, her fists clenched as she snorted her outrage. "Besides, I *never* pay." He caught her wrist as she struck out again.

"You think me a whore!" she exclaimed, her tone seeing a few heads turn towards them. Bray's vision traced her figure suggestively as if to emphasise his point. Her attire was minimal, designed for the sole purpose of drawing attention. His gaze lingered at her heaving chest as she tried to breathe out her frustration, with some difficulty thanks to the corset secured around her waist to present the perfect hourglass figure.

"Well, maybe I can spare a coin, you do have some rather... redeeming qualities." She snatched her wrist from his grasp, her eyes tearing as she turned quickly and rushed away, her cheeks flushed with embarrassment.

Bray gave a martyred sigh. How long would he have to sit here and wait? If he didn't find someone to satisfy his desires soon he'd have to go out and look, and he was comfortable.

Another hour passed. The barkeep's temperament was becoming noticeably sour. He grumbled incoherent curses as yet another empty glass was refilled without profit. What was it about this man? Men and women approached him in what seemed to be an endless stream, each attempting to win his favour, only to be rejected. Some with the promise of another night.

Bray gave another sigh, draining his glass. The barkeep stiffened, releasing a sigh of relief as the man left the glass on his table and made his way towards the exit.

"Well, I guess they're not coming to me," he sighed. He had a very particular appetite tonight, one that not just anyone could sate. He wanted something special, and he could already smell her on the wind. She smelt like cinnamon and apples. He closed his eyes, inhaling deeply. She was close.

"Bray?" The familiar voice snatched him from his musings, also revealing the object of his desire. His eyes traced over the two women before Rob stepped forwards.

"Kitaia and... Stacy wasn't it?" Bray smiled. "I've been looking *everywhere* for you." Rob stepped closer giving a loud sniff.

"Everywhere, or just the taverns?" Rob questioned with a grin, noticing the man before him seemed in exceptionally high spirits. The smell of beer and ale was so heavy it almost seemed as if his clothes had been woven from it. In fact, Rob swore, as they stood outside the tavern, Bray was getting some rather hungry looks from a few who had clearly exceeded their quota and emptied their wallets. "I'm amazed the local drunks aren't sucking on your clothes." He wafted his hands dramatically across his face in a lighthearted manner.

"Well, I went to Elpída," Bray started, pausing to give his clothes a slight sniff before smoothing down their crumpled texture. Perhaps Rob was right, he could do with freshening up a little. "I found out your niece had been sent to Mirage Lake. So there I was, motivated to perform a heroic rescue, only to find out she'd already left. Imagine my embarrassment." Bray gestured wildly as Rob cast a quick glance to Stacy, both of them wondering how he could have hoped to infiltrate such a place alone. "Anyway, I made my way here to drown my sorrows a little, before hunting you down."

"Your sorrows or your liver?"

"*Anyway*, I intended to start looking for you." He stepped around Rob to take Taya's hand. He gave a low bow, raising it to his lips and inhaling her scent. "Once more, it is my pleasure." He placed a gentle kiss on her warm flesh. His eyes sparkled with delight. She would do just nicely, although she may take a *little* persuading.

"Have we met?" Taya questioned, glancing towards Rob through the corner of her eyes.

"My lady, you wound me," he pouted letting her hand fall from his to rest upon his chest in a flamboyant gesture. "Surely our time together was more memorable."

"Bray, I'm glad our paths have crossed. I need to talk with you. Alone." Rob's glare halted his theatrics.

"Now? But I *really* want to get reacquainted with our friends here." He extended his gaze to include Stacy, who seemed to blush under the scrutiny of his stare. Taya felt herself stepping behind her. There was something almost ravenous about the way he looked at them.

"Now!" Rob growled grabbing Bray's arm and encouraging him back towards the tavern's doors. "Why don't you ladies see to our accommodation?" He motioned towards the nearest inn before encouraging Bray back into the tavern. Rob swore as they approached he saw the barkeep's shoulders physically sag.

Bray gestured at the bar before himself and Rob. The barkeep appeared uncharacteristically sombre as he placed two drinks before them.

"These are *not* on the house." Or at least that was what he had *intended* to say. He cursed under his breath before he walked away.

"Thanks." Bray raised his glass in a polite gesture as Rob looked to him with a mixture of jealousy and disapproval. But the disapproval soon faded as he tasted the rich nectar. Even on a good day he would not allow his coin pouch to bear such a burden. Rob savoured the taste for a moment before turning to Bray.

"And *that* is precisely why I need to talk to you."

"Because I get free drinks?" Bray questioned in a tone betraying his amusement.

"No, because you can charm the lock off a chastity belt." Bray flashed him a boyish smile, giving a slight bow. "It's almost like an adaption of Apallagí."

"I don't know what you're—" Bray gave a slight chuckle seeing the stern expression on Rob's face. "Trust me, my good fellow, what I can do makes Apallagí look like a child's trick."

"Look, I don't care what it is, but I have need of your skills." Bray raised his eyebrow curiously. The barkeep remained silent, a defeated look in his eyes as he deposited two fresh pitchers. "It's for Ethelyn." Bray turned, giving Rob his full attention.

"Then perhaps I can suggest a proposition. Tell me what you desire, and I'll name my price." Rob, savouring the honeyed flavour, took a quick draught from his drink before recapping all he knew so far.

"I see, so it appears they devised a method to isolate her mnemonic cues," Bray summarised.

"Yeah, Yuri said something along that vein," Rob agreed before draining the glass. No sooner had it struck the counter the dual thud of the replacements serenaded his ears. But more puzzling was the fact the barkeep had decided to bring them some parchment and a quill. Bray quickly drained his glass before starting on the new one. Rob tried to keep pace, certain that Bray had issued an unspoken challenge.

Bray grinned seeing the game emerge. Once more fresh drinks arrived. Lifting the quill he drew a large circle.

"All right then. Let's imagine this circle's your brain. Hmm I should have probably made it smaller."—He continued ignoring Rob's scowl—"This section here," he drew another circle inside, "is where your memories are kept. Inside is filled with small connections that respond to different topical mnemonics... erm, let me think for a moment." He paused to take a long drink, watching as Rob mirrored his actions. It seemed it may take more than just a few hours for a victor to be revealed, but Bray was not accustomed to losing.

Drinking games such as this were a favourite pastime of his, if he wanted to test the true mettle of a person, learn the truth of their character, this was the easiest way. People revealed all manner of things when their inhibitions were reduced by alcohol. From his willingness to accept, Bray could tell it was a ruse Rob was all too familiar with himself. "Right. Let's say you see a yellow ball, we'll call that the topical mnemonic, that's the thing you're seeing to stimulate the thoughts." He wrote the words 'yellow ball' and drew a bubble around it. "Seeing it you may also think of the sun." He drew a line from the yellow ball and wrote the word 'sun'. "We call this line a trace. It's what makes us associate the yellow ball with the sun. But other things may make you think of it too." He wrote other words like heat, light, and some words Rob was unfamiliar with. From each one he drew lines to the word sun.

"Go on," Rob insisted, he understood so far.

"All right. Now let's say for some reason you don't see the sun for a *very* long time, or anything that reminds you of it. When you next see a yellow ball it may remind you of something but you can't remember what. That's called trace, or mnemonic, decay. It means the line here has begun to disintegrate from lack of use. Think of an unused trade route, eventually nature will conceal it if it lacks footfall."

"Okay." Rob nodded staring at the paper intently, wiping his mouth before his hand clasped around another glass. It seemed the barkeep had taken to refilling their old one while the newest was being drained, along with his hope of any profits.

"It can then go one of two ways. You can remember and, fantastic, the trace is restored and the yellow ball reminds you of the sun." He drew over the line again with the quill making it darker. "Or you can forget completely and the trace is destroyed, meaning the yellow ball will no longer remind you of the sun." He crossed out the line.

"But I still know what the sun is right?" Rob questioned uncertainly.

"Yes, unless I erase every trace that links to it, and thus isolate all mnemonic cues." Bray crossed out all the lines coming from the word.

"But the memory of it is still there?"

"Yes, but you have nothing, no reference, to tell you what it is," Bray explained.

"So how can we restore these models?"

"Well, no matter how well someone erases these traces, there is always an obscure route. An overlooked means to restore what was lost."

"Huh." Rob let out a bemused chuckle. "I didn't regard you as a thinker, pretty boy," Rob mocked lightheartedly, slapping his hand on Bray's back. There was something about this man's presence that put him at ease, or perhaps it had more to do with the free and endless stream of liquor.

"I just make it up as I go along really, that I happen to be correct is just a bonus. I'm not just a pretty face, but thanks for noticing." He winked.

"Is there anything *you* can do to fix it, using your... influence?" Rob asked, finally getting to the matter at hand. He had done his best to keep the mood light and even found himself enjoying the company. But there were still serious matters to discuss. A heavy silence descended, both conforming to the serious tone required for such a conversation.

"On the house." The barkeep's words broke a drawn out silence as Bray finished his drink, concentration lining his brow.

"Eventually I guess, but it'd probably take some time," Bray mused taking a drink. "It's a complicated process, very delicate and specialised." He cast a sidewards glance, the corners of his lips turned up in a smile. Rob sighed. He knew that look well, he was almost reluctant to ask.

"What's your price?"

"We can discuss that later. How about for now you just let me accompany you?" Bray propositioned with a wry smile.

"I'd rather—"

"Either I accompany you and give you a fair price when the time comes, or I give you an outrageous one now *and* you can pick up the tab."

"Welcome aboard," Rob responded without delay, extending his hand to Bray who shook it in a firm solid motion.

They had just finished their conversation when Stacy and Taya entered the tavern. Stacy shook her head disapprovingly seeing the two of them attempting to out-drink each other.

"The rooms are ready," Stacy announced impatiently as she approached. She had grown concerned when hours had passed and there had still been no sign of him. Fearing the worst, but expecting something very similar to the display she beheld, she had decided to check on him. With the weight of events hanging over them she *supposed* they could all use a few moments relaxation, and if the two men could afford this time there was no reason she and Taya should be made to sit waiting. Their time with Amelia had been anything but relaxed as they tried to understand what had transpired, whilst attempting to keep their conversations and concerns from Taya's attention.

"Excellent, so how would you two lovely ladies like to join me for dinner?" Bray gave a smile that made Stacy blush and Taya retreat a step.

"They've eaten. We really should head back to the rooms and get cleaned up," Rob stated firmly. He looked to the pitcher with an expression of disappointment as he realised he'd have to forfeit the challenge.

"Very well. Perhaps I can tempt you to one for the road?" Bray glanced to Rob meaningfully, he gave a quick nod, gesturing the ladies towards a vacant table. "Stay for a drink, I'll grab dinner later." Bray raised an eyebrow, giving a half smile as an attractive woman cast her gaze in his direction. "I'll get the drinks." It was only a few moments later he joined them with a drink in each hand.

"Mead for the lady." Bray smiled placing the small glass before Stacy, aware of the suspicion tracing her features as she was presented with her favoured drink. "The same again for you." He placed a glass of ale before Rob and returned to the bar to retrieve the two remaining items. After placing his own drink down he manoeuvred gracefully to stand behind Taya. His hand rested upon her shoulder as he leaned forward, whispering softly in her ear as his gaze met with Rob's. When next he spoke Taya startled, as if she had been unaware of his presence. "And last but not least, milk for my princess." He shared a meaningful glance with Rob. The slight shaking of his head confirmed Rob's suspicions as Bray approached his awaiting seat.

The twilight lighting did little to deter activity from the busy streets. Patrons meandered, casting their gaze towards storefronts whilst passing time in idle conversations. The sound of small horses and traps transporting people to their destinations echoed upon the cobbled lanes. Collateral was a city beyond comparison, a size beyond measure and, as such, had several methods of internal transport, each coloured to relate to their district of origin. The wide streets allowed ample room for pedestrian and vehicle, neither paying much heed to the other, that was, unless the finery and crest suggested those inside were worthy of a show of respect. People, having heard news of a carriage belonging to The Order, seemed more alert than normal to the sound of hooves, perhaps hoping to catch a glimpse of such elegance for themselves.

Rob stared unseeingly, appearing to watch the people go about their everyday business, his attention often returning to the two women who guided them to their destination. He was trying to organise his thoughts, recalling distant memories in hope to weed out the roots Sunniva had so carefully planted. Taya was not his niece, she was a stranger, yet he loved her as if she were his own daughter.

Bray fastened his arm around Rob's and pulled him aside slightly. An action allowing them to talk in some semblance of privacy as the ladies continued ahead. Given their new agreement he had decided it was better to remain close to them, thus had invited himself to stay with Rob, in his room, while he devised a means to release Taya's inhibited memories.

"I've been giving it some thought. There's a chance I know how to open a trace, but it'd work best if we were in The Depths of Acheron." Bray paused, his eyes fixed upon the two figures as Stacy turned back from the inn, giving Rob a firm 'hurry up' gesture before entering. "You're after The Seed of Nzin, if I'm not mistaken. Well, *I* can get her to take us to it," Bray announced, his chest puffed out in pride. Rob looked to him, his brow furrowing as he questioned how this virtual stranger knew so much of his own unspoken ambitions. But his words had captured more interest than suspicion.

"You can?" he questioned skeptically. Taya's current condition had diminished any hope he'd had of him actually retrieving the information from her, after all, she could not reveal that which she was unable to recall. Bray's words had rekindled a semblance of hope.

"To the place it is stored at least. She will take us to the correct portal. After that it's up to us though."

"Do it," Rob confirmed, his authoritarian tone holding no reservation or delay.

"Are you certain that's what you want?" Rob nodded. "Fine. We can test out my theory tomorrow. In the meantime, now that's settled, there's a lady at the bar I believe capable of sating my many appetites," he grinned provocatively. "Don't wait up."

Taya felt the fear flood through her. Her eyes trained on Rob, crying out to him desperately as the coarse hands grasped her. She felt the sting of their poison as something was buried deep within her thigh. She fought, despite knowing she was no match for them. All the time begging her uncle for aid, his indecision a clear betrayal and wounding her more than those who sought to restrain her. She screamed, panic masking her words as the heaviness from their compounds began to take hold. The world began to darken, and the area surrounding Rob's image grew smaller. Her body flooded with pins and needles and everything slowly turned black.

"Taya!" Stacy's voice seemed panicked. Her relief clearly evident as the young woman's eyes opened. Tears streamed down her pale features as her trembling body took laboured gasps. "I couldn't wake you." Stacy released a long breath. She had been moments away from requesting a physician, but that would have meant leaving Taya alone with whatever torment plagued her sleep. Amelia had warned there would be side-effects from the treatments she had undergone. Even now Stacy herself was not unfamiliar with waking in terror, haunted by images of Mirage Lake, and she had suffered it for far less time than Taya.

"Just a bad dream," Taya whispered steadying her voice and attempting to fight the waves of nausea.

"Do you want to talk about it?" Stacy perched herself on the edge of the bed, placing one hand gently on Taya's knee as she shook her head.

"I don't remember." The tears still streamed down her face uncontrollably, fear still knotted her stomach, but the images that plagued her had almost vanished. There was little point in discussing them further.

"Budge over a little." Stacy gave a comforting smile. Taya shuffled across the bed, giving Stacy enough room to crawl in beside her. She placed her arm gently around Taya's shoulder, pulling her close to offer a comfort her own isolation had denied when she had needed it. Taya accepted the warm embrace, her trembling easing under the soothing touch. "Are you scared?" Stacy asked softly.

"Of my dream? I don't remember it." Taya responded feeling the nervous flutter in her stomach.

"No."

"Of what then?"

"If I were you... if I had just left Mirage Lake, met a fiance I thought was a stranger, and realised there are such important things I should recall and can't, I have to admit I'd be a little scared." Stacy stroked Taya's hair gently as she spoke.

"Yes then, but not of that. It may sound silly but I am scared, I just don't understand why. I feel like there's a crushing burden weighing down on me, but I don't understand it. Does that make me sound foolish?"

"Not at all, I think everyone is scared of something." Stacy stopped stroking Taya's hair, turning her focus towards her own palm. "I'm scared that when the time comes, I won't be strong enough." Taya noticed for the first time the scar tissue that ran across Stacy's hand.

"What happened? Did The Order do it?" Her question brought a new realisation to Stacy, Taya was still under the misconception that she was who she had appeared to be on collecting her. For now it seemed better not to correct this notion. The young lady trusted her, and was being open and honest. To say anything now would only jeopardise it. Although the time for truth would come, for now it was better not to confuse things further.

"No, I touched something I shouldn't have. It was a long time ago now. But you know, for better or worse, if we hadn't touched it things wouldn't be as they are now."

"What do you mean?"

"It's a long story," Stacy answered, staring unseeingly at the small, wooden dressing table.

"I'm sorry, you must be tired."

"Not really, no," Stacy admitted, her hand once more stroking Taya's hair as she spoke. "It was about six years ago. My entire life I had been an outcast, people feared me because I was different. Then one day, a man known as Blackwood approached me, offering to make me normal. I was a fool, but I thought he was helping me.

"He had come to possess an ancient sceptre which could remove my curse. I wanted so much to be like everyone else that I never thought to question his motives. There were four of us, all wanting the same normality, and we would have done anything he asked of us to obtain it. We followed him without question, without thought to the consequences.

"We thought we were using him for our own gains, but we were mistaken. The power of this artefact was so immense it burnt the flesh of all who touched it, feeding on the very thing that made us unique in order to open a pathway into the earth. We didn't see what happened next, truth be told I understand we were lucky to survive at all.

"We should have died upon that island, they thought we had, or they would have ensured it. Those who rescued us managed to stop Blackwood. If they had failed the future would look very different." Stacy lowered her tone to a whisper, realising her tale was not as long as she thought, it just brought with it a heavy burden. "It's strange, if we hadn't acted the world would have been ended by the Severaine. But now, because of our actions, I fear the Mystics won't possess the power to face this n—" A scream pierced the air, severing Stacy's words as Taya keeled over. She buried her hands in her hair, seizing fistfuls in her grasp as she cried in agony. Stacy reached out, placing her hand on the writhing figure, unsure what she could do, unsure what exactly was happening.

The orbs of energy illuminating the room began to flicker, pulsing in time with the soft trembling vibrations. Their light prematurely extinguished with a hiss, plunging the room into darkness. Stacy grasped Taya tightly, pulling her into a firm embrace.

She had experienced Gaea's Stirring or, as most called it, an earthquake, on several occasions, but never quite like this. There was something different, an unnatural energy that caused the hairs on her arms to prickle. The vibrations became deep, rumbling tremors. The room came alive with movement, framed pictures banged against the wall, heavy furniture shifted and groaned as the floorboards lurched first one way, then another. The glass rattled in the windowpanes, cracking as fractures webbed across its surface, imploding to rain shards throughout the room. Grabbing the blanket Stacy covered them, dragging Taya from the bed to the floor as she attempted to shield them.

Taya's agonised screams were almost drowned out by the thundering sounds of movement. Tears streamed from her eyes until the screams died, her body no longer able to vocalise the pain. Cracks chased their way across the mirrors, pictures dropped from the wall, spraying their glass casing across the splintering floorboards. Stacy snatched her hand from Taya's back, feeling movement, watching in horror as ripples of moving bones pushed at her flesh, causing the nightgown to thin against the pressure. She attempted to speak comforting, soothing words, but could hear the horror and panic lining her voice as white shards pierced Taya's flesh from the upper part of her back, tearing the fine cloth, staining its purity with red droplets of spreading blood where the bones seemed to attempt to force their way free.

"Make it stop!" Taya screamed through heavy sobs, once more finding her voice, forcing it through the swelling in her throat as she fought to breathe.

The door was torn from its hinges, crashing inside as Rob and Bray staggered through, pausing to behold the scene of destruction before them. The world around them began to shatter, even the strongest of wood succumbing to the force of the powerful vibrations. Floorboards strained, lifting and splitting across the uneven floor. Cracks chased up the wall as powdered dust from the ceiling above began to warn of a greater danger.

Rob watched in bewilderment as the room around them became reduced to a scene of complete devastation. Bray, recovering from his staggering steps, trained his eyes on Taya. Navigating the debris he dropped to his knees before the cowering women. He reached out pulling Taya from Stacy's fearful embrace. He held her close, whispering softly as his hands caressed her face with a soothing touch. As if hearing the words herself Gaea returned to her slumber, and all became still. Taya's body, once wrought with tension, relaxed as she succumbed to the warm embrace of unconsciousness. The pulsating bones receded. The flesh closing and knitting to leave no evidence of their presence.

"What in Tartarus happened here?" Rob demanded, he had seen but a few things capable of unleashing such complete devastation.

"I—bones were..." Stacy gestured to Taya's back, her mind unable to put into words the horror of what she had seen.

"That's normal, don't worry about that," Bray stated waving a hand dismissively. He still sat beside Taya, his breathing laboured, his hand still resting carefully upon her. "Explain."

"She started gripping her head, then the earthquake started," Stacy answered in a daze, trying to piece together exactly what had happened as she looked over the destroyed room.

"That was no earthquake. Collateral has no such vulnerabilities, it's not part of your world. Before that, what happened?" Bray, having regained some of his strength, lifted Taya gently, adjusting her limp figure to lie across him. He cradled her almost protectively, his eyes closing momentarily as he inhaled her captivating scent.

"She had a bad dream. We were just talking, she asked how I got my scar. I told her."

"How did you get it?" Bray questioned, listening intently as Stacy recapped the story. "Did you mention the Mystics?" he asked sharply, plucking the word from Taya's own mind and gaining some minor insight into what her purpose here had been.

"Yes, how'd you—"

"He's a mindseer," Rob intervened, a little too quickly, earning him a reproachful glance from Bray.

390

"That's how he could stop her." Rob picked his way across the room, approaching the one item which had not been destroyed, the bed. He lifted the bottom sheet, sending a spray of glass and dust through the air before he carefully sat.

He took a deep breath, attempting to distance himself from the overwhelming concern for his niece's safety. She was not his niece, he needed to remember that. His feelings towards her were manipulated, although to what degree he could no longer be certain. It was impossible to discern where Sunniva's influence halted and his own genuine feelings towards the woman took root. He could see the dangers, the complications. If he failed to define reality from deception it could jeopardise the very thing he needed to accomplish.

He could not let anything he felt towards her, real or otherwise, prevent him from doing what needed to be done. He knew he must not forget this, not now, not ever. And if this meant he had to keep himself distant, to reinforce the fact that they had no relationship outside of fabrication, then he would do just that. He could not be pulled into a fantasy which could imperil his very future.

"You mean she did this?" Stacy questioned in disbelief, once more observing the disarray around her. She had only seen devastation like this once before, and that had been when she had not been in control of her own abilities.

"Taya's mission was to find the Mystics, to see if given the shift in powers they would still pose a threat should Kólasi rise. It seems certain things may tempt a memory, this reaction may be a conditioned response. The thing is, Daimons possess impeccable control over their powers. One losing control like this is unheard of."

"Of course it is," Rob observed solemnly. "Taya doesn't know she's a Daimon."

"I never considered that." Bray winced. "Daimon magic is different to that of any other being. They don't have to concentrate to unleash it but to keep it restrained. Whilst we can assume the finer points of control, those gained through training, would have been lost, she should still possess her instincts. They can't have done *that* much damage." Bray seemed to tighten his grip on her, before shifting her weight slightly.

"Shall I help you move her?" Rob questioned, wondering why Bray had yet to place her on the bed he had cleared. He seemed to be enjoying her closeness a little too much given the situation. Rob unclenched his fist, reminding himself that whilst he had an investment in Taya, such things should not concern him.

"Not yet."

"By the Gods' bones, what is going on here!" boomed a voice from the doorway. "Forget me just keeping the deposit, I'm going to bill you for the entire room."

"You bill us!" Rob rose to his feet in outrage as he turned his steely gaze towards the figure at the door. "*You* allow someone to target our friend, and you think *we* are the ones who should pay!" Spittle clung to Rob's angry lips as he turned fully to face the proprietor, who stood beholding the room with a look of horror.

"Really?" The innkeeper folded his arms, shaking his head slightly as he surveyed the room before turning his suspicious gaze back towards Rob. "And just *why* should I believe you? I've heard mute fablers tell a more believable tale." He scoffed at his own comment, his amusement at his wit faded as he saw the rage in Rob's eyes.

"Our friend was on an important mission for The Order," Rob began through clenched teeth. "There are those who would rather see her dead than witness her success." He gestured towards Taya, his angry gaze never straying from the innkeeper. "You think we would allow harm to come to one of our own?" For the first time the man before him looked past the damage and saw the young lady, deathly pale, and limp, cradled carefully in the arms of the other man.

"Gods forgive me," he gasped, raising his hands to his mouth in alarm. Shame filled his voice as he realised he had seen only the damage, blinkered to those who had been injured. Observing now, the entire scene, he saw the truth in Rob's words. The damage seemed to be the result of a targeted attack. He recalled word of The Order's carriage passing through earlier in the day. His mind raced, fervently connecting the rumours with the arrival of these guests. The two women had reserved their rooms soon after the carriage had past. He felt his stomach tighten as the truth of their tale seemed more plausible. He turned his gaze once more to Taya, his concern now evident. "Do you need a physician?"

"She fainted, she should be fine," Bray offered, a weakness to his voice betraying his own exhaustion.

"Please, come with me. I'll see you to another room immediately. We're at capacity, I'm afraid there's only one available." He motioned towards the crumbling door frame, wiping the sweat from his brow as he turned to lead them away.

"It's not like any of us will sleep tonight. I was foolish thinking us safe here," Rob muttered, inclining his head in acceptance of the gesture. The innkeeper turned back to behold the room one final time to settle his remaining doubts. Rob moved to leave, casting a glance to Bray who made no attempt to move.

"You two go on ahead, check the room over carefully before we move her." He gave Rob a meaningful look, one the innkeeper misinterpreted as 'make sure we're not in further danger.' Rob however knew its true meaning. He nodded at Stacy who, with a reluctant glance at Taya, nodded and followed.

Chapter 13

Treasure

Taya opened her eyes to the low murmur of inaudible chatter. Each quiet syllable only served to intensify the throbbing pain radiating through her. Her body felt heavy, unresponsive. Her eyes remained fixed on the brick wall. The view was so contrasting to that of the place she had fallen asleep in that she felt anxiety beginning to build in the pit of her stomach. The picture of a flower had been replaced by a calm ocean scene, and the smooth style walls were now bare. There was no question in her mind, she was not where she should have been.

Slowly she turned over, amazed at the toll even such a simple action took. Just beyond a second bed was a small wooden partition, it stood no more than three-quarters of the room's height, allowing a semblance of privacy. A figure appeared, its form lost in the distortion of light caused by her bleary eyes. It folded back the screen, moving it to rest at an angle against the wall. It was only when the person sat perched on the edge of the opposite bed Taya's sight began to clear.

"How are you feeling?" Stacy's voice was soft, edged with unmistakable concern. Taya pushed herself up slowly, feeling the tightening protests of her stomach as she moved.

"This isn't our room, is it?" Taya questioned hesitantly, slowly moving her head, allowing herself to absorb all the details of this unfamiliar setting. Sweat beaded her skin as the nausea turned her stomach once again. A loud thump startled her, drawing her attention towards Rob and Bray. They were seated at the far side of the room, positioned on opposite sides of a small, wooden table with empty glasses before them.

"No, we had to move in the night. Bray carried you here." Stacy was being deliberately vague, unsure how much Taya remembered of the events leading to their relocation. She knew better than to tempt another reaction.

"Kitaia, you're awake." Bray turned towards them, his attention drawn by the hushed conversation. "How are you feeling?" As Bray stood his hand scooped a rolled up parchment from the table, neither his gait nor his speech betrayed a night of drinking.

Stacy stood as he approached them, crossing her arms she scowled in his direction, excusing herself to the small dressing table found near the door. Upon it was a platter of food, breads, cheeses, and sliced meats, all presented as means of an apology for the events of the previous evening. Stacy busied herself in preparing a small plate of food for Taya. She wanted no part in what they were about to do and had made her position on the matter quite clear. They had *said* it was the best way to help her, but she saw all too well their motives. They were forcing this for their own gains.

"My head feels tender and, I don't feel, quite right. But I'm okay, I think. Why?" Taya questioned. This was the second time she had been asked about her health, and both times had been accompanied by tones of concern.

"Good. Now, close your eyes." Bray unrolled the parchment placing it on her lap. He reached forward, taking her right hand to place it upon the surface of the map and took her other hand in his. He glanced towards Rob, who gave a firm nod. "Where is The Seed of Nzin?" The sound of her nails upon the parchment caused a smile to form on Bray's lips, the damage to her instincts wasn't as severe as he feared. When her finger stilled Bray committed the location to memory, sliding the map from beneath her touch. Taya's eyes opened suddenly, her feet swinging from the bed as her hand pushed Bray aside in one desperate motion as she leapt to her feet. Her trembling legs barely supported her weight as she dashed into the bathroom to empty her stomach. Rob moved to Bray's side, his eyes fixed upon the map.

"How?" he questioned, glancing at the parchment in hope to discern the location Taya had indicated.

"Trust me, that's not the usual reaction I instil in the fairer sex." He winked at Stacy, who raised her eyes to the ceiling in frustration before pursuing Taya, ignoring his words.

"Not making her sick. Trust me, that reaction I understand all too well." Rob lifted the parchment from Bray, annoyed when he could find no new marks upon its surface.

"Defamation of character does not become you. Especially when you still seek my favour," Bray warned with an impish smile, gesturing towards the map.

"You know what I mean, she doesn't remember. How did you get her to tell you?" Rob's stern tone was a clear indication he was not rising to Bray's playful goading, not where something like this was concerned. For six years he had sought this treasure. Six long years.

"She doesn't need to remember. Kitaia Ethelyn is the Sfaíra Fýlakas." He looked at Rob's blank expression and chuckled. "It means she knows such trivialities by instinct. She's a powerful scryer, amongst other things. I used minimal coercion, after last night I couldn't risk another, well you know. I doubt I could restrain her again so soon. As for the sickness, I plead innocence," he added, turning his sight towards the bathroom.

"I see." Rob stroked his chin in thought.

"Anyway, I'm famished. How about we meet up at the Plexus in a few hours?" Bray queried. Rob glanced from him to the platter of food on the dressing table. "I've more than one appetite in need of sating." Bray smirked and, with a slight chuckle, raised his hand in a parting gesture as he left.

* * *

Stacy took a seat on one of the small benches lining the circular tables near the Plexus' entrance. It was the first time she had visited this particular Plexus, and she was impressed by its sheer size. The door led straight into what looked to be a large social area. There were a few hunters sitting around a small table, discussing important matters in hushed tones with bowed heads. But aside from them the remaining chairs were vacant. It was only when the balding man raised the counter to lead the group to a more private location, that Stacy realised he bore the emblem of a Plexus master.

Stacy leaned back against the large window frame, amazed at how peaceful a place like this could appear when empty and bathed in the soft morning light. The warm shades of wooden furniture seemed homely, and the scent of fresh bread and cooking meats from outside only added to the comfort.

Allowing herself a moment of relaxation she let her concerned gaze rest upon Taya, who still clung tightly to Rob. As soon as they had stepped foot outside she had linked Rob's arm, much to his obvious discomfort, and refused to be separated from him. Even at the counter she retained her firm grasp, allowing him barely enough room to manoeuvre. Her closeness to him made him visibly uncomfortable, especially since he had taken it upon himself to keep in mind exactly how inappropriate her behaviour was.

"Here, look, can you hold on to this for me?" Rob turned slightly, using the rolled map to form a barrier between them, forcing her to relinquish her grasp in order to take it. He retreated a few paces before turning to address the task at hand. "I need a few jobs," he announced to the awaiting figure as he straightened his sleeve, where Taya's grip had caused it to ride up. He tossed his emblem on the counter towards Asher. It seemed Barnett was attending to other matters this morning, Rob had caught but a brief glance of him as he escorted a small group into the privacy of the rear area.

"Be right back." Rob watched the figure disappear through the rear door. He returned a few moments later with a hastily scrawled parchment in hand. Fortunately, after years of practice, Rob was all too familiar with deciphering this man's scrawl. "Now, 'ere's what we've got at present. I'll leave yer to peruse 'em. Shout up if yer've any questions." Asher teased his fingers through his scruffy black hair, attempting to smooth some of the wildness from its volume.

"Asher, am I reading this right, Medusa's fork?" The lean figure stepped forwards, squinting at his parchment.

"Yeah, new on' that. Some noble, pays well." The figure stepped back leaving Rob to contemplate the task.

"And... what's this, the Devil's Abacus?" Rob caught movement to his left as Taya studied the parchment before her, making small circles upon its surface with a discarded charcoal marker. He smiled to himself, hearing his stubble grate against his fingernails as he scratched his chin. He thought he had seen her make a similar motion last time, but now he was certain. He glanced to the Plexus master, who rolled his eyes slightly. "You know what, I'll take those two, and—"

"Didn't take yer for a scryer man." He inclined his head towards Taya, whose eyes were fixed unseeingly on the parchment before her. "Seen 'er like before. Good in theory, but I wouldn't trust yer pockets to 'em."

"Scryer, no, no. She's my transla—no, cartographer. My niece, Taya, she's studying topography and wants to apply its theory to—"

"It's your coin," Asher raised his hand silencing Rob's explanation. "Not fer me to judge. Anything else?"

"What's this, a guilded dragon scale?"

"Golden." Rob watched Taya from the corner of his eye, seeing her hand hover over an area just off the coast of Drevera before marking the map.

"Not that one... what's worth the most points?" Rob could feel the sharpness of Stacy's glare, even from across the room. He pushed his shoulders back, straightening his posture in an attempt to ignore it.

"The Darkmore crystal." The Plexus master pointed to the job title near the base of the page.

"Your kind steer clear, since it's a myth and all. I've been trying to get rid of it for years." Taya had already marked the map again.

"Consider it gone."

"Yer sure? If yer fail to deliver within a month we'll reopen it, after six it'll be a demerit. Why not just keep it in mind, it'll save yer alotta bother when yer can't find it." The Plexus master felt pity well in his stomach. At one time or another most hunters resorted to the use of scryers, but this man had one of the leading ranks this year. If he failed even one of these jobs there was little chance he could recover. Whilst it was true he had stated the woman was his niece, and not aligned to that ignoble profession, he had seen too many hunters fall for their entrapment. They charged per scry, and were protected from having their reputation sullied based on the premise that, all treasures, were subject to relocation based on their possessor's movements. In truth, many scryers were simply tricksters.

"No, no, mark me down." Rob felt himself wince slightly as Stacy approached. He had heard the annoyance in her steps, he didn't need to turn to see her expression to know he was in trouble. Stacy yanked the map from beneath Taya's hands, giving Rob her best depreciative look. "Hey, don't you dare. We have to eat and sleep. Who do you think is paying for all this?"

"I was under the impression Bray," Stacy snapped, knowing their room and meals last night had all been courtesy of him. He didn't seem to have the same attachment to coin as most people. She reminded herself to thank him, it wasn't often to find someone of such generosity who sought nothing in return.

"Last night maybe, but I'm normally the one to settle accounts. Besides, they're short detours, and we're at a loss until the next full moon. Am I wrong?" With a reluctant sigh Stacy flicked her wrist, passing the map to him. He took it quickly before she could change her mind.

"Pick *one*," she demanded, her hands finding her hips in an aggressive gesture.

"What'll it be?" The Plexus master intervened with a smile that well and truly told Rob he was not the one in charge. His expression grew serious as he realised he had become the recipient of the cold, stern glare.

"All of them," Rob asserted firmly, his eyes meeting Stacy's. He saw the Plexus master nod in his peripheral vision before excusing himself quickly.

"Fine, since you're the one who's settling accounts, Taya needs some new clothes." Stacy held her hand out impatiently.

"What's wrong with—" he turned his sight to Taya, cringing as he realised that the young woman wore nothing more than a tattered nightgown covered by a lightweight wrap Amelia had given her. "All right, whatever you need," he conceded, pulling on a leather cord around his neck to lift his coin pouch. "Just, nothing too extravagant, and grab some supplies." When the Plexus door swung closed, leaving Rob alone in the strangely empty building, the door from the back once more creaked open. Narrowly at first, almost as if someone on the other side was surveying the area before committing.

"Your wife sure has you on a short leash." Asher smiled broadly, edging through the door before presenting Rob with the job missives and his emblem.

"Tell me about it. Worse still, she's not even my wife." Rob gave a sigh, accepting the papers as he heard the guild master roar with laughter. Rob reciprocated with a slight chuckle.

"No, really?" He studied Rob, his question forced out between gasps of laughter.

"Yeah really. She just decided to tag along. I barely know her." Rob saw the tears forming in Asher's eyes, his amusement so uncontainable he could barely draw breath. He patted Rob on his shoulder while attempting to say something, but each word was masked by uncontrollable laughter. After a few moments, he wiped the tears from his cheeks as he began to calm, but beholding Rob's sombre expression once again stoked the embers of his mirth. Rob gave a heavy sigh, slinking away to the furthest table in hope for some privacy. Every time silence descended he would catch Asher looking in his direction and chuckling as their eyes met.

* * *

Bray entered the Plexus to see Rob sitting at one of the small tables with his back to the wall. He supported his head with his hand as he sat gazing upon the parchment before him, yet he was clearly lost in thought.

"I've just confirmed my suspicions." Bray pulled up a stool, perching himself on it casually. "Our best option will be during the full moon." He paused, looking down at the tattered map, noticing the presence of a number of new marks upon its well-worn surface. This map was a testament to its owner, a story of adventures that only Rob could decipher. "I see you already have an itinerary in mind." Bray shifted his gaze to his surroundings, noticing there were only a few other hunters currently present. "Where've the ladies ventured to?"

"Shopping," Rob muttered, once more feeling the absence of his coin purse. "Hey," Rob started, his posture becoming attentive as he turned his full attention towards Bray. "I thought Taya could pass through boundaries at will."

"She can. But there are others who roam The Depths of Acheron, and they too seek freedom when the moon rises. Some remain, but others attempt to liberate their deities from the hands of the foul and unworthy."

"You mean steal treasures." Rob gave a slight snort, wondering how many times he had recovered something, just for it to be reclaimed.

"Besides, it would be to our advantage if the Daimons remained unaware of our interference. Given what it is you're after, it is best for us to exploit their absence. It's not something they would allow into the hands of another, but it is also away from their vigil. To that end—" Bray rose suddenly, leaving his thought unfinished. He smartened his appearance slightly, turning towards the door as it opened.

"We're back. I *trust* you've behaved yourself?" Stacy narrowed her eyes, her gaze shifting from Rob to the tabletop, relieved when she saw no new missives awaiting their return. Taya followed her inside, her face beaming with happiness.

"Thank you so much for the clothes, Uncle Rob. I love them." She gave them a twirl, reminiscent of a dancer in grace and poise. The two men stared at her, almost unable to believe the transformation. Since meeting her she had always been dressed in the drab, unflattering folds of either the priestess' attire, or nightgown. But to see her now they could almost believe her to be a different person.

Bray looked upon her, his imagination drawing parallels to the forest nymphs. His gaze lingered, slowly tracing the tan, knee-high, ranger boots, before continuing up her bare skin to the shorts. He had removed enough women's clothing to recognise them as such, despite their skirt-like appearance. A dark green, sleeveless linen-shirt hugged her figure in a way which betrayed its supple properties. His gaze lingered at her breasts, disappointed to find a high, circular neckline.

His focus turned towards the leather strap, which ran diagonally across her, supporting a quiver of arrows, and a bow.

Taya stepped forwards, wrapping her arms around Rob. He felt himself growing warm as he once more tried to gently pry himself from her grasp.

"Is something wrong?" Taya questioned when he failed to return the affection. He cleared his throat, managing to gently push her away in the pretence of examining her new attire.

"You can use a bow?" Rob asked quizzically as he moved back to the table, creating a barrier between them. He was finding Taya's familial affection increasingly more difficult to accept.

"I fired a few arrows. The proprietor said I was a natural." Her smile broadened as she caught sight of herself in the window's reflection. She could never remember feeling this beautiful.

"Here." Stacy dropped the coin pouch onto the table. Hearing its weight he looked to her in surprise, receiving only a cold stare in response. He picked it up, hooking it around his neck, thinking better than to question how he had once again managed to annoy her.

"Were you able to get some cloaks?" Rob asked with a slight sigh. He didn't normally bother with the extra weight. He found, whilst warm, cloaks tended to hinder him more than they did aid. But this journey was not about his own comfort. He needed to ensure they could keep moving regardless of the unforgiving elements. The discomfort was a far better compromise than time wasted constantly seeking shelter.

"Whilst you have my gratitude, I find body heat to be the best protection." Bray moved in a single predatory step to slide his arms around both Taya and Stacy's waists. Stacy twisted, thrusting a cloth bag firmly into his chest. Bray gave a forced sigh. He, like Rob, was not fond of such clothes.

"Since we have to wait for the full moon to start our *real* adventure, we'll be taking a short detour," Rob explained, rolling up the parchment and tucking it into his jerkin.

"To Mum's?" Taya questioned enthusiastically.

"No." Rob responded a little too forcefully, a tone he quickly adjusted. "I've a few errands that need to be taken care of. Think of it as practise." He tugged on the cloak, pulling at it in an awkward attempt to make it hang correctly, but only found himself becoming more tangled in the uncooperative fabric. He huffed a frustrated sigh, grateful when Stacy approached, making the necessary adjustments. She brushed her hands down his sleeves, a small amused smile turning the corners of her lips.

* * *

They travelled relentlessly. Resting only as night fell or the paths became too treacherous to continue without adequate lighting. Rob kept himself separated from Taya whenever possible. He would ride or walk several paces ahead, under the pretence of scouting the area. His thoughts were still disorganised. Confusion about where his manipulated feelings for Taya ended, and his real ones began, weighed

408

heavily on his mind. He often berated himself for being lured back towards the comfort of familial connections. It was so easily achieved, something as simple as a look or a smile, would return the feelings of fondness for his niece, and he would once again be forced to remind himself of the truth.

When they first arrived at the forlorn estate an air of uneasy silence descended. The outer buildings showed evidence of ransacking and looting. Doors hung loosely on rusted hinges and climbing flowers and vines strangled the decrepit stone structures. What had once been a tribute of wealth had decayed beyond all recognition. They rode under the boundary archway, where the family name had grown tarnished and barely legible.

"This is the old Malory estate," Bray observed. "I offered some services here some seasons ago. He was attempting to see his daughter married, but even with his wealth he struggled to find a suitor. The marriage contract possessed a clause, no less than two heirs within six years and a commitment to father a male child."

"Why was that a problem? A lot of nobles make such demands." Stacy pulled her horse to a stop outside the main house.

"There's no sensitive way to say this, his daughter was a drassock. No matter the tailors and ornatrix in employ they could not make a leech into a butterfly. The poor man died before finding a suitor."

"What does any of this have to do with Medusa's Fork?" Stacy questioned securing her horse to the hitching rail before helping Taya from hers. Rob tentatively pushed the door, relieved when it opened with relative ease. As he guided them through Bray revealed what he knew of the lore. Rob's ever-watchful eyes saw the gradual increase in mirrors as they worked their way through the ransacked house.

"Well, when Perseus beheaded Medusa, she clenched her jaws severing her tongue and even under her dead gaze it turned to stone. It was rumoured any possessing it would appear as beautiful as the gorgon herself had once been. She was not like her sisters, she was not born in that form. Did you never question why she was the only one thought mortal? She was once a woman of beauty in service to Athena. She vowed celibacy but her oath was broken when Poseidon lay with her, although rumours of consent were ever varied."

"So you think she found it and sought to attract a partner?" Taya asked.

"Coin can buy all manner of information, and I do recall rumours of her blossoming. I learnt of her father's death from a physician, he'd been called to treat one of the servants. A pretty young thing, scarred for life." Bray made a quick gesture across his face. "After that there were only rumours of cruelty and depravity."

"That could explain what we're seeing here," Rob called back. "This hasn't been looted by bandits, it's too methodical. The servants raided the things of value before leaving. If she did have Medusa's Fork it would explain the alteration in persona and vanity."

"Medusa's Fork bestows beauty of the skin at the cost of ugliness to the core." Taya earned a bewildered look as she spoke. "I must have read it somewhere. I used to read a lot," she justified timidly. "For every measure of beauty it reflected on the outside, the inside turned to stone. Emotions were lost, until looks were their sole possession and the only thing of worth. But that which is inside always comes to flesh, and once in its final stages the process of petrification is a slow and painful one."

Rob stood by the windows, wondering how he could hope to identify one corpse amongst the several decomposing forms he had already witnessed through cracked doors. The scenes had turned his stomach. Men and women held prisoner within rooms, bound before shattered mirrors which caused their mutilated features to stare back at them from every possible angle. He searched for something of beauty to ease his mind and cast his gaze past the wooden fences to the overgrown vineyards.

Taya approached the door, stepping through into the side gardens. They showed evidence of their long neglect, but still appeared beautiful in their untamed state. Seeing the solarium within its centre she walked towards it, drawn by an unknown urge to look upon what was within. Alternating panels had been replaced with mirrors, allowing the occupant to gaze upon themselves whilst comparing their beauty to that of nature's perfection.

Within the centre was a statue carved with lifelike perfection. Anguish and torment twisted the beautiful features of the woman. Her recoiled posture portrayed agony, and her eyes were fixed towards the mirrors, as if the final thing she wished to behold had been herself.

Taya wanted to avert her eyes, understanding all too well the scene she beheld and the suffering caused by the punishment inflicted. But it was only as her gaze acknowledged the object clasped within the figure's hands that she could finally look away.

Safe from weathering this statue could have lasted for ages untold. But its grasp upon the treasure had been firm. Stacy escorted Taya in a walk around the overgrown gardens, while Bray and Rob took whatever means necessary to retrieve it, and ensuring their own flesh never came into contact with the forked, burgundy tongue. Bray's vanity warned of the dangers, and he took comfort in the knowledge he had no need of its charm.

When they left the solarium they did so quietly, a single gesture informed Stacy and Taya it was time to depart.

* * *

Rob had planned their route meticulously, and each night he would sit around their fire in the pretence of studying the parchment. His withdrawal became a cause for concern. Even Bray found it difficult to tease a smile from the hunter's lips. For each day that passed Rob seemed to grow increasingly more anxious, his thoughts consumed by what their journey's end would bring.

Their next location had been found upon the gentle gradient of sloping plains. There was no settlement indicated upon his map, yet Taya's markings had led them to a small decrepit town. The crumbling husks of buildings seemed barely capable of providing shelter, yet within the small boundaries the sounds of children could be heard. A single woman, her drawn features holding a smile weighted with worry, watched over them. Their makeshift beds, visible through the broken timbers, were nothing more than old hide blankets upon the floor, allowing them to huddle together against the penetrating cold.

The evening was drawing in, the sun had begun its final descent over the western mountains, bringing with it the cold winds which saw the small group of children, who had been foraging through the broken debris in search of things to trade or sell, returning to the lady. She stood before a large cast iron cauldron, fixing a watery broth for their supper. Seeing the travellers Casie had waved, welcoming them into their shelter so they might escape the biting winds.

While serving them a lean meal she had apologised, informing them food was scarce and they were trying their best to make what meagre supplies they had last until they could next find something to trade. As she ladled the soup into the wooden bowl Rob noticed the white bands, visible through the frayed fingerless gloves, where rings would have been worn. A glimmer of movement drew his focus to a delicate bracelet, a tarnished chain which supported several small charms. Seeing where his attention wandered she tucked it back under her sleeve, holding her hand over it protectively.

Observing their surroundings Rob knew this was probably the only item of any value they possessed, and given such obvious hardships it suggested its value was worth more than any coin. He had been reluctant to ask, but he had recognised one of the charms.

"How much would you take for the bracelet?" He felt the guilt knot in his stomach as he saw the woman before him grow pale. She turned away, wrapping her arms around herself as her gaze lingered on the small shack she and the children shared. Rob tried to divert his attention, pretending not to notice the inner-turmoil he had caused. He looked to his bowl, feeling a further deepening of shame as he noticed that the pale broth she had served them possessed more vegetables than that given to herself.

"I..." she trailed off, she had known for a while now it was time to part ways with this keepsake. If they had any hope of surviving the coming months they needed food more than anything else. The bitter wind stung her face, chilling the forming tears. "Please, give me the night." Her fingers found the silver chain as she twisted it around her wrist. The children knew its worth to her, that was why they foraged through the debris. But Casie had long come to realise that, aside from the remaining iron and metal scraps, everything of value had already been sold. She had petitioned the council for funding, who had in turn referred her to the temples. But no response had ever reached her, and the journey was now too hard for her tiring bones to make.

It hadn't been long after her request for aid that the slavers had paid her a visit. And although there were times—as they once more went to bed cold with hunger burning—she wondered if the life of a slave would be better than what they had here, she could not bring herself to ask it of them. Things needed to change, but people were blind to the plight of others. The answer to their dilemma seemed to have been to simply strike their village from the maps. She could expect no aid, and although each day she gave everything she could, she knew it was no longer enough.

"Of course." Rob nodded his understanding, forcing himself to finish the meal before him. It had been a long time since he had eaten what he referred to as pottage, a watery soup made from a collection of anything edible.

When their meal was finished the sun had already sunk far beyond the distant horizon. Casie, in a somewhat flustered manner, escorted them into one of the rundown buildings where they would be sheltered from the worst of the elements, and there she bid them goodnight.

* * *

When Rob awoke it was still early. His body shivered from the cold breeze which rattled the loose panels and whipped through the crumbling boards. Taya and Stacy were still sleeping soundly, huddled together for warmth. As he placed his own blanket over them he noticed the area set aside for Bray remained undisturbed. Giving a frustrated sigh Rob massaged his forehead, hoping Bray's indiscretion would not influence this morning's negotiations. He rubbed the back of his neck and shoulders before wrapping his cloak tightly around himself. Appreciating its warmth for but a moment he made his way outside, to see if Casie had risen.

Rob gave a fatigued yawn, propping himself cautiously against the door jamb. The predawn light seemed to be playing tricks on his tired eyes. Atop of one of the small buildings, silhouetted by the cold sun's light, sat Bray.

He worked in silence. A cloth was wrapped over a hammer's end as he secured a section of wooden debris over an opening in the roof of the children's sleeping area. Rob could see that already a few of the children were awake. Still dressed in their tattered nightgowns, they hurried back and forth, passing him up pieces of wood from the small pile at the building's base. It was clear Bray had spent some time gathering the materials. Even from his position Rob could see they were of better quality than those which held together most of the ruined buildings.

Looking at the small house's frame, the patching and repairs, it seemed as if he had been working for some time, perhaps even throughout the night. Rob stood transfixed, watching as Bray stopped, mopping his brow with his sleeve before sliding from the roof to a small rusted anvil. Using the same hammer he began to straighten a small collection of nails that he had no doubt salvaged from the debris.

Casie approached him, placing a glass upon the anvil. Even from his position Rob could see the brown hue of the liquid in the glass. Bray accepted it gratefully, drinking it without pause. They exchanged brief words as she gestured towards the debris that had once been the village's centre.

Bray picked his way towards the crumbling stone framework of the well-pump. Appraising it carefully he paced, gesturing to himself in thought before gathering the tools he had already acquired. He stripped and cleaned it as best he could before standing back to examine his finished labour. The water pumped clear, and he was now as dirty as the water had once been.

Bray scanned the area, seeing the rusted tin barrel bath he decided that he would bathe, and then assemble something better for the children to use. As he confirmed his plan of action he noticed Rob stood watching him and, with a smile, gestured for him to approach.

"I never considered you a repair-wright." Rob failed to hide the astonishment in his voice. Bray's actions alone had been enough to pull him from his soured mood of late. He had many impressions of Bray, yet hardworking had not been one of them.

"I'm a man of all trades." He placed his hands on his hips, thrusting out his chest in a proud, yet playful manner.

"Master of none?" Rob quipped.

"Oh, I think you'll find I master them admirably," he winked, turning his attention to starting a small fire in order to heat some stones.

"I was hoping we could discuss my request." Rob turned to Casie as he heard her approach. Bray collected the stones and placed them on a metal grate before dragging it over the fire. Since it would be some time before they were warm enough to heat the water he decided to join them as they sat on the wilting grass near the fire.

For thirty minutes they sat. Each offer Rob made countered by a steeper one, which caused his gaze to occasionally flit pleadingly in Bray's direction as he sat in silent observation. He watched in amusement as Rob's expression became more solemn as Casie extended her hand in agreement. He grasped it almost hesitantly before rising in order to retrieve the agreed amount. She slipped the bracelet from her wrist, placing it within his hand before hurrying away to avoid the spectacle of her tears. After she had left Bray followed Rob, falling into step beside him.

"Hey, couldn't you have helped me out a little back there?" Rob whispered. He saw a flicker of mischief cross Bray's expression. "You didn't?" Bray remained silent in an attempt to stop his smile from broadening further. "You did, I can't believe you!"

"Take a look around you, Rob," Bray gestured. "They need it more than you. Besides, you underestimate its worth." Bray's voice possessed a weight of complete seriousness that Rob had heard him use but a few times.

"I know, but I paid more than the job does." Rob glanced after Casie, given how quickly she had departed after giving it to him he had a feeling he knew its worth better than he cared to admit. He placed his hand into his jerkin pocket, his fingers idly tracing the one thing he knew he could never bear to relinquish.

"It's the only thing left of her son." Rob stopped, turning to look at him. "She's sold everything to support this town. The crops failed, the water... well you saw it. I can't believe you'd quibble over a few coin."

"It's hardly a few coin." Even as he spoke Rob was overcome by the heavy sinking feeling in the pit of his stomach. He turned his sight back to the tarnished bracelet within his grasp.

"Look, I'm going to stay here for a while, help with some restoration. By the time I'm finished it'll be... well, better. I think given the time I could make a difference." Bray looked at their surroundings. This place needed a lot of work, more time than he knew he could give. But his efforts here would not be his alone, would tutor the children, who could learn to make simple repairs in his stead.

"Grayson Bray, could it be there's a hint of altruism inside that arrogant, cocky, womanising—"

"No. I just know a thing or two about trying to make it alone. If I don't stay they have months at most before disease claims them. I can get their buildings patched, clean their water, fix the well, sort out some kind of crop irrigation, and *still* be back in time to meet you at the Plexus."

"Ah, there's the heanling I know so well, the ever humble Grayson Bray." Rob chuckled to himself in good humour. "Fine. Do what you need to. Here." Rob placed the bracelet in Bray's hand having removed the only charm he sought. "I only have need for the gem."

* * *

Taya and Stacy had spent the morning helping in any way they could. When they had seen Rob and Casie engaged in early morning conversation they had decided to attend to breakfast. Taya had rummaged through their supplies, finding a large and heavy bag of oats, which she and Stacy decided would be put to better use in the bellies of the children, rather than on their own backs. Once the oats had been made and served, they helped out in other ways, keeping themselves busy by peeling spoiling vegetables, cleaning the dishes, and resetting snares.

They tried to ensure they kept out of the way of negotiations, Stacy did not trust herself to keep her opinions silent. It had been obvious how much the bracelet meant to the woman, and she found herself once again enraged with Rob's own selfishness. There was no reason for him to take it from her, but for his own greed. By the time Rob was ready to leave she had worked out most of her frustration, finding herself too exhausted to raise complaint against his actions, and her bewilderment at learning Bray would be remaining here for a short time had stilled any intended rebuttal relating to their actions.

She was looking forward to returning to Collateral. This journey had taken longer than she had hoped and her protests had fallen on deaf ears. Taya was excited to be seeing the world after believing herself confirmed to Elpída for countless turns of seasons. For no other reason than Taya's happiness Stacy decided to silence her objections and make the best of the situation. She used the time to become better acquainted with Taya. Rob had once more taken to scouting ahead, leaving the two women ample opportunity to talk.

There was only one job left of those Rob had accepted, and given how much deficit the last one had incurred for him he too was eager to see it concluded. Despite the reward offered his coin pouch would not find balance.

The Devil's Abacus was said to be a gambler's cheat. Anyone in possession of it could trade the white beads for red beads to grant them the gift of luck. It was said the abacus had once been crafted by Tyche to be bestowed upon her chosen hero. The concept being that the sum of a person's luck was measured and could be summoned by the manipulation of the beads. However, when their luck had been depleted and the red beads, representing Nemesis, were dominant, misfortune would befall them and she would collect their due.

This abacus had been passed between hero and villain alike, all twisting luck to their favour, but not understanding the importance of balance. The last known possessor had been a boy who had, by some strange fortune, happened upon it in a crevice he had sought shelter in from the harsh winter storms. Understanding both its worth and danger he used but one bead before concealing it in a place he had hoped none would find it. It was hidden so well that, for decades, it had remained concealed. Howbeit, Taya had directed them to it with ease.

It had taken them several days, and Rob had initially led them to the base of a spectacular waterfall, where Taya's marks upon the map had suggested the item would be found. The cliffs were steep, and when asked, Taya raised her arm to point to the place the cascading water fanned from. There was no means by which to scale the falls, no trail which rose to the path they must walk. Despairingly, Rob had asked how she expected them to reach it, and much to her own surprise she had known.

She led him far from the falls, to a place the waters could no longer be heard. As the sun began to sink she sat to rest upon the base of a hillock. The mound itself was covered with beautiful blooming flowers and clover, a tranquil and wondrous sight for any to behold.

As darkness descended Taya clasped her hands together, bowing her head, as if in response to her actions the clover raised their leaves pressing them together, the poppies, hibiscus, and crocuses closed their blooms becoming small against the night air. Taya stood, gesturing towards a small opening previously concealed by flowers and leaves which grew on vines, to create the illusion of solidity where none had been.

"What did you just do?" Stacy questioned in awe.

"It wasn't me. It's a part of nature, a ritual known as nyctinasty. The plants, and all things attuned with the spirits show respect in this way. I remember reading it somewhere."

"You certainly read some unusual books," Rob observed. He had never considered nature itself could work to conceal things in such a manner. In his time he had uncovered many secret walks, but nothing like this.

With great care they parted the multiple layers of sleeping plants, and descended into a small natural stone tunnel. Fireflies played near shallow brooks and the scurry of wildlife down small and hidden tunnels echoed from every direction. As they reached the passage's end they once again weaved through roots and vines emerging within a forest, protected by steep shale valley cliffs. The mountains arched overhead, creating a protective canopy. Whist the curving stones never met, they shielded the land below from the view of those unaware of its existence.

Taya led them through the trees, their path was nothing more than a trail left by all manner of animals. Delicate fragrances of evening primrose, jasmine, and moonflower filled the air. While the trees slumbered, nature's nocturnal flowers bloomed in soft shades of pinks, whites, and purples. The scene was one of radiance, and exquisite beauty.

Rob had long believed he had seen all the places of worth and wonder within his world. He had walked hidden trails and dusty paths. He had thought there was nothing left to discover and was now amazed at just how wrong he had been. This area was an untouched paradise, something explorers such as he only dreamt of discovering, and yet, he had been guided here. The magnificence of the scene was forever jaded by the ease in which its discovery came.

When they reached the outer borders Taya once again paused, extending her fingers she touched the vines upon the wall. Her gentle caress caused all the leaves, and the small pink petals within the twisted vines, to droop, and the sound of a waterfall beyond its wall grew louder. She gently reached through into a small crevice. When her hand retracted it was holding an object wrapped in cloth.

"Touch-me-nots," Taya explained in response to Stacy's bewildered look. Behind her the leaves and blooms were once more beginning to open.

Rob had looked upon it with great consideration before lifting it from her grasp. As the abacus left her possession she raised her hands to her temples, surveying her surroundings as if in a daze. Rob said nothing, he simply led them back the way they came.

On the return to Collateral Taya sensed a further shift in Rob's temperament. He remained distant, and whilst he should have been celebrating another successful acquisition he, instead, seemed strangely disheartened and unfulfilled.

"What's wrong?" Taya questioned drawing level with him to link her arm in his. She noticed he startled slightly at her touch before pulling his arm away in the pretence of adjusting his cloak. "Shouldn't you be happy?"

"I suppose, but it all seemed a little too easy," he admitted. The tasks they had completed, whilst worth varying amounts of coin, would be considered great accomplishments. He had seen items of myth brought to life, and discovered a hidden oasis of natural splendour. The retrieving of artefacts with such lore and legend were told by epic tales of hardship and trials. They were stories of the wit, intellect, and luck that saw the hero succeed, where countless before had failed. They were not supposed to be tales of scryers and a path without challenge and strife.

"Perhaps that's because you don't normally have a location handed to you," Stacy interjected knowingly, her voice still disapproving. "Quite simply, you cheated." Rob, as much as he wanted to, could not argue. Normally he invested great amounts of time to research. He followed clues, myths, and even coerced information from those with knowledge. He would create compendiums of facts and fiction to be studied and investigated. He worked diligently and, if he was successful, he knew he had earned each moment of recognition his deeds afforded. But this time it was different. The thrill of a successful hunt was lacking.

Stacy was right, using Taya as he had robbed him of the joy, and there was so little in this world still capable of invoking such feelings, and as fleeting as the emotion could be, he craved it. He would, however, use her once more. He still had one treasure to retrieve, and exploiting her to these ends would be more rewarding than any of his past escapades. When The Seed of Nzin was within his grasp he would want for nothing.

"We'll rest in Collateral tonight," Rob stated changing the topic rather than admitting Stacy was correct. "Bray should meet with us tomorrow."

"Oh heavenly delights! I must have accidentally acquired a charm that renders me completely invisible!" Bray exclaimed, extending his hands dramatically. "Oh imagine the..." he looked up in a display of mock astonishment as they all turned their sight towards him. He stood at their flank, a playful glimmer in his eyes. "Alas, it must have expired." He gave a heavy sigh before shrugging. Not one of them had noticed when Bray had joined them. "I must say, ignoring me for the better part of a mile was rather rude."

"Ah, if only you were more memorable. I guess we forgot you were with us." Stacy shrugged, her arm linking Taya's gently as they continued walking leaving Rob and Bray behind.

"Now that's just hurtful," Bray sulked, quickening his pace as his comrades continued to walk. He drew alongside Rob. Their shoulders touched as he leaned in to say something. Rob raised his hand before he could speak.

"I've seen them too," he whispered softly. For some time now Rob had been aware of the movements in the shadows and their distant surveillance. He had made minor adjustments to their route, ensuring they remained clear of any terrain where an ambush could be employed. He knew they were exposed, vulnerable, and possessed no means to defend themselves should their pursuers advance. Yet despite their advantage they remained concealed, silently observing, never acting, giving Rob cause to believe they were being followed for an entirely different reason. "Have you really been with us for the last mile?"

"Further, I picked up your trail just after you got the abacus, but I was keeping vigil on our friends. I'm unclear of their intentions."

* * *

The hustle and bustle within Collateral had come as a welcome reprieve to the strained silence which had accompanied the last few miles of their journey. Even Bray had conformed to the weight of Rob's sombre mood. When they reached the market square, close to the Plexus, Stacy hesitated. It had been some time since she had last relayed a message to Amelia, and much had come to pass. Amelia's insistence that she only used the Herald service in Collateral had only served to complicate matters. Privacy had been a concern given the contents of their communications, and only those within

427

this city were afforded her unquestioning trust. After a moment of deliberation she advised them to continue without her, and that she would reconvene with them later at the inn.

As Rob entered the Plexus he was unable to force the smile which normally so naturally appeared when completing his tasks. With a slight sigh he placed the three parchments beside each other on the counter. Barnett, having no doubt heard of Rob's prior exchange with Asher, chuckled slightly peering over his spectacles at him. Shaking his head in slight amusement he noticed the hunter carefully placing items upon each of the parchments, and given his solemn mood decided not to make idle conversation. This hunter seemed strangely melancholy, especially given the completion of three requests. Barnett looked to the parchments again, scanning the directives. His eyes widened in disbelief before narrowing objectively to examine each of the three items. If genuine, it seemed this man had done, in less than a month, what many had failed to do in years.

Barnett removed the first two items, Medusa's tongue and the Devil's abacus. Deliberately leaving the third on the counter. He excused himself for a moment, returning from the rear rooms within minutes to produce payment.

"Are you sure you want to complete this one?" he enquired, subtly pushing the parchment back towards Rob.

"Of course." Rob placed his finger on the paper, pushing it back his lips curling slightly in a strained smile.

"You're claiming this to be the Darkmore crystal?" Barnett picked up the small charm studying it carefully. He shook his head slightly at the trinket. The small stone had been poorly cast in silver, he had seen many similar items for sale, spread across small trays in curiosity counters. But even compared to those, this one seemed poorly crafted, as if made by uncertain hands.

"I'm not claiming anything."

"It's smaller than I expected. Are you sure—"

"Just go and validate it." Rob sighed in frustration. "If it isn't—"

"Yes, yes, I know, dishonour, fines, and wrath." He raised his hands, gesturing Barnett away.

"It'll take an hour, there are several tests we'll need to perform to confirm its authenticity." He looked to the item once more. "We'll have to remove the casting."

"I'll wait," Rob shrugged. As he watched Barnett disappear once more into the rear area his stomach lurched. If he was mistaken he would lose his ranking, there was no question that the harm this could do to his reputation would not be salvageable. He looked to Taya, she had led him with ease to each. His nerves calmed as she smiled sweetly, surely there could be no question to its authenticity.

"Uncle Rob, since it's going to be a while, might I practice my marksmanship?" Taya asked warmly as she saw him look to her.

"Sure. Bray, you go with her. We'll meet back at the inn." Rob's meaning was clear, he was uncertain of the danger if she were to be left alone.

Bray followed Taya from the Plexus, his nostrils flaring as he caught a heavenly scent from the bowyer.

Taya failed to notice Bray's absence. She had been casting cautious glances in his direction since arriving, but soon was so engrossed in her practice that when he slipped away, arm-in-arm, with the middle-aged bowyer it went unnoticed. The drawing and nocking of arrows quickly became a smooth motion. Her arm grew sore, the darkening bruise caused by her improper positioning remained concealed by the lightweight wrap she wore over her clothes. Each time the bow string grazed her she flinched, but slowly adjusted her positioning until the stance was almost perfect. Time passed quickly. Her confidence grew, and her arrow struck the target more often than not.

"Let us depart." Bray's voice startled her as she was pulling the final arrow from its position just left of its intended mark. Bray peered over her shoulder as she returned the arrow to her quiver, disappointed to find the straw concealed any evidence of where her shots had landed. Her expression, however, told him she was pleased.

Everywhere Taya looked were crowds of people who seemed to fill the busy and towering metropolis to capacity. The tall buildings stood like giants, looming intimidatingly overhead, and the individual sounds of chatter faded into a single roar of noise. Taya walked cautiously, questioning if she was even heading in the correct direction. People shoved and bustled past, bumping into her with little to no regard. She stumbled into Bray, losing her balance as a brutish figure shoved her unceremoniously from his path, and continued without so much as a glance behind him, treating all before him with the same disregard. She pulled herself from Bray's grasp, thanking him as she lowered her head slightly, seeming to retreat into herself.

"Do you know the way?" Taya asked uncertainly, now feeling intimidated and overwhelmed by their busy surroundings. She rubbed her side where the figure had struck her as she watched the darkened streets cautiously.

"Don't let that unmannerly fleck bother you," Bray stated staring after the foul tempered noble. "I know him. His birth was actually recorded in the form of an apology." Taya smiled slightly, remaining close to Bray as he guided them towards the inn, it almost seemed as if the crowds now parted before them.

Rob rose as they entered the room. Taya hurried across to Stacy to converse in lowered tones.

"How'd she do?" Rob asked, as Taya excused herself to the bathroom to prepare for bed. It was only now he realised how late the hour had grown. A quick glance towards the windows confirmed the sky had long grown dark.

"A natural."

"So, I'm guessing returning the bow is out of the question?" Rob said with a gentle smile. He moved to take a seat at the table, kicking the opposite chair out with his leg as an invitation for Bray to join him.

"She's better in a position where she could defend herself. Did you doubt her skill, she's Daimon after all."

"And that makes a difference?" he questioned as Bray sat.

"It should. They're trained in defence and weaponry as basic education. She'd have been holding a bow, dagger, maybe even a sword since she was coordinated enough to wield them." Bray, produced a bottle of strange green liquid from inside his coat and filled their two glasses. Rob glanced up briefly before turning his focus to the rolled out map before him. Even now he could feel the nervous fluttering of his stomach. Tomorrow would mark the day of the full moon, and the quarry he had dedicated himself to acquiring would be within his grasp. Glancing towards Taya, who was sharing her bed with Stacy, he wondered if this acquisition would be as easy as the others. He drained his glass. The potent fluid burned his throat causing his eyes to tear as Bray suppressed a slight chuckle.

"Do you think they're still tracking us?" Rob questioned before securing his parchment. He hadn't observed the small group since they had entered Collateral, but there was no reason to think they had not been followed here.

"The streets were crowded, but I can't say I've noticed anything untoward. It could be they can't reach this city," Bray replied. Hearing a short hiss from Stacy, as she warned them to be quiet, he lowered his voice to a whisper. "We should remain vigilant and, if need be, grasp the nettle when the time comes."

Chapter 14

Sacrifice

The Cartographer of Collateral had once had his services sought tirelessly. More often than not, before the first hint of morning appeared on the horizon, he was awoken by the low conversations of those gathered outside his home in search of direction.

He lived on the outskirts of the residential area, bordering the farmlands. The militia often patrolled, encouraging any loiterers before dawn to be on their way. But even despite this, the man knew little peace. He had dedicated his life, as had those preceding him in his family, to the exploration and recording of where each portal in Collateral could be located, and where they led. He was thought to be the only person to hold such wisdom.

There had been rumours that his family, for generations, had been born somehow connected to the city, that they knew when new portals arose and when those once working failed. His ancestral name had once been uttered alongside powerful mages, and it was often theorised that his lineage still possessed some innate abilities. He was a family man, and longed for those sheltered moments of peace where he would close his doors and relish in privacy, no matter how short lived. There were times he accepted only emergency requests, but adventurers had differing theories on what an emergency actually entailed.

Eventually, he had commissioned one of the board-wrights to fashion a case for the main, central cross-roads. Inside he had secured a map detailing many of the portals and the coordinates of their exits. Of course, not all his secrets were written upon its surface, there were some too dangerous to reveal. Those seeking such a path were permitted to request an audience with him. He would sit in judgement of them, measuring their worthiness to access the lands concealed, and discern if the portals his family protected should be revealed. They could not be accessed without his presence. Few passed his scrutiny.

Additional maps had been sold to the taverns and were often found hanging behind the bar or mounted upon a table and shielded with glass. Thus this man, once plagued by request day and night for as long as his door was open, could dedicate his time to his wife as they entered their golden years.

Rob, familiar with this map, had found a portal which brought them close to their intended destination. They emerged upon the barren sands of a wasteland. This desert, however, had not been formed by the sun's blistering rays, and no life thrived there.

Tall orchards of petrified trees littered the surroundings. Their dark forms the only variation from the nearly white sands. Behind them, masking the horizon, a huge sandstorm raged ceaselessly. It was one of the world's unexplained marvels, and those digging deep enough into the history of this land would discover a tale of magic and woe.

Taya rubbed her temples as a dull ache began. She was unfamiliar with these surroundings, yet something within seemed to call to her, welcoming her.

"Uncle, where are we?" she questioned, shielding her eyes from the sand carried upon the wind, despite having their backs to the distant sandstorm strong winds still chased across the land.

"The Forgotten Plains. But we don't need to go too far," he assured. By his calculations, even fighting against the winds, they would reach their destination within the hour. Shielding his eyes Rob looked up towards the sun in a purely suggestive gesture, allowing him to track the progress of the small group following them. Bray had detected their presence not long after emerging from Collateral, but the exposure of the plains was unforgiving to covert actions, meaning the small group had been given no choice but to attempt to track them using the natural cover of the bordering mountain range. Bray gave him a gentle nudge, inclining his head slightly towards the flicker of movement Rob had not yet perceived, and whispered something in lowered tones.

"Huh, that's... unusual." Taya abruptly stopped, wiping her hands down her face. She drank deeply from the leather skin before focusing ahead of them once more. It was still there. Several paces ahead of them stood what appeared to be a solitary sinkhole within the desert. Sand blew over its surface, never resting upon or falling within. She took a few more steps, aware now of the questioning glances from her friends. The closer she became, the more form and substance this hole seemed to possess. She could see dark chiselled stones, creating large uneven steps, descending into the darkness below, they were free from any sand and dust she would have expected the winds to deposit. Even the sand remained steadfast, never spilling into the opening below.

"What's wrong?" Rob glanced around. The sun's position had not long past the meridian and, whilst the shade offered from the cliffs had completely receded, the temperatures were not excessively hot. Disguised by the cool winds, both sand and sun had burnt their faces but not enough to cause discomfort. Taya rubbed her temples. The dull ache she had been experiencing since their arrival had been growing more intense with each step. She reached out for support as a wave of nausea enveloped her. Waves of heat rippled across her flesh, darkening patches of her sight. She sank to her knees, vomiting violently onto the sands and gestured, through heaving gasps, towards the anomaly they seemed oblivious to.

"I'm fine. Truly." She glanced sideways, letting out a sobbing breath as the strange image remained. "I'm sorry. I'm so sorry," she whispered. "I thought I was better." Hearing this Bray crouched beside her, placing his hand gently upon her shoulder. Seeing the stairway beside her he adjusted his position rapidly. Helping her to her feet he whispered soft words of comfort. Closing her eyes she leaned into him, the pain and confusion receding as feelings of calm serenity enveloped her. She turned within his grasp, sliding her hands up to his shoulders as she held herself against him knowing he was safety. She could trust him completely, she would do anything he asked. She raised herself to her tiptoes, placing her hands upon his face.

Bray moistened his lips breathing in the delicate aroma of the woman before him. He lowered his head, brushing aside her hair as he drew his lips level with her ear.

"Escort us inside," he whispered, lingering a moment longer, savouring the scent of apples and cinnamon. Taya nodded, releasing him with one of her hands to gesture above the ground. Rob and Stacy watched in awe as the land before them altered instantly, revealing the staircase in the sand.

"I thought we couldn't enter until nightfall." Rob glanced skyward, the sun was still many hours from setting.

"It is the day of the full moon, and Taya can enter The Stepping Realm whenever she pleases. It just so happens, we can accompany her." Taya looked up to Bray almost hesitantly as they stood before the dark and descending stairway. The familiar wave of comfort washed over her. He leaned closer. His cool breath tickled her ear, sending goose pimples chasing across her flesh. "Take us through," he whispered, a little more forcefully than before.

* * *

"Damn it!" One of the men cursed as their feet met with solid ground at the place they had moments ago seen their target vanish. They had been given a very specific set of instructions; no one was to see them claim their prize.

They had hunted them for too long now to give up, but their passing into the Daimons' realm before the hour permitted was not something they had anticipated. There was no choice now but to wait for the sun to set. Pursuing them into The Depths of Acheron was less than ideal, but their employer had stated that the retrieval had to be completed today, without fail.

There had been ample opportunity to act. They had skulked in the shadows, following them through forest and plain, busy streets and deserted alleys, for a very long time indeed. Watching their movements, reporting back, all the time being instructed to remain vigilant. There had been times when their target had been alone, and still they had been told to wait, to observe. Today, they had been instructed otherwise.

* * *

Rob, producing his flint box, skillfully lit one of the wooden tapers and held it to ignite his lantern. Using its pale glow he made a quick assessment of their surroundings. Despite knowing there was daylight above them the seal remained dark, absorbing any light.

In Rob's experience, the entrances to The Depths of Acheron, more often than not, were of similar design. There seemed to be only the occasional instances where a portal had delivered him directly into open areas, vistas, or ruins. Typically there were sections he referred to as areas of transition, be they waterways or large stone corridors they led the traveller to the true Depths. There was rarely any warning of what would await once the area of transition had been traversed, and this was no different.

Grey stone walls surrounded them, the weathering upon the surface more indicative of a natural design than a skilled hand. He traced his fingers down the stone's rough grain noticing the fine powdery residue left upon his skin when he pulled away. The corridor's floor consisted of the wall's dust and darker, compacted earth.

"I never imagined I'd walk The Depths in the daylight," Rob acknowledged, briefly glancing to Taya. Bray released her, still talking in softer tones.

"I imagine those following us didn't believe we would be either." Bray flashed Stacy a quick smile. She regarded him cautiously before turning her focus to the area they had entered through.

"We were being pursued, why didn't you say something?" she questioned sternly.

"It was better you acted as naturally as possible. We still don't know their motives, but I can't see anyone risking a journey here, regardless of the compensation. Well, except him." Bray gestured over his shoulder towards Rob. "I could think of worse places to be trapped." A half smile traced his features, appearing almost sinister in the yellow hue of the lantern's light. "Just me and two beautiful women, lost in The Depths, clinging to each other desper—ouch!"

"Oops, sorry." Stacy feigned an apology as Bray retreated slightly to remove his foot from beneath hers.

"Stop acting like children," Rob scolded. "Let's get moving, we've things to do, or have you forgotten our purpose here? I'll lead, Bray, you can take the rear." Rob sighed, shaking his head as he saw Bray grinning. "Honestly?"

Rob led them carefully, his lantern extended before him to guide their path. He knew whilst they had managed to bypass the rules of entry, doing so brought with it further danger. Bray strolled casually behind them, knowing that most of the creatures here were not only nocturnal, but knew to fear the Daimons. With Taya amongst them it was unlikely they would encounter any *real* difficulties. "Stay close, these places are often notorious for traps."

They proceeded with guarded steps. Stacy turned to frown at Bray as his hand brushed against her, or his foot caught her heel. Each glare met with a shrug, an impish smile appearing on his lips the moment she turned away.

Taya bumped into Rob as his pace unexpectedly halted. The corridor before them opened into a small square room. He gestured to Bray, who handed him one of the torches he carried. Each of them had been given two, along with a flint and tinder box in case they should get separated. Rob dimmed his lantern, passing it to Taya as he lit the oil-soaked rag wrapped around the torches' tip. The roar of the flames were the only sound as he passed the light across the floor in front of them, before raising it to look further afield. He fumbled in his pocket, pulling out a piece of white chalk before he entered the room. Signalling for them to remain still. Once every nook and cranny had been searched, he gestured for them to enter.

There was but one exit from this room, and Rob knew from experience that once they passed through they would truly be within The Depths of Acheron. In the centre of the room he drew a large arrow with the chalk, pointing in the direction they would be heading. He always left such markers, they were one of the reasons he never found himself lost.

"Does anyone need to rest?" he questioned, aware their pace had been brisk and continuous since they had first left Collateral. Normally once entering this domain he would not rest until the request was completed, but today he had a safeguard. Time was not the enemy as long as they had Taya. Both Taya and Stacy shook their heads as Rob looked to them in turn, his gaze passing over Bray without concern.

"Oh sure, don't ask me," Bray complained in a martyred tone, trying to bring a lightness to the heavy mood. Neither of the women, whose faces were weighted with concern, smiled.

"Bray, I'm sure if *you* wanted to rest, we'd already be sitting." Bray lifted his shoulders in a slight, acknowledging shrug. "Then we proceed with caution," Rob warned. He stepped through the darkened opening and abruptly stopped.

They had emerged on a narrow ledge, high within a multi-layered chasm. Its sheer size was difficult to comprehend, as was its complexities. Several feet below, mushrooms, reminiscent in shape of those Rob knew as Dryad's Saddles, lined the almost wooden textured walls. The cream mushrooms were larger than any he had ever before witnessed, their brown scaled markings alone appeared to be wider than anyone in his group. These enormous fungi lined the walls, to create a descending pathway to the landmass below. There were several such fragmented lands, some seeming to be formed from the wooden textured walls, others appearing to have grown upwards from the unseen world below. Small luminescent areas littered the fog-shrouded islands, the light reminding Rob of some of the more familiar fungi he had seen within The Depths. It was by these gathering of lights alone the scope of the area could be visualised.

Rob extended his arm before Taya, noticing the almost invisible bridges of vine linking the separated lands. Dropping his torch he rolled it in the dirt until the flame was smothered. He was not foolish enough to believe these lands were uninhabited. There seemed to be something precise about the groupings of light, reminding him of small villages seen across a plain.

At the very heart of the extensive circular cavern was an unusual sight. Extending upwards was an enormous cylindrical platform. It stretched from the darkness below. Its knotty and gnarled bark suggestive of it once being the trunk to a glorious and unearthly tree. There were no branches now, no foliage or signs of such life. The manner in which the level platform at its peak had been formed spoke of deliberate craftsmanship.

From their vantage point Rob could just discern a dark blemish near its centre. He knew, without a doubt, that was the place they sought. The darkness was an entrance into something he knew he could not even imagine. The Seed of Nzin would be found within. Where better to contain a seed than within the heart of an ancient tree?

"What are you thinking?" Bray moved to stand beside Rob, critically surveying the area. Rob's features hardened as he adjusted his jerkin slightly.

"I say we improvise," he responded in all seriousness. "If I've learnt one thing about The Depths it's that procrastination will get you killed." With those words, and a slight fluttering of anticipation tightening his stomach, Rob turned and lowered himself from the ledge onto the first mushroom.

* * *

He watched her talking with Aidan through the eyes of his Epiales. Their union had been something he had not anticipated when carefully orchestrating the abduction. A more fortuitous outcome could not have been expected. He had been contemplating how to breach The Stepping Realm to the lands of the divine, but the capture of a god was beyond his means. She, however, bore the curse of one and her longevity was tied to Kronos, albeit discretely, but it was a manner he could exploit for his purpose.

For too long had he been bound here. Cycles upon end sealed from The Stepping Realm and confined to the Forest of the Epiales which dwelt within but a fragment of The Betwixt. His banishment was a twisted reward for doing what the gods of old had once asked of him. He had sacrificed all, and in the end had been cursed to become the forest's master, and all methods of leaving had been denied to him. The long-fallen deities had given him a purpose, ensuring it would remain an obsession regardless of time's passage. Even now, despite the rise and fall of gods beyond count, he craved to satisfy their will. His masters had long fallen, their powers lost to The Star of Arshad, but he lived, and as long as he did, so did the desire to complete his task.

He created his own domain within the forest, but it was not enough to sustain him. The Perpetual forest—or the Forest of the Epiales as it was known in Darrienia—had once been a thoroughfare, a place where beings from one realm could visit those of another. But his imprisonment within had given it a new purpose, and he had twisted it to his needs. He found just as he could tempt humans, he could also send his Epiales to bring dreamers to him. But he himself could never leave.

He had not always been confined in this manner. Once he had walked amongst the divine. He had been their hunter, their arbitrator of deeds. His actions were as noble as his esteemed position, and he had been promised the hand of Lavender, elevating him to a position of prestige and power as the chosen son of the one who ruled all. Many had sought her hand, for she was as powerful as she was beautiful. When she had discovered her father's intention to present her to the one he deemed had most to offer, she had fled, forcing herself into a mortal incarnation to be born to Gaea's star. As her betrothed, and the enforcer of divine laws, he had been the one to pursue. But the Gods had insisted he too would need to be reborn mortal to complete his task. For only a god born of flesh could hope to apprehend and return her divine gifts.

They gave his forming embryo a blessing, allowing him to retain knowledge of his appointed task, ensuring it became the cornerstone of his existence. Everything he would do as a mortal would be to bring him closer to returning Lavender's powers. His mortal parents had named him Íkelos. Had they possessed an aptitude for the arcane they would have known to fear their child, for he possessed the ability to sever magic and claim it for his own.

Those opposing Lavender's father, and his decision to return only his daughter's divine powers, rebelled. In secret they crafted a new soul, one who would be invisibly tethered to that of the mortal Lavender. It would die and be reborn in cycle with hers.

The soul of a god, once born as mortal, could never find rest in the underworld, it could only be reborn in unending incarnations. Íkelos had not known of this deception, believing he would regain his divine status, but he soon discovered their betrayal. He gathered magic and power, growing stronger, more formidable, as he searched for his missing bride. He knew she was being protected, and sought to ensure those within the world had no choice but to present her to him, or perish. He had thought no one would dare stand against him. Yet someone had.

Íkelos' arrogance had been his downfall. He believed that even should he meet with failure he, like Lavender, would be reborn. But the gods had been cunning, ensuring the soul they had created to protect her possessed the means to sever his ties to The Stepping Realm, and banish him to the one place they thought could restrain him, The Perpetual Forest.

But instead he had twisted this forest to his will and nightmares were born.

The trees became his servants, sustaining him with the magic they drew from others imprisoned within. He corrupted their essences, giving rise to the Epiales and discovered these servants, whilst like him were unable to breach the waking world, could use The Stepping Realm to gain access to Darrienia. The Oneirois were forced to create a divide between light and darkness, protecting their kind and the dreamers as much as possible. They named him the Melas-

Oneiros, for he had tainted the sanctity of dreams with darkness and became the bringer of nightmares.

He had grown in power since the beginning, and still he had not managed to enter The Stepping Realm. But all things change, and old magic was dying. Each of the gods had their own affinity. The primal deities, those who were the founders of life and still lived, such as Nyx and Chaos, had utilised Grand Planetary Magic. But their children, and those born of other gods all found their own source. Some used elements, others channelled power from the underworld and the souls of the dead or living. The forms of magic were varied, and when he had been sealed here they had used a very specific invocation, one which bound him by all the magic that was and would ever be. But most of the magic that was, no longer existed. With the release of the Severaine and the return of the Spiritwest the last traces of this ancient restraining power had vanished, weakening the hold upon him.

Magic was faltering, a shadow of that which it had once been and things once believed impossible now threatened the distant future. He just needed to ensure things remained on their current course. When events turned to his favour he could call upon his prisoners, using their essence to force open the doors to their respective realms. But their essence alone would not be enough to ensure he could make the step. He would need power, and they were the means to discovering what the worlds still had to offer to suit his needs.

Elly's presence had been an unexpected fortune. In the waking world she was protected by Night, but here she was vulnerable. If he could concentrate his efforts on her, then it was possible he would have no cause to seek inhabitants of the other realms. In her current condition she could be the key to them all, she was a divine, mortal-dreamer, who bore the rune of boundaries.

* * *

The climb down the mushrooms to the humid terrain below had been made more difficult by Rob's constant impatience. Every slight delay or hesitation had been met with a frustrated sigh. Why they had insisted on accompanying him this far was unknown. He had explained that he could proceed alone. He was familiar with the dangers and used to operating at a far quicker pace than was possible with their company. Of course, there remained the distinct possibility that Taya's presence would be of further use, as Bray had argued when Rob had broached the topic of parting ways.

Taya grasped his arm, steadying herself as her boots met with the soft boggy terrain of the land. Before them stretched a forest of mushrooms. Giant Morel provided eerie shelters to things unseen, whilst the flat tops of honey fungus clusters provided predatory ledges and vistas, perfect for concealing an ambush. The types of mushroom were as varied as their forms, from Horns of Plenty, whose gaping mouths collected water from the terrain in their hollow stems, to the strange and unnerving shades of the tall amethyst deceivers. Bioluminescent lights reflected from the forest's dark and humid mists to cast unnerving illumination and shadows to accompany the echoing, damp dripping sounds of the world around them. Nature here had its own order, its own thoughts and design.

Muffled and distant shuffling sounds caused Rob to raise his hand, gesturing a complete halt to all movement. With his hand suspended in mid-air he concentrated on listening, to hearing the sounds previously disguised within the natural environment. He heard it again, the damp, padded footfall of something growing closer, its movements cushioned by fog and terrain. He rolled his shoulders, glancing from left to right before committing to a decision. Grasping Taya's hand he led them towards a dense area of honey fungi, impatiently pushing her upward onto the lowest platform before promptly following her, spurring her onward and upward leaving Bray and Stacy to follow behind.

The heavy earthy smell of the terrain seemed less overpowering from their altitude, and the small group took a moment to rest. Rob approached Bray, who stood sentry, surveying their surroundings.

"I have to say travelling with you is all manner of mirths." Bray jerked his head towards the distant illumination. Beyond the forest lay the vine bridge to the heart of the chasm. The area before it was filled with cep mushrooms, small illuminations from within the thick structures betrayed the signs of life Rob had feared would be present. In the centre of, what they assumed to be, the village were several cage mushrooms housing unusual and unfamiliar wild beasts. "Let me guess," Bray whispered before Rob could speak. "We improvise."

"We need only make it to the other side of the vine. Every island here has similar vine-ways connecting them so we can always find an alternate route back, but severing this bridge once we're across would delay their pursuit."

"And you think you can guide us through that?" Bray stuck his thumb out towards their destination.

"I've not seen its likes before, but I have more reason than any to succeed."

"That only serves to make you just as dangerous as the things down there," Bray muttered, his brows knitting together as he watched the small village gradually becoming more animated. "Whatever we're going to do, we better do it soon. I'd say the sun is near to setting." Bray glanced towards Taya, her dark hair glistened with water droplets as she spoke in lowered tones with Stacy. He forced the corners of his mouth to turn upward in a slight smile as the two women looked in his direction. He heard Stacy give a sharp snort, her head shaking disapprovingly as their eyes met.

"We'll stick to the border, we can't risk being noticed. When we reach the bridge there will be no shelter, so we're going to have to keep moving." Rob announced, gesturing Stacy and Taya to their feet. "Ethelyn, you stick with me, Bray—"

"Got it, I'll cover the flank." Stacy's shoulder jostled against his as she walked past, leaving him questioning what he had done this time to earn her wrath.

Once they had descended the mushrooms Rob led the way, his hand in constant contact with Taya. From their closer vantage point he had seen the shimmer indicative of a seal, since this was her people's treasure it made sense he would need her to open the path. Bray fell into step beside Stacy casting furtive glances in her direction.

"What?" she hissed, glancing to him through the corner of her eye, trying to ensure Taya remained in sight.

"That's precisely what I wanted to ask you," he whispered in an equally lowered tone. "Since we've arrived here you've been nothing short of an ass."

"I'm the ass?" Stacy seethed. "I'm not the one dragging Taya down here on the pretence of restoring her. The only thing I have witnessed since arriving is her exploitation. First the jobs for the Plexus, and now this? You men are real jackasses, you know that don't you? She's not your own personal dowsing rod," Stacy fumed, her features hardening as she blanched, her concerned gaze lingered over Bray's shoulder. He closed his eyes, realising how loud Stacy's words had become. He barely dared to breathe, he didn't want to look. He turned slowly, hearing the rustle of hurried footfalls as he saw the flashes of rapid movements within the shadows.

"Run!" he yelled, Rob pushed Taya before him, thrusting her forwards in the direction of the bridge. Concealed shapes and figures swarmed from the shadows, snarls and growls filled the air. The creatures were on their heels almost instantly. Small hatchets whistled through the air narrowly missing their targets as Bray thrust Stacy one way, then the other as he half dragged her along beside him.

Rob had reached the bridge and, crouching slightly, he hoisted Taya over his shoulders, one arm wrapped around her thighs, the other holding her arm as he began to run across the unstable walkway. It was nothing more than a thick weave of vine, with a finer one running nearly parallel. He kept his gaze focused on the vine at his feet, trying to ignore the bottomless pit of darkness beneath.

Bray staggered as he felt the burning pain of a hatchet deep within his shoulder blade. Stacy glanced back, aware that his sudden movement had been an attempt to shield her as she started across the precarious bridge. She clung desperately to the parallel vine, her body swinging wildly as she fought for balance. Rob had nearly reached the centre island now, and Bray, having shielded her from several attacks was only now joining her on the bridge. Arrows sailed past, hatchets dug deep into the thick vines behind her, she dared not turn her gaze to see how Bray fared, she could only focus on placing one foot in front of the other.

Bray yelled a warning as a hatchet struck the thinner vine. The taut sound of its rupture causing his heart to beat rapidly, his breathing hitched as he watched Stacy fighting for balance. She slipped, her hands clinging desperately to the remaining vine as she wrapped her legs around it. Panic washed over her as she saw the creatures. Her pale face glistened with fear and sweat, but slowly, she began to pull herself along, deaf to the encouraging cries from Taya as she pleaded them to keep moving. Bray walked backwards, light-footed, gripping a section of the loose vine within his hand, he swung it wildly in an attempt to throw their pursuers off balance. His left arm hung unresponsively at his side and he felt the numbness caused by the latest arrow spreading through his legs, making his movements heavier, less graceful, and unbalanced.

Glancing behind him Bray saw Rob and Taya seizing Stacy to pull her to the safety of the island. A place still so far from his position. Reaching behind him he grasped the handle of the hatchet, the warmth of blood erupted from the wound, soaking his back to mingle with his sweat.

"Rob," his voice reflected the weight of his thoughts. He stepped back, his footing slipping on the blood from his wound. He turned to face his friends, looking upon them knowingly with the hatchet clutched tightly in his hand. His focus turned to the vine at his feet.

"Don't even think about it!" Rob growled in a tone that carried the threat and warning of thunder itself. He watched as Bray lifted the hatchet striking the vine. "Don't you dare!" Rob demanded as Bray struggled to free the hatchet before bringing it around for a second strike. The air above him grew darker, filled with arrows.

Stacy reached out, pulling the short-sword from Rob's belt. Tears flooded her eyes as Bray faltered, the force of the arrows peppering his flesh caused his balance to fail. She could only watch as he was lost, swallowed by the darkness below. She swung the weapon, the sharp blade singing through the air as it sliced the vine with ease. She turned from the canyon, unable to bear witness to the death her own actions would bring.

* * *

"Damn it Bray!" Rob cursed through clenched teeth watching helplessly as his friend's figure plummeted from sight. He froze, unable to think, unable to act, watching as the darkened forms continued their advance across the partially severed bridge. He willed himself to move, to encourage the two women to safety, yet simply stood, staring at the place he had last seen Bray. His hand fell to his hilt as his mind returned to the severity of the situation. Feeling its absence he glanced around in alarm to see his weapon clutched within Stacy's hand as the bridge collapsed.

"Psáltis," Rob spoke her name in acknowledgement of her actions. She turned towards him with a hateful glare moving to hold Taya close to her. Stacy's body was rigid with rage, her eyes burning with the tears she refused to shed and the blame she so willingly placed upon him. "We'll raise a glass in his honour when we leave, but now is not the time. It won't be long before those things pick up our trail. There's more than one place to cross. There will be time enough to grieve when we have completed our task. Let's not waste the gift he gave." Stacy's eyes narrowed further, her lips parting ready to unleash her venomous comment. Instead she pulled Taya closer, prying her gaze from Rob to her. "Taya, I'll need your help here." Rob spoke softly, placing a firm hand upon her shoulder. She turned from Stacy, burying herself in her uncle's chest for a moment, seeking his comfort. He held her briefly, pushing aside and repressing all the forced feelings of love and sympathy for the stranger in his arms, reminding himself their relationship was nothing more than tales weaved from malicious intentions.

A moment of regret filtered through as he cast his gaze backwards. Bray had been certain bringing Taya here would have allowed him to restore her, but Rob had insisted they first retrieve The Seed of Nzin. His thoughts returned to his prize, his spirits lifted, casting aside the familiar self-vilification. Everything he was doing was for a greater purpose, obtaining this treasure would mark the start of his redemption.

"I can't," Taya whispered as Rob guided her to the large opening in the very centre of the island. Even from a distance he could feel the aura of magic surrounding it. A barrier or seal of some description barred their path. Taya lowered her gaze, seeing the thick beautiful rings which created the ground. It reminded her of the age rings within a tree. Nausea built within her, cool sweat trickled down her already damp flesh. Feeling her fear Stacy's arm once more wrapped around her.

"Ethelyn," Rob breathed through a shallow sigh, not looking back from the darkened pit. "It's simple, trust me, okay?" His shoulders stiffened as he turned back to meet her gaze. "Come, you need only touch it." He extended his hand.

Taya slid her hand into his, allowing him to guide it towards the unseen seal. The ground creaked and groaned as her flesh met with the invisible barrier and dispelled it. Below, sounds of echoing, grinding movement could be heard. Lighting a torch Rob looked down, his vision barely able to discern the large wooden cogs that rotated before their view was concealed by the emerging floors. At the base of the island something slowly began to emerge. Rob dashed to the edge, watching carefully, his mind trying to make sense of the strange motions and movements and the effects upon the structure on which they stood. The gears halted suddenly, reversing their path and the island lurched, dropping several feet. Taya reached out, pulling Rob from the edge.

"It's a giant lock?" Rob pondered, his mind racing. He knew The Seed of Nzin must be near the base. With each passing moment, on the outside of the island, large smooth pillars continued to emerge horizontally. He was almost certain for each one that fully extended the island would drop lower until the path to The Seed was sealed. He rushed back towards the central opening, his frantic gaze observing and contemplating each movement below. Pressure built within his mind. He knew they could not allow this strange and complex lock to seal before he had claimed his treasure.

A ripple of movement from below drew his attention. Wooden beams extended and contracted forming a precariously moving staircase coiling below. Grabbing Taya, and casting a backwards glance towards Stacy, he stood watching for a moment, counting.

"On my mark." With a firm nod he dropped, pulling Taya with him to land on the retracting ledge beneath the opening. Stacy followed, landing beside him. He moved quickly, guiding the way for the two ladies who followed close at his heels. The movements of the pathways were slower and easier to navigate than any of them had anticipated.

They traversed broken and splintered beams, barely slowing their pace until their feet met with the wooden floorboards of the solid floor below. Rob glanced up, marvelling at the sheer distance they had already descended. Narrowing his eyes he turned his attention to their surroundings, feeling the slight vibrations from underfoot. He surveyed the room, his sight falling upon a large silver crystal which reflected the entire room with perfect symmetry. Taya grasped his bicep sharply, pulling against him to prevent his advance towards the seemingly out-of-place object. Rob turned to her questioningly, his posture stiffening as he saw the movement of her eyes as they followed something within the reflective surface.

"Taya?" Stacy questioned.

"What do you see?" Rob asked. Taya glanced behind them before turning her focus once more to the crystal.

"It's moving," she whispered, watching the movements of the boards beneath their feet as they altered and shifted, revealing pitfalls unseen in the room itself. Large panels slid over and under one another, with only small islands of safety, such as the one on which they stood.

Seeing Rob raise his eyebrow, almost doubtfully, she tugged the base of her quiver removing a number of arrowheads and cast them across the floor as the pitfall opened before them. To her dismay they remained scattered in place. Turning her attention back to the crystal she saw the silver glints of metal, but they were not in front of them as she had expected, but behind them. She gave a wry smile as the pitfall appearing to be before them closed, and one to their rear opened, causing the arrowheads to seemingly sink beneath the floor. "Where do we need to go?" Taya questioned returning her gaze to the crystal.

"There," Rob advised confidently, gesturing towards the crystal. He had seen enough of this world to know, that which was out of place was usually the means to progress.

"You can't see any of it can you, the movement?" Taya observed, looking at the puzzled expressions on her friends' reflections. They both shook their heads.

"Will you help us?" Rob asked, flashing a warm smile towards her as he reached out, touching her arm tenderly. "Please?" Taya nodded, taking his and Stacy's hands in her own. With her eyes fixed firmly on the crystal she took a step backwards, pulling them with her. Rob's lips parted as if to speak, but seeing the concentration he decided to still any questions. But the further she led them from their destination the more the question would not be silenced. "You're taking us the wrong way," he whispered in a low hiss.

Taya ignored him, pushing and pulling their arms as she guided each backwards step until they reached the far wall. She released them, turning to face it, extending her hands to touch its rough surface. Rob, still watching the reflection in the crystal, felt his brows furrowing as the image refocused, showing Taya to be stood before it with her hands upon it. The wall rippled as he turned to face it. The wooden grains became transparent, then dissipated before his bewildered gaze to reveal a wall fitted with wooden footholds. The grinding sounds of cogs halted, reversing in a familiar fashion. The floor above retracting back into the wall just moments before the entire structure lurched violently. They clung tightly to the wall before hastening their descent.

"Anything?" Rob questioned abruptly as Taya dropped the remaining distance to the floor. Stacy huffed a sigh muttering something about ignorance and gratitude that Rob just about caught. "Yeah.

Thanks, Ethelyn," he acknowledged almost sheepishly. "Do you see anything unusual?"

"Aside from the stone tiling? Nothing." The room they found themselves within, like the structure itself, was large and circular. Giant segmented stone tiles fanned outward from a central, circular point to align perfectly with the adjoining walls. Rob scratched his chin, studying the pictographs upon the surface, their presentation seemed to suggest they constructed words, but it was no dialect he was familiar with. With large impatient strides he approached the room's centre, his gaze tracing every seam, every join in the hope of finding a passage.

"Do you think we needed the mirror crystal?" Stacy questioned, glancing upwards to where, without the flooring, she could see the reflective surface through the stationary cogs which had controlled the floorboards. Rob removed his crossbow, firing one of his heavy-weight bolts through the openings. The crystal shattered on impact, sending large shards raining down. Striding over he picked up one of the larger fragments, handing it to Taya who looked horrified by his actions.

"Well?" he asked impatiently. The continuous movement of the unseen cogs below grated on him, counting the seconds. Taya looked at the crystal, passing it over to Stacy as she shook her head.

"Why would you do that?" she asked. "Do you know how rare..." Taya rubbed her temples as a dull ache began. "Why don't you just do that?" she snapped gesturing towards the wall.

"What?" Rob vision flitted from Taya to the unfamiliar symbols, realisation dawning on him. "Ethelyn, take a breath. Do you need a drink?" His tone softened.

"Oh sure, now you're concerned."

"Look, Bray thought this was the best way to help her, so excuse me if I am getting a bit overzealous."

"Sure, that's what all this is about." Stacy gestured wildly, her tones increasing angrily. "Why don't you tell her why you really dragged her to The Depths, what it is you're really after, because it sure as heck isn't helping—" The floor lurched, sending Stacy toppling forwards into him.

"Taya?" Rob questioned, seeing her retracting her hand from the wall before walking widdershins, each step carefully measured. She stopped again, reaching up. Her fingers brushed another symbol, causing a soft illumination to flicker momentarily. "What do you need?" he questioned.

"Quiet." She took a backward step, her eyes scanning the wall quickly. The ground beneath their feet began to hum and several large tiles sank, disappearing into the darkness below. Rob moved quickly, running to Taya as the floor's vibrations began to increase, tiles dropped in rapid succession.

"What are you doing?" Rob demanded, closing the distance between them. He could hear her mumbling to herself as she resumed walking, her eyes flitting from icon to icon. Her fingers brushed another symbol, further increasing the vibrations. "Are you sure you're doing it right?"

"How should I know?" Taya asked. "You've the same reading skills as me." Taya's gaze snapped to Stacy, her features growing pale as she realised the young woman had not joined them. "Move!" Taya yelled, gesturing for her to run to the right. "Uncle, help her to the edge, if you want to survive this then I need to keep going." There was something of a warning in her voice. Almost as if she questioned whether he would act on her request.

Rob glanced to Stacy who seemed paralysed in fear. The floor nearest to her was beginning to fall away as Rob dashed towards her, leaping falling tiles, and pivoting openings. His mind tracked the movements of each tile, planning his return as his wrist grasped Stacy's firmer than perhaps necessary. He pulled her towards him as the section beneath their feet fell, plummeting downward with them upon it. Rob reacted by instinct, securing a tether before firing a bolt from his crossbow. The rope grew taut, leaving the rock to continue its descent while they were swung towards the wall.

He braced for impact, the force of the collision sending him spinning, yanking his grip from Stacy. He averted his gaze from her fall, but he could not silence the terrified sound of her diminishing scream. All around him the floor continued to fall, large pillars outlining the outer edge began to drop, halting at varying levels to reveal a sunken staircase comprised of the outer sections. Above him, he could see Taya watching him in horror.

Rob scaled the rope to the place where Taya stood and, grabbing her arm, began to march her down the sloping gradient, not daring to utter a single word.

"Is it worth it?" Taya questioned sharply in a tone reminiscent of the woman he had first met. Her gaze seemed to scrutinise him. For a moment he felt small within her presence as he stood before the partially concealed stone archway. There was nothing but darkness below them, the structure lurched again, dropping until but a quarter of the passage remained visible. Rob turned towards her.

"It won't change the world, but to me it is price-less."

"It seems you already know what you're willing to sacrifice," Taya observed coldly, her eyes fixed upon the opening. "First Bray, and now Stacy. How many more must die before you're satisfied? I ask again, *Uncle*, is it worth it?" Her emotions had given rise to a state of calculating calm. Rob felt himself growing hot under her accusing stare.

"How can I answer? It's a matter of perspective."

"Why do you need it so badly, why is it so important you would trade people's lives to retrieve it?" she demanded, her fists balling tightly at her side as she tried to push down the overwhelming emotions which now threatened to consume her.

"I wasn't always a hunter. I was a husband, a father. I sought to better their lives, and took work at the Plexus in hope to escape the growing depravity, but when the Severaine struck, when I should have been protecting them, I had been away." Rob's eyes clouded over, he stared at opening before them. Time was running out, another movement would see the passage sealed, perhaps forever, there was no time for this, yet he felt his actions needed to be justified. "Weft had been reduced to rubble, and they were... they were not amongst the survivors." Rob placed his hand inside his pocket, feeling for his daughter's keepsake, his heart swelling with both grief and comfort as his fingers touched it. "For the last six years I've dedicated my life to finding it, and I'm so close. I—"

"Go on then." He looked to Taya in disbelief. "You'll find it on the altar. After what has been sacrificed it would be disrespectful to turn back now. But tell me, why *this* treasure, why The Seed of Nzin?"

"It will grant the possessor a single wish," he answered staring through the remaining section of the archway.

"Are you sure it's really what you want?" Dark patches clouded her vision, her entire body growing heavy as she beheld his eagerness to advance. She questioned how she knew it was there, how she knew it to be atop an altar surrounded by glass and crystal and placed within a container to prevent it from being touched.

"More than anything," Rob answered, his gaze fixed solely within, he was so close he could almost visualise his future. He glanced backwards, looking at the woman who had made this possible. "Come on, let's finish this together."

The dark, dimly lit corridor was a stark and gloomy contrast to the beauty of the small glass and crystal shrine. Even with the limited glow of light emitted from struggling plant-life the tall crystal shards shimmered, almost seeming to glow brighter in response to Rob's every step. He felt his chest tighten, his heart flutter as he drew ever closer, not realising Taya had yet to follow him inside. He had but one thought, to seize the crystal so his wish might be granted.

His breath caught. Even from several feet away his vision desperately searched the inside of the delicate webbing of a crystal cage to see a cylindrical tube. For the briefest moment, he feared it empty. His eyes narrowed, scrutinising further before realising that the cylinder itself was a vessel, a plain and beautiful container protecting the small teardrop crystal within. His eyes lingered upon it, marvelling that something so minuscule could possess such potent magic. To any not knowing its lore it would appear unspectacular, yet to Rob it held the world itself and all its possibilities.

Reflections of the world behind him were cast upon each crystal. The movement from the entrance adjusted his focus to see Taya, her bow poised in his direction as she nocked an arrow. He watched her taking hesitant aim, his senses now alert as he listened for the sound of the arrow being loosed, instead he heard a second sound, once disguised within the ever present churning of cogs, the grinding movements of stone from behind the altar. He adjusted his gaze to Taya's reflection, confirming her sights were trained there, and not, as he had thought, on him. He closed his eyes at seeing the briefest flash of movement behind her. She was so focused on the dangers he faced she was oblivious to those surrounding her.

In but a single second everything changed. The wall behind the altar opened revealing a dark mass of writhing shadows. They seemed to spill over one another like a crashing wave as they fought to reach their deity before the stranger could abduct it. Rob threw one of his needles towards the crystal cage, sending fine sprays of glittering dust into the air, the sound of it beginning to shatter almost, but not completely, drowned out the sound of Taya's cry for help as a calloused hand reached to grasp her from behind, piercing the flesh of her thigh with a tubular stinger.

Taya thrashed wildly, unable to remove the poisoned barb from her flesh. She felt the cool fluid within the attached sac being released into her as the figure holding her squeezed it gently. Numbness began to spread rapidly, her legs grew heavy as her blood forced the inhibitor through her veins. She screamed, begging for aid.

The surrounding walls began to shudder. Hesitation was a luxury he could not afford. Rob glanced desperately between Taya and the crystal altar, knowing soon she would succumb to the toxin. Her weapon was still drawn within her trembling, weakening grip. She twisted, struggling against the overbearing hands, hoping for the opportunity to loose the arrow against one of her attackers. But Rob could see her grasp beginning to falter as weakness took root. The bow released with an almost silent twang. The arrow whistled through the air towards him as the weapon fell to the floor from her limp body. He turned, hoping to evade the silent projectile, yet even as he reacted he felt the burning pain of it pierce his flesh. His agonised grunt was disguised by the grinding motion of cogs and the shuddering walls. As all her resistance faded the figure lifted her over his shoulder, giving him nothing more than a passing glance before vanishing from his limited line of sight.

Rob faltered, knowing if he were to act now he could save her. But doing so would come at a heavy cost, The Seed of Nzin, the very thing he had suffered to obtain. The sacrifices had been great. He knew the choice should be clear, so little remained of his family that whatever action he took would now see its numbers further dwindle.

He stood in turmoil before his feet carried him forwards. He berated himself, his delay, it was all meaningless. How could he have thought there to be a choice? He reached out, his hands clasping around the cylindrical container. His feet skidded in crystal dust as he turned to run back down the corridor, snapping the arrow's shaft as close to his flesh as possible.

The creatures moved fast, faster than he recalled. His own pace severely hindered by his injuries, both old and new. Their vicious snarls echoed, causing the fine hairs to prickle on the back of his neck with their closing proximity. The background noise of rotating cogs and trembling walls all stilled, giving deafening volume to the creatures' enraged tones. The rapid movement in his periphery came too late a warning as something leapt, latching onto him and burying its claws deep into his flesh. He weaved left and right, grasping the creature with his free hand, tearing it from his body only to stagger as another took its place.

The opening before him began to groan, Rob forced more effort into moving. If he could make it through he was certain he could overcome any who managed to pass through with him. He propelled himself forwards, but his body struck the solid stone as the opening before him sealed. He turned, preparing to defend himself but the leaping forms dragged him to the floor, wrestling him down as others scrambled over him to retrieve that which he had stolen.

He felt their combined weight crushing the breath from his body as they pried his grasp from the container, the burning anger of their claws sent fresh agony through him. He felt his grip on the vessel release, he reached out trying to retrieve it through his darkening vision. Each breath became a struggle. He closed his eyes, the heaviness in his chest confirming what he feared to be true. Regret flooded through him, he hadn't made his wish.

He lay alone. The creatures, satisfied their prey had been subdued, fled in mass seeking to protect their deity from further attacks. Forcing open his eyes Rob focused upon the light from the creatures' tunnel. He knew his breaths were numbered, and each had become a thankless burden. He should have wished, instead of trying to flee. His survival had never been a consideration before. Everything he had done had been for one purpose, and he had failed.

The light surrounding him darkened as a shadowed figure approached. Hades had sent an escort, he could see the figure's steady advance, and he recognised the familiar gait. There were other faces he would much have preferred to guide him, but considering the judgement he would face perhaps this was for the best. Where he would reside was a place his family could not venture, for this reason alone, seeing Bray was perhaps the final kindness he would know.

Chapter 15

Agendas

Concealing her torment to the best of her ability Taya wished for the obscurity of unconsciousness. Her body spasmed in a pain that seemed to radiate from the places she felt the pressure of contact from the restraints. She had regained her awareness suddenly and, seeing a glistening pool below her, had thought herself to be falling. Then the agony had started. It seemed to lessen slightly over time before unconsciousness would once again claim her. But her body was tolerating the pain for longer periods before it would grant her release.

The metal shackles dug painfully into her flesh. Her body weight was supported by wide restraints, while her head, torso, arms and legs were secured in numerous locations to the crossing part of a large wooden carving of a rune she knew to be Othala. If not for the triangular point towering above her angled body she would have thought herself upon a sacrificial cross rather than the rune of heritage, ancestry, and nobility. Her body contorted, attempting to twist itself away from the contact with the wood, but nothing she did brought any relief.

Red hot tears burned from her eyes, falling to cause tiny ripples across the tranquil surface below. Her sight desperately searched the reflection for any means of escape, a weakness she could exploit, something, anything, that could ease her suffering. But all she could discern was she was being held in some manner of temple. Given the pool's presence it was one no doubt used to cleanse sins.

It was said gazing into the water of the Gods could drive sinners into madness, but she had been cured, absolved from the actions her madness had sown. Sunniva had raised her to honour and respect the Gods, what new sins could she have to repent for? A dark fear constricted her stomach as she recalled her mother had made many enemies through her success. She had kept Taya's illness a secret, sheltered and protected her, maybe someone had learnt of her past indiscretions and planned to use her imprisonment here as a means of causing disgrace to her mother, or perhaps there was a greater manipulation afoot. Taya knew Sunniva would give anything to see her safe, and feared what her captors would ask.

The sky reflected in the water began to darken, and still the pain was as raw as ever. It seemed there was no further tolerance being built, and no matter how hard she tried she could find no internal escape, even unconsciousness no longer claimed her. Instinct told her to search for something living, a flower, a creature, anything to focus upon but the temple was void of life, and she was being forced to endure every second of agony. Her body was exhausted, her voice hoarse from screaming, and now she suffered in weakened silence.

She was aware of the footsteps approaching, but knew better than to hope for salvation. She searched the water's surface for the face of her captor, but only his boots were visible, and the words he spoke offered no comfort.

"Filthy Daimon." The disgust in the strangely familiar voice was evident, the air surrounding them seemed saturated with hate and malice. Taya's voice caught in her raw swollen throat, her mouth moving yet her speech failed. "Fear not, even insufferable creatures like you have a destiny, a place. I am here to ensure you reach your full potential. You should be pleased, you will cleanse the filth and taint from the world. Even now Remedy is aligning itself with you, becoming one with your essence. Then, finally, my people will be free. Your war saw us flee to the skies, but you have owned this world too long. We shall return in a blaze of glory, and you, my dear, *you* will pave the way for our era."

"I don't understand," her broken and quivering voice whispered. The sound was barely audible, even to herself.

"That's the beauty of it, you won't." His footsteps began to fade leaving her alone in the silence once more.

473

* * *

Rob let out an involuntary groan as his eyelids flickered open. Moments of coherence came and went as his consciousness ebbed and flowed until he could finally keep his eyes from closing. The first thing he was truly aware of was the strange patterns in the stone floor he found himself staring down at. His aching body was riddled with pain as he became aware of his weight resting on something warm and soft. He felt weak, lacking the strength to even lift his head from the carefully designed head support which kept his sight turned towards the floor as he lay on his front. His back throbbed and stung as he tried once more to move before giving a frustrated sigh.

He had hoped to just have one glimpse of his family, just one look to soothe his heart. But he had been denied even that.

"I wondered when you'd join us." Bray's voice sounded uncharacteristically stern as the sound of his footsteps drew closer.

"I never thought the afterlife would be so painful," Rob groaned trying to shift his weight, but only succeeding in triggering another agonising spasm.

"Indeed. You should count your blessings, *your* injuries could be stitched, but mine..." He trailed off. Rob could just imagine him giving a despairing shrug. "And trust me when I say, Phlegethon is not the best means to slake your thirst, although it certainly does put fire in your belly." Bray gave a throaty cough, almost reminiscent of a chuckle. "I imagine it

474

is too late to complain about the misrepresentation in myths. I was expecting glory, beauty, instead here I am with you."

"Heh, yeah." Rob winced feeling the pain course through him. "So what happens now? I'm guessing we've been judged already?" Since Bray had arrived before him he was bound to understand the intricacies of this place a little better than he did. Rob had never really given much thought to death and the afterlife, he could not afford to dwell on such things too long.

"Well you certainly have. I guess we're just waiting until they decide what to do with us." Rob attempted to move again, he needed to get his bearings, to see what awaited him.

"Keep still!" Rob heard Stacy scold, her footsteps approaching from far to his left. He felt her soft, cold hand upon his bare back, and realised for the first time he was naked, covered only by a light cloth. "You'll tear your stitches, though I'm not sure you deserved them after what you did." Her tone held the same measure of annoyance as Bray's had. "Honestly—"

"Psáltis? Surely you don't belong..." he trailed off, aside from the brief time spent with her he knew nothing of this woman, and the Gods rarely made mistakes. Her hands seemed to pass over his skin, examining the areas where the pain seemed to radiate from.

"How are you feeling?" Her harsh tone indicated she asked merely as a formality rather than from genuine concern.

"Okay considering. Did you say stitches?" he questioned, realising Bray had said something similar before. He felt her drop the light cloth over him once more and, for the first time, became aware that one injury hurt more than all the others combined, and that was the wound caused by Taya. He grimaced, recalling his final moments.

"You can thank Bray, he attended to me too."

"Will it really make that much of a difference down here?" Rob questioned, the uncertainty in his voice clear. He had always been led to believe the injuries of the body had no relevance in the afterlife, but it seemed that held true only for the pure souls, those worthy of redemption and peace. The damned and wretched, such as himself, it seemed were to eternally bear their torture, perhaps it was no less than he deserved.

"I imagine your wounds would still fester just the same," Stacy stated, her voice revealing her slight confusion. "I don't see why the rules here would be any different."

"Were you badly hurt?" Rob questioned, guilt etched in his voice. "What am I saying? You're here, of course you were. Was it at least as quick?" Rob recalled the sensation of Stacy's hand slipping from his own to send her plummeting into the darkness below.

"Quick? No. The entire place was operated by water, I was trapped in the current, barely able to keep my head over the rapids. But I'll tell you what, I've never been so glad to see another soul, even if it was Bray."

"Excuse me!" Bray interjected, his mock offence ringing through. "I could have left you there I'll have you know. I didn't have to risk life and limb to retrieve you." Rob felt his head sink deeper into the head support.

"Bray," Rob groaned in sudden realisation. "We're not dead are we?"

"Not quite." Bray chuckled. For a moment it sounded like Stacy had slapped him. "You should have heard yourself."

"Hey, whoa wait a minute. I saw you, you'd been peppered with arrows, your wounds were bleeding out, not to mention the fall." Rob moved his fingers, trying to discern whether or not he felt real, alive, or if this was Bray's twisted humour. He couldn't quite tell. As he recalled the image of Bray falling he knew why he believed himself to be dead, no one could have survived those injuries, that blood loss, or the fall, no one.

"Oh that," Bray stated dismissively with a wave of his hand.

"What do you mean '*oh that*'?" Rob challenged.

"Well, the thing is, I just don't die very easily." He gave a shrug. "I've been told I'm quite stubborn in that respect." His eyes briefly glanced towards Stacy, he had managed to avoid her questions thus far, after

477

all, there seemed to be people here interested in talking with her. It afforded him some peace. He, on the other hand, had decided to stay and watch over Rob.

"Easily!" Rob exclaimed in disbelief. "Your wounds were pouring with blood, there's no way you can tell me it was a flesh wound! That aside, the fall alone—"

"Hermes and I have an understanding, in case you haven't noticed I could charm even Hestia into forsaking her oath," he boasted.

"There's charming and then there's—"

"Rob, Bray's an Empusa," Stacy intervened sharply, stopping what could have been a long drawn out conversation. Bray turned to Stacy, his face flushed with genuine amazement. He hadn't been sure how to explain his recovery, but he had invented many believable reasons, and had planned to embrace whichever one Rob had accepted. Besides the Empusae were a myth, even people in this time doubted their existence, and although Stacy was, in some ways, correct in others she was mistaken. He wasn't exactly a thoroughbred.

"What about Ethelyn?" Rob questioned hopefully, trying to hide the shame in his voice.

"You took that well." Bray shrugged. "As for Kitaia Ethelyn..." He shook his head, not considering that Rob was unable to see anything but the stone floor-tiles.

"Empusa or not, it still doesn't make sense," Rob announced after a long a heavy silence. "How *did* you survive?" Rob revisited the older topic, diverting his attention from Bray's implication.

"I wish I could boast a marvellous conquest, but the truth is I landed on a lower ledge, and I didn't fall alone. Once I did what I do, I was able to use their walkways. There's a whole complex of cities, not to mention the passages they crafted to pay respects to their gods. I wasn't fully healed, so I was drawn to her." Rob correctly assumed he had gestured towards Stacy. "After I heroically rescued Stacy from the moat of treacherous spiralling rapids, I saw a hoard of the creatures fleeing the passageway. That's how I found you."

"So how'd we get out?" Rob questioned, hearing the weakness begin to consume his voice. His body grew heavier as the markings in the stone shifted in and out of focus.

"We didn't. I treated your injuries as best I could and visited one of the smaller settlements to request an escort to the Daimon Prince. Their faction leader was *very* receptive to the idea," Bray explained. It had not been quite as easy as he had suggested, whilst he had influenced their desire to fully cooperate, he had also been forced to relinquish many of his most treasured possessions.

"The Daimon Prince?" Rob wanted to look Bray in the eyes, even now he couldn't tell if he was being serious.

"About that," he drew the words out a little longer than necessary. "You know how you're not dead, you may start to wish you were." Bray paused for

479

a moment, wondering if now was the right time to tell him. He thought for a moment, deciding there was nothing to lose. "It's Yuri."

"We're in Kólasi?" Rob groaned, his voice barely above a whisper now.

"Eremalche to be precise. We're here until the next full moon, but I warn you, he is *not* happy." Bray crouched down by Rob's ear as he realised he was slipping back into unconsciousness. "How could you do it, how could you value a trinket over a life?"

"I needed to see them... to put things right," Rob whispered.

* * *

Aidan guided Elly with purpose. His pace ever quickening towards the confined storm upon the horizon. He was now certain this was not the result of a dreamer, nor was it a corrupted dreamscape. The rising winds were whispering warnings about the dangers it would soon unleash. In the distance the turbulent clouds spiralled, slowly rotating to form a large tubular tunnel. Its size and majesty enhanced by the flashes of purple streaked lightning. Something ancient had awoken, something which should never have been, and its effects permeated across all the realms. Even here there would be consequences.

Aidan knew how to read these warnings. Only areas of dense energy could be manipulated into such a display. He was certain whatever was responsible for the fluctuations stemmed from the location the tornado now kissed. He felt his breathing quicken as his pace further increased. A distant whisper seemed to warn that this would also be the place Jude would be found. Somehow the energy being unleashed was linked to his abduction.

"What is causing that?" Elly questioned. She had seen many displays of nature's force, yet even from so far away she could feel its darker qualities, and the strange pull of its silent call.

"Remedy." Elly felt her steps falter as she heard the familiar voice. She turned to face its owner, surprised to see the dark-haired man standing directly behind her. He was dressed discretely, attempting to present the guise of a dreamer, but his presence alone betrayed him. She tried to speak, but her words froze in her throat. Instead of feeling comforted by his appearance she found herself taking a single evasive step. "Lain, dangerous curiosities stir. Now is not the time for slumber. Please, put aside your foolish notions of responsibility. Accept what is, and return to the place you belong. Your presence here breeds danger," Night warned, barely acknowledging the other figure. He was taking a great risk even appearing here. Despite some of his more redeeming actions towards the Oneirois, he was still a traitor in many of their eyes. He only hoped he could relay his message before one of them sought to expel him from their lands.

"I cannot. And you, *you* are interfering. What would your peers say?"

"I have left you to your grief, respected your need for solitude as you once did mine. But the time for such things has now past. You must choose a realm other than this, remaining here will only endanger you further." There was a lie within the truth. He had attempted to locate her on numerous occasions, but his presence in Darrienia was not welcomed. If not for the single moment where she had touched the tether, confirming her link to the world was still present, he would have had no means to reach her. He had thought her ready to wake. When, to his disappointment, she had not he felt cause to seek her once more.

"You were respecting my solitude?" Elly questioned in obvious disbelief.

"Do you truly hold me in such low esteem you would think I could blame you for things that had to come to pass?" Night questioned, his concern evident.

"She had to die?"

"She should not have lived as long as she did. Fate corrected its path, or at least it had. Some mistakes have long reaching effects, this"—Night gestured towards the distant hurricane—"is one even we failed to foresee, and I fear its effects will go beyond the scope we can imagine. Please, Lain, you must return. I cannot protect you here."

"You said Remedy?" Aidan interrupted.

"Yes. It has been lost for cycles untold, and yet we only learn of its emergence when it is being aligned for use." Night recognised this Oneiroi, he had observed both he and his partner on many occasions during his search for Elly.

"Is there nothing you can do?" Aidan asked hopefully.

"The Gods cannot interfere in matters of man. It was created by their hand, and the evil that it breeds can only be stilled by those who created it."

"Remedy, is that what is responsible for the disruptions we are subjected to here?" Aidan questioned uncertainly. He did not believe a tool such as that could have a reach this far into the realm. Not unless there was a conduit being used. Worry crossed his paling complexion as his sight returned to the hurricane and he thought of Jude.

"Alas no, your problems, whilst they do seem intertwined with events, are not driven by them. They are merely being used to channel residual energy here for another purpose." Night wished he could reveal more, but after his last interference he had been forced to take a vow on Styx, and no god could break a divine vow.

"To what ends?" Aidan questioned, drawing Night's attention from Elly.

"Is that not what *you* are attempting to discover?" he scolded.

"But you're a god?"

"And I am forbidden from interfering in your realm." Night frowned taking a slow deep breath. He could not allow himself to be drawn into this conversation more than he already had.

"Then what do you call this?"

"I call *this* talking with a dear friend." Night turned his attention back towards Elly. "You need to reactivate your link to the golem. I know it is you who is repressing it."

"I am sorry, I cannot. I have given my solemn vow to Aidan to help him locate his partner. I cannot betray my word." Elly placed her hand above her heart as she spoke, but failed to meet Night's eyes.

"Then fulfil your obligations quickly. You are in more danger than you realise. At least restore your tether, it may save your life." Night placed his hand on her shoulder, understanding her concern. "Lain, there is nothing to forgive. Just know that I am deeply aware of your absence, you are as much my child as she. You are my one true ally, and our friendship has lasted centuries." Elly closed her eyes, feeling a wave of emotion engulf her at his words. She raised her hand to touch his, but his presence had receded.

"You know you made me no such promise," Aidan jibed once he was certain they were alone once more.

"Well now I have."

"Do you not think you should heed his warning?"

"I do," Elly affirmed in all sincerity. "But you would continue without me, and you are not the only one in need of answers. Shall we?" She gestured towards the growing storm, knowing if Night's words were true its presence would soon recede. It gave her cause for concern, if the mere alignment of this ancient weapon could create such a surge in power, she feared what its use could do.

"I thought I infuriated you."

484

"You do. That is one of the reasons I have come to enjoy your company. Now let us follow the storm and see what its eye reveals."

* * *

Rob shifted uncomfortably upon the bed where Bray stood towering over him, silently removing the stitches. The Daimons had all manner of medicinal advancements compared to the limited capabilities of the human race, but their services had not been offered, nor would Bray trust them with Rob's care given the consequences of his actions. The fact they were allowed to reside within the city, and had not been cast into The Depths of Acheron to fend for themselves, had been a blessing, and one Bray thanked Yuri for often. It seemed the general consensus was not to blame the group as a whole and, whilst Yuri cared little for the consequences, he had warned Bray and Stacy that Rob was not to step foot outside, except to leave.

Their accommodation was a modest dwelling. It possessed a large central room, which functioned as a dining and study area, with a few smaller rooms exiting from it. Bookshelves laden with well-read tomes lined the walls, their topics spanning from medicinal and historical to works woven by the imagination. Bray had insisted Stacy take the bedroom, while he himself was content to sleep upon blankets within the kitchen area. Rob was confined to the larger room where a specialised bed, intended to keep him on his stomach, had been constructed. It had come as no small revelation that these dwellings had belonged to Taya. She and Yuri, after their wedding, had lived here, but in her absence Yuri had returned to his own familial residence, unable to remain in the empty shell of what had once been their home.

"How long have we been here?" Rob questioned, as Bray applied a small amount of pressure to one of the wounds. The stitches had been in for far longer than he would have liked, and Rob's injuries had needed treating and redressing daily to combat the infection which had rapidly taken root. They had been confined within Eremalche for six weeks now, when the full moon arrived Rob had been gripped with fever and, despite wishes to the contrary, he was not deemed able to travel.

"You slept away the first month." Bray reminded him. Rob cringed feeling the tug of the stitches being removed. Even now he was still sore. The first four weeks had passed in a fevered haze. He vaguely recalled waking, staring down to the stone floor, his body burning whilst chills chased through him. It had only been during the last week he had been well enough to leave the bed, and only these last few days had his strength been returning.

"What about Ethelyn, has there been any news?" Rob had asked this same question every day, regardless of any delirium. The memory of his actions continued to haunt him. What little sleep he had was plagued with fevered images of their final moments together, each time he would try to force his dreamself to pursue, but he never would. Each and every time he took the crystal. His question normally met with avoidance or, if it were Stacy he asked, silence. She had barely spoken to him since he had first awoken, and took every opportunity to excuse herself from his presence. Today, however, he received the answer he had been fearing.

"They've searched for her, but whoever abducted her took precautions. She's lost to them." Bray's voice seemed solemn. Rob released a sigh, he had suspected as much. Sunniva had discovered the means to keep her shielded and hidden. It only stood to reason that those who had abducted Taya would also be familiar with such methods. Rob winced, feeling the tug of the final stitches being removed. It seemed somehow rougher than the others, sending a sharp burning pain through his back. "All done. There's still some inflammation, but you'll live."

Bray stepped back, observing the pink flesh of new scars. They seemed raw and angry compared to the many faded ones he had seen. It seemed Rob was no stranger to injury. He had found countless wounds across his body, some made by knives and claws, and others from weapons he knew should not exist. There was also the surprise of seeing the strange tikéta, a marking in ink clearly altered from its original image. Exactly who this hunter was still eluded him, more so now. One thing was clear after their more recent excursion, he was not the man Bray had thought him to be. Bray knew himself to be selfish, but even he could not have done what Rob had.

"Now I'm able, I should thank Yuri for his hospitality." Rob pushed himself up from the bed, relieved to be staring at something other than the floor. His legs still trembled, and his balance protested to each minute movement.

"I wouldn't." Bray tossed Rob his tan hide jacket. He noticed the repairs and patches and met Bray's eyes for the first time in a long few weeks.

"Why not?"

"Rob, you were given a choice between a treasure and *his* treasure. You did not choose wisely." Bray's expression still showed the deep-rooted disappointment. They had known each other for but a short time, but Bray seemed genuinely saddened by his actions. Given his demeanour, Bray could tell Rob too was ashamed and despaired by what he had done.

Rob slowly made his way to the table, placing his stone goblet beneath the potted Nepenthes upon the table before tipping some water from one of the red containers. The rolled leaves shuddered beneath his touch, reminding him it was exactly what it appeared to be, a pitcher plant. Once a day someone would replace it with a new one to replenish their supply. He gave a sigh, staring at the water, unable to return his gaze to Bray.

"Look, Bray, I made a bad decision I—"

"A bad decision!" Yuri's voice held the outrage mirrored by his posture as he stood in the doorway. His fists were clenched as tightly as his jaw was set. "You let the so called demon hunters abduct her and all you have to say for yourself is 'I made a bad decision.'?" Yuri took a step forwards, entering the room, his eyes flashed with anger. Bray stepped between them, his hands raised in a placating gesture as Rob rose unsteadily to his feet and looked at the man before him, willing Bray to step aside and allow Yuri the opportunity to vent his anger. He felt he owed him that much. Stepping forwards, Rob gently moved Bray from between them as he spoke, understanding the tension his presence had caused. That Bray thought it necessary to protect him spoke volumes of the prince's feelings towards him.

"Kyne, I—"

"Do you have any idea what they could do to her? To my Kitaia. With such potential for unparalleled destruction how could you not value her safety above your own gains?"

"Unparalleled destruction?" Stacy questioned, appearing in the doorway behind Yuri. She had been sitting outside when she had witnessed Yuri hurrying towards their dwellings, each long stride revealing his anger. Despite her frustration and outrage towards Rob she had hurried back, hoping to quell any inflammatory actions. Those here sought peace. She would not allow Rob to jeopardise what she was working so hard to achieve between their people.

"I am what you would deem a prince by marriage. Kitaia is the Sfaíra Fýlakas, the keeper of the realm, she is our Queen. The powers of our royals are beyond reproach, and hers more so as she walks the barrier. With her birth came a prophecy, one word within it possessed many meanings. In any of her possible futures she would either destroy, recreate, or return the world. We have always been unsure on which translation was intended."

"Then why allow her through the barrier?" Stacy questioned curiously.

"Allow her?" Yuri scoffed. "You assume we had a choice. The Kitaia you know is a shell of the woman I love, and her decisions were set in stone."

"But why would she leave?" There had been many conversations while she walked Eremalche. She had strolled the streets, accompanied by Geburah and learnt of the Daimons, who they were, their history, their growth, and their imprisonment. But whenever the topic of Taya was broached an uneasy silence had descended, until she knew better than to ask further questions.

"Kitaia intended to find the Mystics, to show them our people were not the threat they once believed. With the Spiritwest returned to Gaea the Severaine will never again be sealed, as such the forces holding our lands here will begin to fade. Kólasi is not an underground prison, it was once a great land. The Mystics need to choose whether to reseal Kólasi, or allow it to rise. If they can't decide it will rise wherever it sits, destroying anything which may occupy the place our land once resided. Kitaia wanted to restore our land to its rightful place, to have us experience the warmth of the sun, instead of this cold functional light." He gestured outside.

"Forgive me," Rob started cautiously. "But given that you utilise humans for energy why *would* they release you?" Rob was already on dangerous grounds with this man. He couldn't see how things could become worse, so with nothing to lose he chose to ask. Yuri shook his head, his eyes narrowing to show the extent of his contempt for the man who stood before him.

"Your ignorance truly knows no bounds. We have on occasion taken a human partner, but what you speak of is barbaric. Our ancestors, during the great war, did indeed find a way to weaponise the human life, but only after your kind had taken countless lives of our own in such a fashion." Yuri turned his glare from Rob, willing him to be silent. His voice grated on him, stirring the anger he fought so desperately to contain. The longer they occupied the same room, the more he struggled to rein in his aggression.

"So if your people aren't responsible for the full moon abductions then there's something else happening to make it seem that way—" Rob scratched his chin as he spoke, the tangle of bristles beneath his nails alerting him to the necessity of shaving.

"Rob," Yuri's voice seemingly went unheard as Rob, unaware of the anger smouldering in Yuri's eyes continued to speak.

"—But who would gain from such a thing? Sure I've heard of slavers—"

"Rob!"

"—But the numbers are—"

"Silence!" Yuri growled, his fists slamming into the table. The room fell into an eerie stillness, the tension almost palpable. After releasing a long slow breath

491

Yuri continued, his low voice filled with venom. "Since it is abhorrently clear that you value The Seed of Nzin above *all* else, I offer you this proposal. Find Kitaia, rescue her, and it is yours. I will see it placed without trap or guard. Once she is free, I give you my word, not only as a male but as the prince of these lands, I will do this." The contempt in his voice was tangible.

Yuri had lost any respect he had ever had for this man in a single night, but for now he was his best chance at finding his wife. The humans could travel where he could not. They were unrestricted by time, and the only true allies he had on the surface world. He suppressed a sigh, turning his back to them. The only ones who would help him were those responsible for her being in danger. Hurting him now would not aid his cause. Perhaps the cruellest revenge was to ensure Rob finally received the thing he desired most.

* * *

Time passed ceaselessly in a haze of movement and motions. Routines which once marked the passing of hours became disjointed. The only real semblance of time was watching the alteration of light in the shimmering pool as day turned to night, or night to day.

Her arm burned where a large yellow-beige pulsating cord had been fused with her skin, sending tiny tendrils burying deep within her veins. Each pulse delivered fluid from what appeared to be a swollen, blood-red organic sac to which the cord was integrated with vein-like tendrils. She had been told this substance contained everything she needed to be kept alive and healthy, but she was certain there was something more.

She had fought at first, trying to flinch away from the squirming tendrils as they buried into her flesh, but as time passed, she found she simply obeyed, not wishing to suffer the extra pain her defiance caused. When she was compliant they rewarded her by bathing her and treating her raw wounds. She needed to be good, their rewards were the only kindness she knew.

She stood upon the pedestal, waiting obediently as they lowered the runic carving behind her. Even now she wanted to scream, to run, but if she did that they would hurt her, they would leave her here longer.

Little by little, as her cooperation became instinctive she felt her strength returning, and the strange sacs responsible for keeping her alive were changed more frequently. Her legs could once again hold her weight without being supported by the rough impatient hands of those charged with transferring her to be redeemed. She wobbled, her arms extending slightly in a bid to find balance as she willed herself to remain still. If she fell they would need to rebalance her energies again, something they achieved by holding her beneath the water until she was forced to release her final breath. Many a time she had hoped not to wake, but she always did, only to find herself staring down at the reflection in the water. She had lost weight since her arrival, the shackles had needed to be replaced to ensure her emaciated form remained steadfast. It was during this period the replacing of the strange sac became more frequent. She seemed to have lost more weight than they had anticipated.

After securing her to the rune they lowered her in place, and soon the sound of footsteps echoed through the domed room. Normally she was left alone, but every few days *he* would visit. She could see the legs of the person as they approached. His face, or even his reflection, was never cast upon the water's surface. Normally he would reach out with his gloved hand, his long slender fingers finding her pulse. Occasionally they would slide around her neck to apply painful pressure, as if he could not decide whether he should continue his efforts to redeem her, or relieve her from the burden of living.

The swollen bruising from where he had last attempted to choke her still flared angrily casting an array of reds, blue and purples across her pale flesh. The combination of those colours, with their slight greenish-yellow tint, almost served to remind her of something. Something which remained elusive despite the time spent staring at the markings in her reflection. She had been certain he would kill her, end her suffering, but there was a calculated control to his actions. He would always render her on the brink of unconsciousness, then stop. He rarely spoke, and when he did it was of things she had no understanding of. She wasn't sure what she had done to earn this man's scorn but apologising, speaking even, only resulted in more pain.

Today was different to all the other times he had approached. Glimpses of movement were thrown upon the water, the reflection of his legs and hands brought focus to something clutched within his grasp. The silver metal reflected on the water and for some unknown reason she feared this item more than his approach. No matter how well behaved she was, he always found cause to hurt her. Thus anything within his possession was surely but a tool to that end.

She flinched as he reached out, but he did not touch her as she had expected, instead he removed something from the pointed peak of the rune she was bound to. Taya watched his actions, mesmerised as she saw the reflection of light glimmer from the small item he had removed. She felt an instant relief from the constant pain which had flooded her body. He stood before her, setting the small stone into the centre of the silver object. He extended it, giving permission for her to look. It was a circlet, crafted from a fine silver. Set between two wishbones was the gemstone he had just retrieved.

She felt herself startle as the rune began to raise. Her stomach churned as her eyes met his for the first time, she quickly averted her gaze, knowing she was not permitted to look upon him. But it had been too late, she had seen him. Their eyes had met, and he had smiled a dark and twisted smile. He had seen the recognition in her eyes. He raised his hands, brushing the hair from her face as he slid the circlet into place, his gentle touch a contrast to that which she had expected. She was almost grateful for his tenderness, but then she remembered where she had seen him before.

"Why?" Her voice was raw, unused. She felt the white hot pain starting at the place the metal touched, intensifying as the stone came to rest upon her forehead. His fingers stroked the edge of the circlet, his delicate motions activating a mechanism within. Taya couldn't hold back the agonised cries as she felt the spikes extend to pierce the flesh above her ears. She fought with all her strength, trying to shake the cursed item from her, but she knew it was already too late, it was too deeply embedded. Her body convulsed, the metal shackles sending unrecognised pain as she fought with the renewed strength of self-preservation.

The chain holding the rune released, sending her back down to the water's surface. Red droplets of blood ran from her flesh, tainting the pool briefly before dissipating. The pain gave way to darkness, the final words of her captor ringing clear.

"Remedy is aligned. Let them know where to find her."

Chapter 16

Devastation

Rob sat hunched over the table. He had spent a lot of time here, too long in fact. The curled edges of the map cast elongated shadows across the worn parchment. His brow furrowed under the force of his concentration. He was normally so skilled with dreamscrying, he had even thought himself gifted. He had tried sleeping, tried focusing on his task as he drifted into slumber, but when he awoke there was nothing, silence, no internal voice giving him the answers he needed, pulling him towards the location he so fervently sought.

He dragged his hands through his hair in frustration, groaning aloud. He had to find her. He had to. His guilt weighed heavily. How he wished in this moment that Bray had left him to die. Understanding the consequences of his actions, the choices he made, and being helpless to rectify them, had stirred old and harboured resentments he had attempted to keep buried for too long.

During his time sealed within these rooms he had learnt much. He immersed himself in tomes and fables, hoping they would guide him, rekindle a memory, something, anything which could be of use. But there was nothing, nothing but the truth of a distorted lie. It seemed the specialist hunters he knew as demon hunters were, in fact, just that. They could recognise the subtle differences between a human and a Daimon, and thus knew something of their true heritage. Each month towns would recruit their services in hope to be protected from the threat. It was only as Rob had reflected on this he came to realise the towns with their protection suffered fewer abductions than those unable to pay their fees. He had always thought them to be providing a great service, but now he was seeing them in a different light. If the rumours of human farming were just that, then who was responsible for the vanishing people? It became apparent that somehow, these hunters had to be involved.

As Rob's thoughts raced he added several marks onto his map. It was a time worn parchment, faded and torn, with more circles and crosses than visible landmarks. It was long past time for him to buy a new one, but this told the tale of all his exploits, and he was loath to part with it.

Rob turned a small silver hair clip in his hand, the clear stones catching the light. He clasped it, uttering a silent prayer for aid. He had to find her, not just for her sake, but for his too. He fixed his gaze to the keepsake, begging it for answers, for relief to a burden of guilt he had never managed to shed, only add to.

Bray, watching Rob's internal self-depreciation and frustration continue to fester, poured himself a drink into one of the stone goblets. He noticed the small trinket, his eyes lingered upon it in appreciation as he placed a goblet before Rob. Sliding his hand from it to still Rob's hand he deftly removed the object from his grasp. Rob's expression turned venomous as he leapt to his feet, his hand extending rapidly in an attempt to catch Bray by the wrist. But he wasn't quick enough. Bray had side-stepped around the table, raising the item for closer examination.

"Where did *you* acquire something like this? Bray questioned evading again as Rob tried once more to take it from his grasp.

"My daughter made it. Please, give it me."

"No seriously, where did you get it." Bray, seeing the depths of despair on Rob's face relinquished the item, placing it upon the table where Rob quickly scooped it up, thrusting it back into the safety of his pocket. His fingers traced the hair clip's cool surface, feeling the reassuring warmth of the metal in his palm before he finally brought himself to release it. "I'd love to meet her, she'd make a fine accoutre with some training. There's few alive with—oh." Bray closed his eyes cursing his foolishness, and all at once Rob's reasons for seeking The Seed of Nzin became apparent. "I'm sorry."

"It was a long time ago," Rob muttered sombrely, moving to sit back at the table and emptying the goblet Bray had placed down.

"Tell me?"

"Every time I went on a hunt she'd give me this hair clip, she'd wear the other every day until I returned. She thought me having it would keep me safe." Rob closed his eyes, haunted by images of his family. Bray adhered to the heavy silence, wondering if Rob realised how close in her observation his daughter had been. "While on the last job... I was betrayed, left for dead. I was with my sister, feeling sorry for myself, when I should have been—" His grip tightened around the goblet in an attempt to still the angry tremors. He took a breath, forcing himself to continue. "Because I was late they waited, they were still in Weft." Rob covered his face with his hands, attempting to hide the burning tears which filled his eyes.

"They?"

"My wife and daughter. It was my fault." He shook his head, his eyes reddening. "They were meant to leave a few days before, but Sunniva sent word of my injuries, instead of going... they waited for more news." He closed his eyes, tears spilling down his cheeks as the raw wounds reopened. He drank, as he did whenever overcome by grief or regret, hoping the burning fluids would sear the wounds closed. It was a relief long lost. Rob glared at Bray as he replenished the goblet, realising what he had done.

"So how are you faring with the map?" Bray changed the topic quickly. Wiping his face Rob heaved a heavy sigh, shaking his head.

"Not well, whatever divine aid I had before, it's long gone," he snorted in contempt.

"What eludes you, maybe I can help?"

"It's just... I know these demon hunters. Every time I look at the map I can't help but wonder why they'd keep her alive."

"Those are thoughts best kept to yourself," Bray warned in lowered tones.

"Oh I have a choice now do I?" Rob spat, flinching as he heard someone clear their throat. He turned his attention to the door to find Yuri and Stacy. Rob hoped he'd not been there long enough to overhear his concerns. "Any news?" Rob's weary voice held little optimism.

"You should already be aware that the Kyklos can't trace her." Yuri gestured towards the parchment on the table, wondering if he had realised that they had been the ones to offer him aid in the past. "She's either obscured by barriers or..." he trailed off. He could not voice his fears. There were times he felt only his belief kept her alive, and should it falter his worst fear would be realised. There was no choice but to believe.

"The Kyklos were unable to detect her in the temple either, I'm sure that's all it is." Stacy touched his arm reassuringly. Yuri moved, his gait betraying his fatigue as he approached to sit at the table. Although not a member of the Kyklos, being Taya's husband had bound him to their land. He had a link with Kólasi and to the energy which sustained it, thus he had been giving his aid, in hope they could see further than the veil would normally permit.

There were few people in this Fiefdom who could fulfil the role undertaken by the Kyklos. Even now, they were relentlessly searching, their groups changing as fatigue claimed them. Only Yuri remained a constant, giving all he could to assist their efforts. They had not wished him to be placed in danger, not given the events surrounding Daley, but he had been insistent. They would either let him assist, or he would attempt the workings alone risking far more danger. Geburah had granted him permission, knowing he could not deny him, especially after he himself had risked the dangers of Lathraía. He understood the need, the frustration. It mirrored that which Geburah himself now suffered as he tried to finalise the archaic rites they needed to free Daley from his captor's embrace, and return him to the sanctity of Kólasi. Until Kitaia was found, Daley's rescue could not move forward. Yuri needed the Kyklos, and finding Kitaia had to remain their priority.

"You must have made *some* progress?" Stacy prompted sternly. "Other than through the bottles," she added noticing Rob's bloodshot eyes lowering towards the table.

"Demon hunters have numerous safe houses." Rob sighed, unable to raise his gaze to meet hers or Yuri's.

"I've marked them. I came to realise they wouldn't want to be seen abducting a human, so I checked off all the ones inside towns or on trade routes." Rob gestured over his heavily marked map indicating the ones he had crossed off. Unfortunately, to anyone but him, one line looked very much the same as the next.

"So what does that leave us with?" Bray questioned, briefly placing one hand on Rob's shoulder as he refilled their goblets to drain the last remnants from a bottle of clear fluid. He crouched, pulling a pale blue bottle from a large crate beneath the table, ignoring the look of contempt as Stacy shook her head in disbelief. Yuri reached for the Nepenthes plant, his hand hesitating by the pitcher before diverting to the bottle and pouring himself a drink.

"These three." Rob drew darker lines under each of the remaining safe houses. Seeing Bray emptying his goblet he instinctively kept pace.

"This one's too close to Collateral." Bray pointed to one of the three, earning himself questioning looks. He flashed a smile, being a Misorian had its advantages, he was versed in so much forgotten knowledge he could seem like a genius by revealing even the simplest of facts. "I'll explain. Think of their 'holy' barrier like a collection of iron filings. Collateral's portal is slightly magnetic and would pull on their protection creating small imperfections, enough for the energies within to be revealed. Given the trouble they went to in order to apprehend her unharmed it's also wise to assume they somehow know of this flaw, either that or it's just coincidence. Either way you would have known if she was being held there."

"So that leaves just two." Yuri's shoulder's seemed to drop slightly in relief. They were finally making progress. He sipped gingerly at his drink, glaring intensely at the map as if demanding it to reveal her location to him. The room fell into a tense silence, all eyes upon the map. Stacy remained standing, pacing slightly, her light steps barely registering to any within the room.

The sound of hurried footsteps upon the cobbled stones outside drew their focus towards the door, in time to see it flung open, revealing the flushed face of a lithe, balding man. He leaned against the door jamb, drawing in deep breaths as he scanned the room quickly, locking his gaze on Yuri.

"They've found her!" he gasped, perspiration clung to his flesh, glistening in the low lighting. Yuri slowly rose to his feet, his hands gripping the table's edge as if he barely dared to believe the words to be true. He glanced towards Stacy and Bray, as if to ensure they too had heard these words. "There was a disruption in their shielding. It was brief, barely long enough to trace her. But she was there."

"Is she all right, could they reach her, is she safe?" Yuri fired the questions in quick succession. His relief was only slightly clouded by his fear. If she was alive it was because they needed her. Questions haunted him. Demon hunters were well-versed in the ways of torture, an involuntary shudder passed through him, his eyes begging the man for answers.

Would the woman they rescued still be alive within the prison of her living flesh?

"I'm sorry, the disruption was brief. They barely had chance to detect she lived," he reiterated, shuffling his feet slightly; his gaze turned towards the floor as he saw the grave expression worn by his prince.

"Don't apologise, if not for your efforts she would remain lost." The man raised his head, noticing as he did so the parchment on the table before them. Yuri once more took a seat, motioning for the man to approach.

"You have a map of the outside world?" His eyes traced the surface as he whispered to himself almost incoherently about longitudes and latitudes. He glanced around, his fingers lifted the quill from Rob's grasp, making a mark on the small island where his sight had come to rest.

"That's Afthonos. The demon hunters don't have a safe house there. There's a few cities and mines but, as I recall, little else." Rob voiced in concern. The man's brows furrowed as he rechecked his calculations, looking to Yuri he nodded his assurance the marking was correct. Rob thought for a moment, scratching his chin. "I think I remember hearing there's a collector of antiquities there." Recalling this Rob groaned in realisation. "She's a collector of blessed relics."

"That would make sense, it explains why the breach was so minor. From what was seen, she was inside a temple. But there is little else I could tell you, they saw only its image."

"A temple?" Stacy questioned receiving a nod. "Tell me, did it have a clear domed roof?" The man once more nodded in response. Stacy glanced to Yuri, she had heard rumours of this place. It had once been a home to oracles and people would journey far and wide to hear their words. Prophetic rites and visions came with a price to humans, and this was said to be the only place to possess a relic substantial enough to drive away the Maniae who plagued those with premonitions. It was thought to have been a safe haven for any with futuresight, until the day all within vanished without a trace. Meals had been left upon tables, and drawn baths were abandoned with discarded garments still beside them. To this day no one knew what became of those once sheltered within its walls.

* * *

The sun entered its final quarter. It was the night of the full moon and preparations were underway. With Remedy affixed to the Daimon there had been no further need to secure her to the rune, it and the waters had completed their intended purpose in allowing the stone to fully attune itself to her. Since then they had permitted her some rest.

When first she was brought to them it had been essential for her to remain in a weakened condition. Strong enough so the gemstone would recognise her, but too weak to resist its alignment with the vibrations generated by her life-force. She had been unable to refuse the power, and now she had become the bearer of it.

Once the circlet was in place nothing but her death would see it released. The barbs that had secured themselves to the bone, which in earlier evolution would have penetrated the skin to form horns, would remain embedded until such a time a new host was required. But he would not require a new host, his plan had been perfectly crafted, and she was all he required. That was the beauty of his scheme, but his aspirations were far more complex than simply the activation of this ancient weapon. They were far greater than even those in his employ understood.

It was essential to his plan that this woman now be allowed to regain her strength. A weapon without energy had no purpose. She needed full access to her power.

There had been a fleeting moment of concern as this day approached. The week following its alignment the Daimon had still not awoken. He had feared the toll upon her body had been too great, and he would have to await another who had no restriction from The Stepping Realm and start anew. He had summoned his best apothecary and the healers in his employ to treat her, until finally she had roused.

He bound her will in the same manner some would bind servants. For one of her species such a task had not been easy and had required much preparation, but until he released her she was his to control. He made her eat, drink, bathe. Every action she undertook was by his will alone, and despite the stain on life that was her race, he found he enjoyed possessing this kind of power over another being.

Now it was the dawn of his greatest triumph, the power of Remedy would be tested.

* * *

"Move!" A heavyset figure demanded, his hand reached down to grab a fist full of Taya's knotted black hair. Over the last hour she had gradually started to regain control of her body, meaning when this burley man came for her, she found her trembling legs uncooperative to his demands. The figure's hand wrapped around her hair, dragging her to her feet to pull her stumbling figure along behind him as he marched briskly. Her uncoordinated movements saw her tripping over her own feet in an attempt to keep pace.

"Where are you taking me?" she mumbled inaudibly to the one who dragged her from the darkened room. Her room had been a strange place, clearly a sleeping quarters, but the bolts and seals had always been fitted to the outside. It had made Taya question if the room had once housed a prophet, and the scarring of nail marks etched into the walls did little to disprove her theory. Humans dealt poorly with futuresight, and often meanings were lost as images were crafted into words. Prophets, more often than not, were driven insane by their premonitions and the stress they put on the body. This downward grasp

on reality was reflected in the embedded marks Taya
had seen.

The figure continued wordlessly, never slackening
his grip, or casting a backwards glance. There was
something different in his gait, a strange anticipation which caused fear to churn within her stomach.
Each step enhanced the deep-rooted foreboding that
threatened to overwhelm her newly gained awareness. She felt her hysteria building, her teeth chattered uncontrollably as she fought to breathe, terrified of what awaited her.

"Where d'you want her? I mean is there a specific
place this is meant to happen?" The man still gripped
her hair as he addressed his master.

"Anywhere is fine." The familiar voice responded
flippantly. He released her, sending her tumbling
ungracefully to the floor. The man stepped aside as
Taya heard the familiar footfall of her captor. She
could feel the prickling of his hateful stare as she lay
with her back to him. There had been times his demeanour had altered, when he had watched her obey
his every command, his eyes relishing the details of
her body. She shuddered involuntarily, remembering
the hunger in his disgusted gaze.

A fresh awareness washed over her as the final
hold of his binding was released, bringing with it a rejuvenating energy and new fear. He had approached
her once as she bathed, taking the sponge from her
hands and gently caressed her. He had witnessed her
fear even through his control. He had told her there
was no satisfaction to be gained from such acts when

he could simply twist her will to submission. At that moment she had heard his desire. As if remembering himself he had recoiled, and the look of seething anger had returned. He exited abruptly, summoning his servants to return her unceremoniously to her room, still dripping wet from the bath. Her recollection of these words caused her body to tremble further, fearing his intentions.

"Thank you gentlemen, I can see to things from here. Return to your families, I shall send word when I require your services again." There was an excitement to his voice, one that warned of dark-rooted intentions. She pushed herself up, struggling with tremendous effort until she knelt before him. Even then she averted her gaze.

"My lord, what do you wish of me?" she questioned, instinctively addressing him as she had been taught.

"Tell me, Ms Ethelyn, tell me what you know." She raised her gaze, noticing he stood between her and the exit. Her mind whispered to her, telling her if she moved quickly enough, if she surprised him with her sudden disobedience, she could escape.

"Of what, my lord?" Seeing her longing gaze he sneered, stepping aside as if to tempt her.

"Who are you, where were you born, who was your mother?" His hands knitted together behind his back as he rocked forwards and backwards on his heels, his amused gaze fixed upon her. Taya felt the dull ache in her temples, her fingers twitched, longing to massage away the pain, yet she dared not move.

"I am Taya Ethelyn, raised by Iereía Sunniva, my mother and homeland are unknown to me, but I call Sunniva such as she raised me," Taya answered obediently, feeling the warmth of tears well in her eyes. He approached, his steps slow, his eyes reflecting the crooked smile upon his lips.

"Did she now?" His question struck her as unusual. "And what of your upbringing, were you a healthy child?" Part of him wanted her to attempt to flee, if only to reinforce his dominance. While within these walls she was his to control, the freedom he now granted her was necessary for this undertaking, but how he wanted her to try, just so that she would understand she would never be free from him.

"No. I contracted a sickness of the blood, one which plagued me with delusions." The pressure in Taya's head increased causing her to visibly wince, almost as if each time she addressed him it caused her physical pain. Yet she was powerless to remain silent, he had spoken, she had no choice but to answer. She squeezed her eyelids tightly together, her fingers pressed firmly on her eyebrows in hope to alleviate some of the discomfort.

She heard his steps draw nearer still. He patrolled around her, giving her a moment to regain her composure as tears spilt from her eyes.

"Delusions, that sounds dreadful. What nightmares haunted you?" His smile broadened as he saw her flinch.

"I don't remember," she whispered trying to hold back the waves of pain and nausea which threatened to consume her. She felt the bile rise to the back of her throat, her body tensed and spasmed as her hands reached up to clutch fistfuls of hair as she fought against the pain. Suddenly she had a moment of clarity, whatever he was asking was pointless. It wasn't about the questions. He was searching for something, something to do with her past.

"What do you know of Daimons?"

"A myth," she sobbed, her breath coming in sharp gasps. "Please..." she begged understanding now this pain was his will. He removed a small clear gem from his pocket, lifting it to his eye he studied her through it for a moment.

"And the Mystics?" Her world turned white. The searing pain was all that now existed. Her nails drew blood as she clawed at the circlet, attempting to prise the source of the agony from its place. He moved to stand before her. This was the reaction he had been waiting for, he could feel the power being unleashed around her. She just needed a little nudge, and all her restraint would fail. "Tell me Kitaia Ethelyn, what do you know of the Mystics, who are they?"

"Please," she begged through ragged breathing as her body collapsed to the floor. "Please stop, I'll do anything, I'll say anything." The ground around them began to tremble. Small dust clouds caught the light now emanating from the large runic symbol where she had once been bound. "Please just make it stop." Her body convulsed in time with the vibrations, her agonised screams pierced the air as the temperature of the air surrounding her grew more intense. Sweat dripped from her flesh, heat waves now radiating from both herself and the rune, which was charged with such raw energy it could be felt pulsating through the air.

The dome above them shattered, unable to withstand the heat coupled with the powerful tremor. Glass rained down, catching the light only to be subdued by the growing clouds of dust thrown into the air by the protesting brickwork. Her awareness was fading, she was unable to behold the terrible beauty of the falling shards, only feel the agony coursing through her. She felt the bile leaving her throat, almost choking her. She felt his foot on her as he shoved her onto her front, the glass shards digging deeper into her flesh as her weight was forced upon them. He was not concerned, she wouldn't die, not yet. She still had a purpose to fulfil.

"Please, help me," she gasped her hand reaching out desperately, attempting to grab him. She felt her fingers close around something soft, before she felt his foot connect with her jaw, hurling her away from him. "I'll do whatever you wish." But the only response, through the deep rumbling and sound of splitting of stone around her, was his fading footsteps.

* * *

Aidan quickened his pace as they fought their way up the sheer face of the rocky ravine. A downward glance over his shoulder had confirmed his fears; the land continued to alter beneath them. What had once been a valley when their hike began had deepened, until the near-vertical climb they now made had become their only way to progress. Now he could see the once dry desert ravine grow darker mere feet from their position. The rocks above turned to mud as they began to slide, running down the chasm's sides like treacle to form a thick river below. The dark waters bubbled, expelling air and becoming white foam upon a raging body of water.

The sound of the roaring currents was deafening, its growing intensity and ever-encroaching proximity showered them in mists of spray carried by the rising winds as they attempted to out-climb it. Dry rocks would crumble beneath their grasp, causing small rock-slides to cascade, only to be whisked away. If Aidan did not know better, which was something at this moment he was beginning to question, he would think the land itself attempted to impede their progress where and whenever possible. It was a consideration given merit by the lack of dreamers. Darrienia was ever-changing, but usually only in response to the stimuli of those dreaming. Whilst Aidan could sense distant energies of those in slumber, they remained always beyond their reach, beyond his manipulation to calm the hostile terrain.

Elly, whilst a dreamer, was of little aid in that regard. When she had invoked the rune of boundaries to enter this realm she had been granted free rein across the land, but at the price of forfeiting any

514

influence she would possess to manipulate the environment as a dreamer. He spared her a cautionary glance, faltering as the dry rocks turned to grit beneath his grip and the compact texture began to soften. Above, hardened walls changed to sand, cascading down towards them. Aidan paused digging his arm deep into the moving surface, creating a large protruding stone above them, segmenting the sandfall. Their pace quickened, knowing that at any moment the rock they were upon could become as unstable as those which rained down from above them. The water swelled, rising as the sand turned to raindrops beneath them.

By the time they reached the rock formation Aidan had created, the cliff walls had calmed. He turned, extending his hand towards Elly, the water nipping at her heels as she made the final ascent. He pulled her towards him, collapsing on the grass, gasping for breath as he surveyed the relentlessly rising waters, wondering if rest was a luxury they could afford. The violent roar of the current softened as it drew level with the land, shrinking and receding. Large jagged rocks became pebbles before his gaze as a small babbling brook was born from the once deadly rapids. The calmed water was clear, inviting. As he turned to behold the scene before them he gave an exasperated sigh.

"You have got to be kidding me!" Aidan exclaimed. The forest surrounding them stretched, elongating as it turned to stone. Energy saturated the air, moving past them in flashes of colour to join with the rising peaks, moulding its shape as it grew to become the most daunting mountain range he had seen. The jagged, snowcapped summits stood like sentries, denying access to the land beyond, and keeping vigil as far as the eye could see.

Turning his gaze backwards he saw the babbling brook had also altered, entering its resting state. A picturesque meadow, awash with the vibrant colours of wildflowers rolled across the land to the distant horizon, its inviting nature a stark contrast to that which now awaited them. "I need to rest a moment." He sank to his knees, closing his eyes to gather energy from their surroundings. Oneirois did not eat. Whilst they would be seen to do so the items themselves were nothing more than condensed theta waves, the source of all life and energy within Darrienia. For those living within this world, simply being in contact with the ground often provided ample fuel for any given tasks. However, Aidan found the land's unnatural temperament seemed more depletive than restorative.

"I cannot help but feel our progress is being deliberately hampered. Does Melas possess this much power here?" Elly queried. Their journey had not been easy. At every opportunity it seemed their surroundings would alter, giving rise to dangerous challenges and seemingly impassible barricades. She had noticed a few occasions where the transition had been marked by the darkening of their surroundings, and she had felt the unmistakable presence of the Epiales. Their locality seemed somehow to correspond to the energies Aidan detected from the dreamers and, regardless of the increasing presence of both, neither Epiale nor sleeper had crossed their path. Elly could recall no time when her journeys had been isolated for this long.

"This is not *his* doing. His reach is not this extensive, nor does he possess the power to manipulate our land in this manner. He can corrupt susceptible dreamscapes, but this is something different altogether." Aidan rose to his feet, exhaling sharply. "Shall we?" He gestured towards the mountain.

"I am not the old man who needed to rest my tired and weary bones," Elly teased, flicking her long hair behind her shoulder as she led the way towards the towering obstruction before them. Her face grew more serious as she watched the speed of the clouds, now mostly obscured by the mountain, once more quicken. They were close, divided from their destination solely by the monumental force before them.

"Something else is happening, we have to hurry," Elly observed, a mild desperation to her voice. The closer they grew to this anomaly, the more her stomach seemed to tighten.

"Tell that to the land," he huffed, beginning to climb.

* * *

The calm ocean winds whipped at the sails. The blustering of the canvas and the indistinguishable relay of orders were the only sounds as the small island came into sight. Standing beside the quartermaster

517

Bray looked out, watching the impressive peaks of Afthonos appear to grow upon the distant horizon. This island was one of the most affluent mining areas. It had once been a nest of fierce and active volcanoes. Bray remembered a time when people would bring offerings to appease the fiery beast, now people built homes and buried deep into its flesh. The diamonds within were now worth more than the memory of an old god.

Large wealthy cities lined the sloping gradients. Their lords enjoyed the produce grown in the rich fertile soils and the wealth produced by trade. Those working on Afthonos were granted beautiful residence, a motivation to work hard.

The bulk of the island's settlements were upon the contours of the slopes, sheltered in valleys or by cliffs. Only the harbour occupied the single plateau. Large wooden docks stretched out welcoming arms to traders and travellers alike with hidden palms waiting to receive the expected coin. People flocked from far and wide to purchase riches from the mines, or be guided through the glimmering caves of crystals and behold all their glory. Once the volcanoes had shimmered with unearthed gems, but now small children ran and played, gathering the jewels, producing them to the lords' merchants in exchange for coin.

When the temple had been constructed upon the pinnacle of the volcanoes, a quarter of the island's revenue had instantly been required to default to The Acropolis. It towered above all, and the only means for the devout to reach it was to cross the large corridor bridges carved by the labour of sinners into works of beauty. The temple had long been deserted. Its only use, like so many others, was the revenue its presence generated.

The once soothing monotones of the crew readying their approach became panicked. Shrill tones carried upon the sea air causing curious by-standers to rush towards the bow. Crashing particles of energy cast ribbons of lights across the island in a breathtaking display which surrounded the temple and the port, dividing the island. Deep resounding rumbling carried from the cliffs, where stone appeared to run as liquid rivulets into the ocean, pulling with it large shards of land. Spray rose, masking the cliffs and rising waves.

The boat lurched and anchors were dropped in an attempt to still their approach whilst the captain took the wheel, turning against the terror he witnessed before them as they closed in on the small dock. Men secured their lifelines, expecting the currents to rage. Sails were dropped and secured all within a matter of minutes after the chilling command had been issued. The deck was awash with frantic movements, not a single pair of hands lay idle.

The island continued to quake, shedding its flesh and extending its eroding limbs. The earth groaned and split, sending avalanches cascading down its surface destroying everything in its path. The ship rocked violently under the sway of the large swells, their position away from the cliffs, nearing the plateau, was the only thing preventing them from feeling the brunt of the merciless waves.

Bray scaled from the main deck to the quarterdeck, his presence beside the captain apparent by the sudden change in the commands being issued. The order to hold steady near the dock was heard. All hands turned to actioning this new request, attempting to halt their evasive manoeuvre. As a skilled seaman the captain knew these waves were less than they should be, as if diffused by an unseen force. He gave thanks to Poseidon, knowing he watched over them this day.

Bray descended rapidly, a trail of whispered expletives rolling from his tongue as he sprung into action. This could not be happening. People cleared a path instinctively, gasping in astonishment as he leapt from the deck, over the rails towards the dock. His pace unhindered by the sharp, violent lurching of the vessel as its moving weight strained against the pull of the set anchors.

Bray weaved through the fleeing crowds as droves of panicked people flooded the streets with arms full of possessions. They screamed and hurried, trampling over the fallen without a care as they tried desperately to reach one of the moored boats before the owning lord could weigh anchor. Most of the smaller vessels were already on route, people clung to the railings, attempting to pull themselves onto the deserted decks, while others threw themselves into the waters, hoping to reach a vessel.

Opening the doors to the stables he secured the first panicked mare which attempted to flee, heaving himself onto the chestnut steed he spurred it to action, calming it until it feared no danger.

The sound of the island splintering into the sea was one he would not soon forget. He had witnessed such things as a distant spectator, watching as cliffs of ice and stone collapsed, but never had he been so close. Sweat glistened upon the horse's muscular body, mirroring the beading formation on his own brow as he forced it harder, quicker. He knew he should care for the horse's wellbeing, but if he couldn't stop this its life would still be forfeit. Sweat foamed from the horse as he implored it to continue just a little further. When the horse's head began to bow with its staggering stride he knew he could push it no further. Not if he hoped to retreat.

He slid from the saddle at the bridge, examining it rapidly as crevices and splits saw one of the many approaches tumbling into the natural chasm below. Arches groaned and cracked as he ran. Glimpses of the island below were highlighted in quick succession through the passing archways.

His steps slowed, then halted. Below him was a scene of death and carnage. Wails of the dying, those trapped beneath the devastating rock slides, serenaded the skies. But it was not their cacophony which had stilled him. It was the lights; the same ones he had witnessed from the ship. Altitude gave this display a fresh perspective. It was not as random as he had thought. The deep and dazzling shades outlined a border, a meshing of two similar energies. One which expanded from the temple and another, which by Bray's visual assessment, originated from a large antiquated building. The two forces reached out to one another expelling a web of destruction of the likes rarely witnessed.

The crumbling of nearby arches pulled him from his dazed appreciation. Everything below was buried beneath rubble. The dock was the only place, as yet, untouched by the collapse. People swarmed becoming nothing more than a writhing mass. Small figures flailed in the water, desperately swimming towards retreating vessels, while others bobbed with each devastating wave.

Bray moistened his lips apprehensively as he slowed before the crumbling temple. He turned sharply, aware of Rob and Stacy's presence upon the bridge. He gestured them away, calling out a warning he was unsure they would hear. He had seen them pursue, seizing horses he had released from the stables, but he hadn't considered Rob could encourage his horse this far into danger.

"Go back." Bray lowered his head, ducking beneath a fallen pillar as he began to tackle his way through the debris.

"Faster!" Rob commanded as Stacy began to lag behind. "We have to move faster."

"Why, what difference will it make?" Stacy griped. Clearly it was already too late, the death count was substantial. The collapsing mines had buried so many who had fled to their safety from the avalanches. "It's going to get worse," she whispered in sudden understanding. "It's going to get worse unless he stops her."

"And there may be only one way to still this disaster." Rob looked up, but Stacy was already picking her way through the rubble. He watched her for a moment, his fingers sliding into one of the pouches on his belt before he pursued.

* * *

The sound of Taya's pain was all-consuming. It pierced the air with the same deafening roar as the outer walls of the crumbling temple. Bray now understood why this location had been chosen. It was too perfect to be a coincidence. The structure of the domed roof had been essential. Her positioning ensured she was in no danger from the falling debris, but the key to its true purpose lay within the glowing rune.

Bray could feel the powerful blessings of the Moirai upon it. The angled glass, which now lay shattered, had served to elicit a resonance effect from the relics in the dealer of antiquities' possession. The result was the whimsical lights which appeared to mark the verge of the colliding energies, and both were being attuned to the destructive force of Taya's magic.

He picked his route towards her carefully, his heart aching as he heard her pitiful pleas. Her body thrashed and convulsed. Her pain was so paramount the wounds obtained from her movement across the glass-dusted floor were not even acknowledged. He could see the path of each movement she had made in the glistening trail of blood upon the shattered glass floor. He had heard the many ululates of pain, the difference in the cries relating to the suffering experienced. With the sounds she made he wondered how she could even be conscious, how her body could tolerate such agony.

"Kitaia." He spoke her name softly, his voice filled with gentle empathy. There was no question in his mind of the restraint she showed, that the island still remained was a testament to her resistance, to the restraint she still unknowingly held on her power. Even without her memories of being a Daimon she somehow managed to suppress the magic through the pain, but he had to question how much longer she could endure. How much longer before she lost the frail grasp, and all of Afthonos was reduced to nothing.

"Make, it, stop, please," she gasped hoping the approaching steps were those of her captor. "Please. I'll say, anything, whatever you want to hear. I'll do whatever you want. Just please..." Her voice failed as her mind registered who the voice belonged to. Blinded by pain she could barely show enough control to reach out in his direction. "End it, please."

"It's okay, Kitaia, I'm here," Bray whispered, trying to force as much comfort to her as possible, but his thrall failed. The suffering she endured was so intense it obstructed his attempt. The glass ground beneath him as he knelt to reach out, placing his hands upon her head as he had done before. His fingers wove between hers, allowing contact to the place she shielded protectively.

Bray recoiled. The pain he received was overwhelming, on par with that of Zeus as he birthed Athena. The splintering agony threatening to spilt his skull in twain. He steeled himself, trying to maintain contact as he shared the torment. Gritting his teeth he endured, but only for a second. His hands released her, clasping his own head as he sucked in deep and rapid breaths. It was too much. The pain was too great. As his sight returned, he pulled his hands through his hair, looking upon her with a deep-rooted sorrow. He could not help her, not in the way he had intended.

"Why aren't her wings showing?" Stacy's voice startled him. She had bore witness to Bray's failed attempt and knew she had to think of something, another way to silence Taya's magic that did not result in her death. Her panicked mind frantically assessed the options, hoping to buy a small amount of time to find an answer as he responded. "Even last time she had bones," she recalled. Bray glanced towards her before approaching Taya filled with foreboding. Gently he took her hands in his, guiding them from her head to gaze upon her. He closed his eyes, wishing they had deceived him. But now he had seen this he knew there to be no other choice. Her death would be a mercy.

"What is that?" Stacy questioned seeing the haunted expression on Bray's paling face.

"Remedy. Those yaldsons aligned her to Remedy."
Bray's legs lost the strength to support him as he
slumped to sit beside Taya, pulling her close. He
whispered tender words of comfort, knowing that as
long as he didn't try to connect with her the pain
would not return. He positioned himself to kneel behind her, draping one arm around her in a tender embrace, while he brushed her hair gently aside with the
other. He could sense it now, the magic web placed
upon her to ensure her consciousness remained. Her
suffering had been intentional. It was doubtful whoever did this expected her to endure. When she lost
her restraint, with the curse of Remedy aligned to
her, there was no telling the damage she could induce.

"Is that the cause of this?" Stacy gestured around
before clutching herself tightly. She knew what Bray
was preparing for. She could see the guilt and hesitation in his eyes. They both understood the implications of Remedy.

"Partly." Bray took a deep, shaky breath. He had
long craved this experience, but not like this. He
traced his tongue over his lips. As she died the magic
too would fade. Without her being able to succumb
to unconsciousness there was no other way to tame
such power. "I'm sorry, Kitaia."

Bray drew his tongue across his palm, wrapping
his other arm around her, tucking it just beneath her
top to rest upon her right shoulder, just above the col-
lar bone. He spread his fingers, coiling them around
her shoulder and neck before bending forward to kiss

the other side of her throat. Her scent filled his nostrils as he kissed her gently. They were gentle, sensual kisses, like those shared between lovers. He pulled away, raising his other hand to cross her in a similar manner to touch the flesh his saliva had marked. He pulled her torso against his, knowing she would be unable to break his grip. He felt the tingle of anticipation as another desire began to overwhelm him.

He was no longer aware of the figure's identity within his embrace. Even the danger surrounding them had faded into the background of his consciousness. There was only her scent, the enticing aroma which promised him satisfaction. She began to resist, but he was stronger. He was always stronger. The struggle only brought more fulfilment, adrenaline flooded his prey's blood to make the meal all the sweeter. The hormones released by panic and fear were second only to those produced when he brought his prey into the heights of pleasure. He would savour every last morsel.

She grew limp in his arms, her screams silenced. But he no longer understood the implications of this happening. He was beyond rational thought, beyond caring. The power in her blood called to him, robbing him of conscious reason. Her scent drew him deeper, awakening the primal hunger he had suppressed for so long. He would feast. Tasting her was all he craved. The blood was so close, and he knew when it finally began to be absorbed, drawn through his own flesh, he would forever crave and hunt for more. He knew their race would be a delicacy. He had been patient enough.

Something struck him, something large, with enough force to release the meal from his grasp. He turned sharply, a guttural snarl leaving his lips, yet his frenzied vision was still fixed upon his feast. He pounced, attempting to reclaim his delicacy. Something struck him again.

Bray shook his head feeling some semblance of control return. The all-consuming scent faded, replaced by earthy odour of dust and rubble, with the almost overpowering metallic tones of blood. He felt flesh giving beneath his fist. It felt good. He struck again. The mask of hunger and darkness began to lift bringing his surroundings into focus. He straddled Rob, driving one fist and then the next deep into his ribs. He was barely able to redirect his descending strike. His fist smashed forcefully into the broken glass just a moment before he sprung to his feet and backed away in partial retreat.

Feeling the onslaught cease, and the pressure lift, Rob coughed, rolling onto his side as he drew in a painful but much needed breath, only to find himself once more choking. Spittle, coloured with blood, clung to his face as he tried to spit the ruby fluid from his mouth.

Bray visually searched the area, trying to gain some understanding, some insight, into what had happened. He turned to Stacy, who was painstakingly dragging Taya through large unstable stone pillars towards the exit, while Rob had bought her time to flee. Seeing his almost feral gaze upon them she froze for a moment before attempting to increase her pace. Her clumsy steps becoming noticeably hindered by the rubble she attempted to navigate whilst dragging the cumbersome weight of her friend further from his reach.

Even from his current position Bray could see the welts of blood trapped beneath the surface of Taya's skin, welts that were reminiscent of bruising. They were something his normally controlled and measured touch never left behind. He dropped his gaze to the floor before turning away only to be stuck by Rob's dazed charge. Bray raised his hands as Rob recovered enough to stumble forwards, grabbing him weakly to prevent his further advance. Bray wanted to speak, but he could find no words.

Rob raised his trembling fist, regarding his adversary through a swollen eye and released him with a weak shove before keeling over to clutch at his side. Bray knew from the bruising on his own hands the punishment Rob had taken. He helped him to stand, partially dragging him across the broken floor to approach Stacy. Taya remained unconscious, and still the world around them continued to crumble.

Stacy cast an alarmed glance to Rob when Bray lifted Taya from her grasp, relieved when the bloody figure gave a slight nod. Bray studied her, searching for the reason her consciousness had faded when such measures had ensured it to be an impossible feat. A single metal needle was embedded in her leg. The projectile had been fired so expertly it had struck the very start of the invisible web, severing the ties to Taya allowing her body to finally surrender to the pain. There was barely a trace of the weave upon her now, just the diminishing threads of the magic which had so expertly bound her. Bray looked to Rob in wonder, as a flash of memory returned the events leading to Taya becoming limp in his embrace.

Bray, in his frenzied state, had been only partially aware of Rob's intervention. The hunter had released the small needle, clapping his hands together slightly as he dusted his palms in a final gesture of self-appreciation. But even this sound had not been enough to break Bray's animalistic desire, by then he had only sought fulfilment.

Rob had been proud of this accomplishment, and with due reason. Bray had never seen anyone succeed in doing what he had. The action alone suggested Rob to have knowledge beyond that of this time, and there was only one place he could have obtained it, The Courts of Twilight.

If Rob had indeed been there, it explained some of the scarring he had seen. It would even establish the source of the tikéta, which Rob always kept concealed. Bray could see now how it could have once been their crest. But those of the Court rarely left, and *never* mingled with those from outside it, which begged the question, what was he doing here?

Chapter 17

Revelations

Geburah sat in silence, his intense gaze turning to each one of the Kyklos members in turn. They did not meet his eyes, their vision remained fixated on the table before them. Some staring at their hands, others at the complex diagrams carefully designed upon the tattered parchment. Their lack of response was as disquieting as the suggestion itself. Every small movement made drew their attention to the other people who sat around the large table, and each person wondered who would be the first to speak.

Geburah breathed out a long sigh. He had said he would allow them some silent reflection, but he had not expected their deliberation to take quite this long. He knew they were meticulous, that each member of the Kyklos was mentally testing each part of his theory, the symbols, the invocations. It was an undertaking with no parallel, no groundwork in practice on which to build a solid foundation, but it all came down to one thing, and it was Meredith who slowly rose from her chair to speak this thought.

"My lord, it could work, in theory." She swallowed in an attempt to suppress her nervousness. "The ideas have a solid root in application, but I have never seen them combined in such a manner. There is no certain way to know how the different invocations will correlate with each other. Your suggestion involves the manipulation of energies from many sources, and whilst the method you have theorised for ensuring their compatibility is, in *theory*, viable, until we attempt the workings we will have no way of knowing for certain. Therein lies the secondary issue." Meredith glanced to the members of the Kyklos for support, yet they continued to avert their gaze.

"Please, continue." Geburah extended his hand in a polite gesture accompanied by an encouraging dip of his head.

"Well, my lord, *if* we do this it is going to take more than just the combined power of the Kyklos, we're going to need access to a tideway. The closest one within our territory leaves much to be desired on a protectional front. The invocations you have suggested have ensured you're central to the process, but you're going to need something else."

"Go on," Geburah encouraged. He believed he already knew the direction of this conversation, and was interested to discover if they had reached the same conclusions as himself.

"In order to combine the Daimon, Moirai, and human magics, you're going to require a conduit for each. You can be the beacon for the Moirai invocations, but in order to fully harness the powers you require you would need Yuri to be the Daimon representative."

"Why Yuri?" Geburah enquired. This too was an understanding he had reached, in fact, before assembling the Kyklos he had first spoken with the prince.

"Because he is the one the land knows, the spirit bonded to the Sfaíra, it will grant him more than it would any of us, and it would also protect him. There is, however, another problem. You will require a human, and it is unlikely they could survive the energy being drawn through them. Their bodies are frail, they have no means to tolerate such large forces of raw power. More concerning, whilst there are those here who would offer their life to our cause, those who have been in our realm for any length of time have already adapted to the energies here and cannot be viable. But even if they could withstand the energy you'd still need a..." Meredith swallowed, biting her lower lip as she tried to find a less distasteful word.

"You need a sacrifice," Eadward announced, finally finding his voice and rising to stand beside Meredith. "You're invoking the ancient blood rites which were practised by their race, the human would, either way, have to die to complete the process."

"Leave those concerns to me." Each head rose to look towards the doorway as they heard the voice of their prince. Only Geburah knew how long he had stood beyond their sight, listening. "Their kind took my wife from me and, if this is what is required to see Daley returned, I know just the person to aid us."

"You know a human who will give their life for us?" Eadward queried in disbelief.

"Who said anything about *'give'*?" Yuri growled bitterly. "Lord Geburah, you see that things are prepared, leave the human to me. Are there any other concerns?" All within the room fell silent. "Very well." Yuri nodded towards Geburah before taking his leave.

* * *

Bray stood in one of the larger of the ship's cabins. A space kindly 'offered' to them by the captain's quartermaster. The slow rhythmic groans and creaks of movement, like the ocean, had calmed since their return. One of his hands rested tentatively on Taya's forehead, whilst the other grasped the neck of a spirit bottle. Since his altercation with Rob his hunger burned painfully, and alcohol was the only method he had found which worked to temporarily inhibit his needs.

Taya's limp body swayed with the subtle movements of the vessel. She lay in the higher of two large hammocks which overlooked a copy of the ship's nautical chart. It seemed this vessel had made many journeys, it was one of the more complete maps Bray had seen, and some of the areas this crew had passed through had been treacherous indeed.

Bray nodded his head in silent contemplation, this was indeed a fine vessel, with a worthy crew and captain. Their earlier reactions sang their praises as they had all worked together as one. The captain, once realising there was no immediate threat to his vessel and crew, had shown the true colours of bravery. The barrage of waves, that in all rights should have grown more violent and powerful, battered the ship merely as large swells mostly void of their initial strength.

Seeing Poseidon was clearly watching over them he, along with four seasoned officers, manned longboats with a small crew braving the waters to give aid. Their small boats fought against the currents, rescuing those who had pursued the near-empty boats of the lords. These vessels had quickly fled and were now but distant glimmers on the horizon. Even now, Bray knew they were still on the water, searching.

Across from the hammocks was a small table where the quartermaster would host private meals, or ponder over paperwork and orders. It was at this table Rob could be found. He sat in silence, drinking. Unlike morale, liquid spirits within this room were not in short supply.

It had been many years since Rob had so desperately longed for intoxication's sweet embrace, and as always it eluded him, forcing him to sit in reflection of his actions. He had only known this level of physical pain but a few times, and it was nothing compared to his inner turmoil. He had wrought this, he could feel the accusing stares of the dead watching him through hollow eyes. He wondered how the fares for the unburied dead would be paid, and in a distant part of his mind allocated another pouch of coin towards his final amends.

He had watched aghast as the island they had once stood upon crumbled into the depths of the ocean leaving only the sturdiest peaks standing. The island's slow devastation had been a sight to behold.

As they fled, Afthonos continued to crumble. Upon one of the longboats Rob had turned back, watching the glisten of unharvested diamonds and stone cascade into the water. He had feared the island itself to be lost. It seemed stone turned fluid, dragging large rocks down into the water. They had boarded the vessel and Rob had stood at the rails, simply watching.

When finally Afthonos stilled he beheld the steep shimmering cliffs. Its image was that of an abstract pinnacle, a twisted spire. Small fragments had continued to fall. Squinting Rob could still see the ruins of the temple atop the remaining landmass. But his sight, in earnest, had sought survivors.

Rob drained the bottle, wincing as the potent fluid continued to burn his swollen lips. He grabbed two more bottles from the box. Partially uncorking them he passed one to Bray, stifling the groan of pain his movement had caused.

"Are you sure this will help?" Bray, hearing Rob speak for the first time since the island, glanced up certain he detected a slight slur in Rob's speech.

"Whoever did this to her possessed extensive knowledge of the Daimons. It's therefore likely the same person who designed the glamour ring given the level of skill these things would require. To this extent we could even go so far as the assumption it was the same person, or organisation, who treated her at Mirage Lake. I don't like the implications." Bray realised his tone and dialogue had become overly formal, it was a mannerism he often returned to when lost in thought.

Bray pried the cork free from the bottle and took a deep draught, attempting to wash away the unshakable foreboding. There were times being a Misorian allowed him to connect seemingly unrelated events. He hoped he was simply jumping at shadows, but he knew all too well these shadows concealed more than just darkness.

"You can't just remove it then?" Rob pinched the bridge of his nose, and gestured extravagantly towards Taya with his free hand before sitting back down. He couldn't even muster the strength to look in her direction. He shifted uncomfortably, trying to relax his rigid muscles. How could he have done this? He had wanted to save his family, and in the process had been responsible for the death of countless more. Tonight, wives, children, and fathers would mourn their losses as he once had.

Rob slammed the bottle on the table, releasing it for but a second before pulling it back and once more drinking deeply. It didn't help. Nothing ever helped. Not then, and certainly not now. He shifted again, the pain of his injuries lost in the rage of his own frustration.

"I am loath to admit it, but this is beyond even my own capabilities. Perhaps if we could find one of Hectarian blood, but the last I know is long deceased, and those once dead cannot aid the living in any form. No sorceress cou—" A loud knock disturbed his train of thought. Stacy, opening the door barely wide enough to squeeze through, entered quietly before closing it. Her fingers slid the small lock across by instinct. She tossed a bundle of cloth-wrapped ice onto the table, not sparing Rob a single glance. He removed a few pieces, placing them inside an empty cup. He pushed the bag aside knowing he had no right to seek relief.

"How is the—erm... re-establishing traces going?" Stacy seated herself beside Rob. He forced the corners of his lips upward in the effort to offer a smile. His gesture failed, sending only a small trickle of blood from his lip. He pushed an unopened bottle and the cup containing the ice before her, unwilling to part with the one he protectively nursed.

"I've not yet begun." His response saw Rob glare towards him in frustration, only to avert his eyes as the act saw his sight also fall upon Taya. Bray understood the meaning and attempted to explain. "I've been trying to find a way to remove Remedy, and getting her prepared for what will follow. It's not going to be an easy undertaking. If I act in haste she may never wake, or worse, become an empty vessel for a power her consciousness will no longer restrain. I'm really in no rush." He pulled his hand from Taya's forehead, flexing his fingers several times to force blood through to them.

For the first time Stacy noticed the quantity of empty bottles. She twisted the top off the one Rob had given her before working the cork free.

"What use does this even serve? If she remembers, she will remember all she has lost, her husband, her home, all places she's unlikely to return. Why bring her this grief, why not spare her?" Rob muttered pulling his hand through his ruffled hair before once again drinking.

"*If* she's able to remember she might be able to hold back the power," Bray answered.

"So it's not for her own good then, it's really just self-serving. Isn't that his role?" Stacy questioned venomously, glancing towards Rob. She poured a small measure in the glass before her. She sipped it, unable to suppress the shudder.

"Hear, hear." Rob raised his bottle in a bitter toast to her words. One she drank to, emptying the contents of her cup.

"I suppose at least what *you're* doing will save lives." A long uneasy silence descended, Stacy's brow furrowed in thought as the alcohol brought a rosy hue to her cheeks. "Does that mean the reason this didn't occur before was because Sunniva was using Apallagí to keep her calm?" The warmth from Stacy's stomach began to radiate through her chest, chasing away the chill of the sea air. She had been assisting the crew with housing the survivors. It was only now she realised how cold it had been. She carefully poured herself another drink.

"That, and the fact she was never truly convinced she was human."

"So when you're done, will she be herself or delusional?" Stacy slurred, there were a few moments delay as Bray interpreted her unintelligible words. Stacy squinted at the bottle, trying to realign the fragmented label to see what exactly she was drinking. She wiped beads of sweat from her burning face, blinking several times in quick succession in an attempt to steady the room.

"I don't know... I've not exactly done it this way before. Normally I'm masking memories, rather than returning them." Bray moved, quickly lifting the bottle from her reach before her hand had managed to grasp the correct one of the many overlapping images she saw before her.

"You don't have to kill?" She closed one eye in a vain attempt to bring his image back into focus.

"No. Little but often." He managed a half smile, watching Stacy frown as she tried to make sense of his words. "I think you should sleep." He would have put some power behind the suggestion, but she had needed no encouragement. He tried to hold the hammock steady as it evaded her. When he could no longer watch the pitiful display, he lifted her from her feet, depositing her within. It swayed wildly for a moment as she wriggled, but before he'd even covered her, she was asleep.

Bray had already explained the complications associated with his current undertaking, and how he needed to distance himself from his actions as much as possible. The living form could work miracles upon itself when damaged, he simply needed to attempt to stimulate the correct areas, and for the most part it would take care of the rest. He would be but a catalyst. His mental distance, during the beginning phases at least, was essential. It would ensure his own thoughts did not interfere, or influence her own as they attempted to reintegrate through whatever method had been used to isolate her mnemonic cues.

Partially understanding the complexities of Bray's attempts, and the need for some diversions presented Rob an incentive to talk, and in doing so he hoped that he too would find his mind strayed from his own discord. He needed a distraction from his self-loathing.

"So were you born this way?" Rob questioned as Bray returned his hand to Taya's forehead to begin work.

"You mean was I born a monster? Yes, you could say that."

"I always thought you were a bit on the pretty side." Rob tried desperately to force humour and merriment, hoping the facade would trick his mind into that state of being. Bray looked at him quizzically as if to challenge his words. "Come on, even I know Empusae are *always* female."

"I imagine that explains the sisters," Bray grimaced. "Lots and lots of sisters, nieces, and not forgetting the aunts." Rob chuckled, it was a forced and hollow sound, but still brought a slight smile to Bray's face.

"So why are there no males?" Rob asked, opening a fresh bottle of spirits. His hand fumbled to place the empty one back into the crate. Bray decided to indulge Rob's questioning. It was unlikely, given his growing intoxication, that anything would be remembered of their conversation anyway.

"I'm not a thoroughbred. Empusae by nature crave the affection of males but have none of their own. Their brief dalliances serve to lure food. Once over they consume the flesh and blood of their lover, but sometimes their meal gives them something more than sustenance.

"Almost all pregnancies result in the birth of a female, a daughter in the image of their mother. On the rare occasions a male is conceived, they take their father's image, but they rarely live past birth."

"And you just happen to be the exception?"

"Yes and no in equal measure. Males are born incomplete. You see, it's part of the female design which allows them to feed. So males starve. A little known fact about the Empusae is that the reason they require blood, and not just flesh, is to replace that in their own veins.

"It is something instantly apparent in boys, but not emerging in girls until they reach an age capable of conception. Their bodies stop being able to produce new blood cells, thus they devour those of others to replenish what they need to live.

"If not for my older sisters I never would have survived. Mother, after birthing me, did that which all Empusae do when presented with a male, she left me to die. But my sisters liked the idea of a brother. They hid me away, feeding me from their own meals.

"By the time Mother realised what they had done I was already a young boy. She cast me from the nest. I did not resemble them and having a human child running around would eventually draw unwanted attention and endanger the whole scare.

"It was cold, time had not long moved from the age of ice and humans had started to craft towns. I had only ever known the scare, I didn't realise the differences and sought a new family. Just as I didn't realise they were different from me, nor did they realise I was not of their own kind." Bray paused, his regretful gaze burning into the wall. "They fed, clothed, and sheltered me. But the hunger grew. Then one day I became frenzied.

"I can still hear their screams. Arteries and veins tore from their flesh to obey my hunger. I couldn't feed through intercourse like my siblings, but the call for blood was still answered. I hadn't even touched them." Bray closed his eyes at the recollection, the images even now were burned into his mind. After he had killed this new family he had stumbled onto the street. Hearing the screams crowds had gathered in fear. Seeing a young boy soaked in blood they attempted to protect him. He had killed them all. He looked to Rob, who sat propped with his hands against his head, listening intently.

"So you didn't just take what was needed?"

"No. I had no control. It was the first time I had fed myself. It was wasteful, unsatisfying. I took everything and moved on seeking more." Bray's voice was quiet, barely above a whisper. "That's the thing about some monsters, when they think food to be scarce they gorge to ensure they can survive a famine."

"What about now? I've seen you feed by touch." Rob's voice seemed so intrusive against the sombre silence his words had pierced.

"Now I take what I need, but never more than a pint from a person, and never the same person more than twice a year."

"How d'you measure that?"

"As a species our kind don't always hunt to kill. We appreciate fine dining and when we find a human appealing to us we scent them."

"Like a dog?" Rob jested awkwardly, instantly realising the inappropriate nature of his comment.

"No!" Bray snapped. "The blood we consume has to be human. My relatives also require a certain amount of human flesh to survive, but the need is not as frequent as the blood. Perhaps another benefit of being a male is that I can eat on par with yourself. I don't have the need, or the craving for human flesh the rest of my family does.

"When we feed our saliva leaves a marker for several months so any hunting know the human has been claimed. I can tell how recently someone was fed upon by its potency."

"But you never explained why you can now feed by touch," Rob interjected, his speech heavily slurred. Bray went silent for some time, basing his decision to continue on the level of Rob's intoxication.

"It was a massacre. After I had gorged myself on the blood of those who had wanted to protect me I moved on, tracking human settlements. They were fewer in number back then. I was wild, lost to the frenzy. Maybe they took pity on me, or perhaps they simply wanted to spare the humans. I don't know their reasoning but the Misorians intervened."

"Misorians?" Rob questioned, his slur lost slightly as his interest piqued. He had heard mention of these people before, but no one had cared to explain them.

"They watch the cycles of the world and store all of its knowledge. They used the wisdom of past generations to study me. They discovered my saliva had altered when I reached puberty, and it would allow any of my flesh to mesh with another's. It's not quite how my sisters feed, but it allows me to draw the blood safely." He gave a slight chuckle, Rob was unsure if it was amusement or contempt.

"Why'd you kiss her," Rob's slur returned as he remembered himself, and he deliberately asked something Bray's explanation had already answered. Hearing this Bray smiled, impressed Rob could even talk, let alone ask such probing questions. He had never spoken to anyone about his past, not even within Misora.

"In simple terms, my saliva allows the blood to travel through the skin to the flesh I temporarily bind to my—the human. It ensures they experience very little pain. The blood is then absorbed directly into my body to replenish me." Bray traced the contours of Taya's shoulders with shame as he beheld the large bruised welts. "It rarely leaves a mark, and when it does it is minor. Not like this."

"Then why—"

"If I don't feed often I risk becoming frenzied, but her blood, that of her people is ripe with magic. It would be the ultimate feast, the most dangerous addiction." Bray moistened his lips, looking longingly at Taya's bruising, he had been so close to savouring her taste. He inhaled deeply, her scent was intoxicating. He tore his gaze away quickly, lifting the bottle to his lips. "If I indulged I am not sure I would have the clarity to acknowledge the danger of overfeeding, or even bring myself to stop. Why the sudden interest?"

"I wondered if you'd tell me," Rob revealed sitting a little straighter to rest on his arms and take another drink.

"A little honesty is the least I owe you, especially after trouncing you completely." Bray grinned, lightening the mood.

"You had an advantage," Rob protested a little too loudly.

"What was that?"

"You were winning." Bray heard himself chuckle, amazed at the sudden realisation that he had grown very fond of this man, flaws included.

"Now it's your turn," Bray's eyes met with Rob's for a moment. There was something he wanted to ask him. This time, unlike when he had learnt about Rob's wife and daughter, he would not use any persuasion to gain the information he sought. "Tell me about The Cou—" Bray's posture grew rigid, his eyes darting towards Taya as he turned his attention to her alone. The alteration had been so instant Rob sprung to his feet. "Those rutterkins!" he exclaimed. He glanced to Stacy, relieved to see she had slept through his outburst.

"What is it?" Rob questioned abruptly, shedding his guise of intoxication.

"Under no circumstances can we return her to Kólasi. That's exactly what he wants, he wants her with her kind. He seeks to eradicate them all in unison. Her presence alone would be damning, but when they questioned her—"

"What's the invocation?" Bray hadn't noticed Rob's approach, but he now stood at his side, his alarmed gaze looking over Taya questioning.

"I can't tell, it's too well concealed. I'm willing to bet it is something someone in Kólasi is certain to say in her presence. He will have picked it very carefully."

"Will we be in danger when she wakes?" Stacy asked stifling a yawn roused by the raised voices.

"I sincerely doubt it," Rob assessed soberly. "The person who did this to her wanted her found. They timed this for the full moon, they wouldn't consider anyone but her own people would attempt to retrieve her. If they had, given who she is to them, it is likely both Remedy and its nature would be overlooked.

"We were wrong to assume the destruction outside was the intention. He knew they were looking for her. That's why they allowed the shielding to fail. It's not something they can just bypass since it's generated by an artefact. They would have needed to deliberately create the breach to grant that insight. Everything was too timely. You saw how the only thing remaining after the damage was where she would be found. They wanted her found, they wanted her returned to Kólasi," Rob summarised forcefully. "Its effects on her people even before activation would be felt, but when they activated it in their land—"

"Then it falls to us to remove Remedy," Stacy interjected sternly. Bray looked towards Rob, wondering if he would care to be the one to explain.

Rob's focus was elsewhere. On the back of her hand there was a small blackening cord, held only in place by the dying tendrils still rooted into her veins. Rob had seen something similar before. He reached out, taking her hand in his, noticing a strange fibre stuck within her shredded fingernails. He removed it carefully, the delicate barbule dissipating almost the instant it came into contact with him. "What was that?" she demanded, staring at Rob's empty, pinched fingers.

"I'm not sure. I thought it was a strand of feather but..." he shrugged releasing his fingers, studying the surroundings carefully for the strand. "You did all see it, it wasn't just me right?" While he spoke Rob,

548

with a well-practised hand, eased the fibrous cord from Taya before pressing a lint rag upon the bleeding wound. Bray stiffened, his gaze drawn longingly towards the reddening cloth. "I've been meaning to ask," Rob announced seeing Bray's distraction. "When we were in Kólasi, what did you eat?"

"There were humans, those who had taken Daimon partners." He wiped a bead of sweat forming on his forehead, attempting to tear his gaze away. It remained transfixed, the smell of richness quickly becoming overwhelming causing saliva to pool in his mouth. "Better a vice I can control than a craving I can't."

"So how do we remove Remedy?" Stacy moved to stand between Bray and Taya. She could see the sheer will it was taking to hold back the primal urges he had unleashed at the temple. His hand, still resting upon Taya's forehead, began to tremble.

"The Mystics, we need to talk with them," he stated, swallowing with difficulty. He released Taya, forcing himself backwards a few paces as he did. "She'll be asleep for a few hours," he advised backing towards the door. "Excuse me, I need sustenance."

"What would happen if you didn't get it?" Stacy questioned.

"It would mirror events at the temple, only I wouldn't be able to restrain myself," Bray admitted, his shaking hand fumbling with the bolt.

"You were holding back?" Rob questioned in disbelief.

"If I hadn't been, I'd not have touched you." Bray turned towards them, pulling the door open to take his leave.

"Then we're lucky there's a full crew, and survivors," Rob stated, only now realising how fortunate he had been.

"And wenches." He winked, his sight turning towards Stacy. Rob positioned himself between them. "Don't worry, she's not my type." Bray forced a chuckle as Rob raised an unamused eyebrow. Bray, assuming this response meant his play on words had been lost, explained. "Blood comes in different types." He huffed a sigh. "It's just not funny if I have to explain," he muttered pulling the door closed behind him.

* * *

Elly had not known she could tire in this land, howbeit, the higher they climbed the more her body began to ache and protest against the strain of their ceaseless efforts. They had moved without pause, picking their path carefully up large crags, stumbling and fighting against the scree which seemed to transition each plateau to their next rise. Given her earlier goading of Aidan, when she finally requested they take a short break at the mountain's peak, it came at the expense of much lighthearted ridicule.

"I did not believe dreamers could tire," Elly admitted. Pulling herself up onto the ledge which she thought to be the summit. She cursed quietly beneath her breath. "Oh why did we not suspect this?" Elly questioned in disbelief, realising they stood atop a false peak, a small icy lake circled the newly revealed peak's base. Aidan placed his hand upon the water's partially iced surface, causing frozen steppingstones to push through the icy water to create a path to their next climb.

"Perhaps I am becoming complacent, this surprised even me," Aidan admitted, patting the ground suggesting Elly should rest before they continued. "As for tiring, you are correct. Dreamers normally do not tire, but nor do they experience such temperaments of the land. The climb we have completed took somewhere in the region of three of your days. That's not to mention the time expended in reaching here. There's also the added burden of you needing to maintain the rune." He gestured towards her arm, where he knew the scarring of the rune was concealed beneath her clothing.

The effort of maintaining such a minor invocation was normally barely noticeable. However, like all magic, it had a cost, and the longer it was maintained the more noticeable it became, especially in times of great labours. "Now you've acknowledged your weakness, it'd help a great deal if you'd partake in sustenance. I've been channelling my reserves to aid you, but the energy here is weaker, that's why you're tiring now."

"You have?" Elly's posture straightened as she turned towards him.

"Yes. Did you honestly believe an Oneiroi could tire from simply walking the land?" Aidan brushed his fingers across the ground, causing a small dust cloud to rise. Manipulating the currents he rotated the air between his hands, altering the particles, condensing them until a piece of fruit rested within his grasp. He tossed it towards her before repeating the process.

During their travels she had seen him perform many minor feats, such as the steppingstones which now protruded from the lake's surface. She had hoped his manipulation of the land could be turned to their advantage and that, with enough time and energy, he could revert the land to a peaceful state to allow ease of travel. Unfortunately there were few who could attempt such a thing, he could create minor aid, vines within trees, climbing holds, but the ability to create bridges and reshape the world was a talent belonging solely to dreamers, and a few very powerful Oneirois. It was during this time he had explained that only certain Oneirois would become Outcasts, those adept in discrete and subtle magics which allowed them to remain unobserved by the Epiales. Condensing energy into food was just one of these abilities. Most Oneirois were unable to create sustenance and relied on the land itself to provide it.

"I am uncertain that *this* could constitute simply walking." Although she beheld it skeptically, Elly raised the fruit to her mouth, relieved when her teeth broke the supple skin to discover a soft and juicy flesh inside.

"Whilst I admit it seems the land is hindering us—"

"Hindering us? That climb took us days of my time. Reaching here weeks, and despite all we have done, the terrains and trials we have faced, I can see clearly where our journey began. Despite what our bodies may think, we have not travelled far at all." Elly rose to her feet, appreciating the view over the area they had climbed. The land below seemed warm and inviting, full of thriving life, flowers, and peace. She turned her sight towards the snowcapped peak. A small waterfall cascaded down parallel sections that were separated by a small scalable cliff face, which Aidan's path led to. The waters spraying against the rocks had frozen, creating a spray of ice and icicles that shimmered in the sun. It looked beautiful, yet at the same time cold and uninviting; it was a complete contrast to the land below.

"We will talk more at the summit, it should give us a good vantage point to ascertain what awaits us." Aidan rose to his feet, carefully navigating the frozen stepping stones. He cast a single backwards glance towards Elly, "Thanks for doing this."

"Now is not the time to become sentimental, old man."

"Come on, get moving. More sopor work, and less jaw work," he teased, smiling as he heard Elly chuckle. "Honestly, if you weren't so chatty we'd be there already."

Chapter 18

Reunion

At some point the darkness had given way to morning. Rising, for the first time on an altered world, the sun's kiss tickled across the water's surface. Uncovered gems reflected the fiery light, appearing like small red droplets upon the wounded land. The surrounding waters burnt with the same fierce and brilliant shades. Light created the illusion of movement and, for this brief moment, Afthonos appeared to bleed into the crimson water of the dawn sea.

Birds circled the ship, while other creatures scavenged the water and Afthonos' remains. Those not preying on the abundance of death kept their distance from the noise rising from the heaving decks, hoping for food as the scent from the ship's galley lured them closer.

Many of the longboats had now returned, and most had done so empty-handed. Those still out there, searching, migrated towards the circling birds, interrupting their feeding in the hope of rescuing just one more soul. The land parties had returned first with precious few survivors. The scenes they beheld, of countless bodies dashed upon the new jagged shore of the towering islet, would haunt their lives for years to come.

The dead outnumbered the living, and those who had survived had spread amongst the crowd a whisper of demons. Broken families huddled together near the railings. Their tear-streaked faces red from the ocean's wind, hoping the next boat to return would bring better news. They knew the truth, those still lost to the waves would never return.

The island had been home to over two thousand people. Many of whom were born and raised on their isolated land. Most had died before realising the need to flee.

Stacy pulled the door closed behind her with an exasperated sigh. She leaned against it, allowing her head to fall back and her burning eyes to turn towards the ceiling. She was exhausted, having spent the night tending to the wounded and dying. Never before had she seen so much death. She felt the warm tears forming in her eyes once more and attempted to blink them away.

"You okay?" Rob enquired softly when Stacy remained rooted in place.

"They're saying it was the work of demons. Who would start such rumours? How could they even know what happened, let alone where to point a finger. I fear not everyone aboard can be trusted. We cannot let anyone realise she's with us." She glanced towards Taya, who still lay sleeping upon the hammock. Her gaunt features were deathly pale. The dark blemishes of bruising and abrasions seemed to provide the only colouration to her flesh, and despite countless remedies still seemed raw. Stacy shuddered at the sight.

Taya had clearly been bound for long periods. Her wrists, and other parts of her body bore the signs of long-term incarceration. The wounds on her skin had broken and healed countless times. Their varying degrees of healing showed near her rescue such methods of imprisonment had been thought unnecessary. Given some of the injuries Stacy had seen it was apparent they had controlled her through fear. The lashings across her upper back and legs would likely scar, as would the worst of the marks clearly left by shackles. The rest of the bruising would fade, in time.

"It's likely some of those responsible found refuge aboard. If nothing else it proves, yet again, that evil always finds a way to claw to life at the expense of the innocent." Rob gave a snort of contempt, his comment clearly intended to include himself in his observations. His empty stare remained transfixed on Taya.

"Says you, hiding yourself away in here. If you protected her as much as you did that bottle this would never have happened. At least I've been out there, trying to make a difference. All you've been doing here is nursing your self-pity." Stacy felt her stomach churn as she caught the scent of the liquor Rob drank. He had almost finished yet another bottle. If she wasn't so frustrated she probably would have warned him he should stop. Besides, she knew he wouldn't listen. "Even now, after all this, it amazes me you can still be so self-centred."

"Better I stay here than make things worse out there." Rob took another drink, forcing himself to swallow before he pushed the bottle aside in disgust. Stacy was right, what was even the point of drinking? He needed something to deaden the guilt, and it could not be found at the bottom of a bottle.

He slumped further back in his chair. Stacy had said they were blaming the disaster on a demon, but it had been an event of his own making.

He raised his head forcing himself to look upon Taya, to fully behold each and every aspect of the suffering he had caused. His eyes migrated to the circlet. There was a part of him that hoped she would continue to sleep peacefully for some time. When she woke, when she realised what the current situation meant for her, she would probably never sleep soundly again.

"Worse, how can it possibly be worse?" Stacy spat. "You at least owe it to them to look upon what your actions wrought."

"Do you think I don't know the devastation?" Rob's voice was thick with remorse. "You want to hear me say this is my fault? Fine. I take all the blame and then some. You want me to admit I acted in my own interest? Very well. I put my needs above hers.

But don't you dare assume I am ignorant to the consequences. I can see them right here, on the flesh of a woman I love as my niece despite knowing her not to be such. Damn Sunniva, damn her to Tartarus." He drank again, trying to drown the images of his own family rekindled by the pain and guilt of seeing Taya in this condition.

"You blame your sister now? Take a good long look, Rob. You're the one who made this choice, not her. Your actions brought her this pain, no one else's." Stacy approached Taya, stroking her hair. Since they had met it seemed this woman had known nothing but suffering. "Damn you," Stacy whispered, glancing over her shoulder towards Rob.

Stacy's fingers moved to the circlet, tracing its silver surface. The contact alone caused the sleeping figure to wince, a small whimper leaving her lips as she shied from the touch.

"Bray called this Remedy," Stacy said, her voice losing its former abrasiveness. "It's hard to believe something this size is capable of such devastation. He said it feeds on her life. Is it killing her now, even as she sleeps?" she asked with genuine concern before covering Taya with another blanket.

"I don't know. I imagine there is something to ensure it can be utilised to its fullest potential. I mean otherwise what's the point? There must be more to it, something we're missing."

"Nicely deduced." Bray's voice startled them. He stood leaning against the wall, listening to the exchange between them as they remained oblivious to his presence. Stacy stepped aside to allow him to check on Taya's condition. He unwrapped one of the bandages on her wrist, wincing at the sight. He had hoped the ointment he had applied would have taken some of the heat from the injury. But it still seemed to burn as angrily as ever. The last thing they needed was for her to contract an infection, and she had no shortage of injuries where one could still take root. What she needed, more than medicine and sleep, was food. "The dilemma we now face is that Remedy itself is so ancient, aside from the primordial deities, only the Mystics even have any knowledge of it. Their spirits are the only ones old enough to know its secrets."

"How about Misora? You said your people were the keepers of knowledge from all cycles." Stacy's voice held reasonable optimism. She had to hope she was correct, after all, she already knew the Mystic approach would prove fruitless.

"You are not wrong. But in this instance we are blind. The information we need was destroyed some time ago. Most was recovered, but not this." Bray removed what appeared to be a small crystal lattice from his pocket. "It is the only one remaining incomplete, and the reason for my being here. I was tasked to retrieve it."

"You think it stolen, from a place no one knows even exists?" Stacy scoffed.

"It *was* removed, although we don't believe it was with malicious intent. We would expect such things to find themselves in the hands of the aristocracy."

Bray looked to Rob. "You know yourself how rich people like their unique trinkets. But nothing, not even a whisper."

"What about the piece you do have, are there any clues?" Rob enquired, knowing anything would be better than their current state of ignorance.

"It's useless incomplete." Bray studied the fragment of the crystal leaf that was woven from fine and delicate threads. It was beautifully crafted. Rob could understand why Bray believed it would be coveted by the rich. He had never seen anything like it. It pulsed with an aura of life and magic, as if wind and ice had merged to create this mesmerising item. Seeing Rob's fixation he placed it away. "It has to be whole. To be fair, I volunteered for this because it meant I could leave Misora. I never imagined we'd need the information. Knowledge is never truly lost, but by the time this is regrown it'll be too late. We have to rely on the Mystics. I was hoping not to have to involve them. Truth be told, I don't even know where to look."

"I doubt the Mystics could be of much help anyway," Stacy asserted. She paused briefly committing herself to her decision. "What I mean to say is... I know nothing of it."

"Why would—" Bray looked to her in awe. "Of course, Holder of the Sacred Chord," Bray groaned in realisation. "How could I have overlooked something so painfully obvious? She as good as told me who you were." Stacy smiled slightly giving a slight nod. "So that means Ms Amelia..." Bray snorted in mild amusement. "Well I guess that explains a few things, like how she knew I was Misorian. *You* might not know, but perhaps she could tell us something." Bray recovered from her revelation quickly, scolding himself for not realising it sooner. He looked to Stacy once more, seeing her in a whole new light.

"Amelia sure does seem to know everything," Rob agreed. His face grew concerned as he gestured towards Taya who seemed to be stirring. "Hey, how're you feeling?" he whispered softly, moving from his chair to crouch beside her.

"Where am I?" Her voice was weak, weaker than he had expected. Seeing her squinting against the light Rob moved to cover the porthole. Darkening the room seemed to bring her some relief. Her eyes now searched the cabin, finding each one of them in turn. Her gaze lingered on Rob until Stacy stepped between them in the pretence of handing her a cup of water.

"You're aboard a ship," Bray responded softly, taking a seat at the table to give her some semblance of space. His body was tensed, ready to react should the need arise. There was no way to discern the effect his actions would have had. It was possible she would not even remember them, or she could even believe that they themselves were her captors.

She moved slowly pushing herself to sit. Before anyone had time to warn her the hammock twisted, tipping her from its unstable embrace to fall heavily upon the floor. She let out a pained groan, committing herself to remaining there, doubting she had the strength to move. Stacy assisted her, wrapping her arms around Taya, and escorting her to a seat at the table. She was unable to hide the concern at feeling the protruding ribs concealed beneath her loose and tattered clothing.

"What do you recall?" Bray questioned softly, briefly turning to Rob, who kept his distance by remaining at the porthole. Bray tilted his head, gesturing towards the jug of water not far from where he stood. He moved guardedly, pouring a glass before he approached only to notice Stacy had already placed one before her. Taya took a slow sip, relishing the feeling of the water on her dry lips.

"We were looking for a treasure. Then"—her hands shot to her forehead, finding the circlet—"spirits, that actually happened!" Her unsteady fingers traced the metal desperately. Her fear welling until the boat began to tremble. She remembered him securing it to her, a cursed item.

"Calm down." Bray's soothing tones came barely a moment after Taya had already regained control. She clasped her hands before her on the table while attempting to ignore the pain breathing caused. It seemed impossible, but she grew paler. "It's very important you try to remain calm." He reached across the table, placing a comforting hand upon hers.

"What do you remember from before that?" Rob watched her stiffen. Her eyes seemed to move rapidly from side to side as she searched her memories.

"I remember everything now. But after what he did to me I don't understand how that can be possible." A clear image of the figure looking at her through a crystal surfaced, causing her to take a startled breath. He had severed her memories, replacing them with the lies Sunniva had been telling her all these years. She tightened her grip on her hands before releasing them. Her fingers rotated her ring. Feeling the familiar ease of movement she glanced down to it, taking comfort in its presence.

"You can thank Bray for that little miracle." Stacy nodded towards him. "For your current predicament however you can thank—"

"Did you recognise the person who did this to you, or the one who imprisoned you?" Bray questioned, casting a warning glance towards Stacy. Now was not the time to incite hostile emotions. "There has to be a link somewhere. If we can work out who they are, we may be able to find some answers."

"It was the physician, from Mirage Lake." Taya revealed, closing her eyes as she took another deep calming breath. When she opened them again she was looking at a spirit bottle. She reached out as if to take it, her hand hesitating just inches from the glass. She closed her eyes, looking away as she lowered her head and retracted her hand. In that moment she looked as if the weight of the world was upon her shoulders. "I can't go home, can I?" she questioned suddenly, her hand once more touching the circlet. A tear leaked from the corner of her eye, she brushed it away quickly.

"It would be better if you didn't." She felt Bray squeeze her hand as he delivered the news. "The circlet," Bray expelled a long and difficult sigh. He didn't know how to deliver this news. Part of him felt, given the severity of her expression, she already knew what he was about to say. "It acts as a setting for..." he hesitated, unable to force the word which would cause her further pain,

"Remedy." Her voice caught in her throat as the words came back to haunt her. '*Remedy is aligned.*' Her fingers once more traced the circlet with a new understanding. The last two months had passed in a haze of pain and distortion, but Bray's words had restored some clarity. She knew what she wore, and what this meant. Bray looked away, seeing the pain and realisation flood her eyes.

"We still don't understand how it works. But, Ethelyn, we'll do everything we can." Rob was unable to meet her eyes as he spoke. His internal monologue constantly berating him and condemning his actions.

"I see." The resolve in her voice came as a surprise. "We have time." She placed her hand on her stomach, feeling the nausea stir. "It may feed on my life, but since it wants to use me as a medium to destroy my people it won't risk depleting me until it can accomplish those ends." Stacy looked to her in surprise, the calm tones were something unexpected. She noticed that, even despite her injuries, Taya seemed to sit a little taller, and held herself with an air of confidence.

"How can you not be angry?" Stacy questioned, glaring vehemently in Rob's direction. "He's made it so you can never go home. He did this to you. How can you be so calm?"

"Ethelyn, I'm sorry." Rob spoke when it became apparent Taya could not find the words to respond. He met her eyes for the first time, speaking some of the hardest words he had ever voiced. The sincerity was apparent through the weight with which they were spoken.

"I'll stay away from other Daimons. Remedy needs me alive, as I say, we have time yet. I know you'll figure this out." She reached across the table, her hand touching his lightly. She would never understand the difference that single gesture had made to him.

"Our next port of call is Amelia."

"Amelia," Taya repeated, thinking for a moment before recalling the elderly lady. She remembered her now, from *both* the occasions their paths had crossed.

* * *

The climb had not been as daunting as it had first appeared, but reaching the peak brought a whole new realisation. The tumultuous clouds had been almost completely shielded from view by the towering giant they had been climbing. Now they beheld the sight once more they could see how much they had swelled. The heavy clouds had once more extended to impact the ground with its devastating fury, changing the column's shade to one of dust and debris as the violent winds attempted to draw the land up and into itself. The ionised clouds became thick with impurities, the rapid succession of lightning growing more intense, as if feeding on the offering from the land below.

The land below them was dead. Through the dusty fog, cracks split the barren landscape, spanning outward from the rising funnel. The damage, spreading as the ground crumbled, opened sinkholes to reveal the void beneath. The fracturing of the land could be heard even from their altitude, deep and rumbling like the thunder which should have echoed in succession with the ever present lightning. Aidan's hands covered his mouth, his eyes portraying his horror. The land made no attempt to heal itself despite the funnel now receding. A circular span of death extended scarring the landscape in a place where no energy survived.

The effects were far and wide, a clear transition could be seen giving scope to the influence of the horror. A border of life abruptly ceased, and all which lay beyond was death. All but for a small oasis, a small point of life where the eye of the hurricane had come to rest. Aidan paced, noticing that the mountain they stood upon bordered this death, the sloping descent becoming a sheer and savage escarpment where the mountain's structure should have extended.

Aidan remained transfixed, unable to tear his sight from the extensive damage. His mind raced, never before had he witnessed destruction of this magnitude. He concentrated on Remedy, trying to piece together fragments of ancient lore, lore predating his time and relating to a world which he was not native to, or even interested in. He questioned how such a thing could relate to Jude's abduction, knowing, without a doubt, his circumstances were somehow central to everything witnessed.

He could feel the trace of energy emitted by his partner, a cry of distress only Aidan could recognise. The amassing energy did little to disrupt the plea. No matter how faint, their separation created a wave of conflicting energy, alien and disturbing to all surrounding them. Partners could always find one another, and he vowed, surveying the awaiting danger, that he *would* find Jude. The last time the clouds had met the earth had been when Night said Remedy had been aligned for use, he feared to think what this more recent display depicted. All he knew for certain was that the energy was being drawn into and from his realm, otherwise the land would not appear as depleted as it did now. Something was using events of the waking world for reasons he could not even begin to fathom.

"What are we missing?" Aidan questioned, tearing himself away from the scene below in an attempt to calm his mind.

"What can be found there?" Elly questioned, gesturing towards the small oasis. She took a step forwards, noticing, as Aidan had, the abrupt stop in the peak's shape. Below them, Elly could see the wasteland and realised it wasn't that the land no longer attempted to delay them, there had been no more means by which to extend their journey. All the energy beyond this point, but for that within the small sheltered area, had been absorbed, leaving only desolation and decay spanning for miles.

"To the best of my knowledge, nothing." Aidan narrowed his eyes hoping to obtain a better view of the distant haven.

"What now?" Elly asked, picking up a loose stone from the ground. She threw it over the edge, watching it rotate slowly as all that created it turned to dust.

"We proceed with great caution. But first, I need to gather supplies. It looks like energy is a luxury not afforded beyond this decline."

"Decline?" Elly scoffed, quizzically examining the nearly smooth, vertical cliff. "And how do you propose we descend?"

"Do you honestly expect me to believe that one of your vast imagination cannot think of at least several methods we can employ?" he challenged with a knowing smile.

"None of which are plausible," Elly observed sternly.

"And why not?"

* * *

Amelia had been expecting their arrival since she had first heard about the disaster on Afthonos almost a week ago. Stacy had been keeping her abreast of developments whenever their path had crossed into Collateral, and had sent news of their pending arrival when the vessel had finally docked. Many days had been spent stationary upon the water, and news of their arrival had arrived a day before they had.

Taya's weakened condition had made the travelling slow, and whilst she attempted to disguise her pain it was apparent to any who looked upon her. Even horseback proved no easier. Eventually Bray had taken to carrying her upon his back. His movements were far smoother than that of the horse.

The expression on Amelia's face as she opened her door to the small group betrayed her concern. She knew Taya had suffered, but she had been unprepared for the extent. Her eyes looked with sorrow upon the exhausted Daimon being carried upon the Misorian's back. Wounds, which should have healed, burnt ferociously and Amelia feared there was little even she could do to alleviate her obvious distress. Taya had looked enfeebled when last they had met, but Amelia had spoken to phantasms who possessed more colour and substance than she did.

"Bring her inside, get her seated. I'll put the pot on to boil." Amelia left for the kitchen, pulling Stacy along with her where the two of them shared a hushed conversation before Amelia poked her head through the doorway to look at Taya. "Stacy tells me you're feeling much better than when last we met?" Amelia called through, cringing at the near falsity of her words. She was not looking better physically, but her mental fractures had been mostly repaired.

"Yes, thank you. I am no longer confused. I'm not so good on boats it seems. My legs are still weak." Taya forced a weak chuckle. She had seen Amelia's expression, the horror at witnessing her current appearance, and was grateful for its lack of mention.

"I am afraid I owe you an apology." Amelia entered the room with a tray in her hands. Her vision fixed onto the ornament Taya now wore as she placed the sustenance upon the table. "I thought myself beyond her meddling. I was a fool. But you're feeling well?" Taya's trembling hands took the cup from Amelia, giving a polite nod.

"It's my own fault, I delayed approaching you. I thought I may gain some insight by observing. I never considered I was being watched as well. I had heard whispers of demon hunters, but given that they only seemed to seek payment from settlements we paid them less heed than was required. The fault is my own."

"Sorry to interrupt," Bray stating showing no such remorse. "But there are more pressing matters to address." Bray inclined his head towards Taya.

"Remedy," Amelia acknowledged. "I may be old, but I'm rarely a fool. I recognised it. But Taya, it seems you have recovered nicely. Pray tell, did our Misorian friend offer some assistance?" Bray felt his shoulders slump, his arms hanging loosely at his sides as he bowed his head. He knew by that question alone he was in trouble.

"Yes, Ma'am," Taya confirmed. Amelia turned towards him with a sly smile, her eyes twinkling with youthful vigour.

"Well, Master Bray. Since you've shed the robe of observation and already breached one of your laws, would it hurt to extend a little further courtesy?" Amelia raised an eyebrow quizzically.

"You assume they haven't asked this already?"

"I make no assumptions, but I *do* know you have information on this matter." She placed a cup from the table in his hand, searching him for a reaction.

"No longer. Marise Shi's attempt to prevent The Chosen from completing their quest saw one of our archives destroyed. We did locate the information you mention only..." Bray pulled the broken crystal leaf from his pocket, sliding it across the table towards her. She lifted it carefully, turning it over in her fingers as she scrutinised it. The missing segment was acutely apparent.

"What is it with that boy and picking up things he shouldn't touch?" Amelia scolded shaking her head, although she couldn't suppress the slight smile that played on the edge of her lips.

"You know who has it?" Bray slowly lowered his cup, his posture stiffening.

"I can hazard a guess." She tapped her finger on the table as if in time to another thought. "He doesn't know when to leave well alone." She paused for a moment, her attention straying to the window. "You know, it was Zo's friends who finally returned the Spiritwest to Gaea."

"Zo?" Bray questioned in confusion.

"My granddaughter." She motioned towards the window. They looked in the direction she indicted to see the darkened silhouettes of two gravestones upon the borders of her land.

"She died? I'm so—"

"Spare it no thought." Amelia gestured dismissively. "She's happier now, of that I am certain." The words struck them as odd. Her tone was sharp, but there was nothing to indicate this was meant to be as harsh as it sounded.

"You knew the saviours?" Rob questioned, wincing as he leaned forward slightly on the table. Amelia cast her gaze over him, noticing the dark purple facial bruising which was now devoid of any swelling.

"At one time or another I put most of you sorry waif and strays on your path. Honestly, sometimes I swear nothing would ever get done without me." She gave a slight shrug, her expression was one of good-humour. "I can tell you where to find two of them. If you're interested?"

"We're going to meet the heroes who returned the Spiritwest?" The tone of Bray's voice bordered on excitement.

"If you think it's worth your time." She smiled again, having Bray present made things easier. He understood her intention to guide them. "You should find Eiji without trouble. He's akin to Stacy here, but he's also an Elementalist. He will have not long finished his offerings. You've probably even crossed paths with them if you've spent any great time in Collateral. They attend to Venrent's former store. They divide the year between Collateral and Eiji's home, but I believe you'll find them there."

"Venrent?" Rob questioned. He could almost remember the name, certain he had once sold a few of his more unique items to him. But placing him now, after so many other names and faces, was impossible.

"Just ask around, someone will point you there. If he's not back, Acha should still be there. They tend to spend most of their time together these days." Amelia smiled a knowing smile.

"I thought Elementalists couldn't be near people for too long?" Bray questioned in surprise.

"Every rule has an exception. He just happens to be one of them, but it's not something accomplished alone." Amelia turned to Taya with a smile. "How about some food? You could use some meat on those bones, dear."

* * *

Amelia, ever the polite hostess, had fed them well before she sent them on their way. She could have told them exactly where to find Venrent's store, but it was her job to guide, not direct.

The Daimon's condition concerned her. It seemed Taya had come to these lands to negotiate a peace, and instead had been abducted, tortured, and now had been forced to bear the very thing which could destroy her race. It did not reflect well upon the people of this world. If the small group were unable to remove Remedy it would create another problem, and she knew from experience that when one artefact of destruction was uncovered, another soon followed.

Amelia shook her head, tidying away the dishes. How could she not have foreseen this? When powers of this magnitude were born or uncovered she always felt the disturbance in energies. Their presence would normally permeate through the world around them. Something had prevented the cry from reaching her, as if it had been diverted elsewhere to silence its call. This failing she could not direct towards the power of Apallagí. Somehow the entirety of Remedy attuning itself to a host had gone unnoticed.

Something had upset the natural order. There were but a few who could hide such intentions, and the implications seemed beyond consideration.

* * *

Beyond the main trade district, close to one of the dividing walls, stood a small, almost out of place looking establishment. Being on the far outskirts of the trading area saw there being little in the way of illumination, but the flickering light from the open windows caused a warm glow to spill onto the cobbled path. There was something inviting to its presence, especially in the hours of twilight.

Outside, sheltering some of its wares from the elements, was a semi-circular, maroon tent. Within stood numerous tables displaying oddities and antiquities, protected from theft only by a worn and faded handwritten notice, warning thieves of curses. The remaining goods were secured behind an open casement window. Yet the assortment of items inside seemed of little worth compared to some of the rarer artefacts displayed outside.

A woman sat just inside, twisting and braiding a selection of materials into a length of rope. Her long brown hair fell in finely crafted ringlets, the ease of the hairstyle's appearance betraying the effort of her nightly preparation in order to achieve the desired effect. Eventually, they approached the small window. She glanced up, there was a friendliness to her smile which set them at ease.

"I am Acha, serving in the stead of Mr Venrent. Might I be of some assistance?" Acha had so many patrons specifically request the old merchant that her introduction now rolled from her tongue effortlessly.

"That's a lot of rope," Rob commented with a long whistle, for the first time appreciating exactly how many rolls were situated behind where the young woman stood. He chewed his lips, disguising a smile as he remembered why the merchant's name had been familiar.

"One for every occasion. Mr Venrent is particular when it comes to that type of thing. The right selection of rope can be the difference between life and death." Acha heard herself laugh, realising how much like Venrent she must sound. She had almost quoted him word for word. "Were you looking for something in particular?"

"Actually yes. We were hoping to speak with you and Eiji." Acha's eyes narrowed slightly, but her smile never faltered.

"Oh?" Her light tone did not conceal the bid for further information.

"Amelia sent us," Bray interjected.

"Ah, so comes the day I am recipient to those words. The door's just inside, please." She gestured them towards the tent, unhooking and closing the shop's windows. She opened the door, her slender frame blocking their entry. "It seems you have me at a disadvantage. You know my name but..." she allowed her words to trail off, prompting them for a response.

"Forgive me," Rob stated. "I'm Robert Raymond, she's Stacy Psáltis, he's Grayson Bray and the other one is..." Rob looked to Taya with a questioning glance, unsure how he should be addressing her.

"Kitaia Ethelyn, but I've grown accustomed to Taya." She nodded politely at Acha, who stepped back granting them entry and extending her hand to Rob as he stepped inside.

"Oh you're a treasure hunter." She smiled releasing him to take Stacy's. "Hmm, you're just like Eiji." Taya extended her hand next as Bray lingered in the doorway, hesitant to approach. After taking Taya's hand Acha pulled back a little quicker than intended. "Kólasi, I'm unfamiliar with." Her eyes focused on Bray. He looked cautiously to her hand, trying to decline the gesture he raised his in a form of surrender, but all this did was encourage Acha to reach out and grab him. "Oh, I've visited Misora." She leaned in slightly to share a quiet word. "My type would kill you," she whispered, smiling as she heard Bray's low, appreciative chuckle as he stepped inside. Acha had no qualms in revealing her ability. If they had been sent by Amelia there was no need for secrecy, and she only touched a fraction of them, enough to ensure she was in no danger, and to understand their needs.

"Psychomancy?" Rob stared at Acha's hands in bewilderment.

"You don't, in all honesty, think I would let just anyone simply speaking a name cross my threshold do you?" She looked to Stacy with recognition, but doubted her guest would remember their paths crossing. "I used to believe my gift was a curse too, until I embraced it. You've come a long way since..." Acha glanced meaningfully towards Stacy's hand.

"You were the ones who returned us from the island." Acha dipped her head in confirmation, despite it not being a question. "Then it seems I owe you a debt already."

"Nonsense." Acha gave a dismissive wave, motioning them towards the fireplace. "Please, sit. Eiji is due home shortly, but shall we begin, he has a habit of getting... distracted sometimes."

"I can't believe I'm sitting with one of the heroes who returned the Spiritwest. I never imagined you'd be working in such a place, or at all," Rob observed, staring at the woman before them. He had long dreamt of meeting the heroes who had prevented other families suffering the same losses he had.

"Heroes, is that what they're still saying?" Acha laughed. "What nonsense, we just did what anyone would have done."

"But anyone didn't, you did. Just like anyone didn't release the wyrms, or search for the knowledge needed. It was you, you all deserve the title."

"It was a difficult journey." Acha's eyes hazed over for a second as she was lost in thought. The silence broken as the door slammed closed.

"I'm home." Eiji's voice seemed a little more forceful than it needed to be. Acha never closed the store early. Despite knowing she was capable of defending herself he still worried for her safety.

"We have company," she called, already sensing Eiji's tension. "Amelia sent them." Her voice dropped in volume as he appeared. He raised his hand in an awkward wave. "This is Rob, Stacy, Kitaia, and Grayson—sorry you prefer Bray don't you?" She gestured to each of them in turn, seeing Bray nod at her observation. But her guests' attention was now elsewhere, their intense stares were directed towards Eiji. Unlike Acha, who was dressed in dull, every day attire, he was the very image of the hero imagined. He didn't normally dress in the manner he did now, only when attending to specific duties. "Did everything go okay?"

"Yeah, I'll tell y' about it later." He removed his long coat. It was a cut and style none of them had seen before except for the artists' representations. The white coat was a contrast to the deep blue trousers and tight fitting shirt he wore. It was not linen, nor was it a material they recognised, it seemed almost elastic. After placing his removed garment on the coat stand he approached, taking Acha's hand in his he kissed it softly. "So what brings y' here?" he asked turning his focus towards their guests.

"We're not sure exactly," Rob answered, shaking his head. He considered how foolish it must sound, to be sent to someone's door with no real understanding of why. "I think she believed you could help us locate something."

"Really, whaddya after?" Eiji questioned cautiously as he moved to perch himself on the chair arm next to Acha.

"It is our understanding you visited Misora. She seems to be under the impression you left there with something you shouldn't have," Bray advised. Eiji's eyes narrowed in concentration as he thought back.

"We were in Misora for a short time, but I dunno that we had anythin' from them. We kind'a caused some problems. Y' hafta understand, the place we'd intended t'visit had been ruined simply because we had t'go there."

"Don't worry about that." Bray waved his hand dismissively. "We managed to repair most of the damage. We just couldn't piece together all the fragments. One was missing." He fished inside his pocket to produce the broken leaf, he rolled it across the top of his fingers before throwing it to an unprepared Eiji. His fingers fumbled the catch, and it broke free from his grasp, twice, before he finally grasped it firmly. He studied its surface, a slight look of recognition crossing his brow as he scratched his chin.

"It's important?" He carefully returned the item back to Bray, after receiving an encouraging nudge from Acha.

"It's needed to remove this." Taya inclined her head, wearily gesturing towards the circlet. Eiji glanced at it before turning his focus to Acha. She watched his expression alter, growing serious before his vision snapped back to look upon it once more.

"That's... y' a..." But no matter how hard he appeared to try the words would not follow. Acha shook her head.

"Yes. She's a Daimon. It's an interesting group. He's an Empusa, she's a Mystic and—"

Bray cursed as Taya fell to her knees, her hands clutching at the circlet as it sent red-hot waves of pain through her. Her vision fixed on him pleadingly. But he was so far away.

"Bray," she gasped desperately, knowing there was but one way to silence this rising power. Tears streaked her face as she felt the magic within her begin to unleash. She fought against it, holding it back with all the will she could muster. Even then she knew this would buy precious little time. The sounds of shattering glass filled the air as delicate ornaments were shaken from their shelves. The windows rattled violently within their frames. The touch of magic upon the walls caused warded symbols, which even Acha and Eiji had been unaware of, to glow with strange and brilliant colours. "I-I can't," she panted. Bray's approach seemed painfully slow as he attempted to close the distance between them.

Eiji thrust himself forwards, knocking Acha from the path of a falling bookcase, his hand outreached to forge a barrier of wind surrounding Taya. It suppressed the damage for but a moment until the power adjusted, embracing the wind to cause more violence, twisting it to a barrier to prevent further interference as it pulled the conjuring from Eiji's control.

Bray reached out, cloth and flesh began to peel as he attempted to force his arm through the devastating force. His skin began to shed, but still he fought to reach her.

Acha, recovering her balance, touched the barrier. The contact absorbed but a fraction of the power, enough to permit Bray to finally reach Taya. His raw, bloodied fingers smeared a trail down her cheek, but that contact was all he had needed. All became still as she fell the remaining distance to the floor where, for more reasons than one, she was taken in Acha's embrace.

"A hidden invocation?" Eiji questioned sternly. There was no denying what he had felt. As soon as it had been spoken it was almost as if a floodgate had been opened to unbridled power.

"Mystic," Bray confirmed, concealing his mangled flesh behind his back in an attempt to disguise the agonising damage. He looked regretfully towards Taya, who now rested on the floor within Acha's arms. "Sorry, I wasn't expecting that," he winced, setting his jaw tightly in an attempt to suppress the pain.

"You knew what the invocation was?" Rob demanded in outrage.

"No, but I had a feeling."

"Perhaps you should have sha—"

"Did I hurt anyone?" Taya opened her eyes to see Acha above her. It took a moment for her to realise she now lay on the floor with her head resting on this young woman's lap. She pulled herself to sit, massaging her throbbing temples.

"No, you're fine," Acha whispered with a passing glance in Bray's direction. He gave an appreciative nod, subtly sliding his arms from his sleeves in order to reverse his linen shirt and conceal at least some of the already healing injuries. He would need to feed before he could completely recover, something he would attend to as soon as he could slip away for a moment.

"It's my fault," Eiji apologised. "I was surprised. It's quite an unusual group y've here." He looked to Rob, his eyes filled with excitement. "So what are you a Ceto, a shade? Oh I know, a Lycanthrope?"

"A treasure hunter," Acha intervened before he could embarrass himself further. "A human one."

"Oh, sorry." Eiji's tone seemed almost disappointed. "That happen often? Oh wait, it wasn't y' that sunk—" Seeing the harsh look being directed towards him by Acha, Eiji fell silent.

"Sunk? It sunk?" Taya covered her mouth as she looked to her friends in horror, fresh tears welled in her eyes. "It sunk?" she questioned again, a little more forcefully when no one answered her. She looked to each of them in turn. Her intense stare lingered on Eiji, who shifted uncomfortably with the need to respond. By the time he realised Acha had shaken her head the words were already tumbling from his lips.

"Well, not all the way, just a little. Okay a lot but—sorry." Eiji raised his hand to briefly shield his eyes as he shook his head. "I thought y'd have known."

"I—you mean—all those people?" She glanced between her friends from her position on the floor. Their expressions and silence told her everything she needed to know. She lowered her head, cradling it within her hands.

"Ethelyn, it wasn't your fault." Rob looked to Eiji feeling he owed some manner of explanation. "It's a long story, but the brunt of it is a physician used some deceptive thrall to make her think she was human, abducted her, secured that to her"—Rob gestured towards the circlet barely visible beneath Taya's forward falling hair—"and used an invocation to release her power. His plan, it seems, is to wipe out the entire Daimon species." Eiji looked to Acha both apologetically and expectantly.

"It's true," she confirmed with a slight dip of her head. She had gained an understanding of their problem from the moment their hands had touched.

"Such power, are all Daimons that strong?" Again he directed his attention towards Acha.

"She's the Sfaíra Fýlakas, that's their version of royalty. She has the power of her predecessors and came here to seek the... old spirits and ask for their freedom. That's probably why she was targeted." They looked to Acha in surprise. "I touched you, I know a lot now." Acha had spent a long time learning control of her skills, but once mastered what she could do with this gift became astounding.

"So what we just saw," Eiji prompted.

"Was Remedy unleashing her power. I'd have to guess if any Daimons were here they would have been killed." Acha once more answered.

"That's why we need the fragment. We can't understand what we're facing without it. We need to know how it works and how to remove it," Bray concluded, Acha gave Eiji a nod. He stepped back from them a few paces, pulling a chain from beneath his shirt.

"Hey, Daniel." As Eiji spoke their guests looked towards the door, expecting to see another figure. But the room remained empty. It was only when a voice responded they realised Eiji held a crystal within his grasp.

"Eiji, how are you? How's Acha? Is everything all right?" The questions were fired in rapid succession, not allowing Eiji time to respond. "Hey, how was your journey, you've just finished your offerings?"

"Yeah, I'll tell y' later, right now I could do with some help." Eiji glanced towards the four strangers. They were watching him intently, wondering what exactly was happening. It was little wonder, gossip crystals were a rare commodity. Eiji continued to speak, as if having received an affirming gesture from the unseen source. "Remember Misora? Well, did y' take anythin'?" There was a slight pause during which Eiji offered something resembling a pained smile. "I've a Misorian here they need it back in order t'find a way t'deactivate Remedy." Eiji looked up, noticing Bray slipping out through the door.

"Can you repeat that? It almost sounded like you said—"

"I did, and the one aligned t'it is sittin' right here."

"I'll be right there." Eiji dropped the crystal back beneath his shirt. He turned, only to find himself almost face to face with Rob who seemed to have approached at some point to watch over his shoulder.

"You've got a gossip crystal." His voice was filled with surprise and awe. Rob, being a treasure hunter, had heard about such things. But even he had never actually seen one before.

"Yeah, me, Daniel, and Zo," Eiji answered without pause for thought, his hand resting upon the place the crystal now hung.

"Zo?" Stacy looked to Eiji sharply as she helped Acha right the bookcase and began collecting the tomes. "The same Zo Amelia knew?"

"Yeah why?" he responded, a frown tugging at his brow.

"Isn't she deceased?" Stacy thought back, she remembered the graves clearly. Hearing the door pull quietly closed she glanced towards it, only to see Bray reentering leaving her to wonder when exactly he had stepped outside.

"Can you talk to the dead on this thing too?" Rob's voice filled with excitement. Surely Eiji would not begrudge him a moment with it, if that were truly the case.

"Well, she's not exactly dead. It's a long story."
They looked to him with interest. "Too long. Daniel
will be here shortly."

Chapter 19

Knowledge

Daniel hurried through the streets of Collateral. Ignoring the strange looks his attire made him recipient to. It was rare for those aligned with the Eortháds to traverse these streets. They were known to travel by way of wyrms or irfeláfa. Hushed whisperings followed him wherever he walked, but his pace remained brisk, unaltered.

His knee-length brown hide coat billowed behind him, weighted down slightly by his old, battered satchel. His supple trousers were laced on the inner leg, creating a form-fitted appearance before disappearing beneath the upper buckles of his laced highwayman boots. The shades and cut of the material were recognised instantly as that of the Eortháds, for no beast known could produce hide so durable yet supple.

He made his way to his friends' home, stealing inside and closing the door quickly behind him. A small crowd had followed to see where one such as himself would take his business. Normally he would not be dressed so conspicuously when visiting Collateral, but his own curiosity had seen his rapid departure from Kalia.

The sound of his light, eager footfalls drew the attention of his friends, but Daniel's eyes saw only the woman seated amongst them. Perhaps there had been something to the manner in which she rose to greet him, or the unusual paleness of her complexion against the darkness of her hair and eyes. But she had captivated him completely.

He approached with purpose, unaware of the crunching of broken ornaments beneath his boots, his steps stilled only briefly before her. He rubbed his chin, inclining his head slightly as he walked around her, his dark eyes absorbed her every detail. He grabbed a nearby stool, pulled it towards the centre of the room, and motioned for her to sit. The room conformed to the silence that had accompanied the intensity of his presence.

"Seldcúþu," he muttered, tapping his lip with his finger before moving to stand behind her.

"What about me do you find strange, my lord?" Taya swallowed, she could only imagine him to be of noble birth given the presence he radiated. His inclination to attend to matters quickly did nothing to dispel this belief. But there was a wisdom in his eyes, suggestive of a seasoned scholar.

"Daniel's fine. I'm nobody's lord." He waved his hand dismissively. His words almost autonomous as his eyes bore into her.

"But y' *are* the Eortháds' Wita," Eiji countered, but his words had been unheard. Daniel was too absorbed in his examination. Hearing this Taya regarded him once more, recognising now the language he had spoken as that known to the Eortháds. His alignment with them also served to explain his brashness. Hearing the title allowed her to see the path of greatness before him. He was not yet all he could be. He was still learning, or he would have already devised the means to remove this headpiece, should one exist.

"Are you sure you're a Daimon?" He placed his hand upon her chin, using it to turn her head first to his left, then right.

"Many have tried to convince me otherwise." He released her showing no sign of having heard her speak. He rubbed a strand of her hair through his fingers, it felt just like human hair. He frowned slightly.

"Ic ácnæwe," he stated, placing his hands on her back and began to feel her ribcage. He felt her tense beneath his touch. "Incredible," he whispered.

"Daniel!" Acha snapped, causing him to startle.

"What? Oh, sorry. I've been around the wyrms too long," he justified, realising that what he had just done was in no way the correct way to examine a human, or Daimon as the case seemed to present.

"Did y' bring it?" Eiji interrupted as Daniel's fingers started to trace the circlet which bore Remedy. He pulled back sharply.

"Here." Daniel reluctantly stepped away from Taya, but before he could place the crystal shard down Bray had lifted it from his fingers. He watched in fascination as Bray twisted and interlocked the fine threads of crystal weave, smoothing them with skill and precision to reform the crystal leaf. He approached the nearby window, holding it to the light as if to examine its surface.

"Can it be removed? Or at least, can you tell me how it works?" It seemed strange to Daniel that, given the information was now in Bray's hand, Taya had directed her questioned towards him. He closed his eyes for a moment, listening.

"It emits and amplifies a reverse resonance pulse to—"

"I'm sorry, but how would you know?" Stacy intervened. She had understood nothing of the title introduced. Thus failed to understand the reason Taya now looked to this man for answers, instead of the one who held the information within his grasp.

"I live in Kalia," he stated in much the same manner as Amelia had advised Bray was a Misorian, as if it should answer all her questions. It did not.

"And?"

"I have access to history known only by the wyrms," he explained, matching the same curt tone of her voice.

"What can you tell us?" Rob questioned, his posture tensing. He glanced towards Bray who was still examining the crystal, seemingly oblivious to their conversation. Daniel paused again before answering.

"Only that the stone emits a pulse on the opposite spectrum to the Daimon essence. When the two meet they would negate each other, leaving nothing. But I would assume it reacts differently to the wearer though." Daniel extended his finger to trace the stone's surface. He paced for a moment, nodding his head slightly. "I see." He glanced towards Taya bearing an expression of pity. "It uses her essence to generate the resonance, thus although she is in contact with it, the pulse surrounds her, rather than consumes her." Daniel paused again his face growing sombre as his flesh turned cold. "Really?" He scratched his nose, wondering if he should continue. "It was designed to work in unison with something in order to be capable of covering the expanse of the world. The premise was to use the life of one Daimon to erase them all. But—" Daniel shook his head, he'd lost the voice.

"What about Sunrise?" Taya questioned, not quite managing to feel guilty about pushing him. She could see he would become a great sage, but he was only now coming to understand his ability. It was clearly difficult and tiring for him to retain such strict focus.

"It uses the same principal. But the human essence is different. While the Daimons have a dense lifeforce, we possess a sparse one, and between the two all other life can be found." Daniel felt his head be-

591

gin to ache. He had been practising with Alessia, but he was still struggling to gain control. When he had chosen to remain amongst them she had explained why he had been referred to as their Wita. He was only now beginning to truly awaken these skills, and it was exhausting. The Eortháds had not known of the birth of a Wita since they had been sealed, and Daniel was the first to assume this role for a very long time. His responsibility to them was that of a Sage, yet he would grow to become so much more. In time he would be able to commune, at will, with the spirits of the ancestors who would impart their knowledge upon him.

"So what was the danger if the two were activated?" Taya pushed, she could see him losing the connection to the other world, and there were still so many questions left unanswered. She knew whatever answers he gave were likely to be correct, but sometimes even the great spirits had to resort to debate and hypothesis.

"Between the two all other life is found," Daniel tapped his temple as he formulated an answer from what he understood. "Combined, any life within the frequency would be nullified. The power alone could see the planet itself reformed."

"Like what happened on—" Eiji caught himself, even before feeling the stern glare from Acha.

"No. That was not Remedy or there would have been no need for rescue parties. I believe it was magical energy transmitted through it, a test of its capabilities perhaps." On hearing Daniel's words Taya became the focus of their stares as they all turned to behold the seemingly innocent circlet she wore. Bray returned from the window, having heard the entire conversation. He was first to notice all remaining colour had drained from Taya's complexion.

"You have it in your possession, don't you?" Bray's eyes locked with hers as she shifted uncomfortably.

"Yes." She barely forced the whisper through her rapid breathing. Bray covered the distance between them in but a few long strides, his eyes burning with anger, and his hand extended.

"Relinquish it!" he demanded through gritted teeth. All this time she had implied to have been on a mission of peace, and yet she carried the very thing which could bring this world to heel. None would dare deny her request, not with the devastation she could bring.

"I refuse." Her voice trembled. "I will not be responsible for it binding with another." She gestured towards the circlet. "There's always a human, a compatible life, in our vicinity. My giving you Sunrise would be no different from you sending me home. At least while I remain here *I* cannot deliver their demise. The same cannot be said if I were to break the seal restraining Sunrise. I will *not* be responsible for such destruction. I refuse," she panted, sweat beading on her brow from the effort of talking.

"You're the seal," Bray whispered in understanding. "You're aligned to both." His extended hand dropped. "Damn he's clever."

"Who?" Daniel intervened not missing the importance of what was now occurring.

"The one who did this to Ethelyn." Rob grimaced. "He must have known how the two powers would react."

"Where is it Taya?" Bray demanded.

"I can't tell you."

"Kitaia!" he snapped.

"I can't tell you because I don't know. I was only an infant when they bound it to me." The stool scrapped across the floor as she tried to retreat from the anger in his gaze. Acha placed a comforting hand on her shoulder. "As long as it stays inside me it remains sealed," she repeated, her voice trembling.

"Kitaia, I can probably find it." Bray understood all too well the danger removing Sunrise could cause. But with Remedy aligned to her, and Sunrise somewhere within its host, it would be possible to create an invocation to unleash both. Sealed or not the two forces would be at war with one another, in some ways aligning Remedy to her had caused the binding to weaken, both tools would seek to preserve themselves, and the stronger Remedy grew, the weaker the force restraining Sunrise would become. With both aligned to her in such a manner it was really possible she could bring forth the end of life.

"But then what? You'll cut it out, break the seal, and kill anyone who comes near you. I think not." She rose to her feet, her unsteady legs barely supporting her. She understood the situation all too well, but if she agreed then countless deaths would be unavoidable. At least this way they had time to find another way. She placed a trembling hand to her forehead, noticing the beads of sweat lining her brow. She backed away slightly, using the table to support her effort to remain standing.

"The person who did this to you already knew the consequences. We were erroneous in concluding he was solely targeting the Daimons. There is only one essence we are aware of that is sparser than that of a human, and if all life here were to be purged they could return in the isolation they so desire, remaking the world to their every whim." Bray understood. It all made sense now. The methods used on Taya had been those even he could not fathom and, for that to hold true, it had to come from something no longer touching the surface of the world where the Misorian tree of wisdom could store its design. If such evidence was not damning enough, the fading barbule they had found on Taya proved his theory. All of this, everything, suggested a single race, the only one to benefit should the powers now within Taya be unleashed.

"The Moirai?" Daniel questioned. "How?" Bray looked to him in bewilderment, he hadn't expected anyone to know of whom he spoke. He had only just realised it himself, then again, it seemed this man knew of many things long forgotten.

"Infiltration and subterfuge. One needed only to reveal themselves as a messenger from the Gods to invoke adoration and unquestioning loyalty. Perhaps this could explain why Sunniva so willingly deceived both Taya and Amelia. The Moirai needed only spin a fable of good versus evil, with themselves regarded as the benevolent. Perhaps even fabricate it with some lies about human abductions, and The Order would do all they could to stave off the threat.

"By having Sunniva watch over her, when the time came to implement his plan he only needed to devise a method to dissolve the seal that bound Remedy to enable it to align to a Daimon. The Acropolis may have even given him access to it initially, in exchange for his promise to see the Daimons remained restrained. After all, he only required Taya, and who else would approach the... old spirits as an emissary of peace but one from the royal house?"

"Why did we create Sunrise?" Taya questioned shaking her head, the room began to close in around her as she fought to control her breathing. "No one needs that kind of power, no matter how strong the enemy is. It has to be destroyed, if, we—" She blanched, gripping her stomach as she fought to inhale, drawing a sharp, ragged breath as she sank to her knees. The room twisted around her as the pain consumed her, each rapid beat of her heart seemed to flood her veins with vitriol.

"Taya!" Stacy touched her gently, checking her temperature. Her skin was clammy and burning with fever. She tried to nod. She gasped for breath, inhaling sharply until she choked, blood dripped from her mouth as she fought to breathe. Daniel placed his hand on her forehead before checking her pulse with a tender touch.

"How long have you been in this much pain?" His voice sung of a bedside manner he had previously forgotten.

"Since they attached this curse to me," she admitted. "It's okay, it'll pass. It always does. I can normally—" She winced keeling over. The pain had been getting increasingly worse. Her natural healing had soothed it, allowing her to repress some of the symptoms to keep her suffering from those closest to her. She touched her stomach gently, she remembered everything now. Everything about who and what she was, which meant she also knew why this was happening. "Spirits, forgive me, I didn't know." Taya whispered to herself, unaware of the conversation continuing around her.

"Is this Remedy's doing?" Stacy crouched, seeing the tears running from her friend's eyes. She looked to Daniel.

"Given we now know she has Sunrise, I'd have to say yes." He looked to Bray for confirmation, but his face remained stern, clouded in his own thoughts. "One must be removed but—"

"Even removing it would be of little use unless it was aligned to someone else," Bray interrupted. "It was never activated in the past, so all we have is hearsay," Bray studied the crystal again. "From what I've been able to understand, the stone's just part of the weapon. It was believed the Daimon would be in proximity to something able to project the resonance, channelling it through attuned relics."

"Attuned relics?" Rob questioned scratching his head.

"Remember how the Moirai relics create an area of blessing? If correctly attuned a relic can temporarily mimic a more powerful effect.

"What we saw on Afthonos was a test. He wanted to be sure they possessed the power needed. He activated the relics in the antiquity store via the one in the temple to test its viability. All he'd need to do is position the most potent blessings to ensure the effects of Remedy could be carried. Think about it, temples are everywhere, and they are not the only places to hold such relics.

"He'd need a specific location, and things in place to gain momentum to start a chain reaction. Somewhere that could activate several close relics and expand their reach."

"But if that's what they wanted to do, why let me go?" Taya questioned, her arms wrapped protectively around herself as she took long deep breaths.

"I don't know, that's all I got from this." Bray waved the crystal leaf at them before he slipped it into his pouch.

"Well we know one thing for certain," Rob deliberated. "It was never their intention for her to return to Kólasi. They orchestrated events to ensure her rescue. They had no cause to think it would be any but her own kind who would attempt to retrieve her, and yet their actions now seem to suggest otherwise. So they either intended to return for her when her magic was depleted, or they believe they can re-obtain her when the time is right."

"And I suppose he'll just wave his hands and she'll reappear at his feet?" Stacy's snapped scowling at Rob. "I'm sure even you can't find an excuse not to protect her *this* time." She placed her hand on Taya.

"Stacy's right," Bray announced. "I mean about needing a means to recover her. Although your suggestion perhaps bordered on the sarcastic, there are wizards and mages still capable of such feats. I think it is best to keep her isolated. But the real question is, how would he know where to find her to begin with."

"I'm marked," Taya advised flatly. "The demon hunter who attacked Elpída said I was marked."

"Hunter?" Rob questioned.

"He set fire to the temple in order to find me. Although Sunniva almost had me believing it never happened. It was strange how much clearer things had seemed, I think it was the Kyklos reaching out to me. That's when I ran."

"And that's when you bumped into me," Rob groaned, wishing he had simply agreed to part ways with her there and then. If he had none of this would have come to pass, of that he was certain.

If they had *never* travelled together they would *never* have spoken of The Seed of Nzin. He would *never* have had cause to hunt it down, or return her to Sunniva in order to force her aid. The trip to Mirage Lake would not have occurred, and in turn he would not have found himself making the wrong choice between saving her, or reaching The Seed. He rubbed his forehead, Stacy was right, everything that had come to pass was on his shoulders. "Sunniva," he whispered suddenly snapping to a state of vivid alertness. "She ensured I'd be there when you fled. She was also the one who first spoke to me of The Seed of Nzin. Somehow my sister is at the core of this." He looked up, suddenly remembering himself and where they were. "Uh, sorry. Thank you so much for your help and hospitality," he acknowledged sheepishly rising to his feet.

"No problem." Acha rose to escort them towards the door. She glanced over her shoulder, seeing Daniel and Eiji at the far side of the room in hushed conversation. "It brings back memories of the old days. Let us know if we can be of further assistance, or if you need a safe haven."

Rob approached Taya as she struggled to stand, scooping her up into his arms despite her objection.

"Shouldn't we have offered t'help them?" Eiji questioned as Acha pulled the door closed. Her face was weighted with concern as she looked upon them.

"Technically we did," Daniel advised, his brow crinkled in thought. "I wonder if we were like that."

"I'd say y' more likely t'be wonderin' if y'll get another chance t'look at Remedy."

"Well, that too, but that Daimon is interesting. I wonder what further examination would reveal."

"He doesn't even realise does he?" Acha shook her head. Only Daniel could trace his hands over another woman's body and be thinking solely of discovery. Sometimes she felt sorry for Alessia, and wondered how she and the other Eortháds managed to tolerate him.

"Same old Daniel." Eiji shook his head. "Hey y' know, I bet Zo could'a removed that Sunrise thing from her, maybe even Remedy."

"Not possible. Although you're right, it would have responded to her magic, before she died that is. I can say with certainty she was the last Hectarian, and the magic which could have displaced it died with her. Besides, I get the feeling it's something they have to do on their own." Daniel frowned at his answer, shaking his head defiantly. "Of course, I see no reason I can't investigate further. I'll speak with Nemean. It may yield nothing but it's worth trying."

"Just tell us what y' need."

"Eiji, for reasons you already understand you cannot be involved in this, and Acha's presence here could be critical. If something were to happen," he shook his head. "Imagine the devastation her power would cause to a place such as this. You could be the only means to quell the threat should something happen to that Misorian."

* * *

The Epiales tasked with retrieving the divine, mortal-dreamer had once more failed. Their efforts thwarted. Íkelos had focused his attention to other concerns, Elly was, after all, already committed to reaching his conduit. She had been coming to him, with no need for further temptation and yet, she was delayed. He had watched in disbelief as Darrienia herself impeded their progress, screaming warnings unheard by Oneiroi and dreamer alike. Of course, such a failing was by the Oneirois' own hand. They could no longer hear the call of their goddess. He could. Of course, the fact that Aidan had not realised the gravity of the land's actions, distracted by his own desires to find his partner, served his interest. But it was taking too long.

He had dispatched envoys specifically to facilitate their journey, yet Darrienia had created barriers, ensuring Elly's journey remained always within a divine dreamscape. A dreamscape even he could not corrupt. He had lured dreamers there, in hope the Oneiroi would utilise their presence to manipulate the terrain, and yet the force of the barrier was too much for even the innocent to pass. Contact saw them waking, just as it had seen the death of some of his most trusted Epiales.

Darrienia had not intervened in the fate of her world for a long time. The creation of the seals, which had once bound the Severaine to Darrienia, had also acted as a syphon and subdued her divine influence. When they had been released, and the Severaine was unleashed, she awoke once more from her slumber. But even she could not stop what he had begun.

Íkelos beheld the faltering of Darrienia's influence as Aidan and Elly neared the lands central to his ambition. Just as she had created a border he could not breach, it seemed her influence could not extend into the area his actions had depleted. She had delayed them from reaching his conduit, but she had failed to prevent their arrival.

Through his unseen windows, he observed as their descent from the cliffs took them from the safety of the goddess. Events were accelerating. What had once been a slow labour now approached its climax. There was but a single purpose for Jude remaining, the initial reason behind his abduction. In order to fully shatter the lock, between himself and the gateway into Darrienia, he must first offer a sacrifice.

Until the remaining magic from the Severaine's seal dwindled and faded, he had never realised this act to be possible. However, ancient ways were often fallible if the magic sustaining them faltered, as it had now. In order to succeed he would need a vast amount of magical energy at his disposal and, with the exception of the power he had once known, there were few magics stronger than that granted in exchange for a life.

The Stepping Realm was complex, but the rules were simple. In order to be able to walk between realms there had to be two adjoining gateways. Thus a simultaneous sacrifice of two tethered beings on either side were needed to dispel the blockade. With this, no more would he be the sole person denied freedom; no more would he remain a prisoner.

Jude and Aidan's link to one another had made them the perfect candidates. Elly, however, if she were to take the allotted role in Darrienia, could pierce the veil itself. Her unique existence would result in not only the gateway to Darrienia opening, but the path to them all.

Chapter 20

Complications

Taya allowed her head to rest on Rob's shoulder. The sounds of the city faded into nothing more than white noise, and the rhythmic movement of his steady gait almost lulled her to sleep. Closing her eyes she allowed the warmth from his body to comfort her, and ease just a fraction of her pain. There was a conversation which needed to be had. It was an important one, and the thought of it filled her with dread.

She didn't remember reaching the inn, or even entering their room. The absence of his warmth sent shivers through her as he placed her upon the bed. She winced, her body objecting against the movement, whilst her eyes reflected a pain no courage could disguise. Rob turned his gaze towards the floor as he stepped away. He was unable to bear the sight of her like this, unable to conceive how so much pain could have been masked for so long. The cold glare from Stacy did little to alleviate his guilt as he slunk away towards the table at the far end of the room.

"I'm fine," she reassured. Stacy folded the covers over her noticing her body still trembled from the earlier exertion. Taya was exhausted, but even through heavy eyelids she had seen the concern, and felt its overbearing presence enveloping the room. She did not want to add to the air of unease, but she knew what she must tell them would do just that. "There's something I…"

Stacy looked to Taya, her voice nothing more than a murmur as she tried to impart some further wisdom but her eyelids had closed, and her body surrendered to a fitful sleep.

"She can't travel in this condition," Bray asserted as Stacy moved to join them sitting around the small table. "Her condition is unlikely to improve from here on in. Not given what we know."

"It works in our favour really," Rob interjected. "We need to speak with my sister, and no good would come from her knowing Taya is with us."

"Sure. Let's just abandon her here then. That would work well. It's bad enough she's only suffering because—"

"I get it." Rob interrupted before Stacy could once again voice her opinion of blame. "What I meant was, given that she's not tried to contact me via the Plexus I assume she believes that we have her. It would do well to divert that thinking elsewhere. This all somehow comes back to her, we need to discover what she knows." It sounded simple enough as he voiced the words, but he knew the task was anything but. Extracting information from someone so versed in not only concealing, but reinventing the truth, would be no simple deed. Sunniva's ability to deeply alter his perception towards Taya served as a potent reminder of how dangerous she was. He feared to consider the ramifications on someone who could not guard against her assault.

"Fine, you two should go. I'll stay here and watch over her. At least *I'll* not be distracted from my duties, and Bray can make sure your carelessness won't put her in further jeopardy."

"But what if—" Bray began, but Stacy's firm voice addressed his approaching concern.

"I have no intention of using the invocation. If something should happen I'm certain I can rely on Acha. Why else tell them where we were staying if not to enlist their aid if needed?" Stacy paused looking between their unconvinced features. "Look, you'll be gone a matter of days at most, right? Even you can't find too much distraction out there."

"Fine," Bray conceded after a short pause. Stacy had made a valid argument through her animosity. He glanced across to Taya, given her condition it was unlikely she would cause Stacy any trouble. He could only hope her rest would become less fitful. His face contorted as he watched her body jerk in reaction to her unvoiced pain. Although momentarily lost to slumber she was now feigning sleep for their benefit, that much was apparent. "On one condition, you stay in the room. We still don't know how he plans to retrieve her, from this point on she must always have someone with her. I'll arrange for the innkeeper to deliver sustenance to you until our return." Stacy nodded, lifting their backpacks from the floor to place them on the table.

"Agreed. Off you go then. Although procrastination seems a well-practised skill amongst *some* of you, there's no time for it here."

"She's right, besides, hostility has no place at the bedside." Rob rose, snatching his bag from the table. "I may have wronged her, but at least I'm trying to do something about it. You don't even see it. This animosity"—he gestured towards her—"is only for your sake. Whatever wrongs I committed, I committed against her, not you, and when she chooses to confront me I will accept her judgement. But only hers. Do I make myself clear?"

"Enough, the pair of you," Bray interrupted before Stacy had time to counter Rob's berating. "We've all got things in our past we aren't proud of, but it's what we do about them that gives the measure of a man, or woman. On that note, we shall depart." Bray glanced over his shoulder as he pulled the door open. "Be careful."

"You too," Stacy whispered, hanging her head as the door closed softly behind them. Rob was right. She did blame him for all that had befell Taya, but she had her role to play as well. She looked to her hand, giving a snort. Whilst she had objected to Rob taking her to retrieve The Seed of Nzin, she had not prevented him from doing so. But nor would she have made the choices he had. As the door closed she quickly slipped the latch into place before making her way across to Taya. "It's okay, they've gone." Stacy stroked Taya's hair affectionately, even after all this time she could not understand why she felt so deeply bonded to this woman. But she swore a silent oath she would do all she could to ensure her safety.

Taya, with some difficulty, struggled to push herself into a seated position. The worst had subsided for now, but even the simplest of movements triggered painful spasms. "Do you want to tell me what's bothering you?" Stacy had been aware of the dark mood encircling her for some time, and had a feeling there was more to it than just Remedy.

"Sunrise," Taya stated, pulling her knees to her chest in an attempt to lessen the pain. "If I were to surrender it, it would only be a matter of time before my blood binding faded and it aligned to one of them. It would kill them, Stacy. Its power is such that it would be transmitted from person to person. With your numbers, even when it was forged, longevity of its host was never a concern. Bearing it is agony, and I wouldn't wish it on anyone." She gestured towards the circlet, tears flooding her eyes. "I would rather endure than pass this suffering to another. Our ancestors should never have created it, and I will withstand this as long as I am able, in order to accept the punishment for their mistake."

"You lied. You know where it is don't you?" Stacy whispered in realisation, taking Taya's hand in her own.

"Don't misunderstand. I'm not saying I am happy to sacrifice my life, but I will do so if it is necessary. Howbeit, if there's another way I hope we can find it, and before my daughter is born."

"You're pregnant?" Stacy whispered, her hands instinctively covering her mouth. "How long?"

"Five months." Stacy's brow wrinkled at this news. "When—"

"When I first spent the night with Rob we—"

"He's the father? How—I mean..." Stacy's gaze burnt into the door through which he'd made his escape. Her body grew tense with outrage at the thought of him preying on her in such a manner. It was no wonder he was ashamed of his actions, he'd thought her his niece, and still lay with her. "When I get my hands on—"

"No. Although you may have reason to question it, he has been kind to me. He gave me hope where I thought there was none." Taya reached out, touching Stacy's arm to calm her. "When I first spent the night with Rob we were forced to make camp. I delayed our journey, and as a result I was abducted. But those who took me intended no harm, only to return me to my home, to my husband."

"Oh, I see. Does Yuri know?" Stacy sat back down on the edge of the bed, but relief was far from what she felt. With this realisation came another, Taya's pregnancy had occurred before she had been sent to Mirage Lake, before Remedy had been aligned to her. What chance did her child have to survive the very things that almost killed its mother?

"I don't think so. When we met again, at Mirage Lake, I don't think he could have known given our limited interaction." The signs had been there for her to see, but she had not been herself. She had no cause to think her nausea and fatigue were anything but a result of the treatments that had cured her.

As a male Yuri would have noticed the changes in her first. The subtle alteration of her scent would have been the first indication. But she had been absent so long before her return, and they barely had time to familiarise themselves with each other again before she left. When they had retrieved her, her body had been flooded with opiates and for weeks she would have smelt only of their abuse. Taya felt the warmth of tears streak her face. She wiped them away quickly with the back of her hand, hoping they had gone unnoticed. She placed a hand to her spine, leaving her concerns unvoiced. Still unborn, and already this child had been forced to suffer.

"But you don't appear to be carrying." Stacy lifted the cover, confirming her words as she saw Taya's slightly sunken stomach.

"Carrying?" Stacy made a rounded gesture over her own stomach as if to explain. "Oh, no, I wouldn't. If our females had that shape when carrying young it would make us vulnerable."

"Then how do you... you know?"

"Our young grow near our back. Female Daimons have hindwings which span down from the lower back. The bones for these sit within and below the ribcage finishing close to the pelvis." Taya ran Stacy's hand down her back as she spoke. Beneath her skin she could feel the presence of what felt to be a secondary ribcage. For a moment Stacy thought back to when she had witnessed some of these bones trying to emerge, and shuddered.

"Can you fly?" Stacy asked frowning.

"No," Taya stifled a slight chuckle despite her morbidity. "They only look like wings. Like the Moirai the bones are structured to enhance our magic. For us they serve only as a conduit, a means to channel and centre the power. Our magic stems from within us, as such we maintain a level of control to keep it restrained. Your magic users would gather and release an energy. The Moirai harvest it and store it as plumes. For us, as it is intrinsic, the bones remain concealed until the forces are unleashed. Their form is one to facilitate the magic's release. The extra bones a female possesses creates a protective cage around our reproductive organs. When we are with child it serves to protect them, not only with the shielding of bones, but with the magic they store within us. Our organs, and our children, are much smaller than those of your kind. That's why we appear the same externally."

"But you're not eating more either," Stacy continued. Since her rescue Taya had resorted to small but frequent meals, a necessity given the conditions she had been forced to endure. Her stomach still seemed unable to handle larger quantities of food.

"We don't need to. We are beings aligned with nature, and whilst some of our sustenance does indeed feed our unborn, so too does our magic. We do tire quicker than normal though."

"Why didn't you say anything sooner?" Stacy questioned trying to keep her tones soft so their conversation felt less like an interrogation. She couldn't believe that through everything she had suffered Taya had been—and perhaps more amazingly still was—with child. Stacy bit her lip, willing her doubts to remain unvoiced. She knew even if the child still lived, with Remedy so close, and the suffering Taya endured, its continued survival seemed implausible. She looked to Taya, wondering what the chances of having two miracles within her bloodline were. Her presence in their realm already proved her to be the first.

"You have to remember, I thought myself to be human." Taya's gaze became distant. "It was only as I spoke with the Wita that I realised," she whispered, her voice losing what little power it possessed. "I needed to tell you, mainly because of the complications it causes." Taya blinked away a few tears, steadying her breath for what she knew would follow.

"What complications?" Stacy cringed hearing her own solemn tone. News of a child should be a joyous occasion, yet the mood surrounding them was anything but elated.

"Because of the phase I'm entering my body's natural defences, and my magic, are moving to the child to protect it." Taya paused for a moment, gathering herself before continuing. "It means the friction between Remedy and Sunrise is taking more of a toll."

"How long do you carry for?" Stacy questioned. She knew Taya's condition had been weakening, but she had assumed it was solely due to Remedy. If it was having this much of an effect on her now, how could she be expected to complete this final phase? Stacy closed her eyes as the realisation struck her.

"Six moon cycles, but—"

"But?"

"In the six weeks leading up to the birth my magic gets channelled into my daughter. Once she's born, for a short time, I will become stronger. Such is always the case, it will allow me to heal and gather the extra energy needed in order to feed her."

"Oh no," Stacy whispered, her eyes meeting with Taya's as she understood what was being suggested. "That must be what he's waiting for, why you were allowed to be rescued. He can't use Remedy because your power is weakening, but once your daughter's born he'll have more power than he could dream of." All of a sudden it made sense, a person with enough knowledge to align Remedy to her would surely have known she was with child, and the effects of the pregnancy. That had to be why he let her go. He knew he could find her again, so all he needed to do was wait.

"That would only be true if the baby's born." Taya looked to Stacy seriously, her features holding an expression that showed her true age.

"What do you mean?" Stacy felt herself stiffen slightly.

"At the moment, the two energies are negating each other within me," Taya explained. "If I remove Sunrise before the full channelling of my own magic to her is complete, she's likely to die." Stacy felt the warmth of tears down her face as she felt the burden her friend carried. To remove Sunrise was to kill her child and release her alignment to it, thus sealing the fate of humanity. But leaving the conflicting energies in place would kill her. Stacy felt a gentle squeeze on her hand, noticing Taya offered her a weak smile. "Do not worry. Our people were born to endure, and I have more reason to do so than most."

"But... the only reason you've managed for this long is because your magic has been healing you, isn't it? So when—"

"Yes. The transfer has already started, which is why I'm struggling to continue concealing it." Taya met Stacy's gaze. "Listen, I need this to remain in confidence. If Rob or Bray were to discover the truth—"

"It's only fair he shoulders the burden of his actions. He should be made to realise the position he has put you in."

"Stacy, I encouraged him onward. I gave him my consent, and I told him where he would find it."

"You think he would have turned back if you'd not approved?"

"That's an answer I don't need to know. I believed I had lost you, my friend. I saw the lives he was willing to sacrifice for his own gain. Had I really cared, I would have prevented his advance. The Seed of Nzin is not the blessing he thinks it to be. I am as much to blame as he. I told him to continue," Taya admitted, darkness clouded her vision as the fatigue once more began to consume her. Soon she would be taken by sleep, but she would find no rest.

"I'm not sure how long we can keep something like this from them." Stacy shook her head, feeling Taya's hand grow heavy in hers.

"Just, a little longer. Please," she mumbled. Stacy tucked the blanket in around her before moving to sit at the table, pulling the bottle of spirits towards her.

* * *

Taya tossed and turned. Even in her dreams she felt the burning agony her body had become. The pain heightened her senses even in slumber. But what she witnessed now was more than a dream. She had once been told that these fragments of insight were delusions. Now she recognised this precognition for what it was. A warning of things to come.

Rob steadied his hand, his gaze fixed upon The Seed of Nzin. He had waited years for this moment, and now it had come to pass. It was finally his. His trembling fingers removed the cover from the glass cylinder, the weight of the object barely registering as he tipped it into his palm. Stilling his breath he closed his eyes, his grip tightening on the fragile crystal as he made his wish. A wish he would give anything to see fulfilled. A wish for his wife and daughter to be returned to life.

The Seed shattered within his grasp, the shards embedding deep within his flesh. Its fragments, as if alive, burrowed deep within his flesh, leaving pinpricks of blood upon his skin. The pain was immense and, somehow, he knew his wish had been granted.

His hand reached out, steadying his fatigued body against the cold, stone wall as his balance wavered. His blood streaked its surface as he fought to breathe. His agonised cries remained unvoiced as he sank to the floor, gripping his stomach, fighting, and failing, to draw breath.

Blood and acid left his mouth in rasping heaves, scorching his throat as The Seed's dust penetrated his bones. The once solid structures became soft, almost fluid, to flow beneath his flesh, reforming into something new. Each movement caused him a pain like nothing he had ever known. Nerves began to sever and regrow, bringing fresh raw agony to the vomit soaked figure. White bones pierced his flesh, hardening, altering his physical appearance. Few would recognise this figure as once human, but many would see a Nzin, a creature of terrible power.

Hours of agony passed. All that this man had once been now lost amidst the madness. Perhaps still remembering a distant dream about walking in the daylight. A single thought remained, an overwhelming grief. The memory of having lost something important. From the hollowed eyes a single tear was shed, becoming a crystal as the last shred of humanity, the final memory of the being it once was, drained away, leaving only the creature in its stead. A dark hunger begins to stir—

"Kitaia." The voice penetrated the premonition, distorting the images into fragments that crumbled like sand. Taya startled. Her dreaming-self became solid, giving her a presence within this realm. She was in the world of the dreamers, staring out through a closing window into the future. Its wisdom was sealed from her by Yuri's appearance, leaving her staring through a gateway into The Betwixt. Her pulse quickened knowing his presence here was an ill-omen. The Kyklos would not risk contacting her in this manner unless there was no alternative. Premonitions were sacred, and to interrupt one this way was strictly forbidden.

They stood almost opposite one another, separated by the gateway that would soon diminish. Their images remained unclear, distorted despite their closeness. Even being so near to his ethereal form brought her some small comfort, she had thought she would never see him again.

He extended his hand, placing it upon the divide that separated them from one another. The relief in his eyes was immeasurable. "Thank the spirits. The Kyklos feel your presence fading, if not for your vision we could never have hoped to reach you." Yuri wanted to reach out and touch her, to take her within his arms and whisper comfort. He wanted to tell her that soon she would have no cause to fear, he was finally doing that which he should have done so long ago to protect her. But he could not cross into Darrienia, not in this form and this had been the only means to reach her.

The Kyklos had acted quickly when they detected her premonition. They were busy with preparations for Daley's rescue. Everything needed to be organised before Full-Moonday in order for Geburah's plan to work. Given Taya's deteriorating presence, when Meredith felt the future window open she knew who would be there, and their concern for her health was great. They had reacted at once, explaining what he must do while leading him to their cavern. He could see her, he could speak with her about why they felt her magic fading, but only if they acted quickly.

He looked upon her with concern. Even here he could see her frailty. He felt the swelling of his throat as his sight confirmed what the Kyklos had feared. His wife was dying. He had just found her again, and now it seemed he would lose her forever. Her hand moved to his, separated by the thin barrier which divided them with all the vastness of eternity.

"Yuri, you're everything I ever wanted. We should have just been happy, but I wanted to give you the sun. Forgive me, my love," Taya whispered, raising her eyes to meet his. He looked upon her, seeing the curse that had followed her. His heart ached, filled with regret, he was unable to touch her, to reach out and offer her the comfort often sought in his embrace.

"You bear their poison, and still retain ours?" His gaze burned into the circlet before lowering. "They did this to you. You owe them nothing. Is it not clear what action you must take?"

"Yuri—"

"No, Kitaia, hear me well. Remove it, bind it with blood. We will come for it. You cannot bear both curses," Yuri growled. "I would see their race extinct before I would sacrifice you for them."

"Yuri, this isn't how I wanted this to be. Please know that. I can't remove it, not if—Yuri, I carry our heir, our future. The only reason our daughter is still alive is because of Sunrise."

"That's why you're... oh, Kitaia." He placed his forehead to the barrier, painfully aware of their diminishing time. "Damn them," he whispered.

"I will do what is expected, what is necessary." Taya forced her voice to become stoic, but she had been unable to deceive him.

"If I have a choice, I would rather it be you who survives. Please, Kitaia, you're the one thing I can never replace," he pleaded. Soon Full-Moonday would be upon them, but he would be unable to take his wife into his arms, unable to feel the life of the child he had longed for. All he could do now was focus his attention elsewhere. He would force Daley to become his sole focus, otherwise he would not continue to survive their separation, not knowing what he now did.

He looked at Taya, wishing more than anything to hold her. The window was nearly closed, and the Kyklos could keep him here no longer. Given the task they would soon undertake he could not ask it of them. "I love you, Kitaia," he asserted softly as her figure became shrouded with darkness.

Taya awoke with a deep intake of panicked breath. Ice cold water ran from her face as her arms flayed trying to fend off her invisible attacker. It took a moment to realise Stacy stood over her with an empty water pitcher in her hand.

"Thank the Gods." Stacy sunk down to sit on the bed, her features showing her clear relief. "I've been trying to wake you."

"I was dreaming," Taya advised horsely, taking the sheet Stacy had offered in order to dry herself.

"You've been asleep for days. You were crying out, fighting, and no matter what I did you wouldn't wake." As Taya became more aware of her environment she felt a magical charge in the air, it was a few more moments before she recognised it as her own. She glanced around, seeing minimal damage and heaved a sigh of relief. For a moment she had feared the worst. "You should eat something," Stacy lifted a small plate from the bedside table pushing it towards her. The smell alone made Taya's stomach churn, but she accepted it gratefully, nibbling on the crust of a piece of bread. Stacy wrapped another blanket around her.

"Has there been any word?" But even as she asked she knew the two men had not yet returned.

"Nothing yet, but it's only been a few days. They're probably on their way back as we speak." Stacy looked to her hands. "You were calling for

Yuri." She rubbed Taya's back lightly before pulling her close.

"For the first time, I am no longer sure of my path. I came here so that I may offer the man I love the sun itself. Free our people. Instead of the sun I give him a daughter. A child he will likely never see, never hold and, in discovering her, he learns of my fate."

"You speak as if it is already over."

"Isn't it? There is no known way to remove this curse. If, by some miracle, the combined energies don't kill me, I can hope only for a life of solitude. I cannot herald a new dawn, when to bring my people here would be to expose them to Remedy. I have no choice but to ask they remain bound to The Depths. As for my daughter, if she survives being birthed, the immediate proximity to Remedy guarantees her death. You've thought it yourself, I see it reflected in your expression every time you look upon me."

"Just because we don't have an answer yet doesn't mean there isn't one. You can't give up hope."

"Stacy, you don't understand. I dream in prophecy. Whilst *he* may have had them concealed I know my own mind. Since my first visit to Mirage Lake I have been nothing but a tool, helping him to devise his scheme to such a degree that there is no future where he fails. I've seen it all, here." She tapped her forehead. "You speak of not giving up on hope, but what if there is none? There is one thing I know with certainty, and that is his victory. I am not subjected to everything, just glimpses of the end, that's where his focus lay. I don't know the fate of my child, but I do know, if he succeeds in retrieving me, there is nowhere you could hide."

"Then he could still fail."

"There's only one thing you can do to ensure that." Taya glanced across the room towards the table where the joint of meat stood, she inclined her head towards the knife.

"Absolutely not," Stacy asserted.

"One for many, how is that even a trade?"

"When will this future happen?"

"Given my condition we have a month where I will be of no use. So we can assume after that."

"Okay, then I give you my word, if in a month's time we still have no answer, I will do whatever you ask of me. But for now, please, let's just see if Bray was successful in gaining some insight."

"I don't see how he could make a difference."

"He's Misorian," Stacy stated firmly. "He shouldn't be interfering. Perhaps your futures don't take him into account." Taya offered a weak smile before lying down. She couldn't find it in her heart to tell Stacy that Bray's presence had been predicted. No matter the future, he was the one who killed her.

* * *

Íkelos could not help but congratulate himself on his own creativity. The closer events drew, the more easily everything had seemed to fall into place. He had expected this to be difficult, yet it was proving to be anything but. He cautioned himself against becoming complacent, yet there was a part of him celebrating his impending victory.

Acquiring the Daimon had been nothing more than a twist of fortune, but given how events were unravelling it would allow him to achieve the one thing he would be otherwise unable to. With Daley in his realm he could breach the human world. His plan had been a stroke of genius. With the magics thinning he had seen the opportunity to weaken the seal that prevented his exit from the Forest of the Epiales. He had long known that the drawing of energy through the barrier from other locations weakened this realm's hold on him, but it had been a feat impossible to sustain. His trees could rarely take root in a world other than his, and over the centuries he had tried countless measures to cultivate them outside his land, and only on occasion would he succeed. Better yet, no one recognised them for what they were.

When cracks between the realms would form—something to be expected since most magic no longer held any real power—his seeds would sprout. People capable of wielding magic would flock to his saplings in droves, drawing upon their power, unaware their doing so also sustained him. They thought they received a boon from the tideways, and to some degree they were correct. Those with magic could draw on the powers harvested by the stone, but their actions drew more of their world's magics to the sapling's location, and it in turn channelled it to him. Tideways were nothing more than his trees, and he had taken great pains to weave a favourable legend to inspire and encourage their use.

Unfortunately the lifespan of a sapling was limited. The world's energies would always work in unison to correct any fracturing, and eventually a balance would be restored and the tideway would crumble. But they served their purpose. The Daimon realm's susceptibility to his seeds had grown since the release of the Severaine. Little by little he was weakening the forces which kept them constrained, creating an instability that would eventually result in the collapse of their realm and their lands being restored to their original location. Events were already on course, and they needed only a small amount of encouragement to grant him permanent passage to their world. He was close to unlocking their domain, but he had to ensure his motives remained concealed.

He had been using the Daimon to scry the human lands. To fully return and take a physical form would require tremendous power, and he would need to acquire it before anyone who would oppose him realised what was occurring. It would take time. His deeds had to go unnoticed, his breach undetected, but he was patient. Opening the Daimon realm was merely the first step. When he had been banished to the Forest of the Epiales it had been ensured he could never overpower the separation between his domain and the physical world. However, if he could open the passage to the Daimons' land, and Kólasi were to rise, the two realms would become as one once more, and his access into that domain would transfer, paving the way for his return.

Its execution, however, had been more difficult. Until he had seen the Moirai spying within his domain, thinking himself to be shielded, he'd had very few ideas on how to ensure his success. Geburah's ethereal form was not the only thing to return with him from the forest. He had used the Moirai's own magic to implant an idea, a means to rescue their lost comrade, one that would ensure when Kólasi rose he could once again use The Stepping Realm to walk between worlds.

There were three plans in place, and if only one bore fruit the world itself would have cause to tremble in fear. He had no further use for Daley, he had already revealed everything he would need to make his return, but as yet, all the powers were not in alignment.

* * *

The last time Rob had brought someone with him to Sunniva's doors had been many years ago. As a hunter Rob undertook many challenging tasks for those of wealth. He sought at the time to provide a better future for his family. After a completed task Rob and his partner, Aglaca would visit Sunniva in order to have their wounds dressed and partake in her hospitality. Over the years it seemed their partnership had been a blessing of the Gods. None thought he would forsake Rob in the manner he had. Not after being allies for so long.

There were whispered rumours that Aglaca had fallen in love with Sunniva and, for reasons unknown, thought Rob would object to their partnership. During their last task he had betrayed Rob, leaving him for certain death. By some strange fortune Rob had been found, and the Plexus had transported him to Sunniva's temple for healing as per his information's instructions.

Those of the temple knew Rob had sworn to never again take a partner or place his life in the hands of another. The fact he arrived with another man had stirred unrest, especially since Sunniva had addressed them regarding her recent misgivings surrounding her brother and his intentions.

Sunniva had spoken to them at length about her brother's stirring evil. She theorised how his time hunting within The Depths of Acheron had corrupted him, twisting him from the truth. Then she revealed his deception in plucking Taya from Mirage Lake and disclosed, for the first time, Taya's true nature. How she was a creature of evil sent to purge all life from the world. Her actions prevented only by the watchful gaze of herself and those at Mirage Lake.

There was a small part of Sunniva that thought perhaps The Order really had come for her. But if that *was* the case, she wondered why she had not been informed of their intentions. She had kept watch on Taya for years, she had obeyed every order. She had to blame Rob, otherwise it would seem she had now been deemed unsuitable. The absence of her guardian did little to instil confidence, he had been strangely silent since Taya's last attendance at Mirage Lake. That was a thought she cared not to study further.

Sunniva had been given news of her brother's approach from one of her children who had been returning with the horse and trap from the town. Before he had arrived, both the acolytes and clerics had been requested to take the children on an outing, so she and her brother may talk in peace. But the stranger concerned her. He had an air of authority about him, a confidence she rarely saw. She feared he was here to judge her, and expose her crimes.

She stood before them in feigned innocence. Deep frown lines wrinkled her forehead as they refused her gesture to be seated.

"I've brought my donation," Rob began, feeling the hairs on the back of his neck rise under the scrutiny of her gaze. She was assessing him, trying to discern what he already knew. He could see their arrival had unnerved her by her guarded posture. "I was hoping I could see my niece while we're here. She *has* returned hasn't she?" Rob's hand fumbled with the small coin pouch as he passed it to her, carefully ensuring their fingers did not touch. Her eyes narrowed slightly as she took it from his grasp.

"I'm sorry, Brother, she was returned to Mirage Lake. She made another attempt on my life." Sunniva rubbed a hand down one of her arms as she shifted uncomfortably, not able to meet his gaze.

"Do you not wonder if such trips are responsible? A girl as fragile as my niece surely needs to feel safe, how can she when at the first sign of trouble you have her sent there?"

"Perhaps you should have tried watching her these years and see what you would have done differently, since you're such a wonderful father yourself," Sunniva spat bitterly. He was testing her, of that she was certain. She was in no mood for his antics, she had only one agenda, finding Taya. If he refused to disclose her location he had very little use left. "At least my daughter still draws breath."

"Better dead than living in a glorified torture chamber," Rob retorted, his voice remaining strangely firm despite the impact of his sister's words.

"And what would you know of it? You've been there have you, recently perhaps?" Sunniva challenged, her frustration rising as she failed to reach her brother's mind through her normal methods.

"I know of the horrors. I don't need to have been to listen to rumours." His voice softened slightly. He could feel so many raw emotions fighting for dominance. He took a deep breath, trying to calm himself as he wondered what had come over him. No matter how much he disapproved of her actions he would never normally speak to her in this way.

"And they are just that, Brother, rumours." Sunniva's voice mirrored his softened tone. She extended her hand towards him as if to touch him, but hesitated in the same instant he stepped away. "If not for that place she would be out of control. She needs to see the error of her blasphemous existence."

"And you think deceiving her into believing she is something she is not will achieve that? Or will you now tell me the wings I recall were a delirium introduced by her hand?"

"She knows many tricks. She was born of deception and false promise. I was a fool to think her worthy of redemption. Some people simply cannot be saved." Sunniva covered her mouth, as if surprised by her own words.

"Such words from a person who called herself her mother!"

"There are some people even prayers and the Moirai cannot save. I realise that now, some people are just born evil, tainted." Sunniva stiffened, suddenly aware of Bray's presence, something she had momentarily been blinded to. "But I speak as a mother, what parent wouldn't have such concerns over the soul of their child?" She glanced to Bray, who seemed to be studying her without emotion. "Tell me, Brother, why do you play these games?"

"You speak as if you don't hold your own counters. You have always been honest and open with me. Tell me, Sister, what is going on, what are you hiding from me? Is it really so bad you can't confide in your kin?"

"I hold counters?" Sunniva let out a bitter chuckle. "What use are counters when you're playing cards, Brother? Who is this man, and why do you feel him fit to judge me?" She gestured towards Bray, her arms more animated than she intended.

"This man is my friend. You think I would dare request judgement on a servant of the Gods, one whose work is nothing but pure?" The slight sarcasm in his voice did not go unheard.

"I don't even know what game we're playing now." Sunniva gave a sigh, raising her hand in an exasperated gesture.

"If you think we are playing a game, Sister, I fear to know the stakes."

"My dignity it seems. You strip me bare, putting all I despise about myself, my doubts, my fears, on display and dare insinuate I have my own agenda. If we were playing for stakes, dear Brother, it would be life itself upon the table." She paused, wiping an absent tear from her eye in a bid for sympathy. "Do you think if there was another way I would not embrace it, do you think I would not have Paion ease my burden and remove such thoughts if it were possible? I pray for guidance, but where there was once wisdom now only silence answers my call."

"Perhaps the Gods disapprove of your tactics."

"You think I want *their* consent? *Their* approval?" she raged. "I was tasked with greater things than you can even imagine. I was sent a messenger from the heavens themselves, tasked to conceal and suppress the Daimon uprising. All they asked is that I kept that filthy monster compliant and still, somehow, she slipped through my fingers. Keeping her would have ensured they dared not move against us."

"What are you talking about?" Rob's tone was filled with genuine surprise.

"You're a fool, Brother. You know I speak of that filthy Daimon, my daughter, ha!" She spat to one side revealing her repulsion. "I know the horror they are capable of, the future their kind will create. Creatures of darkness should not walk amongst those of light and purity. And you! You would aid her. Their blight needs to be eradicated," Sunniva's chest heaved as she pulled in breaths between her angered tirade. "We must prove ourselves worthy of Paion, of the return of the Moirai. All who stand in their way must be removed."

She had moved before Rob had a chance to react, the flash of light upon the dagger coming too late to serve as a warning. "That includes you, Brother," she whispered twisting the knife sharply. There was a moment of stillness, complete unwavering silence before she stepped back in a sudden panic. Her bloodied hands shot to her face as she beheld what she had done. Rob stared at her open mouthed, his hand clasped around the dagger's hilt as blood pulsed from around it. He tried to speak, but the words froze within his throat as he sank to his knees.

Sunniva retreated further, her eyes wide, as she struggled against the darkness which encroached further with every failed breath. Heat rolled over her as she looked upon what her actions had wrought. Sweat beaded upon her brother's startled face as his breath stilled. His lips moved with unheard questions as she knelt before him. Her eyes grew wide with terror as he collapsed to the floor, watching as his blood rapidly pooled around his body. "Gods, no! What have I done?" Sunniva beseeched.

She crawled forwards, tears streaking her face as she pushed her hand against the wound, not daring to remove the blade. She looked upon him in desperation. "Please, Brother, for the sake of those who still live, tell me where she is," she whispered, watching for the absent rise of his chest. She was barely aware of Bray moving to crouch behind her. His voice, so loud in her ear, caused her to startle.

"There's nothing to be done, Iereía." Aware of the figure's presence once more Sunniva seemed to freeze.

"No, no, you're wrong, you must be."

"He's breathed his last." Bray helped her to stand, looking down on Rob's motionless form. "Is what you said about him consorting with demons true?" Sunniva slowly nodded her head, her vision not straying from Rob. His drying blood upon her face caused her to appear paler, only the flush of nausea added colour to her complexion. "Then it is my understanding you acted appropriately. You merely did what needed to be done. I may not hail from these parts, but I know of your work. Him, I've barely heard of." Bray inclined his head towards the body on the floor. "It'd be a shame to lose such a valued servant over the life of a traitor. Allow me to attend to this. Aside from yourself I doubt there are many who would grieve his absence."

"Th-thank you." Sunniva looked towards him, attempting to understand this figure's loyalty, then he spoke the words which saw everything fall into place.

"I didn't say I'd do it for free." Realisation, and a small smile, traced her features. With a firm nod she produced the donation her brother had presented. Weighing it in his hands Bray nodded. "You clean up here. I'll ensure even the scavengers won't unearth him."

Bray bent, seizing Rob's ankles in his firm grip. The dead weight slid with ease under his manipulation, drawing with it a trail from the pooled blood. Opening the doors, Bray surveyed the surroundings before looking back to Sunniva. She sat on the floor, staring at the blood soaked surface before her.

Bray gave a sigh, pulling the body over the threshold onto the dirt track. He was unfamiliar with this location, but given the dense forests surrounding them he was certain he could find a suitable place.

Emerging into an area of low scrubland Bray dropped Rob's feet with a groan, placing his hands on his lower back to give his muscles a slight stretch. His friend was heavier than he had appeared.

Leaving the body, he quickly returned to the temple. Peering through the door he looked in on Sunniva who, having recently returned with a pail, sat scrubbing the floor. She looked up to him in slight alarm before directing him to the tools he'd need to finish his task. Securing a shovel he took a slow walk back to where he had left Rob, concealing the bloody trail in such a manner that Sunniva could still follow it to her brother's final resting place. She would no doubt be unable to resist the urge to ensure his task had been adequately completed. As Bray reached the scrubland he couldn't stifle the chuckle as he saw Rob's angry glare.

"By Zeus, Bray. A little warning would've been nice." Bray raised his hands in a placating gesture.

"Do not underestimate the impact of a genuine reaction." Bray dug the shovel into the ground, forcing it lower with his boot before approaching Rob.

"Genuine? She could've killed me," Rob exclaimed. "And you! What in Hades, Bray? You don't just stop someone from breathing! Gods, I nearly suffocated while bleeding a bloody death!"

"Superficial, and necessary," Bray scolded light-heartedly as he examined the wound.

"Superficial? It doesn't look bloody—"

"It looks very bloody," Bray interrupted. "That was the intention. Now are you going to keep still so I can attend to you, or do I need to stitch your lips together as well?"

"But why was it even necessary?" Rob winced as Bray began to treat the wound. The initial surge of confusion and anger was ebbing now, and the true weight of events was beginning to bear down on him. Bray sensed the change in his friend and remained silent. "Why did she... my own sister... she—"

"I'm sorry, Rob. There was no other way. I only assisted in heightening her emotions, her action was her own, something already harboured within her. She has Apallagí, so I can't influence her. The only thing we gained from our encounter is the fact she thinks you're dead."

"And I should be grateful?" Rob growled, the betrayal burning deep within his eyes. He had always trusted her, given her his faith without question. He had never thought her capable of murder. Now he was brought to question if he ever truly knew anything about her at all.

"Well, yeah. Be thankful I anticipated her reaction the moment before she did. Otherwise I really could be digging your grave."

"And I suppose you did get my money back." Rob forced a lighthearted tone to his voice in a failed attempt to lift his spiralling mood. He held out his hand expectantly. Bray let his posture droop, his shoulders slumping dramatically.

"You're tighter than Epiphron's purse strings," Bray complained as the pouch struck Rob's hand with a little more force than had been intended.

"What's the shovel for?" Rob prompted as Bray started to dig.

"A grave. It'd look suspicious if you just vanished into thin air." Bray frowned at him, catching something of a hidden fear. "You're worried about the Moirai?" Bray observed.

"Wouldn't you be? I thought they were only a myth, but her belief goes beyond that. I think she's actually seen one. The Paion she mentioned, he can't be real, or at least still be alive. He was a myth, a hero of ballads."

"Well we have already considered the possibility of the Moirai being involved, and if they are somehow orchestrating this it certainly explains some of the tactics we are witnessing. But it seems we actually know more about their intentions than she does. If nothing else our theatrics confirmed her to be of no further use, to us or them." Bray stopped digging and looked at Rob. "For what it's worth, I'm sorry, she was your sister."

"It seems she's not been that for a long time. I just hadn't realised it until now." He sighed, wincing against the pain of movement. Someone had once told him the only real family was the one he made for himself. It appeared their words had held more wisdom than he had realised. "What will happen if she decides to dig up the remains?" His only response, as Bray continued with his task, was a broad grin.

Chapter 21

Torment

Taya groaned. Over the last day her magic had further receded, channelling almost completely into her daughter. Her health had deteriorated, and with each movement pain tore through her body. Her burning skin was beaded with sweat, whilst chills penetrated her very core. She was exhausted, and whilst she faded in and out of sleep she found no rest. Rarely now did the agony recede, sometimes it was so consuming she was unaware of Stacy's constant presence nearby.

"—cy," Her voice failed her, but she felt the reassuring pressure of her friend's hand upon hers.

"I'm here," Stacy comforted before refreshing the cold compress on Taya's forehead. The icy sting of water went unnoticed. It did little to reduce the red flushing of her pale flesh. Stacy chewed on the cuticle of her index finger, torn as to what else she could do to ease Taya's suffering.

"We need to talk." Taya's dark, sunken eyes were hardly open, squinting against the almost unbearable light streaming through the window. It was a few moments before she gathered the strength needed to push herself backwards. Her face contorted with the strain as Stacy helped her, until she sat with her back to the headrest. Stacy knew by this alone whatever Taya had to say was of grave importance. "Normally, when my kind give birth, our bones extend allowing us to utilise extra magic." Taya attempted to moisten her dry lips. Her speech was laboured, each word an obvious effort. "It is also necessary to allow the baby passage to the outside world."

Stacy tenderly began to dab the cold compress on Taya's face. Taya moved her head slightly, stilling Stacy's action. Their eyes met as she spoke the next words. "Remedy won't allow it." Taya winced shifting her position slightly. "She'll need to be cut out." Taya allowed her head to fall back, resting against the headboard. "And I'll need some yew berries." Stacy sat on the edge of her bed, taking a moment to gather herself. She knew what Taya was asking and the thought alone caused her to pale. Her final words echoed through her mind refocusing her attention.

"Yew berries?" Stacy heard her own question before she realised she had spoken.

"Yes. My people need to ingest a large amount of the seeds after birth." Taya held her voice steady with great effort. "It's vital, especially if she is born in this manner."

"Should I fetch them now, so we are ready?" Taya swallowed with great difficulty before nodding. Whilst it seemed Collateral would have a merchant for all purposes, those who would trade in yew seeds were not the type of character Stacy should have dealings with. Fortunately Taya knew just the place she could safely obtain them. "I'll do whatever you need me to, just know that," Stacy assured softly.

"When we got my bow, I noticed the archery range grew yew trees, they're probably grown for the bowyer." Taya glanced to the window, noticing the twilight tint to the light. "It's almost dark, they'll have closed for the night. They've no use for the berries, I'm sure they won't mind you taking some." Taya took a pained breath, feeling fatigue wash over her. "Just, don't eat any."

"Why?" Stacy frowned, assisting Taya gently as she lay back down.

"They're not so good, for humans," she whispered as the darkness of sleep once more embraced her. Stacy watched over her for a few moments, images of blood and bones warped the figure lying before her. She knew she would do whatever it took to protect her friend and the child she carried, but feared there was only one outcome. A future where one or both ceased to be. Stacy refreshed the compress, her brow weighted with apprehension.

* * *

The disjointed echoes of a quiet, rhythmic, knocking sound conjured images in Taya's mind of standing in her kitchen at home, preparing a meal for herself and Yuri. She attempted to retain the dream, and the feeling of tranquillity it brought. But the image further distorted with each dull impact until she was looking upon the familiar room.

Stacy was sitting at the small table, the gentle glow of a small oil lamp bathed her in its orange hue, casting strange shadows upon the wall. Their swaying movement was almost hypnotic as they seemed to move in rhythm with each dull thumping sound. Straining her vision Taya managed to bring her surroundings into some semblance of focus. Stacy was carefully cutting the berries to remove the seeds. She had clearly been doing this for some time. An almost empty pitcher of water cast gentle colours on the wall. Taya found herself fixated, watching the swirling and expanding rainbows until once more sleep took her.

Taya startled as the door banged closed. Whispered voices offered apologies as their gaze fell toward her. She lay with her eyes closed, her muscles tensed attempting to suppress the spasms and feign sleep to see what may be revealed. With their journey involving Sunniva she was certain their words would be more guarded if they knew her to be listening. There were things they may have learnt they felt the need to shield her from. Stacy placed another blanket over Taya, the extra pressure seemed stifling, but she attempted to keep her breathing calm.

"Well?" Her voice was low and sharp. She studied their expressions eagerly in the hope of seeing a promise of good fortune. It was only as she observed them she noticed the strange gait with which Rob was walking. "What happened to you?" Rob gave a sigh, shaking his head as he moved painfully to sit.

"His sister attempted to sever his ties to the mortal world," Bray announced rather dismissively with a wave of his hand.

"Has news of your deeds reached that far already?" Stacy caught herself as she saw Bray's disapproving expression. "What happened?" Stacy approached, attempting to force concern into her voice and take the actions expected from a comrade. She cringed slightly, lifting his top to examine the injury. "That's what all the fuss is about?" she snapped. The yellowing bruises around his ribs, from his confrontation with Bray on Afthonos, seemed more painful than the small cut she beheld. "The way you hobbled in here I expected... well something." She tugged his top down, shaking her head.

"Despite her intention it was merely a flesh wound." Bray shrugged moving to sit opposite Rob.

"A flesh wound!" Rob fumed. "My blood recounted a different tale."

"You honestly believed that was all your blood?" Bray's voice possessed an amused edge. "Did you even see what she stabbed you with?"

"Well, yeah. A bloody sacrificial knife," Rob retorted unamused. His mind recalled the images of the long bladed, intricately crafted, athame being buried into his flesh. He placed his hand protectively to the wound in remembrance. His frown deepened as Bray tossed something onto the table.

"You mean this?" He gestured towards the small pruning knife. The blade was barely an inch long and still tinted with his dried blood. "If you were a weed then, perhaps, there'd be cause for concern."

"That's not—you cifesboren! You made me see—"

"Her too." Bray slid a drink across the table to Rob, he emptied it in one quick gesture, slamming the cup down a little harder than needed.

"So how much was real?"

"Well, she did attempt to prune you," he shrugged with an amused chuckle, remembering himself his face grew serious. "As I mentioned before, genuineness was essential."

"And the blood?"

"Mostly mine." Rob glared across the table at him before examining his injury, noticing how small and superficial it really was.

"Aren't we getting a little off track?" Stacy snapped. "Well? Tell me you didn't just waste time with pointless games. What did your theatrics reveal?" she demanded, tapping her foot impatiently.

"Nothing we hadn't already considered." Bray's solemn tone revealed his disappointment. Stacy turned her distraught gaze towards Taya. For more reasons than they knew she had hoped for better tidings.

"Taya says we've about a month to figure something out. After that it'll be too late," Stacy revealed, keeping her promise by concealing the reasoning. A heavy silence descended, broken only by the sound of Bray's chair scraping across the wooden floor as he rose to stand.

"I'm going to get some air," He walked to the door, pausing with his hand upon the handle. "We will broach these matters again later." He knew he couldn't bear to remain here much longer. The room was filled with her delicate fragrance. His senses, recognising her weakened condition, urged him to feed. After the energy expended with Sunniva, his hunger began to dominate his thoughts.

"Tavern, in an hour?" Rob suggested.

"Oh there's a surprise," Stacy snapped. "What about Taya?

"You just said we've got a month, we can afford to let her rest." Bray closed the door behind him leaving no further room for discussion. Rob gave a sigh, if not for the intense look Stacy was giving him he would have probably been lost to thoughts of regret and desperation. He ignored her weighted stare for some time before finally looking up to acknowledge her.

"What?"

"I was just considering our options. Why don't you go get The Seed of Nzin?" Rob's brow furrowed as he tried to determine if he had misheard her. Somehow she was aware he already knew where it could be located, and that he could reach it unhindered. As soon as Taya had been retrieved from Afthonos, Rob had been informed, through his dreams, of its location. But how she knew this was beyond his understanding.

"It can wait." His stomach knotted as he turned to Taya, her weak fevered moans bringing rise to fresh guilt. This, everything, their entire situation, the problems they faced, it was all because he made the wrong choice. Part of him still attempted to justify his actions, but it was a voice he had learnt to silence. This was all his fault.

"Can it? You said it was capable of granting a wish, right?" Stacy prompted seeing the shadow of regret taking form in Rob's eyes. If she was careful with her words she could ensure he made the right decision this time. It seemed so obvious, there really was no other path they could pursue.

"That's the lore. Whoever holds it can make a single wish."

"Then surely our course is clear. We should use The Seed to remove Remedy. I'll do it. That way you don't have to concern yourself about inadvertently wishing for the wrong thing. What's the price of the magic?" Even filled with optimism her voice sounded venomous.

"There's so little known of its nature, but I think the price is knowing only one wish can be made. It has to be the right one."

"If that's true, then why do you think she was so against you using it?"

"It's, cursed," Taya whispered weakly, pushing herself up the bed just a little.

"Sorry, did we wake you?" Rob approached her slowly and carefully raised a glass of water to her parched lips. She took a sip, coughing violently until smears of blood speckled the sheets. After several rasping breaths she gave a weak nod, attempting to assure them she was all right. Rob tentatively adjusted the pillows to support her. He offered her another sip.

"It's cursed. That's why it should never be used," she repeated, hearing the hoarseness of her own voice.

"I've been meaning to ask, The Seed of Nzin, is it actually a Daimon's tear? The lore and legends say that demons, well Daimons I suppose, were creatures of little emotion, they could know no grief or sorrow, only revel in the misery of others. But on rare occasions a Daimon could be forced to shed a tear made from the crystallised essence of magic, and when this occurred, if the tear met with earth a powerful Nzin would be born. However, if someone obtained the crystal before a Nzin could emerge it would possess a fraction of the power, allowing the one who possessed it to make a single wish. But I've seen your tears, they are no different to ours, and I doubt I could wish upon them." Rob moved to sit on the edge of the bed, his gaze searching her for an answer.

"You could." She gave a weak tremulous smile. "But I doubt it would come true. Your legend is partly correct, it comes from a creature who knows no tears."

"So how can it even exist?" Stacy questioned curiously.

"It was once thought to be a Daimon's tear because we are charged with protecting it. It has no place in this world. It brings only misery."

"Couldn't you use it to remove Remedy?" It may have taken him a few moments, but he finally understood Stacy's reason for suggesting he obtain it. Beholding Taya in this condition he knew it was unlikely she could survive its effects much longer. He had done this to her, cost her everything. He could not be responsible for her life. If he could retrieve The Seed, he would consent to Stacy using it.

"No. If that were possible it would have already been done, regardless of the cost." She looked meaningfully at Rob. "Besides I doubt it is within its power."

"I thought it could do anything."

"Most things," Taya corrected. "Both possible and impossible, but I've never seen it do either."

"You mean since its creation it has never once been wished upon?" Stacy moved away, discarding the pink tinted water.

"Its predecessors have, countless times, but not this one, not since we were charged with its protection." Taya sank back down the bed as exhaustion overwhelmed her. "I'm sorry, I need to rest. Could I convince you to visit the tavern for a while?" She had heard snippets of the conversation with Bray, and what she needed, more than anything else, was some time to herself.

"Not a chance," Stacy asserted. "I'll not leave you in this condition. Let him go, but I'll stay, you won't even notice I'm here." Stacy turned towards Rob, escorting him quietly towards the door.

He left willingly. He was due to meet with Bray soon anyway. His mind returned to their conversation, causing him to wonder what possible information he had that could not be discussed in Taya's presence. His stomach tightened fearing he knew the answer already. She could not be allowed to hold such power. If they couldn't find a means to remove Remedy from her, they would need to find a way to neutralise the threat she posed. To do that, there was only a single option.

The small tavern heaved with people. The bard sang lively songs, strumming his lute in time with the music of an old piano. Bray, noticing Rob's arrival, beckoned for him to approach. The atmosphere of cheer did little to lift either of their spirits.

"No Stacy?"

"She thought better than to leave Taya alone, given the circumstances I think I'd have to agree."

"That's probably for the best. Besides, I doubt she'll approve of what we must discuss." Bray gestured towards the seat next to him. "She already dislikes you, so I'm sure you won't mind updating her. One of us at least should remain in her good graces."

"You think she has any left?" Rob gave a sigh. "I think I know why you wanted to meet here, but Taya said it herself, we're safe for a month. It's a shame she can't have a premonition on how we can remove Remedy."

"That's actually one of the many things I wished to talk to you about."

* * *

Stifling a yawn, Stacy quietly lifted the glass from Taya's bedside table. Her communication with Amelia since arriving here had been infrequent, but today she had received a reply. The small package had given her a glimmer of hope. She had been detailing information of Taya's worsening condition and fitful slumber, and it seemed Amelia had seen fit to supply her with a temporary solution.

She quietly counted the droplets from the pipette, carefully swirling it into the glass to ensure it dissipated. Amelia's letter instructed her on its use, and the dose administered should encourage a restful slumber. It was something Taya desperately needed, and Stacy herself was exhausted. She could feel her own attention faltering from the minimal sleep she was allowed. This solution would allow them both the chance to replenish their reserves.

She placed the glass beside her own on Taya's bedside table. The boisterous roars of merrymakers passing in the hall caused her to startle from the guilt of her own deeds. Rousing Taya she carefully lifted the glass to her lips. Her rattling coughs only served to further confirm Stacy was doing the right thing. Lying her back down she watched as Taya's eyelids once more began to droop.

Heaving a quiet sigh she picked up her own glass from the bedside table, a puzzled expression briefly crossing her face as she drained its contents. Her face contorted as the bitter flavour of the liquid assaulted her taste-buds. She flushed with heat, realising her mistake as her vision turned towards Taya, who watched her with exhaustion. Stacy tried to explain, but the concoction was unforgiving, and the only sound was that of her body as it collapsed to the floor.

* * *

Slowly Taya pulled herself to the edge of the bed, forcing her legs over the side. The effort sent beads of sweat chasing down her flesh. She gritted her teeth, refusing to recoil against the pain of every movement. She had to do this now. There was no other choice.

Her trembling hands fumbled to pull her boots into place, hoping they would add some support when she attempted to stand. Gripping the edge of the bed she pushed herself up. Her knees buckled, and her feet barely lifted from the floor, but she slowly managed to shuffle down the edge of the bed.

She swallowed in an attempt to repress the coughing fits which threatened to overwhelm her. With short, sharp breaths she stumbled across to the wall, using it to support her weight on the way towards the small dressing table. The distance was mere feet, but to Taya it seemed daunting and immeasurable.

She struggled for breath as her fingers closed around the dressing table's knotted surface. Guiding herself onto the small stool she surrendered to the raw coughs which rattled through her lungs. Resting her head on the small unit she tried to gather her strength. When she finally forced herself upright she was surprised to see the pale and drawn figure staring back at her. The dark rings around her eyes seemed almost like black pits, and her pale lips were dry and cracked. Small smears of blood seemed so dark against her almost transparent flesh.

Averting her gaze from the stranger before her she saw the reflection of Stacy's crumbled and twisted body upon the floor. Whatever the compound she had witnessed being added to the water was clearly potent. Its effects had been almost instant, and she slept with such peace it almost stirred envy.

There was so much Taya wished to say to her. She wanted to apologise, and to thank her. But the unspoken sentiment would have to remain acknowledged only in silence. She needed all her strength for what was to come. For their own sakes her friends could not learn of what must now come to pass.

Placing a trembling hand to her back she took some small comfort in knowing that, if things did not go as intended, Stacy knew what must be done to save her child. Assuming her daughter survived.

Tears welled in her eyes as she thought about the life her child would have. This was not the way she had imagined her first pregnancy. She had held on to the romantic notion of being with Yuri. Watching with a smile as he fussed over her every need with what she imagined would become annoyingly wonderful concern. Never had she envisioned the horrors of Remedy and the complications of Sunrise. She had not even considered her death before their child's birth as a possibility. The transfer of magic between the two of them had been completed in its entirety, she hoped. It was said children were resilient, and those unborn built up resistance to ailments and hostile environments, adapting and developing a natural defence. She hoped this held true, or what she was about to do could kill them both.

Finally her fingers felt the cool metal of the small knife. Relief and anxiety simultaneously flooded through her. She had to do this quickly before fear clouded her judgement and rendered her unable to act. Her trembling hand traced across the front of her pelvis, stopping as she felt the slight lump beneath her touch. Taya held her breath, attempting to steady her hands. Sunrise had been implanted when she was an infant in order to keep the familial blood seal active. When one bearing Sunrise entered the final phase of pregnancy it was customary to remove and seal it. It was then transferred to the child when they were old enough. Taya knew it should have been removed long before now, but it had not been an option.

The small archery knife parted her flesh with ease as she applied gentle pressure. A wave of heat washed over her as she saw the blood begin to flow. It was always implanted in such a way that removal would cause the bleeding required to draw the seals without causing lasting damage. But she had not expected so much. Gritting her teeth, she pushed her fingers into the wound to seize the object.

Lowering herself to the floor she placed the bloodied stone beneath the dressing table, using the blade to etch the runes and seals into the floor, drawing over them with her blood. She could only hope this would be enough to shield it until the Daimons could retrieve it. Looking down at the wound she felt herself blanch knowing she had left its removal too late. Her body was incapable of healing.

Red trails streaked the floor as she crawled slowly towards Stacy, knowing her help was needed to staunch the flow of blood. If this continued, given her already precarious health, she would lose the one life she wanted to protect.

"Stacy, please," Taya implored, grasping her weakly to shake the sleeping figure. Sobs of desperation escaped her lips as she tugged weakly on Stacy's clothes. It was futile. She pushed herself towards the door, pulling herself up to lean against it. Unaware of the smears of blood left by her efforts.

She fumbled with the door, stumbling unsteadily across the hallway to the wall opposite and used the cream coloured surface to support her weight. Her unfocused eyes searched for anyone who could offer assistance. Her body felt cold, her limbs heavy, and sleep seemed to beckon.

Taya heard the concern within a disjointed voice as a rough hemp blanket was wrapped around her, and the firm support of an arm was hooked around her waist. He spoke in soft tones, promising to get her the aid she needed.

* * *

Sunniva had worked tirelessly to conceal the evidence of bloodshed within the temple's walls. After swilling the ruby fluids away she continued to scrub with the small metal brush until the waters ran clear. Only one person had intruded on her ritual, and the tones with which Sunniva had banished him had afforded her privacy for the remainder of her task. Later, she would make an excuse about someone desecrating the temple and apologise for her outburst, but for the moment she had to ensure no one suspected her of the murder should her brother's body be found.

Untrusting in nature, Sunniva found herself wondering why she had so readily believed the mercenary figure, who had accompanied her brother, would attend to matters correctly. He had been paid well for his services, and had seemed unphased by her actions, but she found herself compelled to ensure matters had been correctly addressed. Donning her short cloak, to protect her against the cool night air, she took her leave.

The lantern's light surrounded her in its warm glow, giving her white attire a warming hue as she walked the isolated tracks. Gripped within her other hand was a pail, filled to the brim with water. As she walked she spilt the liquid on the ground before her, scraping her shoes over the grass and dirt to conceal the faint tracks left by the mercenary. It was clear he had worked to conceal his efforts, but her hawk-like gaze detected the blemishes upon her land with ease. The further she walked, the less blood she found and the easier it was to conceal the route. With the last of the water used she discarded the bucket.

She continued to walk, concealing snapped twigs and deep tracks. River smoke had started to form from the lowered nocturnal temperature. It wrapped around the dark trees, obscuring the surroundings with its eerie haze. Tree boughs creaked and clacked together as the wind lifted fallen leaves in dance. The sounds almost seemed to track her every move.

Sunniva shivered as the cold damp air penetrated her clothing. The dense shadows seemed to flicker with movement and the sound of the dead leaves beneath her feet created hushed conversation. Her scrutiny remained but her pace increased, wishing now to find the place her brother's corpse had been laid to rest. Each movement caused her to startle, the crunching of twigs and the sound of rustling foliage seemed to draw ever nearer. By the time she beheld the mound of disturbed earth, within the sheltered scrubland, she was almost running, sweat clinging to her damp flesh.

The mercenary had been true to his word and had left no marker but for the disturbed land. She dragged her feet across the deep indents where her brother's body had been pulled into the awaiting pit. Her movements kicked up dead leaves and undergrowth, giving her an idea of how to further conceal the mound. Tomorrow, by the time the sun dried the detritus, nothing would seem amiss to any venturing this far afield. She took a furtive glance at her surroundings, brushing away the strands of hair clinging to her face. The forest's noises still echoed around her as she approached her brother's grave. She took a moment, and closed her eyes, listening for anything that didn't belong. Confirming her solitude she crouched, placing her hand upon the mound.

"I'm sorry it came to this, Brother, you left me no choice. You have jeopardised life itself on your fools-errand. I can but pray there is time to make amends for what you have done." Sunniva gave a bitter laugh as she rose to her feet. "You always were a naïve fool. How easy you were to control, but I never suspected that creature could turn you against your own kind. Their evil runs deep, I underestimated them. Never again." Casting a critical gaze over her brother's final resting place she gave a firm nod. It was better this way, she had given her brother the one thing he longed for, peace.

Entering the temple she discarded her damp clothes, slipping into a dry gown. Relishing the warmth upon her chilled flesh she breathed a sigh of relief and wondered how long it would be before someone noticed her brother's absence. He was a loner, known to accept dangerous tasks. No one would question his disappearance, if indeed anyone noticed at all. With him removed she now had the onerous task of finding Taya. Her brother had very few havens where he might think to leave the creature, it was only a matter of time before she found her.

Realising the lateness of the hour Sunniva tiptoed to the pantry, securing one of the older, forest-green bottles, filled with wine from Elpída's first harvest. It was well-concealed and for her enjoyment only. She filled her chalice to the brim before returning to the solitude of her rooms with the intention of bathing.

Sunniva quietly pushed the door into its frame. Leaning against it for a moment with her eyes closed she allowed the tension to slowly drain from her body before making her way through to the adjoining area. Steaming water flooded into the sunken bath, the pipes groaning loudly in protest to use at such a late hour. When the water started to cool she closed the valve, knowing her actions would mean there was no warm water until lunchtime tomorrow. As she slipped into the large inset bath, the water soothed her tired muscles. She leaned back, drinking deeply from the wine before setting it aside and allowing her eyes to close.

The sharp, quiet, ringing sound of a coin being flipped penetrated the air. Its proximity startled Sunniva from her relaxation. Seeing a figure emerge from the shadows she pushed herself upright in a hurried motion, grasping for a towel. Rising to her feet she held it before her, drawing a breath to scream. Before the sound had even escaped her she felt the staggering blow knocking her back into the water. She gasped for breath, her vision distorted as her head sank beneath the surface. Two firm hands seized her, dragging her upward. Her awareness ebbed and she became only aware of being moved before darkness claimed her.

* * *

Bray licked his lips, inhaling deeply as the serving wench bustled past, carrying a tray of wonderfully aromatic dishes. He watched her movement, her frustration evident as she placed the meals down before the customers a little harsher than usual. She scowled, berating their disrespect before storming past him again. He closed his eyes, relishing in the slight scent of apple and cinnamon that seemed to be carried with her. It took almost all his restraint to remain seated. He knew Rob was talking. He could hear the muffled sounds of his concerned tones distracting him from the delightful experience. He moistened his lips again, unaware of the low, appreciative growl which escaped his throat.

"Bray!" Rob clicked his fingers trying to gain his friend's wandering attention. As the surroundings once more came into focus he realised he was on his feet. He cleared his throat sitting back down, his eyes searching for the woman. He knew she was near, her scent was getting stronger. It was almost all he could smell. "Are you all right?" he questioned uncertainly, a concerned frown furrowing his brow.

"Someone smells delicious," he whispered huskily, his tongue once more coating his lips with saliva. When he found her again he would certainly not pass up the opportunity to get better acquainted with the little delicacy. Her scent reminded him so much of—Bray swore aloud as his body propelled instinctively to his feet as he scanned the faces of everyone present, searching for threats.

"What?" Rob rose, searching the crowd in a similar manner to Bray, but was uncertain what he sought.

"It's Kitaia." Time seemed to move in slow motion, each action not nearly fast enough as their uncoordinated steps seemed to delay their advance. Bray pushed his way through the tavern towards the rear staircase and into the hall. He shoved aside a figure, pushing past them as he dashed towards the room. Bray was unaware of anything, the scent was more overwhelming than ever before. It took all of his restraint to suppress his rising frenzy.

Rob was on his heels when Bray froze outside their room, beholding the terrifying scene. Rob nimbly stepped around him to see Stacy lying sprawled upon the floor, smeared with blood. While Rob attempted to rouse her, Bray turned to follow the trail smeared across the wall within the hallway. He reached out, touching the congealing fluid before turning quickly to track the scent.

He followed the trail until it stopped abruptly. He closed his eyes, inhaling. He could still smell her, but there was something else, another fragrance in the air, one which overpowered everything else. His feet carried him down the hallway until the new scent became overwhelming. He heard something crunch beneath his boots. Turning his focus to the floor he cursed, seeing the small crushed phials that littered the corridor. He fought his way through the prevailing odours, through the tavern, and into the streets. But any trace of Taya was gone. As he stood, surveying the streets desperately, he pushed his hands back through his hair and cursed.

Chapter 22

Awareness

The desolate land cracked and crumbled beneath their feet. The broken terrain slowed their progress while the violent wind battered them relentlessly. Aidan's exhausted frame staggered, everything he was felt the exhaustion caused by his absence from the lands blessed by Darrienia. Every second he remained in contact with this barren and devoured land only served to tire him, deleting his reserves far quicker than he had anticipated.

The howling of the gale and the further collapse of the land were the only sounds to be heard. They picked their route with care, avoiding the large sinking chasms which descended into nothingness. Aidan, before tiring too much to converse further, had explained that to stare into the nothingness was to behold Chaos itself, and, as when in the presence of any primal deity, it was best to avert their gaze. Elly had many questions, but seeing his fatigue she attempted to offer him sustenance. Her hand reached into the bag, to carefully remove the last of their provisions, watching in dismay as the particles began to dissipate within her grasp, until nothing remained but the dust carried upon the wind.

Aidan's focus never faltered from the horizon. Each weary movement was filled with fatigue and determination. Elly positioned herself before him, his dragging steps halting. He looked to her pleadingly, attempting to moisten his dried lips.

"I will *not* turn back," he asserted. Elly closed her eyes for a moment, taking a long deep breath, weighing their options. If they were to return, she was confident the plain—which now stood where the mountain had once towered—would replenish him. He could gather energy, but the same problem would still await them. They would never reach further than this point. However, continuing would see him deprived of the sustenance his kind needed to survive. He would not live to complete the journey. She on the other hand would, this land did not pose the same threat to her. Her head bobbed subtly with each of her thoughts before she gave a committed nod, hauling him over her shoulder. "What are you doing?"

"This land depletes you as much as Darrienia restores you. I am limiting your contact," she explained wondering how he would have crossed this wasteland without aid had he chosen to come alone.

"I would have brought a dreamer to sustain me, it—" he paused, feeling a strange sensation building within him "You just joined yourself to me. H-how is that possible?" he queried, his confused voice already sounding much stronger than just moments before. Elly continued to march towards their goal, it was a few moments before she decided to offer an explanation.

"I have been suppressing the ties I have to the waking realm, but whether I am awake or here, my body is always in a state of slumber. I am allowing you to utilise that energy, the energy of my eternal sleep," she explained. She was unsure why she had failed to consider this as an option before. The thought had come from nowhere, a whisper to her mind as she considered the options available to them.

"That makes no sense. What are you?" Aidan questioned.

"Cursed. I live neither awake nor asleep, yet I am simultaneously both."

"Sounds like a riddle to me. You mean you're not a sentient golem?" he questioned cautiously. Such had been his presumption, which was why he and Jude had found her so interesting. Long ago, when Golemancy was a well-practised arte, he had heard stories of many such servants gaining awareness and life. He had recognised her age, the tales she had woven in legend, but her absence from Darrienia—with the exception of the times she had invoked the rune of boundaries—had led him to the conclusion she was a remnant of that time, or perhaps proof such practice had been rekindled once more. Golems lived, but they were unable to dream. Thus their presence here was a rarity. He and Jude had spent many months, years, debating the potential nature of this figure. She had been their favoured topic.

"No. I am, I was, human."

"Then how are you alive?" He knew he was not mistaken about her longevity, but no mortal possessed a life-span equal to hers. Perhaps her humanity explained in some way the grief and loneliness he had felt consuming her when they had first met; at once he felt slightly guilty for his deliberate attempts to provoke her. He had not thought her to be human. He had merely wanted to investigate how deeply the soul and emotions of a golem ran.

"I was cursed to the eternal by Kronos to await his vengeance," Elly sighed, adjusting their path a little further from the deep crevice as she felt her limbs beginning to tire. She continued talking, more for distraction than any other reason. "Night used the ancient rites to allow my soul to walk in a vessel. I am tethered to both my flesh and the golem. But my body will never awaken, not while the old magics endure."

"I assume attempts to counteract this have been made?"

"Many. Spanning magics both old and new." Night had tried without reserve to find a means to liberate her from the curse, but in the end, the golem had been his only option. But she knew he had never stopped looking for a way to undo what had been done. Considering it now, Elly realised she was content with how things were. She had lived longer, seen more, than most. But she had also lost more, and sometimes she simply needed time to grieve for all those she had loved deeply.

"I guess that explains why my kind have always failed to wake you," he mused, filling the silence as he felt her mood begin to darken.

"Indeed. You cannot wake me because my body is bound to slumber, and the link to my golem is being deliberately suppressed."

She returned to the silence of her thoughts, the pain of her loss still present, yet not as all-consuming as it had once been. This alone caused her great sadness. The pain was fading, and eventually would be forgotten until rekindled by the future once more. Elly managed a few more staggering steps as she felt the texture of the dry lands change to grass at her feet. Her knees buckled as she sank to the ground, sliding Aidan from her before allowing herself to rest.

"We actually made it," he whispered feeling the full strength of the land beneath him. "Thank you."

"Do not thank me yet. We still have no idea why we are here. Are we likely to expect any aid?"

"From other Oneirois?" Elly nodded at his question. "No. Given the potential for danger before my task we agreed I would send word if this disruption warranted action."

"Then they must still have some confidence in you to entrust a single Outcast to a matter of such importance. What if you were to perish?"

"I think you still misunderstand what it is to be an Outcast here. We are revered. We do not often engage in dream waking, we are responsible for ensuring the security and well-being of these lands. There is much sealed here that cannot be afforded release. My success will be gauged on whether this anomaly is dispersed."

"And was this meant to have been accomplished within a certain period?"

"Not as such, no. As an Outcast those who we report to are aware of our energies. At such a time that mine ceases to be they will assume I have failed, and a larger force will be assembled to investigate."

"Since your task was so important why did you delay, why visit with me?"

"Like I said before, I had intended to exploit your grief. This was a journey I thought myself unable to complete alone. I know that everything occurring somehow relates to the abduction of my partner and, since it was Melas who was responsible for that act, who better to assist me than someone who had already survived his forest twice?"

Elly gave a slight smile in response to his words, but her expression soon grew more solemn. Above them the darkened hue of the foreboding sky spiralled. Lightning lit the dense clouds, forking through the air in fast angry streaks, but the roar of thunder so often accompanying a storm never came. The energy in the air caused the small hairs on their arms to prickle, its oppressing weight bringing a seriousness to the situation.

A blinding flash of light crackled through the air above them, forcing all shadows to retreat under its dazzling presence. The eerie afterglow remained for a moment, scarring the sky, drawing their focus to something previously unseen. The faintest pillar of energy, a thread lost and shrouded by the swirling mass of writhing clouds, descending from the very centre of the storm, extending to touch the land below.

"Explain that," Elly demanded, gesturing towards the anomaly.

"It's some manner of syphon. Something is drawing the energy here for the purpose of forcing it elsewhere, but where in Darrienia could—"

"Not Darrienia," Elly stated adamantly. "I think I understand now why Jude was taken. We must hurry." Aidan looked to Elly in alarm. "I will explain as we move. If my theory is correct we will find a tideway."

"A tideway, to channel energy? But Melas is not an Oneiroi, he'd need a means to draw and convert the energy from this realm to that of his," Aidan gasped in realisation. "Jude! That abomination is using Jude to draw the energy through the tideway."

* * *

Stacy sat upright the moment she felt herself pulled from slumber. Her nostrils flared, protesting against the offensive odour assaulting them. Rob leaned back, granting her a full view of the blood stained room, her mind quickly recognised the dangers. She lifted her hands seeing the drying strains upon them, and her clothing,

"Well good morning, sunshine. Sleep well?" Rob's curt voice rang through her ears. He stood from his crouched position beside her, replacing a lid on a small tin. "Care to explain?"

"Who did this?" Bray interrupted before Stacy even had the chance to speak. After opening the windows he had done nothing but pace. Back and forth, unable to escape the prevailing scent. It was overbearing. "Out with it," he snapped.

"I-I wanted her to sleep. She switched glasses. I mean, that's what must have happened." Stacy didn't sound convinced. She was certain she would have noticed.

"Oh so *you* did this, and then what, Ethelyn decided to—I don't even know what's happened here. Last time she did something like this was to avoid... you don't think my sister had something to do with this? Kyne said she was hurting herself to retain focus when she was in The Depths, there's no reason she couldn't be enthralled here."

"Unlikely, Rob." Bray placed a reassuring hand on his friend's arm on his way towards the open window. "Whatever sway your sister had was lost the moment Taya accepted herself and recovered what had been repressed."

"So why do this? You were here. Surely you must know something." Rob could hear his own desperation.

"I don't know," Stacy stammered, her sight transfixed upon the smears of blood.

"Don't know what, if she did this to herself, or why she would?"

"Either."

"I can answer one of those. The blood loss and smearing are all consistent with it being something she did. It's doubtful someone attempting to apprehend her would allow her to reach Stacy, or the door. The condition she was in would have made it easy to subdue her. We can firmly assert these actions were self-inflicted. As to the reasoning—"

"If she was bleeding like this then surely she'd seek help, have you tried the medics?" Stacy reasoned.

"Why? There's no reason she would hurt herself in this manner just to seek aid. Did she... did she discuss attempting to remove Remedy?" Bray lifted the bloodied archery knife from the floor near the dressing table.

"Bray." The severity in Stacy's tone saw all movements stop. Both Rob and Bray gave her their complete attention. "Can you tell what kind of blood it is?"

"It's Taya's."

"No I mean... Taya was pregnant. Can you tell if this blood is—"

"Pregnant, why are you only telling us this now?" Rob fumed. Questioning how anything could survive what was done to her. He looked upon the blood again, a sinking feeling spread from the pit of his stomach.

"She only told me because she needed me to get the yew seeds. She said they're an essential part of the after birth care otherwise—"

"Well?" Rob prompted impatiently as Bray slid his fingers across the surface of the knife before touching the fluid to his lips. He felt the pressure of their eyes upon him.

"It's not... that's to say, if she was with child there's no reason to believe she is currently otherwise. But it may answer our second question. It's no wonder she was suffering."

"What do you mean?"

"For her to bleed this much would suggest her to be in her final phase. Perhaps a month from birth?" He looked to Stacy, who dipped her head confirming his theory. "Her body wouldn't heal, and with both Sunrise and Remedy the internal conflict would be—"

"You're saying this is because she attempted to remove one of them," Stacy summarised.

"I'm saying this is because she removed Sunrise. The question is, what became of it." Bray's vision scanned the room again, returning to the area where he had found the discarded knife. He frowned, seeing something out of place. There was blood beneath the dressing table. Crouching, Bray used the tip of the weapon to pull the congealed mass towards him. By the time he saw the symbols etched into the wood's grain it was too late. He lifted his face towards the ceiling, uttering some inaudible words.

"You just broke a seal didn't you?" Rob observed gravely, crouching to look at the object. "She'd safe-guarded it so we wouldn't do what we're doing now."

"If only your hindsight was as quick as your wit," Stacy huffed. "Now what? I assume we can't just put it back."

"Pass me that glass." Bray instructed gesturing be-hind him. Using the knife he pushed the object into the glass before taking it to the window. He looked through the container to the blood-soaked, medal-lion. It was of simple design. An eloquent golden ring surrounded the circular bezel that carefully se-cured the almost flat quartz in place. For something so deadly, it was remarkably beautiful in its simplic-ity.

Studying it further Bray was granted some insight into its nature. It was as Daniel had speculated. The danger it posed was indeed great. Within the clear crystal of Sunrise lay infinite possibilities, all frequencies within the visible spectrum. Whilst the black crystal of Remedy was the absence of colour and represented an equal amount of the frequencies in the invisible spectrum. Each crystal had been de-signed to alter the vibration generated through it to create an opposing wavelength, and when opposite wavelengths combined they cancelled each other. If the joint frequency of both Remedy and Sunrise were to be released the frequencies and vibrations would encompass almost the entire spectrum. Almost all life would be nullified.

"So answer me this. If he already had everything he needed, what did he gain from her release?" Rob mused. His posture stiffened as Bray spoke the words he himself had just considered.

"A distraction."

* * *

Paion stood within the very centre of Napier village. For years untold he had listened from the shadows as people speculated the reasoning behind its unusual terrain. It was the only place in the world where they thought four primary elements visibly met. It amazed him that some human tribe had once thought it wise to construct a town upon this great convergence.

Marsh, plain, stone, and desert all met within its centre. An ever altering divide as each fought to obtain dominance over the others. The town had suffered many hardships as a result of the elemental feud. It mattered not if they had been built to withstand tremor or flood, for wild forces had more at their disposal than even the wisest man could prepare for.

There was something else at work here, an invisible hand which reined in the power and held the sanctity of the land in place. It ensured the devastation such a meeting could create would not come to pass. It was an element long forgotten, lost through time. Its essence had been forcibly splinted and the Elementalists, who could once wield it, had met with misfortune before being able to pass on its powers.

Such was the deliberate execution of the Moirai, for they alone wanted to harness the wild power of the entity known as the Spirit Elemental. Its imprisonment within the converges ensured their longevity and continued isolation from the lands below. They exploited it, using its essence to bind the land and harness magic, while acting as an anchor to something no mere mortal could comprehend.

This entire area acted as a tether, and there were several, both visible and unseen, across the surface of the world. This one however was linked to something unique, something forgotten, and it would suit his needs perfectly. This was the only location he could achieve his desired result without risking exposure or interference.

Paion slowly unsheathed his sword. Widening his stance he lifted its tip to the heavens. Archaic symbols and obscure pictographs seemed to burn from within the tarnished metal, reforging the ancient blade to its pristine condition as it began to glow.

Small gasps could be heard from the gathering crowd as they bore witness to a star appearing within the morning sky. Awe became silence as the light from Paion's blade spanned upwards to touch that of the descending star, momentarily shattering the glamour he had forged to conceal his wings.

People sobbed, falling to their knees in worship, believing they beheld a messenger sent to them from the Gods. The star above grew larger, swelling and flickering as if communicating in unheard tones with the being before them. It was only as the land itself began to tremble that they thought to show fear.

Brighter and brighter the star grew, as if a heavenly body was descending to address them. Some fled, while others averted their eyes, and awaited in fearful excitement as the figure of one of their gods drew nearer. They prepared themselves for the message they thought they would bear witness to, and offered silent prayers and blessings while extending their hands upwards as if to touch the light which bathed Paion. He alone knew such things would serve no purpose, for while it was indeed a heavenly body, it was not what they anticipated. It was not a god but a relic.

Chunks of ice and rock tore away, creating bright siblings which seemed to hover near their parent briefly before breaking free of the controlled descent. They rained down upon the land, spewing dust and debris into the air as even the smallest created enormous craters. Fires burnt from the areas of impact, yet frost swept across the land instantly freezing all within its reach. Screams of terror and agony were masked by the sheer volume of the devastation as Paion returned a relic of an age long forgotten.

The Moirai had been nothing if not ostentatious. Their buildings reflected their love of adoration and glory, built in a manner which revealed their own superiority. They would not settle for a monument one-hundred feet in height, not when they could make it one-thousand and ensure all could behold and admire it.

The jagged rock formation of its base pierced the earth at the place Paion had only moments ago stood. The descent stopped only as the enormous plinth became level with the fractured ground, and upon it stood an object people knew they should fear, yet due to its nature they were unable to feel anything but adoration and love.

Four gigantic columns, forged from smooth minerals and crystal, rose high into the sky. They were joined together at three-quarters of its height by large, glimmering arches to support a single domed building. Its gentle gradient was smooth, with no breaks or crevices through which to gain entry. Upon the dome's tip was a thick spire, a figure of a winged person standing with their arms outstretched benevolently as if to bestow blessings across the land.

This impressive structure had once been used as a prison. Its sole purpose had been to absorb the magic generated within a disgraced Moirai, and use it to send blessings and fortify their own invisible boundaries.

Had any been able to see inside they would have seen Paion, small against the simple grandness of the chamber, looking out to survey the devastation he had caused with a look of satisfaction. This would be his sanctuary, his haven. A place none could gain entry to without his blessing.

When first he had devised this plan he had never imagined bringing down part of their land, and this outer area of Talaria had long been abandoned. If not for Kitaia Ethelyn he would have overlooked this possibility. With its presence here, on the land from which it had originally been constructed, the future he had vowed to create would now be a certainty or, what his people called, a bound prophecy. All that remained was to have the Daimon brought to him, and the return of the Moirai would begin at last.

He looked out over the horizon and imagined what the Seraphim thought of the future he now offered them. They had banished him for his ideals, and now his return would be celebrated with a thousand times more joy than the disappointment he had received at his sentencing.

* * *

Taya heard the distant murmur of chatter and breathed a gentle sigh of relief. Around her she could see the draping of a physician's tent. The privacy screens shielded her from unwanted eyes, and for a moment she allowed herself to relax. The pain of Remedy was still present, but with Sunrise removed she could breathe. She closed her eyes, focusing on the small life within her and relished in the slight stirring her daughter returned at their brief connection.

Slowly she pushed herself up onto her elbows in the hope to better understand her surroundings, but lay back down as she felt the tender pressure of her newly stitched wound. She hoped she would be able to find the person who had brought her here, and offer thanks for his assistance. Without his aid she would have surely died.

It took a further few moments for Taya to realise the movement she thought was due to her own disorientation was actually that of a carriage. They were travelling.

"Ah good, miss, you're awake." One of the screens folded back slightly to allow a young woman entry. "You sure were fortunate, we almost couldn't still the bleeding." The figure pushed her sandy-blonde hair behind her strangely shaped, almost flat ears. "You must be a little confused, how much do you remember?"

"I was stabbed," Taya whispered. It was better to lie than admit she had inflicted the injury herself. "I tried to find help, but everything after is a little hazy."

"Yes. You're lucky we were passing through. Quite frankly it's not every day we see someone like you. The other physician didn't quite know what to make of you. Luckily we're accustomed to dealing with living curiosities, shall we say? Our band used to be quite the crowd pleaser at one time."

"Curiosities?"

"Well you're a little less obvious, bones where they shouldn't be. How you expected to give birth is beyond me."

"But how..."

"We spoke with someone who knows of your condition intimately. They advised us on how to proceed. That's actually why we're travelling. To be honest, we don't have the facilities we need to help you birth the child and they're preparing the area for your arrival. Your injury caused some complications and, whilst there's no immediate threat, we will need to deliver early. They're going to meet us there, but we couldn't risk any other mode of travel with you. Now, you really should rest." She raised a glass of water to Taya's lips. "Drink," she insisted.

Once Taya had finished the offered fluids she rested her head back. The figure at the base of her bed seemed to alter slightly. Taya watched in confusion as she draped her hair over her face and secured it in place before turning. It was then Taya saw another face, that of a man. The figure's shoulders and limbs seemed to alter, twisting to give him dominance. He walked forwards exiting through the screen and the hushed conversation between a man and woman once again resumed.

Taya had heard of people from the tribe of Hermaphroditus, but this was the first time she had met one. It explained why they were so desensitised to her differences. As the carriage movements lulled her to sleep, she wondered briefly if Stacy had told Rob and Bray of her condition as well.

Chapter 23

Manipulation

Rob gestured towards the map assertively, mentally imploring it to reveal an answer. He had thought fortune had smiled upon them when they discovered a woman matching Taya's description had been taken to a nearby physician for aid. After that the trail became complicated.

The person who had brought her to the physician appeared to have done so solely in order to utilise their tools. The proprietor had been reduced to passing the items being requested, while the stranger staunched the bleeding. While he worked he had insisted a messenger be sent to alert his tribe so they might transport her in order to provide the more specialised care she needed. Given the abnormalities the physician had noticed when he had initially attempted to examine her, he had been inclined to agree.

"I can't believe you'd be so stupid!" Rob growled. "People expect a certain level of support from people like you. How could you just let someone walk off with her?"

"Well-I... to be fair, it was their patient. It was an emergency, they just needed my facilities. How was I to—"

"Don't insult us. You don't believe that and neither do we," Bray interjected. "The least you can do now, is *try* to help. The woman they've abducted is important. Someone considered an equal to royalty. Do you understand the situation?"

"Yes." He nodded his head rapidly. "But it doesn't mean I know any more than what I've already told you."

"You've told us nothing!" Stacy snapped. "We've had better accounts from passersby who claim they overheard conversations about Therascia. You helped move her to be transported. Tell us what you know."

"They may have said something about going there. But I wasn't really listening. It was hard to when they looked like they did. They were all miscreations. Given her own abnormality I thought she belonged with them." He mopped his brow uncomfortably.

"What do you mean miscreations?" Bray asked, frowning.

"They weren't like us, not like Méros-Génos either. They were... monsters. The man who brought her in was surely cursed by the Gods. He was two beings in one. Man and woman, front and back.

"The tribe of Hermaphroditus, I thought they were extinct. What else, were the others the same?"

"Gods no. There was a headless man. Headless! His eyes were where his nipples should be. His whole face was on his torso. I've never seen the likes. He wasn't like the pictures I've seen of the Acephali, I'll tell you that. The centre of his torso from nape to navel was held together with teeth. He could swallow a man whole. I know I've a reputation, but I swear, I've not touched anything in years. Not a word of a lie, their driver... he was a one-eyed goatman."

"Okay, we've heard enough." Rob rolled up his map, placing it back within his jerkin. "Let's go."

"No, I swear, I'm telling the truth. Someone said they used to be a travelling act, that is, until The Order sought them out."

"The Order?" Rob's posture stiffened.

"Yes, apparently they wanted to make use of their uniqueness. They heard a force is coming that could challenge even their rule. And we all know how the Acropolis hates to lose coin."

"What force?"

"That's all I know." A loud commotion outside drew their focus. The disturbance had been increasing in volume since their conversation first began. The door opened with a thump, revealing an adolescent female dressed in beige tunic and shorts that were cut in a style which made her instantly recognisable as a Herald.

681

She halted seeing the gathering, and removed her busker hat briefly to display her guild emblem. When the physician nodded, to confirm she could proceed, she unrolled her parchment and read aloud.

"Call to aid. All members of the Physicians' Plexus not attending to critical care must report immediately for relief aid."

"What's happened?" Stacy questioned, stepping into the young lady's line of sight. The figure stepped around her, retaining her focus on the message's recipient.

"You are to bring your field kit and report to the main Plexus. You have been selected to join the convoy to Therascia, where a field hospital is being erected. Said Convoy will depart in," the figure glanced outside briefly, "twenty minutes. Those with critical cases can attend the secondary deployment in order to allow for their patients to be transported to The Medic who will maintain critical care within Collateral. End of message. Do you acknowledge?"

"I... yes, thank you," The physician answered somewhat flustered. The figure turned, placing the scroll in the small roll strapped across her front, and departed at speed to the next name on her list.

"What was that about?" Stacy wondered aloud as the physician grabbed an over-sized canvas bag. He flung it onto his back before securing his physician's bag from inside one of the counters.

"Excuse me." He hurried them through the door before locking it behind him.

"I don't remember when last the Physicians' Plexus mobilised like this," Stacy observed, seeing several people with similar bags pushing their way through the gathering crowds.

"I do. It was when the Severaine began its reign of terror," Rob advised solemnly. "They created outposts to treat the critical and ready them for transport to castles." He remembered visiting several such sites. After returning to see the ruins of Weft he had immediately searched Albeth Castle, in the hope that his family had escaped unharmed. When his search had been unsuccessful he had turned his focus to both the mobile and field based physician units. The number of injured and dying had been immense.

"So what has happened on Therascia that's resulted in this?" Stacy asked, looking to Bray as he began to speak.

"We had better make enquiries. Quickly. It's surely no coincidence those giving Taya's aid were recruited by The Order. Something has occurred to further Paion's plan, and we must find out what."

* * *

Íkelos had been patient. Timing was everything. There was little that occurred in or adjacent to his domain that he was unaware of. With Daley in his possession he believed nothing now escaped his attention, inclusive of how close Paion was growing towards fulfilling his agenda.

Long had Íkelos been manipulating events to Paion's favour; be it a stray thought planted in slumber, or complete manipulation through dreams mistaken as prophecy. He had ensured things had been easy, unchallenged. One thing was now becoming abundantly clear, with the Daimons' Sfaíra Fýlakas within his grasp Paion could very well achieve his goal. This was something Íkelos could not permit, and thus this was where their paths would part.

Paion had been unaware of Íkelos' covert aid. He had been a silent partner, assisting from the shadows cast in dreams. However, if Paion were to succeed, if he were able to erase all life upon that world, but for that of the Moirai, his own ambitions would be forfeit. He could not allow this to come to pass.

Even now the Daimons were preparing to start their ritual in a daring attempt to retrieve the essence of one already lost. When they began he would be granted exactly what he needed to ensure his success. By the Daimons' own actions he would be given passage back into the world from which he was denied. They had no understanding of what they would unleash, what the archaic languages woven unseen amidst the grand design of the magic convergence would achieve. Yes, it would indeed send their regent to Daley. But it would also prepare and execute so many other things, things ingrained and woven so intricately that they would go unnoticed.

The Kyklos were preparing, resting in isolated meditation to harmonise their energies ready for the task ahead. Now was the opportune moment to relay his message through The Betwixt, and into the subconscious of the human they had opened to their messages, the one they had allowed entrance to their great city and even aided through The Depths of Acheron. He could not risk failure should even one detail go awry, and so the treasure hunter would have to find a means to retrieve the one bearing Remedy. Fortunately, for the sake of his ambitions and all life, he knew just how to achieve this.

Íkelos had knowledge of pacts and rites that people now living could scarcely imagine. All had come to pass as he had intended. Now was the time to turn things to his own favour. Paion would indeed be paving the path for a return. Just not the one he had intended.

* * *

Rob sat within the convoy of physicians alongside Bray and Stacy. They had deemed this the best way to obtain the information they sought. To gaze upon the cause of panic, with their own eyes, would instil more understanding than the barely coherent mutters of rumour. He allowed his eyes to close. People seemed to want to talk to him, about anything and everything, in nervous bouts of excitement. This pretence would grant him some semblance of peace.

His thoughts were focused on Taya, hoping if he could achieve a near-dream state the Kyklos would connect with him. He had been surprised to discover that it had been this group who had been feeding him information on the portals he had needed. Although he did understand their reasons for doing so. They knew at one point his path would cross with Taya's, and perhaps even the part he would play in her life.

Taya had been with Sunniva for ten years, yet it was only recently their lives had become intertwined. Rob's visits over the last six years had been infrequent, and it was only recently he had brought himself to once again cross the temple's threshold. Given the time he had spent there before, he had to wonder how Taya had escaped his notice for the four years before his family's death, especially when he had stayed there following his near-fatal injuries.

The conversation within the wagon became a dull, incoherent mumble. He felt the weight on the seat alter and half opened his left eye, startling slightly when he saw a shadowed figure beside him. The carriage was quiet, empty. Just Rob and the figure remained. The voice was a whisper of nonsensical words which conjured images in his mind. A golden coin rotated in the air before a brown-haired woman. The image shifted and distorted to form an immense tower reaching into the heavens, with no discernible point of entry. Their perspective grew closer to reveal the interior. He saw Taya, captive within, and the unmistakable glow of a portal.

"But we're far from the full moon. Even if I knew the path, we can't access The Depths of Acheron to reach it." The image of the woman flashed before him again and a single coherent word whispered within his mind. "I don't understand."

The carriage hit a bump in the road, startling Rob awake. The hum of chatter became loud once more. He surveyed the carriage, earning himself a concerned look from Bray who, at Rob's beckoning, made his way over to crouch before him.

"I think I know what we're about to see," Rob advised in hushed tones, noticing Stacy had also joined them, and now perched on the seat someone had offered her. "The Kyklos just reached out to me. They've told me how to get to Taya. But we'll need to use The Depths."

"What do you think we're going to see?" Bray asked, the carriage was completely sealed, affording no vision to those within.

"A tower as high as the heavens, without a means of entry. Taya's inside. It's where Paion intends to activate Remedy's power."

"And Sunrise's." Bray patted his breast pocket where the crystal had been secured within a fine glass case.

"But she's not got it. He can't."

"You're wrong. She sealed it with her blood. So although it's no longer present it's still bound to her. If Paion activates Remedy, the power of Sunrise will be transferred via the blood seal. It will still use her as its conduit since the alignment to a human is not needed for the use he has in mind."

"So what's the answer?"

"I've a possible option. But I need to consider it more."

"Well don't take too long. From what I saw Paion is preparing to birth Taya's child." Rob's mind filled with the brief glimpses of saw-like instruments and blades lined upon the altar where Taya lay. He failed to suppress the sickening shudder.

"Was the image you saw to be, or current?" Bray asked desperately, seeing his friend pale at the thought.

"I couldn't say."

"Wait you said The Depths right?" Stacy questioned shuffling closer to Rob. "Then surely we've got until the full moon, otherwise why show you something you can't reach?"

"Because I'm meant to find someone who can open the way for us."

"Who?" Stacy demanded.

"Wita." Rob repeated the only word he had recognised.

"Daniel? What's he got to do with this?" Stacy questioned. Bray clicked his fingers gesturing excitedly.

"Why didn't we think of this before? Paion's Moirai. He will have been using prophecy to guide his actions, to manipulate the future until only his success remains. In order to confront him successfully we would have to use the influence of a person who lives in a different reality to our own, one who sees things differently."

"How does that help us?" Stacy frowned.

"A person who sees things differently could also potentially alter things unseen. Daniel's the Wita of the Eortháds, a sage who lives askew to our world." Bray banged urgently on the wagon giving the signal to stop. "We shouldn't waste our time here. We must contact Daniel, but only him. If we speak of this to anyone else it could alter our advantage."

"Really, you're concerned about this *now*?" Stacy's face contorted as she gestured wildly around the carriage, where all conversations had fallen silent.

"Show me *some* respect, I'm no fool," Bray retorted. "They didn't hear what you think they did."

* * *

Sunniva's weeping figure lay within the inscriptions surrounding the tideway. Great care had been taken to ensure the etchings on which they stood were exactly as Geburah had marked. Each symbol, each rune, had been carved with precision, spanning out from the central point. The area was immense and only Geburah, Yuri, and Sunniva could be found within its complex design. Members of the Kyklos stood in their designated rings, separated from them, yet still connected to the main workings by a fine weave of runic symbols. Ensuring their safety, scouting teams and hunters patrolled at a distance, keeping vigil for any signs of danger. This new tideway was deep within their own domain, and whilst it had been some time since their enemies had ventured this far, it was best to remain vigilant.

"Everything is ready, Regent," Yuri relayed as he saw Meredith and Eadward both confirm things were in order.

"Very well. You all understand your roles. I alone will seek Daley, events here will unfold as intended."

"My abduction, your treatment of me, all will bring the wrath of the Moirai upon you," Sunniva asserted, but she already knew there was no hope of rescue. She had been a fool to believe herself protected, but she had never thought a demon could enter Elpída. The blow had come quickly, and when she next awoke she had found herself here, surrounded by demons and weakened by their etchings. She had tried to stand, to resist, but the fear binding her was too strong. Instead of acknowledging her words those around her simply continued as if she had never spoken. "It's already too late to save your wretched whore, you filth." One of the figures stopped, she smiled smugly knowing her words had reached him. He turned, stepping carefully over the markings until he stood towering over her, she opened her mouth to speak, her words lost as he grabbed her hair, pulling her upward to strike her in the stomach.

"The *whore* you speak of is my wife, and you have no worth to even utter her name." Images of Kitaia and their unborn child filled his mind as Sunniva doubled over, gasping for breath. She attempted to speak again, his foot connecting firmly with her jaw to send her sprawling upon the stone markings. She cowered against his relentless barrage. His foot raised once more, his anger burning. Meredith gripped him, pulling him back with gentle assertion.

"She serves no purpose dead, know that she will suffer more this way." Yuri nodded, accepting her council, before turning his back to the sobbing figure to take his place.

Geburah reached out his hand, placing it upon the tideway. He felt the flow of energy being channelled through him. As his ethereal form separated he saw the colours of magic invoking and charring the etchings, he could hear the screams of the human as the energy seared her from within, and her pores bled to soak the runes surrounding her. He felt only the slightest margin of pity as he found himself drawn towards the place he knew Daley awaited rescue.

Daley's presence within the prison convulsed. Geburah reached out, his hand penetrated the bark of the towering tree in a desperate attempt to grasp him. Daley's image was faltering, fading and solidifying before Geburah's very gaze. So little time remained but his attempt to retrieve him met only with air. His hand passed through the figure, who looked upon him with a tortured expression. Removing his hand he tried again as the figure appeared to grow more substantial, he felt the pressure of contact for but a fleeting moment. Daley's eyes pleaded for aid, before being overwhelmed with a desperate fear. His mouth moved, relaying a message which remained unheard as the final wisp of life faded, along with his image.

Geburah covered his face with his hands for a brief moment before composing himself. They had been too late. A glimmer of movement caught his attention. A great influx of light bathed the area behind him. For a moment he thought he could see another world, another plane where dark clouds circled with angered lightning. A wave of power breached the window. Momentarily blinded he felt his ethereal form grow rigid, as if the storm itself had struck him, threatening to consume all that he was with its wild fury. The danger to his living self forcibly expelled him into The Betwixt, propelling him back to The Depths of Acheron, to where his consciousness belonged.

When he caught his breath he found himself standing before the crumbled remnants of the tideway, with the weight of many eyes upon him.

He turned his focus first to the human, her body was covered in still-damp blood. All life had left her, yet he felt no regret.

"What of Daley?" Yuri questioned breathlessly. The power that had united them had been like no other, rejuvenating yet exhausting in the same breath. Their invocation had lasted mere minutes, but within the first several seconds half of the Kyklos had collapsed from the effort. Only Yuri and Geburah now remained standing.

"We were too late," Geburah whispered. "There was not enough left of him to retrieve. He faded before my very eyes."

"We tried, that is what matters," Yuri comforted.

"And what of her." Geburah gestured towards Sunniva's body.

"Let her rot." Yuri spat in her direction. "Daley may be lost to us, but our actions have surely removed any remaining influence on Kitaia, and we must focus our efforts on her." He recalled the last conversation he had shared with her. Out of necessity he had confided the news of her pregnancy with Geburah and the Kyklos, beseeching them to keep the news, which should have been a joyous and celebrated occasion, unannounced. Before all else they had to find a way to remove Remedy, but with the pregnancy transferring her magic there was no longer any hope to reach her through dreams. He had been trying.

"Something doesn't feel right about this. This entire task seemed an endeavour in pointlessness. What did our actions here achieve?" Geburah questioned quietly, his vision returning to Sunniva's lifeless body.

* * *

Rob crouched outside the window to Acha and Eiji's residence. It was dark, and a low mist seemed to chase the deserted streets. The occasional footfall of patrolling militia would echo through the veiled silence, forcing him to seek cover while he waited for the opportune moment. The store's window shutters were fastened, and their other wares were sealed inside for the night. The small flicker of the low embers of a fire teased the window, casting shadows from within.

It had been several minutes since he had heard their muffled conversation fall silent. The subtle fragrance now surrounding their house suggested his small projectiles had successfully penetrated the chimney. They had something within their possession he needed, and he couldn't risk them discovering his actions.

Rob carefully slid under the tent's canvas, covering his nose and mouth with a cloth in case any of the inhibitors remained. Removing his small, leather roll he carefully picked the lock, giving a barely audible groan when the door failed to open. Probing one of his pouches he secured a small shard of enchanted mirror from within. Holding it to the entrance he drew the mirror down slowly, watching the reflection of the door's reverse side appear upon its shimmering surface. At the first bolt he paused, pulling a small length of wire from his belt. He carefully threaded it over the door, manipulating it into place before using it to release the lock. Finally he removed another object from his pouch. Placing its round surface on the wood opposite the hook-latch and slowly raised the cabin hook until it cleared the eye plate. Returning his items he quietly pushed the door, granting himself entry into a place he had once been welcomed.

He cringed slightly, beholding the two unconscious figures. They had been enjoying supper together on the small chairs in front of the fire. He felt almost guilty for disturbing their intimate moments.

With light steps he made his way over to Eiji, deftly relieving him of the small pendent around his neck. Rob marvelled at it for a moment. He could not do this in their presence, but he knew better than to leave their property with it in hand. Despite how it may seem to any onlookers, within that scrawled notice upon the tent was a warning which held true. It warned of curses on thieves, and it was no mere threat. Rob could see the enchantment surrounding their residence and, when last he had been here, he had witnessed but part of the protection scribed upon its walls. He would have to conclude his business quickly, and within their borders. He could only hope there was no one around to overhear his whispers.

Chapter 24

Stratagem

Rob sat near the ruins of Maxwell Radillion's once glorious mansion. Lord Radillion had been appointed by the, now deceased, King of Therascia to be the governor for the Northern regions. He had sought to elevate himself above the common-folk and had requested this residence as a sign of his superior status.

Since his assassination, many years ago, no one had cause to visit this location. His once fine manor had been reduced to stone and cinder, and lay now weathered by age and stripped of anything of value. People had gathered like carrion birds to pick through the remains. The foundations, and three of the lower walls, remained standing, turned black from the fire's caress. The windows and doors had been incinerated, creating yawning dark holes, and the far wall had crumbled into ruin, pulling with it a mass of debris. The earth around the mansion was scorched, but small shoots of plant life attempted to pierce the darkened ground. Even after all this time, the area was heavy with the stench of charred wood.

Despite the sight, it wasn't the shell of the structure belonging to the former governor that held Rob's focus. Maxwell's residence had once overlooked Napier village, and now its ruins beheld a vision that defied belief.

The land below had been razed to the ground. Ice and fire blanketed the crumbled debris of all that remained of the settlement and its surrounding areas. Small groups searched the outer area of the devastation with caution and difficulty. They knew from the destruction alone the survivors would only be those furthest from the impact. Try as he might, Rob could not keep his gaze averted from the tower for long. It was everything he had glimpsed, and so much more.

He remembered the feeling of utter amazement when first he had stood before The Courts of Twilight. Even *its* magnificence was eclipsed by this masterful construction.

Although partially obscured by the sun rising on the horizon behind it, the craftsmanship defied any comprehension he could imagine. It reached beyond the means of man in a daunting display of grandeur. The movements of shadows as the sun's light began to grow in intensity drew his awareness towards the finely carved depictions surrounding the upper area of the widening supports. The intricate details of knots and symbology, lost due to the structure's sheer height, cast small shadows where the sun touched. But even with the aid of such illumination the meanings or representations were still impossible to discern, making him question their relevance. The dome, where he knew Taya to be, seemed so close and yet so desperately beyond his reach.

The structure cast a shadow of unimaginable terror and darkness across the land, but those affected by the blessings of the Moirai thought only to bask in its magnificence.

If there was one thing he remained grateful for from his past, it was the training of his mentor. Ultimately it had been for her own ambitions. He had been a mere tool in her agenda, but that was why their relationship had worked so well. They had both needed something the other could provide.

Lady Elaineor had required his loyalty and a means to remove something from The Courts without raising any suspicion. Rob had wanted his freedom, and in order for that to be possible he had needed to master skills and techniques it seemed only she possessed.

"It truly is spectacular isn't it?" Daniel approached slowly, to stand behind Rob, looking out over the ancient structure. They shared a moment of reflective silence before Daniel moved to position himself against one of the rock faces, turning his vision from the tower. It stirred too many tales to allow him the focus he assumed he'd need. "So tell me, what was so important that you would seek to steal something that would freely be offered had you asked?"

"Obscurity." There was a short moment of silence before Rob spoke again. "I'm ashamed to admit, now

I have you here I don't know where to begin." Daniel adjusted his position against the rock, making himself more comfortable as he waited in silence. Seeing this Rob let out a tense, yet relieved chuckle, understanding the meaning behind the gesture; the figure before him would wait as long as it took. Not many in his position would show such patience. "I was contacted by the Kyklos. Kitaia Ethelyn, the Daimon you met, was abducted... again.

"We discovered too late the only reason Paion released her was to distract us from this." Rob gestured towards the tower. "Ethelyn is in the final stages of pregnancy and is preparing to give birth. Although, I suppose, it would be more accurate to say Paion is preparing to remove the child in order to allow him access to the power at her disposal after birth.

"I've been shown how to reach her, how to gain entry to that, and to do so I need to gain access to The Depths of Acheron."

"I understand the implications so far. So where do I fit into this message?"

"Well, that's when it gets a little more complex. You see, Paion is Moirai and has been manipulating future arcs to ensure all paths lead to his success. This stronghold must have been the final phase. By bringing this here, and sealing them inside, he has ensured even our most valiant attempts would fail. We can't scale it, and even if we reached the top where the dome is situated there's no means to gain access.

"Bray theorised that the reason I was told to seek you was because you live unaligned to our plane in both body and sight. How did he put it? Those who see things others can't can also alter things unseen, or something like that. As the Wita your presence is negated in prophecy because you yourself are beyond the sight of fate."

"You devised all this from the word Wita? Impressive. It certainly explains your reluctance to reveal your intentions. To do so would be to potentially create a path already witnessed."

"There was something else, something within the message that didn't belong. I heard your name, but it wasn't you I saw. It was a woman—"

"And a coin?" Daniel questioned knowingly. There was but a single person he knew with the ability to do what he was asking. "I'll make enquiries. What you ask requires a master of archaic arcane. The person you witnessed, I have no doubt, would be Adelpyro Elfreda, the Thegnalar of Drȳcræft. She and those of her class are the only beings still capable of what you are asking. I have my own conditions to aiding you, so it is better we discuss them now. I hear the Mystics will soon gather and I will be asked to be in attendance. When next we meet we will be unable to talk on such matters, the coin will be here"—Daniel patted his pocket—"it should prove no challenge for you to retrieve, but speak of this to no one. You alone will know of this in its entirety."

"Thank you." Rob noticed Daniel staring far into the distance and allowed him a moment of silence. He was uncertain what his conditions would be, but he would adhere to them.

"They're proud of you. I hope you realise that," Daniel stated suddenly. "Tabatha still wears it and prays for your safety." Rob's hand slid into his pocket to touch the hair clip as tears misted his eyes. Daniel blinked, his eyes showing an important realisation. "We buried them on the borders of Weft," he recalled. "A mother and daughter, and so many more. We didn't know their names, but we paid their passage."

Rob hadn't realised Daniel had approached until he felt his firm, comforting grasp upon his shoulder. Despite himself, Rob wept. For six years he had prayed his family had found passage across Acheron and Styx. For six long years he had tried to deceive himself with the notion of this truth, knowing that without a fare there was no passage. This was the very reason he carried so much coin on his person so, when he finally met his end, he could pay the ferryman and finally grant them, and maybe some others, peace.

* * *

Daniel watched as Rob left through the portal of Collateral before once more making himself comfortable. This time he sat where Rob had previously, but with his back to the tower.

"So, is this the manner by which you Misorians observe?" Daniel asked, looking at the crumbled wall before him. "The watchers watch the Chosen," he recited. "But that's not what you're doing, is it,

Grayson Bray?" Bray stood from his crouched position behind the wall and hesitantly began to approach.

"I'll admit my presence presents many conundrums and contradictions. Accept my apologies, Wita, but I too find myself in need of your council. And, thank you, your words brought him the comfort I fear he'll need if we're to succeed."

"The truth to the right ears is worth more than any riches." Daniel gestured for Bray to sit beside him. "So, what need for obscurity brings you to me?" Daniel prompted.

"There is something I keep returning to, but my instincts and logic are contradictory," Bray explained. "I fear I will not get the objective clarity needed if I speak of this to any other. It's regarding Sunrise."

* * *

Stacy stood with Rob and Bray outside the familiar residence. This morning's first light within Collateral had been met with a summons from Amelia, requesting her immediate attendance in Acha and Eiji's home. Now she stood here and had no idea what to expect, but noticed at least Bray, who had invited himself and Rob along for this gathering, had shown the courtesy of fully buttoning his shirt. He, at least, looked presentable.

Now she was here she felt a little apprehensive. Her delay in knocking would have normally encouraged Rob to step forward, but he was still concerned about his last visit, and the implications of this invitation. Bray rolled his eyes, reaching past them to strike the door. He seemed to flinch as the knock echoed.

"We have no time for procrastination. We need answers, and I have it on good authority that one within these walls can tell us what we need to know." His voice seemed quieter than normal, almost soft.

"And how do you plan on getting such information without it falling on unwanted ears?"

"You've travelled with me all this time, and still you question me?" He forced a smile, causing Rob to frown.

Bray hadn't seemed quite like himself in days, not since Rob had met with Daniel. Bray had been absent when Rob had returned just after dawn, and he hadn't returned until the early hours of the next morning. Without a word, to either Rob or Stacy, Bray had stumbled straight to his bed, and it was the first time Rob had ever recalled seeing him sleep, and still be lost to slumber past midday.

"One within these walls, who?" she demanded, her shrill tones caused Bray to wince. "Don't tell me you're finally suffering cropsick. Now, of all times?" Stacy had been watching Bray for the last few days. He had been sleeping more than normal and seemed more sensitive to the noises around him. Given how much he indulged, and that he had seemed to abstain from drinking these last few days, she could only imagine he was finally treating this situation with the severity it warranted. Of course he was now suffering the consequences of his overindulgent lifestyle.

"The Herald said the Mystics are in attendance, all of them. In order to better grasp our situation I need to speak with the Seer of Misfortune."

"Peter?"

"If that's his name. Then ye—hello." Bray adjusted his shirt, smartening his appearance as the door opened to reveal Amelia's somewhat flustered figure. She motioned them inside quickly, casting a glance through the tent down the length of the street.

Stacy walked through into the main room, feeling instantly more at ease as she saw Helen, Marc, and Peter amongst the familiar faces. Helen sat closest to the fire, her straightened posture, and polite acknowledgement of their arrival betrayed the sheer amount of time spent within the company of royalty and nobles. As always, her short blonde hair was impeccable, but there was regret within her eyes as she looked to Stacy.

Beside her sat Marc. His normally pale complexion possessed hints of colour. Whilst he was still the strawberry-blond she remembered, in health he looked almost like a different man. He had been talking to Eiji, who sat opposite with his hand interlocked with Acha's. Peter stood at the far side of the room, distant to them all, and seeking his habitual solitude. Stacy smiled to each of them in turn. It had been so long since last they had been together like this. Amelia blustered in behind her, gesturing her further inside.

"You all know each other, we've much to discuss and not the time to do it," Amelia announced before turning her attention to Rob and Bray. Rob smiled awkwardly as Eiji raised his hand in a polite greeting. "What are you doing? You've other things to attend to." Amelia intercepted Rob as he moved to approach one of the vacant stools.

"How'd you—"

"Do what you must, but do not play me for a fool. We're gathering like this to discuss what we'll do if you fail, and how to do it. We can allow you two days. You don't need to know our intentions any more than we need to know yours. Am I making myself clear? Good."

"What about me?" Stacy questioned rising to her feet. She shook her head as Rob brushed past Daniel in an attempt to excuse himself from the gathering. Even now, amongst people of such standing, he seemed to show such little respect.

"You're one of us. Your journey with them ends here. They are seeking to save the Daimon, we must prepare to prevent what will occur should they fail." Stacy looked towards her friends with a guarded expression.

"Do you think they will fail?"

"Do you think they can succeed?"

"What has Peter said on the matter?" In response Amelia simply shook her head. Stacy glanced in his direction, noticing his hand was grasped tightly in Bray's. She couldn't help but wonder what was being discussed. She strained her hearing, attempting to discern their conversation but heard nothing. The harder she tried to focus, the more consuming the absence of sound became. She saw Bray glance towards Rob with a nod before excusing himself.

"What did he want?" Stacy inclined her head towards the door once the two figures had departed. Peter gave a half-hearted blow in an attempt to lift some of his unkempt hair from over his eyes.

"He asked about my scar," he replied flatly. He was used to people staring, but not to them openly asking about his disfiguring branding. When he had been young his home town had branded the rune Gebo across his third eye, scarring his cheeks and forehead. They had hoped to silence his seer's blood. The only benefit their actions had was people tended to avoid him. Stacy looked down, noticing he now wore gloves.

"Do they help?" He shook his head. They made no difference. He had recently discovered it wasn't the touching of flesh, but the crossing of his aura with another living person's, that activated his visions. "How long do we have?" Stacy questioned as Amelia cleared her throat, gesturing towards the chairs.

"It starts at sunset, but as to the day the sights I have witnessed grant us three days." Peter looked between the group, over the last few hours he had become comfortable in their presence. "There's another thing, before he left I saw the Misorian's end. He was killing the Daimon, but it was already too late. It was unusual, the vision was overlapped by others, all revealing this same end."

"Then we have no choice but to intervene. I know only of one option, and I doubt it will sit well with some of us. We have to banish the tower. I have already said it once, and since we have found no way to prevent this, we must act in accordance with how we quelled the threat before."

"You mean banishing it into The Depths of Acheron?" Helen questioned.

"Yes. We will give them two days while we prepare, but if they fail to signal their success by then, we must act," Amelia confirmed.

"But doing that, if Remedy and Sunrise are still activated, won't it kill all life within The Betwixt?" Stacy gasped.

"Yes, but only that of The Betwixt, its power will not breach The Stepping Realm," Amelia revealed.

"You're condemning the Daimons to save the humans, again." Daniel rose to his feet, barely able to believe what he had heard.

"Well, boy, do you have a better suggestion?" Amelia demanded deliberately emphasising the name by which she had referred to him since their first meeting. It had the desired effect, she saw him cringe slightly.

"The tower is inaccessible by land, but how about by sky? I can lead the Thegnalars on an assault. If we can fracture the structure we should be able to mount a rescue."

"Then why didn't it work in Peter's vision of the future?" Marc interjected sceptically.

"I doubt there's a future he can see that has witnessed a wyrm siege. We're the only force outside of fate."

"And that, boy, is where you are mistaken. *You* are outside of fate, the actions of those by your command can be witnessed. Especially if they are acts of great power."

"Then my instructing Adel means..." Daniel sat once more and cradled his head.

"Yes, we are aware of the coin's existence, and even the order you gave to Thegnalar Adelpyro to deliver it. Things which generate such power by their rite of creation cannot be forged unseen. I'm unsure how you conjured such a plan, but it was for nought, and now you see we have no choice.

"Let them pursue their leads, but when she gives them the coin we're back to the witnessed prophecies." Daniel kept his head lowered for a moment to shield his relief. It seemed the ancestors he had sought for council had been correct in their assumptions. Despite Amelia's words there was still something they were unaware of, something important. So what had differed between his exchange with Rob, and the one between himself and Adel? Daniel glanced over towards Acha, who averted her gaze. In fact, now he considered it, she hadn't even acknowledged his arrival.

"So, we hope for the best. I'll gather the Thegnalar. If there is the smallest chance we can still prevent this from occurring we should take it."

"I understand your need to save her, but even if you could take her from Paion, how would you remove Remedy?" Daniel blanched at Amelia's words. "You see, boy, ideals have no place in war. We all must do things we would otherwise be ashamed of. You have two days. We will be travelling to the tower to begin preparations. But if you have no answer we will do it my way, regardless of the cost." Daniel rose to his feet, excusing himself. He cast a concerned look towards Eiji, who sat clutching Acha's hand so tightly he could see her fingers turning purple.

"Have y' not considered raisin' Kólasi? If we raised it first there'd be no life for it t'destroy," Eiji suggested once Daniel had left.

"I have." Amelia asserted with a slight shake of her head. "If we did that the power needed to banish the structure would cease to be. No, Kólasi must remain where it lies in order to permit us to channel the forces initially used when we created The Betwixt and The Depths."

"Then, by doing this, does that mean we could never facilitate Kólasi's return? Stacy questioned.

"I know you've grown attached to them, but I need you to understand. While you have been travelling, I have been training the others. This I did because the moment that Remedy was aligned to her there was only ever going to be one outcome. There is no one capable of wielding Hectarian magic. The one person who could, died. There is no way to remove it. Why is this so difficult for you to understand?"

"So when Yuri sat in your home and asked you, even before Remedy was—"

"I turned him back to the subject at hand. I knew this was a possibility. We are not known to be fallible, I could not promise something I knew may not be. This does not sit well with me either, but it *is* what must come to pass."

"So Taya will be forced to suffer through the death of her people, of her daughter, all because we failed to protect her when she first came to us in peace?"

"No. She will suffer, and she will live to unleash the power expected of her. But she will not witness its consequences. Ironically, it seems hers will be the one essence that survives what Remedy will do. The timing of her death means she will remain tethered to Kólasi, never to know rebirth because that which could once hold their essence will no longer be. Perhaps that in itself is the crueller of fates."

"How can you have known all this and still have said nothing?" Stacy demanded.

"Because the prophecy was bound. Kitaia Ethelyn will destroy the world. The only thing we *can* control is which one."

* * *

Daniel stormed from the building, his brow furrowed with concern. Eiji was being forced to become part of something his very morals would object to. If he were to do this, regardless of the reasons, he would find it difficult to live with. There had to be something he could do. Something he had overlooked.

Rob had taken the coin from his pocket, and the Mystics were still none-the-wiser. That in itself had to mean something. Besides, Amelia never actually said his own plan wouldn't work. If he could breach the tower and retrieve Taya perhaps removing Remedy could be a secondary concern. Daniel hung his head, perhaps insisting Bray had accompanied Rob into the Depths of Acheron had been a mistake.

It didn't matter what Amelia said, he was going to do it. He would gather the Thegnalar and lay siege to the tower. There was something else she had no knowledge of, something which could possibly ensure that if he could rescue Taya, and protect her for long enough, the threat itself would cease to be. There was no way to remove Remedy from her, this much was true, but there was no reason she couldn't live in exile from her people and still know some measure of happiness.

Alessia was waiting for him as he returned to the irfeláfa. Those of Kalia had their own means of travel outside of Collateral, and Alessia insisted he used this, rather than the portals whenever possible. Seeing the severity of his expression, and the frustration in his gait, she fell into step silently beside him.

"Tell Adel I need her. Gather the Thegnalar, we have a realm to save."

Chapter 25

Preparation

The horses' hooves thundered across the plains leaving a cloud of dust in their wake. Their pace was as aggressive now as it had been nearly two hours ago at the journey's start. These stallions were no ordinary beasts, they belonged to the Collateral stables and had been bred for endurance and speed.

Rob and Bray knew there was one purpose to the Mystics' gathering. Amelia had said it herself, they were preparing a plan of their own, and they both feared they knew what it would be. The Mystics had been responsible for the sealing of Kólasi, so their intentions towards the tower were painfully clear. Bray shifted uncomfortably on his saddle wondering if Rob had come to realise they would not be as patient for their success as they had implied.

The horses' pace slowed to a trot. A large forest loomed before them, and what they sought would be found within. The boundary was lined with thickets and brambles and they had agreed with the stable master to take their mounts no further. They dismounted slowly, dismissing the stallions with a firm slap, and fought their way past the thicket and began hiking through the forest.

After a further hour of walking, they beheld the low, stone, masonry well that stood at the side of an overgrown path. The roof and rafters were covered with flowering vines in a manner revealing both age and beauty. The sweet aroma of the flowers was as warming as the sunlight, which streamed through the nearby trees to dapple the land. A fine mist appeared to rise from the well, adding a whimsical haze to the surrounding air, in which small glowing orbs seemed to shimmer in the light. Their movements and size were reminiscent of fireflies, but whenever either Rob or Bray looked upon them they appeared to blink from existence.

Rob approached the well, cautiously peering into its depths. He could see the dark reflections on the water below.

"I used to read to Tabatha tales of the Fey each night before I put her to bed," Rob reflected. Bray offered his full attention, realising this was the first time Rob had spoken his daughter's name aloud. "This looks to be straight from their pages."

"It must offer some small comfort to know for certain they are at peace." Bray shifted, tugging slightly at his shirt before adjusting it. "Do you have it?"

Rob pulled a small coin from his pocket, looking at it for the first time. It was a pressed metal disc, aged and worn, with freshly engraved symbols covering older ones. He turned it over, appreciating the weight in his hand.

"So, how many of your Fey tales started with a wish?"

"More than you would imagine."

"And... do they all end happily?"

"Let's find out." Rob closed his eyes, recalling the exact words Daniel had whispered to him when they had met on the mountain. His conditions had been few. He must wish precisely as instructed, and Grayson Bray alone must be with him. At the time it had seemed a strange request but, given that Stacy was a Mystic, perhaps it was understandable.

Rob turned the coin, splitting it into two parts before releasing the first. He listened for it to reach the water. He turned suddenly to look at Bray, realising he had discussed nothing of his meeting with Daniel, or of his plan to open a portal. He opened his mouth as if to address his thoughts, but before the words could be spoken a deep rumbling drew his focus back towards the well. Movement stirred within. A writhing mass of shadows rapidly ascended, its sight caused Rob to stagger backwards in alarm just moments before hundreds of roots spewed from within, erupting powerfully from the well to coil their thick, woody tendrils around them, and haul them down into the darkness below. They dragged them through darkness and water, soil and stone, as if they had no substance. When the roots recoiled the two figures were left alone, heaped upon the floor of a masonry tunnel.

Rob recovered quickly and instinctively surveyed the area for danger. He produced his tinder box, lighting his lantern in order to provide a better understanding of their darkened surroundings.

Bray slowly pulled himself up, using the wall for support. Rob studied his friend, aware of the exhaustion lining his features. When Bray noticed him looking, the signs of fatigue vanished. He stood tall, removing his hand from the wall to dust himself down in the pretence of smartening his appearance. As he adjusted his shirt Rob thought he saw something beneath it catch the light, but it was concealed too quickly for him to be certain.

"You were there, weren't you? When I met with Daniel." Rob inclined his head in the direction they needed to walk and began to lead the way. There was no time for delay, not if they hoped to stop this before the Mystics did something regretful.

"You know I was. Although I wouldn't call it a meeting, you barely had time to pick his poc—"

"That's not when I mean and you know it. I knew something was going on when you weren't with Stacy, and you've been acting odd ever since."

"Odd? I've barely spoken."

"That's what's odd. Is there something I need to know?" He glanced over his shoulder, seeing Bray attempting to control his laboured breathing.

"All right, I admit I followed you. But I didn't intend to overhear. I was in need of his council," Bray admitted falling into step beside Rob, while maintaining proximity to the wall.

"About?"

"Nothing that concerns you. It bears no relevance to what we must do."

"Bray, you can barely stand straight. What's going on?"

"I'm fine. Those roots were a little rough. I'm embarrassed to admit they knocked the breath from me."

"Sure, okay," Rob conceded softly turning his focus back to the tunnel before them. The hairs on the back of his neck prickled, something about this wasn't quite right.

* * *

Dwarfed upon the enormous plinth, sheltered by the shadow cast down from the midday sun, Amelia stood. She had brought them all to the very centre of the tower's base so that they may better understand its enormity, power, and its threat. Standing beneath the giant structure it was impossible to suppress the trembles stirred by the fear, and power, of this location.

The Mystics stood in a circle around her, linked in communication by Helen's gift of mindsight. All understood their task, and their expressions were solemn. They had once condemned the Daimons to exile, now they would condemn their race to extinction. With a nod of Amelia's head they each mounted their horse and began their long rides towards their designated positions.

716

They had come to an agreement, albeit it one none were happy with. There was, however, no room for discussion. It was simply something which had to be.

Stacy spurred her horse into action. Whilst the group were connected, only that which they wished to be known was heard. Each of the Mystics seemed lost in their own private reflections. Except for Eiji. His thoughts seemed unguarded, forming a continuous monologue of questions and thoughts. Some of which made sense to their situations, others seemed to divert on seemingly random tangents.

For the first several minutes of their individual journeys they had reminded him his thoughts could be separated from the group. With embarrassed apologies he would fall silent. However, soon after his considerations and internal debate would intrude again. Their decision seemed to weigh heaviest on him, despite understanding that this was how it must be, he was still unable to accept it as the only course of action available to them. He had conceded to their choice, but he neither respected nor approved of it. Something his projected monologue made abundantly clear.

When they neared their destination he had fallen silent, his words replaced by feelings of intense remorse. He had proclaimed one thing which Stacy thought both apt and wise. Suggesting in his own way, that if it were death alone they brought, it would be a mere transition, but Remedy would not simply take their life, it would destroy the very essence of the Daimons, and cause the end of their race, ensuring no rebirth could ever arise from the ashes of their decision. It was a thought that had briefly given them all pause. But it changed nothing.

Each of the five, now situated at the outer reaches of the tower, sent their horses to graze. The web of energy between them both depleted and replenished them simultaneously, as they prepared for the momentous and devastating task.

* * *

The further Rob and Bray ventured through the tunnel the colder it became. Their breath began to mist as the first signs of frost glistening upon the cobbled stones became apparent. Each step was slowed by the need for caution. Even Bray, who normally walked with grace and poise, seemed to struggle to find his footing. As the ice grew thicker Rob motioned for them to stop near a large oval opening. He pulled two objects from his bag. They were almost identical, crafted from leather and chain. He tossed one to Bray who, understanding the crude design, slipped it over his boot and secured it with the laces while Rob did the same with the other one. The chain would afford them some grip on even the most slippery of surfaces.

"One each, it's better than nothing." Rob eyed him cautiously, aware of the extent Bray attempted to mask his shivering. "You good?" In response Bray simply gave a short nod.

Shimmering ice coated every surface beyond the oval. The walls dropped in a steep gradient to a ledge below where wooden walkways zigzagged in descent. The wood was so thickly encased in clear, glass-like ice that their every imperfection, their every spilt and break, was visible to the naked eye. There were places where it seemed this unbroken ice alone created the path which they would ultimately walk.

Bray looked down, a feeling of vertigo consumed him. Reaching out he steadied himself, moving slowly until he sat beside Rob on the opening's ledge, and looked down at the platform below. He had been about to ask the plan for descent when he felt Rob's hand shove him forwards in a sharp motion, sending him over the edge. His breath caught as they skidded down the slope, gaining speed as they hurtled towards the platform below. They glided across its surface, careening down into the crater and up towards its edge. Bray clawed at the smooth surface, attempting to further slow his momentum. It was only due to the steep rise created by the platform's concave shape that they found themselves safe upon the surface, sliding back down into the depression, rather than plummeting to their death. Bray raised a hand to his chest as he finally managed to breathe.

"How are you still alive?" he demanded struggling to his feet with difficulty. Rob grinned, offering him a hand. "Honestly, please explain what part of that seemed like a good idea!"

"It worked didn't it?" Rob gave a half shrug before climbing the slope towards the start of the walkway in order to better survey their surroundings.

Large, almost semicircular shapes jutted from the glistening wall at strangely uniform angles, curling down to almost meet with similar arcs rising from below. These dark forms never touched but for the ice, which spanned the gaps to create enormous segregated sheets. Upon ledges, lost deep into the transparency, frosted white structures of curved design gave the impression that something sentient had once crafted homes and shelters, structures that were now forever preserved beneath the transparent surface. Whatever happened here had immortalised all that had once been. The only noticeable thing of absence were the remains of things that once calling this area home.

"So answer me this, since you're the expert in all things Acheron, who do you think built all this, and for what purpose?"

"I've always found it best not to dwell on such things." Hearing Rob's answer Bray gave a slight chuckle, his face growing serious as he caught the slightest hint of a familiar fragrance in the air. At first he thought it was his mind deceiving him, but it was gradually becoming more noticeable. By this alone, no matter how improbable, he knew they were on the right path.

The lower they descended the more apparent the previously unnoticed tunnels became. Like everything they had so far beheld, these too were encased in ice, yet the suggestion of movement from within had quickened their cautious steps. Little by little their strides grew longer, always leading with the boot adapted to provide some traction.

Bray considered offering Rob some comfort by explaining that the creatures within the walls appeared to be an evolved form of Osedax. Given that it was doubtful Rob had even heard of these sea-dwelling bone-eaters, or imagined they could evolve to live within ice instead of water, he decided against it. These creatures possessed no threat to anything living.

This thought, however, caused Bray to reflect upon the path they had walked, and he beheld it in a new light. With the exception of the walkway, the entire outer structure of this cavern was comprised of the ice-coated bones of a large and ancient creature. Their entrance, the large black eye socket, stared back at him with its dead gaze. For a moment he marvelled at the sheer size of its overbite, and the enormity of the molars which supported the first stage of the walkways. Standing here, he felt small in the presence of such a giant. He coughed suddenly as the scent he had started to become increasingly more aware of once more caused his nostrils to flare.

"You sure you're good?" Rob questioned. Bray released a jittery breath, feeling a surge of adrenaline rush through him. He gave a nod, as they drew to a halt, not daring to speak. The walkway had finished abruptly to rest upon a large floating dock. Water lapped against the swaying platform, and the slight difference in temperatures caused a light steam to rise from its surface. "You can swim, right?"

* * *

Daniel stood beside Alessia as they relayed his strategy to his chosen few. For practicality alone, a large scale attack would prove of no benefit. They had to be precise and focus their efforts in one location. When the assembly finished Daniel searched the dispelling group for Acha, inclining his head as an invitation for her to join him.

When Amelia had revealed her knowledge of the coin she had unknowingly also supplied him with the means to ensure his further actions remained veiled. There was only one reason Amelia, and fate, had remained unaware of his other deed, and that was because something else had absorbed the energy the act itself created.

At first, he had thought it was possible that the proximity to Paion's tower had veiled both the draw and expelling of energy, but Acha's inability to look at him had suggested otherwise. A conversation, shared in private using Eiji's crystal, had revealed it was as he suspected. When Rob had taken the gossip crystal from Eiji, she had not been as subdued as she implied.

She had overheard his request to meet and, in order to ensure his safety, had scouted the area before their planned meeting, concealing herself in a similar manner to Bray. Daniel had been unaware of her presence, after all, she absorbed life from nature around her as a means to live. This act caused her presence to become almost undetectable, even to the sharpest of senses. She had witnessed his every act. She was also the reason his interference had not been witnessed.

Daniel led her through the crowd into Adel's residence. There was something of great importance he required, and it was something Acha alone could achieve. For his plan to proceed another coin was required, and her presence during its enchantment was critical to ensure fate remained blinkered to his actions.

Alessia had called him an idealist when he had explained what was needed from Acha. The events he had already inspired would be enough, but after hearing his reasoning she too had to concede it was essential. It was unlikely the Daimons would react well to the discovery that the Mystics had been willing to sacrifice them. If they were to then discover there had been a chance to save their Sfaíra—even if it meant a life of exile for her—and they had refused, retaliation would be their only logical response.

Kitaia Ethelyn's importance was being overlooked because of Remedy. She had approached the Mystics in search of peace, and all that had followed had been a result of their own actions. They had been responsible for everything that had happened to her, from the moment Amelia first entrusted her to Sunniva's care. Kitaia's bloodline had ruled the land of Kólasi since the beginning. Their position unchallenged because they alone had succeeded in forging a pact with the land itself. The land, and her people, would not respond well to her loss.

* * *

Taya wrapped her arms around herself as the warmth of tears streaked her face. Unsure of what had transpired, she knew only her belief that she had been safe was far from accurate. On rousing she had expected to still be within the carriage, or perhaps even surrounded by the familiar faces of her friends. Taya had indeed awoken to a familiar face, but it was not one she had expected.

She had not been bound, or weakened in any form, and during her attempt to flee he had simply watched her. Her instincts told her there was a portal nearby, but something suppressed it. Standing beside the familiar energy she begged it to respond, to open for her as they always did. She had never tried so hard to achieve a single thing in her life.

Deep burning pains expanded from her back, and she knew her daughter stirred. She recalled the Hermaphrodite had warned that they would need to deliver her child early, and it appeared they had already forcibly started the process. Her fear deepened as it became just apparent how much Paion knew.

Taya sank to her knees, overwhelmed by grief. There was no visible means of escape, no seams within the smooth wall, or weaknesses of any kind. Her only hope had been the portal, and somehow she had been denied even that.

"Now that you have familiarised yourself with your situation, might I suggest we begin?" He gestured towards a large marble altar within the room's centre. Taya stared at him in horrific realisation.

"I'll not let you do this."

"You have no choice. One way or another I'll rip that thing out of you. But if you cooperate I'll grant you the pleasure of seeing it before you complete your purpose. Given that it has survived this far, there's a chance it may even survive the purge."

"And if she does?"

"Well that depends on you. If I have to force you to cooperate, I give you my word, I will destroy it, and I will make you watch before using you to unleash devastation. Take your time, think it over. I've waited this long, a few minutes will make little difference."

Taya's burning gaze turned towards the floor. Paion knew too much and, given the prophecies she had witnessed due to his manipulation, she knew the future he would craft. There was a single inevitability. As soon as this tower had touched the land's surface his victory was assured. Nothing mattered now. Nothing she could do would make a difference. But there was still one life whose future had not been determined, her daughter's. The visions she beheld provided no insight into whether or not her child would survive.

"If I cooperate you must swear an oath on Styx my daughter will be cared for and treated well." Throughout time, for gods both old and new, a vow sworn upon Styx had always been considered unbreakable. Long had it been decreed that any who broke such an oath, be them man, immortal, or god, would be forced to suffer beyond anything even the greatest minds could imagine. It was an oath never uttered lightly and never requested but for in the gravest of situations. Such power, such commitment, was never to be invoked for frivolities or simple declarations. It was a solemn and standing contract of the highest order.

"*If* it survives, I swear on Styx, she will live a life coveted by my kind. After all, it will share your skill for prophecy, and such a gift affords a certain lifestyle amongst my people." A smile traced his lips as Taya rose hesitantly to approach the altar. He gestured for her to lie down, and she did so willingly. "On your front." His words caused the tremors of fear she worked so hard to suppress to become visible. "For you, this will be anything but painless."

"You don't need to do it like this." Taya's voice held no power, understanding all too well his intention. After checking his gloves were flawless, he moved her arms to the top of the altar and, taking a knife, cut through the fine layer of cloth to bare her back. He studied her bones. His firm touch applying pressure on the lower areas.

"You're correct," he sneered. "I don't." His lip curled in contempt as he looked down upon her. After adjusting her legs to ensure they remained together he removed a glove briefly to place his hand upon the marble surface.

Taya gasped as her flesh grew cold. Channels in the altar pulsed to unleash a viscous fluid which,

on contact with her flesh, rose to cover her forearm, extending just beyond her elbow. A secondary
stream extended up her legs, terminating above her
buttocks. Paion stepped back, examining the shimmering fluid critically before placing his hand down
once more. A thin band extended below her shoulder blades, restraining her completely. "Now, unfortunately for you, the tools I have at my disposal are
rather primitive." He placed a thin-bladed knife and
a saw within her line of sight, smiling as her pupils
widened in fear. He wondered if she realised his reason for this method went beyond his disgust for her
race.

He would take great pleasure in hearing her tormented screams as he snapped and sawed through
her bones in order to gain access to the child. The
pain was crucial, and he would ensure she remained
conscious throughout the entire, lengthy ordeal. He
would inflict damage to her beyond repair, and by doing so would know exactly when he could proceed
to pave the path to his people's future. Her magic,
the magic he needed to assist in carrying the spread
of his destruction, was suppressed at the moment,
channelled into the child so that it would survive any
complications associated with birth. When her body
attempted to heal he would know the power was returning. When the blood stopped, the end would begin.

Chapter 26

Complications

Water had always been thought of as a conduit, an amplifier for certain magics and senses. Predators within the ocean could smell blood from miles away. Bray could not breathe underwater, he was not native to such an environment, but from the moment his skin first touched its surface he could almost taste her. How it was possible through portals and realms was beyond his knowledge, her blood simply called to him. Its promise was intoxicating.

In contrast to the frozen chill of the air the water seemed warm. They knew it was but an illusion as a result of the extreme cold they had descended through. Bray kept his distance from Rob. It was taking an unbelievable restraint to force coherence and purpose to his actions, especially when all he wanted to do was stalk and feed. Rob was not a suitable meal. It was one of the reasons Bray had found travelling with him so agreeable. The years of drinking had poisoned his blood to a degree beyond palatable, and Bray would be lying not to admit he had encouraged it further. He liked company, but could not always suppress the nature of what he truly was.

He forced himself to remain slow, allowing Rob to lead the way despite knowing he could track her with ease. Below them he could just discern an underwater complex of ice caves. The water seemed impossibly clear, and the ice shimmered blue as it stretched into darkness. Through them was where she could be found. As expected Rob signalled a descent. Before submerging he emptied the contents of his leather skins, refilling them with air. Bray would have normally marvelled at this man's resourcefulness, but the longer they delayed the more his friend seemed like an obstacle. Bray briefly ducked his head beneath the water, hoping to dislodge the unpleasant thoughts.

He surfaced again, taking a sharp breath, and noticed Rob's concern, but he said nothing and simply dove down and swam through the large opening. After several seconds Bray followed, attempting to distract himself by examining the breathtaking structures below the surface.

Brinicles spiralled down from the frozen surface above in beautiful and twisted formations, some extending to the frozen floor itself. He watched Rob approach one to examine it, an action which proved this was not the undersea killer of their own world, but a strange adaptation of this one's. Bray, like Rob, cast his gaze upward, noticing the tops were opened to air rather than sealed by ice. He continued to follow Rob, surfacing further along where the strong disruption of a waterfall had made the freezing of the surface impossible.

Bray inhaled deeply, regretting it the instant he did. His teeth chattered as he pulled himself out onto the rocky formation near the rapid moving waterfall. It was a narrow cascade, falling from a yawning hole in the rocks and ice formed far above their heads. Its force was immense, disrupting the water's surface to send fragments of ice surfing upon its waves as it filled the small enclosure with the loud roar of gushing water.

"If you get into trouble the tubes you saw are hollow. They shouldn't be too difficult to fracture if you find yourself short on breath," Rob advised after they had taken a few moments to recover from the exertion.

"They're called brinicles," Bray whispered, turning away as Rob approached. "We should keep moving." Rob nodded taking several long deep breaths before once more submerging.

Bray pushed his hands through his hair. His vision had altered as they were beneath the water, he knew his eyes had taken on a red hue. He no longer saw things in the same manner as others, he saw the warmth of blood pulsing through veins and arteries, the pooling of the fluid his hunger cried out for. Whilst Rob was dark and poisoned, a brighter ribbon called to him and, in one moment of clarity, he realised he must remove any obstacle that might stand in his way.

* * *

Rob surfaced, inhaling deeply before pulling himself up onto the warm stone ledge. Lying back he allowed the strange heat to soothe his freezing limbs as he waited for Bray. The slow sound of melting icicles from the cavern above echoed softly. Their music seemed almost hypnotic, causing his eyelids to droop. It was only as he realised he had been lost in the natural melody he noticed the absence of other noise, the absence of Bray.

Rob sprung to his feet, freezing in place as his vision beheld the dark form below the ledge. It moved at speed, so quickly he barely had time to react. It sprung from the water, wrapping its arms around him and dragging him back down into the freezing depths.

Rob twisted, trying to pull himself free from the clutches of his attacker. His struggle persisted, even when he realised it was Bray's grasp he found himself within. Even beneath the water he could see the murderous intent, the red tint to his eyes. Rob struck out desperately, his attempts to prise himself from Bray's grip hampered by the water. He pushed against him and, for the first time, caught sight of the object Bray had been attempting to conceal beneath his shirt. Fused to Bray's sternum was something easily and instantly identifiable. It was Sunrise. Rob saw the air expel in streams from his own mouth as his back collided with one of the larger brinicles. Their pressure of impact caused the ice to crack. While Rob's movements seemed hindered, somehow Bray's were not.

Bray pulled him away before propelling him back into the ice, again and again, until it gave beneath his weight. Bubbles filled the water, the alteration in current caused by the fracturing pulled Rob inside the structure, forcing him upward as the once hollow tube flooded. He struggled to pull himself out, watching through the icy surface as Bray's dark figure below grew smaller.

"Gods be damned, Bray! What did you do?" he gasped through chattering teeth.

* * *

Daniel's appearance beside Eiji was marked by the heralding cry of wyrms. The enormous forms circled the great tower, led by Alessia, the Master and Commander of the Eortháds. When Daniel had spoken of his plan she had refused to allow him to be placed in jeopardy by participating. Ultimately instructing him the only assistance he could offer, given he had no skill in Drỳcræft, was to speak with the Mystics.

The Mystics' decision had not been wildly accepted by the wyrms, not when other options were still available. Part of the unease perhaps stemmed from their own sealing by Zeus' plan. They sympathised with the Daimons and perhaps viewed the Mystics actions as a warning of things that could come. After all, The Daimons weren't the only race to live unaligned to this world's reality. What was to say, next time such a threat reared its head, that Kalia would not be considered an acceptable loss.

"I'm correct in assuming my words reach you all," Daniel began. "You agreed to allow Rob and Bray two days before you would take action. This marks the end of the first, and I beseech you not to act."

"I hate t'hafta tell y', it's not somethin' we can just—" Eiji relayed hesitantly.

"Please listen. Long before they departed for The Depths of Acheron I aligned Sunrise to another. This alignment has been completed. There is no threat. The host will remain in The Depths where he can harm none, and Remedy can remain here, or upon Kalia. We will offer the Daimon refuge if you will not." Daniel paused seeing his friend pale.

"Amelia wants t'know who y' aligned it t'," Eiji queried.

"The male Empusa. Amelia, you probably only observed him to be a Misorian." Daniel placed his hand upon Eiji's shoulder, knowing the contact would allow him to hear the Mystics as they heard him. "I couldn't tell you before the alignment was complete, in the risk of Paion becoming aware of my actions in time to negate my efforts. No matter what he does now, he can cause no harm to either world."

"Daniel, it's t'late," Eiji whispered, for the first time veiling his thoughts from the rest of the group. "We didn't come here t'prepare. It was decided the risk was t'great for delay."

"You had no intention of allowing them a chance to succeed?" Daniel whispered in horror. "You've already prepared the passage to The Depths. By all the Gods and Spirits, you people are not only the reason this came to pass, but the reason he succeeds."

"Whaddya mean?"

"My idea worked because The Depths of Acheron and this world would remain isolated from one another until you started the process. You were meant to allow them two days, but you gave them barely two hours. Bray was to part ways with Rob before the alignment completed and the frenzy took hold. The only way for them to enter the tower was the other half of the coin I had Adel craft. Rob would have saved her, and Bray had agreed to remain in The Depths until such a time Sunrise could be removed. Your actions have linked the two realms. Bray won't be able to control his instinct."

"And what instinct is that?" Stacy's thoughts echoed.

"Daimons used to have a mutually beneficial relationship with the Empusae. In order to spare humans from some of their more aggressive rituals they made a blood pact. Whenever possible an Empusae will feed on a Daimon, they will instinctively be drawn to them.

"Their virile relations negated the need for the flesh aspect due to the difference in blood. There was one problem though, it was euphoric, a feast like no other. Fortunately females possess a greater control of their libido and can exert control a male could not.

"Until I met him I did not believe a male could survive past birth. Given the physiological difference even should one be born they would be unable to feed, they lack the correct organs. Grayson Bray is indeed a rarity, and your actions have made him possibly the most dangerous being in existence. He will hunt Kitaia, and in doing so deliver the newly aligned Sunrise to the one seeking to exploit it, and perhaps more concerning, he will kill anyone or anything that attempts to come between him and the blood which calls to him."

"Why is that a problem, it just proves we must complete our task," Stacy interjected.

"Because, I'm sorry, Eiji, I sent Acha to The Depths with a second coin forged by Adel." Daniel offered his friend an apologetic look.

"We know of her powers, she need only touch him and he'd no longer be a threat." Stacy once again answered the concern.

"You assume she'd be able to reach him. I have told you, Grayson Bray does not feed like normal Empusae, he simply calls the blood from them to him. The moment their paths cross, if she attempts to stop him, she will die."

"She is unimportant. Her life does not matter," Stacy asserted. In that instant each of them felt Eiji's connection with them begin to sever, and the burden his absence caused.

The Mystics had anchored the tower to the energies aligning with Kólasi, binding them together in order to draw the tower inside The Depths to rest

alongside their land. Eiji's absence caused great unbalance, but this disruption caused a minor inconsis-
tency to be revealed. As they forced this tower to
become unaligned with their plane, it seemed Kólasi
was being separated and displaced from The Depths
of Acheron. It was starting to rise.

"Why not let it?" Helen proposed, knowing that
Eiji's link to them was still active. With the right
temptation she was certain they could regain his aid.
But Amelia's response dissolved all hope.

"We need it as a winch," she asserted. "We can
rebalance the energies afterwards. It will not rise, it
cannot. But first we must focus on banishing this
burden. Eiji, we can't do this without you. I know
Acha is important. I know what we are asking you to
sacrifice. Our success will bind the lands. You will be
unable to retrieve her amulet, unable to save her. But
that does not mean she would want you to condemn
all. Help us, I promise I will do whatever is necessary
to see her returned to you, once we have staved off
the threat."

"With Sunrise and Remedy in proximity, you know
as well as I the amulet will lose its power. Acha's
essence won't be transferred. It, like the Daimons
you have condemned, will simply cease to be." Daniel
relayed through their fading connection.

"Tell me how t'help," Eiji instructed completely
severing his ties to the Mystics. Daniel gave him
an appreciative nod and, placing his hand upon his
shoulder, led him away.

There was so much Bray had wanted to say to Rob in the moment he had thrust him through the ice to be swept up and away from him. He wondered if his friend knew his action had been one of mercy, of great restraint. He wanted to justify why his ability to fend off the encroaching frenzy had finally failed, and explain that his real reason for meeting with Daniel was so he would perform the alignment rite for Sunrise.

Bray had wished to confide in Rob. To tell him that, despite how it may appear, since the Empusae essence was denser than that of a human he had been in no danger. But he couldn't lie. He had known, from the moment it had been affixed to him, that maintaining his control would become more difficult. So had Daniel. The alignment had taken hours, and they had discussed the consequences at length, and the actions he must take to stave off his frenzy for as long as he could.

When he felt its claws clouding his reason he was almost relieved. Daniel had advised the alignment's success would result in his baser instincts conquering his rational thought. Whilst he was able to he had done all he could to keep his friend safe. His final thought, as he watched Rob be pulled from his reach, had been one of relief.

He knew Daniel would have told the Mystics of his solution now. It was too late for Paion to react to the circumstances their actions had created. They had no need to banish the tower, to condemn the Daimons to extinction. Remedy alone could pose no threat to their world, and without the other half of the coin there was no way for Bray, or Sunrise, to leave The Depths of Acheron. In his current condition he lacked the sentience to locate a portal, and when his frenzy finally ebbed, he would remain true to his agreement. Both Remedy and Sunrise would be trapped in the places they could do least harm. It had been the most obvious solution.

Bray pulled himself from the water and inhaled deeply. Her scent left a visible trail in the air. She was all he could think about, her blood was all he longed to taste. He moistened his lips and began stalking through the caverns.

* * *

A tideway was a monument. Its sole purpose was the alteration and diversion of natural energies. It allowed a person attuned to the power it harnessed to draw upon it, fortifying and enhancing their own potential for as long as they could contain it. It was a fleeting energy. A person could only store as much as their body could withstand, but they could return, gathering more whenever they wished. In ages past great mages would gather upon distant hills and misty moors, all united in purpose to draw from these stones in preparation for powerful workings. Few today knew of their existence.

Tideways were not monuments built for the purpose of drawing on the power, rather they were created from its excess within an area. The condensing of energy created shifts in the environment, raising obelisks as the world around this saturation found the necessary means to once more create a balance. They were places of power, the likes seldom seen in a world where the old roots to magic had long been forgotten.

The obelisk towered over them, its matte surface seemed to absorb light itself. Lightning flared violently overhead, unreflected upon its stony grain. The small syphon of energy reached down from above, piercing the stone's apex. It flared, growing more intense with each successive bolt, and highlighted the webbing bound within the clouds to harness the storm itself.

Elly turned her gaze desperately to Aidan, noticing the increase in the violent displays above as the stone itself began to pulse giving off waves of energy, all of which seemed to gather at the stone's centre. The central area burnt white-hot, turning to liquid to form a gaping hole at its very core. Within this the power built, becoming almost solid as it shone with burning intensity, gathering and pulsating before being unleashed as a single focused beam, a beam which seemed to halt abruptly in mid-air at the oasis' edge.

The area surrounding them grew hot. Ripples spread, rising in cylindrical patterns around them to reveal an unfocused image imposed upon the barren wasteland. The dusty dead-land became green and shimmering giant trees blinked into existence. Elly turned, seeing the entire area beyond the oasis overlap with a location she knew all too well, The Forest of the Epiales. The death and desolation of magic from the land had clearly been caused by the infringement of that domain upon their own.

"Jude!" Aidan side-stepped around Elly, as the image before them refined, becoming more focused to unveil an ancient, colossal oak within the forest. Beneath the transparent prison of bark he could clearly see Jude. The small figure's energy cried out to him, revealing the true distance between the seemingly close realities. The light from the obelisk intensified, burning the air itself. The focal point distorted once more, glowing orange as the light pierced the veil between the worlds. A voice cried out, Jude's voice, audible only in the brief seconds of the breach, wracked with pain yet intent on relaying his warning. Aidan's gaze turned slowly towards Elly in horror, and time itself seemed to slow.

Aidan's quickened steps halted, raising clouds of dust from beneath his feet as he turned sharply towards Elly. Ripples of movement traced the obelisk's surface, shifting in strange intangible ways. Darkness extended, and colours formed granting depth to the stone's base. Shimmering scales of shadow tensed and relaxed, uncurling gradually, causing the light to trace the emerging form.

"Run!" he yelled, gesturing wildly towards her as she became aware of the invisible, looming presence.

The figure continued to uncoil. A shimmering of iridescent light distorted around the moving form, revealing its height through its natural camouflage as it emerged to tower above them, its hungry glare transfixed on Elly. The warning had been clear to Aidan alone. Since Jude was not human the tones in which he spoke could only be understood by others of his race, or those who had trained to converse with their kind. He had called to Aidan, warning if the general succeeded in tethering Elly to the obelisk he would draw on her essence, using the rune and her position between so many realms to sever Melas' bindings to all.

"Ah, the divine, mortal-dreamer, our master has been waiting for you," hissed the serpentine voice. Elly span, the voice echoed around them, coming from everywhere and nowhere simultaneously. She turned, in time to witness its jaws and teeth emerge from concealment, extending and drawing focus from the writhing shadows now amassing at her rear. Aidan launched himself the remaining distance as the creature's second tail emerged, striking with unnatural speed and precision. He tackled Elly, dragging her to the ground as the blow sailed above them. The appendage retracted, once more fading from view as parts of its form returned to the unseen camouflage. "The realm of Daimons' is ours but you, you will grant us them all." Light once more began to ripple before their view as Elly struggled to her feet, her attention constantly shifted as she tried to perceive the next attack.

Pushing himself to his knees Aidan reached out, placing his hand upon the base of the obelisk. He could see the general in all its horror as he drew on the tideway's energy. He saw the unseen tether beginning to form between Elly and the obelisk as the creature distracted her awareness of the joining with another attack. Aidan focused his efforts on doing the only thing he could, the one thing all Oneirois were tasked to do when faced with such consuming danger. Before the strike could connect, before she was bound by the tendrils of energy expanding from the tideway, he forced everything he had into a single act. He woke the dreamer.

The general let out a cry heard only within the deepest recesses of nightmares as Elly vanished. Aidan had no time to relish his achievement, the swift redirection of the general's strike staggered him, catching him off-guard as a secondary blow struck him from behind. His body grew rigid as he felt the root of power flood through him and the warmth of Jude's presence relayed by their adjoining energy. He could feel the prison which bound Jude absorbing the power his body had channelled, and at once Aidan realised the brilliance of Melas' plan. The nature of the forest ensured Jude's capacity for energy was endless.

The power he had already harnessed was beyond measure, but alone was insufficient to permit him to breach The Stepping Realm. He needed sacrifices, one each side of the gateway, and now he had them. But there was more, something from the human plane was disrupting the very fabric of The Betwixt, causing discord and unbalance to an already fragile domain. Aidan, in his final moments, realised the true depths of Melas' plan, and the horror about to be unleashed. The Father of Nightmares had never needed to open the gateway to the mortal plane. It would be done for him.

* * *

Taya's dark hair glistened with sweat as she lay upon the altar surrounded by bone fragments, blood, and vomit. She could no longer feel the warmth of her blood as it trickled from her injuries, but she knew it was present. She was bleeding more than Paion had expected, or so his seemingly rapid actions implied.

The pain had been beyond anything she had felt before. It was numbing now, fading like her own awareness. Whilst he wanted her bleeding, it seemed Paion was making some efforts to staunch the flow, and he made minimal repairs with sharp and hasty tugs in order to prolong her life until her own magic began to return. To her left she could hear the cries of her daughter. A few moments ago her vision had more focus, enough to see the bundle wrapped in a towel upon the floor. Now she could not even discern that.

Taya had never once stopped shaking, but now she felt as if ice filled her veins. Her legs had long grown

743

heavy. She could no longer feel them at all. Her fingers had also started to numb. She focused on moving them, her index finger responded with a sharp, jerky movement.

Through the sound of her daughter's tears she thought she heard a sigh. The cries grew louder until she felt a slight warmth at her fingertips. With great effort she refocused her gaze to look upon her daughter as Paion placed her between Taya's bound arms. Taya moved her fingers, vaguely aware of the sticky fluid which coated her child's skin. She was filled with relief to see, even this close to Remedy, her daughter lived. She bit back a cry as the raw pain began anew. She would not allow her daughter's first, perhaps only, memory of her mother's voice to be that of her agonised screams. Her magic was returning. It stimulated the severed nerve endings in an attempt to understand the damage her body had suffered, in order to attempt to repair it. She felt her flesh rejoin over the jagged shards of bone, but even with this she knew there was little guarantee she would survive.

Something had gone wrong. Paion was too quiet.

Chapter 27

Damages

Bray crouched low, stalking almost silently as he emerged through the portal into the tower. He did not understand the implications of being able to gain entry, only the hunger. His nostrils flared as his senses were assaulted by the sweet scent of liquid ambrosia. Part of him knew he should be feeling something else at this moment.

There were two food sources within the room, but only one he craved. It lay upon an altar like an offering, and the slow retreat of the secondary figure suggested it was just that. Bray's tongue traced his lips as his mouth flooded with saliva. He knew it was wrong. The part of him that recognised her fought to regain control from the frenzy. He should have been able to do so, he had been told as much, and had been certain he could suppress his nature, but then her scent had overpowered his faculties.

A sound of pleasure escaped his throat as he stood beside her. Tracing his hands over her exposed flesh he savoured the warmth of blood which glistened invitingly upon her skin. He pushed himself up onto the altar, moving to straddle his meal, unaware it could not flee, even had it wanted to. There were things he liked to do to his prey before feeding, things which flooded them with delicate flavours. But this offering was already everything he could ask from it.

He heard the muffled cries as he sat upon her and lowered his lips to the blood upon her flesh. The taste was more satisfying than the scent had promised. It was all he could do to stop himself feasting; this meal had to be savoured. He moistened his lips, his mouth overflowing with fluid as he kissed the silently sobbing creature. His hungry tongue drew thick trails of saliva across her bare flesh, and he placed his hands upon her glistening shoulders. He felt the excitement build as the blood responded to his call and their flesh knit, fixing his hands to her shoulders, as the exchange began. He could consume her in less than a minute, her entire volume of blood would have passed by their connection three times in just those sixty seconds, but he wanted to savour it. To draw out this delicacy.

He moaned in delight as the blood entered him, feeling its power and magic. The offering had been flooded with hormones from both childbirth and fear, adding to the irresistible palate. He savoured the slow exchange, but he wanted more, more than his hands alone could draw. He noticed the manner by which she was restrained made what he had in mind impossible, besides, he refused to release himself from her. He lowered his head to her neck, tracing his tongue across the weakening pulse before pressing his lips to it. Her warmth filled his mouth, his breathing quickened and he drank deeper as waves of ecstasy flooded through him. The longer they were connected the more he hungered. There was only her taste, her scent. Nothing outside them mattered.

* * *

Eiji's complete absence created rifts and weakness in the formation, causing Amelia to mount her own steed and position herself at the place he had once stood.

"Did he really just do that?" Stacy demanded as Amelia made haste. She could only hope that she was right about where Daniel would take him. If their formation remained in near alignment she could still draw on some of his energies. Consensual or not. All she need do was take his place. She was certain Daniel would have him join the skyward assault.

"Your words gave him the excuse he needed. He never agreed on this course, we forced him by majority."

"But he walked away," Stacy objected.

"I should have expected this. Eiji's essence has always possessed the purer of morals. In some respects he has always been my equal. I govern by logic, he by heart. We once balanced each other well," Amelia advised, taking his former position. She cast her gaze upward seeing, as expected, a new wyrm joining the aerial display.

The wyrms had been circling one focal area of the tower, using choreographed assaults of magic and wyrms' breath to target one specific area in the hope of creating a weakness in the structure. Fýrwyrms coordinated with Íswyrms in hope their alternating siege of fire and ice would yield results as their riders, under Alessia and Adel's commands, attacked with arcane magics. Yet, as far as the Mystics could tell, their assault made no difference to the integrity of the structure.

"He is also the only one aside from you who remains undamaged. Can we still do this without him?"

"He has not abandoned us as much as he would believe." As Amelia relayed this they each felt a surge of his energy fortifying their own. "He remains tethered to a degree, until *I* choose to release him. We are fortunate he is joining their efforts." Amelia felt the regret. She had nothing but respect for him, and for Daniel as well. His plan had been brilliant, something she should have suspected given the title he was preparing for. Her long time upon this world had shown her how little she could trust people. How much influence and persuasion they needed to embark on quests that heroes would have once rallied to be involved in. Times had changed. Her reaction to this threat, given the awakening of all the Mystics, had been instinctive.

Amelia found herself touching unconsciously upon Peter's skill, and for a moment she felt a weakness consume her. Despite all their actions, nothing had changed. She could not fathom how banishing the tower into The Depths of Acheron would not alter the outcome. They would succeed before Paion could act, the fates had advised her so. It was then Daniel's words returned to haunt her. In their haste to act they had created a join between the realms. In their haste they had overlooked something obvious.

Paion's tower had sealed the portal within, its use negated by the Moirai blessing. The coin Adel had crafted would have only allowed a bypassing gateway to run parallel to the join. By design it did not unbind the portal, it merely created a brief and obscured weakness alongside it. Rob could have entered the tower, and the portal would have remained closed.

When the tower became aligned to The Depths of Acheron the Moirai magic surrounding the tower, and sealing the portal, would cease to be. It would be open to manipulation, and Kitaia's presence would provide a wedge, ensuring it could not be sealed. It made no difference to Paion which realm the tower was in, not when he had Kitaia. As both Rob and Yuri had proven, she was not the only thing able to pass through something her presence activated.

The Mystics' thoughts all fell into silent disarray as they understood Amelia's revelation. The tower was already between the two worlds. It possessed a presence both in their plane and The Depths. Whatever they did now would ultimately have no bearing.

"What now, do we stop?" Helen questioned.

"We continue as planned and hope Master Bray's nature contains the situation."

"Isn't it better to hope it doesn't? The moment he enters the tower Paion once again has Sunrise and Remedy at his disposal."

"He's between realms, he already has them both at his disposal. He only needed the tools aligned. He already positioned his relics to ensure his reach was all-consuming. Ultimately, with such resources, it makes no difference where this event took place. When the tower descended the network of relics was complete. It is likely that Kitaia's presence was to ensure that if we did act in this manner he could still claim victory."

"That, and he needed to birth her child," Stacy added. "He couldn't use Remedy until her magic recovered from the birth, and Remedy prevented it from being possible as a natural process."

* * *

When Paion had first realised something other than Remedy was destined to take the Daimon's life it had been a cause for concern. In every vision, no matter the future, this lone figure had found her. He had needed to behold this person in the flesh to witness their aura, and understand how she would meet her end. Prophets could never witness their own demise.

When he beheld the hunger for blood he knew his presence would be of no consequence. He would let the Strigoi feed. It took their species a little under seven minutes to drain a litre of blood from their food source, and the Daimon's magic would have peaked long before he could inflict any meaningful damage. He viewed it as a kindness, one last meal before total annihilation. The power of Sunrise and Remedy would extend outward from the tower. Those within would survive until the network was completed. As long as the power had been unleashed, how she met her death was of no consequence.

He watched the ritual of feeding with interest. Alarm spreading across his features as he realised the being before him was not feeding in the traditional way of his kind. He saw the knitting of their flesh, the rapid paling of the Daimon's features as her eyelids fluttered on the verge of unconsciousness. It was with deep horror he realised his mistake. He was unsure what this creature was, but he was not Strigoi. He could not be allowed to continue to feed.

Paion gathered a fraction of his remaining magical energy. Dragging the tower from above had depleted almost all of his magic. He had hoped to retain some, but as long as enough remained for him to activate the tools, and exit the tower, he had to take whatever action was needed to ensure things progressed as planned.

He released a charge of energy, the jagged form streaking from point to point, consuming the magic between them with crackles as it grew. It struck the

751

blood-drinker's skin with a resounding clap. The impact had the desired effect, instantly separating his flesh from the Daimon's and propelling him backwards to fall heavily, where his body remained, wracked with spasms. Paion approached the altar scrutinising the Daimon, and was satisfied that she could still perform her purpose adequately.

He picked up the sleeping bundle from the platform before its mother, placing it within a small reed basket. He was ready to begin the rite of activation, and given his oath it made sense to try to ensure the child was struck by not only the initial discharge of energy, but that of the completed network as well. Otherwise he would be bound to his oath. He had expected her to negotiate for the child's life, and if it did survive he would be true to his word. It would indeed live a life coveted by his kind. Of course, most of them did not realise the true horror forced upon a prophet that was not Moirai.

Paion approached the Daimon. Ready to speak the invocation he raised his arms. But not even the first syllable could be uttered before something charged, colliding with him as it grasped his arm and thrust its body over and around him, briefly clinging to his back as it dragged Paion down with an angered snarl. It wrapped itself around him, using its weight to increase the force of impact with the floor. It was only when Paion shed his disorientation to behold the assailant, whose weight now pinned him down, he realised it was the blood drinker.

Raising his knee Paion connected a strike with Bray before dropping his legs and turning to thrust the weight from him. Standing quickly he trained his eyes to the feral creature. Bray was wild, dangerous. How he had not seen this before was beyond him. The thing he looked upon was a true monster. Drawing his sword he focused on every twitch of its muscles. Even then, when Bray charged he was unprepared, the solid impact of the shoulder burying itself within his stomach thrust him backwards, jerking the weapon from his grasp.

Paion cried out as areas of his flesh mottled. Blood pooled below the surface of his skin, answering the creature's call as it rose through his veins to be expelled from his body in streams to coat the thing before him. It licked its lips, thick strings of saliva dripping from its open mouth as it watched him hungrily. He found himself paralysed, as Bray circled him, slowly closing the distance between them. If he had been able to speak he would have asked what he was, or maybe, begged for mercy.

The creature inhaled, its tongue tracing against Paion's flesh as he stood enraptured yet terrified. The touch of this being stirred feelings on par with that felt by humans in the presence of Moirai relics. But it was not a feeling of love that intermingled with his fear. It was something far more base in nature. Recognising it allowed him to shatter the thrall. He staggered forwards, already weakened from the attack. Backing away he felt his legs upon the altar, and used it as a barrier between them.

The monster's gaze darted from Kitaia to Paion. Taking his dagger Paion drew it up her flesh. Saturating the air with her fragrance, hoping to offer temptation. But there was not even a glimmer of interest. Paion had disturbed his meal, and as such the predator would not continue its feast until all threats had been neutralised.

Raising his arms Paion attempted to defend himself as Bray once again pounced. His arms flailed as he fought, tearing at Bray's clothes in an attempt to push him away. It was then he felt the call of something. His hand had brushed against the being's chest and, recognising the familiar sensation, he laughed. Thrusting his hand forward he focused his energy on stimulating just a fraction of the power within Sunrise. The creature recoiled, retreating to the burning pain now surging through its chest. Standing, Paion extended his hand, the channel of energy keeping his attacker bound. He had planned to use the Daimon to complete the rite, but this monster would do just as well. Regardless of what they were aligned to, the crystals themselves still contained all waves of potential life from Daimon to human. He would just have to amend the rite slightly to ensure it still did all he desired.

"Well now—" Paion's mocking sneer became pained and twisted, the vein in his extended arm ruptured tearing from his flesh causing him to cry out and disrupting the binding inflicted through the gem. The creature charged, its feral movements seeming more controlled than moments ago. Paion focused on suppressing the blood loss. He knew that despite its reaction to Sunrise this thing remained beyond his power to control, but he only needed a short amount of time to complete the rite of the purge.

For now, it would be better to retreat and complete the rite at a distance. But in order to do so he needed to complete the joining between the two stones, and find a means to divert the creature's attention long enough to make the step from the tower. His eyes flickered towards the baby, perhaps a secondary offering would quell its aggression.

* * *

Daniel sat behind Eiji, offering him what little support he could. It had been many years since the Elementalist last had cause to ride such a beast. Last time it had been Osgar, the wyrm joined to Alessia. The one currently in Daniel's service was a female known as Eirlys. Whilst smaller than Osgar, she was no more difficult to ride upon. Eiji's difficulty came from the fact that she was an Íswyrm. With Eiji's primary attunement being to water he needed to ensure he did not, inadvertently, harness the energies or elemental powers being presented by this creature. The act of doing so would be catastrophic.

The siege had, thus far, done nothing more than create charring and ice upon the outer shell of the tower. Something which to Daniel made sense, especially when considering the extreme conditions it had already survived.

Alessia had relayed instructions for the Úhtfloga to stand ready, awaiting twilight, when they would be able to harness the devastating power of storm and star fire. These wyrms were of a rare breed, but Daniel feared that, given the Mystic's deception, they would not be granted the time or opportunity to attack.

The Úhtfloga could only utilise their talents between twilight of dusk and dawn during the six days surrounding the new moon. The three days both preceding and following this time were the only instances that the stars, gravity, and atmospheric energies aligned in such a manner that they could be harnessed. Daniel knew that given the Mystics' progression with their task, that by the time twilight came it would already be too late. The tower was already beginning to appear less substantial in their plane. Time was of the essence.

Eiji gave the agreed signal, and Eirlys began to climb, readying herself to assist the attack. Closing his eyes he prayed to the Elemental spirits, and beseeched all those who had walked as an Elementalist before him to aid him and guide his strike.

The world surrounding them seemed to descend into chaos. Thunder crashed through the cloudless sky chorused by the roar of wyrms as they retreated from the building energies. Shadows and light became piercing until everything seemed only black and white. Winds from the four cardinal directions rose, meeting in this central force to collide. The earthen north trailed streaks of gold across and over the mountains whilst the southern wind brought with it fire. Ice streaked from the west and twin storms from the eastern clouds trimmed with yellow vapours spiralled rapidly around each other in their approach. All were driven to one place, to the one who had called them with such force, such desperation, that the summons could not go unheeded.

The energies collided above the tower, their potent strength further enhanced by the land's own attunement at the place Napier village had once stood. From the sky itself a piercing light struck down, combining and carrying the amassing forces to deliver one clean blow against the tower.

The roar of impact was deafening. Stone cracked and crumbled cleaving the uppermost section of the dome in twain, as if Zeus himself had taken up arms and delivered a mighty blow.

Eiji watched in astonishment, the fatigue caused by his actions staved off by pure awe. He felt the firm grasp of Daniel's hand upon his shoulder, both complimenting and steadying him.

"It wasn't all me," Eiji whispered. As he had prepared to unleash the energy building within him he had felt another force, two in fact, join with him. One seemed to have been channelled from beyond The Betwixt, it was strangely familiar, yet he could not identify its origin. The second however he recognised with ease, and *her* interference in matters outside her own world was bound to result in a reprimanding, again.

"And yet, it was," Daniel advised spurring Eirlys onward towards the opening Eiji's actions had forged as he prepared himself for what would follow.

Eirlys turned sharply, releasing an ear-splintering bellow. She veered from course as the tower appeared to fade before their eyes. "No!" Daniel protested vehemently. "We were so close."

"But y' ve still got the portal right? That's what y' said. If the tower goes the link between our planes remains open." Eiji's exhaustion struck him with force and he felt Daniel reach out steadying him.

"We'll get you to ground first. Then I'll head back. Eirlys is too large to enter through the portal, so I'll need to be precise." Things had become dangerous. The tower had been drawn into The Depths of Acheron and its position would overlap that of the portal leading to this plane. He had no knowledge of the terrain that side, and could only hope that anyone who could be of aid was already in position.

"Y' kiddin' right? I'm comin' with y'."

"Not this time. You're in no condition to be of aid. I've a feeling you'll be of more use to us here." Daniel's words were supported in action as Eiji grew limp, slumping forwards as exhaustion claimed him.

* * *

Rob gasped with angered exhaustion as he leapt through the portal into the tower. His jerkin was torn, hanging from his shoulders limply with gaping holes and shredded stitching. Dust and debris covered him, streaking his face where the only lighter sections had been caused by him running his hand down it in frustration. Bray would pay for this.

Anger had been his fuel for so long that, when he entered the tower, the only thing he could see was the source of his aggression. Pulling his darts from his belt he charged into the fray, soon realising his efforts were not alone. A blond-haired man crawled desperately away from his assault, nursing ghastly wounds. His retreat leaving trails of blood across the floor.

Sharp spasms caused Bray to grow rigid, but created only the briefest of hesitation as he advanced. His clothes were covered in blood, his skin glistened, but all traces upon his flesh soon faded, drawn within him to feed his hunger. In that moment, Rob was unsure who posed the greater threat. But given the struggle between the two it appeared Bray possessed a far greater advantage.

With his weapon in hand Rob threw himself on top of Bray, burying the needle into his throat before being thrown from his back. For the briefest moment the figure looked towards him and, as if seeing him unworthy of notice, returned his efforts to Paion.

The figure shuffling backwards from Bray was a bloody mess. His swollen face was barely recognisable as human, one of his legs was twisted at a sickening angle, and yet he still attempted to retaliate. Bray growled, the charge from Sunrise becoming more intense the more the figure stimulated it. Slowly, Paion was activating the device buried into his sternum.

Rob charged again, grappling with Bray for mere seconds before being flung aside. He struck the altar with force, expelling deep, barking coughs as he fought to draw breath. His arms trembled as he pulled himself up, his hand slipping on the fluid upon the altar's surface. Turning slowly he witnessed the extent of Taya's injuries for the first time. He glanced towards Bray and Paion before fervently scanning the room.

A small basket drew his focus near where the two struggled. Staggering to his feet he moved cautiously to secure it, dragging it towards Taya as he nursed his ribs. With great effort he hauled the sleeping bundle from within, and placed the infant between the motionless arms of her mother. He was almost certain he had seen Taya's fingers twitch in response to the tiny presence.

Taya's body spasmed in time with Bray's as Paion made another attempt to free himself. Seeing this Rob understood the true danger. Paion was not losing as badly as his injuries implied. He was being beaten, but the reason he failed to retaliate was because, while all this occurred, he was doing something much larger. He was working to complete the rite and, as Taya's reaction to Bray's pain suggested, he had already succeeded in joining Remedy to Sunrise.

Rob began to run towards them, unsheathing his dagger. This had to end. The pain being endured by Bray was becoming noticeable, as were his slowing reactions. The last shock had sent him staggering backwards as Paion continued to pull himself along the floor, gasping for breath. His hand struck Rob's foot, his gaze looking up fearfully as the dagger descended.

The tower began to tremble, the dome fractured above them, raining down large broken segments. Rob felt something collide with him, thrusting him away from danger as a bolt of blinding light struck the place he had stood. Bray growled from atop his friend, leaping back towards Paion, weaving amongst the falling debris with a gait more feral than man.

Fighting for breath, Rob turned his gaze to the fracture. Hope swelled within him as he saw the wyrm beginning its return. But as quickly as hope had kindled it was smothered. The sky above turned dark and but a single window to the world outside remained. Rob groaned, he knew this feeling, they were in The Depths of Acheron. The only escape from the tower shimmered at the location he had entered, a portal which no longer looked out into The Depths but upon the place in their world the tower had once stood.

* * *

Bray dashed through the debris, darting from side to side as he attempted to pick up the scent. Each successive attack by Paion had weakened him, but as a result had also weakened the frenzy. He had seen him, staring up into the opening with a look of realisation as a wyrm descended towards them. But the continual collapse from above had shielded him from sight, now he was gone. But the threat was far from over.

It would take very little for Paion to complete the rite, and with the portal ajar between The Depths and the human plane it would make no difference where the activation took place. Paion had joined Sunrise to Remedy, and tethered them to his own magic so that he could unleash their fury. For the safety of all Bray knew he must find a means to close the portal, and he knew of only one way to do so.

His gaze returned to Taya as he stalked towards her.

"Don't even think about it," Rob snarled, positioning himself in front of Taya.

"Move," Bray growled. Rob had no concept of how fortunate he had been. During his assault on Paion, Rob had not been viewed as an immediate threat. His blood was too toxic to consider the normal method of rendering something helpless. Now, however, he would do what must be done.

"No."

Bray charged forwards, driving his shoulder deep into his friend's injured ribs, forcing him backwards before shoving his hands firmly against Rob's chest, propelling him backwards through the portal. He watched with regret as Rob's limbs flailed helplessly, but he could not be allowed to interfere in what must be done.

Moistening his lips Bray once more climbed to straddle Taya and, whispering a word of apology, he began to feed. The portal started to flicker as her heartbeat began to weaken and to slow.

Chapter 28

Decisions

Daniel clutched Eirlys tightly as she climbed high into the sky, closing in on the area the great tower had once stood. Above he could see the slight distortion caused by the gateway into The Depths of Acheron. Hesitantly he rose to his feet, his arms extended for balance as they approached. The portal itself was too small for a wyrm, but *he* could still make a difference.

There was one thing he had neglected to tell Bray when he had spoken of remaining within The Depths of Acheron. It had bore no relevance for the situation surrounding Taya, but he could offer Bray salvation from Sunrise. His failure to mention it had been a deliberate test of Bray's resolve. It was essential his commitment remained unwavering. The one who affixed the tool, could also remove it. That was why, despite the protests, despite the danger, he would take this risk. As long as the portal stayed open the threat remained. But if he could neutralise Sunrise then he would need only find a suitable haven for the Damion to live out her remaining days, away from her own kind.

Daniel's knees buckled slightly under the motion of the wyrm. He released the tethers which Eirlys, given Daniel's inexperience of flight, had agreed to wear for his extra safety. His gaze locked before them as the shimmer of the portal raced ever closer. Eirlys dipped her head as Daniel tensed, preparing himself for the jump.

Something stirred in the air before him. A ripple within the shimmer of the gateway as something was expelled from within. A screaming figure struck Eirlys' back, rolling as it connected with the solid form, grabbing desperately to her scales as he slid, knocking Daniel from his feet. Eirlys rolled in the sky, turning and diving in an attempt to still the movement upon her back and prevent the Wita from falling. Daniel seized the tethers, and reached up to secure the figure, grasping him tightly until the wyrm's movements calmed.

Rob looked to Daniel in grateful relief, but instead of a word of thanks, he surveyed their surroundings and swore. Eirlys circled, her vision searching the sky for the portal. She retraced her flight path, but found nothing.

"It's gone," Daniel whispered, a heaviness encasing his chest.

"That cifesboren!" Rob cursed, understanding all too well what the absence of the portal signified.

"Was Paion still present?" Daniel prompted as Rob fell silent. "Was he still within the tower?"

"What difference does it make?"

"If he was, he could still activate Sunrise. This plane isn't the only one to take human partners. The death of their Sfaíra and heir will be difficult enough, the land will grieve the loss of the ancient pact, and its eternal binding. View this grief through the eyes of those who also lost their partners, friends, and maybe even children, and I can see no possibility of a lasting peace between our races." Rob looked to him in disbelief. "Do not underestimate the power of that land, and the reach it possesses even when bound. Something cannot be sealed within The Betwixt without touching all within The Stepping Realm. Lest you forget they guided you through such means. Imagine what grief and anger could turn such skills towards."

* * *

Amelia approached Eiji hesitantly. He sat upon the ground partaking in the provisions offered to him by the Eortháds. They had marvelled at his skill, praised his efforts, but finally, when it became apparent he wished solitude, they let him be.

"You see, there really was no choice."

"What I see, Ms Embers, is somethin' that could'a been avoided if y'd just done what y' promised." Eiji rose to his feet, turning to behold the exhausted woman. "Was two days t'much t'ask? Even one would'a seen somethin' better than this."

"We cannot undo what has been done. But perhaps we can ease the burden? If Paion was still within the tower when the Daimon died then there is a chance he could still trigger Sunrise and kill the humans who have partnered and bred with the Daimons over the years."

"Whaddya suggest?"

"I think we should raise Kólasi." Eiji let out a bitter chuckle at her words.

"C'mon, surely we're past this game. It's rising ether way, despite y' saying it could never be so." He had felt it when they began to banish the tower, the energy of Kólasi was being used to pull it within, yet in the same instance the same force was expelling it. They had started a reaction, one which they had deemed impossible. It had been thought Kólasi had to remain for the tower to be bound. Yet for some unknown reason not only was the energy syphoned from it more than sufficient, it had caused such disharmony that it had forced Kólasi to be expelled from its existing alignment. This in turn left the land no other choice but to slowly return to the plane it had once belonged to.

"Yes," Amelia conceded. "But if we offer our aid, suggest this was our intention, it could quieten the discord of the land. We would save lives."

"I remember makin' a similar argument for our delay."

"Eiji we need you. We cannot do it safely without your aid. Does our reason behind needing to do it matter?"

"No. But I understand all t'well it's a reaction t'ensure y' still appear infallible. Y' know I wouldn't condemn them t'death. That was my reason for walkin' away, and it's the reason I'll help y' now." He tossed a small cloth parcel at Amelia, she looked inside at the food parcels and nodded.

"Then let's make haste. They will know by now their land is in motion. We should give them no cause to doubt it was always our intention."

* * *

Acha had not needed to use the remaining piece of the coin as the tower was no longer within her native plane. She had stood for barely a moment, looking down upon the crumbled cliffs and huge crevice that fractured the tower's domed roof, and gave silent thanks. Had the structure not been damaged she would have had no means to gain entry. The tower was expansive, but from her altitude she was able to scramble down to walk upon it before descending inside with great care. The shrill piercing cries of a screaming infant were all Acha could hear as she made her descent.

She instantly beheld the scene before her, and with much apprehension began a slow approach. The person she knew as Bray sat straddled upon another figure. The air was rancid with the smell of dirt and bodily fluids.

She knew he was aware of her approach, but he made no attempt to acknowledge her. As she grew closer she saw the subtle shaking of his shoulders. She approached with caution, picking her way through broken debris at a slow and careful pace. By the time she stood beside him the despair was a tangible force, roiling from him. Hesitantly she raised her hand and, with all the tenderness she thought was owed, placed it upon his flesh.

Acha's body collapsed to the floor in the instant that they touched. She had used this particular gift several times, and mostly to no good ends. But this time she hoped it would be different. Acha, as a life-force, was not traditional. All that she was had been displaced into an amulet by her father.

With skill and practice she had learnt to shift all, or part, of her essence into another being, allowing her to control them as if their body were her own. For what she had in mind she would need to use everything she had, all her concentration, and stave off the need to replenish until she could reunite with Eiji. Their relationship was mutually beneficial, each protected the other from the ramifications of their own differences.

Bray's lips raised in a soft smile as she thought of Eiji before turning her focus to the difficult task at hand. Daniel had discussed countless scenarios, but he had never predicted this. She raised Bray's hand, releasing the painful grasp upon the object within. Lifting it, she examined the circlet. The dull stone of Remedy reflected the light as she turned it over. His memories suggested he had intended to feed until there was not enough life to keep Remedy aligned. He had torn the circlet from her, doing as he had intended, the portal had sealed, and Remedy was removed, but he believed he had exceeded the point of being able to save her. Acha touched the stone, focusing upon it and drawing the energy stored within into herself, something that had been impossible while it had been affixed to Kitaia. The crystal cracked beneath her touch before she dropped it to the floor beside them.

Reaching forwards she placed his hands upon the dark welts caused by his touch and focused on rejoining their flesh. She sat still and even the baby, as if understanding the need for tranquillity, fell silent. With the attachment in place Acha became aware of a weak, rapid pulse. It was barely detectable. She cringed as she felt the movement of bones and tissue. Suddenly, his position on top of her made sense. The damage to the area behind him was extensive. His position, be it an attempt to preserve her life or ensure less blood was wasted, had applied pressure to slow the blood loss her own healing had been unable to staunch due to her weakened condition.

With great effort Acha transferred a fraction of her energy into the blood which pulsed through Bray's veins, and slowly guided it through his hands and back into Kitaia, performing an exact reversal of the feeding ritual. Something Bray himself would have been unable to do. It was an agonising process that she suffered in his stead, and one she needed every ounce of focus she had to control.

* * *

Thunder breached the cloudless sky as lightning fractured the air to leave tears across the heavens and ocean. Waves rose and parted while barriers and boundaries, once unseen by the human eyes, webbed across the horizon. These scars pulsed with light and magic, as if shedding the blood of the world itself in mesmerising displays.

There was a moment of complete stillness. Even the waters grew tranquil and the choir of circling birds grew silent. Six figures crouched upon tall cliffs and small rocky islands, their positioning forming the closest approximation to a circle the natural environment would allow. Their hands were extended outward, palms down towards the ocean floor below. All took a moment to breathe.

Between the six an iridescent film began to form upon the surface of the ocean, stilling the waves beneath it to an eerie calm never witnessed upon this surface. Brilliant shades of primary colours began to merge, intermingling to create exquisite combinations of shimmering beauty. The colours chased and changed, forming an image upon the surface of the ocean until finally they became still, revealing the enormous island of Kólasi as it broke away from the vast land mass known as The Depths of Acheron.

Slowly they stood, their hands aglow with magical strands of colours unseen for time immemorial. Anchors and tethers uncoiled at their will as they pulled upon the corded tendrils, each unravelling and releasing them in unison. The portal rippled as the enormous land grew closer, to slowly permit the emergence of the rising, colossal form.

Eremalche pierced the boundary first. Water cascaded from the protective barrier surrounding the land, pouring from it in enormous waterfalls to create spectacular circular rainbows. The ocean water roared and swelled, but extended no further than the Mystics, its energy harnessed and channelled back towards their task. The city's ancient petals shuddered in response to the first touch it had known from the sun for eras untold.

The frost-blue petals slowly began to twist, sending further sprays of water and mist as they gradually began to uncurl. They released hues of magical light which blazed across the sky in a spectacular display once referred to as the Dance of the Spirits. The ocean and rising lands reflected the ribboned lights from this stunning array, as if the world itself exchanged silent words to welcome Kólasi home.

The flower continued to bloom, revealing the wondrous city within, and granting the inhabitants their first glimpse of the sun as it lowered to touch the horizon, in a final farewell before night.

The Mystics looked upon this land with grief and awe. And all was still. The sun sank beyond the horizon and the protection of the city once more wrapped around Eremalche. The breath-taking lights traced the sky and continued their dance, celebrating their release from captivity. Amelia looked on in amazement. Despite its disappearance she had never realised the Aurora had originated from the Daimons, she had missed its sight greatly.

She made a vow upon these lights. Many times she had questioned the act of banishing the Daimons, but too soon had she been willing to condemn them to save the humans. She had returned to old habits. Her actions over the last few days, whilst she stood by their premise, had been made in haste. This alone showed her the need for faith. She had taken the prophecies seen by Peter to be accurate. She had forgotten people had a way of surprising even the fates. She, more than any other, should have known this well.

* * *

Rob had been unable to believe it when the familiar prickling caused the hairs on his neck to rise as he and Daniel had begun their descent on the wyrm. It was a sensation he only felt when near an open portal. A glance upwards had confirmed his suspicion, somehow the portal had been reopened.

At first he thought Paion had found a means to fulfil his plan, but the more he thought on the question Daniel had posed, the more convinced he was that Paion had not been within the tower after the attack which had damaged it. He had witnessed the look of defeat upon Paion's face as he observed the wyrms, a look which suggested he knew his prophecies had no meaning. He had seen Daniel and recognised the unmistakable armour bestowed upon the Wita by the Eortháds. It made sense he would have fled.

"Bray!" Rob's enraged voice penetrated the air as they entered the tower, causing the once quiet child to startle and scream. He lunged forwards, seeing the crumpled figure of Acha lying upon the floor beside the altar. He would not allow this. Daniel reached out, catching his arm and sidestepping around him to block his path. Bray raised a hand in their direction, panting heavily. Rob grimaced, expecting to see Daniel's blood streak the air, but instead Bray's figure slumped forward, uttering two single words.

"Help her."

Rob looked to Daniel questioningly, frowning as he caught the briefest glimpse of his armour receding to be contained within a gemstone. He stepped aside, nodding to Rob, who resumed his approach, a little more guarded than before.

Acha sat slowly with a groan, raising her hand to her head, ensuring Bray remained unconscious and her leaving his body had not caused his weight to shift.

"His weight is slowing the blood loss," she explained. "I transferred what I could back to her, but the injuries aren't healing as they should."

"I need to remove Sunrise, if he wakes in this state he's likely to frenzy again." Daniel glanced to Rob questioningly. "You trained in The Courts of Twilight, do you know much of their medicine?" Daniel caught the bewildered expression cross Rob's face. "Your tikéta," he explained gesturing dismissively towards Rob's torn garments.

"Some."

"Good. You do what you can for her. I'll remove Sunrise."

"You can do that?"

"I aligned it to him, as such my hands can remove it. I had no cause to mention it before since it seemed unlikely Paion would reverse his actions. Here." Daniel removed a beaten satchel from his shoulder. "It should have most of what you need. Anything you're unsure of I can talk you through, but I really must get started. You can do this, right?" Daniel questioned sensing his hesitation.

Rob looked to the disfigured flesh and cringed. The wound had been sealed in several places by both her own magic and hurried, careless hands. Her skin bulged, seeming thin across jagged splinters of bone, even witnessing it for the second time was nauseating.

"I-I don't know where to start."

"Reopen it, carefully remove any shards and stitch or burn anything that bleeds. At this point we're unlikely to cause any more damage, so do whatever you can. Acha returned some blood, but if we don't stop its flow it'll be for nothing. Have you got this?"

"Yes." Rob flexed his fingers before searching the bag and removing everything he thought he would need. Slowly and carefully he cut along the pink scar where her flesh had attempted to knit across the fractured bones. Acha stood, stepping away to give them some room to manoeuvre. She lifted the baby from the altar as Daniel struggled to adjust Bray into a position he could utilise while keeping the pressure his body applied upon Taya.

Time passed and Daniel was finally able to safely remove Bray's weight, resulting in a flurry of activity from Rob as the pressure's release caused smaller unseen wounds to bleed. But her body's natural healing magic was helping them a little now. Some of the bleeding, triggered by the removal of splintered bones, stilled of its own accord before he had time to react. Daniel stood beside him, assisting with the final repairs. They had done all they could with the means at their disposal. Anything more would have to wait until they could get further aid.

"We can't move her like this," Rob observed glancing towards the portal. With the sheer number of broken bones, and shards still within her, moving her seemed too dangerous. "So what do we do?"

Daniel pulled a cord from around his neck, tossing it to Acha.

"Get Eiji. Tell him to get to Kaila's irfeláfa, Alessia will know the best course. We'll need to get her home, to her own healers, but let's concentrate on getting out of here first."

Chapter 29

Aftermath

The Eortháds had very little in the way of holding areas but, when considering the condition Bray could wake in, they had fashioned something under Daniel's instruction. It was nothing grand, just a small cave overlooking the coast, sealed with iron bars. Rob never strayed far, and at all times it seemed one person or another was keeping vigil upon him whilst Taya was prepared to be moved.

Bray let out a long groan before springing quickly to his feet. His unfocused eyes searched the area desperately until they fixed upon Rob outside the small prison. He was standing, watching and studying Bray intently with apprehension. His eyes still possessed the reddened hue, displaying his need for food, but he seemed rational and in control.

"Kitaia?" Bray questioned desperately lunging forwards to grasp the bars. He covered his face with his hands as he recalled distorted memories, the hunger, the taste, the figure growing limp under his weight. Looking at Rob's expression he cursed. He paced within the confines of the small area, running his hands through his hair. Bray's voice became quiet, haunted as he spoke again. "I had Remedy in my hand, but still I could not release her." He remembered the sound it had made on the altar as her life was fading. He had picked it up, attempting to prise his other hand from her flesh, but he'd been unwilling, unable to resist the sensation of her blood being drawn into him.

"Bray, she's been moved to Kólasi. I don't know what will happen, but you didn't kill her." Bray was still pacing, lost in his distress. "Bray, did you hear me? She's not dead."

"Not yet. She'd just had a child, and the injuries... I thought *I* was a monster, I *am* a monster, but what he did to her—and then I..." Bray crouched down, moving to sit with his back leaning against the bars.

"Don't you go claiming the blame. This all comes back to one thing, I chose a treasure over her life. Everything that has happened, with her, with you, it's my fault. Do you understand? The blame is mine to own." Rob moved to sit as near as the bars would allow. "Here." Rob passed through a bottle of what he assumed to be some manner of liquor. He had retrieved several from what appeared to have been a storage area.

"Yeah, that stuff doesn't work on me," Bray admitted.

"Me either, but we can always pretend right?" Rob knocked the bottle against Bray's arm, he took it taking a long drink.

"Is this your way of punishing me?" Bray coughed passing it back, his face twisted with disgust. "I've had merrymakers more palatable than that."

"See you feel better already." Rob gave a half-hearted laugh. "So, what you going to do now?"

"I think I should return to Misora." He looked to Rob with a grave expression. "They have resources at their disposal I need access to."

"You're going after him aren't you?" Rob questioned.

"People like him are dangerous. Somehow they always find another means to forward their ambitions. One setback won't still his desire."

"Look, just promise me something, if you do go after him you won't do anything until you let me know. We started this together, we should finish it that way too." Bray looked to Rob in surprise.

"All right." He nodded his affirmation. "What about you, what's your plan now?"

"I plan to examine the bottom of these bottles, then I'll go find the thing that started all this mess."

"The Seed of Nzin?"

"Yeah."

"Listen, Rob, I understand it is not my place, but maybe you should consider reducing your alcohol consumption. I was frenzied, and still wouldn't consume you. That alone should tell you something. You're only mortal, and I can count my allies with

779

a single finger. I don't want to see you destroy your-self. Besides, I'm famished and your scent is destroy-ing my appetite," Bray added, attempting to lighten the sombre mood.

* * *

Through the darkness Taya was aware of a small warm presence resting beside her. She felt safe. The softness of where she lay seemed to embrace her weary body. The low murmur of voices faded in and out along with a gentle tugging sensation around her lower back. For the first time, in a long time, she felt no pain. She knew she lived; but how and why was uncertain.

Unclear images of Rob flashed through her mind, and his distorted words echoed through her con-sciousness. He had said something about Remedy. She tried to raise her hand to confirm its absence, but her body refused to obey. Even her eyes refused to open. A fresh wave of panic consumed her as she realised her entire body was numb. Her breathing quickened, she heard the blood rushing through her ears as her heart sped in response to her fear.

"Shh, you're safe." She felt the gentle caress of a familiar touch. His hand softly stroked her face, calming her. Even had he not spoken she would have recognised his touch. She tried to speak, but her mouth and tongue were dry. She felt something cold and damp moisten her lips as if in response to her body's demand. Even enveloped in darkness she could feel the perceived movement of the world around her as it spun. Her body radiated heat, and sensations across her skin consumed her forcing her eyes open. She found no focus. She gasped for breath before beginning to heave, expelling yellow bile tasting of strange energies and magic. Yuri spoke softly, his tone comforting while his words went unheard. He removed the bowl, replacing it with another as she fought back the waves of nausea.

"What's happening?" Her hoarse voice stung her throat, sounding gruff and raw to her own ears. She felt movement returning to her arms and pulled against the invisible restraints.

"Don't fight, you've been bound. Our shamans and naturopaths are trying to reverse some of the damage, but we need you still." Hearing the concern in his voice she managed to lift her head from the downward facing support, resting it on its edge to turn her unfocused vision to Yuri's grave expression. Seeing her looking at him he tried to disguise his apprehension with a brief but weighted smile.

"Is Catrina—"

"She is fine. Erin has been nursing her," Yuri assured, placing his hand on hers.

"How long?"

"A few days, we've both stayed with you." Yuri took his wife's hand and placed it on their daughter, who lay sleeping in a small cot joined to the top of the bed on which she lay. Taya felt the warmth of tears flood through her. "Catrina Kitaia," she whispered, once more naming the child as she traced her daughter's face with her trembling fingers. Yuri saw her shoulders start to shake as Taya began to weep uncontrollably. Her deep sobs shattered the binding spell, causing all movements of those healing her to still.

"Should we calm her?" a sympathetic voice from behind questioned. Taya's eyes widened in fear. She shook her head, her gaze pleading with Yuri as she was unable to find the words.

"Just give her a moment," Yuri requested, mirroring the same soft tone. As her sobs calmed she felt the binding magic once more creep over her until the healers' movements slowly resumed. Eventually one of the naturopaths moved to stand before her. He crouched, lowering himself to meet her gaze with his.

"I won't lie to you, Sfaíra, the damage is extensive." Taya felt her mind wander slightly, thinking how long it had been since someone had addressed her by that title. He gave her a moment until her attention returned to him. "It has been a long time since our kind has resorted to such archaic methods, but given how this was done there was little choice."

"Tell me." She composed herself, trying to suppress the fear and anxiety rushing through her veins. She was alive, her daughter was alive. Already she was more fortunate than she had dared to dream when she had first become aware of Remedy. Yuri squeezed her hand reassuringly, nodding to confirm he should continue.

"We've had to reopen the incision to remove the bones. The damage to your right side was extensive, whilst the left was... less severe." The naturopath swallowed. He had never seen such wounds before, bones snapped like twigs, their jagged shards threatening vital organs. She had been fortunate to have been treated and bound so well before being relocated. "The aid you received following the delivery was handled with a care not shown during the birth, and it's due to that care you're with us now.

"We have assisted the shamans in the repair of the spinal damage. It will be some time before you'll regain use of your legs, but with extensive therapy we are hopeful it will be a possibility." Taya nodded, she could only imagine the extent of her injuries. Such a lengthy recovery was rare given their species' natural healing abilities, and their advancements in medicine.

The naturopath paused a moment, allowing this information to be absorbed before continuing. "Whilst future conception is, most likely, possible, with the bones we have had to remove further pregnancies will carry a risk to both yourself and the child." He paused again, glancing to Yuri, who looked behind her and gestured for the healer to proceed. "Since your return we have worked nonstop to correct the damage, but you will still require multiple invasive surgeries. There are many fragments we cannot risk removing until some of the damage has healed, and we cannot risk moving you again until we are certain it will cause no further harm."

"Thank you," she whispered feeling a strange warmth flooding through her. Yuri squeezed her hand again, her expression growing alarmed as she tasted the unpleasant energy in the back of her throat. Her vision blurred, and she felt herself drifting back to sleep. Her hand gripped his weakly just before sleep took hold of her. He knew it had been against her wishes, but it was essential. He leaned forward kissing her tenderly on her forehead.

* * *

The return of their Sfaíra Fýlakas had been a cause for much celebration. Details relating to Kólasi's rising had been discussed at length, but when Taya was finally permitted to return home, the sight of the clouded sky above them had reduced her to tears.

Geburah visited her often, updating her with the events following the raising of their lands. When first she had heard the Mystics had raised Kólasi she had thought herself suffering from delirium. There were many rumours to the motive behind their action. The most accepted being that following Kitaia's sacrifice they could see no other way of ensuring those living in Kólasi remained safe, if Sunrise had been activated following Paion's preparation. Kólasi had risen before news of her recovery, and both Remedy and Sunrise's removal and destruction, had reached them. Kitaia often questioned if the result would have been the same if things had turned out differently.

There had, however, been an unforeseen problem with their return. Whilst the lands above had been ravaged by the Severaine, eliminating development and wisdom across the cycles, Kólasi had been unaffected. Such things had allowed her land and its people to thrive and develop in ways the human mind could not even begin to comprehend. This posed a problem, one first addressed by Taya. Whilst not wanting to appear supercilious, she was aware of the rift such a gap in knowledge could create. The people of this time were not yet ready to be enlightened in the things their race had taken cycles to understand. Their ways could be turned to war, and result in a situation similar to those responsible for their initial banishment.

The negotiations were long, sometimes heated, and often Taya would be forced to excuse herself and ordered to rest. During these times she had gladly left the discussions in Geburah's capable hands. Finally an agreement was reached. The Daimons would work closely with trainers from the Physicians' Plexus, and assist them in the development of tools and techniques to enhance life-saving skills. But this would be the limit of what they would share, at this time. Kólasi's energy was generated through nature, and so, there was no need to request the Research Plexus to supply them with a means to harness Dynamism, thus allowing their development to remain unnoticed by outside forces. It also allowed them a measure of privacy.

The land directly above where Kólasi physically resided was covered by the ocean, a place bathed in darkness whilst the mapped world was awash with light. This served to ensure their reappearance was easier than had been expected. The only real concern was Collateral. As islands rose and sank the magic relating to each portal reacted to seal or grant access to areas. This meant that Kólasi's return would re-activate sealed portals, and this was something even the Mystics could not negate. Fortunately, none of the gateways intruded on Eremalche, only the lands outside of the great city.

There would be much adaption needed to their new environment, as such, the suggestion that their race remained segregated, for a short time, was wel-comed. Until recently, only Yuri and Kitaia had ever felt the warmth of the sun's light. It would be a time of great change and adjustment and Kólasi was filled with excitement. The Sfaíra had not only returned but had liberated their land and delivered an heir.

* * *

Taya sat at the table scowling. The pressure of the chair and brace against her spine was irritating her more than normal. She tried to ignore it, but today had been challenging. Yuri had taken Catrina outside to give her some peace and quiet. She was angry by her lack of progress and by the praise she received as people told her how well she was doing. She didn't feel like she was doing well.

She took a calming breath, reminding herself of her accomplishments. She thought of Yuri, his end-less patience with her. He knew how much having to rely on the chair's support frustrated her. A knock at the door startled her from her self-reprimanding as she reminded herself why she was lucky to even be here.

"It's open," she snapped, her tone a little harsher than intended. Her vision fixed on the door, watching impatiently as the brown-haired figure hesitated at her threshold. His eyes reflected guilt as his gaze fell upon her for the first time since she had been carried from the tower by the Eortháds. "Well, don't just stand there, come in already. Sit." He walked awkwardly inside, pulling out a small chair from beside the table.

"How are you doing?" Rob asked softly, meeting her gaze with difficulty.

"Don't!" she snapped again.

"What?" He looked away, averting his eyes, studying the book laden shelves in an attempt to divert his focus elsewhere.

"Don't look at me with pity. I'm alive. I get to be a mother, a wife, and the ruler of my people. Don't you, of all people, *dare* look at me like that." The harshness in her tone chilled him. She filled a goblet with water from the pitcher plant on the table and pushed it towards him. Her eyes briefly rested on the front pocket of his jacket, she tried with difficulty to suppress the shudder she felt building.

"I'm sorry," he apologised into the water as he took a sip, watching the light reflect upon its surface.

"Spirits!" she muttered in frustration before raising her voice slightly. "Pity and apologies? Honestly, Rob, I expected more from the man who saved my life."

"What?" He looked to her in astonishment, seeing only her belief in the truth of her words.

"If you'd have visited us sooner you'd already know. The things you did to heal me, they are the reason I am still alive." Taya flinched as she instinctively placed her hand upon her back. She had heard everything that had happened from everyone except for the one person who should have told her. She had started to wonder if he would ever visit. The guilt he carried was tangible, and some of it was unfounded. "To that end, Yuri and I have discussed it at great length and, although in reality you may not have been my uncle, we would be honoured if you would be Catrina's."

Rob's shock was clearly evident from the manner his jaw slackened at her words. There was a long silence as he stared, dumbfounded, almost trying to convince himself he had heard her correctly. "Rob, I'm asking you to be the guardian of this land's future ruler, something other than silence would be appreciated," Taya prompted sternly.

"What's the catch?" he questioned hearing the betrayal of a hidden condition in her voice.

"You don't use that." She gestured towards his pocket where she knew The Seed of Nzin resided.

"Do you know what you're asking?" Taya moved, positioning herself so she was behind him. She reached forwards and placed one hand over his forehead, and the other on the crown on his head. With great effort and energy one gifted in prophetic dreams could share the premonition with another.

Closing her eyes she gathered all her strength and focused on recalling the memory.

"I know what I'm asking, but I don't think you do. I think you need to see to understand." Taya took a deep breath. She'd had variations of this prediction countless times in the last few months, but it always ended the same way. She pushed the vision into his mind. A vision of the moment he made his wish upon The Seed of Nzin. The first time she beheld this vision it had been a bitter blessing, whilst revealing Rob's fate, it had also allowed her to see Yuri for what she had thought would be the final time.

Taya released him as he fought for breath. His panicked hands quickly traced over his body for signs of harm. She moved away, positioning herself back at the other side of the table as he regained control over his breathing. He refilled his water, but found it difficult to swallow.

"I'm asking you to live," she advised softly. "The wish will be granted, but you'll become a Nzin, a being who knows only the desire to condemn others to your own fate." Rob looked at her in horror, his muscles ached as he fought to suppress the shivers from the horrific sight he had just witnessed.

"But the wish is granted?" he pressed. If he had to sacrifice himself so they could live there was no question to his choice.

"In the worst imaginable way. Imagine you wished for the return of a loved one from the grave. Their life-force would be taken from Hades' fields, where it was at peace, and attached to their old body riddled with decay and pain. Even if their bodies had been burned to ash the wish contains enough magic to partially reconstruct their form. Those returning in such a manner usually remain buried until the next full moon. Daimons once opposed the necromancers, to this day we still seek out souls that need quietening. Those who claw their way from the grave are hungry, insane from the pain, and hunted like monsters until we can release them, but their acts forever stain their essence." Taya's gaze fixed upon his pocket. "There are some evils that can't be vanquished. It's best for all if you return it to those who worship such things."

"If it's so dangerous why let me take it?"

"Because you needed to, and Yuri gave his word. Even if we denied you, you would have kept pursuing it. You understand now the price attached to wanting something more than anything else." She placed her hand on his across the table. "You need to let them go. While you still pursue them they will never truly be at peace. The dead still watch over the living, and they have earned their peace. They kept you safe, and your quest brought you to me. Without them, without you, no one would have known what was happening, and no one would have stopped him." Rob looked to her in disbelief, and his free hand found the hair clip in his pocket. His fingers traced its smooth surface affectionately, and his mind was filled with thoughts of his wife and daughter. He relished in their image, and with a resigning sigh presented the small cylinder containing The Seed of Nzin to Taya.

"You're right, they've done enough."

Íkelos surveyed all within his domain, the trees themselves thrummed with such energy the leaves themselves were aglow. Aidan had thought himself resourceful in the waking of Elly, but it was of no consequence. Although access to the Gods would have made his tasks easier, the divine realm had never truly been his focus. Aidan had taken her place as the sacrifice he had originally intended. The divine was out of his reach, but both Darrienia and the Daimon realm were accessible now. But it was not there his sights were set. His ambition had always been to bypass the block to the waking world and soon he would have the means to do so.

The energy from his tideway within Darrienia had been consumed, taking with it the life of the two Oneirois, but now, none would think to investigate. Everything had been cleanly executed with the precision he had required. The attempted rescue of Daley had ensured that when the Mystics acted Kólasi would be displaced, and now it had risen, aligning to the physical world where once it had dwelt.

When the merging of energies was completed, there was only one thing preventing him from taking physical form there. He needed power, a very specific kind, and thanks to Daley he now knew where to find it. Soon he would have harnessed enough energy from the forest to emerge and take form within Darrienia, and when that occurred, nothing could stand in his way.

Epilogue

Elly cried out, her screams unheard through the silence of the chamber. Raising her fists she pounded at the glass above her, drawing laboured breaths. Her hands came into focus as they struck against her prison. All movement ceased as she witnessed the black material which covered her flesh completely. Her mouth grew dry as her focus shifted through the glass to see the endless spiral of tomes. She knew this room, it was filled to capacity with ancient and forgotten literature, shelves upon shelves, books upon books, to the point she thought perhaps the tower itself had been constructed from them.

"No, no, no, no, no." Her voice broke more with each repeated word as she resumed pounding on the surface, attempting to force the glass lid from the metal casket. This was not where she should be. This was impossible. "What did you do?" she cried, her strength failing as tremors consumed her body. She felt the warmth of tears upon her cheeks, the warmth of her flesh, the beating of her heart, and the small shocks generated by the strange clothes which had served to ensure her muscles had never atrophied.

The glass case opened slowly, her body grew light as she felt herself lifted into someone's arms. But the light outside the case was different. It hurt too much to keep her eyes open, and each sound was deafening. Even this person's gentle touch brought pain. She felt the pressure ease as she was placed upon something soft, draped in warm silken sheets.

"But her hair, it's—"

"Thank you, Elisha, that will be all." Night's voice echoed through her head. He was speaking in a tone barely recognisable as a whisper, yet to her, to the senses unused for centuries, it all seemed so loud. Her chamber had been designed to filter the light and mute sound. She had wanted this day for so long, and now she would give anything to find herself within the golem. Her mind raced, unable to comprehend all that had transpired. She felt confusion wash over her, strange sensations long forgotten resurfaced with the warmth of tears as they spilt involuntarily from her burning eyes. "Welcome back." She felt his hand pass over her eyes, dulling the pain. "You can open them now." She did so warily, finding herself looking directly into Night's blue eyes as he crouched before her. "I must say, this is most unexpected. How are you feeling?"

"What happened?"

"I am afraid I have no definite answer. What has occurred was thought to be impossible, the strength needed to wake you in this form is beyond any I can comprehend," Night answered. "I can tell you that the tether to your golem decayed long before you awoke. In earnest I feared you lost."

"The Daimons," Elly whispered, straightening herself.

"The Daimons did this?" Night questioned uncertainly.

"No, Melas has breached The Stepping Realm to their world, Kólasi cannot rise."

"I'm afraid your warning comes a year too late."

"What?" Elly gasped. "How is that possible, Aidan just woke me." Elly felt heat rush through her. He had achieved something no other Oneiroi had, he had woken her. The image of him touching the obelisk flashed through her mind. He had used what she had told him to push her here, to her flesh.

"Lain, you were expelled from Darrienia quite some time ago. Given that you had suppressed your tethers we feared the worst, more so when the anchor to your golem decayed. We thought you lost, like the Oneiroi you travelled with. Given events, I can only imagine you were expelled to this form, but it has taken until now for your mind to realign."

"I'm mortal?" Elly questioned, raising her hand into her line of sight.

"Well, that remains to be seen. But part of your curse has indeed been broken."

"Which part? How can you be certain?" Night reached back, grasping one of the many mirrors from within this room. He raised it, allowing her to see her reflection. She stared in astonishment at the mousy-brown shade of her hair, she looked now as she had in Darrienia. "Your eyes remain altered, even I cannot be certain what all of this suggests."

"We have to warn them, if Kólasi has risen, that means he can access the human plane through The Stepping Realm, just as he can Darrienia."

"Lain, this is one matter in which I must not intervene," Night asserted, pulling the mirror from her grasp.

"Your promises are meaningless if there are no mortals to protect."

"It is not that which binds me in this matter. Íkelos, or Melas, whichever name he goes by now, before being known as such, was a god, and he was birthed by Nyx."

"He is your brother?" Elly looked to him, she had long known he had siblings, but never had he admitted to such, not even to her.

"For me to intervene now, when Nyx forbade the offer of aid, would create strife between the Gods themselves. Do as you must, but know that I cannot be the one to guide you."

Dear reader,

We hope you enjoyed reading *Remedy*. Please take a moment to leave a review, even if it's a short one. Your opinion is important to us.

Discover more books by K.J. Simmill at https://www.nextchapter.pub/authors/kj-simmill

Want to know when one of our books is free or discounted? Join the newsletter at http://eepurl.com/bqqB3H

Best regards,

K.J. Simmill and the Next Chapter Team

The story continues in:

The Dream Walker

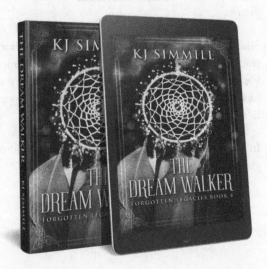

To read the first chapter for free, please head to:
https://www.nextchapter.pub/books/the-dream-walker

About the Author

K.J. Simmill is an award-winning British author with books released in both the fantasy and non-fiction genres.

She is a qualified Project Manager, Herbal Practitioner, and Usui Reiki master, with certifications in various fields of holistic therapy. More recently she has completed training and qualifications in Special Education Needs and Disabilities (SEND).

In her free time she is an avid reader and a passionate gamer.

Acknowledgements

There are many people who have continued to support me in my writing career, so I would like to take this opportunity to thank them.

First of all, thank you to my wonderful husband, who has been with me since the beginning of this journey and has offered more support, patience, and understanding than I could ever have asked. Without him my dream of being published would never have become a reality. He is my muse, my heart, my everything.

Secondly, I want to thank the amazing and talented Stephen Drake, author of The Displaced Series, for his support, friendship, and dedication. Not to mention his valued assistance with the beta reading. Again, thank you.

Thirdly, thank you to my family, especially my father, Stephen, who kindly beta reads my work and supports my writing, and my Nan, Alma, who has supported both me and my dream since I was a child. I love you more than I could ever hope to express.

Last but not least, my thanks to you, the reader. Thank you for choosing to read my book.

Remedy
ISBN: 978-4-86752-723-8 (Mass Market)

Published by
Next Chapter
1-60-20 Minami-Otsuka
170-0005 Toshima-Ku, Tokyo
+818035793528
9th August 2021